To my wife, Catherine, for her love, dedication, support, and that patience.

Acknowledgments

I want to thank my friends and colleagues at Sail Magazine and in the sailing industry who encouraged me to write this story; Nancy Scott of Cruising Guide Publications; and all the government officials in the Caribbean who were helpful in providing information about their islands.

Prologue

Island Drummer is an adventure story that takes place in 1985. While most of the free world was enjoying peace, the United States was at war in many of its cities and towns; a war that was being lost. The nation's primary enemy had unlimited funding plus unlimited resources for equipment and distribution. This enemy struck from the air and sea with its deadly substances, drugs.

In the Soviet Union, the Kremlin, embarrassed by being defeated in the war with Afghanistan began to bring their troops home. The Communist Party started making major changes in their ranks as younger men moved into power bringing a new kind of leadership. This became evident with the death of Konstantin Chernenko on March 10,1985. The Kremlin wasting no time announced his replacement, Mikhail Gorbachev. Gorbachev, age 54, was little known in the Soviet Union and in the free world. Another major Kremlin announcement soon followed. Edouard Schevardnadze, a younger and very popular moderate, had replaced Foreign Minister Andrei Gromyko, one of the last hard-liners of the Communist Party.

On the Communist island of Cuba, Fidel Castro did not expect the changes in command taking place in the Soviet Union would bring about new policies that would deeply affect his country. These changes would add destruction to his decaying economy, limit military supplies and eventually affect his personal status within the Kremlin and the Communist Party.

In the spring of 1985, Fidel Castro felt the first taste of the Kremlin's new policies. He was backing a political movement on the island of Grenada supplying materials and labor to build a new runway large enough to land modern heavy jets. At first the Soviets endorsed the project, but by that spring the Kremlin retracted their support when Castro suggested that a military installation should be built and manned by Russian and Cuban military units.

Castro, seeing that his relationship with the Soviet Union and Mikhail Gorbachev was deteriorating, began thinking about alternatives. To stop the cancer of economic failure in Cuba, he had to find new ways to finance his government, protect his military and feed his people. He befriends a young Chinese engineer, Nan Hi Chen, working in Cuba for the Soviets. Chen supports Castro's frustrations with the Kremlin and presents Castro with an idea that could provide financial security for Cuba. The idea excites Castro and he makes a dangerous decision. It would mean dealing in drugs. The Kremlin had made it clear to Castro that Cuba was off limits to any kind of drug trafficking as long as Soviet military or civilian personnel were on the island. The KGB sent special agents to Cuba to police such activities.

The United States Drug Enforcement Agency, CIA and Customs Department always suspected Fidel Castro to be directly involved in drug trafficking. Cuba, a well guarded island and a stone's throw from the United States and the Bahamas was a protected haven for drug runners who could easily reach any part of the United States, especially the Gulf states from Texas to Florida.

Unknown to Fidel Castro, his secret police, or the KGB, two Cubans, a Colonel serving in Castro's secret police and his brother-in-law, a senior pilot for Cubana Airlines were making plans to escape the island with their families. They make contact through the Cuban underground and inform American agents that they want to make a deal, high level military information for protection and asylum. In a matter of weeks, a master communication network is in place at key airports throughout South America and Mexico served by Cubana and Eastern Airlines. The system is tested and proven valuable. It is code named "Christmas Tree."

On a Friday afternoon in July 1985, a coded message is received at Eastern Airlines Customer Baggage Service at Miami International Airport from Maracaibo, Venezuela. The message is immediately sent to CIA Headquarters in Langley, Virginia. Two hours later, a meeting takes place in the Oval Office of the White House. The message is clear. Fidel Castro is not only involved with drugs, he is about to become a major player. He has contacted key drug lords throughout South America, Mexico and Panama and invited them to a demonstration of a new delivery device. This device offers minimum detection, little or no risk to personnel and can be obtained for a moderate investment. He calls for a meeting to be held on December 24th at a small island near Guadeloupe. His plans are to sail from Cuba incognito aboard a private motor yacht. His guests would arrive on chartered yachts from neighboring islands, Guadeloupe and Martinique.

The President of the United States agrees with his advisers. It would be an opportunity they could not ignore. Castro would be cruising on open seas on what appeared to be a personal trip. Based on information received from Cuba, there would be no type of military or civilian escorts involved, however no information on the type of protection on board. The President gives the order to activate a plan to destroy Castro. One man, Daniel J. O'Brien is selected to design and execute the plan, code named "Operation Yuletide".

This is the story of Dan O'Brien's plan and the men and women who get trapped in it. It is a story about a seventy-five foot luxury sailing yacht that is converted into a killer-hunter with one mission, to find and destroy Fidel Castro. It's the story of a Captain and his crew who have orders to capture and secure Castro's "device". It is the story of a dictator, who sees himself as the last true Communist leader desperate to save his country and his people and bring his most hated neighbor, the United States, to its knees.

Sail aboard the super yacht ISLAND DRUMMER with her determined crew. Explore the beauty of the Caribbean, its many romantic islands surrounded by the mysterious and unpredictable Caribbean Sea. Go ashore on the largest island in the West Indies, Cuba, and meet its famous leader, Fidel Castro. Learn of his goals and fears. Meet the dedicated men who will follow him to his end.

Live the adventure of the hunt aboard the ISLAND DRUMMER as she stalks her prey. Spend Christmas Eve on anything but a Silent Night, Holy Night.

CHAPTER ONE

The Christmas Tree

Guanajay, Cuba
Sunday, March 17, 1985
1300 hours

Carlos Lucia stood on the front porch of his modest home looking down the narrow dirt road that led to the Havana-San Julian highway. The mid-day trade winds from the east felt cool against his brow but he could feel beads of perspiration running down his spine as he nervously checked his watch, it was fourteen minutes past one. He could hear music and children laughing coming from behind the house and knew his wife Teresa, would soon be calling him to join the family for their ritual Sunday luncheon.

He was about to enter the house when he noticed a cloud of dust rising over the poinciana trees that lined the road from the highway to his home. Through squinting eyes he watched the vehicle moving swiftly up the hill and to his relief he identified the square silhouette of the rusty Willys station wagon that belonged to his close friend and brother-in-law, Colonel Luis Navarro.

Carlos got in the wagon and motioned to Luis to continue down the drive where his sister, Teresa, her three daughters and five grandchildren warmly greeted him. After explaining that he had business to discuss with Luis, Carlos kissed his wife on the cheek took a bottle of wine from the table and got back into the wagon.

"Luis, drive down to the shed".

Luis drove slowly down the dirt road until he reached the shed that housed a rusting tractor and a 1949 Ford flatbed truck.

They left the wagon, entered the shed and sat on the dusty flat bed of the truck. It was cool there and the view looking back to the house was spectacular. The small white frame house trimmed in light blue glistened against the deep blue cloudless sky. The women were colorfully dressed and the children appeared like small cotton balls being tossed in the wind as they danced to music played on an old record player.

Luis leaned back on his elbows and took a deep breath.

"Carlos, if only we could spend all our days like this."

He pulled himself up and placed his arm across the broad back of his friend. They silently stared into each other's eyes for a moment. Carlos reached for the bottle of wine and pulled the cork with his teeth.

11

"I drink to you, my friend, in hopes that you have brought good news." Carlos took a long swallow from the bottle.

Luis took the bottle from Carlos and studied the bubbles foaming around the surface of the wine.

"Contact has been made my friend, they have worked out a communication system for us, now we can start to exchange information safely."

Carlos grabbed the wine bottle out of Luis's hand. He lifted the bottle as if making a toast. "To freedom, to our families, to Saint Christopher".

Luis laughed, "Saint Christopher?"

"Of course, who do you think navigates my plane?"

Luis slid down off the truck, turned and looked up at his smiling brother-in-law. "Carlos, you must have your flight schedules ready to pass on as soon as possible."

"Flight schedules? What the hell do they need my flight schedules for?"

"They need to know what airports you will be flying to in the next few months and which airports are also served by Eastern Airlines. This is very important, Carlos, you will be carrying coded messages from me and passing them on to agents at these airports disguised as maintenance or baggage handlers."

"I don't like this, Luis, how do they expect me to make contact with people I don't know?"

"Easy, my friend, you need two identical flashlights. You carry one in your flight bag, right? Well, you need to match that one, or find two new ones."

"Flashlights? I'm going to be sending messages by flashing a light at someone?"

"No Carlos, The messages will be in the flashlight, that's all I know right now." Have you said anything about our plans to my sister?"

"No, I don't want to say anything until the time comes. I don't think it is wise for you to talk to Melinda, either. What we are doing is too dangerous, especially for you."

"Yes, my friend, but we may need their help to exchange our messages back and forth. They see each other more regularly then we do. One thing you and I can't do is start changing our family habits, like meeting more often."

"Luis, do you think we are being watched?"

Before Luis could answer, the ground beneath them began to tremble and loose windowpanes in the garage began to vibrate. Carlos looked up the hill to check on his family. They were standing motionless on the lawn looking towards the south. Before he could step outside the shed to investigate, ear splitting reports, like thousands of firecrackers forced him to cover his ears. A roll of thunder vibrated over and then through them, before it then continued echoing off the hillsides.

"Jesus Christ," Carlos screamed as he ran up the hill to his family.

Luis stopped and looked up just in time to see the underbellies of three MIG-29 Fulcrums in tight formation flying north at 4000 feet. About a thousand yards ahead he saw another chevron of MIG's a little higher and turning to the northwest. Luis stood and watched the sleek jets disappear. He looked up the hill where Carlos stood holding his wife, Teresa.

"Those are the new MIG Fulcrums, Carlos. They must be the new squadron out of San Julian. They are flying to Havana to show off."

Carlos waved his hand at Luis, turned around and led Teresa towards the picnic table where their family sat waiting for them. Luis got back into the station wagon and started up the hill. He blew the horn and the children yelled "Buenos dias, Uncle Luis." Carlos and Teresa just waved, he knew that the sight of the MIGs burned deeper scars in their hearts and increased his sister's concern for her husband of twenty-two years.

Luis was about to drive onto the highway when a convoy of Soviet-built Ural two-ton troop carriers moved swiftly past him heading south. A few soldiers gave friendly waves from their dusty olive drab transports. He recognized the insignias and standards on the vehicles as the 55th Artillery Brigade, probably reservists heading for the new firing range at Camp Batabano. Luis waited patiently until the last truck passed then pulled onto the highway that headed north to Mariano, his hometown.

The White House, Washington D.C.
Tuesday, July 9th, 1985
0830 Hours

The door to the Oval Office opened and Dorothy Cox entered.

"Mr. President, Mr. O'Brien is here."

"Fine, Dorothy, please show him in, and when Admiral Koster arrives let me know and have him wait in your office."

"Yes, Mr. President." Mrs. Cox eased the door open, turned and spoke to the tall middle-aged man standing patiently next to her desk.

"The President will see you now, Mr. O'Brien."

Dan O'Brien hesitated for a moment, reached to check if his tie was properly centered, tightened his grip on the handle of his attaché case and stepped into the bright Oval office. He noticed that, to his left a number of men were seated around a large table, but his eyes were fixed on the large mahogany desk a few yards ahead of him. At first he could only make out the dark silhouette of a man standing behind the desk, framed against large windows where sheer white curtains filtered the morning sun that brightened the historic room.

The President's raspy voice broke the silence.

"Good morning, Mr. O'Brien, I have been looking forward to meeting you."

O'Brien responded as he slowly walked to meet the President for the first time.

"Good morning, Mr. President." Much to his surprise, the President was taller than he expected. His light gray eyes seemed lost in his pale skin and he was much older that he pictured.

The President put out his hand and they shook hands. The President put his big hand on O'Brien's shoulder and directed him towards the center of the room where a group of men were rising from their chairs.

"Gentlemen, I want you to meet Daniel Patrick O'Brien, better known to this club as Santa Claus."

A burst of laughter filled the room. O'Brien smiled as he scanned the six men now moving towards him to shake his hand. He shook their hands and greeted them in his best baritone voice. "My pleasure, pleased to meet you."

O'Brien recognized two of the men; Ian Billings, Director of the CIA, and General William Boyce. The President began making the formal introductions.

"Dan, meet Charlie Ingram, Attorney General". The rather short, overweight man smiled at O'Brien but said nothing.

"You probably know this fellow, Ian Billings, Director of CIA".

"Yes, sir, how are you? We met last October in Annapolis at the Air Force Navy football game."

"Of course, good to see you again, Dan."

The President continued.

"This is Roger Weijlard, State Department, Carlton Simms, Director FBI, Lou Bollman, Miami Bureau Chief and last but not least, Jesus Souza, Eastern Airlines, who I understand you have already met."

O'Brien smiled as he studied Souza.

"Yes, we have spoken a few times. Pleasure to meet you Mr. Souza." Souza was much smaller and younger than he had imagined and very athletic looking. His dark skin was accented by neatly combed straight black hair, dark brown almond shaped eyes and a large broad smile.

"How are you, Dan?" Souza asked.

"Nervous," O'Brien responded.

The group laughed at O'Brien's comment and returned to their places around the table.

"Gentlemen, be seated", the President said, as he pulled a nearby wing chair into the circle and motioned O'Brien to sit.

The sound of a distant buzzer came from the President's desk.

"Excuse me, I believe the Chairman of the Joint Chiefs has arrived". The President went to the door leading to Dorothy Cox's office, and walked out.

Before O'Brien could bring his attention back to the table, a loud raspy voice spoke out.

"Mr. O'Brien."

O'Brien scanned the faces not knowing who had spoken to him.

"I understand you spent some time under the command of my old friend Paul Tibbets down in Florida during the sixties?"

O'Brien, relieved to see who was talking to him, answered. "Yes, General. I was once attached to a wing that he commanded at McDill in Tampa."

"You boys were pushing B-36's around the skies for SAC back then, that was some flying machine. I always wanted to get a shot at flying one of them big-ass birds."

"I'm afraid I came after the B-36, sir. I was in a B-47 wing, Sir. I believe the 36's left around '56." O'Brien responded.

"Yeah, old Tibbs was quite a guy. I spent some time with him in Europe after he came back from the Pacific in '45. Do you know where he is now?"

O'Brien wondered if he was being tested.

"I believe I read somewhere that he was managing a fleet of corporate jets somewhere out in Ohio, sir."

"Oh really? Well, did you know they have his famous B-29, the ENOLA GAY sitting in a warehouse just a few miles outside of D.C.?"

"Yes, sir, I believe I read they are getting it ready to be displayed in some new museum?"

Roger Wiejlard tapped his pipe in the large ashtray, as he interrupted the conversation.

"Never happen, Dan. Too many politicians and organizations won't let that happen, mark my word. That plane represents an important time in our history, but it also represents an event that many Americans still feel ashamed of. Personally, I think it should be scrapped."

"I'm sorry you feel that way, Roger. The ENOLA GAY was a very important instrument of the war and should be displayed as a reminder to those..." General Boyce did not finish his sentence. The door to the Oval Office opened and the President and Admiral Thomas J. Koster, Chairman of the Joint Chiefs of Staff, walked in.

O'Brien was surprised and impressed at the physical size of the Admiral. He was somewhat overweight, but his six-foot plus frame countered his bulkiness. He had thick white hair, and white bushy eyebrows that nearly hid his small deep-set eyes. On his chest a cluster of decorations displaying his service record of four decades. In 1942, he was a carrier pilot flying off the USS Yorktown and was credited helping to sink the Japanese carrier "Hiryu" during the battle of Midway on June 5th and damaging the battleship "Mikuma" on June 6th. Before the war ended, he was credited for shooting down eleven Japanese planes and was shot down twice, the first time flying support for the invasion of Guam in a F4F Wildcat, the second time in a new F-4U Corsair over Iwo Jima. When the Korean War broke out in 1950, he served as commander of a carrier air wing. During the Viet Nam conflict, he was Commander in Chief of the Pacific Fleet. Now at the age of sixty-four, he was the President's closest friend and Chairman of the Joint Chiefs of Staff.

"Good morning, good morning," the Admiral said as he walked swiftly around to his chair. He patted General Boyce gently on the back as he dropped his brief case and hat down on the table and sat down.

"Be seated, gentlemen, please. Let's get this show on the road, the President and I have plans to go fishing later today," Koster said winking at the President.

The President chuckled then introduced O'Brien.

"General, this is Dan O'Brien, the reason why we are here, or I should say, you are all here today." He glanced at his watch.

"I hate to leave, but I have a country to run and a press conference in nine minutes to give my report on the new trade agreements with Japan. By the way, the Vice President sends his regrets that he can't join you. He is tied up on the hill."

The President left the room to a barrage of "good-lucks" and "Give them hells."

16

"O.K., Dan O'Brien, we are here to see what you've got in your bag of tricks."

The Admiral never looked at O'Brien, he went right into his brief case, pulled out folders and started flipping through them.

O'Brien's stomach tightened, he was nervous and he didn't want to open his mouth until he knew his brain was in gear. He opened his attaché case and pulled out a stack of hard covered documents, neatly typed and labeled. As he spread them out for distribution, he responded to the Admiral. "Sir, here are my ideas I feel might work for this operation."

Admiral Koster looked up at O'Brien with his piercing green eyes. He pushed away from the table and sat back deep in his chair.

"Mr. O'Brien, being there are only a few of us here who know what's going on involving this operation, how about bringing us up to speed."

O'Brien cleared his throat, then began. "Yes, well, you see, when I was first contacted by Mr. Harris from CIA Headquarters, I was asked to join him and General Ross at the Pentagon and was briefed on what was going on in Cuba."

Ian Billings interrupted O'Brien.

"Excuse me, Admiral, in all fairness to Mr. O'Brien, to you and to members of this committee, I think that it would be best for me to give you a report first, on how this operation actually started."

O'Brien smiled at Billings. Billings knew O'Brien had only been partially briefed, there were many things that he had not been told.

Koster pulled himself back to the table and gave his attention to Ian Billings sitting directly across the table from him. "Fine, Mr. Billings. I agree, I think it's best we all know how this whole thing got started."

Billings began. "This operation began last January. We received a message from one of our agents in Cuba, that one of Castro's top security officers wanted to make a deal. He wanted to trade secret information regarding military strengths, equipment and locations of new surface to air missile sites for protection and assistance for his family coming out of Cuba. After approving his request, we learned he was Colonel Luis Navarro. We also learned that his brother-in-law, Captain Carlos Lucia, was a senior pilot for state-owned Cubana airlines and he also wanted to leave Cuba with his family. During our investigation we learned that Colonel Navarro is a member of Castro's secret police and has family living in Homestead, Florida. His father is terminally ill and his mother lives in a nursing home. The family's only income comes from his youngest sister, Catherine, a telephone operator at a hotel on Miami Beach." Billings glanced down at an open folder and continued. "In 1957 at the age of sixteen, Navarro joined

Castro's army as a runner operating between the mountain camps in eastern Cuba. When Castro took over the country, Luis was one of his front line fighters and given the rank of Captain. In 1982 he was promoted to full Colonel and picked by Castro to serve on his elite secret police force and became one of Castro's personal guards and security adviser."

Billings closed the folder and opened another, continuing. "Carlos Lucia, age 49 is married to Navarro's oldest sister, Teresa and has three children. Lucia, a childhood friend of Navarro, got his private pilot's license when he was fifteen. He moved to Miami when he was nineteen and trained for his commercial pilot licenses. He flew for a short time for a Miami based cargo company, flying DC-3's, C-46's and DC-4's all over South America. In the spring of 1957 he returned to Cuba to join his friend Navarro, and to serve Castro. He was assigned to fly small twin engine aircraft supporting Castro's supply lines throughout Cuba carrying weapons, supplies, food and sometimes Fidel himself. Soon after the revolution, Carlos was flying commercial again for Cuba's new state airline, Cubana. Once again, he found himself flying old DC 3's and a DC-6 that was abandoned at Havana Airport during the siege. After the takeover, Luis and Carlos stayed very close. Carlos lives in Guanajay and Luis lives in Mariano."

Admiral Koster picked up his pen and pointed it at Billings.

"Excuse me, Mr. Billings, I don't want to sound like some smart ass politician, but just how much trust are you putting in this source of information that you hope to get out of Cuba, I'm impressed with these bios, however..."

Billings interrupted.

"Sir, our sources in Cuba have given us no reason to doubt them. We have agents in Cuba for over twenty years and have been very successful getting sound information out even if we have to meet on the open seas. We will not use radio communications for this operation, the Cubans have very sophisticated listening devices and can locate signals in minutes, it's too risky for our informants. Setting up a dependable communications system for this operation is the sole creation of Mr. Souza, and at this point I would like Mr. Souza to continue."

Souza smiled. "Yes, sir, thank you sir. It seems that over the past ten years, Luis and Carlos became concerned about the direction that Castro was leading the country. They resent having so many Russians living on the island and more important, they were concerned about their families and their future. It was decided that they would put together a plan to get all of them out of Cuba at the same time. Carlos, a senior pilot for Cubana Airlines, has been flying Soviet-built Antonov 24's, a turbo prop medium size passenger plane to various South American countries and Mexico. His plan was to fly his family out of the country to Chile, or Mexico on special visiting visas. He would fly later to the city that they were visiting, pick them up and hijack his own plane and fly to Panama. This plan inspired his brother-in-law Luis to come up with a better plan. He knew someone who could make contact with our agents and get word out to American authorities for help. This was done through one of our agents posing as a commercial fisherman fishing out of a village on Cuba's northeast shore."

Billings excused himself and interrupted Souza.

"Sir, we were having a brain storming session at Langley on how we could help these two Cubans. We definitely wanted their information, that was our first priority. Then, someone came up with a brilliant idea. The Cuban pilot, Carlos, flies into countries and cities that a couple of our domestic airlines serve. So, we did some research and were surprised at how many cities in South America and Mexico we did share, especially with Pan American and Eastern Airlines. We ended up selecting Eastern, who had the most flights to airports that Carlos flew into. We had to work out a communication network, so we started scouting Eastern to see if they had any Cuban employees who held management jobs in customer services like ticketing. During the screening process one name kept coming up, Jesus Souza. Souza was the manager for customer services dealing with baggage complaints out of South America, Mexico and Caribbean bases. He looked perfect on paper, so we had Lou Bollman out of the Miami office bring Souza in. They learned that he was a nine-year veteran at Eastern, single, no police record and a active volunteer in the Liberation Army and has family in Cuba."

Billings took a drink of water and continued. "Mr. Souza was asked to report to the FBI office in Miami. After briefing Souza on the story of his two countrymen, and the plan to set up a dependable communications system, he agreed to help anyway he could. In less than twenty four hours, Jesus Souza marched back into Lou Bollman's office and laid out a plan he felt could work. As it turned out his plan was perfect."

Lou Bollman smiled and shook his head.   "You know, you just have to love this guy, Jesus Souza. Not only did he come up with the idea on setting up the communication network, he did all the interviewing and helped hand pick the teams that would be sent into the field. Then, he went to Eastern's president to make all the arrangements we needed."

Souza interrupted Bollman.

"Well, you needed Eastern, you needed a team of Latin men who could be trained to do the job. I personally know the president and every airport we would be using. You could not have done it without me, yes?"

"No, you're right, Jesus." Billing said laughing.

Bollman continued. "Here is how the plan works. We made a deal with Eastern to hire a number of new employees, all Latin men, as mechanics and baggage handlers. These men went through a crash course at the FBI school, then were sent out in the field for a couple of weeks to learn the basics of their new trades. Two weeks later they were sent down to airports in South America and Mexico. Each of them had the description of Carlos Lucia, and when possible, his flight schedules to their airports. When Carlos arrived, he had a procedure he would perform that would tip the agent off if he was carrying a message from Cuba."

Bollman turned to Souza. "Mr. Souza, why don't you explain how the exchange works."

"Yes, sir." Souza said and continued. "There is a mandatory inspection that Cubana pilots must do after they land. After the passengers, co-pilot and stewards deplane, Carlos will leave the plane. If he is holding his flashlight in his right hand that means he is carrying a message. The message is actually inside the flashlight. His next move is to go directly under the left engine and enter the landing gear wheel well. He pretends that he is inspecting the gear. He places the flashlight on a ledge just over the landing door and continues his inspection. When the post flight is completed he goes to the pilots' waiting room to join his crew. Before leaving for his next flight, he will return to the wheel well and retrieve his flashlight. While the plane was being serviced and baggage removed or stowed, our agent carefully exchanges the flashlight with one that he carries. The messages are exchanged. The airport agent then goes to our Eastern counter and sends the coded message by telex to me at Eastern's baggage claim department at Miami. I send it on to Mr. Billings, who has it decoded."

"Brilliant, absolutely brilliant, young man. I congratulate you on your plan, which I understand is working very well?" Koster asked.

"That's why we are here, Admiral. Three weeks ago, we received word about Castro and this strange voyage he is taking aboard a private yacht in December."

"O.K., thank you, Mr. Souza. Now, can we get back to you, Mr. O'Brien? Let's hear about your plan of how you expect to catch Castro at sea, but before we do, is anyone besides me hungry here? Would someone please go out and tell old lady Cox we need some coffee and donuts in here?"

Lou Bollman volunteered and went to the door.

"Mr. O'Brien? You have the floor," Koster said as he fell back into his seat.

"Well, as I said earlier, when I was being briefed by Mr. Harris and General Ross, they asked if I could design a plan that could be used to trap Castro on the open seas. I told them I would need a few days to think about it. They gave me two hours. Later, I met with them again and told them that I thought a plan could be designed that might work, but it would take some serious investigating. At this time they briefed me on the Cuban intelligence network, and told me that Mr. Souza, who I would be working with, would contact me. I was given an office in the Pentagon, a new secretary whose name I still can't remember, and told that I was to report only to Mr. Harris and General Ross as soon as I had a plan put together. That same evening, Mr. Souza called and briefed me on the communications network."

O'Brien took a drink of water, checked his notes, then continued. "I called Mr. Harris at the Agency at 0900 hours yesterday to advise him that I had a plan for consideration. He called me back within minutes and told me to meet with him and General Ross at 1400 hours in the General's office. We went over the plan and they both agreed to take the next step. Last night I received a call from General Ross asking me to meet with him at his office at 0700. He handed me these copies which outline my suggestions, briefed me about this meeting, then drove me here to The White House to meet with the President, and this committee."

O'Brien's throat was dry, he took another long drink of water. He looked at the faces around the table. Nobody spoke, their eyes were on the Admiral, who thumbed through his folders, pulled one out of the stack and opened it. He leaned forward on his elbows, clasped his big hands together, and looked into O'Brien's nervous eyes.

"O.K., son, I apologize, I'm somewhat in the dark on this operation myself, and personally I think it's too damn risky, however, my friends here feel differently. They believe it can be done with the right man at the helm." The Admiral paused, then relaxed back in his chair. "After hours of research, Mr. O'Brien," he continued, "your name came up many times, mind you, with a few others. However, you got the job." He picked up a manila folder and studied the document inside. "You had a very successful sixteen years with the Air Force. You hold the reserve grade of a full bird Colonel, spent four years at MIT, three years attending two war colleges and now you work as an adviser over at the Department of Defense under General Harry Copeland, a Marine."

O'Brien smiled. " A damn good Marine, sir."

"Yes, but he will be a pissed off Marine, when you resign today. But, not to worry, I will make the duty call to Harry and get you off the hook. You can go back as soon as this operation is over."

O'Brien nodded, "Thank you, sir."

"One thing on a personal note. I see here that you lost your wife in 1970 while she was in labor with your first child." The Admiral looked over the top of the folder directly into O'Brien's eyes."

"That's correct, sir. My wife Carrie and my unborn daughter died in an Air Force hospital."

"Yes, I see that. You went through some therapy, and that worked, correct?"

"Yes, sir, I.."

Koster interrupted. "That's alright, son, no need to explain. Now let's look at your ideas, and would somebody, please, check on old lady Cox. How long does it take to get a cup of coffee around here?"

O'Brien passed out the copies of his plan to each member of the group. He had two left over, both labeled OPERATION YULETIDE in bold red print. One read "President of the United States", and the other "Vice President of the United States." He moved the portfolios across the table to Admiral Koster, who slipped them into his brief case.

For the next few hours, the plan was reviewed and scrutinized carefully. The group only broke briefly for lunch that was brought in. Each member of the committee continued to remind O'Brien that under no circumstances could any part of this operation be traced back to any individual, department or agency of the United States Government. All participants would have to pass a rigid security clearance, and if at any time there were an information leak, or even a suspicion that the operation might be exposed, it would be terminated.

The operation's code name, OPERATION YULETIDE, made it easy for O'Brien to use code names connected with the holiday season, like Christmas Tree, Rudolf, Santa Claus and Blitzen. He would use code names throughout the operation. He code-named the communications network, "Christmas Tree.

Each airport where agents were planted would be assigned a color of a Christmas tree light, as in blue, amber, yellow, red, green. This would be the code name of that base. He felt that because Souza came up with the ingenious plan that he should be given the code name "Star".

Admiral Koster flipped O'Brien's brief proposal closed and covered it with his hand. He looked around the table looking for doubt on the faces of the committee. He glanced at his watch. "Gentlemen, let's take a fifteen minute break here, so we can all do what we have to do, but be back here on time so we can finish this up."

The Admiral stood up, arched his back, put his hands on his hips and moved his head back and forth to exercise his neck muscles. Meanwhile, members of the committee were heading for the door to Dorothy Cox's office and the executive restrooms. O'Brien remained standing at the table putting his proposal back in order.

"Dan, let's you and I step out and smell some of the President's roses in the garden."

O'Brien looked up at the Admiral who was already moving around the table and heading for a pair of French doors across the room. He knew the Admiral was going to cross-examine him on his plan. During the session Koster had asked few questions, but had taken more notes than anyone.

"Yes, sir, should I bring..."

"Yes, grab a couple of those unripe apples that Dorothy Cox brought in."

The air was still and the scent from the roses along the walk was refreshing, but the heat and humidity were too much for O'Brien. He removed his jacket loosened his tie and unbuttoned the top button on his shirt as he walked in stride with the Admiral.

"Hope you don't mind, sir, but I don't take to the heat that well."

"Not at all, make yourself comfortable, but you better get used to the heat, son. If this plan gets off the ground, you could be in for the fires of hell, do you understand?"

The Admiral stopped beside a small concrete bench and motioned to O'Brien to sit. O'Brien placed his jacket beside him, fished out a handkerchief and blotted his face.

"Yes, I know this whole thing could blow up in my face, and I also know that I would be left to hang by myself, because the Government ain't coming to the rescue. However, I am certain I can pull this off, sir."

"Tell me, O'Brien, just how much do you know about Cuba today?"

"Do you mean politically, its military strength, its population demographics, its economic value to Moscow or who is who in government?"

Koster chuckled, and looked down as if checking the condition of his high gloss oxfords. "Let's start with the military."

"Yes sir, let's see. Cuba has a minimum of 300,000 troops under arms, well trained in offense and defense. Currently, Castro is spending nearly one billion dollars annually to update his military, in the air, on land and sea. Two weeks ago for example, Castro received six more MIG 29 Fulcrums, bringing a total now of over seventy in his air fleets. He has also taken delivery of four new Antonov 72 Coaler transports, bringing that fleet number up to sixteen. Last September, another Mariel class frigate was added to the fleet, now numbering three, and four new Osa II missile patrol boats were delivered, bringing that total up to twenty-two. Sixteen new SA-10 and SA-12 installations are now in place as they phase out the old SA-2 and 5 systems and it is estimated that no less than twelve hundred SA-14 and 16 sites are now in place. There is new construction taking place in Baracoa, including new docks, warehouses and barracks, which is a bit frightening. This is their major port for troop dispersal. One more item of concern is the new runways and hangar development going on at Antonio Maceo. I would guess this will be one of the largest fighter bases in Cuba shortly."

Admiral Koster's eyes widened as he studied O'Brien. He was really impressed, but refused to let on. "How deep is the Havana Channel between markers twenty one and twenty four?"

"Fifty-four feet at mean low tide, sir."

"O'Brien, is there a marker number twenty one in the channel?"

"I really don't know, sir, but I know its depth."

"How did you know about the new construction going on at Baracoa?"

"I read about it in Newsweek, two weeks ago, sir."

For a few long seconds, the two men sat silent, occasionally glancing at each other.

"Listen, Dan, let me tell you where I am coming from, and some of the nightmares that I must live with."

"Sir, I don't mean to interrupt, but, I was just about to bring the Committee an update on the situation with Castro down there, I mean about Castro's voyage, when you called the break. We received some very important news regarding Castro's trip last night that answered some major questions. Souza brought the message with him from Miami and General Ross advised me this morning."

"Is Ian aware of this?"

"I'm sure he is, sir, Souza went right to his office when he arrived. Two of the main questions we were in the dark about, regarding Castro on the high seas were finally answered. First, was Castro going to be escorted by other vessels and if so, would it be the Russians? The message says, no escorts. Castro will be sailing solo on this voyage, no escort vessels of any kind. He is going to be traveling on a luxury yacht, a rather large one at that, over 100 feet heading to the island of Guadaloupe. It appears that whatever Fidel is up to, the Russians are either against it, or they don't know about it. He appears to be doing this on his own with only a few of his elite officers aware of his plan, including, I might add, our contact, Colonel Navarro.

Navarro says that Castro is bringing some kind of a "device" on this trip to show to his buyers, what ever that means. This might also explain why he chose Christmas week for his trip. It makes sense. He could easily slip away then."

The Admiral took a deep breath, then asked. "What do you think this "device" could be, Mr. O'Brien?"

"I don't know, Admiral. Maybe guns, or some new kind of super electronics, it's anyone's guess, sir. But all the more reason why we need to know what he is up to and try to stop him if we can."

"Well, Mr. O'Brien, your Christmas tree is bearing some good fruit, but that tree has many lights, and at anytime, they could all blow out. From what I heard this morning, this plan would be like taking the USS Kennedy up the Mississippi without a chart."

"I know it sounds weak, sir, but you have to think like I do, sir. We are going to have Castro off his island. He is going to be cruising in the Caribbean for days on a luxury yacht without an escort. He will be stationary at one point, anchored somewhere around Guadeloupe."

"I know how you feel, Dan, believe me. Shit, a chance to drown that bearded bastard, hell, if I was twenty years younger, I would love to be the kid that plants some plastic under his ass."

O'Brien jumped up, startling the Admiral.

"What the hell's with you, O"Brien? Something bite you on the ass?"

"Sir, what you just said, about the attaching plastics on his hull. I, ah, there is nothing in my proposal that, how did you know I was thinking of using plastic?"

"It makes sense doesn't it? I mean if it was my call and my mission that's what I would do, find a way to get under that yacht and plant some CR-12 under his hairy ass."

O'Brien was speechless. He sat and looked at the Admiral as he rubbed an apple up and down his sleeve, giving it a satin shine. "What the hell is CR-12, sir?"

"None of your damn business, unless you need some."

O'Brien walked in tight circles, shaking his head and thinking to himself. "This guy is not only tough, but ten paces ahead. How did he know that this was my plan, it wasn't in the proposal, unless Ross or Harris tipped him. I mentioned to them I might use explosives, but there is no mention about plastics or how I proposed to kill the man."

"Stop trying to figure it out, Dan. I just put myself in your shoes and went for it, ok? Maybe I got lucky and gave you an idea you didn't have. There are a few other things you missed, O'Brien, like the United States

Navy, for example. Did you know that there were two carrier groups scheduled to go on maneuvers in the Caribbean in December? Of course not. Did you know that no less than four Ohio Class attack subs were going to be working out of Guantanamo in December? No, of course not, but the Russians do, Dan. That might be the reason why they don't want to play in Castro's game."

O'Brien felt like a lead foot just stepped on him. "Sir, I didn't even think about the Navy being down there."

Koster raised his hand. "Relax, Dan, neither does the Navy Department. Oh, they know we are planning the exercise, but the budgets are not completed and if I must, I can send them around into the Gulf of Mexico. The boys will have to trade in San Juan and St. Thomas for New Orleans and Mobile for their shore fun."

The Admiral checked his watch, stood up with O'Brien's jacket in his hand and threw it to him. "Come on, let's go hear the rest of your Charles Dickens story."

"Right, sir. Sir, would you mind telling me just what is CR-12?"

"You tell me, O'Brien, just how do you plan to approach Castro on the open seas? Do you plan on releasing a Harpoon missile from a Caribbean airliner?"

O'Brien chuckled, then looked the Admiral straight in the eyes. "I plan to use a sailboat, sir."

The Admiral laughed. "Of course, I should have known, it was in your 201 file. You are a romantic sail-bagger."

Koster turned his large frame away from O'Brien and walked through the open French doors into the Oval Office. He stopped and grabbed O'Brien by the arm. In a low voice he said, "Do me a favor, if anyone asks, as I just did, don't say anything about a sailboat. Just say you're still working on a plan. We'll save that news for when you present your total plan. Let's not give these guys a reason to keep us here until the Johnny Carson Tonight Show comes on, understand?"

"Yes, I understand, sir." O'Brien said with a smile.

As they walked up to the large table, O'Brien looked across the room and caught Souza's eye. A wink from O'Brien told Souza the operation was on.

CHAPTER 2

White House
1723 hours

The dark blue Chrysler sedan eased past the White House guard post onto Pennsylvania Avenue. It was rush hour in Washington and every government employee was scrambling for lane position to get out of the city and into the suburbs.

O'Brien sat motionless in the passenger seat, trying not to show any nervousness to the driver. He finally spoke.

"I really appreciate this lift, Ian, I completely forgot that General Ross drove me over this morning."

Ian Billings smiled as he pulled at his tie and loosened the top collar button of his shirt.

"Glad to help, Dan, and it's not out of my way. Besides, it gives me a chance to talk with you privately. I still have a few cobwebs hanging around inside my skull. You sure blew some socks off today with your plan, you know that?"

O'Brien knowing he was sitting beside one of the most brilliant minds in Washington did not want to appear intimidated. He sat relaxed watching the traffic. He knew Ian Billings had only been two years in the driver's seat of the Agency, but was already a legend within the intelligence community and one of the President's closest friends and advisers.

"Well, I was most happy that I was not recommended for a mental institution. Admiral Koster had me sweating through my briefs all day. Is he as tough as he looks?"

Billings glanced at O'Brien with a boyish grin.

"Dan, he is just cautious, he doesn't like to mess around in pastures where there are no trees to hide behind, if you know what I mean. He's a good man and will get you everything you need to get this operation completed, but a word to the wise, don't under any circumstance run around his stern, that's where he carries the big guns, and he will use them to blow you out of the water. Do like he told you. Let the experts do the thinking, you just do the planning."

The car phone rang, and Billings responded. "July one, go scramble." Billings ran his finger over the receiver buttons and watched the scanners blinking lights. Three lights flashed on. "Go ahead."

O'Brien turned his head and tried to concentrate on the outside world without success. He was riding next to the number one man in the CIA.

"This call could be coming from anywhere," O'Brien thought. "It could be a serious emergency, or a national tragedy. We could even be at war with Russia, and this could be the final call before the flash."

"I have him right here, George, yes, that's affirmative. Give me those times again. Right, you will pick O'Brien up on the way? right, I'll be back to you in a few minutes."

Billings replaced the phone on the receiver. "Well, they're not wasting any time. I sure hope you don't have any plans for tonight or tomorrow, that was George Harris, he just informed me that you're to be at Andrews Air Force Base at 0700 hours with your final plans and plenty of Tums. You are going on Air Force One for a few hours."

"Air Force One? I thought that the Admiral and the President were going....."

"Oh, they still plan to, but the President feels that Operation Yuletide needs to be thoroughly discussed and wants all the players in place, pronto. We will have all the people you need on board to get this operation off the ground. You will need to fill in all the details that were not covered today, and be prepared to have answers for Koster. He is not sold on your preliminary plans. He feels there are be too many people involved, outside people, the kind we have no control over. For example, you mentioned today that you needed to contact Senator Gordon Hauser. Why do you want a senator from Florida involved, especially one that opposes everything the President does?"

O'Brien was embarrassed, he never thought about Hauser's political position and needed to cover his ass to impress Billings that he had given this problem some thought.

"Oh, I understand there is no love lost between Hauser and the President and I don't plan to have Hauser involved as a player by no means," O'Brien continued. "Gordon and I go way back when I was stationed at McDill in Tampa. He was a young struggling attorney then and we met at a sailing club and did quite a bit of racing together. He grew up in St. Petersburg were many sailboat manufacturers are located and knows every boat builder on a first name basis. I need his advice to find the right yachts I need to pull this operation off and he can save me a lot of time and trouble, he is the only person I know in Washington with that kind of knowledge and contacts."

"Alright, Dan, but be careful this could get a little sticky with the President. Tell me something, why a sailboat? I would think that a power boat would be more practical for the intercept, plus you would have speed and..."

O'Brien interrupted. "Innocence, Ian, a sailboat has the virtue of innocence. I can make a sailboat look like it's in distress using a few phony props, like torn and ripped sails, broken rigging and spray paint. I have to sell a disaster at sea to the captain and crew aboard Castro's yacht, the sailboat can play this role."

"Dan, if I recall, your plan is to be on the same course as Castro's yacht?"

"Correct, I am counting on the law of the seas. I want to have that sailboat adrift looking like it was damaged in a storm or disabled by a minor explosion in her engine room. She is going to be posing as a charter yacht with a captain, crew and a number of charter guests, shaken up, but none requiring medical aid. When Castro's yacht is in radar range, we will start broadcasting very weak SOS radio calls on the standard VHF emergency channel. When Castro's yacht gets closer to take a look, they will see the damage we created to the yacht. The crew and guests will put on a stage show, screaming and yelling, doing anything to get attention. The idea is to get Castro's yacht to stop, which it will do."

Billings smiled and shook his head. "What makes you so sure he will stop and why would he let some old sailboat detain him?"

"Law of the seas, Ian. No captain is going to ignore another ship in distress, especially on his course. Another fact, in 1956 Castro was returning to Cuba from exile aboard an old American-built yacht that nearly sank, luckily, an American fishing boat spotted them, gave them food, water and helped repair their boat from sinking. I know Castro will order his captain to stop and give aid, I've studied this man, he does have compassion and I'm betting he won't ignore a distressed vessel, he will ask his captain to respond. When they do, we will immediately advise them that we are not sinking and do not require medical assistance, we just need a few supplies, that's important. This way they won't have to worry about assisting us or picking up any passengers, but we do need them to stop. I don't expect or want them to send a boarding party, I just need a verbal exchange. We will have a dinghy in the water with our Captain already on his way to Castro's yacht before they can react. Meanwhile, our mate will be radioing emergency needs, like food and fresh water they can spare, plus electrical parts, like fuses. Our captain will tell them he is working off his batteries and can't start his auxiliary generator, he needs a couple of fuses. He will tell them a fire damaged his fuse panels."

Billings loosened his tie. "Dan, you didn't bring any of this up at the meeting earlier. How will you know that his electrical system will have the type of fuses you need?"

"I plan to know everything about Castro's yacht, especially his electrical systems. We will pretend we have the same type fuse's, all we have to do describe to their crew what type we need. Keep in mind, Ian, they want to get underway as soon as possible. I'm positive they will give us what we need and possibly make radio calls to confirm who we really are and this is important, we need them to verify our existence. We will ask that they make radio calls to advise all ships in the area of our location and situation and further more, the reason I did not go into this earlier, I just now put it together."

Billings shook his head and smiled.

"You see, Ian, once we have them dead in the water, that's when we attach the charges to the hull. We have to keep that yacht idle long enough to get two or three divers under them and set time-delayed charges on her bottom.

"Whoa, Dan, you're in crystal clear Caribbean water, divers will easily be spotted.."

"Nighttime, Ian, we are going to do it at night. Castro is going to be traveling nearly a 1000 miles to reach Guadeloupe from some unknown port in eastern Cuba. I figure his yacht will be cruising between sixteen to twenty knots, tops. That gives us a sixty-hour envelope to work in, which means we have about twenty-five hours of darkness. We just need some luck that we can intercept them at night a good distance from any shoreline and hopefully out of sea lanes away from traffic, except our support freighter."

"Support freighter? Dan, what the hell do you need with a freighter?"

"I need a support vessel in the area to carry men and equipment like the UDT team, their gear and explosives. The freighter is the key vessel that will respond to Castro's yacht when they begin to radio advise to other near-by ships that there is a vessel in distress that may need additional assistance. The freighter will respond to Castro's message asking for location of vessel, then advising they are close and will head their way. This will also prevent other ships from coming to aid the stricken yacht. The freighter, idling ten to fifteen miles north of the intercept will advise that they can be there within the hour. Am I making sense?"

"I think I follow you, but why would Castro radio for additional help?"

"Our Captain will ask him to, remember, we don't want to appear that we are sinking or need any additional help, but our Captain will ask that Castro's Captain put out a immediate advisory on the yacht's condition, not a May Day call. This is important, we need our freighter at this point to get involved in communication so that Castro feels he can get underway and let the freighter take over.."

"I see now, when the freighter responds, this will also discourage any other vessels to come to the scene, right?"

"You got it, Ian." O'Brien had not noticed they just passed through the Pentagon's main gate.

Billings took a deep breath exhaling through his puckered lips in a light whistle.

"Phew, tell me something, Dan. Did you put all this together just now?"

O'Brien gave this question plenty of thought and opted not be completely truthful here.

"Oh, hell no, I have been thinking about this since lunch."

"Well, Dan, I don't know anything about sailboats and even less about the Caribbean, but I do know I am running late for dinner, so, where did you park your sleigh, Santa Claus?"

"Oh, ah, in F lot and by the way, I'm not Santa, I'm Rudolf. The captain of the sailboat, YULETIDE?, he is Santa Claus. Ah, right over there, Ian, that rusty old yellow Volvo wagon."

Ian parked beside the Volvo, put his car in neutral and addressed O'Brien.

"O.K., Rudolf, here is the plan. Get your act together and plan for a long day tomorrow. You will be meeting with a few key people you will be working with on your operation. Simms will have his man there, I will have my man there, and Koster has a Navy man coming, plus the President. Here's the plan. You leave your apartment at 0555 and start walking south down Wisconsin. A Dodge van will pick you up before 0600. You might want to pack some casual stuff and a shaving kit. You're going to California to the President's ranch and may be there a day or two, or you may be sent right back, so be prepared."

Billings offered his hand, O'Brien shook it, opened the door and stepped out of the car.

"Oh Dan, I like the code name for your sailboat, the YULETIDE."

O'Brien smiled and closed the door. He watched Ian's car speed across the tarmac and vanish behind the Pentagon. He turned and looked at the familiar landmarks towering over the trees and the city of Washington. The dome of the capitol building and the Washington monument reflected in a pink glow from the setting sun against the fading blue sky. He took a deep breath. For the first time this day he thought about his emotions and how he felt about the operation. He felt good, confident. Most of all, he felt like a young boy again waiting for the next adventure. He reached deep in his pants pocket and found his keys.

Dan O'Brien's apartment
Wisconsin Avenue
Wednesday, July 10th

O'Brien glanced at the glowing red numbers on his clock radio. It was 3:06. He reached over and pushed the button for the radio, the music was welcome. He concentrated on the song that was playing, it was an old classic, but he could not remember the name, then it came to him, it was an instrumental of the Beatles' classic hit, Hey Jude. He lay there enjoying the music that took his mind off the project. He had worked on the plan until midnight, went to bed but sleep would not come. Visions of problems kept him searching for alternatives. "It will take two identical sailboats to pull this off," he said allowed. "One would be a decoy that would be sacrificed, destroyed and the other, the real YULETIDE would have to be special. It would have to be super fast with hull speeds twice the norm that would cover normal cruising distances in half the time. Jesus, that's it, he cried out. "A sailing yacht with speeds of a motor yacht, maybe more. It would act as a normal luxury yacht, a charter yacht working out of the Virgin Islands."

He leaped out of his bed, picked up his robe and entered the small kitchen and switched on the lights over the island counter. He paused for a second staring at all the debris covering the counter where he had been working. He found the remains of a legal pad, sat down and started writing down his ideas.

"Two sailing yachts, one a super yacht called YULETIDE, that can reach speeds of twenty-five knots at least." He rummaged through all the papers on the counter until he found the nautical sectional charts he had bought on the Caribbean and Cuba. He studied the pencil lines he had made from eastern Cuba to Guadeloupe, which showed the shortest route. He measured the distance to scale, it was nearly 1000 miles. He then took measurements with his ruler at points from St. Croix and Guadeloupe to the route line he penciled in. He drew more lines from these islands to act as intercept locations. He pictured in his mind, two sailing vessels and the support freighter. He would place the freighter due north of the interception, out of sight. It would pose as an innocent island trader with phony cargo making passage from San Juan to one of the Windward Islands.

Next he set up the plan for the two identical sailboats. Yuletide, the super yacht, would be a charter yacht working out of St. Thomas. The second yacht would be working a charter from a different down island port like St. Vincent or St. Lucia. She would take on a special charter group provided by one of the agencies. He studied the chart carefully then made his decision. "They would charter out of St. Lucia, sailing westward towards Jamaica, that would put the yacht on a course in the vicinity of the proposed interception with Castro's yacht."

O'Brien looked at the clock on the oven. He had an hour and a half before pick-up. He needed to get his plan finalized quickly. He set up the Mr. Coffee machine, and went back to the legal pad and started to write down his plan.

The yacht, Yuletide, is in St. Thomas and takes on a charter of two couples plus her crew. These couples would be recruited by one of the agencies. She would leave three days before Christmas, destination St. Martin, a normal charter destination. The captain would file a float plan with his clearinghouse, making sure they were advised of the time of YULETIDE'S departure and the ETA (estimated time of arrival) for St. Martin. This would cover the yachts normal sailing time for a couple of days. Yuletide would depart at dusk, head east and sail past St. John on its southern shore. Once out of sight of landfall, Yuletide would change course and head due south at super speed to be in at the rendezvous position nearly 100 miles away where she would meet with the support freighter and her lookalike sister yacht. The freighter would have all the materials needed to disguise the YULETIDE including new name plates to be installed to cover her stern and bows, plus ragged and torn sails and any other props they would need. Last but not least, the UDT team with their gear and explosives would be standing by on the freighter to board the Yuletide.

The sister yacht, O'Brien decided to name "Seaduce" would sail out of St. Lucia, or St. Vincent as a charter yacht. Like the Yuletide, she would be registered with the local clearinghouse and would advise them of her destination, Jamaica. The charter guests would also be selected by one of the agencies. On the appointed date and time, Seaduce would leave port and sail straight for the rendezvous point and meet the freighter and Yuletide. This rendezvous point would be ten to fifteen miles due north of the actual interception point with Castro's yacht.

Once Yuletide is modified to look like a damaged vessel, she would take on the name of her sister-ship, the SEADUCE. She would sail south and take up position for the intercept on Castro's course and wait. The real Seaduce would stand-by in the vicinity of the freighter, hiding in the freighter's shadow to avoid a radar image. When Castro's yacht is fifteen to twenty miles west of the Yuletide and confirmed on radar, Yuletide, now called Seaduce, will broadcast low powered MAYDAY radio signals on the VHF emergency channel. When Castro's yacht responds, the trap would be set. The Captain on SEADUCE would plead for help. He would appeal for water, food and electrical fuses. He would explain that he was a charter yacht with guests and that his yacht was not in danger of sinking and had no injuries aboard. This should relieve Castro's crew from the worry about having to pick up or tending to injured passengers.

Yuletide's captain would have to accomplish a few important facts in his first communications with Castro's crew. He would advise them not to come alongside, but to keep a safe distance. He would explain there had been a fire on board, that it was contained, but there was still suspicious smoke in the engine room. After Yuletide's captain explained what his needs were, he would advise them he would be in his dinghy and waiting for them to arrive in the area. He would also ask Castro's crew to broadcast to other vessels in the area and advise them of his location. He would tell them that he lost his main sail in a freak gale, then had a fire in the engine room that destroyed his electrical fuse panel. He could make repairs if he had a couple of 30-50 amp fuses, this would enable him to start his auxiliary generator, charge his main batteries so he could start his main engine. Once under power, he could easily make port at San Juan.

"That's it, this will work," O'Brien said out loud. "We just need to find a captain who can make all this sound plausible and a sailboat that goes twenty five knots."

O'Brien began to write down the items that should be requested by the captain. Fresh water, food, a fire extinguisher and most important, fuses. These fuses would have to be the same type that are used on Castro's yacht, one item that O'Brien had to find out about. Next, he would need a UDT team. They would have to be in the water when the dinghy was launched, and stay with the dinghy until Castro's yacht arrived. They would submerge and head for the target once it stopped, plant their charges and timing devices, and move out. "I wonder how much time this is going to take?" O'Brien asked himself, and made a note.

Once Castro's yacht was dead in the water, the captain on Yuletide would go alongside and pick up the supplies. It will be up to the captain to delay the pick up as long as possible to give the UDT time to get their charges attached and swim clear before Castro's engines were engaged.

O'Brien leaned back against the counter top and closed his eyes trying to visualize the situation from his captain's perspective, talking to the Cuban crew. He opened his eyes and continued writing.

When Castro's crew sends out the call for help, the freighter will have to respond, give their position, and advise they were making way to the distressed yacht. Castro would continue towards his destination satisfied that they helped provide for the stricken yacht. At a point of time, maybe 30 minutes after the rendezvous, there would be a large explosion that would be seen by Castro's yacht in the area where they had stopped to help the sailboat. A radio message would be broadcast immediately by the freighter, claiming that the distressed yacht, the "Seaduce", had just blown up, and that they were heading to look for survivors. In reality, the real Seaduce, sailboat number two that was sailing in the freighters shadow, would actually be destroyed, leaving plenty of debris for recovery by the freighter for evidence. The next radio report from the freighter would announce that there were no survivors. Meanwhile, Yuletide has removed her disguises and is headed at full speed to her scheduled destination, where she would arrive within normal cruising period and report her arrival. The crew and charter guests of the Seaduce, along with the UDT team would be on board the freighter heading back to San Juan with the remains of the Seaduce's unfortunate crew and guests.

O'Brien, pleased with his idea so far, hoped that he could convince everyone on board Air Force One that he had covered all the bases. If everything was done right, there would be no possible way that any investigation could connect the sinking of Castro's yacht to the United States Government. The only contact that Castro's party made prior to his meeting, was a distressed sailboat that was lost with all on board.

Now it came down to the explosive package. Is there a device that can be set to go off many hours later? Can a device be placed against a fast moving hull subject to many hours of water pressure? How many divers would be needed? Where can two look-alike yachts be found? Can a sailing vessel be converted into a super fast yacht? Where would the mission be headquartered? Where will he find the captains he will need and the support teams? These were the questions, if asked, O'Brien did not have answers for.

He wrote down a list of the questions that he needed answered. What kind of surveillance is going on over Cuba? How accurate is it? Can Castro's yacht be tracked so his route can be established? Does the Navy have, or can they get, a small freighter, or commercial trawler to use for the supply ship?

The clock on the stove told him he had forty minutes before he was to be on the street. He took his coffee and a cigarette and went into the bathroom where he prepared to shave. A long look in the mirror disclosed the face of a tired troubled man. As he ran his hand over the rough stubs of his day old beard, he noted the deepness of the crows-foot lines around his eyes and the silver hairs that appeared throughout his light brown hair. At fifty-two, he thought of himself to be in pretty good shape, even somewhat attractive, but not this morning.

O'Brien walked out of the apartment house entrance exactly at 0553 hours, according to his watch. He walked slowly south as instructed. The air was warm, still and humid. There was absolutely nothing moving on the broad avenue. When he reached the corner, he noticed a small mini van moving quite fast towards the intersection. He stopped and waited until it passed by, then crossed the street. He took about a dozen strides, when he heard the sound of a car from behind. He turned and saw a large dark van pulling up to the curb beside him. The van stopped and the passenger door opened and George Harris stepped out.

"Morning, Dan."

Blocking O'Brien's view of the van, Harris took hold of O'Brien's arm and led him away for a few feet.

"Listen, Dan, we have Senator Hauser in the van. He is not happy one bit. We notified him last night that we wanted to meet with him this morning and he pitched a fit, claiming he was up to his ears in work and had a meeting at seven this morning he couldn't miss. He is cleared as far as security is concerned, but the President does not want him to know what is going on under any conditions and definitely did not want him on board Air Force One this morning. Needless to say, the press would have a ball if they found out he was and that would raise too many questions. As it is right now, we have the press squashed on the President's trip to California. Can you find out what you need from him without tipping your hand?"

O'Brien thought for a minute. "I will explain to him I need help locating a sailboat company building large yachts in Florida that can build a custom yacht, a "Spook ship" for the DEA. We can say it's for use in south Florida and the Bahamas as a disguised luxury yacht, electronically equipped to monitor targets and do patrol work."

Harris thought for a minute, not understanding one thing O'Brien just said. "Yeah, O.K., but even that sounds like you're saying too much, Dan."

"Naw, I know Gordon. He will buy what I have to say. I have to tell him that the yacht is going to be rigged for speed so he can recommend the right guy to contact, or the yacht type I should be looking for."

"O.K., Dan, but I'm warning you, he is some kind of pissed off right now. We made him get up early this morning and he is wondering what the hell the CIA is doing involved with you and him, so be on your toes."

They walked back to the van. Harris slid the large sliding door back, and even in the darkness of the van, O'Brien could easily recognize the Senator's profile outlined against the large window behind him. O'Brien stepped in the van, Harris closed the door and returned to the passenger seat next to the driver. The van pulled away from the curb moving fast down Wisconsin Avenue.

O'Brien sat down next to the Senator in the plush velour captain's chair. "Gordon, good to see you."

The Senator interrupted. "Dan, what the fuck is going on here? I get a fucking call from that asshole up front at three o'clock this morning telling me I have to be ready to leave my house at four-thirty to meet with you. He says that it's a matter of national security? I told some other asshole last night from the State Department that I had a full calendar today. He also wanted me to meet with you. I told him I couldn't, not today, and hung up. Next thing I know the damn CIA is on my ass."

The Senator was rocking around in his seat, throwing his hands and arms around like a wild man.

"Calm down, Gordon. Hey, I apologize about this inconvenience, but..."

Hauser flew into O'Brien again. "Inconvenience! Shit, Dan, I ain't no kid anymore. I work my ass off, and right now, I am in the middle of hearings on the way some asshole military jokers at the Pentagon are spending big bucks on toilets. I was up until after midnight last night with Congressman Wayne Peters looking at over-runs on contracts that would blow your mind."

"I know, Gordon, I read the papers, and I know you're under pressure, believe me, but you're the only man in Washington who can help me right now, and I need your advice."

The Senator swung his chair around to face O'Brien and sat back. "O.K., what the hell do you want, O'Brien?"

"Gordon, I have been given a job to do by the DEA. They want a spook ship built that can help them in south Florida and the Bahamas. It has to be big, maybe sixty feet or more. It has to be a sailing vessel. It has to look totally harmless, but it will have to do things no other sailboat ever did before, like have twice the speed of a standard yacht of her size. She's going to be rigged to the teeth with surveillance equipment."

"Whose harebrained idea is this?"

"Mine, Gordon. I was given the job. The sailboat idea is mine."

"Speed? what kind of speed are you talking about, twelve, fifteen knots?"

"Ah, more like twenty, twenty-five knots."

"Never happen. Shit, you should know that. Damn, you spent enough time on sailboats for Christ sake to understand their hulls. Have you ever seen a sailing hull that would go twenty-five fucking miles an hour?"

"No, Gordon, I haven't, but that doesn't mean they can't. Senator, you know all those designers and builders on the West Coast of Florida. All I need is someone to talk to, you know, a designer, like Charlie Morgan, or that guy that builds the Gulfstars, ah, Lazzara, yeah, Vince Lazzara."

Hauser was quiet for a moment looking out into the black night.

"Collins, Ted Collins, that's who you need to talk to, but he will tell you you're fucking nuts."

"Ted Collins, Citation Yachts? He's in St. Pete, right?"

"Yup, and he's really into performance cruising hulls. If there is anyone who might be able to help you, it would be him."

"Collins, yeah, that's good, Gordon. He designs and builds all his own yachts, doesn't he?"

Hauser began to lighten up, and started to rattle on. "Sure does, and he just came out with a new seventy or seventy-five footer, so I hear. He is building a whole new breed of mega-yachts for the crewed charter industry."

"Perfect, Gordon. He could be the man I need to talk to. How soon can you call him and ask him to come to Washington?"

"Are you nuts? What reason would I give him to come to Washington?"

"Tell him you're interested in buying one of his new yachts."

"I already have one of his yachts, Dan. I bought a forty-five nearly two years ago at the Annapolis boat show. I had some problems with it and even though we are sort of friends, I may have bruised that relationship last year when I was screaming for some service, or I would go to court."

"Then use some other excuse. Tell him there's some super benefit you want him to invite him to, you know, a party thing. He is a member of your party isn't he?"

"No, that's another sore spot. But maybe I could get him up here on a tip that one of my asshole friends in government wants to contract a boat builder to build some special boats, right?"

"Now you're cooking, Senator. Will you call him this morning and set it up, then call me, ah, shit, I'm going on Air Force..."

Harris turned in his seat and deliberately interrupted O'Brien.

"Senator? You want to go straight back home, don't you, sir?

Harris just saved O'Brien from a major disaster.

"Of course I want to go home, you dumb twit. I'd look silly as shit walking into the Capitol in this outfit. Jesus, where do you guys get your training, at some fast food service school?"

"I was trying to say, Gordon, that I have an early flight on US Air this morning. I'm going up to Jersey to talk to some electronics folks. If you can just call my office and leave word with, ah, better yet, call General Ross's office at the Pentagon and leave the message with Debra, Ross's secretary? She knows where I will be and advise me how you made out with Collins."

"Ross, huh? He's one of my prime targets, you know? I'm going to get a piece of his ass on some of the shit he bought that he claimed he needed."

The van pulled up in front of a row of attractive townhouses and stopped. The senator got out of the van, still complaining about his morning ordeal. The driver of the van, Frank Rossi, opened up before anyone could comment.

"Jesus Christ, is he a piece of work, how long has he been a senator?"

"Too long," Harris growled. "And we haven't heard the last of him either. He will be all over Ian Billings' asking questions as to why the agency is mixed up in this. I guarantee you."

"Ian will handle him, I'm sure. Ian can't stand the old bastard from what he said last night," Rossi said laughing.

"Hey, Harris, thanks. I damned near got caught on Air Force One. Thanks."

"Don't mention it, Dan."

Andrews Air Force Base
O715 Hours

O'Brien got out of the van onto the hardstand. Standing before him was Air Force One. "She is beautiful," Dan thought. He slowly studied the graceful lines of the aging Boeing 707, as it stood glistening in the breaking sunrise. Harris motioned to O'Brien to join him as he walked towards the boarding ramp.

O'Brien was greeted at the door by an Air Force Major. "Welcome aboard, sir. I'm Major Hirshburg, and this is Sergeant Griffin, who will take you to the conference cabin."

"Thank you," O'Brien said, and followed the young airman with Harris close behind down the aisle dividing three rows of large plush seats. They entered a small cabin, which appeared to be a communication center. It had numerous phones, desks, typewriters and telex machines. The next compartment was large and decorated in tasteful light blues, creamy ivory and grays. The Presidential Seal was posted on everything. Swivel lounge chairs were neatly arranged around small mahogany tables. Towards the rear, O'Brien could see the President's desk just forward of the rear bulkhead, on the port side of the cabin. The mural on the bulkhead wall was spectacular. It looked like a scene right out of America's heartland. Standing in the cabin, towards the rear, O'Brien saw four men in shirtsleeves talking to a Navy officer. O'Brien did not recognize any of them.

Suddenly, the sound of a helicopter with its blades slapping the air, caught everyone's attention. Through the cabin window O'Brien could see the ground crew scurrying around to meet the incoming chopper.

"It's the President's bird," Harris said.

O'Brien looked to the rear and noticed the five men watching out the windows.

Harris whispered to O'Brien. "It's the President alright. Look at those guys back there straining to see who else is on board this morning."

The helicopter finally touched down off the port wing of Air Force One. O'Brien could see a number of legs and feet running around the other side of the giant olive drab painted machine. Then he saw them. The President, Vice President, Admiral Koster, the President's chief of staff, and three other men all fighting the down blast of the giant rotor blades as they made their way to the ramp.

When O'Brien straightened up, he looked aft again into five smiling faces. They had put their suit coats on and were walking towards him. He recognized Lou Bollman, the FBI man from the Miami office. He looked forward and saw at least four Air Force uniforms standing near the flight deck door, looking out the open entry. The five men joined O'Brien and Harris.

"Hello, Mr. O'Brien," said Lou Bollman as he got into position in front of his group to make introductions. "Dan, this is Commander Art Buckland, Navy Intelligence. Ralph Steele, Professor, Georgetown University and John Kilpatrick, DEA. Gentlemen, meet Santa Claus."

O'Brien smiled, looked at Harris and said, "You tell them, George, I ain't Santa Claus."

Harris looked at O'Brien in total puzzlement. "You're not?"

"Nope. I am Rudolf, Santa Claus has not been found yet."

"I'll be damned, I thought yesterday the President called you Santa?"

"He did, shows you how much he knows, right?" O'Brien said laughing.

"Gentlemen, the President," Lou Bollman announced.

O'Brien turned and saw the President as he entered the cabin. He was grinning from ear to ear and looked far more cheerful than he did yesterday, and in much better color. He was wearing a bright red sweater with the Presidential seal over the left breast.

A barrage of "good morning Mr. President" filled the cabin as he greeted each man with a two-handed handshake. He went directly aft and took a lounge seat in front of his desk. The small group followed. The President indicated to O'Brien to take the seat directly next to him. After an exchange of greetings, the rest of the President's party entered the cabin led by the Vice President.

The speakers in the cabin overhead suddenly came alive. "Good morning, gentlemen, and welcome aboard AIR FORCE ONE. I am Colonel Phelps, your pilot in command, and with me up here on the flight deck, Major Donald Hirshburg, second in command, Captain Sam Rice our Navigator and Communications officer, Master Sergeant Oliver "fingers" McGee, our flight engineer. Your two flight attendants today are Airman Don Bowers and James Lasiter and your cabin steward, Sergeant William Griffin.'

The President leaned over and whispered into O'Brien's ear, "This is the part Colonel Phelps likes to do best."

The speakers broke the silence again. "Our flight today, gentlemen, will take us across the sunny south-land to not-so-sunny California. Estimated flight time, four hours fifty-five minutes. Weather en route is severe clear till we reach Dallas-Fort Worth, where we may encounter some thunderstorm activity, but we should be able to ease around most of it. Once airborne, we will be serving the President's favorite breakfast as soon as we reach our cruising altitude, that being, eggs Benedict on English muffins with Canadian bacon, and hollandaise sauce, whole wheat rye or raisin toast, sweet rolls, fruit, juice, coffee, high and low test, and milk. If anyone would prefer to order anything special, please use the white intercom phones located throughout the cabins, and place your order with Sergeant Griffin. Now, if everyone is comfortable, please put on your seat belts, and observe the bulkhead signs. No smoking, please. Andrews tower has told us that we are cleared for immediate take-off. Sergeant McGee says we are ready to start engines. We hope you have a comfortable flight, and we thank you for flying Presidential Airlines."

The President chuckled. He turned to O'Brien and said,

"You know, last year we had the President of Brazil on board heading for Toronto and Colonel Phelps makes an announcement that we had to return to Andrews, because somebody forgot to put the Colombian coffee on board. Man, this old bus shook with laughter. Thank God, our guest and his wife did not understand the joke, but they joined us laughing anyway."

41

O'Brien smiled as he looked into the President's cheerful face. "What is so funny about forgetting Colombian coffee, sir?"

The President studied O'Brien's puzzled face for a second. "The TV commercial, you know? There's this airliner, and it's up in the sky. Then this female voice, you know, a stewardess type, tells the pilot "Captain, we forgot the Colombian coffee. Next you see this jet do a sharp 180 degree turn."

O'Brien could not hold a straight face. The President saw him straining to keep from laughing. He put his hand on O'Brien's arm and gave a light squeeze. He smiled, and said, "O'Brien, I like you. I like your Irish style. Now, tell me, do you think this plan of yours will really work?"

O'Brien leaned over close to the President and in a whisper, asked. "Do you know for sure if this plane really has Colombian coffee on board?"

Nearly an hour and a half into the flight, the remains of the morning breakfast were being collected by the three attendants. The large conference table was in place and the President assigned the seating. He had the Vice President on his immediate right, and Admiral Koster on his left. Sitting directly across from him, O'Brien, flanked by Lou Bollman and Commander Art Buckland. Professor Steele, expert on Cuba, sat at one end, facing John Kilpatrick at the other. Roger Weijlard, State Department and Ian Billings took up seats together, as did Carl Strauss, President's National security adviser, and his Chief of Staff, Sam Gaylord.

The President called the meeting to order.

"Gentlemen, we are here today to make final decisions on OPERATION YULETIDE. Most of you have been briefed on this operation. Before this flight ends however, everyone will know all there is to know. If we decide to proceed with this operation, some of you will be the key players throughout the operation. Some of you will be advisers, but each of you will be a contributor, finding all the necessary personnel, equipment and funding it will require. I feel we have a responsibility and duty to our country and our Cuban American brothers and sisters to pursue this opportunity of removing a malignant growth from our hemisphere.

The President cleared his throat, and continued. "Last night, Admiral Koster and Mr. Kilpatrick worked up a organizational chart that shows who is responsible for what during this operation. Commander, will you be so kind to distribute the copies."

The young Commander stood up and placed the notebooks in front of each man. As they opened the cover, an organizational chart was displayed with boxes connected with colored lines.

"You will note some of your names are in boxes on the chart, and you can read where your responsibilities lie, who you report to, and vice versa.

Read this chart and study it well, memorize it. Each of them are numbered, and they will be collected at the end of the flight and destroyed."

"Mr. O'Brien?"

"Yes, Mr. President?"

"Let us take it from the top, shall we?"

O'Brien opened his brief case and removed a very abused yellow legal pad. He removed two sectional charts, and after some agony, he managed to unfold them so they would lay flat on the table surface. He stood up and eased the charts closer to the center of the table, then reached into his inside jacket pocket and produced four small metal objects, which he removed from a Monopoly game before he left his apartment. He held up a small thimble.

"This is the yacht, Seaduce." He placed it on the chart. Next he displayed a little top hat. "This is the yacht, Yuletide." He then picked up the small racecar. "This is the freighter, Red Sleigh." Then he picked up the small shoe. "This is Fruitcake, a motor yacht sailing from Cuba."

O'Brien carefully placed the little metal objects on the lines that he had drawn, and continued to explain his theory on how he felt the operation could work, why he needed two sailboats and the freighter.

Somewhere over New Mexico, at 34,000 feet, during one of the welcome breaks, Admiral Koster led O'Brien forward to the first cabin, where a few secret servicemen were sitting around relaxing. Koster pinned O'Brien against a small bulkhead where two lavatories were located. He spoke in a low voice.

"O'Brien, I wasn't going to say anything in front of those very respectable intelligent men back there, but I think you're fucking nuts. Do you actually believe you can pull this off? Do you have any idea how much damn money this is going to take? Have you looked at the date on this morning's paper? Christmas is almost here!"

O'Brien knew he had to keep cool and convincing. "Don't let him see you sweat" he kept telling himself.

"Sir, If you asked me to take the helm of the USS Kennedy, and drive it up the Mississippi, I would do it in a wink, as long as you were on the bow calling the headings, sir. Its called faith, sir."

Koster studied O'Brien for a second. O'Brien did not give way to Koster's cold staring green eyes.

"Tell me something, Daniel Patrick O'Brien. Your old man didn't happen to own a used car lot outside of D.C. on route 50, oh, sometime in the late forties, did he?"

"No, sir, why?"

"Cause another O'Brien, a Tom O'Brien, also sold me a bucket of shit." Koster shook his head, turned his back to O'Brien and walked into the nearby rest room.

CHAPTER THREE

Dan O'Brien's Apartment
Washington, D.C.
Thursday, August llth
0846 hours

O'Brien heard the faint sound of a telephone ringing in the distance. He opened his eyes and saw a glass partially filled with water. Through the glass the outline of a brown bottle. As his vision became clearer he could see the label on the bottle and the letters VO. He lay motionless trying to get his thoughts together. The ringing began again. He lifted himself slowly, and attempted to reach for the phone on the nightstand. The bottle of VO and the glass went crashing to the floor, along with an ashtray and an answering machine.

He located the receiver and heard a voice calling his name. He brought the phone to his ear only to hear his voice on the taped message. "Hello, this is 544-2l2l," O'Brien tried to override the tape recording.

"Hello, I'm here." The recording kept going, but he could hear another voice responding.

"Dan, it's me, George." The tape ended with the beep before O'Brien could find the button to cut it off.

"Sorry about that, George, I knocked the ..."

"Dan, listen up. Senator Hauser is trying to reach you. He just called Billings. Did you get his message?"

"Message? No, I haven't. What's going on?"

"You have to get your butt over to Annapolis pronto. The Senator is picking up Ted Collins right about now at National Airport and heading for Annapolis. He has set up a meeting with you and Ted this afternoon. Billings told Hauser that he would have John Kilpatrick and Commander Buckland there also. I'm picking up Lou Bollman on the way over."

O'Brien sat on the edge of the bed massaging his scalp vigorously, trying to get rid of the throbbing pain between his temples.

"Jesus, George, I thought we were supposed to keep Hauser out of the plans. Why is Billings inviting everybody to the meeting?"

"Billings feels it may be wise to include him in on the operation, for the moment. He thinks that we are trying to build a special yacht for the DEA, and that's all. If Collins thinks he can build the damn thing, we may have to let Hauser in on the whole plan. The Admiral and Billings are worried about the funding for the operation. Sooner or later Hauser is going to know about the dollars going out for the project. If we have to cut him in, better now than later, but that's not your concern. Billings, Admiral Koster or the President will make that decision when and if the time comes."

"It's beginning to get crowded. Where is the meeting being held?"

"The Senator plans to go sailing this afternoon. He says the meeting can take place while we're sailing around the bay, plus he wants Ted to sail his boat."

"Shit, all Hauser wants to do is trap Collins into getting something fixed on his damn yacht."

"Yeah, we already figured that, but we're going along anyway. Some good news, Hauser did tell Billings that he had to be back in D.C. for a dinner party tonight. Billings suggested that you and Collins should spend the evening together in Annapolis, so you can talk in private."

"Yes, that would be a good idea." Dan said.

" By the way, Dan, Ted Collins has been cleared by the FBI. I took the liberty of getting him checked out when you and Hauser mentioned his name the other morning."

"Good, now, I'd better get my ass in gear. Should I bring the plans with me?"

"No, don't bring anything except what you need for staying over. Leave all your papers locked up somewhere. Billings is a bit concerned about your papers. Do you have a place you can keep them safe?"

"Not to worry, tell Billings I keep them under the front seat of my Volvo."

Harris laughed. "You have exactly two hours, Dan, and it's drive time in downtown D.C. and you can expect heavy traffic on route 50 heading to Annapolis. Go directly to the Hilton Hotel, it's in the heart of town. We will meet you in the lounge at the rear of the lobby around noon."

"Hilton, downtown at noon. By the way, thanks for the lift home last night. That flight yesterday was one for the books. I haven't spent that much time in the air in twenty years, and it was the first time I ever crossed this damn country twice in one day."

"Tell me about it, my ass is still dragging, so is everyone else's, but you got the job done. The President and the Admiral seemed pleased, I'll see you at the Hilton."

O'Brien put the phone down, pushed the rewind button on the Phone-Mate and waited. The green light came on. He pushed the "Listen" button. There were three messages. The first was Karen Meyer, his new secretary. She had a few names and numbers for him to call. The second was his sister Terri, reminding him that he was to be in Summit, New Jersey next weekend for a reunion. The third was Senator Hauser, explaining his conversation with Ted Collins; he said he had told Ted that he had an opportunity to sell some boats to the Government, and that Collins would be planning on spending the weekend. He left his home number and his answering service number. O'Brien figured he had better at least try to reach him and left word with the Senator's office that he had received his message.

Hilton Hotel
Annapolis, Maryland
1230 Hours

Harris was right, the traffic in D.C. and on route 50 was miserable. As O'Brien pulled into the parking garage at the Hilton, he glanced at his watch, it was 12:30.

O'Brien walked into the smoky jam-paced cocktail lounge. He passed through the patrons standing around the bar looking for a face he knew. He felt a tug on his elbow, turned and looked into the smiling face of Commander Buckland.

"Mr. O'Brien, you made it, follow me, sir, the troops are out back."

O'Brien followed Buckland as he wove through the crowd. Buckland looked like a model for Brooks Brothers. He was dressed in a blue oxford button down short sleeved shirt, tan tailored cotton slacks, web belt, Topsider loafers and no socks. His short light brown hair had a few silver hairs at the temples that hinted he may be older than he looked. O'Brien estimated he was 35, but learned later that he was 40. Buckland was becoming one of the key players in the operation, and O'Brien liked him.

"Is everyone here?" O'Brien asked, as they walked down the dock to the rear of the hotel.

"Yes, sir, they are already on the Senator's yacht, just around the corner."

"Commander, I know I have a few years on you, and I know you're trying to be polite, but can you dispense with the "sir" and just call me Dan?"

"Of course, and you can call me "Buckwheat", until we start the code games, then I'll be "Evergreen".

"Buckwheat? Was that name branded on you by an ugly sister?"

"Nope, my C.O. on the Eisenhower. He tagged me two days out of Norfolk heading for Nam. He told me I looked like something right out of the Kansas wheat fields. I had to agree, I was really skinny and all my flight gear floated on me, including my helmet. It was my first tour, I was pretty green and guess I did look a bit strange."

"What were you driving, F-4 Phantoms?"

"Naw, A-6's. Couldn't have any fun in those fours. They kept them off the deck. We could go anywhere." Buckwheat stopped and pointed to the yacht a few steps away. "There they are."

O'Brien wanted to ask a few more questions, especially about Nam, but they had reached the yacht. The Citation yacht was sloop rigged with an exceptionally tall mast with double spreaders. The low silhouette deckhouse tapered gracefully into the foredeck suggesting she was designed as a racing cruiser.

Senator Hauser stepped up on the dock and greeted O'Brien and Buckland. He looked like a cartoon in his bright red shorts, blue and white rugby shirt and Greek fisherman's cap. He was short and carried a healthy spare tire around the waist.

"Welcome aboard," he said as he shook their hands and motioned to them to step aboard.

O'Brien and Buckland stepped down into the cockpit and were greeted by the crew. O'Brien noted that everyone was there except Ted Collins. He was about to ask about him when Collins appeared in the companionway. He stood on the steps, still inside the cabin, resting his arms on the cabin roof. O'Brien was surprised at his size and youth. His dark brown wavy hair framed a broad well-tanned face, accented by deeply set brown eyes.

"Hi, I'm Ted Collins. You must be Dan O'Brien."

Ted stepped into the cockpit, towering over O'Brien by two inches. O'Brien shook his large hand, and introduced Commander Buckland. Senator Hauser, standing behind the helm set the throttle and clutch levers and started the diesel engine.

"Ted, if you will be kind enough to take the bow, and O'Brien the stern lines, we'll be on our way."

The sleek yacht moved silent along the row of yachts tied to the Hilton's dock. As they approached a large sport-fishing rig, the Senator started yelling at the crew sitting around in the large cockpit. They were a mixed group of men and women, thoroughly enjoying themselves. As the Senator's yacht passed by, they all raised their drinks in salute.

"That's Charlie Downs and his partner Fred Zimmerman," Hauser remarked. Nobody had to ask who they were. Everyone knew the two famous Washington lawyers.

Commander Buckland caught Hauser's eye and asked, "Senator, how come you don't have one of those fancy sport fishing boats, that yacht must be fifty-five feet?"

"Oh, but I do, young man. Only mine is fifty-nine feet and lives in Florida."

The Citation was clear of the moored yachts and passing east of the Naval Academy. The Senator turned the yacht into the light wind, throttled back and asked Ted Collins to take the helm. He then asked O'Brien to help raise the sails.

Hauser and his crew enjoyed the next couple of hours sailing under the Bay Bridge and skirting the eastern shores of Maryland. Running out of time, Hauser decided to motor across the bay to Annapolis, which gave O'Brien the first opportunity to talk to Ted alone. They sat near the bow away from the crew, who were still partying in the cockpit.

"Ted, just what did Gordon tell you about meeting with us today?"

"Not much, he told me that you were some big shot in the Defense Department, and you were looking to build some special spy boats for the Coast Guard."

O'Brien shook his head and laughed. "Well, he told you one thing that was right, I do work for the Defense Department, but I'm not looking to build spy boats for the Coast Guard."

Collins looking out to sea, leaned back on his elbows against the cabin. "You know, I had a feeling he was jerking my chain. I thought he got me up here to throw this yacht back in my lap. He has been wanting to trade it back for a fifty-two."

"Ted, what I am about to tell you is totally confidential, and not to sound dramatic, it is also top secret."

Collins turned his head and faced O'Brien. He could see that he was deadly serious.

"Buckland as you know is Navy, Kilpatrick is DEA, Bollman is FBI and Harris, CIA. We are part of a special team. The senator is not aware of what we are doing, he just knows who we are and he is not involved in our project. If he starts asking you questions, try and be creative, if you cant, pass him on to me."

"Where do I fit in here, Dan? I have never dealt with the government before."

"Well, the Senator told you I was looking for a yacht, right? Well, I am, a big yacht, maybe seventy feet or so. And it must be a sailboat."

Ted grinned. "Ah, Gordon told you I just came out with a new seventy-five footer and you're thinking of leasing it?"

"Ah, not exactly, we may want to buy it though, or one like it."

"Now we're talking, my friend, I like it when you say you want to buy one, or did you mention two?"

"Just how fast is the new boat, Ted, I mean under power?"

"Well, I have never red-lined her, but with the present power plant she will easily do her hull speed, around nine knots"

"Could you get her to do twenty-five knots?"

Collins began to laugh and became so loud he caught the Senator's attention.

"Hey, you two," Hauser yelled. "If you're telling jokes, get your asses back here and let us in."

Collins immediately apologized to O'Brien for his outburst.

"That's alright, Ted, I expected a similar reaction. However, I am serious, and I want you to think about it. After the Senator leaves for Washington, the six of us will go somewhere and I will explain why I need a twenty-five knot sailboat."

After securing his yacht at the marina, Senator Hauser bid his crew farewell and left Washington. Collins had a room at the Hilton, and O'Brien was able to book a suite. It was decided that they would freshen up meet in the lounge and have dinner at one of the local eateries. After dinner they would return to O'Brien's suite.

O'Brien stood staring at the plans of the Citation seventy-five. "Ted, I know a little about sailboats, as does Buckland and Harris, but would you mind going over these plans?"

"Sure thing," Collins responded and he spent the next half-hour explaining special features and its hull design.

"Now that we all have a better understanding of this particular hull, Ted, can you do the impossible and convert it to go faster? If you recall, earlier today I mentioned to you that we needed a sailboat that would cruise twenty-five knots. Before I explain why we need to know, is it even possible?" O'Brien paused and waited for Collins to react.

"Let me put it this way, Dan, it would be impossible for this hull. I would need to design a new displacement type hull."

Nobody spoke, they stood studying Collins, waiting for his next words. "There are some motor-sailers around that are fast, not twenty-five knots fast, but fast for sailboats."

"I don't want a motor-sailer, Ted. I need a regular sailboat, a ketch, like this one." O'Brien put his hand down on the blueprints.

"Dan, even if I had the horsepower, all the Drummer would do is leave a big hole in the ocean, her hull would never get up and give you those speeds."

"The hull you have now won't, but what if it were modified, or had a displacement bottom, like a big power boat?"

"It would probably roll over, Dan. You forget, we have tons of rigging above, and without the counter weight of the keel, you couldn't raise a sail."

"Ted, please think about it, there must be a way."

Commander Buckland interrupted.

"Ted, you make models of your hulls and test them, right?"

"No, not really, Commander."

"Why not make one, or better yet, let the Navy make one. How would like you to come up to Groton to the Naval Underwater Laboratories. We have the computers, test tanks, and some of the best naval architects at our fingertips. Maybe we can come up with a modification that could work."

"Well, that would be one way to find out," Collins said.

O'Brien turned and addressed Collins.

"Great, how soon can you get your ass up there Ted? I don't mean to be pushy, but I have a problem with time."

"Time? I don't understand..." Collins remarked.

O'Brien looked at Harris who offered no help. O'Brien made up a fictitious story on the spot about a known voyage a major drug lord was making in the Caribbean.

"Ted, we five warriors here are working on a special project that calls for two identical sailboats. They are going to be playing the role of charter yachts. One of these yachts has to be a super yacht and has to cover distances at twice its normal speed. Why, you ask? Because it has to be in two different places at one time, that is all I can tell you at this point."

Lou Bollman raised his hand.

"If I may, Dan. Ted, we have already cleared you through both agencies this week. As O'Brien just said, this is a very confidential project that is stamped Top Secret. If you get involved, and can make this project work with the use of your yachts, we are home free. Keep in mind, you will be paid for everything, and paid well. You need to understand, Ted, there is great deal riding on this project, and if it works, it will add a page to our history books. Our major enemy, right now, is time. We need your "Island Drummer," isn't that the name of your yacht? Or did I misunderstand you earlier?"

"No, you heard right, I call her the "Island Drummer.""

Buckland raised his drink.

"I like that, the Island Drummer."

O'Brien was grinning. He looked at the smiling faces of his team and picked up his glass. "To the Island Drummer."

Ted raised his glass then addressed O'Brien. "You mentioned time, Dan. I take it there is a schedule involved here?"

"Ah yes, and a tight one. We will need both yachts ready to go no later that December lst."

"Jesus Christ." Collins exploded. "Do you know it took me nearly fifteen months to complete the Drummer and you want two of them built in fifteen weeks?"

"You can do it, son," O'Brien said, as he finished his drink.

Buckland stood up and walked over to Collins. "Ted, let's take one step at a time. First, how soon can you get up to Groton with all your plans?"

"I, ah, I guess I could be up there Tuesday or Wednesday."

"Good, I will make all the arrangements, you just let me know when you can leave. I'll call you Monday afternoon and give you the details of your flights and I will try and be up there myself to make introductions. Ted, one thing, we are working on a special "spook-ship" for the Coast Guard and the DEA, that's all you tell them."

Bollman stood up. "Hey guys," he pointed to his watch. "I don't know about you single fellers, but I have to kiss two tots good night and I'm ninety minutes from home."

Within ten minutes, the room was cleared out, except for Collins and O'Brien. "Interesting group you have there, Dan, known them long?"

"Oh, a couple of days longer than you."

"Are you serious, you mean you just met these guys?"

"Yup, how about a night cap?"

"Make it a double."

O'Brien and Collins spent the next three hours getting to know each other. Before Collins went to his room, he was feeling more positive about the project, but he was still doubtful that the hull conversion or modifications would meet O'Brien's demands. He did get O'Brien to agree to stay and have breakfast with him in the morning and face Senator Hauser who was coming over for one reason, to learn more about what they were really up to.

CHAPTER FOUR

Washington, D.C.

The next few weeks were hectic for Dan O'Brien. It was decided between the President, Vice President and Admiral Koster that September 15th would be the termination date for Operation Yuletide if certain goals were not reached. O'Brien's request for a later deadline was refused.

As the first days of September passed, O'Brien became confident in the progress of the teams, which began with positive news from Ted Collins at the Groton Test Laboratories. Tank tests being conducted on models with the modified hull designs were performing above expectations. A message to Ian Billings sent by Jesus Souza disclosed that a luxury yacht was being purchased in France by one of Fidel Castro's closest friends who resides in Spain. Information on the type of yacht and its location in France would be contained in the next message.

Commander Buckland called O'Brien from Jacksonville, Florida. He located an old Navy vessel that could pass as a coastal freighter for the mission. It was a WWII minesweeper that was used as a work boat at the Jacksonville Navy yard. AG 521 was one hundred and ninety feet long and powered by two large GM diesels and could cruise at speeds up to twenty-two knots. Its yard name was "Sonar". Buckland felt it could easily be converted to look like an island trader and recruiting a crew should be easy since there was unlimited retired maritime manpower in the Jacksonville area.

Collins was concerned about the modifications needed to be made on the Island Drummer. He felt that it would raise too many questions from his employees and visiting customers. It was decided by O'Brien to look for a new location. Lou Bollman, familiar with most of south Florida, was assigned the job of locating a facility somewhere in south Florida, preferably on the west coast that offered the requirements of solitude and had access to launching facilities.

Within a week, Bollman located the perfect site. Collins drove to Ft. Myers, met Bollman and proceeded to the town of Immokalee, a small community thirty miles south east of Ft. Myers. Bollman found a small, uncontrolled airport just outside of town, used by a few private pilots and crop-dusters. Located at the south end of the field was an old hangar filled with wrecked planes, old cars and junk. Built in the early forties, both the hangar and the small airfield served as a training base for the U.S. Army Air Corps. After checking out the facility, Collins agreed that it would work.

The roads leading to the major interstate highway and to nearby launching facilities could easily handle the Island Drummer's wide load. After a short tour of marinas along the Ft. Myers' waterfront, a major boat yard was selected that had lifting equipment that could handle the Island Drummer.

O'Brien was given permission to assign the Immokalee project to Lou Bollman who was to recruit the qualified personnel and make the necessary arrangements on leasing or purchasing agreements of the properties. Ted Collins suggested that the project could be set up in his company's name, until such time when the proper fronting company name was established. Collins would also be responsible for hiring all the workers he would need, laminators, carpenters, electricians, and fabricators. They would be screened by Bollman's office, sworn to secrecy and given housing. They would be advised that the work they would be doing on the Island Drummer was classified, that the yacht belonged to the DEA and was being refitted for surveillance duty.

Ted Collins was also investigating marine engine manufacturers. He was looking for a particular system he felt would provide the power the Drummer would need to reach the speeds needed. He located a custom engine company in Houston that looked promising, so he flew to Texas and met with their engineers and in a few hours came up with the power plant and drive train system he needed.

Admiral Koster suggested to O'Brien he should move to Florida to be closer to the project. O'Brien agreed. He also advised the Admiral that it was time to tell Ted Collins the truth about the operation. Koster agreed.

Commander Buckland asked he be assigned the task of putting the team together that would be setting the explosive charges on Castro's yacht. He had served in Nam with an instructor at the Navy Seal School, Captain Jack Chen. Buckland felt Chen could put the underwater demolition (UDT) team together, design the plan and know what devices and types of explosives to use, plus how large a team he would need for the operation. O'Brien, confident in Buckland's abilities, gave him the go ahead.

St. Petersburg, Florida
Wednesday, September 9th

Ted Collins helped O'Brien locate a comfortable apartment on St. Petersburg Beach close to his residence in Pass-A-Grille about a twenty minute drive to the factory.

The phone rang at 0715 on the morning of O'Brien's first day in his new apartment. It was Ian Billings at CIA Headquarters with news from Souza in Miami. The motor yacht that had been purchased by Castro's friend, called "Unicorn" was berthed in Marseilles. It was one hundred and twenty-four feet in length, built in Holland by the Feadship Yacht Corporation in 1978. It was scheduled to leave Marseilles on September 14th with a fuel stop in the Canary Islands and continue on to the French West Indies, arriving at Fort-de-France on the island of Martinique, September 30th. The yacht will change crew, receive a new Panamanian registry and continue on to Maracay, Santa Marta Venezuela, arriving in Santiago, Cuba, sometime between the 12th and 15th of October.

Billings informed O'Brien he had a man in Milan, and would dispatch him immediately to Marseilles to locate the yacht, take photos and obtain as much information as he could.

As soon as Billings hung up, O'Brien contacted Bollman, George Harris and Ted Collins asking them to come to St. Pete Beach as soon as they could. O'Brien called an old yacht broker friend in Ft. Lauderdale to inquire about Feadship Yachts. He was surprised to learn there was a Feadship Yacht representative with offices at the Bahia Mar hotel. O'Brien called the representative giving a false name and inquired about the "Unicorn." The representative, familiar with the yacht quoted O'Brien the asking price, location and the condition of the yacht, plus all the specifications and equipment that was on board. O'Brien was able to learn everything he needed to know about the Unicorn, including the type of power plants, electronics, cruising range, speed and fuel capacities. After a quick shower and a cup of coffee, he drove into St. Petersburg to find a bookstore and purchase the best world atlas he could find. On his way back to the apartment, he started thinking about the route of the Unicorn. The information from the Feadship rep gave O'Brien substantial firepower to lay on the Admiral. He prayed the next two days would be as equally as rewarding, since the deadline was almost at hand.

O'Brien rolled out the stained and battered charts of Cuba and the Caribbean on the small kitchen table. "Santiago, huh?" O'Brien said aloud as he studied the chart of Cuba. "O.K., Fidel, now we know your departure point." He took his ruler and worked out the shortest route from Santiago to Guadeloupe. From the chart's scale, he marked the probable route in fifty-mile increments. The route would take Castro south through the Jamaica Channel, then eastward passing south of Haiti, Dominican Republic, Puerto Rico and the Virgin Islands. O'Brien marked an X on the route line, after connecting another line that ran due south from St. Croix in the U.S. Virgin

Islands. The mark was located in the middle of the Caribbean Sea far from any landfall. He took the pencil and printed "BOOM" on the mark.

Sand and Sea Apartments
St. Petersburg, Florida
Thursday, September 10
1920 hours

The doorbell rang. O'Brien got up from the table and went to the door to find a grinning Ted Collins standing on his doorstep.

"We got it, Dan. The boys in Groton did it."

O'Brien smiled, reached out and shook Collins large hand. "Thank God, I have been sweating it out since your call this morning. Come on in, the guys are waiting for you."

Collins walked into the living room. Lou Bollman was sitting on a couch. Stacks of folders were on the coffee table in front of him. George Harris was sitting at a small desk wearing a walk-man, typing on O'Brien's typewriter.

"Hey, look who's here," O'Brien shouted. "Guess what he's got?"

Bollman stood up, causing a cascade of folders and documents to scatter all over the floor. "Hey, tiger, you got the word?" Bollman asked.

"I got the word, I got the plan and I got the solution."

Harris had not heard Collins when he first came in. He looked up to see Collins and Bollman laughing. He pulled the headset off and walked over to join them.

"George, Teddy here just gave us the word, Operation Yuletide is for real."

O'Brien appeared from the kitchen with four glasses and a bottle of champagne. "I bought this bottle today knowing that we would be celebrating tonight, I knew, somehow, that today was the day." The cork was released and the champagne flowed.

"Hey, we have to get hold of Buckwheat, he's gotta know," Bollman said.

O'Brien looked at his watch. "Shit, he's somewhere over the Carolinas by now. He left D.C. an hour ago with Captain Chen. They should be on base at Key West by nine. I'll call base operations and leave word." O'Brien went to the phone.

Collins gave his report on the hull tests at the Underwater Laboratory at Groton. He explained that the results proved his theory based on the

56

present hull design could be modified. There were two options to work with. One would require building a plug and putting it into the mold. The second choice would mean cutting out part of the hull's bottom and rebuilding a new one. The latter would be faster to complete. The major problem was installing larger fuel tanks, positioning two big power plants, and pulling as much weight out of the yacht as he could.

O'Brien disappeared into his bedroom and returned with a sealed legal size envelope and dropped it in front of Ted Collins. Collins stared at the large brown package. He looked up and scanned the three faces staring at him.

"For me? Is this the brown bag with all the taxpayers' loot to pay me off?"

O'Brien laughed. "No, it's not the loot I'm afraid. However, it is the plan for "Operation Yuletide" and before you open it, Ted, we have to ask you one question."

O'Brien pointed to the entrance door. "Ted, if Fidel Castro walked through that door over there, and you had a loaded 45 sitting on the table in front of you, would you use it?"

Collins studied O'Brien's face, then looked at Bollman and Harris. They were not smiling. Collins became a little uncomfortable and squirmed in his chair. "I take it you are not kidding, you want a serious answer?"

O'Brien nodded yes.

"No, I could not shoot him."

"O.K.," O'Brien continued. "What if he had a gun and was aiming it at Lou or me. Would you shoot him then?"

"Possibly, I, I don't know, hey come on, what's all this shit about anyway?"

O'Brien stood up and walked over to Collins. He rested one hand on the back of his chair and the other on the brown envelope. Collins lifted his head inches from O'Brien's broad, hardened face.

"This package contains the plan to kill Fidel Castro, Ted. You're going to provide the means to do it. You won't be pulling the trigger of a 45, but you will be responsible for delivering the gun, therefore, you will be part of the kill. How does that sit with you?"

O'Brien straightened up and walked to the credenza and poured a double VO. Collins sat patiently, arms resting on the table. "Is this what it's all about? All this nonsense about building spook ships is all a front to kill Castro?"

"Afraid so, Ted," Bollman said in a saddened voice. "Sorry we couldn't tell you earlier, but we didn't have the authority. Dan just got the authority, but we decided to wait until you were sure we had the hull problems solved. This entire operation was going to be terminated in four days if we did not have your good news tonight, now all you have to do is build it in time."

O'Brien sat down, lit up a Winston and relaxed back in his chair. He spoke slowly. "Ted, we are not going to hold a gun to your head. None of us know how you feel about this right now and you can get out of this project with no questions asked. But first, I want you to listen to what we have to say and why Castro has to be taken down. Then you can make up your mind on what you want to do, is that fair?"

Collins looked into the face of each man. They all avoided his eyes and sat motionless occupied with their own thoughts.

"I appreciate the option, Dan, and I can almost understand your reasons for keeping me out of the circle. I just, well, I've never been in a position like this, making a decision on being part of what I understand now is a plot to take another man's life. I guess it's easy for you guys, you're in business to plan these things and for all I know, may have had some experience in, a..." Collins found it difficult to say what he meant.

O'Brien interrupted. "Taking lives? We know what you mean, Ted. And you're right. Speaking for myself, I know I was responsible for taking lives during Nam and Korea. I never saw the people being hit by my gunfire, or saw them blown up from my rockets and bombs, but I knew they were there. How many were the real enemy, how many were innocent women and children? I will never know. I was doing my job as a soldier. Do I live with it? You bet. Do I regret it? You bet. Would I do it again if asked by our country? You bet. That is why I'm here. I have been asked to do it again. If my plan works, it will cost lives, hopefully only those who are the targets. You see, Ted, I'm still a soldier, hell, we all are and we are still at war with thousands of Castros. You can help win this war and nobody will ever know you even took part."

O'Brien, Bollman and Harris took turns explaining the entire operation to Collins and answering all his questions. The communication network and how the information was getting out of Cuba dumbfounded him. Without saying he would stay with the project, Collins reached for the envelope and held it in front of him. He looked at O'Brien. "Should I open this now?" Collins asked.

O'Brien, gave a sigh of relief, glanced at Harris and Bollman and said, "No, you can look at it later. There is a lot to be discussed about that plan. I hope after reading it, you can add some recommendations and ideas." He walked back to the bar and poured another drink, "One thing I have to ask you. We are going to need a very special crew for this mission. We need a captain who is exceptionally good and needs to know the Caribbean. He will have to be able to handle the Drummer and all its new systems. Since you are very close to the charter industry in the Virgin Islands and you know many of the skippers, I'm counting on you to find this man."

Collins thought for a minute. "I may have the perfect guy. He's a close friend, licensed captain, single and knows the Caribbean. You did not mention where this, ah, event is going to take place with Castro, but I would guess that it will be somewhere at sea?"

O'Brien chuckled. "You're right, however, we are not positive exactly where, we only know it's somewhere around Guadeloupe."

It was close to midnight when Collins left the condo. O'Brien and Bollman stayed up and went over some of the problems at Immokalee. Harris went to bed after he made his call to Ian Billings to report the good news about Ted Collins' decision.

CHAPTER 5

St. Petersburg Beach, Florida
Friday, September 11th

The next morning Bollman left for Immokalee and Dan O'Brien took Harris to Tampa Airport. O'Brien called Ted Collins from Tampa Airport to make sure he had not changed his mind and to meet for lunch. O'Brien drove over Tampa Bay on a causeway that took him right to the St. Petersburg-Clearwater Airport. He stopped at Tropical Aviation located on the west side of the airport. Tropical Aviation was a franchised Cessna dealer that leased aircraft. After O'Brien filled out the necessary paper work, he showed his pilot's license and medical certificate and told the receptionist that he wanted to get checked out on a Cessna 172 Cutlass that they had in their fleet. He went up with an instructor pilot for an hour of orientation and was signed off as qualified to fly the aircraft. He left the airport and drove to the Citation factory. He was about to get out of his car, when he noticed Ted Collins coming towards him. Collins got in the car, closed the door and ordered O'Brien to head north to the traffic light.

"Anything wrong?" O'Brien inquired.

"Nope, just hungry. Oh, here you are." Collins reached in his inside blazer pocket and handed O'Brien an envelope.

"What's this, your resignation?" O'Brien asked.

"Nope, it's your captain for the Drummer."

O'Brien took the envelope and placed it over the visor. "Is this the right guy? I mean the one you were telling us about last night?"

Collins looked at O'Brien and smiled. "Let's put it this way, Dan. He is the right man. All you have to do is convince him that he has to leave his new business, chase around the Caribbean on one of my Citations, find Fidel Castro on the open seas, blow his ass out of the water, then return to a normal life. Right?"

O'Brien chuckled, "Well, let's hope we can get him cleared through security pronto, otherwise you may have to volunteer your services."

"He'll pass security. I just can't wait to see how you are going to convince him to volunteer for the operation."

"You really think he's going to be difficult?" O'Brien asked.

"Difficult? Naw. Impossible? Yes."

O'Brien and Collins spent nearly two hours at the Bardmore Country Club where they had lunch plus a few wines. They came up with a brilliant idea for a business front for the Immokalee site. They would set it up to look like a repair and overhaul depot for yachts and small boats. This would be a natural cover for bringing in supplies that would be needed for the project. Collins felt it would be easier to sell this idea to his captain friend, so he would have an excuse for being in Immokalee over the next few weeks.

When O'Brien and Collins got back to the Citation plant, Collins let O'Brien use a private office where he made calls to Washington and Miami to advise everyone of the plans for setting up a yacht repair company at Immokalee. He also gave Bollman the information on the Drummer's new captain, Phillip Avery, Sarasota, Florida, and told him to rush his clearance.

When O'Brien got back to his condo later that afternoon there was a message on the machine to call Ian Billings. It was more good news. A message had come in to Miami early that morning with the information on the mystery island Castro was going to. His destination was Grand Islet, one of three small islands known as Isles Des Saintes just south of Guadeloupe.

O'Brien immediately got out the charts and began to look for the island. His chart showed some small islands just below the island of Guadeloupe, but gave no names. He almost tore the apartment apart looking for the only cruising guide he had on the Leeward Islands. After he found it, he turned to the section on Guadeloupe, found a decent map of the area, and found the small island. The cruising guide gave little information about the island, except that there was no one living on it, and it had a small hill that reached an elevation of 553 feet.

In the excitement of receiving the good news, he forgot to give Billings the name of the man he hoped to recruit as YULETIDE's captain. He called Billings back and Billings suggested that they needed a name for the new business and needed to know how much money would be needed to support the program.

September 12ᵗʰ
0345

O'Brien was awakened by the ringing telephone. He turned on the nightstand light and looked at the small alarm clock. It was 3:45 a.m. He knew it had to be bad news as he picked up the receiver.

"Dan, it's Ted, we have a serious problem."

"Ted, have you been drinking? Where are you?"

"At the plant, I may be wiped out, Dan."

"Ted, for Christ sake man, what the hell?"

"I was torched. They burned the R and D building down."

O'Brien swung his legs out of the bed and stood up, knocking the phone to the floor. He grabbed his pants that were hanging over the nearby chair. "Ted, don't move, wait there, I'm on the way, I'm coming right over."

Still climbing into his clothes, O'Brien jumped into his rental Grand Prix. When he got within in a block of the factory, the police stopped him. There were all kinds of fire equipment parked on the road along with utility trucks and even a television remote van. He convinced a roadblock policeman that he worked for the company and was allowed to go inside the barrier. He arrived at the main office door being held open by a chair. The halls and offices were filled with firemen and policemen moving in and out. He was stopped three times trying to get back to Ted's office. He found Ted with his wife Connie, and Chuck Gold, the company's accountant sitting on folding chairs in front of Ted's desk. A detective in a yellow slicker was talking to Ted and taking notes.

O'Brien had never met Chuck Gold so he introduced himself to him then turned and faced Connie. He could see she was in shock. He asked if she knew just how bad the damage was but she couldn't answer him. Chuck Gold told him that it looked like the entire lamination, research and development buildings were destroyed.

When the detective left, Ted Collins took O'Brien by the arm and led him out a side door into the smoky back yard next to one of the large production buildings. The smell of burning chemicals and the density of the smoke forced them back inside. They went into a nearby sales office. Collins closed the door. He was a covered in dirt and ringing wet.

"We are fucked, Dan."

"Take it easy, Ted, what do you mean?"

"There are two seventy-five foot hulls back there completely destroyed, and the molds are gone too."

O'Brien said nothing. At this point, he did not understand what Collins was trying to tell him.

"There's no way we can build that second yacht, Dan. No way in hell. I would have to build a new plug and a new mold from scratch, or take a mold one off the Drummer. We would never make it for a December date."

"Well, we will just have to find something that looks like the Drummer, that's all. There has to be something around that can work, we just have to find it. Come on, let's get you out of here for now."

They joined Connie and the accountant who had left the building and were standing in the parking lot next to Collins' Cadillac. O'Brien suggested to Connie that she take Ted home. He would hang around with the accountant and keep an eye on things and call Ted in the morning. Connie appreciated O'Brien's concern and helped Ted into the car.

After Collins left, O'Brien turned to the accountant, "Mr. Gold, is there a chance this was deliberate?"

"Hard to say, could be. They hire and fire a lot of loonies and druggies around here. Could be some asshole got the axe today out in the plant, and came back tonight to get even, it happens in this business, Mr. O'Connor."

"O'Brien, the name's O'Brien."

An hour later, O'Brien lay still clothed on his bed, smoking a cigarette and holding a glass of watered down VO. He stared at the ceiling like he had many nights before, waiting for the sunrise. But tonight was more disturbing than before. Tonight's setback could be a final blow that might kill the operation. He only had three days to solve this new problem.

It was 7:12 when the phone rang. O'Brien answered, it was Ted Collins.

"Dan, I was just informed that the fire started in the R and D shop, they believe it was started by an overheated exhaust fan. Somebody forgot to turn it off when they left last night."

"Well, that's some relief, at least it wasn't arson, right? How bad was the damage?"

"Bad enough to put me out of production for a few months. I lost all the tooling on the seventy-five, along with a bunch of small part molds, and the two other hulls are beyond repair."

"Well, Ted, we have three days to..."

"Listen, Dan, I was thinking. I designed the Drummer's lines based on a wooden yacht I saw two years ago. She was a little larger and built nearly forty years ago, but she had the traditional features and the styling that I really loved. I sort of copied her, a little."

"You mean she looks like the Drummer?'

"Well, yes, except she's longer, made of wood and lower in profile."

"Where do you think it is now?"

"I don't know. I saw her in the Bahamas during Abaco race week a couple of years ago. She was anchored in Hope Town when I first saw her. Her name, was either "September Morn or September Song." I met the owner, he was some big time doctor in Palm Beach."

"Ted, do you have any contacts in the yacht business in Palm Beach?"

"Sure do, Mike Middleton, he's a yacht broker, works for Royal Yacht Brokers, at least he did last year. He sold a number of my yachts over there."

"Ted, see if you can locate him, now. I'm going to call Tropical Aviation and charter a plane. You get your ass ready, I will pick you up in forty-five minutes, we're heading for Palm Beach."

When O'Brien pulled up in front of the Citation plant, Ted was standing outside waiting. Ted got in the car.

"We are in luck, old man. I got hold of Mike. He knows the yacht and it's at the Palm Beach Yacht Club. He said he would check out its status, locate the owner, and when we get over there he will take us over to the Club to see it."

"Terrific, now all we have to do is pray it's for sale."

"Dan, if that yacht is for sale, they will be asking a small fortune for it."

"Well, it would still be cheaper than one of yours, right?"

Collins laughed. "You don't know much about this business, do you, Dan? This is a classic yacht, my friend, a one of a kind."

"Well, we just have to buy more insurance, right?"

West Palm Beach
September 12th
1345 hours

O'Brien was lucky, Tropical had the 172 Cutlass available. It took them a little over an hour to reach West Palm International Airport.

They arrived at Royal Yacht's offices in Palm Beach right on schedule. Collins introduced Mike Middleton to O'Brien, who was impressed with the youthful looking man. He sat and listened to Ted and Mike as they talked industry talk, mostly about Ted's new Citation.

"Now, what is this interest in September Morn all about?"

Collins and O'Brien looked at each other, waiting to see who was going to do the explaining.

"Well, Mike, you see I saw this yacht two years ago, and it was the yacht that gave me the ideas for the new Citation line, and..."

"We want to buy it," O'Brien said.

Middleton laughed. "Buy it? Man, do you know who owns that yacht?"

"No, we don't, Mike, but we would like to. You see, we need..."

O'Brien interrupted Collins again. "We really don't care who owns it, Mike, can it be bought?"

65

Middleton studied O'Brien and could see he was serious. He picked up his phone. "Patty, get me Sid Workman, thank you." He put the phone down, and turned to his computer keyboard. He typed for a few seconds and watched the monitor, which was out of sight to O'Brien and Collins.

"Ah, there she is, September Morn, 78 foot ketch, built at Kelsey Shipyard in Maine, 1947. Designed by Hans Kroeger for Mr. and Mrs. Ronald J Hemmings, of Chicago. She is double planked oak and Philippine mahogany, with walnut and cherry interior. A master stateroom, three guest staterooms, three heads, stainless galley. She was repowered with a 653 GM diesel in 1975, plus a new Onan generator, new teak decks, along with extensive interior changes. She was on the market in 1979 and priced at $1.5 million. She came off the market in '80. She is presently located in West Palm Beach at the owner's residence. Huh? I heard she was at the Yacht Club, that's strange."

Middleton's phone rang. "Yes, put him on, thank you." He pulled up to his desk and flipped a page on a legal pad, picked up a pen and began to write. "Sid, how are you? Yes, things are great. Listen, Sid, I have a friend in my office that may be interested in the old September Morn. Oh? No I wasn't. Well, it's not the Hatteras, it's the ketch. Listen, can the doctor be reached? O.K., Sid, thanks, yeah, I'll let you know what he says, right, yeah, let's do lunch, right." Middleton replaced the receiver, pushed a button on the phone and gave instructions to his receptionist to look up the name of Dr. Hemmings in Palm Beach.

"Alright, gentlemen, here's what we have. Workman, who once worked here, had a central listing on the yacht originally. Doc Hemmings took it off the market when he decided to take it to the South Pacific on a cruise. Mrs. Hemmings became very ill and they never got past Hawaii. They came back to Palm Beach, bought a long range Hatteras, named it September Morn II. Mrs. Hemmings died in '83. Dr. Hemmings sold their Palm Beach estate and moved into a condo on the beach. That explains why the yacht is now at the yacht club. Sid says the last he heard, Dr. Hemmings was very ill. His son has the Hatteras up in Virginia Beach. He doesn't think the Doctor will sell the ketch, feels he may have already willed it to some charity."

Middleton's phone rang again. "Thanks, yes, I have it. Listen, I will be out for a couple of hours, if you need me, I'll be on the pager, thank you."

The three men departed the building and got into Middleton's Mercedes and drove up to the yacht club. Fifteen minutes later, they arrived at the Club where Middleton checked the dockmaster's office and learned that a Captain Spencer was on board the yacht. They strolled down the docks between some of the most valuable yachts in Florida. They found September Morn, stern in, near the end of A dock.

Middleton walked out on the finger pier and called the captain's name. The yacht appeared to be in use as the main cabin doors and all the hatches were open. A VHF radio was broadcasting conversations. Middleton called again. "Anybody on board?" He leaned over an knocked on the varnished rail. Suddenly, a massive bearded face appeared from the aft cabin hatch.

"Can I help you?"

"Hi, I'm Mike Middleton, Royal Yacht Sales, and these are two of my clients, mind if we come aboard?"

"Just a minute." The head disappeared below. A few seconds later, the captain came up though the main cabin doors and into the cockpit. He was tall, at least six foot, trim and muscular. Evidently he was working in the engine room, his white shirt and jeans were covered in grease or oil. He was wiping his hands with some paper towels. "I received no word to expect you, ah, Mister.."

"Middleton, Mike Middleton. I didn't have an appointment, are you Captain Spencer?"

"That's right, but unless you're an expected guest, or I get a call from my boss, I can't let you aboard, besides, I have the engine room torn up right now, and she's messy below."

"That's fine, Captain, I understand, but may we just come on deck and walk around topside, we won't touch anything, just want to admire the workmanship, you know, you don't see many....."

Captain Spencer had been studying Ted Collins and he interrupted Middleton. "You're Ted Collins, right?" he asked.

"Yes, sir," Collins replied.

"I'll be damned. We met, oh, two years ago over in the Abacos. I was racing a Soverel, called Green Hornet, you nearly sunk us at the start of a race in Marsh Harbor, remember? You were driving that new half-ton you designed, called Shot-puts, wasn't it?"

Collins face lit up and he laughed, "Of course, I remember. I'll be damned. You were trying to squeeze me into the start boat, a real gutsy move considering I had right of way, but you guys got away with it, and we didn't even protest."

Collins and Captain Spencer exchanged a few more minutes of their experience on their race adventure that week. Finally, Captain Spencer asked the visitors aboard, and offered some cold refreshments. They sat in the comfortable cockpit and drank cold beer. Middleton asked the Captain's permission for he and O'Brien to walk around the yacht, while he and Collins talked racing. Twice, Middleton tried to find out from O'Brien what his interest was in the yacht. Twice, O'Brien avoided answering him.

They spent an hour on the yacht and learned from Spencer that Dr. Hemming was terminally ill with cancer. Collins was able to persuade Spencer to call and find out if they could meet with him and talk to him about selling. Spencer, knowing that Dr. Hemmings would probably enjoy meeting Ted Collins, made the call and set up the appointment for 3:30 at his condo on the beach.

Dr. Hemmings was seated in a recliner chair near a large bay window overlooking the Atlantic Ocean. The large room was bursting with overfilled bookcases, numerous models of famous sailing ships, and a large brass telescope on a tripod near the window. He was quite interested in Ted Collins and very well educated on modern sailing yachts and their construction. He even criticized Collins about the lack of quality in his yachts and told him that he should build them better and charge more money for them. When he asked what their interest in September Morn was, Collins simply told him that he would like to own a classic yacht, especially this one, since it was the one that inspired him to design the new Citations.

The doctor did not buy Ted's answer. Somehow, he saw right through their smoke screen. O'Brien decided to take a gamble and asked if he could speak to him privately. The Doctor agreed and O'Brien asked his two companions to wait outside. Middleton was confused, but left the room with Collins.

O'Brien explained to Hemmings what Operation Yuletide was all about with a few reservations, mainly about Castro. He explained the disaster at the factory and the need for the second yacht. O'Brien had learned much background on Dr. Hemmings from Captain Spencer earlier and from information the Doctor disclosed about his own life, O'Brien felt it was worth the gamble.

An hour later, O'Brien found Collins and Middleton sitting in the small courtyard outside of the Doctor's town house. When asked how he did, O'Brien simply told them that Hemmings would think about it and let him know. Middleton was promised that if the deal was made, he would be the acting broker. He offered to drive them back to the airport.

On the flight back to St. Petersburg, O'Brien gave Collins the rundown on the meeting. Dr. Hemmings would not sell the yacht to them, but would donate it for the cause. But that created problems to work out, like a commission for Middleton and how they would explain the situation to Washington. Most important, September Morn would need some rework on her cabin profile and would have to be painted. He gave Collins the Doctor's unlisted phone number and told him to make the arrangements for moving the yacht to a repair yard. A new, phoney registration and her new name, "Seaduce" would have to be assigned.

Washington, D.C.
Sunday, September 13th
0740 hours

It was raining in Arlington. Ian Billings had taken his pet beagle "Sneakers" out for a walk to retrieve the Sunday papers. Doris Billings called him from their bedroom window and advised him there was a phone call for him. He checked his watch, it was 0750.

Billings went into his study and picked up the phone. It was O'Brien. They spoke for nearly an hour. O'Brien told him about the Citation fire, the trip to Palm Beach and the deal on the yacht September Morn. Billings told O'Brien that he would take care of passing the information along and advised O'Brien that he should plan to be in D.C. first thing Monday morning to make the final decisions on the operation. He warned O'Brien that Koster was making waves and they were not in his bathtub.

O'Brien spent most of Sunday morning talking to Harris, Buckland and Collins, briefing them on his trip to D.C. and the strategy he would use during the meetings on Monday. Each man had some positive news for O'Brien, especially Harris. The work at Immokalee was on schedule. Collins had already started to de-commission the Drummer and could have her in Ft. Myers, hauled out, put on a truck and in Immokalee by Tuesday, the 15th. The new engines were ready to leave Houston and work crews could be on site as soon as they were all cleared by Bollman's office.

Washington, D.C.
Sunday
1930 hours

O'Brien caught a Delta non-stop into Baltimore-Washington airport. He arrived at his Wisconsin Avenue apartment at 2230 hours with about six hours to put together his final notes before meeting with Admiral Koster. What troubled him most was the request he had to make for a quarter of a million dollars in cash to set up the new yacht repair company.

At the time that O'Brien was boarding his flight in Tampa, the phone rang in Admiral Koster's den. His aide reported on the latest surveillance photos taken over Cuba earlier by a Air Force SR-71 Blackbird.

Koster phoned General Richard Kratz, Air Force Chief of Staff, and told him he wanted to increase Blackbird SR-71 and U-2 surveillance immediately over Cuba because he was seriously thinking of sending a battle group into the Caribbean Sea for maneuvers. He removed a ledger from his brief case and opened it. He carefully examined the inventory of all ships currently in port on the Atlantic coast and he made notes as he reviewed the status of each vessel. The carrier Eisenhower, CVN 69, at Mayport Navy Base in Florida, was on a thirty-six hour alert status, no major work in progress. Frigates, CGN 39 and CGN 40 on standby status. Destroyers, DDG 46 and 24 were on stand-by as well as the FF 1096 tanker "Valdez". He closed the ledger and noted that he could order up a standard carrier attack force built around the carrier, Eisenhower. Now all he needed was three subs. He reached for the phone, then checked his watch, it was too late. He would have to call Norfolk at first light and speak to Commander Shock to get the update on readiness reports of all ships in port. He also needed to contact the Commander of Atlantic Fleet Sub Forces and see what units were active in the Caribbean and what he could borrow for the carrier group.

What was troubling Koster about his aide's report was the sighting of a Soviet C-6 Kara Class Cruiser and a Kivak Class II destroyer escorting a AGI intelligence ship, most likely the "Krym", towards the Port of Havana. It was unusual to see the Soviets bring down any first line war ships to Cuba. He wrote another note. Check on recent position reports of all Russian\Cuban cruiser and destroyer traffic in the Caribbean for the past year. Also confirm position of "Gigrometr", the Russian survey ship hanging out between St. Martin and Antigua all summer. Also, a track record on the other spook trawler "Krym", where had she been hanging out for the last six months?

Havana, Cuba
Sunday
1910 hours

At the time Admiral Koster was enjoying a simple pot roast dinner with his wife Marlene, two young Cuban altar boys were lighting candles in a small Roman Catholic Church in old Havana. Evening services were about to begin at Holy Trinity. Kneeling together in the first pew, two women prayed in silence beneath their black lace veils. At the end of the service, the two women would walk to a near-by cafe. When they parted, one would take a taxi to her daughter's apartment in Havana, the other would be picked up by her son-in-law and driven home over thirty miles away. During their visit together, their identical purses were exchanged. In the purses were identical flashlights.

Before the sun rose over Cuba the next day, one of these flashlights would be in the flight case of Captain Carlos Lucia, who was scheduled to command Flight 411, Cubana Airlines, departing Havana at 0830 hours non-stop to Maracaibo, Venezuela. Before the sun set this day, a message was sent to Eastern Airlines Customer Services at Miami International Airport. Within minutes, Admiral Koster knew its contents. He called O'Brien and told him to bring back some Cuban cigars for the Pentagon's Christmas Party.

White House
Monday, September 14th.
0830 hours

Outside the Oval Office, unseasonable winds and heavy rains threatened the fragile gardens. The dark gray skies hung low, moving rapidly west to east. Occasionally heavy volleys of thunder would roll through the stone corridors of Washington. Inside the Oval Office, all the indirect lighting was turned on as well as the chandelier that hung above the round conference table.

"Mr. President, Mr. Vice President, as you can see by this rough progress chart we put together, Mr. O'Brien's Operation Yuletide is close to schedule and he has met the demands that we placed on him two weeks ago. There are a few problems we still face and I personally feel that it's still a 50-50 ballgame. However, I'm pleased with O'Brien's reports and I would like to let him pass this deadline tomorrow and continue the operation." Admiral Koster looked over at O'Brien and smiled.

The President stood up and turned to O'Brien. "Dan, I just heard your major critic, you just got his blessing, that's good enough for me. You have done a commendable job, considering some of the setbacks you have faced. However, like the Admiral said, it's still all uphill for you. If you see any signs that the Yuletide operation is in any kind of trouble, for any reason, you shut it down, am I clear?"

"Yes, sir, and thank you, Mr. President."

"Now, for the funding of your ship repair company in, ah, Emamalee?"

71

O'Brien laughed. "That's Immokalee, sir. We feel we will need at least $250,000.00 to cover our costs from now until the tests. I know it's a lot of money, but we will have some assets we can sell and be able to recoup about half."

The President laughed, "Dan, it's not the amount we are worried about, it's whose little fund are we going to raid to get it. Not to worry, that's my job. You will have it when you're ready to leave for Florida."

"Gentlemen?" The President smiled. The Vice President reached over and shook Dan's hand and stood up. The meeting was over.

O'Brien stood with Admiral Koster beneath the small awning at the west entrance of the White House. "That was easier than I thought it would be, Admiral."

Koster smiled. "It was not so easy at 0545 this morning when he woke me up to hear my opinion."

The Admiral's limo arrived and the White House doorman opened the rear door for the Admiral. Koster turned before he entered the limo and faced O'Brien. "Call Commander Buckland, he wants to see you. He is flying out to Ardmore, Oklahoma tomorrow to watch some tests on the new CR-12 plastic. Oh, almost forgot. The message that Mrs. Cox came in and gave me an hour ago? It was from Ian Billings. Mr. Castro is expecting his "device" to arrive on a freighter sometime around the 30th. He has code named his operation "DOLPHIN"."

O'Brien was puzzled. "Why didn't you tell the President about this, sir? He would have been even more pleased."

"I was holding it as a trump card, just in case I needed it. Have a nice day, O'Brien and let's plan a few minutes before you head back."

The Admiral got into the back seat of the black Cadillac Fleetwood and the car drove away. O'Brien was left standing next to the dripping doorman, whose transparent raincoat was boiling him from inside out. He looked at O'Brien like a worried father. "Sir, your car? Has your driver been called?"

O'Brien laughed. "My car is a ten year old Volvo and is parked at the Pentagon and my other car and driver just left with the Admiral. I guess he forgot I arrived with him."

"Would you like me to call you a cab, sir?"

"Why, do I look like a cab?"

"I beg your pardon, sir?"

"It's a joke, yes, please, if you wouldn't mind?"

The doorman walked over to a small box attached to the inside wall of the doorway and opened the door. O'Brien could hear him calling. " Hello, hello, is anyone there?"

The noise of an engine caught O'Brien's attention. He turned to see the massive front grille of a Cadillac approaching. He recognized the Navy officer behind the wheel and the arm with all the gold bands waving frantically from the rear door window. "Terribly sorry, O'Brien, I forgot we gave you a lift over this morning, please get in."

O'Brien got in the limo and sat next to the Admiral. He suddenly realized that the doorman was still on the phone and had not seen the car pull up. Before he could yell, the young officer at the wheel pulled away.

"By the way, as you requested I called Dr. Hemmings in Palm Beach on Friday and had a good long chat. I agree with you, Dan, the man is a team player and can be trusted. I told him we would appreciate if he would keep his name on the yacht until after we do the modifications, or whatever. It would look like he wanted to have the work done. You will see that he gets the bill and we will reimburse him later. I take it that these modification expenses on the September Moan are not in the quarter mil you asked for?"

O'Brien chuckled. "It's September Morn, sir, and you're right, I did not include the new modifications in my budget. The bright side is that Ted Collins is doing all the mechanical drawings saving us a bundle and he found a yard close to Palm Beach that can take her in and start work immediately. Collins figures it will take at least six to seven weeks to make the changes needed and will cost between eighty to a hundred thousand."

"Did you tell Dr. Hemmings that you plan to destroy his yacht in this operation?"

"No, sir. Collins and I both agreed it could affect his health , he is not well and.. "

"I agree. He told me he hopes that he can make it to Christmas." The Admiral picked up his car phone and pushed in a few numbers. "Commander Buckland, please, this is Admiral Koster. I will hold, thank you." He looked at O'Brien and grinned. " Here, when he gets on, invite him out for dinner tonight, and don't forget to include his wife, Peggy, or Meggy."

O'Brien took the phone and put it to his ear while eyeing the Admiral. "What's up, Admiral?" Buckland's voice came on the line.

"Ah, Buckwheat, it's me, O'Brien. No, he is right here. Listen, everything went fine, the Chief and the VP are pleased, ah, what are you doing tonight? Oh, well, I was wondering if you and your wife would like to join me for dinner later? Uh huh, yes.. fine. Ah, let's say, eight sharp at The Den, in Georgetown? Great, see you later."

O'Brien handed the Admiral back the phone.

"He's going to hit you for a favor, Dan."

"A favor? Buckwheat wants a favor?"

"Yes, he wants on the mission. He wants on the Drummer when it goes to war."

21,000 feet above Ocala, Florida
Saturday, September 19th

"Mr. O'Brien, sir, would you like to come up and take the right seat? We are about to contact Tampa approach."

O'Brien looked up into the face of what he thought was a teenager. It was actually the co-pilot who was leaning out of the small cabin door that led to the flight deck of the Lear jet.

"Ah, no thanks, son. Thank the pilot anyway. I have some things I have to read."

The young pilot smiled and closed the door.

O'Brien looked at his watch, it was 06:50. He looked out the small window for any landmarks he could see. It was still fairly dark, but he could see off to the west pure white smoke clouds climbing into the atmosphere from the nuclear power plant at Crystal River. He sat back and studied the package that sat on the seat opposite, neatly wrapped in brown paper and tied with postal string. He had to strain his eyes to read the black printing on the top, even though he knew what it said. AVERY'S YACHT REPAIRS, IMMOKALEE AIRPORT, IMMOKALEE, FLORIDA. It seemed such a small package to carry a quarter million dollars in twenties, fifties and hundreds.

The Lear gracefully banked west and reduced power. O'Brien could feel the pressure change in the small cabin as the aircraft started to descend. He glanced out again, the white clouds were to the north now. He closed his eyes, trying to figure out what was taking place in the cockpit. He guessed that Tampa radar approach was vectoring the jet to set up a landing approach to St. Pete Clearwater Airport, his destination. He relaxed again and closed his eyes as thousands of voices echoed in his mind. Suddenly he sprang upright, eyes wide open, his heart felt like it was coming out of his chest.

"Sir, I'm sorry if I woke you, but we are cleared for St. Pete. Please check your seat belt, we should be on the ground in ten minutes," the young man disappeared again behind the cabin door.

He checked his watch, it was 0710. He began to think about the next few hours. Souza should be at the National FBO if his flight into Tampa was on time. We can be at Tropical by 0800, in the Cessna and airborne by 0815, and landing at Immokalee no later that 0930. He closed his eyes again, this time concentrating on the past week. The last four days in D.C. had been productive. O'Brien had nothing but positive reports from all his people. Buckwheat had been out to Oklahoma and was pleased at the results of the tests on the new plastic, CR-l2. He had made arrangements to have some of the new material sent to San Diego to the Navy Seal school and to Key West where UDT experts could experiment with it.

Souza reported that according to new messages out of Cuba, Carlos Lucia was scheduled to make four trips the coming week and expected to have some final information on the arrival of the "device." He planned to have more information on Castro's new yacht and hopefully for Admiral Koster's sake, some information on the arrivals of two new Soviet war ships in Havana.

September Morn was moved to the ship yard and turned over to Eugene Massey, owner of the yard, who had already met with Ted Collins and gone over the new modifications. Captain Mel Spencer had delivered the yacht himself. Collins reported that Spencer was asking all kinds of questions, but Massey, as instructed, ignored him. According to Dr. Hemmings, he had terminated Spencer with one year's salary, but advised Collins that Spencer was quite bitter about being let go.

O'Brien had called Collins and Bollman and told them it was time to get Phil Avery on board and that he should be brought down to Immokalee next Saturday morning for indoctrination.

Collins also reported on the progress of the DRUMMER. The two super engines had arrived with their crews and were already assembling the engines to the new hydraulic V-drive transmissions. Work crews had begun gutting the Drummer's interior and major surgery was started on the hull sections where the new drives would be installed.

St. Petersburg\Clearwater Airport

O'Brien was wakened by the sudden hard shock he felt when the Lear touched down. He held on to the small arm rests as the plane rumbled, shook and vibrated as the brakes and reverse thrust was applied. He stepped down out of the Lear onto the hardstand. The fresh air felt good. All he wanted now was to see Souza and get a cup of hot coffee. As he picked up his B-4 bag, brief case and the small carton, a voice came from behind.

"Have a nice day, Mr. O'Brien."

He turned and saw the young pilot standing in the small door. He smiled and waved a salute. "Ah, right, thank you, tell Mr. Billings I appreciate the lift."

The door closed and the two engines began to wind up as the small jet began to roll and turn towards the taxi strip. O'Brien made note of the numbers on the side of the aircraft. N 3002 H. He turned and headed towards the National Flight lounge about twenty yards ahead. He looked at the two glass entry doors and saw the familiar smile of Jesus Souza, who was dressed in a red banlon shirt, white cotton slacks, a Panama Jack hat, sunglasses and white loafers, no socks.

CHAPTER SIX

Sarasota, Florida
Saturday, September 19th
06:45 A.M.

The vintage 1962 Thunderbird pulled out on Midnight Pass Road and headed north on the resort island of Siesta Key. The clock on the dashboard read 6:40. Phil Avery tapped on the plastic face of the clock; it was running, it was just slow. He glanced at the temperature and oil pressure gauges and did more tapping; all the needles were working. He noted the gas tank had a quarter tank of fuel but figured it was enough to get him to Sarasota-Bradenton Airport.

The alpine white sports car attracted the attention of a number of fishermen standing along the drawbridge connecting to the mainland. For years Avery dreamed of owning a classic Thunderbird, now with his business accelerating he began fulfilling his dreams. He had his classic car, a small a condo in Ft. Lauderdale, a modest bayside home on Sarasota Bay and his most recent purchase for his company, a used Piper Archer II, four place airplane.

Avery turned the Thunderbird into the parking lot at Dolphin Aviation at 7:07. He parked the car, put the top up and proceeded to the pilots' lounge where Corky Riggins, the Dolphin's service manager, greeted him.

"She's ready to go Mr. Avery, both tanks topped and you're about a pint low on oil, she's parked on the..."

"Thanks, Corky." Avery interrupted. Avery walked past the service counter and through the door leading to the ramp. Riggins, a tall lanky African-American was disturbed at Avery's strange attitude; he always stopped to double check on how much fuel and service his plane needed.

As Avery walked towards his plane, he noted bright sunrays beginning to break through the purple cumulus clouds on the eastern horizon. A cool breeze drifted across his face and in the distance he could hear the whine of jet engines coming from the main terminal. He looked towards the airport's terminal and saw the silhouettes of two tail sections, a Boeing 757 and 727, rising above the terminal. The 757 had all its lights on, preparing for departure.

When he reached his plane the wings and cabin top were glistening with droplets of water from the wash down that Corky had given it earlier. For the next ten minutes, he carefully performed a pre-flight check on the plane and prepared for the short flight. After putting on his headset he reached for the sectional. He knew roughly where his destination was but wanted to confirm its location and establish the course and mileage. He found the small uncontrolled airport that was named after the town it served – Immokalee. He estimated it was eighty to eighty five miles southeast and would take twenty-five to thirty minutes to fly there. He tuned in the local airport information (ATIS) on his VHF radio to listen to the pre-taped information on weather, temps and runway use, then started the engine and switched his radio to "ground" frequency for taxi information.

"Sarasota ground, Archer November eight-three zero-two Sierra at Dolphin with information Bravo, ready to taxi three four."

"Zero three-two Sierra, proceed to three four, hold short two-two."

"Roger tower, proceed three four hold short two-two, zero-two Sierra." Phil glanced around the ramp then eased off the brakes and taxied his way out to the taxi strip that paralleled runway three-four.

"Zero two Sierra, Eastern seven-fiver-seven departing terminal, use caution, you will be number two for departure."

"Roger tower, have Eastern in sight". Suddenly, Phil was totally blinded by the sun's reflection bouncing off the silver body of the Eastern jet turning onto the taxi strip. While fighting the blinding rays he reached for his sunglasses on the passenger seat.

A loud intimidating voice broke through his headset.

"Zero-two Sierra, hold short for two-two, there's traffic departing, do you copy?"

Phil over-reacted slamming both feet hard against the pedals. The Archer responded like a lassoed wild bull, slamming down on the nose strut sending groaning metallic sounds throughout the airframe. Phil's worse fear was confirmed; he was sitting in the middle of runway 22. He looked up and saw the underbody and landing gear of a Cessna 150, its wheels spinning as they flew past him banking away.

"Eastern one-one-seven, tower frequency one-two-zero one-zero have a nice day. Archer three-zero-two Sierra, proceed to three four, use caution."

"Roger tower, three-zero-two Sierra." Phil eased the throttle and released the brakes; his eyes fixed on the large jet fifty yards ahead. He was embarrassed at his performance and angry because he was about to break all his rules on taking to the skies. He was flying to an uncontrolled airport he had never visited with no filed flight plan because he was ordered not to tell anyone where he was going or when he was coming back.

"What the hell is Ted Collins doing in Immokalee? It's a damn farm town, and what does he want with me? Why would he ask me not to tell anyone about this flight and not to file a flight plan?"

The Eastern jet turned onto runway three-four and without hesitation began its take-off roll. Phil turned the Archer into the wind, locked the brakes and switched to tower frequency. As he began his run-up check, he could feel the Archer tremble as if it had caught a chill. It was caused by the vibrations coming from the two powerful jet engines swung under the wings of the 757 as they reached maximum power. The big Eastern jet took little time and runway before it was lifting into the clear morning sky.

"Archer three-zero-two Sierra, you're clear for take-off and a left hand departure."

"Roger tower, clear for departure, left turn-out, Zero-two Sierra."

Phil taxied out on the runway and moved the throttle slowly to full power. The Archer flew itself off the runway while Phil made instrument checks and trimmed his climb rate. He had just begun to bank left to fly over Sarasota Bay when the tower called.

"Archer three-zero-two-Sierra, say your intentions."

"Sarasota tower, zero two Sierra, climbing to fifteen hundred and heading south along beaches to Venice."

"Roger zero two Sierra, squawk one-zero-four-zero. Be on alert for a helicopter working around south end of Longboat Key in the City Island area."

"Roger that Sarasota, zero-two Sierra."

Phil banked left when he reached fifteen hundred feet flying above the beaches of Longboat Key. He leveled off and throttled back to cruise. The view outside was spectacular with the morning sun glistening on Sarasota's downtown buildings and Sarasota Bay.

When he reached the island of Casey Key, he banked southeast to avoid any traffic around Venice Airport and climbed to thirty-five hundred feet and set his course on one-fifty-five degrees.

Avery began to relax and enjoy the flight, then his thoughts drifted to his office manager, Gail Townsend. "She will be opening the office in a few minutes and wondering where the hell I am. She won't panic until 11 o'clock; then she will start calling my house, all the coffeehouses and by noon she'll be boiling mad. Maybe she will call Dolphin and they will tell her that I took off, which is really going piss her off for not telling her where I was going..."

Phil scanned the horizon, checked his instruments and watch, estimating to be over Immokalee airport in fifteen minutes. He thoughts of the journey returned.

"I thought I knew Ted Collins, had some great times together over the past few years. At times a little self-centered and crude but he was never secretive, at least until two nights ago when he called. Maybe something snapped when he had the recent fire at his boat plant, and what the hell is he doing in Immokalee?"

Immokalee airport finally appeared and as Avery flew over the field he scanned the area and noticed an old hangar with a few planes setting outside. The 5000-foot runways appeared clear with no traffic in a pattern. There was no radio control here, no traffic in the air and the windsock on the field was indicating the wind was out of the west, so he set up his pattern to land on runway 27.

On the final leg, he trimmed for a long approach using no flaps. He was about to flare out and touch down when he noticed a pickup truck swerve onto the runway heading his way along the edge of the runway. At first his reaction was to firewall the throttle and take off, then he saw an arm waving madly from the passenger side of the cab. He let the Archer settle down on the concrete and pulled off the power. The truck turned around and caught up to him and Archer saw Ted Collins waving with his arm out of the window. He brought the Archer to a stop as the truck came alongside. Ted motioned to Phil to follow them.

The long taxi trip across nearly an acre of rough pasture finally ended near the old Quonset hangar. Ted jumped from the truck and ran towards two parked aircraft, waving to Phil to follow him. When Phil shut down the Archer, he was lined up with a Cessna 172, and a Piper Cherokee-six. Phil opened the cabin door and stepped out on the wing. Collins was standing next to the pickup truck, his dark brown hair blowing over his tanned face.

"Hey, asshole, you're late."

"Well, talk to the asshole in your tower here, he wouldn't give me clearance to land." Phil stepped off the wing and the two men greeted each other.

Ted Collins was taller than Avery was, boasting a larger athletic frame. Physically, they shared some similar features. Both had broad shoulders, trim waists and in top physical condition. Ted was a no-nonsense health freak. No smoking, no red meat, taking handfuls of vitamins and he jogged five miles a day. Phil, although five years younger, smoked cigarettes, loved steaks and took vitamin C only when he had a cold. They both had a taste for the finer things, loved to sail and chase women. It was through sailing they first met in Miami in 1979. Ted had a new half-ton racer that he was campaigning and Phil was recruited as crew when one of Ted's regulars didn't show. From that day they became close friends and business associates.

"O.K., you got me down here, now what the hell is going on, Ted?"

"Hop in the truck, Phil, we need to go around the to the front. I will explain when we are inside."

Phil slid in beside the young driver and Ted followed. Before Ted could close the door, the driver put the truck in gear, slipped the clutch and spun nearly 180 degrees. Before the dust could settle in the cab, the truck stopped nearly jerking Phil's head off. Phil looked at the young man hoping to get eye contact. Ted jumped out of the truck and ran ahead to open the gate that was attached to a ten foot chain link fence. He pushed the gate open and signaled to the driver to come ahead. This time the truck moved slowly and stopped in front of an office trailer. Phil stepped out of the truck and joined Collins who was walking towards the office door.

"What the hell is he all about? Is he the mystery down here? Are you developing some kind of new species? He does talk, doesn't he?"

"Ah, he's alright, Phil, his nose is a little bent because, well, he's a gofer and wants a better job to make better bucks, that's all."

Collins placed his hands on Phil's shoulders and looked him straight in the eyes. Phil could see that whatever Ted was about to say was going to be serious.

"Phil, when we walk through that door over there, your whole life could change. You are going to meet some very unusual people inside and see some very unusual things going on. I am not allowed to tell you much right now, there is a guy that will be here within the hour who will be briefing you on everything?"

Phil did not respond. He looked around the front of the building. He saw two white Dodge vans parked near-by and two Chrysler New Yorker sedans by the fence. He noted the large poles that held the fence in place had small mounds of fresh dirt around their bases, which meant the fence had just been installed. It appeared to go completely around the entire hangar and office building.

"I'm going to take a guess, Ted. From the looks of the rented cars, the fencing and lack of anything else around this place, I'd have to say you are involved with a government project, right?"

Ted smiled, his dark brown eyes rolled back in his head, as if he were relieved. "Yep, you hit it on the head, Phil. I am working on a project for the U.S. of A. As a matter of fact, everyone you meet here today is working for the government, under very strict security. I'm afraid you will have to agree to some security terms yourself, providing you want to accept a job offer."

"A job offer? Are you nuts? I can't take on any new job, I'm still getting settled in Sarasota and the Ft. Lauderdale office isn't running as smoothly as I had hoped when I decided to move over here."

"Easy, Phil, this isn't a full time, well, it won't be for ever, just a few months, that's all, and you will be well paid. I'm sure we can find a way to help manage your affairs...."

"Hold it, what do you mean, manage my affairs, what the hell are you talking about? You sound like you're planning to send me somewhere, is that it?"

"I can't say, Phil. Hey, when you find out what is going on, I know you will be excited, and buddy, you're the only one who can pull this off."

"Pull what off? What the fuck are you talking about? Either you start explaining, right now, or I'm out of here and we will forget this meeting ever took place."

Ted could see that Phil was not bluffing and knew he would leave, even if he had to scale the fence. Ted reached out, took Phil's arm and led him towards the fence. He kept looking back at the office door.

"Ah, I don't know where to begin, I just can't tell you anything, but you will be told soon. One thing I can tell you is that inside that building is my ISLAND DRUMMER; I brought her down here a couple of weeks ago. She is going through a total rework that needs to be completed by December lst. If all goes well, she will be the fastest seventy five foot sailboat in sailing history."

Phil studied Ted for a moment. He could tell that there was more, but decided not to push. "O.K. Ted, now we are getting somewhere. You are building a super spy-ship, or a spook ship, right? It's going to be working in Florida and possibly Bahamian waters, monitoring drug runners, or something like that."

"Damn, Phil, how did you figure that out, its classified stuff, but your right, its going to involved with drug surveillance."

"Fine, now where do I come in?"

"Ah, we want you to be her skipper for a while, that's all."

"Uh-huh, you want me to run her around the Gulf and maybe even into the Caribbean, as if I was on vacation."

Ted could hear the sarcasm in Phil's voice building. He had to stall. The door of the office opened, attracting their attention.

"Hey, Ted, where's McCoy and the truck? O'Brien is due on the field in five minutes."

"Ah, he took off, Lou, about ten minutes ago. I think he went over to Ft. Myers to pick up some marine batteries."

"Is that Phil Avery with you?"

"Ah, right, we were just about to come in and meet with you."

Lou Bollman let the door close behind him as he walked towards Ted and Phil. Bollman was built like a bulldog and in top physical condition and looked very much like the movie actor, Robert Duvall. He had a pleasant personality and was always smiling. He was smiling when he reached Ted and Phil and held out his hand. "Hi, my name is Lou Bollman, Phil."

"Hi, Phil Avery."

"Ted has told us a lot about you, Phil, we were looking forward meeting you. Has Ted explained why you're here?"

Ted interrupted. "Well, I was just explaining to him about the Drummer and that we hope to have her ready for testing around Thanksgiving week."

"O.K., ah, listen, would you guys mind taking one of the vans and running around and pick up Rudolf? He should be landing any minute." Bollman asked.

"Sure, come on, Phil. This is the guy who will be briefing you on the project, right, Lou?"

"Right, nice meeting you, Phil, I'll see you a little later."

Ted and Phil walked over towards the nearest white van. Ted located the keys beneath the seat and started the engine.

"What does Lou do?" Avery asked.

"Ah, he's the Bureau Chief, Miami, ah, FBI."

"FBI? Whoa, I'm impressed, and Rudolf?"

"Ah, he is sort of in charge of the project, you know, like the chairman of the board? His name is really Dan O'Brien, his code name is Rudolf for the project."

"Oh, you have a code names for the project? If I agree to come on board, do I get a code name?"

"Ah, would you mind unlocking the gate, Phil? The combination of the lock, is zero, zero, seven.

"'Zero-zero-seven'?, that sounds familiar, getting a little theatrical aren't we? Hey, I want to be code named James Bond if I'm to be the new skipper of the Drummer." Phil was laughing and shaking his head as he opened the door of the van and stepped out.

"You're Santa Claus, I'm afraid," Collins said.

Avery looked dazed for a moment. He closed the door and walked towards the locked gate, turned and looked at Ted's solemn face. Santa Claus? he said silently. Ted easily read Phil's lips and smiled. The door of the Cessna opened and Avery watched the large man struggle to get out of the cockpit. On the passenger side, a small Latin man got out of the plane and was removing a carton from the back seat. Collins was standing behind the wing waiting to greet the pilot. Avery could not hear their conversation, but could see in their faces that they were pleased to see each other. The Latin man joined them and they headed for the van. Avery opened the door and stepped out facing them.

"Phil, this is Dan O'Brien and Jesus Souza. Gentlemen, Phil Avery". They exchanged handshakes and got in the van for the trip back to the hangar.

"Mr. Avery, I understand that you have built a very successful business managing private yachts here in south Florida?"

Phil, knowing it was O'Brien's voice from behind, answered in a military response, "Yes, sir."

Ted pulled up to the chain link gate and stopped. Phil jumped out, unlocked the gate and swung it back.

"He appears to be a little feisty, Ted, is everything alright?"

"Yeah, he's fine, he's testing you. I told him we were building Drummer into a spook ship and wanted him to play captain. He knows you're going to be the man to make the deal."

"Are Buckland and Bollman here?"

"Yeah, they're waiting for you."

"O.K, here's what we do. Let's turn Phil over to Bollman for the briefing first. I will meet with him after, matter of fact, we will all meet with him later, but first let's see what his reaction is to Bollman."

The four men entered the mobile office trailer. Phil was amazed how much bigger it was inside. He counted five men working at various locations. One young man was seated with a headset on looking at a computer monitor. Another man was sitting on a high stool working on a blue print. Towards the rear of the office, a large man sitting at a desk had a phone tucked under his chin, and was chewing someone out.

Phil followed O'Brien, Collins and Souza as they snaked their way to the back of the trailer. When they reached the man on the phone they stopped. There was a door there that evidently led to a private office. Another door with a window obviously led outside to the hangar.

"Listen, you asshole, I already gave you all the credit information I can, are we going to get some kind of credit line or not? Well, fuck you too." The large man slammed the phone down hard enough to send a glass of pencils and pens flying off the cluttered desk. He looked up at O'Brien through his smudged thick horn-rimmed glasses. "Man, we've got some fucking twits down here, O'Brien. How do you expect me to keep this place going without cash flow? Nobody in this fucking wilderness is going to give us credit without some kind of...."

"Here, Sam, this will take care of your problems for now." O'Brien motioned to Souza to hand Sam the well-wrapped carton that came from the plane. Avery saw printing on the carton with what he thought was his name written in large letters.

Souza placed the carton on top of the messy desk and smiled at Sam. Now Avery could clearly see the black print. It read AVERY'S YACHT REPAIRS INC. IMMOKALEE, FLORIDA

The office door opened and Bollman stepped out. " I hope you brought Sam some cookies, this son-of-a-bitch is driving us nuts with his screaming and yelling all day."

O'Brien smiled, "Sam's got his problems, but he is the best, right, Sam? When we need action, there isn't a better purchasing agent this side of Little Rock."

"Fuck you, O'Brien and the Irish steamer you came over on. By the way, is this the man?"

"Yep, Sam, this is the man and you can have him just as soon as Lou finishes with him." O'Brien motioned to Avery to enter the office. "Phil, Lou here is FBI, and he needs to spend a few minutes with you, O.K.? Lou, we are going to be in the hangar, give me a call when you're ready." O'Brien gently placed his hand on Avery's shoulder. He studied O'Brien's large square face and for some strange reason he already liked this man they call Rudolf. Bollman closed the door as the three men left.

The room was badly lit. There was a desk and chair to one side and two large boards attached to the wall. On another wall was a chart of Florida, the Caribbean and parts of South America. In the opposite corner was a split sofa with a table and lamp, a coffee table laden with and overfilled ashtray. A brief case was open and a number of folders were spread out on one of the couches.

"Phil, let's sit down, would you like a coffee or a coke or something?" Phil said no and sat down on the sofa. He watched Bollman as he pawed through the folders. He picked one up and put the rest in the case, sat down, reached for a pack of Camels on the table and offered Phil a cigarette.

"Ah, no, prefer my own brand, thanks." Phil reached in his pant pocket and located a badly crushed pack of Winstons and an ancient Zippo lighter.

"Boy, that's a classic flame thrower."

"Yeah, sure is, I've had this baby since flight school in '71.

Looking in the folder, Bollman corrected him. "Seventy-two, you completed flight training at San Antonio in '72."

Phil lit a cigarette and sat back against the foam cushion. "Yeah, you're right, it was 72."

"Born in Toms River, New Jersey, September 18, 1950. Mother, Agnes and father Richard, both deceased. Your older sister Mary lives with her husband and two children in Bay Head, New Jersey. Your younger sister Eileen recently divorced a lawyer in Scranton and is planning to move to Florida. You graduated Toms River High School with a scholarship in sports, a three-letter man, football, baseball and hockey. You attended University of Pennsylvania from 67 to 70, majored in business and economics. Joined the Air Force in October '71, trained in multi-jet transports, flew with Military Airlift until your discharge in '75. You joined your dad in Toms River to help him with his charter fleet. In '78 your dad died and you took over the charter fleet, which consisted of three sport fishing boats. In '80 you sold the business, including a bait and tackle shop. You set your mom up in a small apartment in Toms River and you moved to Ft. Lauderdale. You purchased a 1978 Bertram 38 sport fishing yacht and became a professional charter boat captain at Bahia Mar. By January '82, you had four charter yachts and doing quite well. You had a client, Mel Rosin, also from Toms River, who bought you out in May '83. You went to work as a broker for while, then opened your own charter and management business. In 84 you became one of the largest yacht management companies in Florida. You have two offices, one on 17th Street in Ft. Lauderdale and one at City Marina in Sarasota. You have sixteen employees, most of them in Lauderdale. You have one in Sarasota, Gail Townsend. Your personal properties consist of a condominium on 15th Street south east in Lauderdale and a three-bedroom two-bath frame house on Siesta Key, Sarasota. You purchased the condo in '83 for $79,000, and owe $18,945. Your house in Sarasota has a current mortgage of $105,889.87. You purchased a 1962 Thunderbird in Miami for $12,500 last January, and a 1978 Piper Cherokee, amount unknown, which the C&S bank in Sarasota holds a note on for $46,000. Presently, you are drawing a $75,000 annual salary from the Company, plus. You have three business accounts – Avery Yacht Management Inc., Avery Charter Service, Inc. and Suncoast Yacht Management, Inc. Currently in business accounts you have roughly $103,357.00 in cash. In personal accounts in Lauderdale and Sarasota, you have a little over $8,200.00 cash. You have some stock in ATT and two ten thousand-dollar c.d.'s. You're not aware of it, but you're about to be audited by the IRS, a field audit. How am I doing?"

"$68,350.00."

"I beg your pardon?"

"That's what I paid for the Piper."

"Oh, I'll make a note of that."

"O.K., I'm impressed, you guys did your homework, shit, I have nothing to hide and I am aware of the IRS, my lawyer has it taken care of."

"Yeah, we know you're clear. Phil, there is one very personal item that I need to discuss, as it could interfere with this operation, if you accept our offer."

Phil lit another cigarette. "Where is that coffee you offered?"

"I'll have to have Sam get it, how do you like it?"

"Little cream, no sugar."

Bollman went over to the door and stuck his head outside. Phil could barely hear him talk to Sam. Bollman returned to the couch. He reached over and picked up another file and started flipping through pages. He stopped, "Nancy Barnes."

Phil became uneasy. He rested both elbows on his knees and clasped his hands as he stared at Bollman. "What about Nancy?"

"Well, we know she's your lady, Phil. You have been seeing her, or I should say, living with her for nearly two years."

"Not quite, but what business is that of yours?"

"Well, we learned that you wanted her to come to Sarasota, but she wants to continue working for a while, and this may be causing some problems."

"Hey, you fucking guys got a nerve, you know that?" Phil stood up and walked from behind the table stood face to face with Bollman. Bollman stood at ease looking at the fire in Avery's eyes.

"Phil, when we were checking you out we learned about Nancy and your disagreements, that's all."

Avery turned and walked across the room towards the desk. "Nancy has a senior position with Island Airways. She's been with them nearly ten years and loves the job. She's not ready to give it up, that's all there is to it."

"Yes, Phil, we know, however, we also learned through our surveillance, and I don't know how to say this tactfully, but Nancy is sharing your condo with might be another lover."

Phil faced off again with Bollman. This time he could feel his heart beating down to his fingertips. He curled his bottom lip over his teeth and clamped down, trying to hold back an outburst he felt coming from the pit of his stomach.

"Get Collins in here now, I want out of here. You and your government pimps take a flying fuck for yourselves, for two cents, I would..."

Bollman stepped aside and went to the door. He spoke again to Sam, closed the door, threw the folder into the briefcase and walked over to Phil who was leaning against the desk, staring at the dingy gray linoleum floor.

"Phil, I am really sorry about this, I wish there was another way, but man, this operation is, well, it's like nothing I have ever been connected with and we can't let anything or anyone cause any problems. Phil, you are the main player here, you do realize that don't you?"

"The hell I am, pal, get yourself some other jock who won't give you any problems, o.k.? You know the only thing that's stopping me from re-arranging your nose? I want to get out of here, now."

The door flew open and O'Brien appeared. He was breathing heavy and perspiration was running down his face and bleeding through his cotton shirt.

"What's going on here, gentlemen?"

Sarasota City Marina
1000 hours

Gail Townsend parked her Firebird in her usual parking space in the marina parking lot reserved for Suncoast Yacht Management Company. As she walked down the sidewalk on the way to her office she sensed that there was someone walking close behind. When she reached the first store front of a gift shop, she glanced over her shoulder and saw in the reflection of the glass window a figure of a man in a white shirt and blue trousers behind her. She immediately recognized him as the assistant dockmaster, Bill Chew. Without turning or missing a step, she addressed her follower. "Oh Billy boy, someday I'm going to mace your face if you don't stop coming up behind me like a pole cat."

"Hey darlin, mace my face, sit on my face, do anything your heart desires, just give me a chance to get you into a v-berth and show you what a real anchor feels like."

Gail stopped, turned and faced Chew. Her long auburn hair swirled around her deep tanned face as her dark almond shaped eyes widened in protest. Chew stood boldly stared at her body as it moved in slowly towards him. Her round tanned breasts would rise and fall with every step inside the low cut blouse hanging from her shoulders as her long tanned legs escaped through the wrap around skirt with every stride. Before she could reach him, Chew began to dress her down.

"C'mon baby, show me what you got, you got to be tired fucking that old married man you're seeing or are you giving it all to Phil Avery now? Honey, you let me in your pants one time and you won't have to look no more."

Gail stared into Chew's eyes just inches away. Her heart was pounding so hard she thought it would explode. Chew stood working his mouth into a twisted smile while his steel gray eyes fixed on her breasts.

"Chew, you're a piece of shit and if you want a piece of me, you're going to pay for it, I ain't cheap." She quickly scanned the area around them and noted they were alone. Chew's lips parted into a smug smile. "Baby, I'd sell my old lady's new Chrysler LeBaron, if.."

Those were his last words before he felt his knees buckle. He started hyperventilating as the pain became more intense. He was physically drained and helpless.

Gail released her vice grip on his genitals. Chew grabbed himself with both hands and started falling towards her. She put a hand on his chest and pushed. He slipped downward falling knees first on the sidewalk and rolled over in the grass, curled up with hands buried deep in his crotch. All she heard were small groans as his legs folded up tighter to his chest. She took a glance around the area; nobody was there. She turned and walked the few yards to the office and unlocked the door. Once inside she leaned her back against the door and slid down to the floor. She rested her head on her knees, wrapped her arms around her legs and openly cried.

A phone rang in the distance. It took a few seconds for Gail to gather her senses, then lifted herself and reached across her desk and lifted the receiver.

"Suncoast Yacht Management, this is Gail."

"Hi Gail, Ray here, can I speak to Phil?"

"He's not here, but I'm expecting him."

"I'm checking to see if he got the tickets for tomorrow's game and what time he's flying in."

"He's got the tickets, Ray, they're on his desk. He also told me the Colts are going to trash the Dolphins."

"Over Shula's big ass." Ray responded. "Have him call me when he comes in."

"I sure will, Ray, have fun at the game tomorrow."

Gail put the receiver down, walked over to Avery's desk and checked his appointment book. The only note he had made for today was to call

Dolphin aviation to have his plane topped off and on the ramp for an early Sunday departure. She saw the four green tickets for the Dolphin vs. Colts game in Miami. She checked her watch and the phone mate; there were no waiting calls. She began to get concerned and started making calls to Phil's home, and then to a number of coffee shops he frequented. Finally, she called Dolphin Aviation where she learned that he had taken off earlier but did not say where he was flying. She called Flight Services at St. Petersburg\Clearwater Airport only to learn that he did not file a flight plan. She called Dolphin again and left word for Phil to call her at home. She also called his home and left a message on his recorder. All she wanted to do now was to leave, get out of the marina and go to her apartment. She began to cry, knowing there would be no one waiting there to comfort her, it was Carlton's weekend to go camping with his two sons on the St. Johns River.

Immokalee Airport
Immokalee, Florida

"Lou, leave us and tell Buckland, Collins and Souza to, oh, just tell them to keep busy, I'll see them later?"

"Right, Dan."

Bollman went over to the table, picked up the folders and stuffed them into the briefcase. He looked up at Phil as he walked towards the door, but Phil would not look at him.

"I started to tell him about the girl, Nancy? That's when he..."

"Alright, Lou, I'll take it from here."

Bollman left the office. O'Brien went behind the desk and stood with his hands in his pockets looking at the back of Phil's head. Phil was leaning against the desk, head down, eyes focused on the imitation tiles printed on the linoleum.

"Ever been to Cuba, Phil?"

"You know goddamn well I have."

"Yeah, you're right, you were there in 59 with your dad and some of his fishing buddies. Do you remember much, I mean how beautiful the island was?"

"What do you want, O'Brien? What the hell does Cuba have to do with me, or Nancy, cut the shit, o.k.?"

"O.K. tough guy, I'll cut the shit. Turn around and I'll do one better." O'Brien went up to the map on the wall displaying the entire Caribbean. He put his finger on the island of Cuba and looked at Phil as he watched O'Brien's index finger tearing into the map.

"There is a nasty bastard running this beautiful island, Mr. Avery. He has been ducking our bullets for twenty-five years. Presently he is facing some new hard political times. He has problems with the Soviets and our new friend, Gorbachev. Gorby doesn't like Fidel and doesn't like bankrolling him. He has been critical of Fidel's ideas on agriculture, cattle programs and Cuba's economy. We have reason to believe that Fidel is going into business for himself, so he won't need to depend on the Soviets. As a matter of fact, we have positive proof he is about to do just that. Phil, please, sit down."

Avery reached over and moved a small folding chair in front of O'Brien's desk. O'Brien took a pack of Winstons from his pocket and threw them on the desk.

"Go ahead, they're your brand, right?"

Phil nodded, picked up the pack and removed a cigarette. O'Brien offered a light, took a deep drag and blew the smoke upward.

"Phil, Castro is in the drug business. He has or will have some kind of a new device that he is planning to introduce to some folks we think are key members of drug cartels. We have no idea what the device is. Right now, what we do know is that Fidel Castro is planning to take a trip out of Cuba during Christmas week on a luxury yacht to meet and demonstrate this device to his guests near an island south of Guadeloupe. We already know the yacht he will be on and hope to know when and where she will be leaving. Our job is to intercept Castro on the high seas, plant some plastics on his ass and blow him out of the Caribbean, hopefully while he is entertaining his friends. We also need to find out what this so called device is he is marketing."

Phil sat back in the small chair, almost enjoying this man before him. O'Brien appeared relaxed, calculating and carefully confident. He was talking about assassinating a leader of a country as if planning a vacation trip somewhere.

"Mr. O'Brien, let me get this straight. You are here with one of my best friends preparing to execute Fidel Castro because you have reason to believe he is selling some kind of device to drug dealers. You think he going to be sailing from Cuba to Guadeloupe, a thousand miles away on a yacht, and somehow you are going to blow him up, right?"

"You got it, Phil."

"This is definitely a typical government project, a super catch twenty-two in the making."

"Who told you it was government?"

"Collins did, when I arrived."

"This operation is highly classified, Phil and you will be sworn to secrecy whether you're on the team or not."

"Tell me, O'Brien, whose authority are you really working under? I mean, what agency, CIA, DEA, HUD?"

"I'm working directly for the President of the United States, as is everyone here, as you will be, if you take the job."

Phil moved up towards the desk, planted his elbows down, clasped his hands and put his two index fingers together and pointed them right between O'Brien's eyes.

"Just exactly what is my job, if I take this job?"

"You will be taking the Drummer down to meet Castro, intercept his passage, set charges and disappear."

"That's it? That's all I have to do is find Fidel's yacht, stop it on the high seas, plant some charges to the hull and, did you say disappear?"

"That's the plan Mr. Avery? You see, we have all the details worked out, all you have to do is play captain for a few days, maybe two weeks, that's it. You get well paid and even inherit a new business right here in Immokalee, Avery's Yacht and Ship Repairs."

O'Brien stood up and walked around to the front of the desk, leaned back resting his buttocks on the desk. He looked down at Avery, his arms crossed, chin resting on his chest and staring at the large chart.

"You're absolutely right, Avery, it's not that simple. We have been working night and day on this project since for months. There are many lives involved here, some in very dangerous positions within Cuba. We are not playing a game nor are we taking any chances on anything, equipment or people. There is much involved in this project and a big piece of its success is just behind us in the hangar next door. There is risk involved. We don't expect any danger or confrontation; however, you will be well trained. We feel you're the man for the job. You have all the qualifications, experience and from what I have seen today, you have a pair of brass ones, and you will need them on this operation. So, what do you say? Do I bring the team in and present them with their Santa Claus, or do you want to go back to Sarasota and.."

"I'll do it, I'll take the job, but I need to get my business straightened out first. Jesus, what do I tell my people?"

"Easy, you're just expanding. You have bought a fix it shop here in Immokalee. Ted suggested you say that you and he bought it as partners, or something like that. As far as the voyage on the Drummer goes, just tell your folks you're going on a delivery-vacation, hell, you have done plenty of them to the Caribbean in the past."

"Shit. I'm trying to break in a new girl in Sarasota. She's not ready to handle things alone yet. No, man, I can't do it, O'Brien, there's just too much to lose here..."

"Ah, you're talking about Gail Townsend, right?"

"Yeah, of course, she's new."

"Ah, Gail will be going with you, Phil, she has already been screened, she's highly qualified. You'll need her as crew while you're posing as a charter yacht, she will be registered as your cook."

"Are you're fucking nuts? That's it, man! Avery leaped up from his chair, turned and stomped off towards the door.

"Hold on a minute, Phil. Townsend has three years of experience on charter yachts in the Virgin Islands. She holds a Captain's license. She also holds a reservists rank of captain in the Army Reserves as a registered nurse. She was raised on a farm in northern Louisiana, where her daddy taught her to hunt. She's a champion skeet shooter; did you know that? Plus, she holds two degrees and knows how to shoot stars with a sextant. Her only personal problem, we learned, was a love affair she had with a buddy of yours down in St. Thomas. We were told he beat her up and left her high and dry. You came along as a friend, brought her back to the mainland and gave her a job. She seems to be headed down another dead end again; all mixed up with some married big time lawyer. Need I go on, Mr. Avery?"

"I gave her this job because she is bright and knows the yacht trade and yes, I did feel bad for her when she was kicked around by a friend of mine. Her personal life is her business, O'Brien. Carlton Tucker is a nice guy; I met him a number of times. I believe he loves Gail and I believe he will do the right thing, eventually. No, I am not dragging that woman into this operation; she's had enough problems in the past two years. She stays, I need her to run the office if I am taking this job."

"Phil, I want you to take a few minutes here to think. Think about what it is going to take to pull this operation off. Think of what it will mean if we pull it off. Now, tell me, who do you want as your wingman out there? Who do you want in that fox hole with you when the shit starts to fly? Now, do I call in the troops? They're outside waiting for your answer. We need you and Gail, Phil. What do you say, do we bring them in and let them give you the nickel tour?"

Avery walked around the desk and stood in front of the large chart on the wall. With his finger, he ran an imaginary line from Cuba to the island of Guadeloupe. He stood and studied the chart for a few minutes.

"Tell Sam, I take one cream and no sugar in my coffee."

For the next two hours Avery was briefed on OPERATION YULETIDE, with only one interruption. One of Bollman's men came in and talked to O'Brien and Bollman privately. They excused themselves and left the room. At the end of the briefing, O'Brien and Bollman briefed the team on a serious problem. It seemed that the young man who was hired as an errand boy, Mike McCoy, had managed to get into the hangar and discovered what was going on. He had brought two large marine batteries to the rear door of the hanger when the security man was absent. One of the workers who let him in did not know he was not authorized to be inside the building. McCoy wandered around for nearly fifteen minutes before he was spotted. He had plenty of time to observe what was going on in the hangar and had simply figured it out. He could see that major modifications were in process on the Drummer. Two very large power plants with mysterious looking drive systems were waiting to be installed into the remodeled hull.

"Gentlemen, the worst case scenario has just happened," Bollman said. "As soon as we learned of McCoy's adventure, we ran a make on him, just in case. It seems our friend has had two scrapes with the locals down in Ft. Myers. One a moving violation, the other, more recent, possession. We found three other reports on him. A DUI in Dade County, a drunk and disorderly arrest in Davie and he was charged in an accident that put two teenagers in a hospital with life threatening injuries, in Jacksonville. We got a call from our Miami office a few minutes ago, the local Sheriffs Office reported they presently have McCoy under surveillance along with a dozen others who hang out at an old farm house not too far from here. They want to know what our interest is in him, Dan."

"Jesus, O'Brien, who hired this guy?" Collins asked.

"Sam Levin did. He liked the kid. He told me the kid appeared to be honest, shit." O'Brien slammed his hand down on the desk.

"Where is he now, Dan?" Buckland asked.

"They have him outside cleaning the office, keeping him busy until we learn more about him. One of us is going to have to find out just what he thinks he saw inside."

"Hell, Levin can do that, Dan. He's the only one that talks to him anyway. McCoy likes Sam."

"I guess you're right, Lou. At least we can start there."

O'Brien went over to the desk phone and called Levin. He explained the situation to him. Levin told him he could handle the problem. O'Brien also told Levin not to let McCoy out of his sight and to keep him busy in the office.

"You know, Dan, we are going to have the Sheriff and his deputies out here, especially now that they have been tipped we are interested in their man. They know he works here, they have probably been watching us all along. Last week, they stopped one of our vans down the road and asked the crew what was going on here."

"You're right, Jack, we better cover our ass. You get out to the Sheriff's office right now. Show him your credentials. Tell him only what they need to know. Tell them we are building a special ship for the Coast Guard. Ah, say its highly classified, and they will be getting formally briefed in a few days by Lou Bollman, Miami office of the FBI."

"Fuck, there goes the neighborhood, O'Brien. The Sheriff will tell the locals, and I'm sure he has friends at the local Highway Patrol barracks."

"Yeah, you're probably right, Jack. But, I knew sooner or later that we were going to have to get the locals involved. We just have to be careful."

"I don't like it, Dan, these guys out here are all part of the "good ol' boy network", you know, country boys? They talk to each other."

The phone rang. Collins picked up the receiver. "It's Levin, Dan." Collins handed O'Brien the phone.

"Yes. O.k., thanks, Sam." O'Brien hung up the phone.

"Well, Mr. McCoy appears to be very sharp. As a matter of fact, he has pretty much figured out the whole fucking operation. He told Levin what we were doing here, knows the Drummer is a new Citation and knows that the two big holes are for two four-fifty-four Chevy engines attached to special vee-drives. He told Levin he could smell government here and figures that the sailboat is being modified to be a super fast yacht that will be used to track drug runners. Our front is a joke for this guy and claims we are all agents with the exception of Ted Collins. He told Levin that he would bet his paycheck on it."

"Listen, Dan, you have enough to worry about, I will take my team and work out a solution. We will contain him here for the rest of the day, and will come up with a plan on what to do later, o.k.?" Bollman headed towards the door.

"Thanks, Lou, keep in touch."

"Dan, I'm anxious to show Phil the Drummer. Why don't we go next door to the hangar and give him the real fifty cent tour." Collins asked.

O'Brien looked at Collins. "Yeah, you're right, come on Santa Claus, let's go look at your million dollar sleigh."

"Jesus Christ." Phil shouted, as he stood looking at the hull of the ISLAND DRUMMER. The massive yacht dominated most of the hangar floor and was surrounded by a network of tubular frames and scaffolding.

There were workmen climbing all over her like bees. Most frightening were the large crude gaping holes that were cut on both sides of the keel, exposing the entire bilge area beneath the main stateroom.

Avery could smell the familiar scents of acetone, resins and burning woods as he studied the horrifying sight before him. He felt a slight tug on his arm, it was Ted Collins, motioning Phil to follow him. When they got just below the transom, Avery could see that the entire aft stateroom, that once offered a beautiful king sized bed, a full bath including a whirlpool, was gone along with most of the cabin floor. Phil also noticed that the original diesel engine and auxiliary generator had been removed, plus all the electrical and plumbing that dominated this compartment.

Ted led Avery over to where the two huge power plants were setting on makeshift stringers. Attached to the large black engines were massive transmissions and gearboxes. These were the vee-drives that would drive the yacht to super speeds. There were four heavy-duty hydraulic cylinders attached to large struts the two drive shafts ran through.

"Phil, this is Larry Keen, Chief engineer of Aero-Tech Marine out of Houston."

"Hi Phil, pleased to know you."

Larry Keen looked like a line backer for the Chicago Bears. He was a big man, a fit man. He wore a white jump suit with a colorful embroidered patch on the right chest pocket, the logo of the Aero-Tech Company. The left pocket had more embroidery on script that read "Bear". He had a youthful broad face, pale skin dominated by freckles, and topped with thick curly red hair.

"I don't know how much Ted has told you regarding my two orphans here, but I will tell you this. If they do what we tell them, they will give you all the power and speed you need, but they are going to be hungry, Mr. Collins, I would think about larger tanks."

"Well, Bear, we don't really know that yet, and won't till we get to the sea trials."

"All I am saying, Ted, you're going to need some huge tanks to feed these kids if you're going on long cruises."

"Just what are the kids, Bear," Avery asked.

"Oh, just an old pair of Chevy 454's that we modified a bit with superchargers. Then we married them to these two custom built Walter-Vee-Drives, added hydraulic struts and bingo.."

"The hydraulic struts, what's their purpose?"

Keen went over to the nearest power plant unit and crouched down. He looked at Avery and Collins. "Well, get down here and I'll show ya." They went over and joined him.

"You see standard shafts running off a Vee-Drive, or straight drive for that matter are at fixed angles, right? Well, these units are equipped with movable struts, that move the shafts for variable angles, ideal for tunnel drive hulls."

"Yeah, but the Drummer isn't a tunnel hull."

"Well, Phil, it will be somewhat. We need to tuck these shafts up close to the hull for performance as well as concealing the big props from view."

"How do you know this whole idea will work?" Avery asked.

"We don't, well, not really." O'Brien said as he stood up.

"Ted took my plans up to Groton, to the Navy's, whoops, should I be telling him this shit, Ted?" Keen asked.

"Oh, of course, but to make a long story short, Phil, let me put it this way. It works on paper and in tank tests, so far. Our biggest problem right now is getting the weight out of the Drummer. We are replacing all the wood bulkheads with aluminum, as well as floors and furnishings where we can. We are pulling everything out we can, like refrigeration, washer and dryer, except for their fronts, trying to make it look normal to the trained eye."

"Yeah, but these two huge units here are adding considerable weight, aren't they?"

"Yes, and no," Keen replied. "We decided we will take all the fresh water cooling systems off the units before we install them. This takes a lot of weight off the system, and being they are only going on a one way trip, we don't have to worry about long term service problems?"

Keen reached over and patted the valve cover on the engine. He looked at Avery and smiled. "Believe me, Phil. They will work. I put two sets of these hogs in two riverboats for the Army fifteen years ago. They were both destroyed in Nam, but I still get letters from the guys who ran them, telling me how dependable they were, and how great they performed."

Phil smiled and offered his hand to the Keen. "I'm looking forward working with you, Bear."

For the next two hours, Ted Collins took Avery through the entire hull and to the drawing boards that displayed all the plans and modifications that were taking place. Phil, although impressed with the plans, still questioned many of the stress and strength problems that faced them when the yacht was pushed at high speeds. His main concern was the new laminated hull parts that were going to be constructed and married to the original hull. Collins kept convincing Avery that it could be done.

Meanwhile, back in O'Brien's office, another meeting was taking place. Bollman presented O'Brien with a solution for the McCoy problem.

"It's the only way, Dan. We tell McCoy we are taking him to Miami to pick up a new van. He can stay over at a motel, pick up the truck and head back in the morning. We offer him some extra bucks."

"Shit, Lou, what does that cure? Now he is in Miami, at a motel with a telephone he's not isolated, what's the."

"Dan, McCoy will never see Miami, O.K.?.

O'Brien stood up from his chair, rested both fists down on the desk and leaned over closer to Bollman.

"You're not serious, Lou. You're not telling me that you plan on taking this boy's life are you?"

"No, Dan, we are not going to take the boy's life. We are going to plant some stuff on him and have him picked up by the locals, that's all, o.k.?"

O'Brien sat down. "O.K. Now, tell me, Lou, how do you feel about Avery?"

"He looks good to me, Dan. He's a little quick on the trigger, gets his balls up in a hurry, but he looks like he can handle the project. How did he react when you told him about the Townsend girl going with him?"

"Strange, he was more worried about how he was going to replace her at the office. I think he might even like the idea of having her on board. From what I have heard about her so far, I wouldn't mind either."

They both laughed.

The door opened from the hangar and Commander Buckland came in. "O.K guys, I'm on my way to the East Coast to see how our little project is doing over in Stuart."

"Is Ted going with you?"

"No, he gave me the new plans on those changes to the aft cabin and transom. Ted feels that they can cut the time in half on this modification plan, something that was really worrying the carpenters."

Bollman looked over at O'Brien and asked, "Has there been anymore trouble with that former Captain Mel Spencer hanging around? Last report I had, he arrived shit-faced got into the yard where he screamed and cussed at the work crews for destroying his yacht."

"That man worries me, we should talk to Gene Massey, Lou." O'Brien remarked. "Maybe we can get a restraining order on him, or something, I don't like him hanging around the Seaduce."

"You got it, Dan. Say, speaking of captains. Have you made up your mind about who will be skipper on the Seaduce? You know Buckwheat here, is sorta hoping.."

"No, I haven't, but I will be talking to Avery about this later, maybe he could suggest someone, but I won't forget your, suggestion, o.k. Commander?"

"Thanks, Dan, talk to you tomorrow night. You are still going to the Key West from here, right?"

"Right. I promised Captain Chen that I would watch the UDT team he put together do a practice run. Besides, I want to meet them."

"Roger on that." The door closed.

"He is something else." Bollman remarked. "Are you going to let him skipper the Seaduce, Dan?"

"Don't think so, but I may put him on with Avery on the Drummer as crew. The Seaduce needs a Phil Avery, we are researching all the agencies right now hoping we find the right man and we need to find him soon."

Al Kruger, one of Bollman's team approached McCoy with a coke in each hand. McCoy was sweeping around one of the drafting tables at the end of the office. McCoy looked up into Kruger's square muscular face and stopped sweeping and pointed at one of the cokes. "Is one of those for me?" Kruger handed one of the cokes.

"Thanks." McCoy placed the broom against the wall, put the coke on the corner of the nearby desk, reached in his shirt pocket and pulled out a pack of Camels. After placing a cigarette in his mouth, he offered Kruger the pack.

"No, no thanks, I have my own." Kruger reached into his pant pocket and pulled out a pack of Kents. He lit one, leaned against the desk with his arms folded and addressed McCoy.

"Hey, how would you like to earn a few extra bucks, spend a night in Miami and help us out?"

"Sure, what do I have to do?"

"Nothing strenuous. You ride over to Miami with me and Bollman later, we give you some pocket cash, drop you off at a Dodge Dealer in Coral Gables where you pick up a new van that we bought. You can spend the night on us in Miami, or come home, whatever."

"Hey, that's a deal, but I have to take Angie."

"Angie, who the hell is Angie?"

"My lady, man, I don't go nowhere without my lady. She picks me up, feeds me, fucks me, bathes me, and drops me off, every day."

"Oh, well, I don't think that would be wise, McCoy. We can't allow civilians, you know, non-employees riding in our company vehicles, you know, insurance."

"Well, fuck it, man. Find someone else. I ain't losing this filly to some stud while I'm out of town just to help you guys."

"Alright, what time does she come for you today?"

"When I call, she is off today. She's probably out at the farmhouse where I live, about eight miles from here. What time do you want us to go to Miami?"

"Ah, I'll get back to you on that, probably around five."

McCoy winked at Kruger, spun around grabbed the broom and began to walk away. Kruger felt somewhat uncomfortable as he watched McCoy move away. McCoy was a large muscular young man with untamed long blonde hair. Although he appeared rough, his jeans and rolled up long sleeved dress shirt were pressed and spotless. On his feet were cheap shower clogs, and around his left wrist a leather bracelet.

Bollman pulled the metal chair up close to the desk. He studied O'Brien in the dim light of the desk lamp noting he looked ten years older than a few months ago when they first met.

"Hey Rudolf, you alright?"

"Sorry, Lou, I was just thinking, trying to visualize just how the picture will look when it happens. I mean, when the Unicorn comes up on the Drummer. I can see Phil in the dinghy pleading for help. The underwater guys messing around under Castro's hull not knowing when those two big screws are going to start turning. I wish I was going to be there, don't you, Lou?"

"Fuck no. That's not my thing, besides, I can't swim."

"You can't swim, and you're the Miami Bureau Chief? I thought all agents had to know how to swim?"

"I had some, ah, pull, you know, connections?"

O'Brien pushed back his leather chair laughing. He reached over and opened the bottom drawer of the desk and came up with a half bottle of Mount Gay Rum.

"Ready?"

"Naw, too early for me. Hey, you're flying later, Dan."

"Yeah." O'Brien spun the bottle around with his fingers holding the top. He picked the bottle up and put it back in the drawer. He looked up at Bollman and smiled.

"October 3rd." O'Brien said.

"What's that, your birthday?"

"Operation Dolphin arrives, my friend."

"Come on, Dan, what the hell are you talking about?"

"Fidel Castro takes delivery of his device on that date, Mr. Bollman. The mysterious device is supposed to arrive at Port Havana aboard a Russian freighter."

"Jesus, when did you find out about this?"

"Actually, last week when I met with Admiral Koster. I haven't said anything to anyone, except to Ian Billings. Admiral Koster ordered more surveillance and a SR-71 Blackbird has been photographing a Russian freighter for days heading northeast towards Cuba. She's called the Pechora. She sailed from Kowloon to Hong Kong, then sailed direct to the Canal. It looks like Castro's delivery ship, and we estimate her reaching Havana sometime around Friday, October 2nd, or Saturday, the latest. Nothing of interest on her decks to see, she's a small freighter. What ever Castro is expecting, it's down in her hold".

"Christ Dan, that's great news. Now maybe we can find out what he is up to, so we can better prepare ourselves on what we are dealing with."

O'Brien sighed and slouched back into his chair, rubbing his eyes vigorously.

"I have drained every ounce of imagination out of my brain for the past six weeks trying to figure out just what this device of his could be. The only thing I can possibly think of, it must be some kind of new watercraft. Why else would he code name the operation... Dolphin?"

O'Brien reached for a Winston.

"What about Castro's yacht that his friend bought, the Unicorn? Any word of its whereabouts? It was due last week if I recall, in Martinique wasn't it?"

O'Brien took a deep drag from the cigarette. "I talked to Ian Billings at CIA Headquarters last Tuesday. He informed me that the Unicorn was delayed in the Canaries. She was having refrigeration problems, and also waiting on a depression to clear out that was building up just west of Cape Verde Islands. I have requested that we start watching out for her now, as she may change her original plans due to the delays. My guess is that the Unicorn will still arrive in Martinique for fuel and crew change as originally planned. Ian has the island wired, we will know when it arrives."

Bollman looked at his watch. "Hey, it's tuna time. Let's get the crew and run over to the Holiday Inn on the river for lunch. You round up Phil and Ted, I'll get Kruger and Gerdts."

Winding Oaks, Bradenton
1315 hours

The sound of soft ringing bells seemed far away. Gail opened her eyes and sat up in bed and reached for then phone.

"Yes?"

"Hi, Gail, it's Phil."

"Oh, Phil, where are you?"

"I'm in Fort Myers having lunch with Ted Collins and some friends. I hate to bother you and Carlton, but do you think we can get together for a few minutes in the morning before I leave for Ft. Lauderdale?"

"Sure, Phil, and you are not interrupting anything. I guess you forgot, Carlton has his boys this weekend and is camping with them on the St. Johns River."

"Oh that's right, I did forget. Well, if that's the case, how about joining Larry, Carol Webber and me tonight? It's Larry's birthday. We're meeting at the Summer House. Maybe you could meet me early in the lounge so we can talk. Is that alright with you?"

"Yes, I guess so. Is there anything wrong, Phil? You sound a little strange."

"No, I'm fine, Ted's been busting my chops all morning. I will see you, say at eight? Oh, better call the Summer House and make sure I made reservations, tell them there's four coming."

The line went dead. Gail put the phone down and lay back across the bed. All she could think about was Carlton and praying that he would call soon.

CHAPTER 7

Immokalee Airport
1630 hours

O'Brien, Collins and Avery stood next to the white van while Souza placed O'Brien's briefcase and file jackets on the rear seat.

"We're ready to go, Dan," Souza said, taking a seat in the van.

"Phil, what can I say, except thanks. I know you have hundreds of little voices telling you you're crazy, but think about this, someday the Soviet Union may call you a hero."

"Hey, don't be putting all the freight on my back, O'Brien, that's a big ocean out there full of surprises and nobody mentioned what happens if we run into bad weather, or an engine pukes."

"Phil, we know things can go wrong and when and if it happens, we will handle it."

Ted Collins reached out and shook O'Brien's hand.

"You know, O'Brien, when this adventure is over, I am going to hire you to run my company."

"No offence, Ted, but I think I'll be ready for the rocking chair and oatmeal club."

Avery laughed and took Collins by the arm.

"Let's go bore some holes in the sky, sailor, I have a dinner date and a lot of explaining to do." Avery and Collins got into the van but were detained by Sam Levin.

"O'Brien, wait, Avery didn't sign the checking account card."

Levin looked into the van and handed Avery a stack of papers and file . cards.

"Here, just sign these beneath my signature, Bill."

"Its Phil, not Bill, Sam."

"Bill, Phil, Jill, what the fuck do I care? Just sign."

Phil signed the cards and handed them back to him. "Just get your ass back here to sign the new checks before next Friday like a good little Santa." Levin spun on his heel and walked away.

"Damn, that is a piece of work. How do you stand for his shit, O'Brien?"

"Easy, Ted, he's the President's brother-in-law." O'Brien stepped into the van and sat down next to Avery.

Collins sat in silence, his mouth dangling open. "President of what country?" he asked. The van departed ringing with laughter.

The van stopped at Avery's plane and O'Brien spoke.

"Have a safe flight, Phil, I'll be in touch with you Monday morning."

"Fine, but I'll be at the Lauderdale office. I'm flying over in the morning for the Dolphin and Colts game."

"Lucky you, after I drop Jesus in Miami I'm heading to Key West to the Navy UDI school to see a demonstration on the magnetic device we hope to use for the explosive charges. I should be back in St. Pete late tomorrow afternoon if you need me.

"Thanks, Dan, and good luck in the Keys."

The late afternoon sky was cloudless as the Piper Archer lifted off the runway. At twenty five hundred feet, Phil dropped the nose on the horizon, throttled back then banked northwest to avoid Fort Myers airspace.

"Keep your eyes open, Ted, especially out east. There's lots of sky-kings flying from that direction on a radial out of LaBelle to Ft. Myers."

"What the hell are you talking about, LaBelle radials? You know I hate this shit." Collins was nervous and hated flying.

Avery chuckled. "I don't believe you don't enjoy flying Ted, hell its just as easy as sailing. I would think you..."

"You think wrong, Santa Claus, I hate it up here, especially in these little toy airplanes."

"Ted, take the wheel, go ahead. Put your feet on the pedals and take the wheel."

"Bullshit."

"Come on, what if I have a heart attack? I would think that you would at least want to save your own ass."

Collins said nothing. He reached out and put his hands on the wheel and placed his feet lightly on the pedals.

"There, now you own the airplane, it's all yours." Phil took his hands from the wheel and put them in his lap. "Look out there, Ted, do you can see Boca Grande inlet over there at 10 o'clock? Head for it, all you do is turn the wheel slowly left and push slightly on the left pedal."

It took Avery about ten seconds to recover the plane which nearly rolled over on its back as four hands and four feet fought for control.

"Holy shit, do you know what the word ease means? You have the touch of a rhino in heat. How can you be so sensitive at the helm of a race boat and so heavy handed up here?"

"I hate these little airplanes and I hate instructors. Just get me to St. Petersburg before I lose my lunch."

Avery put the Archer on course to St. Pete Clearwater airport eighty miles ahead and engaged the autopilot then sat back enjoying the view of the Gulf of Mexico in the late afternoon sunset..

"When are you going to tell Gail?" Collins asked.

"Don't know. I invited her to join me tonight for a drink with some friends. I thought I might meet her earlier and tell her, but this will take much time to explain. I don't know how she will react, I know she won't be happy about going back down to St. Thomas and facing old friends, especially Captain Roger Novak. Personally, I think she will tell me to stick the idea where the sun don't shine and walk on me."

"Good, then I can hire her, I would trash half my office staff to have Gail on board."

"Ted, I'm worried about you, lad. Do you realize that's the second time today you offered to hire someone, sounds like you have some problems."

"Yeah. I want to go play, o.k.? I need to get out, like you, be single again and buy me a little airplane so I can take my friends flying and scare the shit out them. Ah, the damn truth is, I want to be the one taking Drummer on this mission, I want to be Santa Claus but don't have the military training."

"Shit, why didn't you ask O'Brien? Hell, you have all the qualifications, you don't need to have military background for this trip; or do you know something I don't? Is O'Brien expecting some action down there?"

"No, at least he never came out and said so, but I guess there is that possibility and that's why you would qualify and I really do believe, pal, he picked the right man. I'm pleased as hell that you took the job."

"I heard the name Seaduce mentioned and the name of some Captain that is giving you a fit."

"Seaduce is a classic yacht I saw in the Bahamas a few years ago when I was racing in the Abacos. I copied her lines for my new Citation series. When we realized that there wasn't enough time to build a duplicate of the Drummer, I had to find the Seaduce and hope it could be bought. I found her in West Palm Beach and her owner, a personal friend of Nixon, is terminal with cancer and dedicated her to our cause after O'Brien explained our mission. Her captain for ten years got his nose bent when he was dismissed and started hanging around the yard where we are doing modifications to make her resemble the Drummer."

"Why do we need a duplicate of the Drummer?"

"So we can blow it to hell. I take it O'Brien did not go over the plan of attack with you?"

"Not that part."

"He will, ol' buddy, he will."

Dolphin Aviation
1835 hours
Sarasota-Bradenton Airport

"I have a message for you, Mr. Avery."

"Thanks, Linda." Phil stepped over to the counter and collected the message that Gail had left earlier.

"Linda, I need the Archer topped off and ready for a nineish departure."

Avery pulled the cover off the Thunderbird, rolled it into a ball and threw it in the passenger seat, got in and headed out to U.S. 41 and home. Two gauges caught his eye, the fuel gauge, which read "empty", and the slow clock that read seven-fifteen. "Shit," he said to himself. "I'm going to be late." At that moment the big four-barrel carburetor sucked the last drops of fuel and sprayed them into eight thirsty cylinders, seconds later the classic car rolled into a small side street four blocks from a Chevron station.

The Summer House Restaurant
Siesta Key
2015 hours

Avery checked with the receptionist to make sure she had his reservations and asked if his guests had arrived. Relieved that he had arrived before anyone else, he ran up the spiral staircase to the second floor lounge. The room was noisy and the bar was full. Avery made his way around to the backside of the bar to his favorite stool to find an attractive elderly lady talking to a well-groomed gentleman standing beside her occupied it.

The bartender suddenly noticed Avery.

"Hey, Mr. Avery, where did you come from?"

"Ah, originally Toms River, New Jersey and still thirsty, can I have my usual?"

"You got it, pal."

"Hello, Phil Avery."

Avery turned to see a very attractive petite blonde looking up at him.

"Hi Terri, am I in your way?"

"You're always in my way, darlin, but I kinda like it."

Avery moved from the service bar and worked his way along the bar exchanging hellos with regulars. Then he noticed her. She was standing alone. Her long silky auburn hair flowed down the sides of her face and over her shoulders. The strapless deep green satin dress clung to her shapely body and her long bronzed legs flowed into black patent leather heels. Phil was speechless as he approached Gail, he never realized just how beautiful she was. A couple leaving the bar offered their seats to them.

"Phil Avery, get that silly look off your face, you're embarrassing me."

"Ah, you, well, you look." He started to laugh.

"I look pretty good when they dress me up, is that what you're trying to say?"

"Yeah, that's about it. No, you look fantastic."

The bartender caught Avery's attention.

"Here we are, folks," he said as he placed two drinks on the bar. "I got you a new one Mr. Avery. Evening Miss Gail, good to see you again. Rob Roy on the rocks, no fruit." Charlie placed the two drinks, smiled and left.

"Rob Roy, good to see you, Gail?"

"Phil, you don't have an exclusive on this bar. Carlton and I come here frequently. However, I do give you all the credit for telling me about this place. Remember, I pay your American Express bills and this place comes up often."

"Right, ah, you don't feel uncomfortable with me do you?" Phil asked as he looked around the bar.

"Don't be silly, Phil, of course not. Most people know I work for you."

"Yes, I guess you're right. Hey, listen, I have some news for you, I bought a new business today that's why I was down in Fort Myers."

"A new business? What kind of business?"

"Well, it was Ted Collins' idea and he is sort of a partner with me, it's a yacht repair service, you know, rebuilding old yachts, restorations, that sort of thing. Ted found this great place, real cheap, in Immokalee, a small farming town a few miles from Fort Myers. It's at an airport, the main building is an old hangar.

"Phil, why do I smell something rotten in Denmark? What are you up to? I know you well enough that you wouldn't fly off to nowhere and buy a new company, an antique car maybe, but a boat repair place? What's going on, Phil?"

A voice came from behind them.

"Hey smiling Jack, you finally got your head out of the clouds and landed." It was his dinner guest, Larry Webber.

"Happy Birthday, stud, where's Carol?"

"She stopped at the ladies room."

"Jesus, Gail, you look fantastic."

"Larry, before you step on your tongue, why don't we all head downstairs, our table should be ready, we'll catch Carol downstairs." Avery checked his watch, signaled the bartender, took out a pen and signed his bill.

After dinner and three bottles of Pouilly-Fuisse, Avery made it a point to look at his watch constantly. Larry Webber picked up the hint.

"Well, folks, it's nearing the magic hour," Larry said.

" Great dinner, Phil, thanks for the party." Carol said squeezing Avery's hand.

The foursome got up from the table and headed for the large glass doors.

"Hey, anyone for a last call?" Avery asked checking his watch again. "Not for us, you kids go ahead, thanks again ol' buddy." Larry took his wife by the arm and walked out the door.

"Well, are you up to it?"

"What time are you flying tomorrow?"

"I will drink coke, I promise."

"I don't think so, Phil. It's really late, and I'm supposed to be getting a call."

"Oh, yes, excuse me, I forgot."

Phil headed for the two glass doors. He opened one and held it waiting for Gail. She stood staring at him for a moment then walked out the door.

The young parking valet attendant came running. "Hi, Mr. Avery, how was dinner?"

"Ah, great, thanks kid."

The attendant ran across the shell drive to where Avery's Thunderbird was parked.

"The kid's name is Chad," Gail said.

"Yeah, I forgot. Listen, Gail, we have to talk. Can we get breakfast or some coffee somewhere?"

"Phil, I have to drive twenty miles to get home, it's nearly one in the morning. Can it wait until tomorrow, or Monday?"

"Yeah, I guess. Sure, it can wait."

The Thunderbird was waiting. Phil walked around to the open door and handed Chad a folded five-dollar bill.

"Thanks, Mr. Avery."

Phil stood watching Gail. Even in the faint light her tanned face glowed. Chad went over and escorted her to the open door of her Firebird. Avery could hear him as he asked where Carlton was. Phil got in his car, closed the door and drove out the winding driveway. He had stopped to check traffic when he noticed Gail's headlights flashing at him. He opened his door and looked back.

With her head out of the window, Gail shouted, "If you got the coffee, I'll make the time."

Phil smiled, closed the door and headed home with Gail following behind.

Avery's house
Siesta Key
0235

"That is the dumbest thing I ever heard of, Phil. No, I won't play cook and bottle washer on Ted's yacht, not for you or anyone. I went that route, my God, you were the knight on the white horse that saved me in St. Thomas over a year ago. Now you want me to go back?" She paused then asked. "What is this really all about, Phil? You're not being straight with me. Your story about this yacht rebuilding company stinks and how come you never mentioned it at dinner to your best friend?"

"Gail, you're right, I haven't been straight with you."

The wall phone rang.

"Excuse me." Phil looked at his watch, it was two forty.

"Hello? Oh, hi honey, I know, it's after two, I was out to dinner with the Webbers. Yes, I plan to be over there around ten. Are you picking me up? Oh, I seem well do me a favor, call Ray or leave a note on his door before you leave, he can come get me. Yes, I understand, I love you too, good night."

"Sorry about that, would you like some more coffee?"

"No, just some water." Gail stood up from the kitchen table and walked out the back door onto the screened porch. She stood in the dark looking at the peaceful waterway. A small white light on a boat was moving north up the channel.

"Here you are." Phil handed Gail the glass of water and stood beside her.

"It's really nice here Phil, you're lucky."

"Yeah, I like it. It's old and needs a lot of fixing up, but that's what I like best, fixing things."

Gail tuned and faced Phil.

"You couldn't fix Roger, but thanks for trying. I'm asking as a friend, please don't ask me to do anything that may ruin things with Carlton and me; I'm just beginning to feel like a woman again."

"Roger was an idiot, everyone knew he loved you Gail, but, well, his mistresses are the sea and the bottle. I certainly don't want to cause any problems between you and Carlton, please understand this is not my doing, I volunteered to do it, but they had already picked you."

"Phil, you're talking crazy, who picked me, what are you talking about?"

"It's the government, they picked us. They want you and I to sail a seventy-five foot Citation to the Caribbean in December and kill Fidel Castro, who is sailing on a yacht from Cuba to Guadeloupe."

"Phil, sit down, I'm going to call Larry Webber, then we're going to the emergency room at the hospital, I think you're having a breakdown and should be in the hospital."

"Gail, I'm alright." He grabbed Gail tightly around her upper arms.

"Phil, you're hurting me."

"I'm sorry, please, Gail, come sit down."

The sky in the east was beginning to lighten. Tall pine trees across the bay stood like silent soldiers against the new morning sky. The only sounds were the herons calling their mates from the mangrove islands nearby. Gail sat, her feet tucked in under her legs. An old comforter lay across her lap. She rested her head on the back of the lounge chair staring at an old ceiling fan barely windmilling. Phil was sitting slouched in a wicker chair, both arms hanging down. In one hand a cup with the remains of instant coffee, the other held the stub of a burned out Winston. His eyes were closed, but he was not asleep.

"Well, I can honestly say, Mr. Avery, you really know how to entertain a girl. I feel like some mysterious force just took over my body. I can't feel anything. My God, I don't believe I'm part of this world anymore, what's happening out there, Phil? What are these people doing to us? My God, are any of us safe from them? They know everything, they really do control us now, don't they?"

"Gail, come on, it's not that bad, Jesus, it's the government at work, they have to know things. How do you think I felt when that FBI man told me how much money I had to the cent in all my bank accounts?"

"Well, what do we do now? What if I refuse to help, what happens to me, do I get a call from the IRS next? Do I have to live with them the rest of my life because I refused to help the government kill somebody?"

"Nothing will happen to you, Gail. You have every right to say no. I have already told them you wouldn't do it. The problem is, it's a time thing, we don't, I mean, they don't have time to recruit and train anyone with your experience. You have all the qualifications they are looking for, and I have to admit, if I had to plan this mission, I would have been looking for you too."

Gail moved her legs out from beneath her, put her feet on the floor, picked up her shoes, stood up and pulled her dress down around her thighs.

"Sun's coming up. I better get out of here before your neighbors start talking."

She walked back into the kitchen and picked up her purse from the table, turned and looked at Phil.

"See you Monday?"

Avery pulled himself up from the chair, put the mug on the nearby table, threw the cigarette butt into it and walked into the kitchen.

"You look like shit, Phil."

"Yeah, but I'm the captain of the Island Drummer, I'm supposed to look like shit, it's part of my cover."

"Call me before you take off later. I will give you my answer, o.k.?"

"Sure, that's o.k., but you don't have to tell me anything now. Talk it over with Carlton, just don't tell him about Castro.. tell him its some big drug lord. See what he says, after all, he is planning on spending the rest of his life with you, isn't he?"

"You know, Phil, you're still a shining knight, don't tarnish that with smart-ass assumptions, o.k.?" Gail went out the door to the carport. Phil watched her get into her Firebird, she never looked back.

Phil went to his bedroom and fell across the bed. He turned on the answering machine and listened to Nancy's message telling him she had to fly to the Bahamas and could not go to the Dolphin game. He lay there thinking about her when he remembered what Bollman had told him only twenty hours ago that she was sleeping with someone else. Avery buried his head into the pillow as his fists tightened trying to fight off the emotions that were tearing him apart. His eyes closed and he fell off to sleep.

0810 hours

The phone rang, waking Avery. He reached over and picked up the receiver. "Hello?"

"Mr. Avery?"

"Yes?"

"Are you still flying this morning? I was about to pull your Archer out, but looking at the weather, I thought maybe you wanted to wait some."

"Huh? Oh yes, the weather. Ah, listen, Corky, let me call you back in a few minutes, o.k.?"

"Yes sir, I'll be standing by."

Phil looked at the clock, it was ten after eight. He had slept a little over an hour. He called Flight Service's at St. Petersburg Clearwater Airport and got briefed on weather, then called Corky back and told him he would take off around 0900. He then called his friend Ray Nickles in Fort Lauderdale and advised him that he should be arriving at Walkers Terminal at Lauderdale airport around 1030 hours. He also told him to find someone to use Nancy's ticket for the game.

Avery was locking the rear door to the house when the phone rang. He walked back in and picked up the kitchen wall phone. "Hello?"

"I'll do it, Phil, for you." The phone went dead.

Walkers Terminal
Ft. Lauderdale International Airport
1045 hours

Avery walked through the door to Walkers service counter. Sitting across the room reading a People magazine was Ray Nickles. Avery went to the counter and filled out a service request form, then went over to the pilot's lounge and called Miami Flight Service to report his arrival and cancel his flight plan.

"Hey, meathead," Avery said.

Nickles looked up from the magazine, nodded and then went back to reading his magazine.

"O.k., so I'm late, sue me," Avery said.

"You're always late, what's new? Say, did you know that Bo Derek actually got hurt screwing with a real lion on this movie she made? Look at this shit." He handed Avery the magazine opened to an article with photographs of Bo Derek on a beach embracing a large lion.

"Lucky Leo, huh?"

"Any weather on route?"

"Naw, a few showers over Andy Town. Sorry I had to ask you to come get me, Nancy.."

"Hey, no problem, that's what pimps are for."

The drive down U.S. 1 to 17th Street went fast. Nickles loved to weave his classic GTO Pontiac convertible through traffic, shifting gears and rattling its big dual pipes.

"Did you want to go to the office first?"

"Naw, let's go to the condo."

They pulled up in front of Avery's condominium and he noticed his company station wagon was parked in his private parking space and wondered how Nancy got to the airport earlier.

"Hey, what time do you want me to pick you up and what do we do with those extra tickets?"

"We'll take them to the club, I'm sure we can give them away down there."

"Got a better idea, pal. Why don't we have some fun, remember old thunder-thighs?"

"The bar-maid at Chucks Steak House?"

"Yeah, the one with the big air tanks. Well, I ran into her yesterday over at the shopping center and she was with her new roommate. Phil, this lady is stacked, blonde, blue-eyed and.."

"And I get thunder-thighs, right?"

"Hell, Phil, I don't care, man. We just take them to the game, and what ever romance is in the cards, well,..."

"You've lost it, Ray, ol' buddy," Phil burst into laughter. "No, let's just you and I wing it, how about you picking me up here in one hour, o.k.?"

Phil got out of the car. Nickles spun around on the narrow street and headed down the road waving.

Avery turned the key in the lock to his apartment, then he heard the door across the breezeway open. He turned and saw Margo Nolte stepping out of her apartment dressed in a lime green tennis outfit. Her short blonde hair was crowned with a matching green ribbon that she tied Indian-style around her head. In one hand she carried two tennis rackets. She was one of the most attractive women Avery ever met, but she played strictly in the big leagues. Avery never saw her at any of the regular haunts around Lauderdale.

"Hi, Phil, are you just getting in?"

"Yes, flew over this morning. You look almost too dressed to be going out on a tennis court, I mean..."

113

"I don't play, you silly, I sit and watch. I'm into more indoor recreation, you know, air conditioned type sports."

Avery did not know how to handle the comment, so he changed the subject. "Do you still have that 450 SL? I bought myself a classic recently, a sixty-two T-Bird."

"I hate Thunderbirds, my ex-lover had six of them. Well, I must be going, it was good to see you again, Phil. Oh, I saw Nancy this morning and did she ever look yummy."

She smiled and walked down the narrow breezeway. Avery's nostrils widened as he took a deep breath. Whatever perfume she was wearing was getting to him. Margo was short, maybe five two, but solid. All her parts were real from toes to nose, she was a classic 10. Avery shook his head, opened the door and walked into his apartment. He couldn't get Margo's parting comment out of his mind. "What the hell did she mean, Nancy looked yummy? She should have been in her flight uniform if she was going on a charter and that uniform was far from yummy."

Holiday Inn, Key West
1050 hrs

Dan O'Brien took a booth at the rear of the crowded restaurant. He threw his room and rental car keys on the table and sat down. Before he could open his Miami Herald newspaper, Dolores was standing over him with a pot of coffee in each hand. "Regular or hi-test?" she asked.

O'Brien looked up into her pleasant attractive face.

"Do you have a jealous boyfriend who would fight for you?"

"Huh? You have to be kidding, government man. If I had a boyfriend I wouldn't be serving you coffee on a Sunday morning. I'd be shining his shoes while making him breakfast."

"Tell me, Dolores, why did you call me a government man?"

"Cause you are, aren't you? At least that's what the hotel desk clerk told me just minutes ago. He says you are some kind of inspector for the government. That's him, sitting at the counter up there."

"Regular, thanks."

"Are you alone?" she asked.

"Yes, well, no, I am waiting for someone. If you see a good looking Naval officer come in looking for someone, it's probably me, my name's O'Brien."

"Damn, O'Brien, I figured you for straight," she laughed and poured the coffee.

O'Brien unfolded the Herald. A small headline caught his eye near the bottom of the front page. YOUNG COUPLE FOUND SLAIN ON ALLIGATOR ALLEY. Broward County: Arthur Mize and his nine year old son were launching their airboat at a public ramp last night about twenty miles west of U.S. 27 on Alligator Alley, when they discovered the nude bodies of a young white male and female floating near the ramp. Mize stopped an eastbound truck and the driver contacted the Highway Patrol on his CB radio. Both victims were taken to the Broward County Coroners office for examination. First reports indicate that both victims had been shot in the back of the head. No identification could be made at the scene. The investigating officer's only statement was that the two victims had long blonde hair and appeared to be in their late twenties.

"Jesus Christ, no, It can't be.." O'Brien slammed his fist down on the paper. He looked up to see everyone in the restaurant looking at him. Dolores was running down the aisle to his table.

"Are you all right, sir, what's wrong?" she asked as she bent down close to him.

"Where's the phone? I need to make a call."

"It's through the door where you came in from the hotel lobby."

O'Brien excused himself and flew past Dolores towards the lobby door. Dolores looked into the curious eyes of the other customers. "Maybe we better take more caffeine out of our coffee."

"Sam, I don't care how you do it, just find Bollman, o.k.? I'm at the Holiday Inn in Key West, in the restaurant. I don't know, I'm at a fucking pay phone, get the hotel number through information, tell them I'm in the restaurant. Yes, it's an emergency, find him."

O'Brien walked back to his table. The newspaper was where he left it together with his room and car keys. A Navy Captain in a pristine white uniform sat waiting.

"Hello, Captain, sorry I was not here, I had a small emergency. Would you like some breakfast, coffee?"

"Ah, the waitress is getting me some, thanks. Are you all right, Mr. O'Brien? you look pale. We didn't get you sick out there this morning, did we?"

"No, not at all, I will be alright, just a little old age setting in..."

"Well, what did you think of the demonstration this morning, sir?"

O'Brien looked into the broad smiling face across from him. Five hours ago, this same handsome face looked grotesque with stainless steel fittings under its nose, black hoses running over his tanned cheeks. Two black straps crisscrossed his short brown hair and strange looking eyeglasses with yellow lenses covered his narrow oriental brown eyes.

"I was very impressed, Captain Chen. Your team is well trained, without a doubt physically fit. How long have they been in training?"

"Well, one of them has been a Seal now for eight years, the others vary from five years to six months."

"About this lark thing?"

"You mean the Lar-Five re-breather apparatus?"

"Yes, that thing you all wear on your chests that doesn't show the bubbles. That's something new, right? I mean, has it been used before? It doesn't look like it holds much air."

Captain Chen laughed. "Not to worry, Mr. O'Brien, the Lar system is most dependable. From what Commander Buckland told me we shouldn't have to worry about a long exercise. I understand that the mission will take place at night?"

"Ah, yes, the mission is short, and we are planning a night maneuver. Just how much has Commander Buckland briefed you on the mission, Captain?"

"All he has told me was we would be setting plastics on a steel hull. We would be coming from a mother ship and swimming to the target which is estimated to be no more than fifty yards out, but could be protected with armed guards. The mission is scheduled for December, possibly around Christmas week, somewhere in the Caribbean."

"Well, I see Commander Buckwheat is.."

"Buckwheat, sir?"

"Ah, I mean Buckland, he seemed to pick up a nickname along the way. Well, he has pretty much covered everything. The only concern I have right now is that young Polish lad, what's his name?"

"Chief Frisoski, Randy Frisoski"

"Yeah, he seemed to have trouble with the new magnetic box. "Is there something wrong with them that we should know about? You know that box is very experimental and was designed just for this mission?"

"Yes I realize that, sir, and we did have a few problems attaching them to the grassy bottom of that old ship, but we can work that out."

"Where is home for you, Captain?"

"Originally, Honolulu. My dad was Navy, thirty years. Retired off the Bunker Hill in San Diego two years ago. Diego is really my home now, have you ever been to San Diego, sir?"

"Ah, Captain, let dispense with the formal stuff. You call me Dan, o.k.? To answer your question, yes, I spent some time in San Diego doing some research for the Navy Department."

O'Brien checked his watch, looked up and caught the waitress' eye and indicated he wanted the bill.

"Well, Captain, it looks like we will be seeing more of each other in the next few months. Congratulations on your team. Let Buckwheat know if you need anything, and tell your boys I enjoyed meeting them."

"Yes, sir, I mean, Dan. Ah, if you are going to continue to call my superior, Commander Buckwheat, it's just a matter of time before I screw up, you know that?"

"Ah, call him Buckwheat like we do, he loves it."

"Well, I have to get up the road to Miami. Got a few more hours of business up there before I head home. Thanks again, Captain. I'll be seeing you."

O'Brien stood up, shook the Captain's hand, took the bill from the table and walked up to the cash register, where Dolores was patiently waiting.

"Didn't eat much, government man."

"Dan, the name is, Dan. Next time I come down, Dolores, you and I are going dancing, o.k.?"

"You got it, Dan. Just don't make it so long between visits."

"Ah, listen, I may get a call in the next few minutes? Would you please tell them I left for Miami and will be in St Petersburg later."

Dolores smiled. "Of course."

Tony Roma's Restaurant
North Miami Beach
Sunday, September 27
1940 Hours

"I still can't understand why Shula put Strock in there, can you Phil?"

"What? of course, Strock, yes, he still has it."

"Shit, when are you coming back to earth? You've been hanging around at ten thousand feet ever since you landed this morning. What's up, Phil, I know it's got nothing to do with the Dolphins getting hosed today, or that you regret not having thunder-thighs keeping you warm, so what is it?"

117

"I am sorry, Ray, I have a lot on my mind and I don't mean to take it out on you."

A leggy redhead in a brief cocktail outfit approached their table.

"Hi, fellers, something from the bar?"

"Ah, yeah, and we both know what we want to eat, bring us two slabs of ribs and some of those onion things, o.k.?"

"Fine, now what would you like to drink?"

"Ah, just a coke for me, what will you have, Ray?"

"Bring me a double Gibson, on the rocks."

The waitress turned and left.

"Hey, Phil, did see that? That waitress has no pants on under that skirt."

"Ah, really? Isn't that against the law?"

"O.k., that's it, pal, let's have it, what's eating you."

"I bought a new business. It's a boat yard, a ship rebuilding thing, you know, repairing old boats."

"Oh, where's it at?"

"Immokalee."

Ray began bobbing his head like a pecking chicken.

"Uh huh, yeah, right, Immokalee, the yachting capital of the fucking world, I think I went through there once on my John Deere tractor."

Avery laughed.

"Do you know how stupid you look right now, you dork? Stop bobbing your head, people will think you're a retard."

"Me, retarded? Me, retarded? You're talking boat yards in Immokalee, Florida and you call me retarded?"

"Hey lady." Ray leaned over to the next table, where two elderly ladies were enjoying their cocktails. "Have you ever been to Immokalee, Florida?"

"Is that near Ocala? There are lots of Indian named towns up around there, right?" One of the ladies responded.

"No ma'am, but it's a long way from water, except when it rains."

The two women smiled and returned to their drinks.

"Phil, get serious."

"I'm serious, Ray. I have a ship repair and refinishing company at the Immokalee airport, called Avery Yacht and Ship repair yard, I think."

The waitress came and put the drinks down, along with a basket of steaming onion rings. Ray picked up the wide fat glass and poured the Gibson straight down. He gave the glass to the astonished waitress, who was shaking her head.

"Tsk, tsk. You won't be able to stay up and play if you keep drinking that way." She took Ray's glass, looked over at Avery and said.

"You are holding up the party."

For the next hour and a half, Avery tried to explain to Nickles why he needed to buy a boat repair yard. After four double Gibsons, Nickles was ready to write Avery a check for it. He was convinced that Avery must have found oil under the property.

Avery's apartment
2200 hours

Avery looked at the clock on the VCR. It was nearly ten o'clock. He went into the bedroom and saw the red light on the answering machine flashing. It was Nancy apologizing for not getting back, that she was staying in Palm Beach because she had to fly to Treasure Cay in the Bahamas first thing in the morning.

Avery sat on the edge of the bed looking at the large pillows resting against the brass headboard. He reached for one of the pillows and held it close to his face. He could smell her scent and began to fantasize. "Why Nancy, why are you doing this to me? I wanted to get married, I asked you to move to Sarasota but you wanted to stay with the airline a little while longer. What do you want Nancy, what have I done wrong?"

He rolled out of the bed, lit a cigarette and walked out on the screened lanai overlooking the canal and docks below. It was unusually quiet for a Sunday evening. The only sounds he could hear were a few loose halyards clanging on metal masts of moored sailboats and the occasional sound of music coming from one of the nearby apartments.

"Hi Phil, sorry about your Dolphins.."

Phil turned towards the silky voice. It was Margo. She was standing on her screened balcony, shielded by a sheer curtain. He could see her tanned face reflecting from the glow of her cigarette each time she inhaled. She stepped closer to the screen and Phil noticed she was totally nude, even though her dark tanned body nearly blended into the shadows. His nostrils filled with the scent of her sweet perfume and pot.

"Hi, Margo. How, was your day?"

"Beautiful, all my days are beautiful, Phil, like your Nancy."

He was about to suggest that they share a drink together when he heard another voice but couldn't figure out where it was coming from, then he saw a tall slim shapely figure move behind Margo. Phil's curiosity ignited when the figure moved closer to the screen where he could see her face. She was extremely beautiful with glossy black hair pulled tightly back around her long oriental face. She embraced Margo, moving her long arms around from behind, her hands resting gently across Margo's breasts. Margo responded, relaxing against her partner and folding her arms tightly over the arms of her companion.

"Phil, say hello to Jessica."

Avery was speechless as he watched Margo turn and arch her body into the hollow of Jessica's frame. The two embraced while their hands moved gently over each other's breasts. They spoke to each other, but not in words, just sounds. Then Margo turned and looked into Phil's bewildered eyes.

"You've lost her, Phil, you've lost your Nancy, your beautiful Nancy. Jessica comes to comfort me when your Nancy can't and I have you to thank for her, Phil, Nancy is my precious."

2305 hours

Avery found himself speeding along the airport service road, when he realized where he was and what he was doing. He continued driving to Walker Terminal. After parking the car, he called his office and left a message on the answering machine for Debbie Young, his office manager and told her he had to get back to Sarasota.

Forty minutes later, at forty-five hundred feet, Avery was approaching the small community of La Belle. He could see the lights of the town ahead and reflections of flickering lights on the waters of the cross-state barge canal. From the corner of his left eye, he caught sight of a flashing collision light and navigation lights approaching from the south. The plane was higher, and one mile away. He watched until he determined it was another small plane heading on a more northerly course than his, and appeared to be at least a thousand feet above. As the aircraft came closer Avery could see that he would cross well under the plane's path. He noticed that the other pilot had turned on his landing light.

O'Brien was fighting fatigue among other things. He reached over and grabbed the thermos bottle sitting on the passenger seat and removed the pressure plug. He drank right from the bottle, which wasn't smart. The lukewarm coffee flowed around his lips, down his chin and down his neck. He cursed and yelled, then realized he had turned left almost forty degrees off course. He checked his chart with his flashlight, found La Belle and returned to his course. He began to compute his airspeed and distance in his head, and figured he should make St. Petersburg\Clearwater airport in about an hour and ten minutes. He reached up and put two more hundred rpms on the engine.

O'Brien was not a good night flyer and with the lack of lights in this section of Florida, he was a little apprehensive. Suddenly, lights appeared on the horizon. He knew it was La Belle. He checked his altitude, sixty-five hundred feet. Then he noticed the flashing collision lights to his right at three o'clock. He watched as they came closer. O'Brien could see the small plane was below his path and would cross under his nose heading on a westerly course. He reached up and switched on the landing light and banked slowly right so he could keep the other plane in his windscreen. As the plane moved closer, O'Brien followed him until he was back on his original heading. When it was clear, O'Brien began to relax. "He must be heading for Fort Myers," O'Brien thought. "Naw, heading too far north, he's probably heading to Venice or Sarasota."

Pitch black filled the windshield again. O'Brien turned the instrument lights down to a minimum, checked his heading, his altitude and adjusted the trim for a little more nose up. He sat back and cursed the black outside, but in a sense it was welcome too. He thought about the morning exercise with the UDT team. He thought about the young captain and how confident he was in his team. Then he thought about the article in the Herald. "Maybe it's just a coincidence," he thought, but the image of Levin's young man at the hangar was burned in his brain. "My God, has this operation already killed innocent people for the sake of keeping the operation secret?" He was not prepared for this. He prayed that the two people found dead on Alligator Alley were not from Immokalee.

Unfortunately, his worst fears would be confirmed before his eyes closed on this day. A message from Bollman was waiting on his recorder at his beach apartment. "The leaks in the roof at the manger have been fixed."

CHAPTER 8

St. Petersburg Beach
Monday, September 21st
0745 hours

O'Brien spent another sleepless night. He lay fully clothed on the light cotton bedspread that he had fallen on exhausted, six hours before. As hundreds of thoughts ran through his mind, the one thought he could not shake was the deaths of two young people who would still be alive if it wasn't for the Yuletide Operation.

The phone rang.

"Yes?"

"Dan, Buckwheat here, did I wake you?"

"Ah, no, I was up, what's going on, where are you?"

"I'm in Stuart, but I am leaving for West Palm and flying home for a few days to clear my desk."

"How goes the work on September Morn?" O'Brien asked.

"Right on schedule, Dan, Gene Massey says he could be finished ahead of schedule, just before Thanksgiving."

"Great, I'm happy to hear good news for a change, I was.."

Buckland interrupted. "Ah, not too fast, Dan. I do have a serious problem over here."

"Shit, take it easy on me boy, it's only Monday."

"It's about Captain Spencer, Dan."

"Spencer?"

"Dan, he must have been tailing me and watching where I go and who I talk to."

"Why would he follow you?"

"Dan, this guy is no fool, he smelled a rat in the wood pile from the day you and Collins went aboard his yacht. He also has friends around the boat yard and he figured out some things."

"Buckwheat, you got my attention, what the hell are you saying?"

"Well, I went to this little waterfront dive last night to get a few beers and some steamed oysters. I heard a voice mention my name and looked up into the bearded kisser of Captain Mel Spencer. He told me that he had followed me there and wanted to talk."

"So, what was on his mind?"

"September Morn. He wanted to know what was going on with her. At first I laughed and told him it was none of his business and I got up to leave, then he addressed me as Commander Buckland. That's when I sat down again. Dan, he knows who I am, and he has pretty much figured out what's going on with the yacht. He may be guessing, but he is damn close."

"Jesus, it seems we can't do anything without someone sticking their nose in our business. How much do you think he knows, and how did he learn about you? You were supposed to be operating as a civilian consultant over there. Did Massey blow the whistle on you?"

"No, it wasn't Massey, I think it might have been a bimbo I was talking to a couple of nights ago at a pub down in Lake Worth."

"A bimbo? What the.."

"I went down to look up an old Academy friend, a retired Admiral who was one of my teachers at the Academy. I stopped at this pub to get directions, and, well, met this very neat lady."

"And you told this neat lady that you were a Commander in the Navy, and your battleship was tied up at the yacht club, right?"

"Well, ah, sort of. I told her I was a Navy Commander and was having my yacht repaired in Stuart."

"What does this bimbo have to do with Spencer?"

"Ah, he told me he spoke to her. I told you he followed me, Dan."

"O.k., so Spencer knows you're a Navy man, so what?"

"Dan, he knows that September Morn is being modified to look like a Citation. He don't know why, but he figured because everybody is so hush – hush around the yard that the project has Government written all over it and I am the watch dog. Those were his words."

"So my young warrior, what do you propose we do with Captain Spencer?" O'Brien asked.

"Give him his old job back as captain when she's ready to leave."

"Buckwheat, did I hear you right? You want us to hire Spencer for this mission?"

"Dan, you haven't come up with a skipper yet and after spending four hours with this guy last night, I am really impressed with him. He has one hell of a military background including serving as a navy Seal, he did three tours in Nam. Claims he's clean with the law and never did drugs. His only vice is too many wives and he gets into the bottle now and then."

"Buckwheat? There is no way.."

"Listen, Dan, why not run him through the mill, I'll call Bollman. Dan, this guy is sharp, honest. He knows the Caribbean too, couldn't we at least look at him?"

"O.K. Buckwheat, we will look at him, but what if we don't like what we see, how do we deal with him then?"

"In his words, Dan, he promised if he did not qualify to meet our criteria, he will accept the rejection and no more said. Dan, we don't have to open the books to him. We hire him as captain and send him down to that island you talked about. He would not have to know the real facts about Drummer. He just wants to get in on the action, and he really loves that old yacht, that's what really hurting him."

"Let me think about it, o.k.? I want to run this by a few more people, particularly Admiral Koster. How did you leave it with him?"

"I told him I had to leave for D.C. and would be gone for a few days. I would call him as soon as I got word if he was approved by Washington."

"You have his address and local numbers, right?"

"Sure do."

"When you talk to Bollman tell him I want a tail on this guy for the rest of the week, is that understood, Commander?"

"Yes, and Dan, I don't think you're going to regret this, he's alright in my book."

"By the way, Commander, when you're home this week you had better start establishing a story to explain why you won't be home for Christmas."

"Dan, are you serious? You're going to let me go on the mission?"

"Looks that way, you will be first mate on the Island Drummer. Keep it under your hat, I have to clear it with your boss and break the news to Captain Avery. There is always the chance you could end up with your friend Spencer, too. Either way, you're going south for Christmas. You might consider letting you hair get shabby, most first mates always look a bit.. loose."

"Thanks, Dan, see you in D.C. later this week, right?"

"Right, and nothing said about Spencer to anyone except Bollman. I don't want Spencer to know anything except what he is told by me, understand?"

"Yes, sir."

O'Brien put the phone down, lit a cigarette and lay back on the bed again. "Well, the captain's job is now settled for the Seduce, but how do we work around him? Buckwheat may have the answer, don't let him know what is going on. If he feels he is on a mission and can take orders, no problem." O'Brien sat back up, checked his watch and started to dial his office at the Pentagon then stopped. "Jesus, how do we handle Spencer when it comes time to blow up the Seaduce?" Another problem added to the many still spinning around in his head.

Admiral Koster's Office
The Pentagon, Washington, D.C.
0915 hours

Paul Stone, Secretary of the Navy sat patiently in the high back leather chair directly in front of the large mahogany desk. Sitting on the desk in front of him, carved out in golden hardwood, was the name Thomas J. Foster in large script. Nearby, a scale model of a F4U-1 Vought Corsair. Stone was too young for World War II, but he was very familiar with the Corsair from his days in the Korean conflict. The room was filled with photographs of great war ships and portraits of famous Naval Commanders. One particular picture, directly behind Koster's chair, was a photograph of Admiral Halsey with his arm around a young naval airman, taken aboard the USS Lexington. There was writing on the picture, but it was too far away to read.

"Sorry to keep you waiting, Mr. Secretary. It seems we have a problem with a memo sent over here from the Vice President."

Barbara Knolls, standing beside the Admirals chair, made a suggestion. "Admiral, why don't I just call over to the Vice President's office and ask his secretary if he means to meet at his office?"

She took the piece of paper from the Admiral's hand. He looked up at her and smiled. "You do that, Mrs. Knolls, that would take the guess work out of this problem. Then, would you call Admiral Werts office in Norfolk and advise him of the meeting place?"

"Yes sir. Mr. Secretary, would you like some coffee or hot tea?"

"No, Mrs. Knolls, thank you."

Barbara Knolls left the office and closed the door.

"O.K. Tom, let's get it on the table. What the hell is going on with you and Atlantic Fleet Headquarters? I got a call from the Vice Chief of Operations last night that you're looking to put a carrier group together?"

"My dear Mr. Secretary, Vice Admiral Shea is reacting to a call I made last week to Norfolk and Mayport, checking on status of our carriers and support groups, I said nothing about putting a carrier group together, well, not officially, mind you."

"Has this anything to do with Operation Yuletide, Tom? Come on, what's bugging you? Are you getting nervous? The President and the new Soviet leader don't meet for seven or eight weeks."

Koster rose from his chair, pushed it back and walked around the desk. "Come with me, Paul, I want to show you something," Koster walked to the opposite side of the office to a long table. On the table were a number of nautical charts, some rolled up and some lying flat. In the center of the table,

126

held down by four miniature bronze propellers, was a chart of the Caribbean basin.

"Here are the positions of all Russian ships in the Caribbean, including three trawlers we identify as spooks."

"All I see, Tom, is a frigate and two destroyers in port at Havana and the same two sub tenders that are almost landmarks. We know of six Russian attack subs working in the southern basin deep water, so, what's the problem?"

"No problem, Paul, I just can't remember anytime in the past few years when it has been so quiet, as if every war ship has been called back to their bases in the past few weeks."

"What's coming out of Sevastopol? Maybe Admiral Mikhailovsky is having problems with the new President, Gorbachev. He is cutting a big bunch of fat out of the military, could be he has put the Soviet Navy on rations, Admiral.   Has anyone talked to their new Naval attaché lately, Captain Smirnov?"

"Nope, but maybe I will learn something in a few days. Smirnov is having lunch this week with Vice Admiral Coons. It seems they both like saltwater fishing and get together occasionally."

The Secretary leaned over the chart and placed his finger on one of the many colored lines that were inked in. "What do all these lines mean here, Tom?"

"Oh, those are O'Brien's intercept courses for Yuletide and the Unicorn."

"How is Operation Yuletide really doing, Tom?"

"As well as expected, we are having an all-hands meeting later this week over at the VPs office, why don't you try and stop in. We are meeting our star player, the captain of the Yuletide, and his first mate, for the first time."

"I will be in New Hampshire for the next few days at a family reunion, keep me posted." The Secretary then headed for the door, stopped, turned and looked back at Koster who had returned to study the chart.

"Take care of yourself, Tom. I will check in with you next Monday." He continued out he door.

Koster didn't respond, he kept moving his fingers around the chart. He traced the pencil line from Santiago de Cuba with his finger until he found the "X" mark. "Boom," He yelled loudly.

"Boom, boom," came a reply from behind him.

Koster turned and saw Barbara Knolls standing next to his desk. She reached down and placed a piece of paper on his blotter. "Everything is all set, Admiral. The meeting will take place in the Vice President's conference room."

"Babs, see if you can locate Vice Admiral Coons, then call down to Atlantic Fleet Headquarters and get me the Commander of Submarine Forces, Vice Admiral, ah,..."

"Halprin, Charles Halprin, sir."

"Yeah, that's him, set up a conference call as soon as you can."

Koster stirred through a stack of papers until he found what he was looking for. "Ah, get me Captain Leonard Mize, he has something to do with recommissioning procedures of Naval vessels, you'll find him in Norfolk or Hampton. Give him the information on "Sonar", AG 521..ah, you have the file somewhere and tell him we need to get working on the paperwork to get her out of the U.S. Navy, ASAP. He needs to call me so I can explain what we want to do with it. Hell, I don't know what to even tell him. Tell you what, Babs, call Vice Admiral Barrett at Mayport...

"Commander, sir. It's Commander Barrett."

"Oh, yes, whatever. Harry will know what to tell Mize, and while you're at it, call Barrett and tell him we need to get the Sonar over to Jacksonville shipyard yesterday for refit and painting, paperwork is on the way. How come you're not writing any of this down, Babs?"

She smiled and put her finger on her temple and smiled. "I got it all up here. By the way, sir, I located that retired friend of yours, Captain Lind? You know, the one you wanted to talk to about being Captain on the Sonar?"

"Oh, yes, what did John say?"

"His first comment was very apologetic. Then he told me to tell you to jam your job, if there is any room left, up your keester. He said he doesn't do tugboats."

"Good, that means he will take the job. He was one of the best tin-can skippers we ever had. Get back to him and tell him to call me when he gets to Mayport, he is to report to Commander Harry Barrett. Tell him to stay at the officers transit quarters for now, and make sure he knows the lid is on, not to talk to anyone till he talks to me, Ah, where is the old fart living, anyway?"

"Fort Walton Beach, near Pensacola."

"Hell, he's practically in Jacksonville, just a stone throw away. We will have to make arrangements to put him on the payroll, find out what he needs and put it on O'Brien's list, you know what to do and keep in mind, he's on full retirement, offer him minimum wage."

Barbara Knoll stepped out of the room and closed the door.

Koster read the memo on his desk from the Vice President and sat down. He wrote a note to himself. "Call John Lind."

Wednesday, September 23
Holiday Inn

Baltimore\Washington International Airport
1930 hours

The hotel dining room was full to capacity. After asking the hostess how long of a wait there was, Phil Avery made a reservation for three and told her they would be in the lounge.

Avery approached Gail Townsend sitting in the small circular booth. "About thirty minutes, according to the hostess."

Gail checked her watch. "That's perfect, your friend O'Brien told you we would meet here at eight, right?"

"Sure did. Are you nervous?"

"Yes, now would you sit down, please?"

Avery opened his sport coat and sat down next to Gail. He watched as she stared into her wineglass, rotating it slowly back and forth.

"Hey, look at me, its not as if you were being sentenced to prison, you're going to like O'Brien, honest." Avery put his hand gently on top of her glass and brought it down to the table. She looked into Avery's eyes and found comfort. She smiled.

"I'm sorry, Phil. This whole thing is, well, so overwhelming, I feel like I am living some kind of a bad dream."

"Good evening, am I interrupting anything?"

Avery and Gail looked up together at Dan O'Brien, who stood towering over their small table. He looked like a college professor in his gray tweed sport jacket, dark maroon vest sweater, oxford button down shirt and flannel slacks with penny loafers. His graying black hair was long and brushed back over the tops of his ears, and his well-tanned face was dominated by a warm broad smile.

"Not at all Dan, here, let me get this chair over here." Avery started to move towards the next table.

"Stay, Phil, I'll get it." O'Brien pulled the chair over to the table and sat down. His eyes were fixed on Gail. She was striking, even more attractive then the photos in her file.

129

Gail was also surprised. O'Brien was handsome and very physically fit, not at all what she had expected.

"Gail, this is Rudolf, better known as Dan O'Brien."

"Mr. O'Brien, my pleasure." Gail offered her hand.

"Ms. Townsend, I have been looking forward to meeting you." O'Brien reached over the table, took her hand and shook it gently.

"What can I get you to drink, Dan? Service here is a bit slow."

"Just a white wine, Phil, thanks."

Phil excused himself and walked over to the service bar.

"Well, your presence here tells me that you have no reservations about the project we have asked you to join?"

"Oh, I have many reservations, Mr. O'Brien, and a great many questions I would like answered. Phil told me you were the only one who could do this. I am here because, from what little I have been told, feel I should support this operation. However, I want you to know I am not in favor of being part of a conspiracy that may cost the life of anyone, regardless who they are."

O'Brien studied Gail's face for a moment. She maintained eye contact with him, never looking away. He knew that there would be no room for maneuvering with her. He decided to tell it like it is, and how he hoped it would turn out.

"Ms. Townsend." O'Brien stopped, looked around the room. He pointed to Phil's seat. "Do you mind?"

"No, not at all."

"Thanks." O'Brien moved around the table and sat down in Avery's chair. He looked over to see Avery still waiting at the service bar.

"I can only hope that Phil told you the importance of this operation. If not, let me tell you in few words. We are losing the war on drugs, Ms. Townsend. You must be aware that Florida, especially South Florida, is still one of hottest areas in the country for drug smuggling. Airports, marinas, barrier islands, even the Everglades. The law enforcement agencies cannot be everywhere. We are dealing with experts, who have the money to buy everything they need. Once in a while we catch a few, but they are the sloppy ones and represent less than ten percent of what is slipping through our fingers. We recently learned that Castro is about to become active in the drug distribution business. We always suspected he was allowing shipments to pass over and through his island, but now he may be getting ready to ship on his own. We have to stop him, Ms. Townsend, before he gets organized or operational. We have a window of opportunity to do this in a few short weeks. We have a plan, we have the equipment and the talent to get the job done. Part of this plan will be to destroy his plan and if there are lives lost during this exercise, it can't be helped, even if it's the life of a world leader. If it means anything, you will be nowhere near the site when and if that time comes."

Gail Townsend went back to playing with her wineglass. She shifted her eyes back to O'Brien and then to Phil Avery, who was nearing the table with three drinks in his hands.

"I'm very excited about tomorrow's meeting, Mr. O'Brien. Will I really meet the Vice President?"

"You will, plus a few other people you may recognize, I'm sure. They are equally anxious to meet you and Phil. I'm very pleased to have you on board, Gail. You are on board, right?"

Gail turned and smiled. In her mind she had to agree with Phil and what he had been telling her all day, she was beginning to like this man called Rudolf.

"Here we are, I'm sorry it took so long." Avery studied the faces of his two companions. He knew Gail had made her decision. He put the drinks down on the table, then lifted his and made a toast. "Here's to a very interesting Christmas."

The Executive Office Building
Thursday, September 24th
0830 hours

The black Chrysler with darkened windows moved through the gates leading to the rear of the Executive Office Building. It drove down into the parking garage and stopped at a elevator station.

"This way, sir."

The agent held the car door open while Phil Avery and Gail Townsend stepped out. Another agent standing by the elevator doors pushed a button and the doors opened. Avery and Gail stepped in with the two agents.

"How are you this morning, ma'am?"

"Fine, just fine, considering I just toured the District of Columbia at six hundred miles per hour."

"Yes ma'am, you had agent Faulkner at the wheel, his hobby is stock car racing on weekends. The agency doesn't give him any real fast cars anymore, he's wrecked four Lincoln Town Cars this year."

The two agents took the lead and Gail and Phil followed for what seemed like miles down corridors until they reached a pair of massive

131

mahogany doors, guarded by two Marines. One of the agents pushed a series of buttons on a call box and a buzzer sounded, he turned the large brass knob in the center of one of the doors.

"How do I look?" Gail whispered

"Fine." Phil responded.

Dan O'Brien was standing with Commander Buckland, Ian Billings and Roger Weijlard of the State Department and introduced Gail and Phil.

"I had no idea how beautiful and how historic this building was, Dan."

"Yeah, that it is, Gail. By the way, may I can call you Gail?"

"Why not, my mother does."

O'Brien laughed and turned to Avery. "You know, Phil, you never told us about the lady's wit."

"I am learning more about her by the minute, Dan."

The doors opened across the room and the Vice President, Admiral Koster, Vice Admiral Halprin, Charles Ingram, Attorney General and Carlton Simms, director of the FBI walked in. The final meeting was about to begin. From this day on, Dan O'Brien would have to report only to Admiral Koster, except for Ian Billings, who would handle all communications dealing with Jesus Souza, Cuba and the Christmas Tree network.

Atlanta International Airport
Delta Crown Room
2110 hours

Phil watched Gail as she walked through the maze of chairs. The room was filled with travelers, some watching the big screen television, others reading newspapers, and a few admiring Gail as she walked by them.

Gail sat down opened her purse and took out a compact.

"I got you another drink, did you reach him?" Avery asked.

"I didn't talk to him. His son answered. Damn, I hate this." Gail threw the compact back in her purse and grabbed her drink from the table.

Phil could seeing frustration on her face and asked.   "What if I called and explained, Gail."

"Don't worry about it, Phil, it's not your problem. Carlton knows that it's impossible to call him at home. We tried codes and phony names but we both get nervous that she, or one of the children, oh, let's drop it, o.k.?"

"Sure, but you know, you're going to have to tell him, Gail. You can't wait until the last minute."

"What time is our flight?"

Phil looked at his watch. "Ten fifteen."

"Boy, this has been some day. I was really impressed with the Vice President, weren't you? He was much taller than I pictured. And wasn't Admiral Koster a trip? You know, I actually felt he was flirting with me sometimes."

Phil rested back in his chair and studied Gail. "I was impressed with all of them but when it comes to personality I have to go with Dan O'Brien. I don't know where they found this guy but you have to admit he has one hell of an imagination. This whole plan as complicated as it seems does make sense when he explains it and I think it will work."

Gail smiled. "I agree, and he mentioned to me that Commander Buckland may be joining us on the Drummer?"

"Yes, he's quite talented but hasn't done a lot of sailing, so we will have to teach him as we go."

"Phil, what do you think it will be like? I mean when we get to St. Thomas?"

"I don't know. We will have to be careful down there. We can't let too many eyes get a close look at the Drummer. I don't know just how much we will be concealing below deck or how she will look below the water line. I told O'Brien we wouldn't have trouble explaining two gas engines rather than a single diesel, but I do worry about those hydraulic struts and their systems, that could start some serious questions if they are discovered. We'll have to tell all our old friends that we can't entertain any visitors because the owners on board want total privacy."

Gail responded. "I understand that our charter guests are actually Navy Intelligence personnel?"

"That's what Buckwheat suggested to O'Brien. They will arrive two days after we do, and we will leave after provisioning. "We need to register with a clearing house, are you going to use Charter Services?"

"Yes, you will need to talk to the owner, Cathy Miller and tell her we are bringing Ted Collins personal yacht down for a few weeks of chartering."

"Phil, I don't want you worrying about a certain captain being interested in my arrival there. I am not interested seeing him, and if it happens, I can handle him."

"I'm not concerned about him, Gail. I just want to get in and out of there with the least amount of socializing with old friends, especially the ones who are curious and will come on board."

"By the way, how and where do we get the props for the Drummer's disguise? We can't hide them on board, can we?"

133

"No, they will be put aboard our support freighter before it leaves for San Juan."

Gail sighed. "There are so many complications on this project and so many things that can screw it up. No one during the meeting today even mentioned the weather. Phil, you and I know that December can be a bastard down there."

Phil looked at Gail and pointed to his watch. "It's time to go home." They left the lounge and boarded their plane.

For the next two and a half-hours they talked about the mission and tried to plan their next few weeks. Nothing they could have planned would have prepared them for the scene that was about to take place at Sarasota Airport.

Sarasota\Bradenton Airport
2350 Hours

Carlton met every plane that came out of the Baltimore Washington area all evening. He was upset and verbally blasted Gail at the arrival gate. Avery tried to explain, but Carlton ignored him. Gail moved fast to prevent a confrontation. She took Carlton's arm, bid Avery goodnight and left. Avery stood and watched them walk away and for the first time had a bad taste in his mouth for the lawyer, and pitied Gail Townsend.

Before the day ended, Phil Avery would be confronted by more depressing news. Two messages waited for him on his answering machine. The first was from Nancy. She called to inform him that she moved out of the condo. She had been promoted to operations manager of the small airline company and moved to Palm Beach. She tried to explain nothing would change, but Avery knew it was over.

The second was from O'Brien. Unicorn had arrived in Martinique. The crew and the yachts flag had changed as did the itinerary. She would be departing 0900 Tuesday for Santiago, Cuba. He also advised him to meet at St. Pete Airport at 0800 in the morning.

Avery mixed himself a light scotch and soda and sat in the darkness of the lanai. He lit a cigarette and took a long drag. His thoughts went right to the ISLAND DRUMMER and his friend Ted Collins. If Collins could pull this off he was a miracle worker. Avery was finding it hard to believe that the Drummer would be able to get up and run the speeds they would need and if it didn't, would the entire operation go down the drain? He closed his eyes, the cigarette fell to the floor and rolled into a crack between two tiles.

St. Petersburg\Clearwater Airport
Friday, September 25th
0815 hours

O'Brien stood on the windy hardstand watching the lone monoplane in the southern sky descending on a right base leg to runway 35. He could see the low wing plane was definitely a Piper Cherokee with a fixed landing gear as it turned on final. He was certain it was Phil Avery. He checked his watch. It was 0820. Avery was twenty minutes late.

The attendant from National Flight services directed the Piper to a parking space between two other transient planes. O'Brien noticed that Avery was not alone. When the passenger door opened, Gail Townsend stepped out on the wing and waved.

"Good morning, Dan O'Brien." Gail yelled, then walked down off the wing. Phil stepped out of the plane, closed the cabin door and joined her.

O'Brien reached the couple, extended his hand to Phil, put his arm around Gail and kissed her on her cheek.

"Morning, you two. I take it you will be joining us today, Gail?"

"I asked her to come, Dan, I thought it would be alright, after all, she needs to understand what's going on with the new systems on the Drummer."

"I have no problem with that, I just wish I thought of it first."

Ten minutes later they were back aboard Avery's plane on their flight south to Immokalee to meet Ted Collins, Bollman and Larry Keen to check the progress on the Island Drummer.

The Manger, Immokalee Airport
1030 hours

Gail stood speechless under the stern of the Drummer.

"Hard to believe your eyes, huh Gail?"

Gail turned and looked into the well-tanned face of Ted Collins. He was standing behind her, watching two workman replacing stanchions on the aft deck.

"You know, Phil tried to explain all this to me, but seeing it, well, it's..."

"It's a mess, that's what it is," Ted responded laughing. "Come on, let me take you upstairs." Ted took Gail by the arm and walked up the ladder to the deck level, then down through the companionway and aft to the master stateroom.

Ted guided Gail over to a large wide board that was used to walk over the floor joists. Gail could see down into the bowels of the Drummer where a number of men where working applying fiberglass cloth soaked with resin, and rolling it flat with small paint rollers. The heavy smell from the resin and the fumes from acetone, was irritating to Gail, but she wanted to see what was going on.

"Ted, I know you're working around the clock, but do you think we can actually get her ready in time?"

Collins flashed Gail his famous smile. "We will have her done, not to worry. Will she hit the speeds we are looking for? We don't know. We are getting a real education on this project, but we have the best brains available helping us work things out, only time will tell."

For the next hour Ted, Phil and Gail went over the systems with each project manager. The new power plants had changed the CG of the yacht, moving weight further aft, so new tanks were being installed forward in the bow section to add ballast. The complicated hydraulic systems for the movable struts were causing many problems, especially where the levers, or switches were to be installed at the helm station. There was no more room on the present console to handle anymore levers, gauges or switches. Gail came up with the idea to install them beneath the cockpit table that was attached to the console. They would be out of sight, which everyone agreed was important, yet the helmsman could reach them.

The idea brought praise from the crew and Collins suggested that a new engineer had elected herself to the project and she should at least buy lunch. Ted suggested they head over to the restaurant across the highway.

Gail went off to the office to round up O'Brien and Bollman. Ted Collins and Avery walked over to inspect the large external patch areas around the shafts that were being glassed in from inside.

Avery moved his hand slowly over the seams that were still visible from where the new molded glass parts were attached.

"Not to worry, Phil, when we get done with those seams you will never know they were there," Ted said.

"Yeah, I know, my concern is the vibrations that will be created between those V-Drives and the engines. Larry Keen says he has the vibration problems licked with new type engine mounts. He is using some kind of new high tech sandwich material, rubber between plastic, something like that."

Ted slapped Avery on the back. "Hey, let's worry about that at the sea trials. Right now, I'm hankering for some hot shepherds pie across the street."

The small group walked across the road to the popular local restaurant. When they entered the eatery, two young Sheriff's deputies confronted them.

"Hey, you all work across the road at the old Wilson hangar, don't you?" the young deputy asked.

O'Brien addressed the young man. "If you mean that hangar over there?" O'Brien pointed to the manger. "Yes we do. My name is O'Brien, Dan O'Brien. This fella is Phil Avery, this big guy is Ted Collins, famous yacht builder who just bought the hangar don't you know?"

"Is that a fact? Are you building any yachts over there now?"

"Naw, just repairs, you know, overhaul and refit work?" Collins replied.

"Well, partner, we hear different. We heard that you may be messing with some real secret shit in there. Man, that place looks like it's deep in secret goings on, I mean with all that fancy fencing and those strange looking workers you got, hell, none of them are from these parts, are they, friend?"

"Would you gentlemen mind joining us outside, please?" O'Brien pushed the door open and motioned for the two deputies to lead the way out.

O'Brien addressed his party. "You folks go ahead and get us a table, ah, Mr. Bollman, would you join us please?" O'Brien walked around the side of the building and headed straight for the two big Chevy patrol cars parked next to the building.

"Hey mister, where do you think you going?"

O'Brien stopped, turned around and faced the deputies as they slowly approached him. Bollman was walking behind them.

Once they rounded the building, out of sight from the road, Bollman challenged them. "Let's hold it here, gentlemen and don't turn around. Keep your eyes on the guy in front of you, and don't move a muscle, I have a forty-five back here, and I can take you both out before you could pass wind." Bollman pulled the breach back on his weapon so they could clearly hear the familiar metallic sound of a weapon being prepared to fire.

"Now, you know, gentlemen, how easily a 45 can separate your mouth from your asshole, so let's not do anything stupid."

"What the fuck you think ya doin, man?" the older deputy yelled out.

Bollman tossed his billfold to O'Brien. O'Brien flipped open the wallet displaying Bollman's FBI I.D. and badge so the two deputies could read it.

"We are the good guys, gentlemen and we want you to know and remember that. Now, if you, ah, Joe-Bob, will be kind enough to open this here car, we can get on your radio and talk to your boss and get this matter cleared up in a hurry."

Bollman put his gun on safety, released the hammer and returned it to the holster under his coat. The deputy opened the door to his car, sat down, put the key in the ignition and turned on his police radio.

The young deputy stood in front of O'Brien and Bollman. "I don't give a good fuck who you guys are, or who you work for, if you think you can pull a gun on me in this county, you got some hard time coming."

"Who's your boss?" Bollman asked.

"Sheriff Goodson, Charlie Goodson."

"Get him on the horn there, Billy-Bob," Bollman ordered.

"Car one-nine-four to base."

"Come in Joe-Bob, what's your..."

"Where's Charlie, Mike?"

"He's up in Arcadia, Civitan luncheon. What's your.."

"Can you reach him on a land line?"

"Hell no, what's going on, where's Mark, is he with you?"

"Yeah, he's right here. We got a problem, and I need Charlie."

"Tell your dispatcher, that we want to meet with Charlie after his lunch, out here at the old airport hangar. Here's our number." O'Brien handed the deputy one of Bollman's cards with the manger number on it.

O'Brien looked at Bollman and smiled. "Let's go eat, little buddy." He looked into the two sour faces of the angry deputies.

"Hey, we'll see you guys later, and we recommend that you keep your thoughts to yourselves until Charlie Bob talks to you."

O'Brien and Bollman walked slowly towards the front of the restaurant. "I think we just got our asses into a bucket of shit, old man."

O'Brien laughed. "Man, I don't believe you pulled your gun. Is that legal? I mean, are you authorized to jump on a local like that?"

"Hell, I don't know, never did it before, but I bet we are going to find out pretty soon, ol' buddy-bob."

Collins, Avery and Gail were anxiously waiting for them to return and to hear what happened with the young officers. O'Brien described the brief encounter with some humor, but he couldn't hide his concern about the incident. The operation was getting tougher to hide by the day.

Bollman went right to a pay phone and called Washington to alert FBI Director Carlton Simms, of the problem and have him contact the County Sheriff's office and Dan O'Brien.

At 1540 hours, O'Brien received a call from Simms in Washington telling him that Sheriff Goodson had been briefed. He was having a meeting with his deputies at 0700 Saturday morning. They would be told that a spook ship was being built for the Coast Guard and DEA for drug surveillance work. It was a classified project, and required maximum security.

Before the day ended, O'Brien called a meeting to set new dates and work schedules for everyone, until the project was competed. Ted Collins and Jack Courtney targeted October 30th for the completion of the Drummer. He pointed out that the work on the Seaduce should be finished on or about the 10th of October, according to Massey and wanted to move her down to the Caribbean as soon as possible. For the first time, he brought up the name of the captain who would take her to the islands.

"Jesus, Dan, I thought this guy had some serious problems?" Collins asked.

"Well, he does, most of it is in a bottle. Commander Buckland spent some time with him recently and learned a lot about his background and told me he thought the guy deserved a shot at it. He's got a clean bill with Billings and Simms, and only one charge in Palm Beach, a speeder that he beat."

"What do you think, Phil?" O'Brien asked.

"Well, I don't know the guy personally, but he's been on her decks for some time, so you say and the guy who owned the yacht, ah, Doctor...?"

"Hemmings."

"Yeah, he had to have some respect for the man, he employed him long enough. Hey, if he's qualified, I see no reason why he can't continue at the helm. But how will he fit in, I mean he will have to know what we are going to do with the yacht, won't he?"

"That's the problem, Phil. I don't know how much I should tell him. Personally, I would rather keep him in the dark until it's time for him to sail from St. Lucia. Meantime, we can just order him to head down as soon as the yachts been provisioned. We need to get him a first mate and Buckwheat is working on that."

"Does he have any idea who he will be working for, Dan?"

"Ted, we didn't fool him a bit, he suspected something from the beginning when you and I first met him. He started to shadow Buckwheat and learned that he was a Navy Commander, that's when he made his move."

"Buckwheat tipped his hand? How?, I mean why?" Bollman inquired.

O'Brien laughed. "I wish I could tell you, but there is a lady present."

"Anyway, Captain Spencer collared Buckwheat and flat told him he wanted to get in on what ever was going on and have his old job back as captain on the old yacht. So far, all he knows is that we are doing surveillance work, and that he will be paid through a private fund. I plan to go over and personally meet with him next week and work out all the details."

"Phew, this project gets more thrilling by the day, doesn't it?" Gail said.

"It sure does, Gail, and can you imagine what it will be like when all the toys are in place depending on split second timing on open waters?"

O'Brien looked at his watch. "O.K., it's three-thirty. Phil, you have some paperwork to go over with Sam, he needs your signature on some checks and some State of Florida forms need to be signed for the business. Speaking of business, I understand that there have been three or four guys who came up with their boats on trailers looking for someone to talk to about repairs. What the hell are we going to do about these guys?"

"Just send Sam out to talk to them, we won't need any advertising."

"I'm serious, Ted. This could be a problem, especially when the sign goes up next week, announcing this place as Avery's repair yard."

"We can stall for a while, we'll tell them we are waiting for our license or approval from EPA. What we need to duck is those advertising folks and newspapers who will be out here trying to sell ads, or worse yet, do a story," Bollman said.

"Jesus, you guys are just full of things I need to lose more sleep over."

Collins laughed. "Dan, you got us this far, you will get us through."

Sand and Sea Apartments
St. Petersburg Beach
Sunday, September 27th
1625 hours

O'Brien was switching through the channels of his small black and white TV looking for the Redskin vs. Eagle game, when someone knocked on the door.

"Hi, Dan, thought I would take you up on that offer you made last night."

"Oh, yes, ah, here, please come in, you will have to excuse the mess, the maid hasn't been here since January."

She was pretty, far more attractive than she appeared at the piano bar. He hair was different and the outfit she wore left nothing to the imagination. The blue halter she barely had on must have belonged to her teenage sister along with the white short shorts.

"Here, have a seat, I was just trying to find the Redskin game, ah, do you like football?"

"No, can't stand it, only because I don't understand it."

"Oh, how about a drink? I have VO and some beer?"

"Do you have a Coke?"

"Ah, no, ah miss, but I will be most happy to run up to the machine at the pool and get you one."

"Eileen, Dan. The name is Eileen."

"Of course, how could I forget, ah, Eileen, from Fitchburg, Massachusetts, right?

She smiled as she reached into her leather cigarette case and pulled out a cigarette. "Do you mind?"

"Ah, no, of course not, here, let me find you a light."

"I have it, Dan."

"Now, let's begin where we left off last night. You said something about taking me over to Palm Beach tomorrow? What time were you planning on leaving? I have to make arrangements with my in-laws to come and pick up Leslie."

"Ah, yes, Palm Beach, I, er, I may have to change plans on that, ah, the plane I normally charter? Well, it's already flying, I mean someone is using it and won't be back until late."

"How far is Palm beach? we could drive over, it's closer than Miami. We could even use my car if you don't have any reservations about riding in a German made convertible."

"Ah, it's a long drive, and we wouldn't be back until late."

"Back? We don't have to come back, silly. I don't leave until next weekend, and John doesn't arrive until Thursday night, so I have plenty of time. My in-laws live over in Tampa, remember? They will love having their granddaughter for a couple of days."

"Ah, John, like in husband John, yes right, now I remember. Listen, Irene, Eileen, ah, I may have had a few last night and said some things out of line and if I did I deeply apologize, but I have been working a lot lately, and last night.."

"Last night you were a darling and a gentleman and were not out of line, that is until you took me to my apartment. You insisted that we make love on the concrete bench outside my door. You would have made it too had you not taken that last drink...the brandy did you in. I tried to help but you just laughed.."

"Ah, Jesus, I don't think I want to know the rest. My God, I am sorry, I don't know what..."

Eileen got up from the sofa and walked passed Dan towards the door. He couldn't believe his ears, and now he couldn't believe his eyes. "Damn she was sexy, what a body, what a pair of legs," he thought as she passed him by.

She opened the door, turned and smiled. "Well, Dan, it could have been great. Maybe next year? I will be here, same time, same apartment and John might not be around at all, who knows?" She went out the door and it closed quietly.

Dan fell back into the small lounge chair. He put his hands tight against his temples, closed his eyes and tried his damnedest to recall his time with Eileen. The phone rang. "Yes, listen Eileen, you must think I am a total ass, the way I am acting."

The voice on the other end responded. "I beg your pardon. Is this Dan O'Brien?"

"Ah, yes it is, Ian, is that you?"

"Sure is. Hey, are you alright?"

"Oh, yes, I thought you were, Eileen, my new neighbor."

"Listen Dan, we got some exciting news from Souza. Two Dolphins have arrived from the Pacific. They are going to play near Marineland. Understand?

"I think so." O'Brien began to unravel Ian's words to himself. "Source in Cuba is saying that there are two devices and they are going to Santiago de Cuba, near Guantanamo, the Marine base known as marine land. Yes, I got it, Ian."

"Also, Dan, a big defensive star is going to a island resort to get well after surgery. More team members already arrived."

O'Brien closed his eyes and translated in his head. "Ah, defense, defense, ah, he could mean the Soviet's Defense Minister, Ustinov, Dimitri Ustinov, yes.. I read somewhere he had some surgery recently. It may be he is heading for Cuba for some R and R. That would explain some of the extra traffic in Port Havana that Admiral Koster was concerned about."

"Ustinov?" O'Brien said.

"Right, Dan. I will call Admiral Koster now; that should stop him worrying about the extra traffic down there. You know, Dan, when this operation is over I just might find a spot up here for you at the agency. You're really good. 007 has nothing on you, my best to Eileen."

"Yeah, right, thanks, Ian." O'Brien put the receiver down and thought about the message. "Two?, there are two dolphins? What the hell has Castro got? Why can't they say more about what they are? 007? What the hell does that mean?"

CHAPTER NINE

The small Russian freighter, PECHORA, was secured portside to the Government dock. A light rain mixed in heavy mist swirled around the eerie waterfront. The only sounds disturbing the chilled morning stillness were the small waves lapping at the decaying sea wall and the freighter's rusting hull. Occasionally the muffled sound of a distant bell could be heard as it swayed on a buoy in the peaceful harbor.

Moving slowly along the pot holed roadway between the aging warehouses and the sea wall, two pairs of headlights probed through the sea fog. Then came the sound of clattering diesel engines disturbing the peaceful waterfront. Two trucks, a Soviet built Ural cab-over tractor pulling a flatbed trailer and a GAZ-51 troop carrier came to a stop beside the freighter. Two Cuban Army officers climbed down from the tractor, while a half dozen soldiers jumped from the troop carrier and started unfolding large canvas tarps that lay on the flat bed.

Another pair of headlights suddenly appeared. With no regard for the water filled pot holes, the fast moving automobile bounced and swerved sending cascades of water into the air until it came to a stop alongside the troop carrier. Two men dressed in suits and raincoats stepped out of the small black Ladaz sedan.

The taller of the two men walked over to the Cuban officers.

"Good morning, Colonel Navarro."

"Buenos dias, Major Kotov." Colonel Luis Navarro tried not to show his displeasure at the sight of the two visitors. "Now, don't tell me, Major Kotov, you're just now heading home from Los Marinos Bar and lost your way?" Navarro said forcing a smile. He was not only surprised at the arrival of Kotov, he was puzzled why. He proceeded to be cautious with his words and actions, Frederick Kotov was the assistant deputy chief of KGB Caribbean operations.

Major Fredrick Kotov, much taller than Navarro, looked down on him and smiled as he flipped the collar on his raincoat around his neck. He was a large man, six foot two, broad chested with a wide flat face accented by deep-set eyes and flattened nose. He had no eye brows, eye lashes or hair. It was said that he had been exposed to gamma rays at a nuclear test site in the Ukraine when he was a young soldier. He was assigned to Cuba in 1976 as assistant deputy for Caribbean operations. After serving under two chief deputies, he expected to be promoted when the new President, Mikhail Gorbachev was appointed, but KGB Headquarters had other plans. They brought in Dimitri Sorokin, a younger agent with deep family roots in the Politburo. Upset that he was still the number two man in Cuba, Kotov had decided that he would prove to his superiors in Moscow that Sorokin could not match his knowledge, contacts and skills working with the Cubans. He decided to intimidate his superior, when and where he could to make him look foolish.

Acting on a tip from within Castro's secret police, Kotov had learned that a shipment of cargo from China was on board the PECHORA addressed personally to Fidel Castro. Kotov was curious since his superior, Dimitri Sorokin, had not advised him of the shipment or its contents. He also learned about the secret unloading that had been scheduled.

"Colonel Navarro, might I might ask you the same question? Why are you here with a military detail? I would guess, you are about to pick up something of substantial size and weight from the looks of your equipment."

"You are right. We are picking up two large crates for our President, and taking them to Holguin to the research farms."

"Holguin research farms? I know of no such farms."

"Comrade Kotov," Navarro said loudly. "I don't believe my ears. You, who knows everything about my government doesn't know about the Ministry of Agriculture's new research farms? Captain Minas, please make a note of this. Advise Dr. Martinez at the Ministry to put comrade Kotov on his mailing list."

Kotov laughed as he wiped the raindrops trickling down his forehead.

"Of course, now I remember. Comrade Castro spoke of such farms to the Central Committee of the PCC last month." He turned to his companion.

"Remember, comrade Petrov?" Ivan Petrov, a special aide to Sorokin and Kotov nodded his head in agreement.

The Russian agent walked over to the side of the flatbed and examined the tarps. He turned to Navarro.

"I still find it a bit curious, Colonel, that you, a member of comrade Castro's elite secret service is out here in this miserable weather picking up, ah, just what is it you are picking up?"

Navarro was prepared.

"I believe it's a new kind of tiller and cultivator machines. They are experimental prototypes designed by the Chinese agriculture ministry and President Castro is very excited about trying them. As you know, comrade

Kotov, our President is putting great emphasis on the development of new farming techniques, and I might add, with the blessings of your government."

"Well, Colonel, I was under the impression that Cuba was restricted from purchasing anything from the Chinese government, especially machinery, unless it comes..."

"Come now, Major," Navarro interrupted. "Do you think that your new President is not aware of this purchase? After all, the machines are aboard one of your freighters, along with the personal belongings of your own Minister of Defense, Marshal Ustinov. As you must know, comrade, he comes as a guest of our President to rest from his recent surgery"

"Of course I know, Colonel, but since my superior is not here, I would like to inspect these implements, just for our records mind you."

"Of course, shall we go on board? Captain Slitka is expecting us." Navarro pointed towards the steep boarding ramp that led up to the deck level.

The four men proceeded up the ramp. When they reached the deck, they walked aft towards the main cabin and entered through a small steel door.

The PECHORA crewman walked briskly along the narrow catwalk between the ship's midship superstructure and the aft deckhouse. He went into a small cabin that housed the master switches for the electrical power needed for deck lights, tower lights, the tower control room and to the large electric motors that operated the huge steel doors over the cargo holds. He pushed buttons and pulled levers, sending electrical current to hundreds of lights that flooded the aft cargo deck. The towering crane with its bright orange painted control booth was nearly fifty feet above the deck. The crewman started the long climb up to the tower. Once there he stepped inside, closed the small door, sat down and began throwing more switches that in turn excited numerous red, yellow and green lights on the display board in front of him. He reached for a headset hanging behind him, and put it on over his ears. He turned on his intercom system, picked up the hand mike and called out to a crewman standing deep in the aft cargo hold 80 feet below him.

The entire hull of the Pechora began to moan as the big steel drums that gathered the cargo door cables began to turn. Slowly, the two huge doors over the hold moved apart. A narrow beam of light shone through the seam, getting larger and brighter as the doors retracted into the hull. The control operator was having difficulty looking down into the brightly-lighted hold. Between the glare of the floodlights and the swirling rain, he could not see well enough to start dropping his lifting boom and cables. He tried cleaning off the windshield, but made matters worse using an oily rag. He called down to the number three hold foreman to shut down some of his floodlights.

A small army of men wrestled with a large cargo net, spreading it out on the wet steel floor. Other crewmen were carefully pulling leather straps underneath two large crates that were sitting end to end. A few orders to the foreman, and a message to the boom operator was passed. The large hook began to take up the slack of the belts and began lifting the wooden crate upward.

Standing against the forward bulkhead of hold number three, trying to keep dry, were the two Cuban officers and the two KGB agents. Next to them the captain of the Pechora, Frederick Slitka, and his first officer, Hans Stocker.

"I can only hope that there has been no damage to the cargo, Captain Slitka.'

"See for yourself, Colonel. Both crates are intact. I personally saw to their loading in Kowloon. My first officer had them guarded for the entire voyage. They must be very important tractor parts."

"Tractor parts?" asked Kotov.

"That is what is printed on the crates and listed on the manifest," the first officer replied.

"You told me, Colonel, that these were machines, you said nothing of parts."

"That is correct, Major Kotov. Why they wrote tractor parts on the crates and invoices is not my concern. I do not question my President. He told me they were cultivating machines, which may mean they are only parts, you know, parts of a tractor."

Navarro glared at Kotov hoping to make him drop the matter, and not discuss it in front of Captain Slitka and his crew.

"Colonel, I am sure these parts, or machines have been approved by the proper authorities, wouldn't you agree, Colonel Navarro?"

"Yes, and I know for fact that President Gorbachev is very interested in our new test farms, I'm sure he is fully aware of this shipment."

"Well then, I see no reason to stand here in this stinking wet hold any longer. We will leave you with your, ah, farm equipment. Have a safe trip, comrade Navarro."

"Thank you, Major Kotov. I'll walk you to the dock."

Kotov started for the bulkhead door, stopped and addressed the ship's officers.

"Captain Slitka, Comrade Stocker, it was a pleasure to meet you."

Navarro gestured for Kotov to pass first through the open door to the stairwell.

"I will join you, Colonel, for final inspection at the truck. You will need to sign for the cargo," Stocker said, presenting Navarro a clipboard with a manifest attached.

The rain began to fall harder as the two KGB officials got into their car. The car window opened and Kotov's face appeared in the opening.

"Where did you say you are taking the crates, Colonel?"

"I am to take them to our test farms outside of Holquin." Navarro responded.

"That's a long journey comrade. I suppose that is why you chose this early hour to unload and for good reason, its best to beat the morning traffic. I have not been to Holquin for some time, maybe I will see you there, soon, Colonel."

"Look forward to it, Major."

The window of the sedan closed slowly. Kotov's face distorted behind the rain-splattered glass squinting his eyes as he took a last look at the cargo on the flatbed truck. The small Ladaz engine came to life and the black sedan departed. Navarro and the young captain watched as the single red taillight vanished into the thick mist.

"What to you make of Kotov showing up here, Luis?"

"I don't know, Antonio. What bothers me is, how did he know we were here? General Vincetta made no mention to Sorokin of this delivery on Castro's orders."

First Officer Stocker arrived at the truck. He looked at his watch. It was 0550. He reached for the clipboard in Navarro's hand.

Navarro reached into the vest pocket of his jacket, pulled out a sealed brown envelope and attached it to the clipboard.

"Everything is looks ready, comrade. The crates are secure and covered for the journey, please give my respects to your captain. When do you sail?"

"On the morning tide, around 1100 hours."

"Well, young man, if I was not on this detail, I would have liked to show you our beautiful city.

"Colonel, I would have liked that. Maybe next time. My parents came here for many years when we lived in Germany."

Navarro ordered the NCO in charge of the detail to return to Campamento Columbia just outside the city. He and Captain Minas climbed into the cab-over tractor and joined the driver, Sargeant Julio Chevesa.

"Sargeant, go to the end of this pier, turn left and drive down to warehouse C-14. It should be the third building on the left."

"Yes, Colonel," Chevesa replied.

Minas gave Navarro a curious glance. "Why aren't we going straight to the main gate?"

"We are meeting another crew at the warehouse who are going to remove these crates, put them in a closed van and give us two identical crates, then we continue our journey. It has to do with countering American intelligence who recently increased their SR and U-2 surveillance just outside our air space.. President Castro personally arranged these hours for off loading to hide from satellite fly overs, and any surveillance flights."

Minas reacted. "I heard that the Americans have stepped up their fly-overs, but why would they be interested in farm machines, if that is what we are carrying? Maybe there must be something else inside these crates that President Castro does not want the KGB to know about?"

Navarro stared at Minas jabbing him hard with his elbow. "We don't question our orders, Captain, remember, we are operating under strict security measures." Minas got the message.

"I am troubled by the visit from Kotov," Navarro said.
"I don't know what I would have done if he had asked to inspect the crates. He really has no authority to make me do anything, I don't think. We must talk to General Vincetta about this."

"I would have been proud to help you, had that red bastard tried to give you a bad time, sir."

Navarro and Minas looked over at the frail dark skinned sergeant. He looked almost comical fighting the large steering wheel and the long gearshift lever with his skinny arms and hands.

"You could have helped by doing what, sergeant?"
Chevesa asked.

"I would have taken this piece of Soviet shit, slammed it into reverse and backed right over those two assholes in their toy car."

Navarro looked at Minas, they both laughed.

"Sargeant, you'd better be a little careful about what you say and who you run over. Those two Russians are KGB."

"Oh, I know that, Captain. It seems that all our Russian guests have a new attitude since Gorbachev has taken over. Is it my imagination, sir? seems this new Russian leader has no use for us."

"Well, I can't answer that, sergeant, but keep in mind, President Castro has outlived many world leaders since the revolution. I'm sure he will survive this one, and so will you."

"Yes, sir."

"There's the warehouse," Minas said as he rolled down his window to get a better look. He could see the large open doors and people moving about in the semi darkness of the building.

Chevesa tugged at the wheel and shifted into low range as he turned to enter the large warehouse. As the cab of the truck moved inside, a man jumped up on the driver's side doorstep and ordered Chevesa to turn out his headlights. He did, and brought the rig to a stop. For a few seconds, the three men sat scanning outside of the cab. They could see dark figures running around but no faces, no noise, only the sound of their diesel engine. There was a loud crashing sound. Navarro guessed it was the large metal doors closing behind them, and he ordered the sergeant to cut the engine.

A booming voice from a mega-phone filled the large open building. "Colonel Navarro, and only Colonel Navarro step down from the truck."

"I don't like this, Colonel, one fucking bit," Minas said as he strained to see where the voice was coming from.

"It's o.k.. Here, let me climb over you. You both stay calm, I'll be right back."

Navarro lifted himself up and slid over Minas' legs. He grabbed the small latch handle that released the door and opened it. When Navarro stepped onto the floor a blinding light shined in his face. He could smell cigar smoke, but could not see the face of the man directly in front of him.

"Navarro, my friend."

The light went out and Navarro recognized his mentor, General Alberto Vincetta, Commander of Castro's Secret Police.

"Alberto, you scared the shit out of me," Navarro whispered.

Vincetta smiled at him. " You up there." The General yelled as he held the flashlight on the window of the passenger door. "Who is with you, Luis?"

"Captain Minas, you know him, General."

"Oh yes, of course. Antonio Minas."

Minas responded as he held his hand in front of his face trying to block the strong beam of light from his eyes. "Yes, sir?"

"Captain, tell your driver to start the engine and wait for my command. You will be relieved at the other end of the building by Major Cunha. He will be in charge of getting this cargo to Holquin. You report back to me back here, as soon as you are relieved."

Navarro and Vincetta walked towards the rear of the truck where the work crews were putting the last tie-downs over the tarps on the new cargo that had been exchanged. Navarro could see the two crates he had brought from the ship sitting next to each other on the ground. A forklift was moving around to get under one of the crates. Suddenly, another engine came to life and a string of yellow lights came on from a large closed commercial van being backed up towards the crates.

"We are ready, General."

"Good."

"Captain Minas, move out," Vincetta ordered.

The truck's diesel started up and without any delay began to move. Navarro heard the sound of the metal doors being rolled open at the far end.

Vincetta led Navarro over to the crates. It was the first time he had a close look at them and he saw the red lettering stenciled all over both boxes in Russian and Chinese, RUSH, FRAGILE TRACTOR PARTS.

Vincetta ordered the entire work force to retreat to the other end of building for a fifteen-minute break. He took his portable radio from his belt and made a transmission. A few minutes later, two sets of headlights appeared in the door and headed towards the crates. The two Russian-built Gaz enclosed jeeps stopped just short of the crates. Four guards stepped out of the first jeep carrying automatic weapons and the passenger door opened on the second jeep and Fidel Castro stepped out.

General Vincetta walked over and greeted Castro. They spoke quietly for a few moments, then Vincetta turned and signaled for Navarro to join them. After greeting him, Castro ordered General Vincetta to open one of the crates. A tire iron was produced and one of the soldiers was given the task of removing a side panel of the crate.

Just as the section was about to be removed, Vincetta ordered Navarro to take his flashlight and locate Captain Minas and join him and the detail of soldiers. Navarro was frustrated. He wanted to see what was in the crates. He tried to stall as the two soldiers fought to get the last nails holding the panel. Vincetta repeated his order to Navarro. He got the message, he was not going to see what was in the crates.

About thirty minutes went by. Navarro was sitting on the concrete floor talking to Minas when a young lieutenant came over and told him that the General wanted to see him right away. When he found Vincetta, the two jeeps and Castro were gone, the crate had been resealed and the forklift was getting ready to place it in the waiting van.

"Colonel Navarro, you will take this small detail of six men and Captain Minas to Santiago." The General looked at his watch. "I will drop you and Captain Minas off at the base. You will be back here in civilian clothes at 0800 hours and begin your trip. I will have all the details when you get back. As you can see, you are moving van experts now, so dress appropriately." The General laughed and put his large arm around Navarro's shoulders. "Today, we will play hide and seek game with the KGB."

Navarro's hopes brightened, now he was assigned to move the two crates. He needed to write a message, code it and get it to his brother-in-law, Carlos immediately. It would say, "OPERATION DOLPHIN has arrived. The device is around 3000 pounds, it measures less than thirty feet in length and six to seven feet in height, and four to five feet wide. There are two of them."

"By the way, General. Comrade Kotov arrived at the dock just as we were getting ready to load the crates."

"Kotov? Why the hell didn't you tell me this before?"

Navarro could see that Vincetta was not pleased with this news. "I did not think it was important. I was surprised to see him there, since I had not been told to expect him."

"What did he say, I mean, about the crates? He didn't open one?"

"No, General. He was told that the crates carried new farm machines for our President. He did not open them, but he seemed quite disturbed that they came from China."

"I am sorry about this, Colonel, and I will look into it. You can go now, my jeep is waiting for you and Captain Minas."

Fidel Castro's Mansion
Varadero
0840 hours

Dimitri Sorokin stood in front of the large open French doors. The view was spectacular. The air was fresh and the breeze coming from the Bay of Cardenas felt pleasingly cool. The long sloping lawn surrounded by groomed hedges glistened in the sun. The sky was cloudless to the south, but Dimitri knew if he looked west towards the Hicacos Peninsula and Varadero Beach, he would see clouds building over the mountains. He took a Marlboro from his silver cigarette case, lit it and walked towards the tall mahogany doors to the patio.

The large wood doors were nearly eight feet tall and he found it difficult to push them open. Their hinges were badly corroded with rust.

"What a shame," he thought as he examined the condition of the windows and the wood frames. The hand tooled mahogany panels that framed the room, once beautifully varnished, were scarred with mildew and dry rot at their bases where they rested on the marble floor. His attention was drawn to the brilliant white mansion in the distance. He had spent many splendid hours there dining with friends, Soviet and Cuban officials, including Fidel Castro. It was once the winter home of Irene DuPont, who in the 1930's invested heavily in properties in Varadero. Called Xanadu by DuPont, it was taken over by the state after the revolution and turned into a splendid restaurant. Facing the Atlantic ocean, Xanadu was surrounded by plush manicured lawns, tropical plants and a nine hole golf course, outlined in towering Royal palm trees. The rear of the estate on Cardenas Bay featured a large dock and seaplane ramp.

"Good morning, comrade, how was the drive over this morning?"

Sorokin turned to face a humorous sight. Fidel Castro was standing in the middle of the room on a small oriental throw rug, dressed in a old worn out gold colored terry-cloth robe, that rose high in front over his protruding stomach. On his feet, a pair of dark green open toed slippers. In one hand he held a large envelope, the other a foul looking cigar. His hair, like his beard, was tossed wildly around his face, and on the end of his nose a pair of half rimmed glasses.

Trying not to laugh, Sorokin responded. "The drive was quite beautiful, comrade, quite beautiful. I appreciate you sending your car, it gave me time to appreciate the scenery."

Castro laughed as he headed towards the tall Russian with his hand extended. "What you really mean, my friend, it gave you time to see some of those Canadian beauties heading for the beach, yes?"

Castro turned and walked over to his large desk at the end of the room. He stepped behind it and sat down on a large maroon leather chair. He placed the large envelope in front of him, and extinguished his cigar in a over-filled ashtray.

"Come my friend, sit, sit," Castro pointed to a high-back chair in front of his desk.

Sorokin walked slowly to the chair keeping eye contact with Castro. Before he sat down, he reached down and pulled his pants up slightly by the pleats. He crossed his right leg over the left. The highly polished Italian loafer on his tanned, sockless foot caught Castro's eye and gave him a lead in to the subject he wanted to cover.

"Ah, comrade Sorokin. You have learned the meaning of living the good life, no? Look at you, you are the picture of a capitalist tourist. Silk shirt, expensive Italian shoes. You make a very handsome model, my friend. Someday, maybe I can fit into nice clothes again, like you." Castro laughed, leaned back and patted his hands on his large stomach.

"My dear President, you should be taking your weight problem more seriously. All that weight is taxing your system, this is not good for the heart. You owe it to your people, if not yourself, to stay as healthy as you can."

"My blood pressure was one-twenty over seventy-five an hour ago, and that was after a two mile swim. I am pretty fit, you need not worry."

Castro sounded defensive, and Sorokin knew him well enough to back off on the subject of his health.

"So, Mr. President, what is so important that you needed to see me this morning? I thought you were taking a few days off."

"Yes, I am, this will be my last day here at Varadero. Comrade Ustinov will be arriving next Saturday afternoon with his family, and he will be staying here for maybe six months to rest. His personal belongings have already arrived at the port."

"It was most generous of you to provide such a personal gift to our Minister of Defense. He will be most happy here at your home."

Castro stood up and walked around the desk. He stopped directly in front of Sorokin and sat back on the desk.

"Comrade, you and I have been friends now for quite some time. I know it's your job to keep a close eye on my administration, and me, and I know you must send reports on my activities to Moscow. I also know that you have become, shall we say, a little spoiled. Life here has been good for you. You have a beautiful apartment, a beach cabana, you drive an American Oldsmobile, and you have Maria and Sonia fighting over you at the Embassy, yes?

Sorokin bowed his head, smiling slightly. He kept watching Castro's small squinting dark eyes. He had studied Castro over the months, and one thing he had learned was that Castro gave away his moods through the movements of his eyes.

Castro stood up, walked a few feet and stopped inside the open doors to the back yard. He turned and faced Sorokin. "Comrade, you are, what, forty six now? You are a widower with a son serving in the Soviet air force. I have no idea what men of your rank in the KGB are paid, but I do know that I can make you a very rich man, and you can live like the DuPonts did. I will even sell you this mansion if you like."

"Why would you want to make me rich? You know the state would never let me accept gifts."

153

Castro moved back to his chair and sat down. He leaned forward and picked up the large brown envelope. He opened it and pulled out a stack of papers and a folded blueprint. He opened the blueprint and spread it out. "Look, comrade, see what can make you rich."

Sorokin stood up and stepped up to the desk. He studied the blueprint in silence at first. "This is a submarine, or a mechanical whale?"

"Yes, you might say that. It has all the characteristics of a submarine, but looks like a killer whale, or a porpoise. It travels well below the surface, but it carries no weapons, and seeks no enemies. It seeks only money, millions and millions of American dollars."

"I don't understand. Why would you be interested in such a machine?"

Castro laughed out loud. "This machine, my friend, can and will sail right up the Mississippi, the Hudson River or even into San Francisco Bay, absolutely undetected, and deliver four to maybe five hundred pounds of cocaine, right under the noses of America's best agents and their satellites."

"Comrade, you should know better than to show this to me, or even talk about drugs. President Gorbachev made it clear to you how he feels about drugs, and he even warned you never to get involved with any kind of drug business on this island."

Castro sprang up out of his chair. "He told me a lot of things I chose not to hear. I see much trouble ahead from your new leader, my friend. He talks about new dialogue with the western world. He talks about major changes within your government. He talks of glasnost, he wants your government to be more open. He talks of perestroika, reconstruction, opening up doors to the west. He talks of new arms control, and has made plans to meet with Reagan in November for summit talks. When he arrives here, I am supposed to accept his new plans to cut off my country's legs. No more aid he tells the Party. Did you know that he took my brother's request for a new MiG-21 training wing, and tore it up? We promised our CDR forces new uniforms and new patrol vehicles this year. No, Moscow says. No more surplus sugar trade, no replacement weapons. He gave us two out of the six new radar installations we need, and approved sending two new Osa II missile patrol boats, instead of the six that we were scheduled to have by March, 1986."

"Comrade, you must realize, President Gorbachev is trying hard to make an impression, not only on our government, but also on the Soviet people. He brings a new breed of leadership to my country, leadership that our people appreciate right now. He will end the conflict in Afghanistan, soon, and he will have to face our people with the truth of what happened there. Our people were lied to by our military. They were not told of the real facts about the war. There are many hard liners this new president has won over in the party, especially some of the older members in the Politburo. He has convinced them that his ideas and new approaches to foreign policies will help the economic disaster we have created building our military strength. Unlike his predecessors, Gorbachev is a more personable man, more of a modern businessman, you might say. He doesn't want the image of a sword-waving monster that strikes fear in our adversaries. He wants to do something for his country, and that means cutting some of the flow of money and equipment to you, I'm afraid."

Castro picked up the cigar out of the ashtray and lit it. He blew a large cloud of bluish smoke into Sorokin's face.

"Chernenko was my friend, Kruschev was my friend, comrade. This man is a pussy. He will ruin you, your country, and the Party, and you can put that in your fucking weekly report. He has no use for my country, or my people. He feels we are nothing more than a financial burden and I have heard some talk that he is afraid that I could become an embarrassment to the Kremlin and the Party. If that is so, he can call back the hundred and sixty thousand soldiers and technicians enjoying my country anytime. I will protect my people and my country with or without Gorbachev, or the Soviet Union."

Sorokin's face was expressionless. Strangely, he felt no anger with Castro. He understood his feelings and resentment for Gorbachev. Most of what Castro said was true. Gorbachev needed to stop the flow of money supporting Cuba and war in Afghanistan. Sorokin was surprised to hear Castro air his thoughts so openly and giving thought to a possible separation of the two countries.

"Comrade President, you know I will not report this. But I will warn you that others on my staff would if they heard you speak in this manner. You must be careful."

"This is my country, I can say what I want. I don't fear your KGB or your President. Nobody tells me to be careful, not in my house."

Castro threw the cigar out the open doors, then eased back into his chair.

"Dimitri, you must come join with me. I know you, Dimitri, I know you would like to stay here forever. Think about it my friend, all the money you could ever want. Nobody would know. I promise you my life on this."

"Why do you need me? What is it I can do? I know nothing of drugs. I know nothing about, these, submarines. I don't want to get into some foolish venture that could get me or my son put in prison, or even killed."

"You would do nothing, my friend, absolutely nothing. You don't see anything, hear anything or write anything. Isn't that easy enough?"

"Come, comrade. There must be more to it than that?"

"Not really. I just need your trust, and, well, protection for the lack of a better word. I will be very busy with my new toy boat here, and will be leaving the island sometime in December. I need you to cover for me. I need you as a friend, and for this, I will make you very wealthy."

"Too risky, comrade. There are too many eyes and ears, and too many..." Sorokin was interrupted.

Castro leaned over the desk and slammed his fist down. "Kotov, he is the only real problem here, Dimitri. He wants your ass and mine too. I have known him for years, and I don't trust him. I don't think even the KGB trusts him. They haven't promoted him since he came here. You are his third superior, no?"

"Yes, I am, and I too have reason to suspect that Kotov may have a plant within your special guards and secret police."

"We know he does, Dimitri, and we think we know who it may be. When this is confirmed, he will be dealt with. We can also deal with Kotov, you know that?"

Castro moved from behind the desk and stood in front of Sorokin. He reached up resting his large hands on Sorokin's shoulders pressing his thumbs gently into his soft skin. Castro was two inches taller, and one hundred pounds heavier than Sorokin. He smiled, showing his yellow teeth framed by his matted gray mustache, his breath was sour and he smelled of sweat.

"Will you come with me?" Castro asked.

"Let me think on this. Regardless of my decision, I promise it will remain only between us."

Castro removed his hands from Sorokin's shoulders. He put his left hand in the small robe pocket, while his right hand stroked his heavy beard. His eyes, barely noticeable under his heavy eyebrows, searched Sorokin's face for some kind of answer.

The telephone rang on the credenza behind the desk and Castro walked over and picked it up. "Yes? Yes, put him through. Buenos dias, General. No, not at all. That is good. They should be in Santiago when? That's fine, very good. Yes? When? Very interesting. Are you returning to headquarters? Call me when you arrive; say nothing to anyone. I will know soon what we are going to do."

Castro put the phone down, turned and faced Sorokin. "That was General Vincetta. Did you give Kotov and Petrov orders to be at the government wharf this morning?"

Sorokin looked puzzled. "I don't understand, what you are talking about? No, I had no reason to send Kotov to the wharf, or anywhere else for that matter, why?"

Castro reached over and picked up the folded blue print from the desk. He held it out on his extended arm as if he was offering it to Sorokin. "My toy arrived yesterday aboard the PECHORA, comrade. It was being unloaded by my secret police earlier this morning when Kotov arrived with comrade Petrov. Can you explain this?"

Sorokin pulled his cigarette case from his shirt pocket and removed a cigarette. He lit it and casually exhaled. "You have a serious problem, comrade President, you have a leak in your secret police. I know nothing of this incident, or anything about the freighter. Major Kotov struck again. He is out to belittle me, make me look stupid, unqualified for the job, he wants to disgrace me to Headquarters. This is a good find for deputy Kotov, and just what is it he has learned about your miniature submarine?"

"General Vincetta says he learned nothing. He was told that the crates contained farm machines from China, which raised more suspicion as to why I was dealing with the Chinese. One thing I do know, comrade, is that I don't have any more time to fool with this idiot Kotov and his puppet. At the risk of our friendship, I must advise you that plans to deal with Kotov are about to be activated before he finds out too much."

"I don't know what you have in mind, but I would be very careful, comrade President. Do you realize the consequences should anything happen to a KGB agent here in your country? None of us would ever see peace again. The KGB will not give up on an investigation until they have all the answers. You, comrade President, would not be exempt if they could prove..."

"Prove what, Dimitri? I did not say anything about destroying comrade Kotov, did I? No, I just said there where plans to deal with him, and those plans will work. You, my dear friend, will have the honor to execute them. All you do is ask Kotov to join us on a short trip to Maspoton for some hunting."

"Maspoton, the hunting resort? Nobody goes there anymore, not since the club house burned."

Castro walked over to one of the large cabinets that framed the huge fireplace. He opened the doors and pulled out a long package, wrapped in a white sheet. He carried it over to his desk, laid it down and removed the cloth. He stepped back and smiled, "Well, what you think?"

Sorokin reached over and picked up the gleaming well-oiled carbine. He rotated it in his large hands, pulled the stock up to his shoulder and looked down the sights. "It's magnificent, it is a Winchester, am I correct?"

"Yes, a very special Winchester, comrade. A model ninety-four, a collector's rifle. It is the gun that won the West, as they say in America. It's a 30-30 caliber, lever action hex barrel carbine."

"It is beautiful, comrade, very beautiful. But what does this wonderful weapon have to do with Maspoton and Kotov?"

Castro returned to his chair. "You, comrade Sorokin, will invite Kotov to go to Maspoton to do some hunting. You will tell him of this magnificent rifle that you received from me. He loves guns. He also spends a lot of time on the practice ranges. I personally gave him a M-l Carbine that was a souvenir from the Bay of Pigs. He loves going down to Maspoton and has joined me there a few times. He also has a woman in Piña Del Rio, just a few miles away. Now, we must move fast. I will lend you my helicopter to save time. You must call Kotov, make up a story that a few of us are meeting in Maspoton later today. Tell him that I will be there too. You pick up Kotov and Petrov and arrive at the old club around five o'clock. I will have General Vincetta prepare quarters for you. You tell Kotov to bring his M-l, tell him you may want to trade for his M-l. He would kill for this Winchester."

"Comrade President, this is ridiculous."

"Go, go, take the carbine. Grab some boxes of those Remington shells in the cabinet. Tell my driver to take you home, wait till you pack, then take you to the heliport at Campameto Columbia. I will have my helicopter there. You go now, hurry, I must make some calls."

Sorokin picked up the carbine and the sheet. He looked at Castro in bewilderment. "What is going to happen down there, Comrade President?"

"Nothing that you will have any control of, comrade. This time tomorrow we will celebrate. Go now, I will speak to you when you return tonight. Tell my secretary that you want to use line two. Call Kotov now."

Sorokin followed Castro's orders. He reached Kotov, told him about the surprise trip to do some hunting. Castro was right, Kotov was ecstatic and said he would bring his gun and Petrov and meet at Campamento Columbia for the one hour flight.

Government Docks
Port Havana
0915

General Vincetta was standing inside the small warehouse office when Navarro walked in. He had just finished his call to Castro. "Ah, now you look like an honest worker, Colonel."

Navarro laughed as he looked at himself. He was wearing a pair of very tight washed out Levis, a sleeveless gray sweat shirt, no socks and a pair of paint stained moccasins. A faded black ball cap covered most of his black curly hair. The faint remains of the initials of the New York Yankee logo were still visible.

Vincetta handed Navarro a white envelope. "Put this in your pocket. It contains the name and address that you need of a friend in Ciego de Avila where you will spend tonight, and the rest of the information you need on where to go in Santiago tomorrow."

"General, I don't want to seem curious, but it's difficult to understand. What is so important in these crates, and why are we playing this dangerous game with the Soviets?"

Vincetta studied Navarro for a moment. "Colonel, we may be on the verge of another historic movement, a Cuban movement, not one that involves the Soviets. Our President is setting up what you might say, new means of survival for us. Should there be any political or financial problems on the horizon with the Soviets, we want to be ready, that's all. The two crates contain what may be the key to our new foundation. When the time comes, you will be shown. Meantime, it's up to you and Captain Minas to make sure the cargo gets safely to Santiago tomorrow.

"What about Kotov, General?"

"Not to worry. He has his hands full right now preparing schedules for his Minister of Defense who will be arriving from Moscow. We know he did not tail our convoy to Holguin. Sometime later today I will be at Headquarters with our President and I will discuss Kotov and our problem."

Navarro climbed up into the cab of the small moving van. Captain Minas was asleep behind the wheel. Navarro couldn't help but laugh at his companion. He too was dressed like a teenage hoodlum, in dirty jeans, Tee shirt and old military boots. Navarro reached over and checked the gearshift. He put in neutral, reached up and turned the starter key and the little Fiat diesel fired right up. Minas exploded into life, eyes as big as golf balls. He looked at Navarro. Navarro screamed, "El camino hacia Santiago?" (which way to Santiago).

159

"Que' hora es?"

"Time to go, Fernando, we are late, estoy apurado."

Minas pushed in the clutch and after a number of grinding guesses, found low gear and started to move towards the large opening doors. The creaking van moved through the huge doors into the bright sunlight. Minas struggled with the wheel cursing and stamping his foot up and down on the clutch while grinding the teeth off the gears in the transmission box.

"Captain, we are trying not to attract attention. Do you think you can get us through the tunnel and out of the city without blowing us up?"

Minas looked over at Navarro. He had one foot up on the dashboard, one arm out the window and the other resting on the backrest and he was smiling.

"Yes, Colonel, I will get us out of the city despite this deathtrap trying to kill us. I don't suppose that you would like to..."

"El almuerzo, amigo, when we reach Cienfuegos," Navarro looked at his watch. "In five hours."

Minas laughed, "Not in this pile of shit, amigo."

Navarro smiled, closed his eyes, rested his head back on the seat and relaxed. His thoughts drifted back to earlier hours at home struggling with his code-book. "Did I code it right? Did I tighten the end of the flashlight. Will Melinda get through to Theresa in time to arrange to meet in church tonight? Where the hell is Carlos flying next?" Navarro could not stop the flow of questions running through his mind. This was the most important message yet, the arrival of the device. He tried to picture who was getting his messages in the United States, and tried to imagine what their reactions were like when they arrived.

Suddenly, there was a loud knocking sound on the small rear window of the cab. Startled, Navarro and Minas turned and looked at a youthful face with large brown eyes and large teeth. Navarro slid the small window open.

"Captain Minas, sir. Ah, we would like to know how long it will be before we stop, sir, some of us had nothing to eat this morning, sir?"

Minas looked at Navarro. "Ah, we will stop after we pass through the tunnel and get out of the city. Ah, tell your men, ok.?" Navarro slid the small glass window closed.

Both Minas and Navarro went into convulsions. Minas could hardly handle driving the truck he was laughing so hard. Navarro, his hand over his mouth, was doubled up with tears filling his eyes.

"I completely forgot about them back there," Minas said.

"Jesus Christ, you must have been killing them back there. You have hit every fucking pot hole since we started out."

"My God, what a way to start a secret mission, Colonel."

Their laughter could be heard in the rear of the stuffy van, but the six soldiers, most of them sleeping on blankets, were comfortable. They were on a special mission wearing street clothes and they were getting extra pay. The famous General Vincetta had selected them, which was a great honor.

New Havana
Revolution Square
0950 hours

Carmen Maceo, Director of the Telegram office at the Ministry of Communications Building in Revolution Square, had just entered his office when his private line lit up. He picked up the receiver.

"Maceo. Uno momento." Maceo put the phone down, went to the door to his office and locked the door. He returned and picked up the receiver."

"Si, I am back. Yes, but it will take some time, General. I will tell my manager I have a emergency. Most of the office here knows my mother is failing. Si, I will have them meet me in Soroa at my campsite. We will head straight for Los Palacios and wait there. General, you must remember, we will be going for the second vehicle, be sure you have no friends on board. Yes, we will come out on the road some five kilometers before the town. Si, we have plenty of ammunition, and we will be using M-16's and American grenades. You must get some distance between the vehicles. If there is any problem, you must keep flashing your high beams in the first vehicle. General, my men are well trained and dedicated. They do not like playing the part of rebels against the state, and they don't want to die in this way either. There is no chance that there will be any militia near by, is there? Gracias, comrade General. Yes, we know the escape route, and we will talk again in the morning."

Maceo hung up the phone, locked his desk and left the office. After explaining to his manager that he had an emergency, he ran across Rancho Boyeros Avenue and hailed a taxi. Fifteen minutes later he was at the Deauville Hotel. He entered the lobby and went to the small cafe overlooking the Malecon. He sat down and lit a cigarette.

"Buenos dias."

Maceo looked up into the face of Juan Latenza. He was tall and thin and his long face and receding hairline gave him a clownish look. His starched shirt was badly stained and his apron was filthy. Latenza was also one of the agents on General Vincetta's secret 753 force.

Maceo continued to look at the tattered and worn menu. In a muffled low voice he gave Latenza his orders. "We go tonight, Operation Vulture. Meet me at the campsite no later than 1500 hours. If you have transportation problems call Julian at Carnival Taxi, you have the number."

Maceo purposely raised his voice. "Señor, I don't see anything on here to my liking." He stood, straightened his tie, buttoned his jacket and left the cafe. Latenza, looked at the couple sitting at the next table, he smiled and shrugged his shoulders.

"Disculpeme, we no have frito conejo," he said, knowing the elderly Canadian couple did not understand him. "Fried rabbit," he said laughing.

The couple looked at each other and went back to eating their fruit salad.

CHAPTER 10

Castro's Mansion
Varadero
1100 hours

President Castro showered and dressed in his regular military fatigues. He put through a call to General Vincetta's office at defense headquarters.

"General, we have Sorokin, he has agreed come along with us. He will be meeting Kotov and Petrov, just about now. I will wait until I hear from my pilot when they are aboard the helicopter and heading down to Maspoton. Do you have your people ready? Good. Remember, General, there must be no survivors. Have you picked your place of ambush? That's good. You will be heading into Las Palacios for dinner, yes? Good." Castro put the receiver down and leaned back in his leather chair. He was pleased. He lit up a cigar and took a large drag. He was relieved at the thought of never seeing Kotov again.

There was a knock on the door and his secretary came in. "Comrade President, communications just called. Captain Ribalta sends his regrets that number seven nine is still out of commission."

Castro smiled. "Thank you, Anna."

Castro relaxed again. He had received the message that Sorokin and his two KGB associates were airborne.

Headquarters, Ministry of Defense
CDR Offices
1135 hours

General Vincetta climbed into his Gaz jeep with his aide and headed out to Jose Marti Airport. They turned off the Maximo Gomez road and drove into a small garage. There they changed into civilian clothes, picked up two small suitcases and three rifle cases and threw them into the trunk of a 1958 Bel-Aire Chevy. They continued out to the airport, where they would meet the pilot who was waiting for them in a vintage Piper tri-pacer to take them down to Maspoton.

163

Maspoton
1145 hours

Joseph Orlando, a wiry thin man in his fifties, pulled the large hat down over his forehead as he left the small cabin and the protection of the shade. He carried a set of rusty battery jumper cables over his bony shoulder. As he passed the old Club de Caza, his nostrils were filled with the smell of smoldering damp wood. The Club had burned to the ground two months ago, but the smell still hung over the charred remains. Just behind the Club was a bungalow, once used by sportsmen from all over the world. Now it was a makeshift garage that protected an old Willys jeep and a rusty old Ladas that were stored there for officials who occasionally flew down to do some hunting, or relaxing with their women. The only use these two relics got was to go into Los Palacios for food, booze or women.

Orlando was lucky, the battery on the jeep was strong enough to turn the engine over and start. He took the cables and jumped the small Ladas engine into life. He made a few adjustments to the linkage to increase the idle and left them running, while he went back to his cottage and got the gas can.

After Orlando received the call from General Vincetta earlier, he cleaned up two of the small cottages and prepared them for the guests. Vincetta had advised him that the President might also arrive, and to be sure his quarters had clean linen and fresh water.

After Orlando put fuel in each of the vehicles, he turned off the keys and tried to start them again. He was pleased that they both fired up. He walked outside, stopped and looked towards the north. He could hear the sound of the helicopter with its blades beating on the wind. He hurried over to the President's quarters, opened the windows and with an old towel, brushed the doorstep off.

Maspoton Campsite
1830 hours

The five men walked slowly up the path from the firing range to the campsite and their cottages.

"Comrade Kotov, you should know better than to bet against a man who holds the gun that won the west."

164

"General, I have seen comrade Sorokin on the range many times. There must be a secret to this Winchester, he has improved his marksmanship tremendously."

"Major, you can't compare your M-1 accuracy against the Winchester. It has a superior range."

Sorokin held the Winchester over his head. "Besides, I'm using a far more powerful load, Major Kotov."

Kotov stopped and rocked back on his heels. He held the M-1 under his left arm while he struggled with the cork on the rum bottle. It finally came out and he poured the remains down his throat. He wiped his mouth with his sleeve and threw the bottle over his shoulder.

"I would like to have another chance to beat you, comrade, only this time we will use just this carbine, o.k. with you?"

"Fine, only let's wait until morning, Major. I'm ready for some hot food. How about you, General Vincetta?"

"Of course. I will have my aide run ahead and see what Orlando has in the icebox. We can build a fire, maybe roast some hens?"

"Nonsense, General, we have transportation, why not drive into Los Palacios. We can all have dinner on me, that's if my friend here, Major Kotov pays me what he owes me for beating him on the range."

Thirty minutes later, the two vehicles were headed down the crude dusty road that led into the small town of Los Palacios. Vincetta's aide, Captain Morales, was driving Vincetta and Sorokin in the jeep. Behind them in the Ladas were Petrov and Kotov. Kotov was singing at the top of his lungs while Petrov fought the wheel to keep up with the jeep.

"When?" Sorokin asked.

"Soon, we should see them soon. I told them to stay at least five kilometers this side of the town," Vincetta answered.

"How much distance do you want me to keep, General?"

Vincetta looked back over his shoulder. He estimated that the Ladas was forty yards behind. "Pick it up a little, Captain, and put your lights on, but don't blink them, that would be the signal not to attack."

Sorokin, sitting on the rear bench seat, was getting nervous. His palms were damp and he could feel sweat running down his spine. He looked at the young captain as he fought the steering wheel and the dust coming into his face from the open window. Vincetta looked calm as he concentrated on the road ahead looking for any sign of the ambush.

Sorokin, Vincetta and Morales never saw them. The concussion from the two grenades tossed all three men forward in their seats. Captain Morales pulled off the road into a soft shoulder and stopped. They jumped out of the jeep and looked behind just in time to see a spectacular explosion that knocked them to the ground. It was like a small atomic bomb complete with a mushroom shaped cloud rising over the blazing fire that was once a Ladas sedan. Reports from automatic weapons could be heard, then all became quiet except for the crackling sounds coming from the fire and occasional puffs of smoke, as glass exploded.

"Come, draw your weapons and follow me, we must look like we are counter-attacking," Vincetta ordered.

The three men started running towards the fire. Vincetta saw three men running across an open field to his left. He raised his 45 caliber Colt and fired off nine rounds well over their heads. Captain Morales kept scanning the road towards Las Palacios but he saw no sign of people or vehicles coming towards them. Sorokin stopped, fired six rounds into the air from his nine-millimeter automatic. Vincetta stopped and ordered Sorokin to catch up.

"Come, comrade, we must chase the rebels."

"Shoot me, General."

"Shoot you? What are you saying?"

Sorokin walked up to Vincetta. "Shoot me here in my upper leg with your American 45, just don't hit anything vital, do you know what I mean?"

"I can't do that, Dimitri."

"I can do it, General." The young captain took the automatic from Vincetta's hand. He pointed the gun at Sorokin's left leg, toward the outside of the upper thigh.

"Pull the cloth tight on your trousers, comrade Sorokin, please."

Before Sorokin could respond, the gun exploded, sending Sorokin spinning like a top onto the ground, rolling over uncontrollably. There was so much pain he could not concentrate where it was coming from. The next thing he knew, Vincetta was rolling him over on his back and holding him down while Morales attended to his leg.

"Good shot. I don't think I did any bone damage. The bullet went through clean, good thing you had old type bullets, General."

Sorokin laughed through his tears and pain. "Nice time to think of what kind of ammunition you had. You could have blown my fucking leg off with the right ammo, I suppose."

Vincetta removed Sorokin's expensive belt. "Sorry about this, comrade, we have to cut the blood flow. I will make a tight tourniquet above the wound. You must remember, every fifteen minutes, you let it open, loosen it to let blood flow, you understand? You must do this to keep the wound clean." He took his jacket off, rolled it up and placed it under Sorokin's neck.

"You stay quiet now." Vincetta stood up and headed for the burning car in the middle of the road. Captain Morales had already confirmed that both Kotov and Petrov were still inside the car. Vincetta dispatched his aide to drive into the town for help. "Call President Castro at Headquarters, he is waiting for the call. Tell him to send a helicopter for Sorokin to take him to the University hospital, advise him both KGB agents are dead and to advise defense headquarters of the raid on us by at least a half dozen rebels. They had American grenades and automatic weapons, two may be two wounded and they are heading south east."

The truth was that Vincetta's rebels were carefully skirting Los Palacios on the east, then turning north towards Soroa where a vintage Piper tri-pacer and its pilot waited on an abandoned road. The three rebels would be home safe in Havana before midnight.

Captain Morales returned with two women and the head of the CDR in Los Palacios. He reported to Vincetta that he had called Castro. He also had a squad of sixteen armed soldiers heading down the road and a fire truck would be arrive as soon as a flat tire was repaired. The two young women brought bandages made from sheets. One had a small bottle of alcohol and a cork in her hand. She knelt down, gently lifted Sorokin's head onto her lap. The other woman was cutting away the blood soaked trousers from around the wound. The woman holding his head put the cork in between Sorokin's teeth while the other took the alcohol and poured it over the open hole in his leg. He jumped, then passed out. Sorokin was lifted and put onto the back bench-seat of the jeep. The two women got in with Vincetta and his aide and drove to the towns train station where they waited for the helicopter to arrive.

University of Havana Hospital
Emergency room six
2140 hours.

Two heavily armed special policemen stood outside the emergency room doors. At each end of the wing armed special police were posted as well as at the front and rear doors of the hospital. Nobody was allowed in or out without the permission of General Vincetta.

In a small room next to the operating room where doctors were repairing Sorokin's leg, Fidel Castro, General Vincetta and Raul Castro waited.

"You did good, General, very good," Raul complimented his Chief of National Security.

"He did better than good. He even shot our friend Sorokin to make it look unquestionably real," Castro added.

"I can't take the credit for that, comrade President. Captain Morales shot him. I had no idea of his talents, or guts," Vincetta laughed.

"What's going on down at the site? Did the local CDR get started on the tracking of our 753 men?" Castro asked.

"Yes. They even called for patrol boats to come into the beach areas and start looking for the rebels' boats. They are convinced that the rebels came by sea."

"You will check later. Make sure all your men got home. Let me know, I will be staying at my apartment tonight."

"Yes, comrade President."

The door from the operating room opened and an elderly tall thin doctor approached Fidel Castro. His blue hospital blouse was splattered in blood. He removed his surgical hat and mask as he stood and smiled at Castro.

"He is fine, comrade President. He lost some blood and had some muscle damage, but nothing serious. He should be up and around in four or five days. He will need some therapy for a while."

"Gracias, Doctor. Can we speak to him now?

"I don't think he will be conscious for a while. We had to give him sodium pentathol. He refused a spinal."

"Never mind. We will see him in the morning." Castro reached out and shook the doctor's hand. "Gracias."   The three men walked out of the emergency room doors into the cool morning air.

"Raul, you and I must talk. We must plan for what the KGB might do when they hear about Kotov and Petrov. How much of an investigation do you think they will do?"

Raul looked at General Vincetta for a response. "I have no idea."

"Comrade President, if I may. I don't think they will do much of anything, except maybe ask Sorokin who he would like to have as a replacement. Remember, Sorokin is a friend of many in the Politburo and the Secretary General. I suggest we have the bodies shipped as soon as we can. We can try and get them on the three o'clock flight to Moscow this afternoon."

"You may be right, General," Castro said. "When you get to Headquarters later, call the Soviet Embassy right away. Advise Comrade Grochenski of the tragedy. Tell him we are sending the bodies home today. Advise him that Sorokin is in good hands, and that all three will receive Cuba's highest awards for their bravery. Also explain to him, that in the interests of security we don't want any word getting out about what happened at Las Palacios."

Vincetta smiled. "Brilliant, Comrade President."

"I will draft a cable of regret to KGB Headquarters and to Gorbachev at the Kremlin. General, you go back into the morgue and tell those interns in there to prepare the two bodies for shipment immediately. If the Russians want to make positive identification, they can do it in their own labs."

"Yes, this is good, this will work. Come Raul, let's go to my apartment and make plans for Santiago."

"General Vincetta?" Fidel looked at his watch. "Please call Colonel Navarro before 1800 hours and give him the address of the marina in Santiago. Tell him he should try to be there by at least 1500 hours tomorrow."

"Yes, comrade President. He stayed with some of my good friends last night and he should have no problem reaching Santiago and the marina by then."

"Raul and I are going to do an inspection tour today. We will leave Headquarters somewhere around noon and fly to Camaguey to inspect the new SAM installations. Then we will fly down to Baymao. We will leave there before sunset and drive down to Santiago. You are to meet us at the field in Baymao, say around 1530 hours, we will need two transports."

"Comrade President, headquarters received word that Yang Lo and his wife arrived in Santiago this morning and have checked into the Casagrande Hotel. He will wait there for word from us as to when he will meet with you to inspect the Dolphins."

"Who do we have contacting our Chinese visitor and setting up security at the marina, General?" Raul asked.

"Major Verelas, Rego Verelas."

"Yes, yes, he is a good man. Now, when Colonel Navarro arrives at the marina, they are to unload the crates and come straight back to Havana, correct?"

"That is so, yes. Major Verelas has his own men there and they will open...

"No," Fidel raised his voice and pointed his finger at Vincetta. "Nobody touches anything until I arrive, General. That's an order."

"Yes, sir."

"Come, Raul, we must go." Fidel raised his arm to get the attention of his driver. The black Mercedes came around the small circular driveway and stopped. The two brothers entered the back seat. The rear window came down, and Fidel's face appeared.

"General, you see that we find some flowers somewhere today to fill Sorokin's room."

Santiago De Cuba
Versailles Hotel
Sunday, September 20th
0645 hours

Major Rego Verelas, dressed as a tourist in walking shorts and guayabera cotton shirt locked the door to his room and walked down the small path leading to the hotel restaurant. He took a table on the veranda overlooking the peaceful Bay of Santiago De Cuba. The restaurant would not open for another half-hour but he wanted to enjoy the early sunrise on Morro Castle across the bay and think about his orders. He pulled two hand written notes from his shirt pocket, and began to read to himself. "Locate Lantana boat works just north of De La Torre Marina. Contact Senior Ernest Rivero, the marina's owner. Give him the sealed envelope and see that he has the boathouse ready for occupancy. Check for electric, table saws, work tables, and see that all windows and doors are blacked out. Make arrangements to meet with Yang Lo in a public place and give him directions to the marina. Set time for him to arrive to meet van and check both crates. They are to remain sealed until President Castro arrives. Make sure Colonel Navarro's work crews are sent back in the van after unloading crates. Place armed guards in street clothes inside boathouse. Estimate time of van arrival between 1500 - 1700 hours." He put the notes in his pocket and checked his watch, it was 0640.

There was no sign of anyone preparing the tables for breakfast so he went to the hotel office and called for a taxi to take him down to the waterfront. He located the marina and the boathouse and found nobody there except three fisherman casting bait nets from their small trawler. He walked along the new security chain link fence around the entire building. Lantana Marine was one of the most modern yacht yards in Cuba. It had a rail and dry-dock that could handle yachts up to a hundred feet and it offered complete yacht services, including mechanics and carpenters. For nearly thirty years it had been host to hundreds of visiting yachts and sportfishing boats and was once owned by an American millionaire, Cayo Smith. He also owned the only island in the Bay, called Cayo Granma. Now the yard was leased from the State, and operated by Ernest Rivero and his oldest son, Tomas, who worked mostly on the local fishing trawlers and occasionally on Cuban Navy patrol boats.

Lantana Marina would soon be the homeport for the yacht "Unicorn" and where the Unicorn would be fitted to carry the mini sub. The aft salon would be entirely gutted and the main cabin roof modified to incorporate two large doors. The two sets of davits on the cabin roof that were used to launch the Unicorn's auxiliary craft would be relocated to lift and launch the sub.

Lantana Marina
1820 hours

The two wooden crates lay almost end-to-end on the dusty concrete floor.

"Señor Rivero, pretty soon it will be dark in here, can you turn on some of these lights overhead?" Major Verelas asked as he examined the crates.

"Yes, Major," Rivero said, then walked over to a large circuit breaker box on a nearby wall. He pulled two levers and a number of long fluorescent overhead work lights came on.

Colonel Navarro and Captain Minas stood by as Verelas walked around the large crates inspecting them.

"Colonel Navarro, could I see you for a moment?" Verelas said. He was holding some documents in his hand.

"Colonel, President Castro has requested that you and your detail return immediately to Havana. You are to take the van back to the warehouse. General Vincetta has arranged transportation for you and Major Minas to get you home. Your detail will be given two days leave. You are to advise your men that this mission is of the highest secrecy. They are to tell no one of their trip here to Santiago, or what they saw. They will also be receiving a bonus when they arrive at the warehouse as promised."

"I understand, thank you, Major. Now, can my detail assist your men in opening the crates?"

"I'm afraid not, Colonel. These orders here, as I mentioned, are for you to leave with your detail immediately. The crates will not be inspected until the President arrives."

"Major, Captain Minas and I have had a long day, as did our detail. We would like to rest here for a while, maybe we can be of some use when the President arrives."

"I am sorry, Colonel, these are General Vincetta's orders."

Navarro was beginning to feel a bit paranoid. He was ordered to be on the detail by Castro from the beginning. Now, for the second time when the opportunity to see what was actually in the crates was at hand, he was being dismissed.

"Major, may I remind you, I am a Colonel in the President's special police, and I..."

Verelas interrupted Navarro. "Colonel, maybe we should speak in private. Captain Minas, you had better get your men together and head for the van, Colonel Navarro will join you in a few minutes."

Minas was not pleased with Verelas' order, and was even more disturbed that he was being separated for some reason from his senior officer, however, he obeyed his orders and walked over to the soldiers in his command and ordered them to retreat to the van.

Verelas looked into Navarro's questioning eyes. "Comrade Navarro, there is reason to believe there may be a problem with Captain Minas. General Vincetta feels he may be an informer for the KGB, Kotov, in particular. He may be the reason why Kotov showed up to greet you at the freighter the other night, plus, there are some other problem areas that are being investigated. What is in these crates is highly classified, as you well know, and is also being kept from the eyes of the KGB."

"Major, I have known Captain Minas since we were little boys. I even helped get Antonio on the special forces. There must be some mistake here."

"I know, Comrade, I know, but General Vincetta as you know is an expert at investigations. He has been checking on Minas for some time now, and has reason to believe that he may have been passing sensitive information to Kotov. The incident two nights ago could have caused many problems had Kotov opened those crates."

"I would not have let him do that, Major, and I don't agree with you or General Vincetta about Captain Minas. I'm sure Antonio will be cleared of this ridiculous suspicion. What does Comrade Sorokin have to say about this? As close as he is to our President, he must know if there is someone inside our government working with Kotov."

"Sorokin is in the University Hospital. He was shot during a gun battle with some rebels last night in Los Palacios. Kotov and Petrov were killed when their car was attacked with grenades. General Vincetta, Sorokin and Captain Morales were in another car and challenged the raiders; that is when

172

Sorokin was shot in the leg. The rebels got away, maybe by boat. General Vincetta says they will catch them and execute them on the spot."

Navarro looked totally shocked. "I don't understand. What were General Vincetta, Sorokin, Petrov and Kotov doing in Los Palacios? When I left the warehouse yesterday morning General Vincetta was going to Headquarters and a meeting with the President."

"I was told they decided to go hunting. They all flew down to Maspoton yesterday afternoon, and were heading into Los Palacios for dinner when they were attacked."

"Major, we have not had any rebel activity in Pinar Del Rio Province in twenty years. Who were these rebels? Where did they come from?"

"Colonel, I don't know, but I am sure you will get a complete report when you return to Headquarters. Now, you must be on your way. I'm sure you will want to drive straight through tonight. Be sure you give this information to Captain Minas exactly the way I told you. Keep your eye on him during the trip. When you stop for food or fuel, make sure you're with him. If he makes any phone calls, check the number on the phone so we can have his call traced, do you understand me, Colonel?"

"Yes, yes, I understand."

"Good. Have a safe trip home, Colonel."

"Tell me something, Major. What do you think is in those crates? What is it that has to be hidden from the Russians? You don't think our President is playing with some small nuclear device, do you?"

Verelas laughed. "Colonel, I don't think our President would be that foolish to challenge our Russian friends by playing with nuclear things. I would guess it may have a some kind of new electronic device, maybe a new satellite receiver, or something like that. Your guess is as good as mine, Colonel."

"I don't suppose you would tell me even if you did know, would you, Major?"

"Only if I am told to do so. Right now you travel with questionable company, but, to put your mind at rest, I don't know what it is either. Good night, Colonel."

Verelas turned and walked away.

Minas saw Navarro coming and sprang to his feet, while calling out an order for the men to return to the van.

"Well, Colonel, can we go now?"

"Yes, and we are going to drive straight through to Havana. Tell your men we will make stops for food and drinks. Remind them again that this has been a classified secret mission. They are not to talk to anyone about where they were or what they did. They will also be getting paid extra when we arrive at the warehouse."

Minutes later while heading out of Santiago, Navarro was about to tell Minas about Kotov's death, when two Russian Gaz vehicles met them at the intersection of Jesus Menendez Avenue and Paseco de Marti Street. The two military jeeps turned directly in front of the van and headed south down Menendez Avenue. Both Navarro and Minas thought they recognized General Vincetta in the first jeep. There were at least four passengers in each vehicle, well concealed by the tinted plastic windows attached to the portable canvas curtains.

"I would bet my mother's rosary that was Vincetta in that jeep, Colonel."

"You could be right, Captain." Navarro turned to watch the two Gaz jeeps in the rear view window. He knew it was the General, and guessed that Castro was also on board.

"They are heading for the Marina, Colonel, and whatever is in those crates will soon be known only to a select few, don't you agree?"

"Well, Captain, it doesn't look like you and I are included, does it. Maybe it's best we don't know. There are many things happening these days that I find strange. For example, do you know what Major Verelas told me just before we left? He told me that Petrov and Kotov were killed yesterday in an ambush down in Los Palacios. General Vincetta, Comrade Sorokin and Captain Morales were also attacked, but got away. Sorokin was wounded, but not seriously."

"My God, Kotov is dead? Who would do that, I mean who would attack them? This is crazy."

"Rebels, they say, and quite a few. They attacked their motorcade just outside of town while they were driving in from Maspoton."

"Colonel, I need a very private favor. I need to go to Kotov's quarters right away."

Navarro could see that Minas was upset. His body was erect and leaning over the steering wheel, as if he were pushing the van from within. He was pumping the accelerator to get more speed out of the straining engine. Directly ahead was a slow moving dump truck loaded with fill dirt. Navarro could see that Minas was going to pass the truck at all costs, challenging the heavy head-on traffic.

"Pull over, Captain, over there in the filling station. I will drive now, before you get us all killed."

Lantana Marina
1710 hours

Castro paced back and forth as he watched the two crates being dismantled by Major Verelas and three of his men. An electric motor came to life high above the floor and a large steel beam began to move on screeching wheels. Ernest Rivero walked slowly beneath the beam holding a control box connected by a heavy electrical cord to the motor. He was positioning the beam directly over the crates. A pulley and block could be seen hanging below the beam, and a large hook, attached to a steel cable began to drop slowly.

"More lights, can we get more light in here?" Castro yelled.

Rivero released the control box and let it swing on the cord. He went over to the electrical boxes and threw a few levers, but nothing happened.

"I am sorry comrade, President, but this is all I can do. A lot of lights are out above, but I can't replace them, I am sorry."

It took nearly fifteen minutes to raise the large crate. Castro joined his brother and Yang Lo as they stood next to the long strange shaped object, now shrouded in dusty burlap wrappings. Two soldiers pulled the heavy cloth away, leaving a cloud of foul smelling dust whirling around. There was silence as they stared at the strange looking machine before them. It was a miniature submarine, shaped like a killer whale. It was painted flat black, with a light gray underbody. The dorsal fin, or the sail, was very streamlined. The two midship lower wing fins were also shaped similar to those of a large fish. The tail featured four fins, two vertical on the upper and lower surfaces, and two horizontal, attached to each side. It was evident that these were moving surfaces, as they had small hinges, and were all protected from movement with flat slats of wood and tape holding them in place. The machine, nearly twenty-seven feet in length and five feet in diameter was very impressive sitting on its wooden cradle. Yang Lo walked over to the port side of the machine and just behind the midship fin, pulled off a protective sheet of cardboard that was taped onto the hull, exposing a large eight inch intake covered by a wire screen. He then went aft to where the tail, or stern of the machine tapered into a point and removed a fiberglass shaped cone that protected an exhaust vent nearly ten inches in diameter.

He motioned for one of the soldiers to bring the ladder that was lying on the ground. Lo took the ladder and carefully placed it on the port side of the machine, just forward of the fin. He picked up a small wooden box and removed a Phillips head screwdriver. When he reached the sail fin, he turned and looked at his audience. Castro, Raul, General Vincetta, Rivero and four soldiers stood watching him.

"Gentlemen, we have built a explosive device into this machine. Even though it is small, it is strong enough to destroy this machine, all of us, and part of this building. Should I make a mistake by not properly disarming this device, we will all be part of your island's landscape. I suggest that you all leave the building until I have disarmed the detonator."

Raul looked at Fidel. "Did you know about this, this explosive thing?"

"Of course. Lo told me they would build in a device that would keep anyone not authorized to open the hatch from learning about the machine, or its contents. I see now he kept his word." Castro smiled at Lo and waved. "We will go outside. You be careful up there. I will leave a runner with you." Castro turned to General Vincetta and told him to pick a volunteer to stay with Yang Lo and report to them when it was safe to return.

"Fidel, this is not good. This safety device, or what ever you call it is too dangerous. Think of the idiots who will be loading these machines, and handling them. All we need is one accident."

Castro ignored Vincetta and walked outside to the seawall.

"Look how the sun sets now on the bay and on the western hills. Remember the days we stood not far from here and celebrated the liberation of Santiago? Remember the small boats out in the bay that were set on fire because the poor fishermen had no fireworks? Look around, this place was once filled with capitalists yachts, Batista's rich friends."

"Yes, my President, and we had work, money to spend and no shortages of food or supplies, like light bulbs."

Vincetta's strong short arm came out of nowhere. The back of his closed fist caught Rivero on the right side of his face, dislocating his jaw, loosening teeth and opening a two inch gash in his cheek from the large ring on Vincetta's pinky finger. Rivero did not fall, but he was stunned and fell into Fidel's arms. Rivero had been a key operative for the 26 of July movement. He was wounded outside the Moncada Garrison when Castro and his rebels were defeated by the Cuban Army, July 26, 1953. Now in his mid-sixties, he was becoming careless with his opinions and resented being used by the government.

"He cannot speak to you like this, comrade President." Vincetta growled. "I will have him dealt with."

"No, General, it is alright," Castro said, as he held Rivero by his bony shoulders and tried to look him in the eye.

"Are you alright, Ernest?" Castro asked.

Rivero bowed his head, both of his hands holding his aching face. "I am alright, sir," he said, in a whisper.

Castro turned to one of the curious soldiers standing nearby and told him to take Rivero to his office, where he could call his son and get some medical treatment. The soldier put his arm around Rivero's back and led him down the narrow concrete walk.

"He was one of my best front line soldiers, General, over thirty years ago. No harm will come to him or his family."

"Yes, comrade President, I apologize for..."

Castro threw his heavy arm around Vincetta's shoulders and started walking towards the building. They both noticed the soldier running towards them. He was the volunteer left behind with Lo.

"Well, the building is still standing and I don't see any smoke and flames, so that must mean Mr. Lo remembered the combination." Castro attempted to lighten the atmosphere with his rare sense of humor.

When the party arrived, the large sail section had been removed from the sub and was sitting on the ground. Lo was standing inside the craft, handing small cartons down to a soldier on the ladder.

Castro and Raul went over to the ladder and took the packages and set them on the concrete floor.

"Comrade President, you must see the inside of this wonderful machine. I think you will be surprised."

Raul and Vincetta were studying the sail section, which was nearly three feet long and at least two feet high. The base was square, with six large pan head screws on each side, and four on the front and rear of the plate. Raul asked Lo if it was alright to move it so they could look up inside. Lo said it was safe, since the charges were not in the sail. Vincetta and Raul lifted the sail by its base plate and laid it on its side. They were both amazed at how light the section was. There was no way to look up inside the structure, as a fiberglass board was screwed into it, concealing the inside compartment. There were a number of female electrical plugs mounted on the board, along with two instruments, an ampmeter and an out-put gauge. Vincetta removed a small canvas dust cover, held on by six snaps. A pair of radios sat side by side, similar in size, but the numbers on the frequency dials were different. They both looked like very old VHF types. There were no ID cards on them, or brand name plates.

Castro crouched down in the small cavity of the sub. He took the small flashlight that Lo handed him and flashed it around the sterile hull sides and bulkheads. There was little to see, just a few plastic tubes and some cables, and a large metal box on the rear bulkhead. What Castro really wanted to see was the propulsion unit on the other side of the rear bulkhead. As he stood up, he felt something give beneath his foot. He shined the light down on the wood floor and noticed that it had screws in it, but it was detached. He kicked the board and noticed the tops of a row of batteries, then he remembered. The sixteen heavy-duty marine batteries powered the sub's systems were located under the floor of the compartment.

Back down on the floor, Castro and Raul watched as Lo removed another panel from the starboard side of the sub. This panel was at least three feet in length and at the front, measured about fifteen inches in height, then tapered back to about eight inches. After a lengthy wait, the panel was finally removed. Lo flashed the light inside, and exposed the three-horse electric motor sealed in plastic. A molded fiberglass tube was actually a venturi chamber that housed two sets of stainless fan blades, or propellers. A stainless steel shaft connected the motor with the propellers. It was a simple water jet pump. Water was drawn in from the vent on the port side, into the venturi chamber then pushed out by the fans under high pressure through the exhaust outlet, propelling the sub at speeds up to eighteen knots.

Lo took Castro and Vincetta on a tour of the small sub, going over the details of the mechanical parts as well as the electronics that would operate the vessel. He was proud of the fact that the engineering on this project was far above most standards in his own country. The construction of this first hull was somewhat heavier than planned, however, he was most impressed with the water tests. The navigational systems, gyro control, radio transmitters and receivers were flawless. The small onboard computer with its pre-set commands and maneuvering functions was more than adequate and it was reliable. Lo explained to Castro that the sub would be subject to damage if not handled with some caution. If the sub was damaged, or jarred, it would have to be checked out before it could be used. In a worst case scenario, a uncontrolled vessel could go crashing to the bottom of the sea, possibly releasing its contents, or worse, it could beach itself.

"Our simple, but very effective safeguard is our code to protecting each sub."

"You mean the explosive device?" Vincetta asked.

"Yes, General. One of our young engineers came up with the program. It requires that when anyone is removing the sail panel from the sub, the holding screws must be turned in a certain sequence. If a stranger decides to, shall we say, take a peek, and he doesn't turn the proper screws, he would be vaporized along with the sub. There are no components on board that can be traced to anyone. Radios have been copied as well as the main motor, which was made in the United States. There are no I.D. numbers, etc. The wires and cables are universal as well as the glass products." Lo turned and pointed to the second crate. "There is a complete set of tooling and molds for your sub, as promised, comrade Castro. I don't know where you will find anyone who cam compete with us."

"I appreciate your advice, Yang Lo. You have done a magnificent job on our project."

Castro called Vincetta over to join him. "General, you have a package for our distinguished guest?" Vincetta removed a large brown envelope from inside his jacket and gave it to Yang Lo.

"You will enjoy our hospitality, and as soon as you have trained our technicians, you will receive the rest as we agreed. Major Verelas will have our technicians here sometime this week, ready to be trained, in the meantime, you should..."

Castro was interrupted by one of the outside guards, who was running towards them screaming, "General Vincetta, there has been a bad accident with Colonel Navarro, hurry please, the police are outside with a message for you."

Jesus Menendez Avenue
1705 hours

Captain Minas drove the van up on the empty dirt lot past the gas station's driveway. He stopped the van, pulled the hand brake and put his face into his hands. His voice was calm, but Navarro could see he was about to break down. Minas began to sob, softly at first, then loudly.

"Comrade, what is it? Why must you do this?"

"He owned me, Luis, he owned me, and if the authorities search his quarters they will find out.

"Antonio, this is me, Luis, remember? What is it, who owns you?"

"Kotov, he has, he has photos of me, pictures that could have me thrown out of the army, pictures that could ruin my life forever."

"Pictures? What kind of pictures could Kotov have of you?"

Minas sat back against the seat looking straight ahead out the windshield. Tears ran down his dark brown cheeks. Then he turned and looked into Navarro's concerned face.

"He has pictures of me with, a young boy, a friend of our families. He also has pictures of me with Petrov. Need I say more, Luis? Somehow, Kotov learned about my problem. He followed me until I was caught. Then he forced me to please Petrov. For my life and career, he made me agree to inform him on everything I saw or heard about at Headquarters, especially

179

concerning the secret police and President Castro's activities. Believe me, Luis, I never gave him anything that was real important. I just kept him happy. The arrival of the freighter and the cargo for the President I felt was not important. It seemed strange to me and to Kotov that machines would be coming from China, but I never felt it could be so important to the President, I am so ashamed, Luis."

Minas started crying again. Navarro left the cab of the truck and went back to the rear of the van where he found most of the six man detail missing, they had wandered off to the filling station to relieve themselves.

Navarro needed to contact General Vincetta. He thought about turning around and heading back to the marina and talking to the General. "Let Antonio speak for himself, Vincetta was a good man, he would forgive Minas, especially after he explained that he had not passed along any top secret materials."

After ordering the detail back into the van, Navarro got in the cab again, only this time he sat behind the wheel. He told Minas that they were going back to the marina so that he could talk to Vincetta. Minas said nothing. He just sat and starred out the window watching the buildings of old Santiago pass by. There was very little traffic northbound on Jesus Menendez Avenue at this hour, and the lights of the historic city were just beginning to come on, as were the headlights of the few vehicles that Navarro approached. Two blocks from Avenue 24, where Navarro would turn to reach the marina, Antonio Minas made a decision. He opened the door and jumped out into the path of a large utility truck. The driver of the large Russian built Ural tractor had no time to react. Minas was pulled under the front wheel and killed instantly before the rear dual wheels rolled over his lifeless body.

Bacanao General Hospital
2015 hours

"I am sorry, comrade Navarro, he was a good soldier and friend, I know. I will take care of everything here, and I will personally search Kotov and Petrov's belongings. There will be nothing left that can soil the life of Captain Antonio Minas."

"Thank you, General. I feel so responsible for this. I wanted to bring him to you and let him explain."

"Nonsense, Colonel. You can't take the blame for Minas' actions. He was in trouble the minute he was in Kotov's clutches."

180

The two men went out the emergency doors where they were met by two military police. Vincetta ordered the two young men to escort Navarro to the Moncada Garrison, where he could rest for the night at Vincetta's small apartment.

"You get a good night's sleep, Colonel. I will call for you in the morning and make arrangements for your return flight to Havana. I have already sent the van back. We will meet in the morning."

Vincetta gave Navarro a casual salute and a comforting smile, then walked over and got into his jeep. Navarro had no choice but to leave with his two escorts. Even with the tragic death of his friend, his thoughts were still on the two crates. Vincetta never mentioned them from the time when he arrived at the accident, nor did he mention if the President was in his party at the marina.

Fidel Castro was not pleased at the news of Antonio Minas' death, he had thought highly of him. He was pleased to hear, however, that the mystery haunting him and Sorokin was solved. As they had suspected, Minas was Kotov's contact. The serious leak in the secret police was plugged, but at the price of a good soldier. Castro instructed Major Verelas to have Minas' body flown to Campamento Colombia and given a full military funeral. The cause of death, an accident, crossing a busy street in Santiago.

CHAPTER 11

Government Palace
Havana Cuba

Monday, September 28th
0920 hours

Fidel Castro Ruz stood motionless gazing out the large window in his office that looked out on the Plaza de la Revolucion and the 300-foot towering monument dedicated to Jose Marti. The sun was reflecting on the brilliant white modern buildings that surrounded the colorful Plaza. In the distance he could hear the rumble of thunder that would bring a welcome cooling rain at mid-day when it came.

"Good morning, Mr. President."

Castro turned to see his old friend Acevedo Rogelio, standing in the middle of the spacious room. General Rogelio, Vice Minister of Defense and a Division Commander, was also Vice Co-Chairman of the PCC, Central Committee of the Communist Party.

"Buenos dias, my friend, come sit over here and let us talk," Castro pointed to a pair of high-back leather chairs in front of his desk.

"Have you read the report about the terrible attack on our comrades, Dimitri Sorokin, Kotov and Petrov down in Las Palacios?"

"Yes, I read it this morning in General Vincetta's office. I can't believe we had rebels working down there. They must have come in from the Pines by boat. We have had no success in finding them so far. We have added more men this morning to make up six patrols. We also have four helicopters and four patrol boats assigned to the search."

"Forget it, General. They are long gone." Fidel replied.

"How did they know General Vincetta and his party were visiting the camp? How did they know they would be coming into town at that time? Doesn't it seem strange to you, comrade President?"

Castro stroked his wiry beard. "It was a random strike, they had no idea who was in those cars. They were not military cars or trucks, or didn't you read that in the report?"

Rogelio could see that Fidel was becoming uncomfortable with the subject, but proceeded to ask questions that had not been answered earlier by General Vincetta.

"What have we heard from the KGB in Moscow? Aren't they calling for an investigation?" Rogelio asked.

"No, I personally talked to one of Gorbachev's aides in Moscow last night and he agreed that there should be no publicity on the matter as it could be embarrassing for both of us. We are shipping the bodies out this afternoon for Moscow. The KGB will officially announce that they died in a automobile accident. We do not want the rebels to know who was killed or hurt in the incident, but Moscow expects to see the murderers in front of a firing squad and soon, if you get my gist, General."

General Rogelio sat relaxed in the large chair, hands clasped. His eyes were difficult to see through his thick sunglasses. His mouth opened showing badly stained teeth. "Evidently you don't think we can capture these rebels, are you thinking that we have to create them? am I understanding you right?"

Castro reached over and placed his hand on the general's knee. His long fingers surrounded his kneecap and began to close like a vice. "You are still the best, General. You will see to this matter, yes? Do it down in Pinar Del Rio, quickly. You will need at least four, ah, criminals. Shoot them, then burn them."

"Yes, sir. By the way, how is Comrade Sorokin?"

"He is doing fine, just fine. I had coffee with him early this morning. The doctors say he can leave on Friday, but he will be on crutches for a couple of weeks."

"That is good. Please pass along my best wishes for a speedy recovery."

"I will be most happy to, General. Now, when you have completed this mission, I have a very special assignment for you. This will also require the strictest security. I'm choosing you now, as I picked you twenty six years ago, when you were, what, seventeen years old when I recruited you in Santiago?"

"Sixteen, comrade President, I was sixteen. I lied to you."

Fidel laughed, reached over to his desk and picked up part of a cigar from an ashtray. "I need you to work with my brother and take care of things around here for a week or so to keep things, ah, looking normal."

"I do not understand. What about General Vincetta?"

"General Vincetta will be with me. I plan to be off the island for a short period of time in December, possibly during Christmas week. I can't tell you where I will be going, that is not important. I will be on a special trip to look into some investments that may be crucial to our future economy."

"Our future economy?"

"Yes, General. I see dark days ahead for us and in our relationship with the Soviets. Gorbachev has put us on notice that we may be seeing major cutbacks in military and financial areas. He seems to be working towards new relationships with the EC, and the United States, especially the United States. This new man scares me, my friend."

"He is highly respected within the party, Mr. President. I have read much about him, there is nothing but praise for him here among the Soviet officials and the military."

"Oh, there is no doubt about his popularity, or his phony loyalties to the party, but he speaks of new relationships with the west to create more stability and trust. What he is after, is to bring about more cooperation with the North Atlantic Treaty Organization so he can open new trade. His only hope, he claims, to prevent his Soviet Union of economic collapse is to stop spending money on the military. He has offered to have new peace talks with the Americans, and discuss cutbacks on the placement of ICBM's. I believe he is going to bring down the Soviet Union, but he is not going to take our country with him, General."

"If what you say is true, what role do we play now? I mean, what about all their military here in Cuba, and all the training that is going on?"

"General, I don't have that answer. I see us as being a bit of a knife in his side right now. We will remain as we are, General, true to our beliefs and loyal to the party. We are not going to go along with his so-called healing programs with the west. We will survive, with or without the Soviets."

Rogelio looked at his watch, then slowly stood up, and saluted. He watched Castro, who was sitting totally relaxed, rolling the cigar between his fingers watching the ashes drift down to the hardwood floor.

"Comrade President, are you suggesting we will be separating from the Soviet Union?"

"No, General. No, I am not saying that. What I am saying is that we need to start preparing for a new source of economic stability without the help of our Russian friends. However, you and I and a few who I have selected must do this without their knowledge. Under no circumstances, can anyone know what we are doing, regarding my future activities."

"Mr. President, what if, well, what if we get caught doing what ever your plans call for? What becomes of our country then?"

"Nothing, my friend. I may get my hand slapped, but nothing will happen to our beloved Cuba, I promise." Fidel stood up. "Now, my friend, can I count on you?"

"Of course, Comrade President. What is it I have to do?"

"For the meantime not a thing. I will be calling a meeting in the next couple of weeks. Then, and only then, will you meet the men I have chosen to carry out this mission. Meantime, General, not even your family must know of this conversation, understand?"

Rogelio nodded yes.

"Good. Now, I want you to go back to your Ministry and call Commodore Santamaria at the Naval Academy in Mariel. Tell him I want one his best patrol boat commanders to be assigned to your division for special operations. I want to see a file on this man first. Tell the Commodore, orders will be sent through special channels and he is not to speak of this to anyone, especially the officer until we screen him. Tell him that this officer will also be selecting a special crew assigned to me, personally."

"Yes, but, the Commodore.."

"No." Castro interrupted. "Aldo Santamaria is not one of my recruits."

There was a sign of relief on the General's face. Castro did not need to question him. None of Castro's army officers were fond of the elderly Commodore.

Fidel Castro had a full day ahead of him. Meetings with a number of Ministers and members of the Council of State. In two days, Ministers from all fourteen provinces were coming to Havana to meet with members of the National Assembly to review new legislation being prepared for presentation. Castro was pushing all the lawmakers to get their business completed in November. He wanted December clear. As President of the Council of Ministers and the Council of State, First Secretary of the Cuban Communist Party and Commander in Chief of the armed service, he had his plate full, and needed to get it clean if he was to be on board the Unicorn in late December.

Old Havana
Plaza de Armas
1415 hours

Carlos Lucia sat on a stone bench in the quiet park of the Plaza de Armas. The sun was bright and the air unseasonably humid and a welcome breeze roamed through the tall majestic royal palm trees that surrounded him. He looked patiently at the slow traffic moving around the plaza and noted that there were very few tourists moving about this once famous Havana attraction.

A voice came from behind, startling him. "Carlos, sorry I am so late."

It was Luis, his brother-in-law, dressed in civilian clothes, jeans, tee shirt and wearing his favorite baseball cap and a pair of tattered and worn out sneakers.

"I don't have much time, Carlos. I have to get back to headquarters by 1600 hours. What is so important that you could not wait to see me on Sunday?"

"We have trouble, my friend," Carlos said.

"Trouble? What kind of trouble?"

"Quevedo, my boss, informed me I must report to the next pilot training class on the new Tupolev-134. The classes begin on October the third."

"Oh, no. That means you will be going to Moscow, right?"

"Yes. The school is fifteen weeks, with at least a month of flying around the Soviet Union before I can return. Jesus, Luis, what are we going to do?"

"I will have to talk to someone, I will help get you out of this, Carlos, do not worry. We have time, maybe I can go right to Fidel."

"Fidel! Are you crazy?"

"No, why not?, he loves you, Carlos. You were one of the only pilots he trusted with his life twenty five years ago, remember?"

"Yes, but, what would you tell him?"

"I don't know, I can just say you want to stay with the old planes until they are all phased out. I can tell him that you want to be home more, I don't know, I will think of something."

They both sat and looked straight ahead not speaking for a few minutes.

"Come, let's go have a beer."

"No, I have to get home right away. Teresa, she is cooking me a special dinner, it's my birthday."

"Oh, I forgot, forgive me, Carlos."

Luis put his arms around Carlos and kissed him on both cheeks. "Oh, here are some cigarettes for you. I smoked a few, but the thought is there, between the cigarettes. When do you fly out again?"

"Tomorrow, around noon. It will be a long day. I go to Maracaibo and Caracas, then back. I should be home around ten o'clock tomorrow night."

"Good, maybe I can come out and we talk for a while. So many things are happening that I don't understand. The message you are holding must get out. It is very long, you must be careful when you put it in the flashlight. If you can talk to the contact, Carlos, explain it is long and important, o.k.?"

187

"Yes, I will do this. Tell me, Luis, so far the plan, it seems to be working, no? I mean, so far the light has been moved when we had the message in it. What is so important in this message, can you tell me?"

"Two KGB were murdered on Saturday evening, and another wounded in an attack by rebels. Also, I helped take the two devices that arrived on the freighter to Santiago on Sunday, to a old run down marina. There was an oriental man there, waiting for Fidel, who showed up later with Vincetta. I still don't know what the hell the devices are, but I think I will be going back soon to the marina, then I hope to see the devices."

"My God, KGB are murdered here in Cuba? There will be hell to pay, Luis."

"There is something very strange going on, Carlos. I know that Fidel, Vincetta and others are deliberately working behind the Russians backsides. Whatever is in those crates, Fidel doesn't want the Russians to know about them, or for that matter, even that they exist. The reason they are in Santiago at a marina is that they are going aboard some big yacht that belongs to a friend of Fidel. This boat is expected to arrive very soon, that's when I hope to be assigned there."

"Time is getting short, Luis. Do you know what plans, if any, the Americans might have working to help us?"

"No, when the time comes, you will be bringing that information back in your flashlight. Right now, I have no idea what they are doing. As the time gets near for this boat to arrive, we should start observing any naval movements around Santiago Bay. I am betting that Fidel is going to slip out of this port at night. Only a few of us will know, except maybe a patrol boat or two, that will have to escort him out to sea. No foreign ships can leave without escorts."

"I can't help us here too much, unless I can get some inter-island turnarounds to the eastern provinces. They give those kind of domestic flights to the newer pilots, and it would be difficult to ask for such trips."

Luis stood up. "I must go, Carlos, take care, give my love to my sister. I will try to drive down tomorrow night. Maybe I will have good news about you not going to Moscow."

Carlos smiled and waved goodbye. "God be with you," he said under his breath.

Government Palace
PCC Headquarter Offices
1730 hours

Luis Navarro waited patiently outside the small conference room where Fidel Castro was meeting with ministers from the eastern provinces. When Fidel left the meeting, he was in a hurry to get to his car and drive down to the University Hospital. He had received a message that Sorokin was running a high fever and was delirious.

"What is it, Colonel? I am in a hurry to get to the hospital, comrade Sorokin is having problems."

" Please, may I join you, comrade President? I would like to see..."

"Come, come with me," Fidel ordered.

The short ride to the University Hospital took the motorcade only minutes to drive down the busy Indepencia Boulevard. Castro's aging Mercedes and three escort jeeps with lights flashing and sirens screaming cleared a path right to the emergency entrance. In less than ten minutes, Castro was standing at Sorokin's bedside with a doctor. Sorokin looked like death, his face was gray, his eyes blackened and sunk deep into his skull. There were two bottles hanging from a steel rack next to his bed with small tubes attached to needles that were tapped into both his arms. Oxygen was being forced into his lungs through a tube that was attached to a plastic pipe and taped into his nostril. Navarro, standing ten feet away with one of the nurses, could not hear Castro's conversation with the doctor, nor could he tell if he was even communicating with Sorokin.

After ten minutes, Castro moved away from Sorokin's side and walked slowly towards Navarro. "Come, we will get some tea next door and wait for a while. Comrade Sorokin's temperature is near normal now. We will wait for him to wake up."

Navarro and Fidel Castro walked into the small adjoining room and sat on two folding chairs. A nurse brought in two cups of tea in plastic cups. Two guards took up their positions outside the door.

"What is it, Colonel Navarro? What is so important this hour that it can't wait, huh?"

"It's very personal, comrade President, but I have no choice, I must talk to you. It's about Carlos Lucia, my brother-in-law."

"Lucky Lucia? That old fart? Is he still flying sheep and goats to Nicaragua?"

"Ah, yes, sometimes, comrade President. He is still with Cubana, and I think once in a while he still has some goats and sheep on board."

"He was one hell of a pilot. When I think of some of the loads that we would give him to take up to the mountains, and some of those terrible planes he had to fly. Do you remember that funny little plane with the two tails and the bubble top cockpit? It was a Taylorcraft, or something like that. We stole it from some rich merchant up in Holguin, remember? Carlos packed me and some bitch he had into that thing and we flew down to Camaguey and ran off the runway. The damn landing gear collapsed and we went skidding into the swamp, damn, he almost killed us all that afternoon."

"Ah, he married that bitch, comrade President. She is my sister, Teresa."

Castro said nothing. He looked straight ahead at the sterile white painted wall. The smile left his lips and the sparkle left his eyes. "Excuse me, Colonel, I did not mean to.."

"Please, not to worry, how were you to know?"

"Just what is I can do for Carlos, is he in some kind of trouble?"

"No, nothing like that, Sir. It's his job. For years, Carlos has been flying those old Soviet turbo-props. Now they want him to train on new pure jets, T-l34's, I believe they call them. They want him to go to Moscow in October and start his training."

"So, isn't this good for him? It will pay more, I'm sure. Why would he not want to learn about jets? Besides, he would enjoy going to Moscow, I am sure."

"Sir, Carlos, well, he is getting on in years, and he likes being close to home now. He loves his flight routes, he hardly ever has to stay overnight. He also loves those, ah, propeller airplanes he flies. He would...."

Castro interrupted. "I think I understand, Luis. You tell him to call my office in a few days and make an appointment. I will personally talk to him and work something out. Not to worry, he will not be shipped to Moscow, o.k.?"

"Thank you, comrade President, thank you. I will tell him."

Navarro stood up and saluted Castro and left the room just as a nurse was about to enter. "Comrade President, your patient is awake now."

"Gracias, gracias."

190

Maracaibo International Airport
Venezuela
Tuesday, September 29th
1430 hours

Carlos Lucia watched the ground crewman as he directed him to his parking space at gate seven. The crewman crossed his arms above his head, and Carlos applied full brakes. The Tupolof 24 bowed gracefully on the nose strut. First Officer Manuel Diaz went through the shut down procedures as Carlos finished his paper work.

"Better get on the intercom and let the passengers know we are only staying on the ground for an hour. We will leave for Caracas at 1530."

"Yes, sir."

While Diaz made the announcement, Carlos looked over the passenger list. He did not recognize anyone, and it seemed there were no military.

Without looking up from his paperwork chores, Carlos spoke. "Hardly worth the trip down for only nine passengers, with a pick up of fourteen for Havana."

"Tuesdays are always slow days for Caracas, Captain. I was supposed to go to Mexico this morning. I wonder why they decided to make this trip so early? And since when do we make special stops on route?"

"I can't answer that. I was called in early too. The stop in Santiago to pick up those two Orientals is a complete mystery to me too. They must be some kind of officials. Anyway, we are here. I will do the post flight, you go ahead and sign us in, check to see how long before we get fuel and I will meet you at the weather office."

"Si, Captain."

Manuel got out of his seat, crawled over the console and took his jacket from the locker behind Carlos. Carlos waited as Manuel combed his hair and fussed with his tie in the mirror. Finally, he left the cabin.

Carlos reached into his flight bag and took the flashlight. He put on his hat and walked down the portable ladder. He looked around the area, but saw no sight of even a baggage conveyer heading towards his aircraft. With the flashlight in his right hand, he started walking around the outside of the port engine and under the wing. He did not have to look hard for any oil leaks, the nacelle was covered with oil streaks. He ducked down and up into the large open wheel well. He placed the flashlight on the ledge over the open landing gear door. He was reaching into his rear pocket for his hanky, when a voice startled him from behind.

"Captain Lucia?"

"Si, senor?" Carlos found himself face to face with a small slightly overweight black man dressed in a one piece faded blue uniform, like a mechanic would wear. His eyes were hidden behind dark glasses. He spoke very good Spanish.

"Wilson, Sam Wilson, ah, Eastern Airlines, Miami. I understand you have a problem with your landing door sensor?"

"Oh, yes, Señor. Sometimes the left landing gear warning light stays on. I think it's the gear door switch, ah, here it is." Carlos put his hand on the small bayonet type switch that opened and closed with the landing gear doors.

"Ah, could I borrow your light, mine seems to be out of power." Wilson banged his light a number of times on the tire.

"Sure, here, Señor." Carlos handed Wilson the flashlight. Wilson fooled with the switch and pretended he was following the wiring.

"Big news, Señor, long message, important it goes fast."

"Roger that, Captain.

Carlos smiled. "Gracias Señor, gracias."

Wilson moved out of the wheel well and walked back to the small Toyota pick-up truck, got in and drove off.

Carlos went up the ladder to the cabin, stepped into the flight deck, dropped the flashlight into his flight case and returned to the ramp. He smiled as he walked in the afternoon sun to the ramp gate and down to the main terminal. He entered the weather briefing room and noticed Diaz on the phone, he was waving to Carlos to join him.

"Not good news, Captain, we have heavy weather moving through Caracas in about an hour. T-Storms with heavy rains and gusts. Winds at six thousand are 45 from zero nine zero, and fifty-five and nine thousand. They are estimating the storms to be through by 2100 hours. We should be getting the front line of them here almost anytime."

"What's it like to the south, can we go down to Merida, fly through the Pico pass and then up to Caracas?"

"I will check, Captain. I too would like to get off the ground as soon as we can. Oh, fuel is on the way, we had to wait, same old shit, they say we haven't paid our August landing fees yet."

Carlos went to the pilots lounge and made a long distance call to Havana to Cubana flight operations. He explained his delays and intentions and also asked to have someone call his home and advise Teresa that he would be very late.

Carlos Lucia, Manuel Diaz, flight stewards Romona Delugo and Angela Rufio would not see Cuba again that day. After three and a half hours of pure terror in the skies over Venezuela, they managed to finally land at Piarco Airport in Port of Spain, Trinidad. Fortunately, their passengers were so happy to be on the ground the delays reaching their destination was of no importance. Two Orientals, however, were upset, but managed to get on a BWIA flight that took them to Caracas. Carlos grounded his aircraft for minor maintenance. He would return the next day to Havana to find a message waiting. He was to report to Government Palace on October 1st, 1000 hours, to the Ministry of Defense Headquarters, room 412. Appointment with General Vincetta. He was to bring all his flight logs.

CHAPTER 12

Dan O'Brien sat at a small table where he could watch the entrance. He had driven over from St. Petersburg Beach early, so he could park his car and have time for breakfast before his flight to Washington.

He checked his watch, he had an hour before his flight departed, and a half-hour before Phil Avery arrived to meet him. Dan opened his tattered briefcase and removed a legal pad, placed it on the table and took a pen from his vest pocket. He printed in large letters, three letter "P"'s , then in script wrote: Problems, Priorities, Progress.

"Would you like more coffee, sir?"

Dan looked up at the young black waitress, standing with a glass pot of coffee. "Yes, thank you."

She filled his cup, smiled and walked off.

Dan leaned back in his chair and stared at the yellow pad. He reached for a cigarette, lit it, then took a sip of the black coffee. He closed his eyes for a moment and his thoughts went immediately to that Sunday morning at the Holiday Inn in Key West, the cute red head waitress, the young Navy Captain, and the haunting article in the newspaper about the young couple found shot on Alligator Alley.

He opened his eyes and began to make notes for the meeting he and Phil Avery would have the next day with the Admiral. This would probably be last meeting with Koster before the mission.

There was good news to report on the "Seaduce". Captain Spencer had checked in from Nassau on October 25th. The yacht and crew were doing fine, and expected to be arriving in the Turks and Caicos Islands around the 28th and leaving for St. Thomas around the first of November, with an ETA sometime around the 10th. O'Brien chuckled to himself when he thought about the new first mate they had assigned to Spencer. Captain Paul Gransaull was an Academy graduate and a veteran F-14 Tomcat pilot, on special assignment by Navy Intelligence to baby sit Spencer. Spencer had been told that Gransaull was an old hand sailing yachts to the Caribbean. The truth was his only training was on his grandfather's classic 60-foot yawl that he sailed on every summer at Nantucket. He was close friend of

Commander Buckland, who had arranged the thirty-day TDY program for him with a little help from Admiral Koster, who got him relieved from duty on the U.S.S. Kennedy.

O'Brien scribbled the name "Seaduce" under the progress column on the pad, then wrote Gail Townsend's name. She had contacted a clearinghouse in St. Thomas, listed the Seaduce with them and sent them all the necessary information including the charter she was booking for the yacht for Christmas week. The charter would originate in St. Lucia, which meant that Spencer would leave the Virgin Islands and head for the Windward Islands no later than December 15th. The charter guests were members of Ian Billings' agency.

Next he wrote down under progress, Unicorn. Information on the yacht in Cuba had not changed since the last report from Navarro and Lucia, October 26th. The yacht arrived in Santiago de Cuba on the 18th and modifications were being made. That was all that was said. Navarro had not mentioned anything new about the "devices" that he had delivered there. Castro, however, was making frequent weekend trips to Santiago. Major Dimitri Sorokin had recovered fully and Dimitri Ustinov, Defense Minister, had cut his vacation short and returned to Moscow on October 20th. In large letters, O'Brien printed, OPERATION DOLPHIN DEPARTING SANTIAGO DECEMBER 21st. He lit another cigarette, scanned the entrance area and looked at his watch. Avery was late. He thought to himself that things were in pretty good shape. The next major hurdle was the sea trials on the Island Drummer. If there were no hitches, the Drummer could be in the Virgin Islands by December 10th, as planned.

"Morning, Rudolf." O'Brien looked up to see Phil Avery standing in front of the small table. He held a hanging bag over his shoulder and a leather briefcase in his hand.

"Morning, Santa."

Avery placed his bag over a nearby chair and took a seat.

"Like some breakfast?"

"Nah, just some coffee, thanks."

"Been waiting long? I see you have already started on your cue cards for tomorrow."

"Yeah, just making some notes. I just know I'll forget some major items in my report tomorrow with the old man, and he will be all over my ass if I leave anything out."

"Ah, come on, Dan, he likes you. He's just pissed he can't get in on the action of the operation, that's all."

O'Brien laughed. "You're probably right. I think he would love to be down here. You know, he has been a basket case for the past two months worrying about the absence of Soviet war ships in the Atlantic and the Caribbean? When he learned from the Russian Naval attaché in D.C. that Gorbachev had called in all the Atlantic fleet back to port, he blew a gasket."

"Why do you suppose they brought their hardware back home, Dan?"

"I don't know. Their attaché told Koster they were cutting back expenses. Gorby is meeting with the President in three weeks, on the 21st. They are supposed to be discussing missile reductions and this may be Gorby's way of saying that he has called in the guard dogs."

"Is Koster still planning on sending a carrier group down as he threatened?"

"No, changed his mind and we have to convince him this is a good move. He has been wanting to put a task force down there since the day this operation started. I have had one hell of a time asking him to keep the Caribbean clean."

"What about the subs?" Avery asked.

"What subs?"

"Hell, we're supposed to have about a dozen attack subs flying around down there chasing Ivan's."

"You ask the old man about that, Phil. I know nothing about sub activities."

O'Brien checked his watch. "Hey, we better start for the gate. Do you have your ticket?"

"Oh, yeah, right here. I couldn't get smoking, only in first class."

O'Brien looked at Avery's boyish grin. "And I suppose you took it?"

"Hey, Santa Claus deserves to fly first class, doesn't he?"

Eastern Flight 901
27,000 feet
1010 hours

"Sir, there is a gentleman in first class who says you should come up to see him. There is a smoking seat open, and we would be happy to upgrade you."

"Sure, why not." O'Brien gathered his belongings and walked up the narrow aisle of the DC-9 to the first class cabin.

O'Brien stood over Avery, who was sitting in his big seat reading a copy of Newsweek Magazine.

"Well, aren't we cozy?"

"Hey, squat and try some of this bubbly, it's great. Who said Eastern was in trouble, look at this stuff."

O'Brien sat down.

"Tell me something, Dan. Where are you going to be during the operation?"

"I don't know yet, Phil. I would like to be with you on the Drummer, but that was shot down by Koster. I thought I might put myself aboard the SONAR when she leaves Puerto Rico, or maybe hang out down at the NASA tracking station at Antigua, where I could at least monitor you, the SONAR and SEADUCE."

"SONAR, that's where you should be."

"Yeah, that would make sense."

"You still have to get things straight with Spencer, right? Just when do you plan to tell him you're going to deep six his yacht?"

"I don't know. We briefed his mate, Paul Gransaull, about what we are going to do, but, no, I have not told Spencer."

"Spencer doesn't know the truth about Gransaull either, does he?"

"Shit no, you kidding? He thinks he's a boat bum, one of your delivery guys. We told him he worked for you a couple of times, didn't we go over this?"

"Yeah, I didn't like the idea then and don't like it now. Spencer is no fool. He knows a lot of crews down the islands, and he will drill old Gransaull on his experience and knowledge, I guarantee you."

"Gransaull will handle it. By the way, speaking of handling things, what's the latest with Gail Townsend?"

"Well, if you mean did she tell Carlton that she is going on a cruise with me, no. She is worse than you when it comes to putting things off."

"No good, junior. She should tell him now and get things settled. We don't want him coming down to the islands and chasing after her. You better get on her butt when you get back from D.C., and I don't mean that physically, either."

"You're right, but I can't tell her what to do. You're going to have to do it. She will listen to you, make it an order. I have had enough problems with her men. I had to threaten the assistant dock master at the marina, who was making passes at her."

The Pentagon Building
Admiral Thomas Koster's Office

Monday, November 2nd
0835 hours

Admiral Koster looked tired. Both his elbows were resting on his desk and the tips of his index fingers were pressing his reading spectacles against his temples. He was silent as he read through the hand written reports that O'Brien had given him ten minutes earlier.

O'Brien glanced at Phil Avery. His head was turned away, inspecting the photographs and ships models that covered the walls and tables in the large room. It finally hit him, this mission was real and just weeks away. He suddenly realized he was the centerpiece and a chill went through his body.

"Well, gentlemen," Koster sprang upright and slipped back into his chair. "It looks good, little late, but good. How are you feeling, Phil? Ready to put the Drummer through its paces?"

"Yes, sir. We will be moving her to the river Thursday night, and if all goes well we'll have all the rigging up and ready to sail, hopefully late Sunday afternoon."

"Now, once she is commissioned, there's no taking her out again, is there?" Koster asked.

"Ah, no, sir, unless she is sinking. Any problems we have will have to be solved at the marina. When she is launched we will keep the lifting belts and the cranes in place. We will do all our water checks, run the engines, operate the hydraulic struts and make sure all the new seams and through hull fittings are sealed and holding. We won't leave the dock until we are certain we have a water tight hull."

"Good, now what precautions been worked out for getting this ship to the river?" Koster asked.

"Sir, we will have the yacht covered from the toe rails to the keel, in canvas. Nobody will see any part of the hull, as the canvas stays on 'til she is in the water. We will be moving at night with escorts provided by the hauling company as well as the Sheriff's Department. It will take about two hours to go from the hangar to the marina, a thirty mile hike, but the best news, we don't have to remove any telephone or electric cables on route."

Koster reached over and pushed a button on his intercom. "Miss Knolls, send in John Lind, will you?"

"He just excused himself, Admiral, he had to, well, I won't repeat it, but he should be back in commission soon."

Koster laughed as he raised from his chair. He stood for a moment, adjusted his suspenders and brushed off the front of his trousers. "You are about to meet someone who just may be as crazy as you are, O'Brien. I took the liberty of recruiting this man myself. He will be the captain on the "Solar".

"Ah, yes sir, I believe, you meant the Sonar?"

"Whatever." Koster responded. "Anyhow, you had not mentioned the Sonar in quite some time and I realized you had a full plate, so I decided to ride shotgun on Sonar's well being. She has been decommissioned by the Navy and moved from Mayport to a civilian yard in Jacksonville, where she is being painted and transformed into a half-ass island freighter. I understand her code name is to be RED SLEIGH?" O'Brien nodded yes.

"Gentlemen, I want you to treat this man with respect, even though he can be total asshole at times. He was blown out of the water twice in the Pacific and has had four tin cans under his command, last one in Korea. He may have a few years on you both, but when the chips are down, this is the guy you want next to you in a fox hole."

The door opened and John Lind made his entrance. He was about average height, five nine, with a squared build, a little pouchey in the mid section. A deep tan painted his nearly bald head, which was accented by blonde and silver threads of hair. He walked up to his old friend with arms outstretched.

"Tom, you old son of a bitch, good to see you."

"Likewise, Johnny, it's been a few," Koster opened his arms and the two men hugged each other.

"John, I want you to meet the two guys who will be depending on you for the next few weeks. Dan O'Brien, operations chief, and Phil Avery, sailboat skipper."

Lind walked over and shook their hands, saying nothing, just flashing a warm smile.

"Sit, gentlemen, sit." Koster ordered.

Lind began to speak before Koster had a chance.

"I just came up from Jacksonville, Tom, and that old mine sweeper doesn't look too bad. She is all but painted out. I went over her engines with a fine-tooth comb with the yard's manager, they are in excellent condition. Now, you wanted to know how soon I can move her out? How soon can I get crew? I will need at least seven."

Koster interrupted. "You will have nine men, John. They have already been recruited. Two of them, your First Officer, and your communications and electronics chief, are veterans off the SONAR. They have all been briefed on the mission, up to a point, they think we are chasing druggers. You will fill them in later. Now, you give me the word and I will have the rest of the crew together and on board in seventy two hours."

"Shit, you mean I don't get a chance to pick my own officers?"

"No, not this time, John, we let the computers do it."

Lind turned and faced O'Brien. "O'Brien, did your daddy have a used car lot one time up on route 50?"

O'Brien was speechless.

Koster broke out in a hearty laugh.

O'Brien smiled and spoke. "I take it, you and the Admiral have talked about my plan?"

"Oh, a few times. Tom, I mean the Admiral, put me up to that, Mr. O'Brien."

O'Brien looked over his recruit with some reservation, but it appeared the Admiral was right. Lind was probably the right man for he job.

Lind began taking charge of the meeting. "O.k., as I see it so far. I will leave Jacksonville at a date to be determined, and head straight for San Juan, correct?"

"Ah, correct, however, we have made a change in your cruising plans, Captain Lind. We need to get a Navy Seal team on board your ship, so we decided to send you to St. Croix after your cargo is aboard. We would rather fly the Seals to St. Croix, where there is good housing at the airport at the Army reserve quarters, were they would be out of the sight. We plan on bringing them down from Homestead on a Air Force C-130. There is a Florida Air Guard C-130 that makes regular monthly runs down to St. Thomas and St. Croix for training. We can load the Seals on board without attracting any attention. We feel coordinating these men and their gear from the airport to dockside in San Juan would be a logistical problem."

"You're absolutely right, Mr. O'Brien, but I still go to San Juan, correct? I mean to fuel up and pick up goodies?"

"That's correct. We are working on a manifest for you through some agents in Puerto Rico. We need to pick up cargo of some nature with Barbados as its destination. I have no idea what kind of cargo they will come up with, but to cover our ass, the Red Sleigh, ah, Sonar, has to look the part of island freighter, right down to the cargo."

"I understand, hell, that's no problem for me, O'Brien. What I would like to do is to get SONAR out of Jacksonville and give her a good shake down before we head off to the Caribbean."

"I see no problem, do you, O'Brien?" Admiral Koster asked.

"Ah, no sir. I will check with Ian Billings on the phony paper work for your ship and the crew, and see how soon all the documents will be in order, after that, she's all yours, Captain Lind."

The three men discussed the entire operational plan and did some fine-tuning.

"Gentlemen, I am afraid I must excuse myself, I have a lunch date with the Secretary and meetings all afternoon with the Joint Chiefs. Make yourself comfortable here if you like. Oh, there is one thing." Koster lifted a few papers and found the one he was looking for.

"You know how paranoid I am about the Soviet navy and their movements? I got this message when I came in this morning. Don't know what it means, but I will pass it along anyway. According to our surveillance, Ivan has made a change of equipment down in the Atlantic off Antigua. For the past few months, the 354-foot "Chukotaka", a Sibir class trawler has been running shotgun on our down range launches. Now, normally," Chukotaka" would be exchanged with the "Sibir", or "Levnskov", ships of her class. However, sometime within the past forty-eight hours, she has been replaced with a much smaller, Samara class research ship, the 190 foot "Kompas." Now, Kompas came out of Havana over a week ago, we saw her leave but lost her in the basin. "Chukotaka", is definitely heading home, but she will need a tanker on the way, so we are watching for more activity heading south in the next few days. It could be that the "Chukotaka" has mechanical or electrical malfunctions and needs to go home, or maybe due to lack of activity with NASA right now, they are getting bored and sending in juniors."

"Sir, is this "Kompas" equipped as well? Maybe she has been updated out of Havana with some new upgraded gear and.."

"No, Mr. O'Brien, it's not the equipment. I'm beginning to believe that maybe there is some truth about this Gorbachev fellow. He just may be pulling in his horns, cutting back on costs. At least that's the impression their new naval attaché has given us."

O'Brien smiled. "Well, whatever is going on, my friends, its good news, as long as they are down-grading, we can't complain. The less we have to deal with down there, the better for us."

Admiral Koster excused himself and left for his lunch meeting.

O'Brien, Avery and John Lind were taken by limo to the Air and Space Museum, where they killed two hours looking at exhibits and having lunch in the cafeteria. John Lind had never seen the Museum before, and had promised O'Brien and Avery that he would buy lunch, if they would go with him.

After lunch, they returned to O'Brien's office and worked until six that evening. John Lind's only objection was to his code name, "Grumpy." He even wanted to change the code name of his ship from "Red Sleigh", to "Red Star." O'Brien would not give in. He told Lind that he just looked like the character and it was easier to remember him that way. O'Brien also advised Lind that he should have all his VHF, UHF, single side band radios checked out, as well as his radar. Red Sleigh was going to be the center of communications during the operation. Commander Buckland was in the process of working with the Navy Intelligence people to decide on what communication systems would be used for the operation.

Andrews Air Force Base
Washington, D.C.
1840 hours

The sleek Gulfstream jet moved silently across the wet concrete surface, about one hundred feet behind the small yellow pick-up truck, flashing a sign "follow me".

While the turbines were spooling down, the passenger door opened and the small ladder extended down to the ground. A tall Navy Vice Admiral dressed in his blues, carrying only a brief case and raincoat stepped quickly into the waiting staff car.

"Evening, Charlie, how are you?"

"I was great, Bob, until yesterday when I got the call to come up tonight to meet the old man."

"Yeah, I know. I was just leaving for Puerto Rico and Roosevelt Roads to join up with Harry Gates and his crew. They are leaving tonight on "Hammerhead." This is Harry's final cruise. He hangs it up in two weeks, twenty seven years."

"Gates, yeah, we are going to miss him, the fleet's going to miss him. Did you know that he is our oldest Nuke driver?"

"Oh yes, he reminds me of that constantly. He just thought it would be fun to have me join him on the run home to Groton, for old times."

"Well, you can tell him that if it wasn't for the Chairman of the Joint Chiefs calling you to D.C. for dinner at his home, you would be there."

The gray Chevy staff car headed across the black Potomac River heading west. In forty-five minutes, Vice Admiral Charles Halprin, Commander of the United States Submarine Forces, and Rear Admiral Robert "Mac" McKinsey, Commander U.S. Forces, Caribbean, would be drinking martinis as the home of Admiral Thomas J. Koster.

Lantana Marina
Santiago de Cuba

Sunday, November 1st
0945 Hours

Fidel Castro stood on the aft deck of the 124-foot Feadship, known as UNICORN. He was uncomfortable with all the dirt, dust and junk accumulating in the main salon and on the once spotless teak decks. His attention was focused on Ernest Rivero, who was standing in the salon directing two workers on the cabin roof, lowering one of the large new doors that were being fitted to the saloon roof. Dimitri Sorokin stood next to him leaning on his crutches.

"It's a shame you had to destroy such beautiful workmanship to get those doors put in, Fidel."

"Yes, but we had no choice. We thought we could launch the Dolphin through the rear salon doors on rails, and hoist it to the water from there, but it could not be done. This way, we just use the portside davit on the cabin roof, open these new doors, pick the Dolphin up and swing it overboard. It will work beautifully. We had to remove a 21 foot speedboat from the cabin top so we could do this."

"Very clever. Now, tell me, how do you plan to explain the Unicorn's presence here in Santiago, especially now that you have the yacht guarded by your own special military police?"

Castro turned and looked at him. "I thought you might come up with a good explanation, my friend. I have no problem with my people, it is yours we must be concerned about."

Castro moved away from the deck rail and looked down the port side companionway. "Come, let's go forward to my stateroom and talk in private."

Castro offered his hand to Sorokin, as he moved the crutches in place under his arms. They walked along the narrow catwalk until they reached a door to the private state room forward of the salon. Castro opened the door and helped Sorokin struggle through the narrow doorway. Once inside, Castro pointed to a small sofa behind an oval coffee table. Sorokin made his way to the sofa, and sat down. Castro took the small desk chair and moved it over in front of the coffee table. He then went over to the desk and picked up an ashtray and set it on the table. Smiling, he raised his right arm around, sweeping it around the room.

"Not too bad for an old retired lawyer."

204

Sorokin looked around the spacious room. The walls were done in rich oiled oak, and trimmed in a glossy walnut. The forward bulkhead had two large built in televisions and two smaller ones. A complete set of instruments, knotmeter, tachometers, radio directional meters, radar screen and assorted compasses were all built in along with an intercom system, two tape decks, tuner and amplifier.

"I take it the previous owner liked electronics, or didn't he trust his crew. That is a monitoring system, isn't it?"

"I don't really know, my friend. I do know he is a Greek, and has a new yacht is nearly seventy feet longer than this one."

"I am a bit surprised there are few furnishings about..."

"I had everything removed when she came in. I had all the paintings, furniture, carpeting, crystal and silverware all removed. As you saw, we even removed all the beautiful wood paneling from the main salon and carefully covered the hardwood floors. I want to put this yacht back in pristine condition when our voyage is over."

"Without getting personal, did you purchase this yacht yourself? I would imagine a yacht of this caliber must be in the millions, no?"

"It was expensive, yes. Did I buy her?" Castro laughed. "No my friend, I don't have that kind of money. I have a friend who invests in me. This is nothing more than an instrument that will be returned to the Mediterranean and sold to regain the investment."

"You continue to surprise me, Fidel. Now, when do you meet with your investors, who are they and where does this demonstration take place?"

Castro leaned back in his chair and put his hands on his knees. "Christmas week, we meet on December 25th. I won't disclose who we will be meeting with yet and it's best you don't know, as it is they don't know I have confided in you, a KGB official. They are aware of the restrictions that have been put on my country by Gorbachev. Now, where do we meet? Yes, I can tell you that, I will even show you."

Castro stood up and went over to a roll top desk and unlocked the cover. He pushed the top up and picked up a rolled up chart. After removing the rubber bands, he rolled the chart out on the coffee table, holding one side down with the ashtray, and other with his hand.

Sorokin studied the chart of the Caribbean from south Florida to Venezuela. There was a large circle drawn around the lesser Antilles, that included Anguilla to the north and Grenada to the south. Another circle was drawn around the islands of Antigua, and Guadeloupe. Castro removed a mechanical pencil from his shirt pocket and put the point on a small cluster of islands just below Guadeloupe.

"It is not shown on this chart, but here in this small cluster of islands called Les Saintes, is a small uninhabited island with a small but well protected cove on its leeward side. That is where we will meet our guests."

"Now, about your guests. How do they get to this small isolated island?"

"The same way we do, my friend, by boat. Two yachts will be joining us. The yachts will leave their ports in mid December and work their way to various ports where they pick up their guests and join us. Of course, like us, they will be traveling incognito. For insurance, I will have one of my own special agents watching over us."

"Well, I am impressed, but I still feel that being on the open seas for all that time is a bit risky. You will be traveling over, what, fifteen hundred kilometers?"

"Eighteen hundred, my friend."

"How fast does this yacht travel?"

"Oh, top speed maybe sixteen to eighteen knots."

"So, we are talking a cruising speed of what, fifteen to sixteen knots, correct?"

Castro put his hand to his beard and started rubbing.

"Yes, I would say so."

"That means you will be on the open seas for nearly three days before you reach.."

"Seventy six hours is what we are planning. You are correct, it will be over three days, but it will be three days of relaxing in the sun, three days away from screaming ministers, Russian Army officers screaming about food shortages for their men."

"Too risky, my friend, I don't like it. What if something serious goes wrong on this yacht, like engine trouble, or bad weather and have to head for some island like maybe in the Virgin Islands, who knows?"

"Dimitri, you worry too much. Where is your sense of adventure? Trust me, we have thought of every possible problem we could run into, and have worked out a plan. We are not amateurs at this, Dimitri, we can have any kind of papers we may need, including passports. I will be changing my looks considerably." Castro put his hands to his face covering his wavy salt and pepper beard. "Picture this face without the beard and mustache." He removed his faded fatigue hat, and bowed his balding head. "Can you picture all this hair gone?"

Sorokin began to laugh.

"I will be a bald Mexican domestic working on this yacht, Comrade. I believe my name is Chino, second cook."

"O.k., Fidel, if you feel it is safe, I guess that's it. However, I think we should work out something, some kind of surveillance and an escape, just in case."

"Oh, but we are working on that, Dimitri. We will have surveillance set up through our own state airline service that will be flying over our route and checking on us daily. Should we have a serious problem, we will have two P-4 torpedo boats standing by to come to our aid."

"P-4's are fast, but with no range. I don't think they can reach you once you are over 500 kilometers out."

"They can and will, at least the two that are being modified as we speak over at Mariel."

"How did you?"

"I didn't. Aldo Santamaria has been screaming to have at least four long range P-4's so he could work beyond the Bahamas into the Atlantic. One of his engineers over at the Academy worked out the plans and they have been under construction since late September. They will have at least a twelve hundred kilometer range. No torpedoes, no missiles, just four pairs of fourteen millimeter guns."

"And I suppose you made a deal with Commodore Santamaria, that the new boats be stationed at Santiago?"

"Just until the new year. Of course, he knows nothing of the mission you understand? But if I call for these two boats to come to a rescue, they will be there. I will work out the explanations later."

"Well, Fidel, it looks like you have all your plans in order. Now all we can hope for is no leaks in the system. I will be able to cover you with my reports, just don't get caught down here, playing with this thing. I guess you could say, that you confiscated the yacht when you suspected it was running drugs within your boundaries offshore."

"You must read my report to Commodore Santamaria some day. That is exactly how we brought this yacht into port weeks ago. It was escorted in here and locked up. The crew has been, well, sort of deported. The yacht remains here under investigation by my intelligence people, indefinitely."

There was a soft knock on the cabin door.

"Yes, enter," Castro ordered.

A young officer stepped into the cabin. "Comrade President. The van is here to take you to the airport. General Vincetta wants you to contact him as soon as you arrive back at your headquarters in Havana."

"Tell the driver we will be right down."

"Yes, Comrade President." The officer closed the door.

"Well, Dimitri. It's time for us to go. This will be our last meeting here in Santiago, I see no need for you to return here. I just wanted you to see the yacht and fill you in on the final plan. Do you have any other questions at this time?"

"No, no questions."

Castor helped his friend to his feet and out of the cabin. When they arrived at the van, Sorokin laughed.

"Look at this, it must be, what, a 1959 or 60?"

"58, sir," the young driver said."

"Don't laugh, Comrade, we keep many of these old Volkswagen vans running, and we can still get parts. I would like to see your automotive geniuses in the Soviet Union come up with something better."

Castro smiled and opened the large side cargo door. "After you, Comrade."

Ministry of Defense Headquarters
Office of General Vincetta

Monday, November 2nd
0810 hours

"This is good, Acevedo, very good. Our President will be pleased.

General Vincetta dropped the report on his desk, stood up and walked over to a side table and poured a cup of coffee from a silver thermos. He turned and walked over to his second in command, General Acevedo Rogelio, who was sitting comfortably in a stuffed lounge chair. Rogelio was a trim taller than average Cuban in his late thirties. A very popular officer among his Division troops and among his fellow officers.

"Now that you have completely covered our asses by capturing the rebels who killed our comrades and have carried out their executions, what do you have to prove this to be fact."

Rogelio pulled out a manila envelope that was between his leg and the arm of the chair and handed it to Vincetta.

"This should take care of any inquisitive red-balls."

Vincetta opened the envelope and removed the contents. There were four large black and white photographs. The first one showed four men with sacks over their heads being tied to poles in front of a tiled wall. The next photo showed the men in various positions as the rounds were entering their bodies. The next photo showed the execution team examining the bodies.

The fourth photo showed the four bodies being prepared for cremation in a large ditch.

"Yes, this will do. You had no problem getting volunteers I take it?"

"These men were already condemned, comrade General. We just accelerated their judgment day. You might note that the wall in the background of the first photograph is the wall of the market place in the square at Las Palacios. We first thought of using the small cemetery at the church, but the locals would have surely given us some grief, so we used the square. We had a good audience, and there were many words of wisdom given to the people of Las Palacios, regarding any dealings with any rebels in the area. We buried them in the square."

"Nice touch. The Soviets will appreciate that, I'm sure. But tell me, did they not cry out to the crowds that they were innocent of these charges?

"General, they were told before they left the prison, that if any of them opened their mouth unless they were praying, their families would be terminated."

"Excellent, the President will be pleased with your performance, General. Now, we must work on the President's travel companions. I have a list that he gave me of the few crewmen he wants on board. What we have to find is technical people to work as crew."

"Excuse me, General. I am not aware of the President's intentions. He only told me he was leaving the country for a short time, sometime around the Christmas celebration."

Vincetta moved back around the desk to his chair and sat down.

"Of course, I almost forgot. You have not been briefed on Operation Dolphin."

"No, I have not. What is Operation Dolphin?"

"General, our President has borrowed, for the lack of a better description, a luxury yacht and will be taking a cruise over to the lesser Antilles. The objective is to meet with some very important businessmen from other countries. This meeting could never take place anywhere in this country without causing serious problems with the Soviets. It was decided to put together this meeting at a specific location near a small uninhabited island. This area is frequently visited by luxury yachts of all kinds, from all over the world. You see, our guests will also be arriving on other yachts from various ports throughout the islands."

"How long is this meeting to be, Comrade General?"

"That depends. We are planning on just one night at the island, no more, if weather cooperates."

"This sounds very dangerous, Comrade, very dangerous. If this trip begins in Cuba, that means the President will be on the open seas for days."

"Yes. Six, maybe even eight days, depending on weather and any mechanical problems that may come up."

"How are we protecting the President? Are we sending an escort of some kind?"

"No, no escorts. We may have some surveillance worked out to keep an eye on us during the day, that is all. We don't want to attract any attention. This is simply a luxury yacht sailing around the islands.

"How much more innocent does a capitalist need to look?"

General Rogelio sat motionless, staring at his superior. He was having difficulty putting the picture together in his mind.

"Relax, General. We have it all worked out. Our toughest problems now are putting the right people together for the mission. We have been doing well working around the backsides of our Russian friends. Dimitri Sorokin, however, is aware of the project and may even be aboard. So far, the KGB in Moscow is not planning to send any replacements for Kotov and Petrov."

"Tell me, General, did Kotov and Petrov somehow learn of this operation? Is that why..."

"Let's just say, they were in the wrong place at the wrong time. I don't expect to hear any more on that subject from you, do you understand, General?"

"Yes, sir."

"Now, so you understand our movements for the next few weeks, the luxury yacht we will be on is presently in Santiago, at the Lantana Ship Yard. It is hidden in one of their large hangars guarded by secret police. It was brought in under suspicion of drug running by two of our patrol boats two weeks ago. This was all pre-arranged of course. The yacht, called Unicorn, is being modified for the trip as we speak. Only a few, and I mean a few selected officers and enlisted men are involved in the plan. We hope to have the yacht leaving on the evening of December 21st. She will be escorted out of the harbor and released to its original owner, that is, as far as the Russians are concerned. I will be traveling with the President. You will take command here in my place. Officially, the President, myself and some friends are going to be in seclusion for that week in the eastern province mountains from where we started our revolution."

"I see, it's like a small reunion of some kind, is that what you plan to release to the country?"

"Yes, it would be something like that. Now, my friend, let's continue. I received this file from Commodore Santamaria's office, at your request, last Friday. He has submitted two officers for review. Of course, he has called every hour to find out what we need them for. You have not told him anything, correct?"

Rogelio smiled and responded. "Nothing, sir, I told him nothing."

"Good. Personally, I like this young captain." Vincetta handed Rogelio a large card with a photograph and personal history of Captain Carlos De la Torre. Age 31. Twelve year veteran in the Cuban Navy, presently commanding a Komar Missile Patrol Squadron out of Punta Ballentos.

"Yes, he looks good. He is single, well educated, attended two Soviet schools on diesel engines, a graduate of the Soviet Fleet Tactical Warfare Institute. I would say this is your man, General. How are his politics?"

"He could be Fidel's oldest son."

The two officers laughed.

"Our President wants you to take charge of this recruiting program, General. You will make all the arrangements to have this Captain De la Torre brought in and screened. Once you are satisfied that he is our man and that he can be trusted, we will then have him meet with our President, who will explain the mission, and the consequences of failure."

"What about the rest of this crew we will need?"

"I recommend that we let the captain pick his crew. He will know what he will need for the yacht, and the caliber of man we seek."

"What about Commodore Santamaria? What do I tell him? He hates my guts you know."

"I will handle the Commodore, General."

"Oh, before I forget, there is one more item, as soon as I can find it here." Vincetta rummaged through the hundreds of papers piled on his desk until he found the folder he was looking for.

"Here, this needs attention right away. This pilot, Carlos Lucia? He is an old personal friend of mine and of the President. Evidently, he has had some problems with old man Sanjenis over at Cubana Airlines. The President wants to have him transferred into the military, preferably the Air arm. Get him papers and give him the rank of Captain or Major, what ever it takes to get him equal pay, understand? Call General Ramon Blenco, Commander Airlift Services, at San Antonio de los Banos. Tell him Lucia will be on special assignment to the President for special duties in fixed wing aircraft. I have no idea what type aircraft he is currently checked out in, so he may need to have some training. The President wants to go back to using his old Convair, so be sure Lucia gets checked out. You may want to do this out fast, as the President will be using the Convair on his more frequent trips into Santiago. The Convair is unmarked, and not many know of its existence."

"I remember this man, Carlos Lucia. He flew much of the supplies for us during the early days of the war. I had no idea he was a civilian pilot. I see here that he is related to our friend, Colonel Navarro. How could I be so stupid. I went to his wedding."

"Well, comrade, he must be very special to our President, so don't fuck around with him. You may want to advise General Blenco the same."

"Is that all, sir?"

"General, I would say that is enough for one day."

General Rogelio stood up, snapped a formal salute and left Vincetta's office.

Vincetta picked up his phone and pushed the top button of his call box.

"General Rogelio just left, comrade President. He will do just fine. Oh, I have begun the proceedings on your pilot friend, Carlos Lucia. I also advised General Blenco that Carlos is to be updated on the Convair and any other non-jet, fixed wing aircraft we are using for official use, correct? Yes, Rogelio did a great job. I have the photographs right here, would you like to see them? Fine, I will bring them over. Is Comrade Sorokin with you? Good, I shall be there in fifteen minutes."

CHAPTER 13

Ft. Myers Shipbuilders Company
Ft. Myers, Florida

Thursday, November 5th
0430 hours

The last of the noisy engines that ran the two monster cranes were shut down, and a welcome peace came over the marina. Only the voices of the work crews could be heard as they carried out the final tasks around the Island Drummer, floating motionless in her new berth in the brackish waters of the Caloosahatchee River, five hours and ten minutes after she was moved from the hangar in Immokalee.

Even without her masts and rigging, the Island Drummer, all seventy five feet of her looked majestic floating in the marina's launching slip, which barely gave her room to breath. On her decks the work crews struggled to release the large lifting rings attached to the wide belts still wrapped around her enormous hull. High above her deck, two large crane booms stood guard with their lifting hooks dangling on the ends of heavy cables. They swayed slightly, patiently waiting in case they were needed to lift the 83,500-pound yacht back out of the water, and return to her to the custom cradle on the flatbed trailer.

Down in the Drummer's dark bilge, Jack Courtney, Larry Keene, Phil Avery and Ted Collins moved cautiously over the huge stringers in the engine room and carefully over the open hatches throughout the cabins with flashlights as they studied hull fittings, gate valves, exhaust systems and most important, the new fiberglass patch work. Their flashlight beams crisscrossed back and forth as they called out their findings. Finally, someone topside yelled down that the portable dockside generator was on line and the yacht should be hot. Ted Collins went to the master electrical panel at the navigation station and threw the circuit breakers on for the ll0 volt system. He turned the selector switch to the shore power position and the interior of the hull was illuminated with numerous work lights that had been installed at the hangar.

"So far so good," Collins said to Jack Courtney.

"Yeah, so far, Phil just went topside to check on how she is sitting on the old water line. So far all the new glass work looks good." Courtney responded.

"We'll know more after we get the engines cranked up and vibrating. How much time before we head out, Ted?"

"Couple of hours. Putting fuel on now, we planned to give her about 100 gallons in the main tank, that should give us enough fuel for a good sea trial."

"O.K. Ted, I'm satisfied with everything down here, let's get topside and cut those two cranes loose." Courtney moved over to the staircase in the main salon and looked up at the companionway. "Mr. O'Brien?" He called.

"Yo, back here, Jack." O'Brien's voice came from the aft stateroom area.

"Dan, we are going topside to cut the crane folks loose. Do you have any objection?"

"No, if you and Ted are happy, Jack, let them go. Tell that tractor driver he did one hell of a job."

"Gotcha," Courtney replied and started up the staircase followed by Collins.

0743

The sun began to break through the overcast in the eastern sky, as the small crew sat around the large center cockpit. Larry Keene was standing at the helm, waiting on word from Ted Collins who was below at the navigation station.

"You should have power now, Larry," came the order from below.

Keene flipped two switches on the instrument panel and the console in front of him lit up.

"O.K. Ted, we are hot up here," Keene yelled. He moved his hand down to two keys in the panel. He tightened his fingers on the right key and turned it.

"Here goes," he said quietly.

From deep in the bowels of the ship came the high pitched scream of a starter motor. The big modified GM V-8 came to life exploding loud reports into the mammoth exhaust manifolds and out through the big rubber hinged flaps on the end of the exhaust pipes exiting through the transom. Keene did not have to wait for the instruments to tell him that the engine was running, the exhaust noise some thirty feet behind him, was proof enough. He ran the RPM's up to the 1000 mark while watching the oil pressure and exhaust temperatures on the two manifolds, then started the other engine. He asked Avery to look at the exhaust pipes and see if water was running out.

Avery reported it was. Meanwhile below, Ted Collins was climbing all over the two huge engines with his flashlight looking for trouble. He found none. All connections, manifold seals, hull intakes and gate valves were dry.

It was decided that they would secure the Drummer and get some breakfast before the sea trials. They all piled into Courtney's Mazda, all but Larry Keene, who wanted to pull the oil filters, and drove off to the Holiday Inn a few blocks away.

Collins, Courtney, O'Brien and Phil Avery were walking through the lobby of the Holiday Inn towards the dining room when O'Brien spotted the public pay phones on the wall. He went over and made one call.

Thirty-five minutes later, a message was handed to Admiral Thomas Koster as he waited outside the Oval office with the Vice President. Koster read the note and chuckled. "Well, looks like the damn thing floats."

The Vice President, looking very concerned asked. "Just what damn thing are you talking about, Tom?"

"The Island Drummer, sir. They just splashed her this morning in Ft. Myers, and she's actually floating."

"Well, are you happily surprised, Admiral, or just shocked?"

"Oh, no sir, I'm very pleased. I had no doubts that what ever they were doing down there to that yacht would work, yes, I knew they could do it."

"Bullshit, Koster," the Vice President laughed. "I don't think you ever thought any part of this operation would really work, am I right?"

"Well, I have to admit, a few times, in the beginning, I was ready to wash the whole thing down the crapper, but that Irishman, Dan O'Brien, he just keeps pulling rabbits out of the hat. He has managed to put quite a team together and I really feel they have a chance, that's if all goes well in the next few days with the tests and sea trials."

"Good, keep me informed. Oh, the President just might ask about the Yuletide Operation at this morning's meeting. You might want to be prepared."

"Yes, sir."

Aboard the Island Drummer
1045 hours

The four men back on the Drummer planed their test run. Suddenly, Avery jumped up. "Courtney, give me your car keys, I need to run an errand."

Jack threw the keys to Phil Avery and he jumped off the Drummer yelling he would be back in fifteen minutes. Thirty minutes later, he returned to find four very stressed out men waiting. Avery had both arms full of grocery bags and called for help. Courtney finally went to give him a hand. Avery went back to the car and came back with a case of Budweiser beer.

"Cast off," Ted Collins commanded.

Jack Courtney was on the bow and threw his two lines on the seawall. Avery cleared the port lines and Larry Keene released the starboard. Collins moved the two clutch levers back and advanced the throttles, the Drummer began to move out of the concrete vault into the murky brown waters of the river. As soon as she was clear of the last dock, Collins spun the wheel hard to port, but there was no response from the Drummer, she held course. Avery reached up and pulled the port engine clutch into neutral, and the large vessel responded. Her broad bow began to swing to starboard.

"Shit, I forgot, we got twins, we don't need this damn wheel."

Collins spun the helm back to starboard, while he engaged the port engine along with the starboard and headed towards the channel markers that would take them down river into the Gulf Of Mexico.

For the next two hours, the Drummer headed out into the Gulf into northeast winds and a three-foot chop. Collins remained at the helm and on Keene's advice did not exceed 2000 RPM on the engines. The Drummer was doing a comfortable hull speed of ten knots. Meanwhile, the crew took turns going down and inspecting everything to make sure there were no problems lurking.

"O.K., Ted, let's see what she's got." Keene yelled as he headed down the companionway on his way to monitor the engines. "Keep them about 3500, no more for now, and bring them up slow."

Collins took one look around the horizon to make sure there were no other boats around. His attention went to the instrument panel, where he watched the tachometers as he advanced the throttles. The Drummer moaned and began to dig herself down in the stern. He put both throttles on the stops, but nothing was happening.

"She's cavitating like hell," Keene screamed from below.

"Put the struts down, move the shafts out."

Collins reached under the cockpit table attached to the console and found the two levers and advanced them forward. He could feel the Drummer straining so he pulled back the throttles until the shafts were extended, then advanced them slowly forward again. The Drummer responded and he could feel the difference as the big brass props began biting into the deep blue water. The bow started to plow as the stern rose, because of the new angle of the shafts and props. Collins pulled the shaft levers slowly aft while advancing the throttles. The Drummer was picking up speed, and the bow was beginning to rise again. The hydraulic struts were working. He brought the shaft levers all the way back while increasing more throttle. The hydraulic struts were trimmed as were the two throttles until the Drummer was on a plane. The Drummer was gaining speed as the throttles were moved up to 3500 RPM's. Collins studied the sensitive instruments, then called out. "We have to be doing at least twenty, maybe twenty five, guys." The Drummer plowed through the rough chop like an ocean-going tug.

Avery was standing next to Collins watching the instruments. Without a word, Collins stepped back and let Avery move in and take over the helm. He immediately turned into the wind and the increasing heavier seas. O'Brien sat quietly behind Avery and Collins enjoying the fresh salt air and the occasional spray that came up from the bows and covered the deck.

"She's going to do it," Collins yelled in Avery's ear. "I'm going down below with Keene, hold her on this these settings, but keep an eye on that port temperature, it appears to be climbing."

Avery turned around and looked into O'Brien's smiling Irish face. He put out his right fist and raised the thumb. Avery shook his head, smiled and returned his attention to the open seas ahead of him.

Larry Keene appeared in the companionway smiling. He stepped up into the cockpit and joined Avery. "O.K., it's my turn, pappy."

Avery gave him the helm and he moved the throttles forward, ever so slowly. The big exhausts were bellowing from the stern leaving a white vapor trail behind as the steaming hot water from the manifolds met the cool waters of the Gulf.

Ted Collins came up on deck, and the three men stood shoulder to shoulder at the helm, watching the RPM's move up past the 4500 marks. Three pairs of eyes straining, watching the small sensitive needles that were telling them the engines were doing their thing, and doing it right.

Phil got Keene's attention and pointed to a vessel just off the port bow about three miles out. Keene started to move the helm to starboard. The Drummer was tracking like a powerboat. He kept increasing the turn until he could hear cavitation building up on the starboard prop, so he decreased the RPM's on the starboard engine, putting all the thrust on the port. He increased the turn and was delighted to find the Drummer was not skidding, but almost banking in the hard turn. When he had come one hundred and eighty degrees in the turn, he advanced the starboard engine again, released the wheel and the Drummer recovered beautifully.

217

"Damn, they said it couldn't be done," Ted yelled.

Keene gave the helm to Collins and went back and sat down with O'Brien. "We got it Dan, she's going to do it. I estimate that at 4500 RPM's we are getting maybe twenty to twenty two knots, at least, and we can go to 5500 anytime when needed, it's there, man."

The Drummer continued at standard speed towards the sea buoy that marked the entrance to the river. With all the excitement going on, nobody paid much attention to the gathering skies overhead, which were getting darker and lower. It wasn't until they found the first channel marker that they realized it would be dark before they get back. Keene increased the hull speed slightly, as Collins started to look for landmarks.

1550 hours

"Hey, Phil, you have been through this pass a few times, what should we be looking for? I can barely make out landfall on the south shoreline."

Phil was not in the cockpit.

"Where the hell did he disappear to, now?" Collins yelled out, but was interrupted as Avery appeared in the companionway,.

"Hey, somebody grab these." Avery held out three bottles of champagne. O'Brien went to the rescue. The sounds of exploding bottles began to drowned out the exhaust noise, as the bottles were passed around. Next came a few bottles of assorted, not so premium, wines, then the warm beer, along with black overcast skies and a light shower.

"Jesus, Phil, you couldn't spring for a bag of ice, this stuff tastes like shit, it's warm," Keene growled.

"Hey, how many bridges have we gone under?" Collins asked.

"I don't know, you're the captain, haven't you been counting?"

"Nope, but here comes a big mother..."

"That's the Interstate, I think we went too far, we've got to go back, man." Avery looked at the shoreline on the south side of the river. "There, over there, see? There's the Holiday Inn, see it, Ted?"

"Nope."

"Shit, give me the wheel." Avery moved Ted away from the wheel, and began to turn hard to starboard.

"Shit, it's really getting dark, keep your eyes out for any markers, I'm going to head closer to that shoreline ahead where all the lights are, that's the Holiday Inn, I think, and we have to go west of there."

Keene was sitting looking up at the dark overcast sky. "You know, we're all fucking nuts. Here we are, on the most important yacht built since the ark, we are all shitfaced, soaked to the balls, we have no anchors, no charts, no lines or life jackets, not even a hand held radio, it's getting very dark, and I have to take a dump."

"You're right, Larry, we are nuts, and if anything happens to this yacht, I couldn't get a job with the Jersey City post office," O'Brien said laughing.

"There are two heads forward, Larry, just don't use the one in the port cabin, it's a fake, and don't forget to flush," Avery said.

"Hey, Larry, while you're down there, wake up mad Jack. We may need him up here to help find the marina."

Keene stopped at the companionway, turned and addressed his companions. "The heads? I don't think they are hooked up, and I don't think they work, and know what? I don't think there's any paper down there. Do you guys have some paper?"

"Damn, Larry, weren't you a boy scout? Use some of those paper bags I brought the booze in."

"Hey, Collins, do the heads work on this barge?"

"I dunno, they used to. Why don't you just go over the side, Larry?"

"Gotta take a dump."

"Oh, well, then do it.. if the head doesn't work, it doesn't work. You can clean up later, right?"

Keene staggered, then holding on for dear life, worked his way down the companionway to the main salon, then forward to the head in the port stateroom.

"Whatwazdat?" Avery yelled out.

A beam of light flashed passed the heads of the three crewman, then came back.

"Over there," Collins yelled, pointing aft towards the starboard stern. "What's going on out there, Phil?"

The red and green bow lights of the twenty-five foot Wellcraft powerboat were just off the starboard stern. O'Brien tried to stand up and hold on to the rear of the lounge seat in the cockpit.

"It looks like two guys in slickers, whoa, lookie here," O'Brien yelled as the beam from the spotlight hit Phil Avery in the back of the head. He tried to look back, but the light was too strong. Then the other lights came on. Blue flashing ones, then came the electronic squawking voice from the hailer.

"What the hell are they yelling at?" Avery screamed."

"Us, you flaming asshole. I got a feeling we have trouble, guys, they are the DEA, I just feel it." Collins tried to whisper to O'Brien as they fought to hold on to each other.

"Phil, stop the engines," Collins yelled out.

Avery responded. He pulled off both clutches to neutral, and the two engines started to wind up and began screaming. Avery reached for the throttles and pulled them back. "Shit, that was real smart," he thought to himself. "Never do that again, never."

Nobody on deck heard the crashing sound that came from the forward quarters when the Drummer reduced its speed and came almost to a dead stop. Larry Keene slid off the hardwood toilet seat, and fell between the bulkhead and the head. He found himself tightly wedged, sitting on the teak grate that covered the shower pan. It took a few seconds to realize that he was really stuck fast. His knees were under his chin, and the teak toilet seat was stuck between his shoulder blades. His pants and briefs were around his ankles. He probed around the floor, then reached for the cabin door handle. He had locked the door and couldn't locate the release. He also discovered that he smelled awful. It was dark, it was smelly and he started to panic. He began screaming to the top of his lungs, but he was no competition for the twin 454 engines that were idling fifty feet behind him. Without floorboards, bulkhead doors, or engine soundproofing installed, they drowned out his cries.

Ft. Myers Shipbuilders Marina
2135 hours

"Well, that was an interesting experience. Now, how do you explain this to the old man, O'Brien?" Collins held the crumpled and rain soaked citation inches from O'Brien's nose.

"Hell, I can fix that thing, not to worry, Teddy boy."

From down below in the cabin, Avery was calling. "Hey guys, I need some help down here. Larry won't come out of the head."

Avery began banging on the small varnished door that opened into the head were Larry Keene was stuck, yelling at him to unlock the door, but all Keene would do was yell that he was ready to end his young life.

The sound of the Sheriff's patrol boat's twin outboards, disappeared into the night.

"Hey, those two guys were not that bad, Ted. They got us back here, right? You were trying to motor us up to fucking Jacksonville."

"Oh yeah, right, Mr. Diplomat. Just when those deputies were getting pleasant and understanding, and buying my story on how we were just celebrating my new yacht, you go and have to refer to them as "uniformed mermaids", that really went over, Dan, that's why we got this $500.00 citation. Man, they got us for everything except sales taxes and a towing charge."

"I think that you should pay the fine, it's still legally your yacht, even though you couldn't prove it to those mermaids just now. I'd say, this is your problem, not Yuletide's, not the U.S. of A, or Avery's Shipbuilding place. Now, if you two will excuse me, I will go down and help pry lard-ass out of the toilet." O'Brien went to the companionway, slipped, and slid down the teak steps bouncing on his tailbone to the floor, where he sat in total disbelief. Collins looked down at him from the companionway.

"Head." Collins yelled out.

"What?" O'Brien responded.

"Head, it's the head, not the toilet."

"O.k., so why don't you get down here and help me get Larry's head out of the toilet, so we can all go over to the Holiday Inn for a drink and something to eat, I'm starved, o.k.?" O'Brien shouted as he began to lift himself from the floor. "You got it, pard," Collins yelled, as he threw his arm over Courtney's shoulders. "We're coming, Larry," he yelled. "Don't break anything, buddy."

Holiday Inn restaurant
2215 hours

O'Brien threw two keys attached to little green plastic cards on the table. "Here, I got us a couple of rooms, go get yourselves cleaned up, I bought some toothpaste out of a vending machine, you will have to use your fingers." He threw the small tube of Crest on the table.

Collins stood up from the table and picked up one of the keys. "You're a real sport, O'Brien. I ordered you a VO and soda. Are you coming, Phil?"

"Naw, I'm alright, just hurry, I'm starving. I need some food in me, fast."

O'Brien sat down and looked around the small dining room. "Good thing it's a quiet night, I don't think they really wanted us to come in here."

"You got that right, man. When you left to get the rooms, that bitch of a hostess asked us if we had been in some kind of accident."

O'Brien laughed. "Well, you both look a little shipwrecked, and you do smell a little rank."

Avery started to laugh. " Can you imagine what she would have said if we dragged Keene in here? Man, you talk about smelling bad, that son of a bitch should have jumped overboard. He had that stuff in his hair."

"Yeah, so what does he do? He gives old Courtney some static, talks him into letting him sit in his car, then orders him to take him to his apartment. Courtney will have to burn that Mazda after tonight." They began laughing out loud.

"Gentlemen, please. Do you mind? We do have decent customers in here. If you have to laugh so loud, why not go into the lounge?"

The tall thin hostess was leaning over the table addressing the two men in almost a whisper.

"We already tried that, lady, they threw us out. They told us we smelled funny and belong in here, with you." O'Brien said, looking into the hostess's thick glasses.

At this point, Avery and O'Brien went into hysterics. O'Brien could not speak and was wiping his eyes with the tablecloth. Avery was doubled up on his side in the lounge seat. The hostess walked off.

"Hey, what's going on guys, what's so damn funny?"

O'Brien and Avery looked up into the shining moon-shaped face of Larry Keene. He was dressed in a fresh cotton plaid shirt, Levis and boat shoes, and smelling like a cosmetic counter. Avery looked at O'Brien and both collapsed in laughter.

After dinner, Keen made a suggestion. "Hey, when I passed the lounge, there was a sign on the door that read it was "Ladies Night, all drinks 50% off."

Phil looked at Ted, Ted looked at Dan and they all looked at Larry.

"So, I thought maybe we would go in and see what kind of fillies frequent the establishment."

"Oh, sure Mr. Hollywood, you went home, showered, shaved, changed underwear and threw on some cologne, and now you're ready to jump on some sweet old lady's bones, right?"

"Well, you should have said something, Dan. I would have brought some stuff back with me. Hell, you guys don't look that bad, besides, it's the Holiday Inn, not the Stork Club. How fussy could these broads be, right?"

"Yeah guys, let's go in with Larry. Hell, we can tell the chicks about Larry's love for teak seats and toilets, and that he has this giant sailboat down the street and will take us all out for a cruise later, but first we have to have the fire department come down and wash out the forward head."

"Very funny, Mr. Collins, very funny."

"Hey, Larry. You weren't really serious about killing yourself in there were you?"

"Cheap shot, Mr. Avery."

"Come to think about it, what happened to Jack? Why didn't he come back with you tonight?"

"He, ah, wanted to go back to the manger and get some, stuff."

"Stuff? You mean air-wick and Spic and Span. That car should be trashed, classed twenty-six, deep-sixed."

The table roared again in laughter. Larry Keene, joined in, he had no choice.

Lantana Marina
Santiago de Cuba, Cuba
Friday, November 6th
1630 hours

The aging unmarked twin engine Convair 440 landed hard on the short runway east of the city of Santiago de Cuba. It taxied to the north end of the field, well out of view of any spectators, where it lowered the back stairs. Four figures, three in army fatigues, disembarked and stepped into the waiting Volkswagen van, which began to move immediately towards a service gate on the airport's perimeter road.

With its engines still running, the stairs were retracted and the plane taxied to the end of the runway and took-off. It would fly north-north-east only a short distance over the mountains and land at Baracoa at a small military base and wait for word to return.

Thirty minutes later, the rusting unmarked gray van arrived at the gate of Lantana Marine, where it was checked by a guard and allowed through.

"Mr. Lo, buenos dias," Fidel said as he approached the small oriental man.

Lo bowed gracefully. His salt and pepper hair was thin and long, giving him the appearance of a much older man.

"You know General Vincetta, but you have not met one of my oldest friends, Juan Luis Cantillo, or Captain Carmen Amador."

Lo bowed again.

"Juan Luis is from the University, he is a professor of physics and a master of electronics. He served with me during the revolution, and he was born in this great city. Captain Amador is also a highly skilled

223

communication expert and electronics genius. He is second in command of our entire military air defense radar network. These are the two men who will be responsible for the electronic installations and the training of the Dolphin's communication and electrical engineers."

"Yes. If you will follow me, please." Lo led the party over to the small sub, fully covered under heavy canvas. He had a workbench nearby that was also covered with a light burlap cloth. He removed the cloth and unveiled a number of black and gray metal boxes, a large instrument panel and some cardboard boxes and coiled wires. A small red plastic toolbox was open, filled with a variety of small hand tools. Four metal folding chairs were neatly lined up in front of the table. Lo invited his students to be seated.

He reached into a cardboard box and brought up a black teardrop shaped device, with a brass threaded pipe attached.

"Do any of you recognize this?" Lo asked.

"Yes, I do. That is a transducer, is it not?" the young captain asked.

"Correct, Captain. And what are most of these devices used for?"

"Well, to the best to my knowledge, all they do is transmit and receive low frequency sound waves to measure water depth or locate matter, like sunken vessels, schools of fish."

"Correct, Captain." Lo picked up a large black box from the table and held it in front of him. "This transmitter and receiver is like a radio. The transducer is the antenna."

"This device is the key to the communications operation of the submersible resting behind me, better known now as your "Dolphin." It is through this device that the Dolphin will be located beneath the sea, then given commands on what to do. What we have done is to design a simple but reliable propulsion system that is commanded by a small on-board computer, powered by a bank of batteries. The system is energized by electronic impulse signals, similar to the Morse code." Lo picked up a board that was under the table and held it in front of him. On the board was a cut-a-way drawing of the Dolphin's propulsion system, which showed the jet pump and the small electric motor that drove it. A number of boxes with numbers were also displayed connected by numbered lines. A small boat was shown sitting on the top of a water line. A diagram, with another box inside it and the transducer was displayed next to the boat. Zig-zag lines led from the small boat to the other boxes, indicating sound waves.

"What we have driving the small sub is a five-horse electric motor, water proofed and sealed in a stainless steel housing. This small shaft connects to the fiberglass worm gear, or propellers that draw the water in from this intake, push it through this venturi and out the exhaust. Down here, above the keel of the Dolphin is the sixteen twelve volt batteries that run the motor, operate various solenoids and valves. Up here, in the sail compartment of the Dolphin is where all the brains to the electrical system are located. Radio receivers, computers, control surface servo motors, antennas and last but not least, the firing detonator that will, on command, totally destroy the Dolphin and anything within twenty feet around it."

Lo reached down and picked up another board with more drawings on it. It showed a large ship off shore of a land mass. A cove, or bay was drawn in. A smaller boat was in the bay.

"Let me show you how the Dolphin will be used. Here, this large boat is the mother ship. The mother ship carries the Dolphin from its source and takes it to a pre-arranged launching point. The Dolphin has already been programmed with its destination, speed and depth. As soon as the Dolphin is launched, the technician on the mothership will transmit a signal to the Dolphin to start the motor and take it away from the ship. The next order the technician will give is to slowly dive the Dolphin to a preset depth, at a given heading and location. When the depth is reached, the motor shuts down. This small gatevalve, forward of the engine intake will open and the ballast tubes will fill with water and the Dolphin settles on the bottom. Are there any questions so far?"

"Go ahead, we will ask later." Amador said.

"Thank you, sir."

"Over here, we have our pick-up boat. He leaves his dock and runs out of the harbor, let's say three miles out. He has on board the standard electronics that most boats or ships would have. One thing for sure, he will have a depth sounder or depth recorder." Lo reached over and picked up one of the large black boxes that was on the table and turned it around. He laid the transducer next to it. "This is a depth sounder. A few days ago, with a little help from General Vincetta, my wife and I flew to Caracas to find a marine store. I purchased this depth sounder for a reasonable price, and brought it back. I am sorry, President Castro, I could not find one here in Santiago, or in Havana. This one, although is labeled by American company, was actually made in Japan."

Castro and his companions laughed.

"Now, we have the small boat cruising out to a designated location, and when the rendezvous position is reached, the boat turns on their depth sounder and starts transmitting the coded order to the Dolphin, down below. Now, how we do this is simple. We have to modify the depth sounder. All we are going to do is to install a small doorbell type button on the side of the

225

unit. We splice, or break into the signal wire that goes to the transducer. Instead of a steady signal going out of the transducer, we have a signal that is being sent in a code simply by pushing the button. Down below in the Dolphin's sail, a receiver is waiting to pick up this code. When it does, the electric motor will start. The valve that opened for the ballast tubes is now closed by the flow of water now being drawn through the intake. Another valve, here at the venturi chamber, is now opened by the water suction in the chamber, and the ballast tubes are emptied. Two valves here in the sub's floor will also open automatically as the water level decreases in the tubes, and lets in air pressure from the hull. When the Dolphin begins to rise, this small device, which looks like a small skid located under the keel, signals the computer that the Dolphin is clear and ready to take commands. You see, this retractable skid is actually a safety switch. When the Dolphin reaches the bottom, this skid retracts into the hull, breaks the circuit to the motor and the control surfaces, but leaves power to the receiving components, the radios and computers. When the signal code is received from the pick-up boat, the motor circuit is completed through another circuit, by-passing the skid. As the Dolphin once again begins to rise and move, the spring-loaded skid returns to its regular position, which closes the circuit to the control surfaces. One other thing now takes place. When the Dolphin is clear and operational, a signal is sent out by the Dolphin's computer transmitter and received by the pick-up boat's transducer. It works visually on the recorder's scope, with a identification pinging sound on the speaker. This will last for 60 seconds and tells the technician in the pick-up boat that he now has control of the Dolphin. In a coded sequence, he can give the orders for speed, depth and direction. One of the best options we offer is that the Dolphin can be put directly under the pick-up boat and guided anywhere, providing there is enough water beneath to operate."

Fidel Castro walked up and stood beside Lo.

"My friends, is this is not the work of a genius? Just think of what this device can deliver. Think of how it will undermine our enemies. Think of this for a minute, the Dolphin can be sailed up any river, enter any bay in the United States. It can be set down anywhere. It will surface, be unloaded and sent back the way it came. It will revolutionize the drug industry's means of delivery. No more loss of expensive airplanes, boats, talented pilots or boat drivers. Just one small investment that can last for years, and we are the only ones who can provide it. Mr. Lo says we can carry a five hundred pound load for a medium range."

"Yes, Comrade President, but how are we going to educate the buyers on how to run these machines, they seem very complicated, don't they?"

"Captain, you find this complicated?"

"Well, yes if I was not an educated man, Comrade President."

"I disagree with you, Captain." Fidel Castro walked around the table. "Comrade Lo has worked hard on this project. He has tested the Dolphin thoroughly, and has designed it so it would not be easily detected. From the air, as you can see, would look like a common whale. He has made it impossible to trace back to anyone or any country. Anyone who does not know what he is dealing with and happens across our Dolphins, won't live to turn the second screw to find out what he has found."

General Vincetta, Juan Luis and Captain Amador could tell by Castro's voice that this was not a time to challenge him or the Chinese creator of the Dolphin.

"Comrade Lo. How many days, or hours can the Dolphin be used? I mean how long will it run on those batteries?"

"The battery system, as it is now, at full charge will run the Dolphin at full speed, which we estimate submerged to be between eight and ten knots, for a period of seven to eight hours."

"Fantastic, Comrade Lo. That should be plenty of time if the distances between the mother ship and the pick-up boats are not too far apart."

"Exactly, General. We also have a reserve built into the system to insure that there will never be a total loss of electrical power. There will always be an emergency reserve to raise the Dolphin, providing the surface rescue is done within thirty days."

"Captain, you are concerned about the technicians who will be setting the radios and codes, right? Is that what you are concerned about?"

"Ah, yes, and of course the crews that are handling the Dolphins on the mother ships. They are very fragile, considering their electronics and gyro guidance systems, and I understand they are going to be built of a very new thin fiberglass material?"

"Captain, these are not your problems. The new materials that will be used to build the Dolphin are stronger fiberglass composites. They are going to be somewhat fragile and will need to he handled with some care. They are also very expensive to replace. I might remind you, gentleman, we are in the replacement business, yes?" Castro said in a slight grin.

"Yes, comrade President."

"Juan Luis, you have no questions for Comrade Lo?"

"No, I have no questions."

"Captain Amador?"

"No sir, I have no more questions."

"Good. Comrade Lo, Captain Amador will stay with you to learn about the Dolphin's systems so he can draw up the new plans and specifications. There won't be a living soul, who will know more about this device then you, Captain, when Lo is finished teaching you. It will be your duty to draw up all the plans and prepare to go into production when we are ready. You see that large crate over there, Captain? Those are the molds for the Dolphin, that could easily be our new financial future, think about that."

Castro turned to his companions. "I think that it is time for us to leave."

Castro pulled a cigar from his vest pocket and put it in his mouth. He smiled as he looked at Lo. "Gracias, gracias, comrade. Is there anything you need? Are you comfortable at the hotel?"

"Yes, Comrade President, very comfortable."

"Good. Captain, you will be staying at General Vincetta's quarters at the fort. You will be transported by security when you need it. You are to call General Vincetta if you have any problems or need anything, understand?"

"Yes, comrade President. I will have everything done as you wish as soon as I can."

"Good, buenos noches."

1811 hours

The van sped through the waterfront, turned up Avenue 24 to Eduardo Avenue, then turned south to head for the airport. Sitting in the stuffy windowless van, the three men strained nervously to see out the windshield, each one wanting to tell the driver to slow down, but no one raised their voice.

1831 hours

The Convair flew in a cloudless sky along the rugged coastline westward to Antonio Maceo. Once there, they would climb over the rolling mountains and take up a heading to Cienfuegos up the coast, then directly to Havana, two hours and fifteen minutes away.

"You said very little all afternoon, Juan Luis. Something troubles you?" Castro asked his old friend.

Cantillo looked over at General Vincetta, who was enjoying his cocktail and chatting with the stewardess.

"I don't like this whole crazy idea, Fidel. It is too dangerous."

Castro twisted in his seat and turned his body to face Cantillo. "My friend, we have no choice, I have no choice. It's just a matter of time now before we get totally shut off from this new Russian snake. I feel it coming, he is going to have us on our knees begging. He has already made cutbacks in our orders for new equipment and is moving his Navy out, except for four submarines and their support group. By the first of the year as many as 25,000 troops will be going back and no replacements. Not that it won't please some of our countrymen. Juan, I have to look to the future. We will need oil and petrol. I can't trade the Soviets for oil with sugar or coffee and fruit anymore, don't you understand, my friend?"

"I understand nothing, Fidel. This move to build these machines for the drug monsters is crazy. You think they will be your friends? Huh, just you let one of these devices get caught, or blow up on them. Do you think they are going to let you get away with that? Fidel, you're dealing with the deadliest people on this earth."

"One million dollars a piece, Juan. One million dollars, and I don't get my hands dirty, no Cuban gets their hands dirty. We just supply the product. Do you have any idea what the first order will be? At least one hundred of those plastic fishes, one hundred million dollars, my friend. We estimate that our total cost to produce a completed Dolphin will be less than twenty five thousand U.S. dollars."

"You think you can build those fish in Cuba without the Soviets getting wind? My god, you have a personal shadow with you now, compliments of the KGB, who wipes your nose every time you sneeze. How are you going to get around him?"

"I already have, my friend. He is a partner. He wants to stay here in Cuba. He too sees the writing on the wall, Juan Luis. Dimitri Sorokin is a true communist. He comes from a hard line family and is a member of the old school. Gorbachev is not fooling him either."

Cantillo turned and looked into Fidel's narrow deep eyes. He pulled his glasses off and waved them in front of Castro's face.

"Fidel, when I leave this plane in Havana, I will go to my apartment and weep for you, I will pray that you come to your senses. You are the President of our country, our savior, and leader. You can't do this, and if you do, it will be your end and the end of this country's existence. All you have done for the past twenty-five years will go back to the Batistas of the world, you fool. Now, let me sleep, I am tired, I am too old to fight with you now. Go, go now and sit with your puppet General."

Juan Luis Cantillo turned his head to the small window and looked out into the dark Caribbean night and the black sea below. As the single tear moved down the deep crease in his weathered cheek, he knew he may have just lost his oldest friend.

CHAPTER 14

Charlotte Amalie
St. Thomas, Virgin Islands

Monday, November 9th
1520 hours

The emerald green island of St. Thomas, with its rolling mountains and soft dark valleys, appeared to be sleeping beneath the gentle low cumulus clouds that were building like giant castles. A light shower was falling on the east end of the island, spoiling the view of St. John, the smallest of the three American Virgin Islands

Paul Gransaull held the wooden helms wheel casually as he maintained a heading of zero seven zero. In the distance, he could see Water Island. "If all goes well, this should be the last reach," he thought to himself. "This heading should bring the Seaduce right to the entrance of Charlotte Amalie Harbor." Like a thoroughbred, the classic wooden ketch moved gracefully over the deep warm blue waters. Her sails were full and her rigging sang as she sliced through the endless parade of rolling seas.

Captain Mel Spencer was standing on the aft cabin braced against the mizzenmast scanning the islands through his field glasses. "Looks like the old Norway swinging on her hook outside the harbor, yes, that's her all right."

"Does that mean the cruise ship docks are filled? Is that why she has to park outside the harbor?" Gransaull asked.

"You know, Paul, for a guy who is supposed to be so damn experienced down here, you're not too observant. The Norway never sails into the harbor at St. Thomas, she's too big, or draws too much, I forget, but the fact is, she never goes into the harbor."

"You're right, Captain, there are a lot of things I don't notice while I'm down here. For example, I never knew that there was an old submarine base down here at one time. Some guy I met in a bar in Newport told me his old man was stationed there."

Before Spencer could respond, a well-tanned shiny face appeared in the small companionway. "Hey, you guys, I just made up a special rum-a-rama treat for us so we can celebrate our flawless voyage."

Gina Wilson stood in her brief black bikini at the top of the companionway steps, smiling. Her pixie styled blonde hair framed her bright blue eyes, and deep dark tan. She was short, attractive and proud of her well-

231

toned body. Her pleasing personality and continuous high spirits had made the long voyage from the Bahamas tolerable for Gransaull, who was under constant verbal attack from Spencer.

"Permission to come on deck, Captain?"

"You bet, princess, and let's have a taste of that rum special of yours. In thirty minutes we will be busting ass getting ready to dock," Spencer said cheerfully as he climbed down into the cockpit.

Gina brought up a tray of cheese and crackers, a pitcher of her rum special concoction, and three plastic glasses. She placed the tray on the cockpit table and filled the glasses, handing one to Spencer and one to Gransaull. She lifted her glass in a salute.

"To the end of our very smooth voyage, and to your new adventures. Good health, smooth sailing and a successful season." Gina put the glass to her lips and downed the entire contents.

"Salute." Gransaull said as he raised his glass. "I sure wish you were going to be working with us."

"So do I, damn shame I wasn't told about the Seaduce sooner, I would have jumped to work on this yacht. But, you guys are getting a great cook and neat lady. I have known Karen Goodson for ten years, she's a great cook and a good sailor. You had her on board as crew before, didn't you, Captain?"

"Yes, years ago when I was running an old Morgan Out Island down here. You're right, she is a great cook, and a dynamite deck hand. She married Sam Goodson, a captain who worked out of St. Thomas. He was killed in Cleveland a few years back, when he went home to bury his father."

"Yeah, that was terrible. Karen told me the story, tough break. Anyway, here's to Karen, and you guys take good care of her. Now, I am going below and get all the laundry together for you and finish packing. Stomp on the deck when you ready to drop the sails, Captain."

Gina took the tray and went down the companionway.

"Going to miss that lady," Gransaull said laughing.

"Yeah, she's special. But, you'll find Karen just as personable and equally talented in the galley. We were lucky to get her, thanks to that girl in Sarasota that works for Avery, what was her name?"

"Gail, Gail Townsend," Gransaull replied. He knew that he was being tested again by Spencer.

"Have you ever met her or Phil Avery?" Spencer asked.

"I told you during our interview we only talked over the phone. I was picked up by Avery's crew placement service out of the Lauderdale office, remember? I never met Avery, or Ms. Townsend."

"Oh, yeah, I forgot. Here, I'll take the wheel now."

Spencer stepped down into the cockpit behind Gransaull. "I'm going to bring her up some, standby on the jib."

"Right." Gransaull moved over to the port side of the cockpit and placed the winch handle in the winch that held the jib sheet, then waited for Spencer to head up into the wind.

Spencer reached around and picked up the main sheet and pulled it through the jam cleat slowly, as he changed course five degrees to starboard. He gave no order to Gransaull. Spencer was satisfied with the jib setting as well as the mizzen sail. The Seaduce coasted past Water Island and Spencer let her fall back off the wind slightly. He planned to make the harbor entrance on this reach. He had a good breeze and wouldn't lose it until he was abeam of Frenchmans Reef Hotel, where the easterly wind would be disturbed and reduced dramatically.

"We will sail in, Paul. Once inside, we'll come up on the wind, drop everything and head for the docks at Yacht Haven. Here, take the helm, I'm going to give the dockmaster a call and see what dock we can tie up to."

Gransaull took the helm as Spencer went down the companionway to the main salon were he went to the navigation station, turned up the volume on the VHF radio checking to make sure he was on channel 72. He picked up the small microphone.

"Yacht Haven Marina, this is the yacht Seaduce, whiskey yankee zulu four-four-seven-six, do you copy?"

"Seaduce, Yacht Haven Marina, welcome, we have been expecting you. You're early, Captain."

"Roger that, Yacht Haven. Is Paul the dockmaster around?"

"Yes, he is on the docks. What is your location?"

"Ah, about a mile out, should be in the harbor in fifteen minutes."

"Roger, Seaduce. Proceed to end of "B" dock. Paul will meet you there. You also have messages waiting at your clearing house."

"Roger, Yacht Haven, will go direct to dock B. Seaduce, whisky yankee zulu four-four-seven-six going back to sixteen."

"Yacht Haven Marina, seven-two."

Gina came into the salon from her rear cabin carrying two duffel bags and a small suitcase under her arm. She placed them on the oriental rug.

"Well, that's it, Captain. Oh, I separated all the laundry for you and put it in pillowcases in my stateroom. Don't forget to take them over to the laundry as soon as you can, or you won't have it ready for your charter on Wednesday."

"Thanks again, Gina, we appreciate you being on board for the trip down, and if you don't have a bunk ready for you tonight onboard your new assignment, you're welcome back here, o.k.?"

"You got it, skipper." She stood on her tiptoes and put her arms around Spencer's neck and a kissed him on his cheek.

"Hey you guys, we are on top of the Norway," Gransaull yelled.

Spencer and Gina went up to the cockpit and turned their attention to the stately ocean liner off the port bow. She was turned into the wind, and they could hear cheers coming from passengers waving their arms trying to draw their attention. The crew waved back.

The Seaduce glided across the calm waters of the harbor, passing the Frenchmans Reef Hotel to starboard. The cruise ship wharf, also to starboard, was empty. There was little activity going on in the harbor, except for a few ferries that were running passengers back and forth to the downtown shopping district from the Norway.

As Spencer moved the Seaduce carefully to the end of the dock, Gina and Paul stood ready with dock lines to secure the classic yacht. Paul Vineyard, the dockmaster stood waiting on the dock. Vineyard stood six feet two, and weighed around two hundred and thirty pounds. He was dressed in his dockmaster uniform, white military styled short sleeve shirt, white shorts, no socks and white boat shoes. A small brass nametag was pinned over his left breast pocket. It read, " Paul Vineyard, World's Greatest Dockmaster."

"Is that you, you old fart?" Vineyard yelled,

"Jesus Christ, I would have thought some jealous husband would have deep sixed your fat ass by now," Spencer cried out.

"I'll be damned, we thought you retired, Spencer."

"I did, until we had a change of command on September Morn."

"This, this ain't September Morn, is it? What the hell did you do to her?"

"Long story, man, you know, one of those chapters over a case of Heinekins?"

Once the electric, water and phone lines were connected and checked, Gransaull helped Gina bring her gear topside and onto the dock. Spencer introduced his crew to Vineyard, then invited him aboard. Gransaull overheard Spencer tell Vineyard that the yacht was no longer owned by the doctor in Palm Beach, and that the new owner wore a high hat and red and white striped uniform.

This concerned Gransaull. He knew that Spencer had been ordered not to talk about the new owners of the yacht to anyone. The only information he was authorized to give was that the yacht was now under contract with a management program, working through Averys Charter Yacht Services in Florida.

Gransaull told Spencer he was going to help Gina with her bags up to the Bridge restaurant and would be right back. When they reached the restaurant, Gina ran into some old friends. Gransaull quickly excused himself, so he could find a public telephone, and report in to O'Brien.

Immokalee Airport
The Manger
1610 hours

O'Brien was in his office, when the call from St. Thomas came in.

"Right, Paul. No, you did right. I have a message waiting for you guys at the clearinghouse. Soon as you can, get Spencer over there for the message. He probably won't call at this late hour even though we are an hour later than you are, correct? How was the trip?, you made it a day earlier than planned, is everything alright with the Seaduce? That's great. If you need anything, let me know. Meantime, keep an eye on Spencer. I will remind him when I talk to him to keep his mouth shut about the yacht and who he is working for. If worse comes to worse, I will send Commander Buckland down and he will deal with Spencer. Don't you approach him, or challenge him on anything, you have to maintain a good relationship, play dumb, stay healthy and for God's sake, keep in touch."

O'Brien put the phone down. He sat back in his chair and looked up into Ted Collins' sober face.

"Problems, Dan?" Ted asked.

"Don't know yet, well, maybe. Gransaull is a little concerned about Spencer's mouth. It seems he just mentioned to one of his buddies at Yacht Haven Marina that the Seaduce was owned by a man with a tall hat and a red, white and blue uniform, meaning Uncle Sam, I'm sure."

"Who was the guy he spoke to?"

"The dockmaster, I believe. I guess they are old friends from the days when Spencer was down there chartering."

"That would be Paul Vineyard. He's alright, and yes, he probably would be a good friend to Spencer, they both like to bend at their elbows at the local pubs. Are you going to advise Billings about this problem?"

"Fuck no. His guys move too quick for my blood. I will be talking to Spencer tomorrow, and I think I can control him for now. It's later on that I'm concerned about, when we send him down to St. Vincent to pick up the charter. God only knows who these folks are that Billings is putting together from the agency. I hope I get a chance to at least talk to them before they meet with Spencer."

Yacht Haven Marina
St. Thomas, USVI

Aboard the Seaduce
1745 hours

Paul Vineyard spun the bottle of Miller Lite beer between his fingers as he sat comfortably on the large sofa in the main salon. Mel Spencer was standing over the small wet bar at the end of the island cabinet that separated the salon from the galley. After mixing his drink of rum and soda, he returned to the small armchair next to the sofa and sat down.

"You didn't screw her up too much, Mel. As a matter of fact, I actually like some of the new modifications, specially raising the main salon roof. It's much more airy in here, and it looks much bigger."

"Does the old yacht remind you of another famous yacht, Paul? Just look at her lines, with the raised salon and aft cabin. Did you notice the new treatment around the cockpit? Doesn't she remind you a little of a whole new series of yachts?"

Paul studied Spencer for a minute. He sensed that Spencer was a little uptight, yet he had a smile on his face.

"No, I can't say she reminds me of any other yacht, why do you ask?"

"Think, Ted Collins, Paul. Think Citation fifty-five and sixty-five."

"Yeah, I guess there is some resemblance in their lines. They both have that neat clipper bow, and the step up sheer. Yeah, I guess one could say they do share something in common."

"They should, you dumb ass. September Morn, or I should say, Seaduce, was the yacht that inspired Ted to re-design all his new yachts, as fast classic looking cruising hulls. He got the idea from this yacht a few years ago when I had her over in the Abacos. Collins came over to do some racing during Abaco race week, and he fell in love with her, so he went home and designed his entire cruising fleet based on the lines of this beauty."

Vineyard got up and put his empty beer bottle in the sink, then took another from the refrigerator.

"So, tell me, what is the mystery behind this yacht. You say you have new owners, but not who they are. Are you working for some kind of super star now?"

"I would say so, Paul. And as a U.S. taxpayer, you may even own a piece of this great ship. Actually, I am sworn to secrecy, Paul, and I can't say much. However, my visit here, and this ship do have something to do with a very popular agency, and that will have to remain here, between us, old buddy."

"Sure Mel, what ever you say. But, what are, I mean why would the government want to own a sailboat, especially a crewed yacht? Don't they know we don't make any money with these things? Shit, all we do is drink, sail and have a good time down here, right?" Vineyard laughed and Spencer joined in as he downed the rest of his drink.

Vineyard stood up and walked over to the companionway steps, turned and looked at Spencer. "Hey, let's go up to the Bridge, there are a few of your old cronies up there waiting to see you."

When Spencer reached the top step of the restaurant, he started walking towards the bar, when he was quickly noticed by two of his old friends, Rick Van Wagner and Hugh Murphy, two of the wildest charter yacht captains in the Virgin Islands.

"Well, if it ain't the old wonder wolf of the West Indies, alive and well," Van Wagner called out.

"We heard you met some Palm Beach socialite and married her for her vintage Rolls Royce and young daughter," Murphy said laughing.

Spencer stood in front of his two friends with arms outstretched. "I have returned to this sacred place, to resurrect this fragile charter industry, and to return it to its once noble reputation, a challenge neither of you two would ever understand." Spencer took a few steps then threw himself between the two well tanned, well salted and well watered down friends. After a few slaps on the back and screams for the barmaid, Spencer, his two fellow captains and Paul Vineyard found a table, took up their positions and started collecting long neck Budweisers. They talked and joked for hours about the old days, which took them well into the wee hours.

Crewed Yacht Services, Clearing House
Yacht Haven Hotel, St. Thomas USVI
Tuesday, November 10th
0930 hours

Spencer and Gransaull entered the clearinghouse and walked up to the counter. A young black girl was on the phone taking a message. A number of people were moving around the large office picking up their mail while others were on telephones maybe talking to family telling them they were still alive and surviving in paradise.

"Can I help you?"

"Yes, I'm Captain Mel Spencer on the yacht Seaduce. You're holding messages for me, so I'm told."

The young girl stood up and moved over to a desk behind her and went through some papers.

"Yes, Captain Spencer. I have three messages for you. One is from Ms. Miller, our manager. One is from a Mr. Rudolf, and the other from Karen Goodson." The girl began to look around the room. "I believe Karen is still here. Yes, there she is over there, on the phone."

Spencer looked at the woman sitting in the small booth. Her hand was covering most of her face as she played with her long blonde pigtail. Spencer walked over and stood in her light. She was talking to someone on the phone and paying no mind to him as he stood directly in front of her. She finally looked up and saw him. Her face lit up. Gransaull could see she was pleased to see the bearded Captain.

After hanging up the phone, Karen stood up and threw her arms around Spencer's neck. She was an attractive woman in her mid thirties, dressed in a plain white T-shirt, washed out jeans and shower clogs. Her deep tan looked rich and smooth. Gransaull was attracted to her immediately. They stayed in each other's arms for a long time, talking quietly to each other, and kissing each other's cheeks. They finally broke away and walked over to the counter where Gransaull stood waiting.

"Paul, this is Karen Goodson. Karen, this is Paul Gransaull." They studied each other for a moment then extended their hands.

Spencer suggested that Paul leave with Karen and help her move her belongings aboard the Seaduce from her car, while he called O'Brien and set up a meeting with the clearing house manager, Cathy Miller. He also suggested that Karen take Paul and do provisioning as soon as possible. He reached in his pocket and took out his wallet and gave Paul three one hundred dollar bills.

238

After Paul and Karen left, Spencer went over to a pay phone and made a credit card call to the States.

"Mr. O'Brien, this is Mel Spencer."

"Oh, yes, Mel, where are you?"

"St. Thomas. We got in yesterday."

"You made good time, I take it the weather was favorable?"

"Yes, ah listen, I have a lot to do. We have our first charter in twenty four hours, thanks to Avery's brokers, and I would like to get going."

"I understand, Mel, and I won't keep you. I just want to go over a few things. First, be sure you have the Seaduce in top shape by the 15th of December. You will have a special charter, as you know that will originate out of St. Vincent or St. Lucia. Avery's people will keep you booked as much as they can for the next few weeks. If you need anything, radios, parts, whatever, call me here at this number and advise. We would like to have you heading down to St. Vincent or St. Lucia no later than December 10th."

"I have no major problems on the Seaduce. We have a little overheating problem with the auxiliary generator, and I have to work on a few leaks that were created during reconstruction."

"How's Gransaull doing?" O'Brien asked reluctantly.

"He has sure bullshitted someone in Avery's company on his sailing experience. He's not too sharp at his job, but he is personable and learns fast, he will be alright. Karen Goodson, our cook, just arrived, she's out with him right now getting our provisioning."

"Sounds good, Captain. Listen, as you know, we have told you that you are involved in a classified operation. We are working with a number of government agencies. If you haven't guessed, we are going after some serious drug distributors in the Caribbean. You will be playing a major role down there when the time comes, Spencer. Right now, you just do as we ask, act normal enjoy yourself and your charters, and keep your mouth shut. You don't say anything to anyone, or discuss anything about your real reason for being there, or anything about the ownership of the Seaduce. As far as you know, the Seaduce is being managed by a management company, and is being put into charter for this season, that's it. I don't want to have anything coming back that you are saying anything different, do you understand me, Spencer?"

"Tell me, Government man, could it be, that my new first mate, Mr. Gransaull, is one of your moles?"

O'Brien hesitated for a second and thought about his response, then decided it might not be a bad idea to keep him somewhat on guard. "Could be, Spencer, you never know who's looking over your shoulder. However, as Avery's people picked him, as I mentioned, you never know. Keep your mouth shut and you have nothing to worry about, right, skipper?"

"Fuck you. You know, O'Brien, I don't like you, buddy. But I will do my job, you just stay out of my face, unless you have good reason."

"I have no problem with that. Have a good charter, Spencer, and keep in touch." O'Brien slammed the phone down.

"Shit, I got a bad feeling about this bastard. I better talk to Buckwheat and Bollman, they need to know about this asshole, maybe they can give me some advice how to handle him."

Mel Spencer walked back though the busy clearinghouse office until he came to a door marked "Private." He knocked twice.

"Who is it?" Came a reply from a woman's voice.

"It's me, Mel Spencer."

"Come in, Mel, it's open.

Cathy Miller was sitting behind her desk as Spencer entered the small office. He closed the door, never taking his eyes off her.

"Looking good, Mel, you lost some weight."

"Yeah, stopped eating junk food and little girls."

Cathy stood up and moved around from the desk. She walked up to Spencer and slowly draped her arms around his neck. They kissed hard.

"You look great, babe. Charlie must be treating you right."

"Always has, Mel, you know that."

"Yeah, but he also knows that I'm waiting in the wings, just waiting for him to mess up one time."

"You haven't changed a bit, Mr. Spencer."

Cathy went back around to her chair and sat down. She picked up a stack of papers and started to read. "Seaduce? I understand it's the old September Morn in drag, is this true?"

"Yep, it's her with a little plastic and wood surgery. Her new owners wanted some changes, what can I say?"

Cathy shook her head. "Why would they want to change one of the most beautiful yachts ever built? Anyway, who is this Gransaull character? I never heard of him."

"That's what I was afraid of. Nobody around here knows him, I'll bet. But he claims he has delivered a number of yachts down here, more recently for the Avery Company."

"Can't help you, Mel. Is he o.k.?, I mean he's not on drugs or anything?"

"Shit no, he's almost too clean. He doesn't even smoke. Ah, he's a nice guy, just not too swift on deck, but I'm stuck with him for awhile, I mean, he will have to do. Besides, I have Karen Goodson on board, she can break his ass in for me."

"What's with the new owners? I see only Phil Avery Management's name on everything, have you met them?"

"Ah, no, and don't plan to either. It's too complicated to get into now, babe. The yacht is in good order, it's legal, well insured and inspected, you got it all there in your pretty little hands. I get paid, you get paid, why ask where it comes from, right?"

"O.K., Mel, all your papers are in order." She put the papers back into the large brown envelope. "I have your mailbox being labeled, you're on the booking board and your charters are posted. By the way, your charter party is due at the hotel around six tonight. They would like to meet you, if possible at the Patio bar around seven? Carol Perot, the broker who booked them at Averys in Lauderdale, says they are two young swinging couples. Sounds like your kind of charter, Captain. Now, can you board them at noon tomorrow as planned?"

"Sure, no problem. I'll go up and meet them later. Will I see you later?"

"Mel, I don't think we should, o.k.? Things are going well now, and I..."

"Hey, I'm a big boy, Cathy. I'll see you in ten days after the charter. Then we talk."

Spencer rose from his chair, winked and walked out the door.

Aboard the yacht Seaduce
1420 hours

Spencer was in the engine room, beginning to disassemble the raw water pump on the engine, when he heard voices topside. He climbed out of the compartment into the walkthrough and entered the salon. Looking through the port cabin windows, he noticed Paul and Karen standing on the dock. They had a dock cart full of plastic grocery bags. They were laughing and joking. Spencer stepped up on the companionway ladder.

"Need any help, you two?" Spencer asked.

"Ah, no, we can handle it. Captain. Ah, we ran through that three hundred I'm afraid; you owe Karen, thirty-six bucks and some change. I couldn't help, I left my money on board."

"That's o.k., Karen is used to me short changing her, right Karen?"

She smiled and lowered her head, trying to avoid eye contact with Paul. She said nothing.

"I keep forgetting, you two have shared a lot of these shopping trips in the past," Paul said sharply, as he turned his back to Spencer and began to lift the bags out of the cart. He watched Karen, but she did not respond. Spencer went back to the engine room. Paul and Karen continued to bring the groceries aboard and stowed them. No more was said.

CIA Headquarters
Langley, Virginia
1505 Hours

"Mr. Billings, you have a call on the green line, coming in from the 809 area."

"Thank you, Sharon."

Ian Billings took a brown book from his top desk draw and opened it to a section marked "area-codes." He picked up the phone and pushed the flashing green line button.

"Billings here. Well, what a pleasant surprise. How are you, Captain Rick? How's that new young wife and baby? It was a boy, wasn't it? Yeah, we are all fine, Rick, all fine. What can I do for you?"

Ian picked up a pen and started to take notes. He wrote down Spencer, Milton, Captain, yacht, Seaduce, arrived on 9 November.

"Ah, what's your interest here, Rick? I see, yes. Listen Rick, do me a favor, I will check him out, meantime, keep an eye on him and that yacht, o.k.? He's going out tomorrow on a ten day charter? Ah, no, Rick, that won't be necessary. Where would he go? Yeah, and he would just cruise around the British Virgin Islands, right? O.k., see if you can learn more about the charter and the guests, like, who they are and were they are coming from, o.k.? Right, thanks Rick, keep in touch."

Ian switched phones and hit the intercom button.

"Yes, Mr. Billings?"

"Get me Dan O'Brien, try the manger first."

"Yes sir."

A few minutes went by, then his phone rang. "Mr. O'Brien on two, sir."

"Thanks, Sharon," Billings switched lines.

"O'Brien?, Ian, here. I just got a call from a friend in St. Thomas. He ran into a Captain Mel Spencer last night, claims they are old friends. Spencer just came in on a yacht called "Seaduce." That's your man, isn't it? Right, yeah, well, it seems Spencer is spreading the word that Uncle Sam owns his yacht and claiming he's working for him. What's going on here, Dan?   This guy sounds like a loose cannon, do you want me to have someone stop in and see him? O.K, but I want to know. Keep in touch."

The Manger
Immokalee, Florida

O'Brien sat quietly at his desk. He picked up a cigarette put it in his mouth and then threw it across the room. He picked up the phone, ran through his rolodex and found the number for Commander Buckland at the Key West Naval Station. He put the phone back down. "Shit, he's already on the way here."

O'Brien called over to Ft. Myers Shipbuilders and asked to have Ted Collins paged. He picked up another cigarette while he waited. This time he lit it.

"Sorry, he doesn't answer the page. Would you care to leave a message?"

"No, thank you."

O'Brien placed the phone down. He sat back and thought of the call from Billings. "Jesus, this guy has spies everywhere. Hell, if Billings has a man there, maybe he's qualified to, damn, I need Spencer, I just need to find a way to get him under control, fast."

City of Havana, Cuba
Vedado District

Habana Libre Hotel
1735 hours

Carlos Lucia sat patiently at the small patio table sipping on a fruit punch. He watched the busy sidewalks laced with tourists and business people who worked in the Rampa area. He looked at his watch. "Maybe Luis could not get away," he thought. Then he saw him, winding his way through the traffic and pedestrians.

"Carlos, how are you? Are you alright?"

"Luis, I don't know how to tell you this, but your friend, General Vincetta?"

"Yes, you met with him some weeks ago. He helped you, no? He told me you would not be going to that flight training school in Moscow. He told me this just two weeks ago, Carlos, did he change his mind?"

"No, no, Luis, he didn't change his mind. But, I don't know how to tell you this, my friend. They are moving me back into the Air Force. I will be made a major, and will be flying for Fidel."

"Carlos, they, you can't. What happens to our messages? How do we get our reports out? Jesus, Carlos, when do you stop flying for Cubana?"

"I'm not sure yet. So far all I got is this letter from General Vincetta's office, congratulating me. I called yesterday morning to reach this Colonel Valsada on Vincetta's staff to find out when I must report, but he never returned my call. I don't even know if they notified my superiors at Cubana. I'm totally lost right now."

"Listen, Carlos. Where will you be flying to for the next few days? You are scheduled, aren't you?"

"Yes. I will be going to Merida, San Salvador and Managua on regular runs all week. Why?"

"I must get some final information together on Fidel's trip, just in case. If I could just get back down to the marina in Santiago, and learn more about the Dolphins and study that damn yacht. I know they are planning to leave on the twenty-first early in the morning. They are going to some islands near Guadeloupe. I don't know about the other visitors, or anything about where their yachts are coming from. I don't know who will be going with Fidel on the trip. I believe General Vincetta will be with him. There is talk that Sorokin may be going too, that's all I know."

"Whatever you can find out, you will have to have it ready no later than Thursday, Luis. I leave early on Friday, and we only have two airports that we can hope to make the drop at. You better put together all you can, and we better advise them of this problem too."

"How will this affect your plans to fly our families out?"

"Actually, Luis, this may be the answer to all our problems. I will have to be checked out on Fidel's favorite transport, it's an old Convair 440 he keeps over at Camp Columbia. It's the perfect airplane. I can fly it without a co-pilot. I can land it almost on any highway, or small field. This may be the gift from heaven we have been waiting for."

Luis reached over and took Carlos's hand. " We are getting close my friend, I can feel it. We now pray for those we do not know, who someday, maybe will give us back our country, yes?"

Luis stood up. "I will have the message brought to you on Thursday, and I will see you on Sunday, if I am not called to duty." Luis turned and walked into the maze of people walking by the small hotel's patio restaurant.

Yacht Haven Marina
St. Thomas
2015 hours

Gransaull stood on the dock holding the tether line to the Avon inflatable, as Karen, holding her skirt and white slippers, carefully balanced herself as she stepped up on the dock.

"My hair must look beautiful," she commented as she walked past Gransaull, who was tying the dinghy to a cleat.

"Wow, this place is neat. What did you say the name of this place is?"

"Gregory's East. At least that's what it was called the last time I was here."

"Well, I have never been here, so, we will call it Gregory's, o.k.?"

The two shipmates walked around to the side entrance of the outdoor restaurant, where a young woman holding menus met them.

"How many, two?" The young hostess asked.

"Yes, and we would like to be down on the rail by the water, if possible?"

"No problem, sir, follow me."

The small restaurant was nearly filled. The waterfront atmosphere was peaceful and the cool breeze from the bay welcome. Paul was like a little boy in the candy store. He glowed with excitement admiring the large motor yachts that were moored nearby, and fascinated by the lights and activities taking place at the new terminal docks just across the small bay.

Karen studied Paul. She liked his youth and enthusiasm. His bronzed tan, accented by his light blond hair and bleached out eyebrows, enhanced his wide blue eyes. His build was slender, but muscular. His hands had long fingers, and his nails were well manicured. This was what bothered Karen most, his hands. They were not the hands of a man who worked on yachts.

"Paul, tell me something. How long have you been crewing on yachts?"

"Hey, is this another drill? Spencer put you up to this? I thought we were going to have a nice pleasant dinner, away from Spencer, away from the boat."

"Hey, don't get mad, I was just curious. Spencer has nothing to do with it."

Karen reached over and took Paul's right hand and gently pulled it across the table. She opened it, palm up, and moved her index finger across the palm.

"These are not the hands of a full time mate, Paul. And you don't have that, well, the rough around the edges look, of a crew member."

"What can I tell you? I, ah, wash my hands in Ivory Liquid, twice a day. Spencer has never complained, why does it bother you?"

"Let's order, shall we?" Karen changed her tone and picked up the large menu. "Maybe some day you will tell me why you are really here, Paul."

"Maybe someday we will both be honest enough to tell our stories. I can't wait to hear about you and Spencer. Will you be sharing his stateroom on the charter?"

"Paul, you just proved my point about you. You definitely have no experience in this industry. I have my own quarters, Paul. I don't share with anyone, especially members of the crew on the yacht I am working."

"I'm sorry, I was out of line." Gransaull reached over and took her hand. "I apologize, forgive me, Karen."

"Apology accepted. Try the coconut battered butter-flied shrimps, they are fantastic."

Bridge Restaurant Bar
2120 hours

Paul Vineyard and Rick Van Wagner were sitting in their usual chairs at the bar, when Mel Spencer walked up.

"Hey Judy, bring a Mount Gay and tonic, and hold the lime."

"Well, how did your meeting with your charter guests go, Mel?" Vineyard asked.

"Alright, looks like I lucked out. The two guys are big time sailors out of Charleston, they do a lot of racing on J-boats."

"Are they with their wives or lady friends?"

"Definitely wives. This is a pay back trip for the girls. Anyway, they seem real nice, it should be a nice easy charter."

The three men continued drinking and telling their tales long into the evening. Paul Vineyard got the call from home, and retreated. Spencer and

Van Wagner left the bar and walked down the dock until they reached "Piccolo", Van Wagner's vintage Citation.

"C'mon aboard Mel, we'll have a nightcap."

The two men sat in the center cockpit, sipping on brandy and smoking real Havana cigars.

"She's still a great gal, Rick and you sure take good care of her. How old is she now, ten years old?"

"Ah, really nine I guess. I picked her up in November 1976. She is hull number four, out of twenty-six that were built, so far. I told Ted Collins last year when he was down, that "Piccolo" has more miles under her keel than any charter yacht in the Caribbean."

"Ted Collins, huh? You know, somehow, he's mixed up in this fucking mess I'm involved in."

"What are you talking about, what mess?"

"I'm involved with some dumb Government deal, Rick. Oh, it's all being painted over by the Avery Charter Company and Avery Yacht Management Group, but it stinks. There's this asshole, his name is O'Brien? He and Ted Collins came over to Palm Beach a few months ago, came aboard September Morn, and started asking questions about the owner. Shit, in less than twenty-four hours, O'Brien and Collins somehow bought the yacht. I couldn't believe it. My boss paid me off and sent me on my way. I got suspicious, I don't know why, just did, so I found out where they were taking the yacht and checked on it. She was motored down from Palm Beach to a boat yard down in Stuart. I asked around and learned that she was going to be modified, and her name changed. But why, I kept asking myself, and by whose orders? I kept my eye on this young guy who was frequently visiting the yard and checking on progress. I learned the son of a bitch was a navy commander. I collared him one night down near Lake Worth trying to make it with a local whore. I told him I was wise to him, and had him on film trying to make it with the hooker. He called this Dan O'Brien character, and I got my job back. I was all but bodily threatened by O'Brien, to keep my mouth shut about Seaduce, and who I was working for."

Rick rested his head back on a cockpit cushion, and threw his legs up on the lounge seat. He raised his brandy glass close to his face and studied the dark liquid as he swirled it around.

"Maybe you should take this guy's advice, Mel. Maybe you are involved with something big, and this feller, O'Brien, he just maybe calling the shots."

"Shit, I had enough of the O'Brien types in my life. If I am doing something for Uncle Sam, like maybe getting mixed up with druggers, or something like that, and putting my ass on the line, I want to know who all the players are."

Van Wagner placed his glass on the small cockpit table, and lit a cigarette. "Mel, I want to tell you something, and I want you to pay good attention, because this will be the last conversation you will have on this subject. It will be the last time you mention Dan O'Brien, September Morn, Commander Buckland, or Uncle Sam, do you understand?"

"What the fuck are you talking about? Who are you to tell me what I can and can't say?"

Spencer stood up and took hold of the console table to steady himself. Van Wagner just sat still. He picked up his glass and began swirling the brandy around. He looked up at Spencer, and said, "I might be the guy who will have to shut your ass up, Mel."

"What? Man, you're pulling my leg, right?"

"Mel, if you want to enjoy some golden years ahead, I would do like the man said and keep your big mouth shut. Take your money, mind your business and let folks do their thing."

Spencer stepped out of the cockpit onto the deck. He stood for a moment staring out into space. Then he walked to the open gate of the lifeline and stepped onto the dock, where he slipped on his boat shoes and walked down the finger dock to the end. He stopped and came back and stood opposite Van Wagner, who was still resting in the cockpit seat.

"I have always wondered about you, Rick. You were never a so-called, big time contractor, were you? All this shit you threw around here about your old lady running out on you, and your company going belly up. Shit, you're nothing but a fucking ex-government pimp, right? You're down here reporting to your friends at the agencies, right? Which is it, the IRS, CIA? You're nothing but a pimp, a squealer for the Feds, right? Son of a bitch, man, I don't..."

Van Wagner sat up, turned and rested his elbows on the varnished teak trim of the cockpit coaming. It wasn't that dark and Spencer was not that drunk. He could clearly see that Van Wagner was holding a large gun in his right hand.

"You want out, Mel? I can help you. You want to run your mouth? I can help you there too. You want to go back to the Seaduce and pretend this conversation never took place? I will swear to it. What's it going to be, Spencer? I have to make a call this morning, and advise them what I feel you're worth. My advice to you, friend, is you hang in there, do what you're told, and keep your mouth shut. I'm sure you were picked because you're qualified, and when the time comes for you to know, you will be told."

Spencer stared at Van Wagner and into the black hole at the end of his gun. "You would use that, wouldn't you, you son of a bitch. I mean, my life means nothing to you. If they tell you to do it, you do it, right?"

Van Wagner sat up and put the gun back into the small compartment on the console, where he kept it. He stretched then stood up behind the large steel helmswheel. He took the lighter from his pocket and lit the remains of his cigar. The glow from the lighter reflected in his deep tanned face. Spencer could see the strength in this man's face, as he took shallow drags on the half-spent cigar.

"You better get some sleep, Mel. You have a long week ahead. I will see you in the morning. You will feel better about things, after you think them out. Good night, Mel."

"I ain't forgetting this, Rick. That gun don't make you a bigger man than me. And don't think you got away with anything here tonight, either. Fuck you, man."

CHAPTER 15

Ft. Myers Shipbuilders
Sunday, November 15th
0805 hours

The Island Drummer was being readied for the trip north to Sarasota. All the shakedown tests had been run and all systems were working perfectly. All that was needed now was the final tuning of the rigging, furnishings, appliances, and bits and pieces the crew would need for every day operations, plus state of the art electronics and emergency equipment. It had been decided to move the Drummer to Sarasota so that Phil Avery could load the rest of the gear and provisioning needed for the long voyage to the Caribbean.

The crew consisted of Dan O'Brien, Ted Collins, Larry Keene, Phil Avery and Gail Townsend, left the marina in Ft. Myers at noon. Nearly eighty feet of sculptured fiberglass, moved silently under her new harnessed power towards the Gulf of Mexico. For the last ten days engineers, sailmakers, electricians and mechanics had swarmed all over the yacht making final connections, adjustments and static checks. The Drummer's new stowaway mast stood ninety-one feet from the waterline to her anchor light, and boasted three spreaders. Her generous beam was one inch shy of being twenty one feet at her widest point, and her stability now depended on the modified full keel with a hydraulic centerboard, large ballast tanks and extended rudder, to hopefully get back most of her original sailing performance. Because of the major hull changes, it was decided never to load the sails or sail hard on the wind to prevent over-heeling. They had not experienced any strong winds during tests all week, but would learn later that any winds near fifteen knots presented a stability problem.

"Where's Larry?" Ted asked.

"He went down below to check on the engines," Avery replied.

"That guy's something else," Collins said. "Hey, Dan, what are the chances of getting Larry on the mission? He would be a great help to Phil and Gail, should something mechanical puke."

"I'll give it some thought, Ted, but right now, I have some bad news to tell you guys."

"I thought you were acting a bit up tight this morning. What's wrong, Dan?" Avery asked.

"I got a call from Billings last night. A message came in from Cuba yesterday. It seems our Cuban pilot is leaving the airline service shortly. He doesn't know when, but it should be soon. He is trying to get as much information together as he can on his next few flights."

"Jesus, Dan. They haven't got wise to him, have they?"

"No, I don't think it's anything like that. He is either being transferred or pulled off flying status. He doesn't say, but he doesn't seem to be concerned about anything like that. Billings has contacted Souza in Miami and told him to put all the agents on alert at all Christmas Tree airports. We can't afford to miss him or any of his messages at this point."

"What do we know now? Is there anything changed in Castro's plans?" Avery asked.

"No. We do know they plan to leave Santiago on the morning of December 21st. There's no passenger list, nor do we know how many on board. We do know that Castro and his number one adviser, General Vincetta, will be on board. We have no description of the other yachts involved, or the parties who will be attending the meeting. Billings is watching all exit doors out of the countries he suspects could be involved. Oh, we did get a better fix on where the meeting will take place. It's a small island close to Guadeloupe. Billings said Koster will be doing a study on what's down there. He also told Billings that he would increase the fly-overs of the area commencing December 21st, so we can watch everything that floats around the area."

"Don't we have satellite coverage there?"

"Not that they are telling me about. I do know that we won't be getting satellite help at all, once Castro gets east of Dominica. The SR-71 Blackbirds are our only source."

Collins noticed Larry Keen coming up on deck. "Ah, here comes Larry, Dan."

"O.K., we will go over this later up in Sarasota, before we split."

"Hi, Larry, how are your two iron ladies doing."

"The port engine has a small gasket leak around the oil pan, and the starboard engine needs a new alternator belt, that's it."

For the rest of the day, the Island Drummer tacked across the warm waters of the Gulf, easing its way north. Ted and Phil played with the sails and worked on the problems the Drummer might face if caught under full sail in high winds. Ted was hoping to be able to see the effect of the centerboard under heavy air, but it did not happen. It was concluded that the Drummer could easily fool anyone who saw her under sail. She was a bit sensitive on the helm, but Avery convinced Collins and O'Brien that the yacht was ready. He wanted to keep his departure date set for the Friday after Thanksgiving, so that he could be in St. Thomas no later than December 10th.

Marina Jacks
Sarasota
1730 hours

Avery slipped the Drummer into her new berth with little room to spare. After tying her up, the crew went into Marina Jack's cocktail lounge where they took a table and ordered cocktails.

"To our valiant ship," Commander Buckland said as he raised his glass of beer.

"Hear, hear."

"Funny how you men need to refer to ships, planes and cars as if they were women. How did all this begin anyway, do you know, Commander?" Gail asked.

"I believe it started with Lord Nelson In the seventeenth century. Most fighting ships of that era were given male names, until Nelson commissioned his flagship the H.M.S. Brucie. That ended the macho era and ships were called ladies ever since."

There was dead silence around the table, then the outburst that led to the party being asked to leave the restaurant.

Varadero, Cuba
Fidel Castro's Mansion
1950 hours

"Dimitri, you don't like your grouper?"

Dimitri Sorokin pushed himself back from the large mahogany table. He picked up the Waterford wineglass and raised it in a salute.

"The fish was exquisite, Fidel. My compliments to Sara, she is the prize of all chefs in Cuba."

"Comrade Sorokin, I do believe you are getting Cubanized. I can remember when you hated our food."

"My dear General Vincetta, there are many things that I did not have a taste for when I first arrived here. I never knew for instance that I would take such a liking to this strange man, you call your President, here. I care for him now, like he was my brother."

"Yes, I know. Many of us feel he is our brother. You should have been here when we fought together to take back our country."

"Yes, I can just imagine how close all of you must have been. So, tell me, General, if you care so much for this man, why do you let him get

253

involved with these drug people? This is dangerous, my friends. These people are very dangerous."

Castro was becoming concerned with Sorokin's remarks, but did not respond. He realized the Russian had consumed more wine than he usually did during dinner. Castro flashed his eyes at Vincetta, a clear signal to get Sorokin off the subject.

"Comrade Sorokin, why don't we all go into the library and enjoy our President's special brandy. It was a gift from another special friend, Comrade Kruschev."

Castro stood up, walked around to Sorokin and put his hand on his shoulder.

"Come, my friend, the General is right, we should have some brandy now, it is good for the gas." Castro patted his stomach.

The three men sat for another hour, sipping on brandy, and discussing anything but the forthcoming cruise and its purpose.

Sorokin lifted his snifter and smiled. "My friends, I would like to make this toast, then I would like to go upstairs and crawl into whatever is waiting for me."

"You will be most pleased, Dimitri. The one who waits you, is one you have long admired, that is all I will tell you." Castro said laughing.

"Comrade President, I toast to your long life, and your long rule. I toast to your wonderful people, and I toast to, ah, to your Dolphin. For your sake, I hope it swims away and never comes back."

Vincetta began to move forward in his chair, as if to stand up. Castro raised his hand as a signal to Vincetta, not to do or say anything.

Sorokin's head dropped until his chin rested on his chest. The snifter slipped from his fingers and shattered on the tile floor.

"Let him be, Comrade. Let him be." Castro stood up and went over to Sorokin's sleeping form. "He's a good man, General, he means well."

Fun and Sun Apartments
St. Petersburg Beach

Monday, November 16th
0842 hours

The phone began ringing, and Buckland, without thinking, picked up the receiver. "Buckland here."

"Buckland? Is this O'Brien's place?"

"Ah, yes it is, he's in the shower. Who's this?"

"Ian Billings. Get O'Brien for me, Commander, it's important."

"Roger, sir, hold on, sir."

Buckland left the kitchen, went down the narrow hall to O'Brien's bedroom. He could hear the shower running, and door to the small bathroom was open. He stuck his head in and yelled.

"Dan, it's Billings, says it's important."

Before Buckland could clear the door, O'Brien flashed by him and crawled over the unmade bed. He grabbed the phone from the small nightstand.

"O'Brien here."

"Dan, late last night we received what could be the final message from Cuba. I'm sorry, but there is not much to it. It appears that our pilot is being transferred to the Cuban Air Force. This is what he had for us. There are two other yachts joining Castro, passengers unknown. Unicorn is ready to sail. Departure date December 21, 0600 hours. No escorts, seven crew including Castro, Vincetta and a KGB agent, Dimitri Sorokin. Island meeting is in Les Saintes, Grand Islet, just south of Guadeloupe. Look for possible defection Christmas week of an unmarked Martin 440 aircraft, six to ten passengers. It will be flying from Havana direct to Key West. That's it, Dan."

"Well, I guess we go with what we have. Have you talked to the Admiral about this, Ian?"

"No, I thought I would give it to you first."

"Thanks, Ian. O.K., when he calls me, I will tell him that I am pleased with the information, and it's enough to go with. We have the name of the island, the count on the other boats and the final time and date of departure, we can go with this as far as I am concerned."

"I read you, Dan. I'll call him now, you may want to stand by down there, I imagine he will want to talk to you right away. What do you make of this KBG man being on board? Think that could change things?"

"Yes, it could, that does bother me, Ian. Koster is going to go ape-shit if he knows there's a Russian on board, he might even cancel the mission. Son of a bitch, what the hell is a KGB man doing on this trip? Listen, Ian, I don't suppose that you could, well sort of miss that part of the message, could you, ol' man?"

"I can't do that, Dan. What I can do is to try and convince him that it makes no difference if a Russian is involved with Castro's plans. If he gets caught, or killed, it may even help the cause. Moscow will not be too pleased that Castro converted one of their own, keeping in mind, Castro is getting into something that we know for fact the Kremlin is totally against."

"Sounds good, let's hope that will convince the old man. Thanks, Ian, I will wait for his call. Oh, by the way, I was planning on putting a meeting together over in Lauderdale this week, as soon as I heard from Captain Lind on the Sonar. He is supposed to be putting into Lauderdale right about now. This will be the last time we can all get together before we take off. I will call and give you the details, in case you would like to be there."

"Roger, Dan, let me know if I can do anything, and good luck."

O'Brien put the phone down and stared down at his bare legs, still dripping from the shower. He was about to turn and talk to Buckwheat, when a towel hit him in the face.

"Thanks."

"Good news?"

"Well, not super, but not too bad. We just lost our Christmas Tree and all the trimmings in Cuba. Our man is leaving the service of Cubana Airlines and joining the Air Force, the Cuban Air Force, that is. We have a KGB agent on board the Unicorn with Castro, which adds a bit of spice to the operation. Other than that, we have enough to go with, that's if the Admiral doesn't put us on hold because of the Russian."

O'Brien got dressed and waited in the kitchen with Buckwheat for the phone to ring. In the meantime, he started writing down the plans for the meeting and who would be attending.

"We need someplace to meet down in Lauderdale, someplace secluded. Have any ideas, Commander?"

"No, but Avery should know where we could all get together in private."

"You're right, I'll give him..."

The phone rang. "Yes, O'Brien here."

"O'Brien?"

"Yes, Admiral, good morning, sir."

"Well, you still think it's a go, Dan?"

"Yes, sir, I feel we have enough to continue our operations, sir. The only problems we face now are bad weather or a major breakdown of one of our machines."

"Well, one of your machines is in trouble. John Lind has some main bearing problems. He is putting in at Miami. Mechanics from Jacksonville already on their way. You should be hearing from him tonight, or first thing tomorrow. He feels at the worst, he will be down for a week, no more."

"Jesus, I hope no more, sir. He needs to be heading towards Puerto Rico, and soon."

"We have no back ups, O'Brien. If one or the other toys screw-up and break down, it's good-bye Mister Chips, remember that."

"Yes, sir."

"Now, Ian tells me you are planning a meeting with the team. When and where are you putting this together?"

"Working on that right now, sir. It will most likely be in Lauderdale, in the next few days."

"Good, keep me informed. I will be down in Norfolk for a couple of days, but I can be reached."

"Yes, sir, thank you."

O'Brien put the phone down. "Shit."

"What's up, Dan?"

"Sonar has main bearing problems, damn, they told me she had perfect engines three weeks ago. I bet that fucking John Lind pushed those two power plants to their limits, shit, he knows how bad we need that ship on this mission, that asshole."

"Easy, Dan, it may not be that bad, let's wait till you know. Where is he now?"

"Somewhere off the east coast near Miami, I guess. He is heading in right now."

"Is Lind supposed to call you?"

"Yeah, what an asshole. Wait a minute, Jesus, it just hit me. The Admiral said nothing about the KGB being on board with Castro. Either Billings did one hell of a selling job on the old man, or he didn't tell him. Whatever, I owe Mr. Billings, big time."

O'Brien moved over to the coffee maker, and poured the rest of the pot into two cups. He went over and opened his brief case and removed a legal pad and placed in on the island counter in front of Buckwheat.

"O.K, let's get organized, Commander." O'Brien picked up the phone and dialed Avery's office in Sarasota.

"Good morning, Gail, is Phil there? Good."

"Morning, Phil. Just talked to D.C. We got our final call from our Cuban friends last night, and I feel we have enough information to go on. I want to put the entire team together over in Lauderdale as soon as you can to go over final decisions, instructions and general information. Can you suggest a meeting place? You don't think we will draw too much attention there, do you? Good. What's the address? O.K., I got it. Now, let's shoot for Wednesday. You take care of getting you and Gail over there. We will set the meeting for noon and tell the troops to arrive at different times in the morning. Are sure you have enough room? Well, there's Collins, Buckwheat, you and Gail, Lind, Bollman and Captain Chen. Unless there is a major change, we will see you at your place at noon."

O'Brien put the phone down.

"Avery has a condo over there, on South East 15th street. Says there is always lots of activity around, people coming and going. There is a parking lot at the end of the block where we can park our cars. Now, we have to call the rest of the team."

"If you don't mind, Dan, I'll fly down to the Keys and meet with Captain Chen and bring him up to Lauderdale with me. I would like to bring him up to date before he meets everyone, o.k.?"

"Sure, I'll pick up Collins and fly over late Tuesday. Say, would you mind picking up Captain Lind? He's going to be in Miami, probably up on the river somewhere, I will have Lou Bollman check on him and advise you where to find him, is that alright?"

"Sure, Dan, no problem. Well, I think I will go and get packed up. It's a four-hour drive to Lauderdale. I will set up some rooms for us, somewhere close to Avery's. There are a few places on 17th street and over on U.S. 1."

"Sounds good, but scatter us around, and no titles. I'm going to call Jesus Souza and thank him. I see no need to involve him further at this time. His system really worked, now he can call in all those unknown troops who made this mission possible."

O'Brien made his calls. He promised Souza that he would come to Miami and see him later in the week. He called Billings and advised him of the meeting, and told him he had dismissed Souza and the support team at the airports. He also called and advised Admiral Koster of the meeting place.

St. Petersburg\Clearwater Airport
Tropical Aviation

Tuesday, November 17
1010 hours

"Mr. O'Brien, when did you say you would be coming back?"

"Ah, I should be back on Thursday, late."

"Do you have any idea how many hours you will be putting on the plane? The reason I ask, it is six hours away from an oil change and fifty-hour inspection."

"Ah, not to worry, I won't be flying over six hours, I'm sure."

Through the office door, dressed in a gray sweat suit with the letters USF printed on the chest, walked Ted Collins.

"Hey, Captain Midnight, are you ready to go? For a guy who hates little airplanes, you're getting to be quite a fan." O'Brien said laughing.

"Oh, I made up my mind, Daniel, I have to put my trust in something, and somebody, so it might as well be a Cessna with a rocket scientist at the wheel."

Collins and O'Brien couldn't help but notice the curious expression on the young woman's face behind the service counter.

"He's not really a rocket scientist. He is really a washed out ass-trow-nut, who flunked his physical."

"Have you got everything, Mr. Collins?"

"Yep, right here in my bag, sir. Can I cut my beautiful wife loose now? She is outside in the car waiting to see if you are sober enough to fly this morning."

"Go ahead, cut her loose. I'll meet you at the bar, I mean, the plane."

Collins picked up his hanging bag and headed out the door to the waiting Cessna. He stopped and winked at the young lady receptionist.

"Not to worry little lady, I never let him at the controls."

Lantana Marina
Santiago De Cuba
1100 Hours

"Well, Captain, what do you think?"

"She is the most beautiful yacht I have seen, General."

"Well, it is still somewhat messy, but in a few days the construction will be completed and clean-up can begin."

"I would like to get my crew together as soon as possible, General, and start going over the systems, especially the electronics. We will be installing new radios and new communications systems, won't we?"

"No, Captain, it won't be necessary. Unicorn has all you need, according to Captain Amadore. He has gone over all the communication gear, and it was decided that it is best for this mission not to use any military equipment. You won't be needing military frequencies. We are a private yacht, comrade, remember that. Captain Amadore told us you have state of the art electronics aboard."

259

"General, I fully agree with Captain Amadore, the electronics are very sophisticated. I just thought, with having our President aboard we would want to have..."

General Vincetta interrupted. "Come, let's move off the boat, Captain, there are many ears around. We can use the marina office over there, it's more private."

The two officers walked carefully along the cluttered deck of the Unicorn until they reached the temporary staircase and landing.

"I couldn't help but notice, General, over there, in the shadows, there are guards standing around two large crates. Do they have something to do with my new assignment?"

"Yes, and you will learn about those crates later in the day."

Vincetta reached the office with Captain De Torre, only to find that it was in use. Vincetta suggested they walk down by the seawall outside of the hangar.

"Captain, you were told by General Rogelio that you were picked for a special mission for our President. You were also told this mission is of total secrecy. Not even Commodore Santamaria will know about it. He will be told that you are going to be training a crew on a new more powerful experimental patrol boat, under my command."

"What about my crew, General? I will need at least five to six men aboard this yacht. We have no experience with these MTU engines."

"We realize this, comrade, but all the technical books are on board, why should our engineers have problems working on them? They should be pleased to get away from the shit the Russians have been giving us. As far as the crew is concerned, they will be picked by you, then screened. Once you have their names, we will issue orders and have them transferred. I will give them strict instructions. You will not have to worry about their security."

The young captain stood on the edge of the seawall. Fifty feet away, tied to the opposite seawall, the stately yacht floated patiently, as workmen put the finishing touches on the modifications.

"You know, General, to be a Captain on such a particular yacht, a Feadship built yacht, is quite an honor."

"I would think you are correct. I know little about capitalist luxury yachts, but our President has said as much."

For the next three hours, General Vincetta and Captain De Torre discussed the mission, its importance to the President and the state. De Torre was also introduced to the "Dolphin" by its creator and given a crash course on its operation.

Later in the afternoon, they flew back to Havana. Fidel Castro was pleased to hear from his general that De Torre accepted the mission.

CHAPTER 16

Ft. Lauderdale, Florida
Wednesday, November 18th
0643 hours

The sun rose slowly over the warm waters of the Gulf Stream as it quietly snaked its way north close to the world famous beaches of Fort Lauderdale. A number of chartered sport fishing yachts were zigzagging over the calm ocean waters trolling through the long weed lines with their outriggers down and hooks baited with ballyhoos waiting for the strike and the welcome battle with the colorful blue and yellow bullhead dolphins.

On the beach, a uniformed policeman was bending over a large colorful bundle covered in sand, poking at it with his nightstick. Within the cloth cocoon, two teenagers had been sleeping. One of them shouting, clearly telling the officer where he could jam his nightstick. At the water's edge, two senior citizens, dressed in colorful sweat suits, were having a jogging marathon, disturbing hundreds of resting sea birds that stood in their path.

Phil Avery's Condominium
S.E. 15th Street
0652

Horizontal rays of light created by the sun leaking between thin plastic blinds, cast strange patterns on the wall over Phil Avery's bed, as he lay blowing smoke from his cigarette through the beams. He watched as the swirling smoke moved upward and formed small clouds that disappeared along the ceiling. It reminded him of the summer storms that build daily over Florida. They start out from low broken clouds that come together, begin to change their color as if they were exploding, then begin boiling upward into the endless sky. He turned and looked at the glowing red numbers on the nightstand clock, it read 6:59.

Avery heard a metallic clicking sound coming from the kitchen area. He threw his legs over the side of the bed, stood up and began walking towards the bedroom door. He was about to reach for the knob, when the door opened. Standing inches away in the doorway was his former roommate and lover, Nancy. It was difficult at first to see the details of her face in the backlight. He could however, see her curvaceous figure. His pulse began pounding in his temples as the scent of her cologne swam around in his head and he could taste its flavor in his mouth. He wanted to put his arms around her and tell her how much he missed and needed her.

"Hello, Phil, I hope I am not disturbing you. I saw your car in the parking lot and figured you were here. I, I just wanted to return your keys."

Avery began to feel awkward, he wanted to touch her and wrap his arms around her.

"Ah, sure, thanks. Ah, would you like to stay for a minute? I would like to talk, why don't you make us some coffee, I'll just throw on.."

"I can't stay, Phil, I have a flight out at eight. Maybe some other time. I'll leave the keys on the kitchen counter."

Nancy spun around and went down the short hall into the kitchen and out the door before Avery could grab his robe. He stood at the kitchen door, opened the jalousie window and looked out into the empty breezeway. He heard a car door close, followed by the sound of a starter motor, then the roar of an engine. He leaned his head against the cold aluminum window frame.

"It isn't over, not by a long shot," Avery told himself. He could feel every bone in his body begin to ache. With his eyes closed, he welcomed visions of Nancy rinsing her long hair in the shower, sitting naked in front of her dressing table playing with her long eyelashes. He could almost feel her long body pressing against his as he inhaled the sweet and spicy scents of her body. Phil closed his right fist and slammed it into the metal doorframe. He felt no pain, just rejection.

The phone rang on the nearby wall.

"Hello?"

"Phil? Hi, it's Gail. I'm about to leave the hotel. Do you want me to stop at Publix and pick up some food or snacks for the meeting? We never did talk about feeding the troops. What do you have there in the way of drinks? Are you going to serve beer or booze later?"

"Damn, I gave it no thought, why don't I meet you at the store. It will take me fifteen minutes to get ready, what time did we tell the guys to start showing up?

"There was no specific time set for them to start arriving," Gail responded. "Buckwheat and O'Brien are having breakfast right now at the Marina Motor Inn. They should be arriving at your place within the hour. Phil, let me do the shopping, I'll get enough stuff to get us by. My only concern is I don't have a car. I'm doing all this by taxi, do you think this will look a little strange when I arrive at your condo?"

"You're right, you had better call me when you're ready for pick up. I will come, or I'll send someone to get you, don't take a cab."

The doorbell rang.

"Jesus, someone is at the front door, call me from the store when you're ready, Gail."

Avery put the phone down and ran to open the front door. Standing in the doorway a giant of a man dressed in white slacks, white boat shoes, open collar blue oxford button down shirt and a navy blue blazer. A white golfers cap, with crossed golf clubs, sat on his massive head. For a few seconds Avery just stood and stared at him.

"Well, Captain? Are you going to invite me in?"

"Of course, sir, ah, please, come in."

"Avery, you blooming asshole, it's me, Admiral Koster."

"Of course, I know, sir, it's just, well, I wasn't expecting to see you, ah, I mean we didn't know you were coming."

"Where's the coffee? and I hope you have decaf."

"Yes, sir, this way. I'm afraid it's instant, sir."

Koster followed Avery through the hallway back to the kitchen, where he instantly took over. He took the kettle from the counter and went to the sink and added water. All Avery could do was watch.

"Sir, the coffee is in that cabinet to your left, there should be some decaf there. Ah, the spoons are over in that drawer next to the stove, milk and sugar in the fridge, and if you don't mind, I would like to get dressed?"

"Do it, I'll find what I need. What time is the crew arriving?"

"Ah, they will be staggering in all morning, We didn't want to draw attention to ourselves. O'Brien wants to start the meetings at noon."

"Go get ready, I'm alright. I'll wait in the living room, if that's o.k. with you? and do you mind if I put the TODAY show on?"

"Ah, sure, sir, the remote for the TV is on the coffee table, I forget the channel, I think it is seven for NBC. If you need me just yell."

Avery returned to his bedroom and closed the door. He started for the phone but remembered that Gail had said O'Brien was already on his way with Buckland. There was no way to warn him, but maybe O'Brien knew Koster was coming.

The doorbell rang again.

"I'll get it, Avery," Koster called out.

He opened the door and was confronted by two men who looked like they just came off Space Mountain in Disney World. O'Brien and Buckland stood speechless and paralyzed at the sight of Admiral Koster.

"Well, just don't stand there like two dorks, get in here."

"Admiral Koster? I had no idea that you were going be here."

"Of course not. The President of the United States doesn't know I'm here."

O'Brien and Buckland stepped into the room. Koster closed the door and walked towards the kitchen. Avery, dressed in shorts and Tee shirt arrived in the kitchen ahead of Koster. He could see O'Brien's puzzled face, but all he could do was shrug his shoulders.

"I have coffee brewing over here." Avery reached up and opened a cabinet and brought out a number of colorful coffee mugs. He opened the refrigerator and took out a quart of milk and a small sugar bowl.

"Ah, anybody want some orange juice, or tomato juice?"

"Naw, coffee is fine," O'Brien responded.

"Well, Admiral, we are pleased to see you. Will you be staying for the meeting later, or are you just passing through?"

Koster leaned back against the sink cabinet and moved a spoon slowly around inside his coffee mug, never taking his eyes off the mug.

"I would hardly get dressed up like some yacht club twit just to be passing through, Mr. O'Brien. No, I am here to listen and learn and maybe even put in put in my two cents. For example, have you had contact with John Lind yet?"

"Ah, no sir. I was not able to contact him last night in Miami. I know that he made it up the Miami River, and he is berthed at a yard called Allied Marine. Lou Bollman had a couple of men watching for him. He called us when Captain Lind got docked."

"That's correct, O'Brien. Lind tied up at 0130 hours. I had breakfast with him at some greasy spoon on LeJeune Road at 0300 this morning. He said he will be here around 1100 hours. The good news, Mr. O'Brien, is that SONAR doesn't have any main bearing problems. All she has is a few clogged fuel injectors. It's not nearly as serious as was first reported. Captain Lind estimates he can be heading out by Monday for San Juan, and could be there about December 1st."

"That's good news, Admiral. We still have to.."

Admiral Koster interrupted. "O'Brien, what I want to know is why you or Buckland were not down there in Miami to meet Captain Lind and look into his problems when he arrived?"

Embarrassed, O'Brien tried to think of a good explanation.

"I did not feel it was necessary, sir. Captain Lind had been sent the information about today's meeting, and he confirmed that he would be here. You advised me he had some mechanical problems but they were being taken care of by some mechanics coming from Jacksonville. I saw no need to be in Miami, sir."

"The point is, O'Brien, you are in charge of this operation, and responsible for its people and its problems. You have a very special sailor in John Lind, and you're treating him with little respect."

O'Brien felt his face turn red. He ground his teeth as he curled his toes inside his weathered boat shoes.

"Admiral, Captain Lind has been playing shake-down-cruise for nearly two weeks. He has not exactly kept in touch with me. I had a hell of a time getting word to him on the radio to advise him of the meeting."

Koster put his mug in the sink. He glanced at O'Brien over his heavy-framed glasses, then walked out of the small kitchen and into the living room. Avery caught O'Brien's eye and winked. Buckwheat reached out and patted O'Brien's shoulder as he passed by him heading for the living room.

The phone rang and Avery picked it up. Gail Townsend had finished her food shopping.

By 1200 hours, all the players had arrived and were gathered in the living room. Admiral Koster, Jack Chen, Ted Collins, Phil Avery, Gail Townsend, John Lind, Commander Buckland, Lou Bollman and Dan O'Brien.

O'Brien opened the meeting. "Today we will try to put all the final touches on Operation Yuletide. If there are any weak spots, mechanical or equipment problems, we need to know now."

Admiral Koster cleared his throat loudly to get O'Brien's attention. "If I may, Dan, I would like to address the crew."

"Of course, Admiral."

Koster sat deep down in the crowded sofa. He rested his large hands on his knees and looked around the room over his thick glasses. "Dan is the only person, apart from the President himself, who knows how skeptical I was about this mission from the beginning. When O'Brien produced his plan on how he thought he could pull this off, I thought he had some porch lights blinking somewhere. However, he convinced me that, with all of you and your varied talents, it could be done. Now, just five weeks away from Christmas, we need to look at what has been accomplished and what is left to be done. Mr. O'Brien? The floor is yours."

"Admiral, I know you have put your neck on the line for us, and we are all grateful that you still believe in our efforts. We will not let you down, sir."

"Hear, hear," came the light cheer from the group, raising coffee mugs, glasses with orange juice and two beers.

O'Brien walked over to the island cabinet and rested against the counter and began his report.

"First let me update everyone on our communications with our Cuban friends. The Christmas Tree is no longer working, it unfortunately burned out. We will not be receiving any more messages from Cuba. I have officially relieved Jesus Souza, our man at Eastern Airlines, and all our agents who were working the communication network at airports throughout the Caribbean have all been recalled and are back on their jobs in the States. The information we have received from our Cuban friends is what we will go with. From now on, all our information will be coming from the eyes in the skies over Cuba provided by the Air Force, their SR-71 Blackbirds and U-2 spy planes, and some satellite service. Keep in mind that they too are limited by weather conditions. Here are the latest facts that we do have."

O'Brien stepped over to the wall between the kitchen and the living room. Taped to the wall above the counter was a standard Omega chart, INT 402, showing the entire Caribbean Sea, including south Florida. Next to the chart was a blow up of a section of the 402 showing the island of Guadeloupe. O'Brien put his briefcase up on the counter, took out an envelope and emptied the contents onto the counter. There were a number of small, brightly colored flags.

"Wonderful what we learn as kids." He held up one of the flags. "Ever make these in school? Wooden matches, straight pins, colored paper and white paste glue."

He began sticking the small flags into the chart.

"Jesus, Phil, O'Brien doesn't have much respect for your wallpaper, does he?" Collins said laughing.

"Not to worry, Teddy old man. I have very sharp pins that leave very little holes."

O'Brien took his felt pen and pointed to a group of islands on the smaller chart. "Right here, just a couple of miles south of the island of Guadeloupe, there are a few small islands known as Les Saintes. This island here, southwest of Terre de Bas and Terre de Haut, is called Grand Islet. It has a small, protected cove on the leeward side that is a popular small hurricane hole with cruising sailors. It is a deep-water cove, but one needs to know how to maneuver through the reefs and sand bar that protect it. This is where the meeting will take place. We know there are two other yachts that will be meeting with Castro's yacht. We don't know, however, where they are coming from, and who will be on them. We can only speculate. Ian Billings is working with a number of international agencies and South American governments to monitor all the ports where yachts belonging to drug cartel suspects are located. Billings is not putting much faith in this however. He feels they stand a better chance with surveillance of the movements of major South American drug lords and their associates during Christmas week."

"Excuse me, Dan, do we have any better details about that cove, other than what's on the standard charts?" Collins asked.

"No, but we are working on that. There is information supposedly in some cruising guides. However, we have, or I should say, Admiral Koster has a good friend who is the Commanding Officer of the NASA tracking station on Antigua. Arrangements are being made to have photography done from the air and sea of the cove, and if time permits, even a scouting visit to take actual soundings and measurements of the cove. This information could be helpful for Captain Chen here. His UDT team will be setting the charges on Castro's yacht and if all goes well, the charges will detonate in the cove. If it's real shallow, the explosives could be twice as effective.

"Fidel Castro, along with his number one General, Alberto Vincetta, KGB agent Dimitri Sorokin and a crew of four to five and an unknown oriental will be leaving Santiago de Cuba on December 21st at 0600 hours."

O'Brien pointed to a small circle on the southeast coast of Cuba. He took one of the flags with a red pennant and stuck it in the circle. "They will most likely run due south here, down through the Jamaica Channel, then head east-south-east directly to Guadeloupe, just off the southern coast of Haiti and the Dominican Republic. This heavy black line is the course we anticipate Castro's yacht will take. Twin 900 horsepowered engines power the yacht, a 124-foot Feadship. She has a four thousand-mile cruise range, and is capable of reaching speeds up to twenty knots. Her cruising speed is around sixteen to seventeen knots. The Unicorn, as she is known, has the latest electronic equipment on board, with back-up systems." O'Brien reached into his brief case and pulled out a large brown envelope. He pulled out a number of 8 by 10 black and white photos. He kept one and handed the rest to Ted Collins, who handed them out.

"Here she is, the Unicorn. She is a beautifully styled Feadship yacht. Study her hard and make notes on her features. One thing you may note, is the special framework, or halo, that supports her large radar dish above the flying bridge. A smaller dish is located just below the open bridge windscreen. Her mast has double spreaders, and the Satnav dome is painted black. Over her owner's cabin, you can see the streamlined funnel. Note the Unicorn cartoon artwork. Over the main saloon she has two pairs of davits that haul her two auxiliary boats on and off her upper deck. The boat you are looking at, under that cover, is a 21-foot Donzi. It's red and white. On the other side, not shown in the photo, is a Boston Whaler, maybe 14 to 15 feet, with a Mercury outboard. On the back of the photo, I have attached the

Unicorn's floor plan and specifications. Captain Chen? At the end of this meeting, I do have some plans for you and your UDT team. We have the complete set of plans that show her running gear, keel and the locations of water intakes, positions of struts, shafts and rudders."

"Dan, for those of us who will come in contact with the Unicorn, and I take it, we are still planning on doing this at night. Is there any lighting or markings that we can spot to make sure she's our target?"

"Good question, Captain Chen, and I don't have an answer for you. We have no night photos on her. My guess though, she will be running with minimum interior lights, but for sure she will have her navigation lights on. It's going to be Phil Avery's call out there to decide if it is Castro, when the time comes."

Avery, sitting on the floor leaning up against the sofa raised his hand. "Dan is right. The Unicorn will be running at that hour with just her required navigation lights. My question is, when I make radio contact, if I make contact, will she give her proper name?"

"I don't see why not," O'Brien responded. "They took no precautions to ever hide her, until she disappeared into Santiago Bay. My guess is that she will respond to her name, Unicorn. Keep in mind, they are cruising and acting like a normal touring yacht. They won't do anything that would attract any attention to them, I am certain." O'Brien looked for any doubtful looks in the faces of his audience around the room, he found none.

"O.k., let me do this." O'Brien took the colored flags one by one and placed them on the chart. He put the white flag at St. Thomas, a green flag at St. Croix, a blue flag at St. Lucia and checked the red flag at Santiago.

"Each of these flags represent our players in this game of finding the Unicorn."

"This flag, the white flag, is the Island Drummer, located in St. Thomas, code name, Yuletide. Just south, on the island of St. Croix, we have the green flag. This is you, Captain Lind, and Sonar, code name, Red Sleigh. Down here in St. Lucia, we have Captain Spencer on the Seaduce, code name, Music Box, wearing the blue flag. Over here in Cuba, the red flag, appropriately I might add, is the Unicorn, code name, FruitCake. Here, in this red circle are the cross hairs, that show where we hope our interception will take place. You might note this vertical line moving down from St. Croix is the route of the Sonar and the Drummer. It is exactly 180 degrees on the course line. Over here, you will see I have a heavy pencil line that leaves St. Lucia and runs northward up to Antigua, and connects with this line running almost due west from Antigua. This is the course that Seaduce will take to intercept Sonar and the Island Drummer. Can everyone see these lines? Good."

"Excuse me, Mr. O'Brien, but as the latecomer into this crazy operation, I have a few questions that I need answered."

"I realize that, Captain Lind," O'Brien said as he reached into his brief case. "Here, let me give you this right now."

O'Brien reached into the brief case and brought out a large brown envelope. "Please pass this back to Captain Lind, thank you. You don't need to open that just now. I will tell you briefly what it contains. Later, you and I will go over the materials in depth. For now, however, let me explain your operational moves. "First, in that envelope you will find all your new ship papers for the Sonar. You will also find your new identification papers, including drivers licenses, Social Security card, a couple of credit cards and your passport. All we need is a current photo. Please, don't shave that beard."

"What the hell do you mean new identity?"

"It's just a precaution. You will also find your manifest for the cargo you will pick up in San Juan. You will be taking on four tons of cedar shakes, destination Barbados, for the American Embassy. You will leave San Juan, and head for St. Croix where you will drop anchor. You will let it be known that you are having mechanical problems and will order parts from the States, that we will eventually ship to you. You and I will discuss this later and decide what mechanical failure we could use. You will hang around the island until you receive the new parts and make repairs. You will await word of when and were to pick up Captain Chen and his team. Your orders will come by phone call through the local clearing house named in your kit. The message will simply tell you when your departure time is. We will give you at least a twelve-hour notice. Upon notice you will leave Christiansted heading west. Your course and coordinates are in your kit. As you can see, from St. Croix to the interception point is approximately eighty miles. You will be cruising at fifteen knots. It will take you about five hours to reach this point, fifteen miles north of the intersection. You will need to monitor your radar and VHF radios, and locate Spencer and the Seaduce as soon as you can. He will be heading for this same location on his westerly course. We will be using standard VHF frequency, channel 72. You will send all messages in code from Sonar using the code names. Once you make contact with Seaduce, you coordinate your rendezvous. Seaduce will transfer its four charter guests to your ship. One of Chen's men will board the Seaduce with Captain Spencer and set explosive charges throughout her hull, then return. The Seaduce is to stay close on your portside at all times, this

271

is very important. When the Unicorn picks you up on their radar, we want them to see only one bogie. Seaduce must stay in your shadow at all times. If the seas are calm, you and the Unicorn will be seeing each other on your screens from at least fifteen to twenty miles out, so keep you eyes open for him. He will be coming from the southwest moving at sixteen knots or better. It is most important you hide the Seduce in your shadow, do I make myself clear?"

"Jesus, this is getting more like D-Day every minute. Isn't there a cleaner way to blow Castro's ass of the water instead of all this cat and mouse shit?"

"Cool it, John, you have been through worse. Let's hear Dan out, but first, will someone get me a drink of water?"

"Sure, Admiral, would you like some ice?" Gail asked.

"Thank you, Ms. Townsend, yes."

"Continue, Dan, excuse the interruption."

O'Brien put a cigarette in his mouth but decided not to light it and dropped it in his glass. He continued. "Up here in St. Thomas, we have Phil, Gail and Buckwheat on Island Drummer, or I should say, Yuletide, waiting for their call. Also on board, their four charter guests. When the call comes through their clearinghouse, they will prepare for departure. Gail, please make a note here. Don't forget to call the clearinghouse and make sure they know you are heading for St. Maarten. Also give them your itinerary, like a stop at Virgin Gorda. Once you have cleared past the east end of St. Thomas, call the clearing house again and advise them that your charter folks decided they want to see Antigua instead, that you're changing course and estimate you will arrive at Antigua in twenty four hours on your float plan. This would be the normal sailing time for the Drummer to cover this mileage according to Phil's estimates, right Phil?"

"Right," Avery responded.

"In St. Lucia, down here in Marigot Bay, we have the Seaduce with Captain Spencer, Paul Gransaull and their four charter guests waiting. This situation right now is my only concern. Seaduce is nearly three hundred miles from the interception point, which could be too risky. What we might do, is move Seaduce with their charter from St. Lucia up to Antigua early. Spencer's destination from there will be Jamaica, that's what he will advise his clearing house when he picks up his charter guests in Marigot Bay. We will move his timetable up, and get him up to English Harbor in Antigua, and advise him when to head out to meet Captain Lind and Sonar from there."

John Lind raised his hand. "O'Brien, I have to ask this. These charter guests, there are eight of them, correct? Four on the Seaduce and four on the

Drummer, just who are these people? Aren't they going to wonder what the hell's going on here?"

"They would under normal conditions, I guess, but these people have been carefully selected by Ian Billings. I believe they are all CIA agency people, am I correct, Admiral?"

"Yes, they are agency people, briefed to play their part as fun loving couples on vacation. They will all carry phony papers, like you, John. I believe they will all be posing as vacationing Canadians. None of them can be traced back to anywhere."

O'Brien continued. "Each of you must be at your points of departure by December 20th ready to sail. All problems, human or mechanical, must be taken care of before this date. You have to be ready to go. If you're not, we are inside a very small time envelope here, and we won't have much time to fix anything, is that understood?"

There was no verbal response, just a little head bobbing.

"Now that you can see where all our players are, let's do a dry run. Let's pretend that it's December 20th, twenty four hours before Castro is scheduled to leave Cuba."

"Phil, Gail and Buckwheat, you're standing by here in Charlotte Amalie, ready to go. Your guests are aboard, and your clearinghouse knows your plans for running through the British Virgins, a stop over at Virgin Gorda, then on to St. Maarten.

"Captain Lind, you are standing by at anchor off Christiansted at St. Croix, waiting on parts for your ship, before you can continue on down to Barbados. Captain Chen, you and your UDT team are living somewhere at the St. Croix airport in the Army Reserves barracks.

"The Seaduce, is now at English Harbor in Antigua.

"Time, 0600 on December 21st. Unicorn is spotted sometime in the next couple of hours heading south. By 1000 hours, a message from a SR-71 Blackbird is sent to McDill Air Force Base in Tampa, Florida. Calls are made and messages are forwarded to all the waiting players. The messages will actually be sent out of Bollman's communications office in Miami. There are also four special phone lines going into this office. Each of you will be assigned one of these numbers, and you will have the only access to that number." O'Brien handed Phil Avery and John Lind a small white sealed envelope.

"These numbers, gentlemen, are to be used only in case of an emergency.

"Avery, when your message comes it will tell you to call your Lauderdale office, it's an emergency."

"That's it? There's an emergency, and to call my office?"

"That's it Phil. Your clearinghouse will get the phone call, and will call you on the VHF and give you the message. You may want to check in with them if they haven't called by 1700 hours on the 22nd. The message, "it's an emergency", is the signal that the Unicorn is underway. You then get to a public phone and call the number I just gave you for any additional information, or changes in the plan.

"Captain Lind, your call, like Avery's, will come from your clearing house in Christiansted. Your message will be the same, as will Spencer's. They will tell you to call your office, or in your case, Captain Lind, call home, that it's an emergency. Again, the word emergency is the key that Unicorn is on the move. Captain Lind, you will also have to check in by 1700 hours with your clearinghouse if they haven't called you.

"Now, what if Unicorn is not spotted or we can't confirm her departure and location? Simple, there will be no messages. However, you make your calls in any case and you will be advised as to what to do. Now, should an act of God occur or for any reason you can't get out on a land phone, use your single side bands, the instructions are in those envelopes on what to do, should this happen to any of you. God forbid that we get into a weather problem down there that could affect any of you, without all the players, we don't have a mission."

O'Brien turned and went back to the large chart. He picked up his marking pen and put the point of it on Santiago De Cuba. "If you all look closely you will note that there are times and headings marked in pencil along the Unicorn's route. Here at the port of Santiago, I marked 0600. Down here, where Unicorn will change course and head east, you will see 1800 hours. Here, just south of Isla Beata, you see 0300. Here, due south of the Mona Passage between Puerto Rico and Hispaniola, 1200. Here, at the intersection where Castro's course crosses the course of Sonar, Seaduce and Drummer, 2200. Needless to say, these are the hour marks where the Unicorn should be, if she's on course and there are no mechanical breakdowns or bad weather. As you can see, Unicorn is going to be right here, in the black of night with no moon, between 2200 and 2400 hours. The ball is in our court and so is Fidel. Once we are certain that Castro is on his way and we get our next report that he is on the predicted course, the rest is easy. We compute his speed, the seas, tide and winds and wait. We can have everyone in place in plenty of time. As you can see, with no complications, it will take Castro 36 hours to reach the proposed intercept point. We know he will be at that point somewhere between 2200-2400 hours. Captain Lind, you need five hours to reach your position. Avery, you will have to calculate your times to work within your twenty four-hour framework. You have approximately six to seven hours of running down to the intercept point, depending your allowable speeds. Prior to getting there you must meet with Captain Lind and Sonar, pick up Captain Chen, his team, all their gear and head out. Your departure from St. Thomas is critical, as it must work out with your time clock to be in Antigua twenty-four hours later, or less, no more. You could even travel close to Sonar, providing nobody sees you under power at fifteen knots. I can't stress enough, that your departure times have to be realistic, and made record of at your clearing houses, or we lose our cover stories, should an investigation ever take place after the, ah, accident. Avery, your log time, times checking in and out with your clearing houses is the most important of all, that is what the Drummer is all about. She has to leave St. Thomas, show up here, one hundred and fifty miles due south, haul ass, and make Antigua in twenty four hours."

"Hold it there, Mr. O'Brien. Again, I am the latecomer here, and I don't exactly understand this check in, check out, be in two places at one time with this Drummer sailboat. Why all this screwing around?"

"John, please, Dan will get back to that later, right Dan?"

"Yes, sir, thank you, Admiral. I will cover that later for you, Captain."

"Jesus, Dan, you sure are putting a lot of faith in VHF's out there, and with little or no discretion. Shit, anyone could pick us up and monitor our crazy Christmas jive talk."

"I agree, and it sounds silly, but I don't think we will have a lot of traffic in the area listening on channel 72. Had we put a lot of military stuff on board, it could be spotted, look suspicious, and could possibly be monitored. No, I think this is safer, at close ranges. We will use our single side bands if and when needed. Each player has his code name, and if we forgot them, here are some cards to remind you. Read them, memorize them, then give them back. They don't leave this room. Ah, Mr. Lind, you are the exception, here is a list of all our names and our code names, plus the yachts code names. Please study, then destroy."

O'Brien took a long drink of water, wiped his mouth and continued. " Now, back to Sonar and Drummer. Before you guys get to close to the intercept intersection, or within Unicorn's radar range, you need to shut down and get your personnel moved. Captain Chen and his team, plus his equipment need to be transferred to the Drummer. I'm forgetting something, what are we forgetting here?"

"The phony props, you forgot about the props, Dan. They are still back in Ft. Lauderdale, waiting for Captain Lind to pick them up." Ted Collins was not trying to be a smartass, but he did make O'Brien feel stupid.

"Shit, I forgot. Ah, Captain Lind. Somehow, we have to get some crates and packages down to you in Miami in the next couple of days. I thought you were coming into port here, and we shipped some props over for you to pick up."

"Props, spares? I have two spare props, what the hell?

"No, not propeller type props, these are, ah like movie props, fake things that we need to put on the Drummer to look like she was damaged."

"What?"

"They have to make the Drummer look like she was in a storm, you know, torn sails and deck damage, plus the new name plates. She is going to be the Seaduce for a few hours, that's part of the plan, ah, you had better explain the rest, O'Brien."

"Hey, Dan?" Lou Bollman raised out of his seat. "Let's take five, I have to get up and move around."

"Right, Lou, let's take a small break here." Dan looked at his watch, it was 1345.

"I'm going to put out some food, if that's alright with you, Dan?"

"Sure, Gail, go ahead. Let's take about thirty minutes. Avery suggests that we don't go out on his back porch, or leave the building."

"Hey, Phil, how do you figure we are going to get out of here?" Buckwheat asked.

"Same way we snuck in, I guess. We go out in intervals."

John Lind moved over and sat next to Admiral Koster. They looked at each other for a long moment, then smiled.

"You sure got me into a fine mess this time, Ollie," Lind said doing a bad impression of Laurel.

"Oh, you can handle it, John. If you could maneuver a sinking destroyer, on one boiler through half of the Jap fleet at Leyte, you can pull this off with your eyes closed."

"That was forty-three years ago, Admiral, and I was young and stupid. I can't help but feel there's an easier way to do this. It seems so confusing and complicated."

"It's O'Brien, he thrives on this shit. But I give him his dues, he has thought it out pretty well. He's not leaving any traces behind."

"This charade with these two yachts, one pretending it's the other, then taking off on some super engines that get it there in half the time? Is all this really necessary?"

"Yep. Dan says so. It's called, "covering our asses." Personally, I don't care how he pulls this caper off. If he gets Castro and a few of those drug bastards, it was worth it. The only troubling news I have heard so far is having this KGB bastard along with Castro. I don't like the smell of that. I know for a fact these guys face execution if they're caught messing with drugs, that's Gorbachev law. Let's get something to eat, John, I'm starved."

It was nearly 1500 hours before Dan got his audience together again. During the break, he told Phil he would call on him to explain what takes place when he meets the Unicorn.

"Alright, now let's get back to our game board here. Let's say its nearing the hour of intercept. Unicorn is on course and on time. Captain Lind, you are right here, about twelve to fifteen miles north of the intersection, drifting at idle, you don't want to be too close to Castro and Avery, too soon. Spencer is in your radar shadow, also idling. Phil, you and the Drummer are about here, just south of the intercept. Let's review your program, Phil."

"Sure, Dan." Avery walked up to the charts and placed his finger in the red circle. "When we reach our position in the path of the Unicorn, we immediately start preparing and converting the Drummer into the Seaduce. We change flags, and put on the new nameplates. We install the torn and tattered mainsail to the boom, run the ripped jib up the spare headstay. Smoke pots are put in place, and the cabin windows are sprayed with black water paint to look smoked. We also have some water paint that we will pour over the cabins to look like smoke damage. As soon as we pick up the Unicorn on our radar, we will begin our SOS transmissions. We will be sending out a weak signal so we don't alert other shipping that may be within range. I will keep sending my distress call until I get a response from the Unicorn. If they get close enough for a visual, and have not responded to my radio call, I will shoot off a shallow flare to get their attention."

"Dan, do you really think that the Unicorn will be listening to their radios?" Lind asked.

"I'd bet my life on it."

"First, the Unicorn has a powerful radar, and it stands about thirty-five feet off the water. In calm seas, he's going to have good eyes well beyond fifteen miles. He will see two blimps on his screen. One moving slowly from the north, and one stationary on his course. Castro's captain will have his radio on. He will hear the weak radio distress signal, and he will advise Fidel."

"Dan, pardon the interruption, but if Castro's yacht can clearly see a vessel on his course, especially a stationary one, and another closing in from twelve o'clock, don't you think his captain would elect to change course to avoid traffic? This is one part of your plan that has always concerned me."

"Admiral, under normal conditions, most probably he would change course, and I have given that much thought. However, I am putting my money on Castro to come to the rescue of the Seaduce. That is why it is so important for Phil to be sending those distress signals out the minute Castro is in range."

John Lind raised his hand again. "This whole operation right now is based on your gut feeling that Fidel Castro, regardless of what we have learned of him and his lack of respect for human rights, is really a sucker for strange distress signals?"

"Like I said, I'm betting on him to respond. You see, Captain Lind, I have read up a little on Fidel, and I know for a fact that in 1956, when he was returning to Cuba from exile to start his revolution, he boarded a leaky old American yacht in Mexico and barely made it to Cuba. A few days from Cuba, Castro's yacht hit a storm and almost sunk. Another American fishing boat found them, gave them food and water and helped pump out their sinking boat. The name of Castro's old yacht was "Granma", and it is a museum piece in Havana today. Castro respects the sea, and I believe, would come to the aid of a ship in trouble. If not him, his Captain certainly would recommend that they do so."

"O.K., Phil, would you please continue?" O'Brien asked.

"As soon as we get a response from the Unicorn, I will advise them of my situation. First, my ship is not in danger of sinking and my passengers, although concerned, are not injured. I will tell them that we were on our way to Jamaica, hit a freak storm and lost our sails. I also had a chemical fire in the engine room. My fuse box was destroyed, along with battery damage. Presently, I am working the radio with a small auxiliary battery. I will ask for 30 and 50 amp fuses, water, and any foods they can spare, that's all. I will convince them that with the fuses and some wire, I can get the auxiliary motor and generator running, pump the bilges and should be able to get the main engine running after a charge on the batteries.

"While the Unicorn is closing, I will put the dinghy in the water. Captain Chen's UDT team will already be in the water on the blind side of the hull. I will jump in the dinghy and start to paddle towards the Unicorn, keeping them from getting too close. I imagine they will have spotlights on and will look over the yacht. Our passengers will all be on deck waving, while the UDT team stays behind or beneath me. When I reach the Unicorn, I will repeat my needs. If they ask me to come aboard, which I doubt, I will refuse, telling them I don't want to leave my guests too long, and I am concerned about the smoke in the engine room. When I get my fuses and food, I will thank them and retreat, and ask them to signal any ships in the area of my position and condition, just in case more assistance is needed. I figure from the time I reach the Unicorn and pick up the supplies until the time I depart, should give us between five to ten minutes. During this time, I have to keep their attention on me somehow, and give Captain Chen and his crew the time he needs to get under the yacht, set his charges and swim clear again. Captain Chen, you told me you would need at least three minutes to work under the Unicorn and attach your charges, is that correct?"

"That's correct, Mr. Avery, all we need is about three minutes to hook up the charges, but we will need some time to get in position and to get clear, I figure six to seven minutes will be plenty of time if you can hold their attention that long, sir."

"You've got it, Captain, I'll get you the time," Avery said.

"O.K. Phil, thanks," O'Brien said as he lit another cigarette and sipped more water. "O.K, here we have Avery heading back to the Drummer, the UDT team has swum away from the Unicorn on the opposite side and standing by until the Unicorn is underway again, heading east. If the Unicorn does as Phil asked, and begins broadcasting a relay message to inform vessels of the Seaduce's condition, they should reach you, Captain Lind. When they do, you respond and tell them who you are, and that you will look for the distressed yacht on your course. At this time, and only if the Unicorn is moving, you go back to cruise speed and begin to close on the Drummer."

"Hold it here a minute. Dan. Captain Lind and Sonar are still in Unicorn's radar range, hopefully showing up as one bogie, correct?

"That's right, Phil, and I think I know what you are getting to, and you are right. Captain Lind can't move up to cruise at sixteen knots at this time, as he will be leaving Spencer and the Seaduce behind. "

Lind raised his hand. "If I may, I would like to make a suggestion. Once we all make contact with the Unicorn, I mean on our radar, I can calculate the speed that would keep Spencer hidden, so we can move together easily on course. Spencer's yacht, the Seaduce, she's capable of eight knots, isn't she?"

Ted Collins spoke. "Seaduce should be capable of at least ten knots, Captain."

"Dan, what I am trying to say is that it would look better if we were moving, even if it was a slow crawl. Remember, Castro's captain is watching and calculating my speed, and on your numbers I would have been a maximum of what, fifteen miles from intercept? If he is closing on Avery, say at fifteen knots, and he's the same distance away that I am, I'd better not be doing any more than ten knots, or less than five, I don't want to be crowding Captain Avery during his visit. If Castro's captain gets nervous of

279

my approach, he may want to get underway before Chen here and gets his charges set. Another thing, don't worry about Spencer, I will keep him in my shadow and direct him where he needs to be out of the radar search when the Unicorn moves eastward."

A sudden chill came over O'Brien. He studied Lind for a second and tried to remember how many beers he had consumed in the past few hours. "Where was Lind a few minutes ago when this was already explained?" He thought to himself.

O'Brien continued. "Captain Lind, Spencer will have to keep as close as he can to you, preferably off your stern on the starboard quarter now, as the radar signals will be coming at you from the southeastern direction."

"Mr. O'Brien, that is not our problem here. My problem, is that I am closing with Castro too fast from the positions you want us to be at. We either need to be dead in the water when Castro is in range, or fifteen miles from you, or further north, sir. Do you understand what I am saying?"

"Yes, I understand, Captain, and I agree, we need to work this out more clearly. Maybe it is best that you and the Seaduce remain stationary at this point here, fifteen miles north, until the exchange is over and the Unicorn is moving again."

"Dan, that would look a little too conspicuous from my bridge if I were Castro's captain. I disagree, I think you should be moving, John, maybe slowly, but be moving in some direction, but not sitting still, that would not be natural out there."

"You're right, Admiral. Captain Lind, just set your speed at a crawl and hide the Seaduce. You can increase your speed after the Unicorn sends out the appeal, that would look natural, don't you agree, Admiral?"

"Yes, Mr. O'Brien, I agree, however, I see at least an hour of cruising before the Sonar can reach the Unicorn even at full speed, providing you're fifteen miles up country."

"Good point, Admiral. Then, this is settled?" O'Brien asked.

Lind nodded his head in agreement.

O'Brien turned to Buckland. "Commander, you and Gail along with your charter guests will start tearing down the props and preparing the Drummer for your exit to Antigua as soon as the Unicorn is safely out of view and Chen's team and Avery are back on board. Phil, as soon as Sonar arrives alongside with the Seaduce, you get Chen's team and the charter folks on board the Sonar. Once the Unicorn is out of sight and hopefully out of radar range, you start your run north." O'Brien put his finger on a pencil line that began at the intercept point, ran northeast then eastward. "You have to follow this course to take you out of Unicorn's radar range, and you're going to have to haul ass to keep your arrival time within the limits of your float plan, no more than twenty four hours out of St. Thomas, this is crucial. The clock is ticking now, boys and girls."

"Captain Lind, after you reach the Drummer, you remain stationary as long as it takes to set up the Seaduce. Captain Chen, after you and your party set the charges on the Seaduce, you retreat back to the Sonar. Spencer and Gransaull will put the Seaduce on her disaster course, under power, jump into the dinghy and return to the Sonar. Now, Captain Chen, it's all in the timing. You will have the remote detonator transmitter. When you feel the Seaduce is far enough away from Sonar, let it go. We can only hope that the atmosphere is such that the explosion is noticed by the crew on the Unicorn."

"That should be no problem, Mr. O'Brien. The way we have designed the sequence and the amount of explosive we will be using, I assure you they will see the explosion, maybe even hear it."

"Good, just as long as it doesn't take us all with you," O'Brien said smiling, but there were no smiles on anyone else's face. They were beginning to appreciate the seriousness of this crucial period in the plan. "Captain Lind, you immediately get on the VHF and report the disaster. Be sure you describe the yacht as a large sailing vessel, and that you suspect that it is the Seaduce, a sailing yacht that had been in distress earlier. You have to keep calling until you get a response from the Unicorn, even call them by name if they had contacted you in the previous exchange of radio calls. It's important that they confirm you reached them at this time. I am betting again, right here, that the Unicorn will respond, they will be curious if nothing else. Once they respond, you can advise them you are heading for the scene to search for survivors. You may want to ask them if they can assist you. They won't, but ask them anyway. Wait a few minutes, then tell them you are at the scene and have found no survivors, only three bodies, and that you are searching for more. Also mention that you will be heading back to San Juan and will notify the Coast Guard and local authorities. At this point, if the Unicorn's captain is a professional, he will enter all of this in his log. If, for some reason, there is ever an investigation, and the Unicorn's log survives, the facts are clear and written in the log. The only contact the Unicorn made on its voyage was a disabled sailboat, under a Panamanian flag, that blew up with all hands lost."

"Jesus, O'Brien, wouldn't it be just as simple just to have me take the Sonar and ram that son of a bitch down there while we have him dead in the water and forget all this fucking around? There's too much going on here, Mr. O'Brien, too many things that can go wrong. You are trying to second-guess all the actions that Castro's crew will take. I cruised through and around half the Jap fleet under fire in the Philippines on a wounded destroyer with less confusion."

"I know, Captain, and your tin-can ended up on the bottom of the Pacific with half of your shipmates, because you thought you could out smart the Japs and their big guns. I don't plan to lose anyone here, Captain Lind, just an old sailboat to cover our ass."

There was deadly silence in the room.

"Now, Captain Lind, if I may continue?"

John Lind glanced over at Koster. Koster clearly sent his silent message through his cold deep-set eyes. "Don't challenge him, John." Lind bit his lip.

O'Brien continued. "Captain Lind, when you get to San Juan, you will sail straight to the Coast Guard station where we will have our people do the off loading of the bodies, and the parts of the Seaduce you recovered for proof. There will be local press there to record your arrival and hear your sad tale. The Navy, of course, will stage all this. The bodies in the body bags will actually be our live charter guests, correct, Admiral?"

Koster threw a shaky salute, and motioned him to go on.

"Captain Chen, you and your crew will remain out of sight on board Sonar, until it's safe to leave, then you will be sent back to Homestead on a military plane. On that same evening, Captain Lind, you will be found dead on a back street in old San Juan, a victim of a hit and run. Naturally, you had been drinking, trying to forget the tragedy at sea you witnessed."

"Just how do I disappear, Mr. O'Brien?"

"Quite easy. You will be met by someone who will escort you into the Navy facility at Roosevelt Roads. You will come out the other side, clean shaven, dressed like a tourist, sporting a new name, whisked off to the airport, where you will board a flight back to Florida. In a few days, under your own name, you can show up in San Juan as the new skipper of the Sonar, and finish your cruise to Barbados."

Phil Avery tried to put some humor into the atmosphere.

"Now you understand, Captain, why we want you to keep your reddish long hair and that beard you grew. When you surface as your handsome clean shaven self, and Sonar's new captain, you want to look you best, right?"

O'Brien went back to the chart and put his finger on the Virgin Island area. John Lind shook his head and looked over at his friend Admiral Koster, but Koster would not meet his eye.   O'Brien continued. "Phil, your time from departure out of St. Thomas to your arrival in Antigua is only twenty four hours. You have your work cut out computing your entire program. Yours is the critical schedule, the reason for those big engines. On paper it looks reasonable to get everything done, with maybe time to spare, but.."

"Don't worry, Dan, we know what we have to do. We will work out the schedule and be in those two places at one time that you dream about."

"You mean, all this bullshit about building this super fast sailboat, blowing up a classic yacht and getting me killed, is all for some stupid smoke screen?"

"You got it, Captain Lind. If the Unicorn goes up with Castro and the KGB guy aboard, who do you think will be called in to find the culprit? The French are good, and thorough, and we are in their backyard, but the KGB are deadly and they won't care whose back yard they are in. They will look under every rock until they find the answer. They will know that the yacht was deliberately sabotaged. Their problem is to figure out when were the charges set, where were they installed, and by whom?"

"Well, Castro is not exactly meeting with members of the United Fund down there. Won't they suspect maybe someone was out to get the other guys? After all, Castro is supposed to be in Cuba, am I right?"

"Yes, you're right, John. I have taken that into consideration. Any of them could be the reason for the execution. What we can't afford, however, is any link, and I mean any link, between our Government and the disaster. Ian Billings is working a plan that could possibly throw suspicion on a particular cartel out of Chile that has big connections in Guadeloupe and Martinique, that may work, making it look like Castro was invading their territory."

"Dan what about Captain Chen's explosives, aren't they some kind of new material or something? Couldn't that be traced to the United States?"

"Ted, I will let Captain Chen answer that one, Captain?"

"Yes, we are going to use a new explosive plastic, but unless it is recovered in its natural state, there would be no way one could tell it wasn't of the same common or garden variety used by terrorists or many governments today."

"What about the Unicorn, Captain Chen. How much time will there be before she blows?"

"That is the tricky part. We are using a new type timer with a maximum twenty-four hour clock, plus a special plastic housing to contain the charges. These containers had to be designed to withstand the constant flow of water pressure on them while they adhere to the hull. All our tests at the lab in Key West have been about 85 per-cent positive. Naturally, we want 100 per cent. Therefore, we are setting four charges with four independent detonators wired in series. We will not depend on one timed detonator. This means we are taking more risk adding three more timer problems, but it's the only way we can feel sure of complete success. We only need one of them to work."

"Whoa, Captain. You said the explosives are not traceable, or at least this type, but what about the plastic housings and the detonators themselves?"

"Mr. Collins, the detonators are also, let's say, available on the open market, anyone can get them. The plastic housings, well, there would be nothing left to find in this kind of explosion."

The young Navy Captain stood up and walked over to the charts. He studied them for a moment. "To get back to when the Unicorn blows. We are going to calculate that problem the minute we make contact with Unicorn in the open seas. We will then know what her average speed has been over thirty some hours. We know how many miles she has left to the island off Guadeloupe. We will compute the time giving all the allowances we can, and place the time of the explosion when we feel everyone will be there. From all indications, just playing with Mr. O'Brien's figures and the ETA's, we could see fireworks about 1900 hours on Christmas Eve, maybe a little later."

"Damn, it would be great if we could catch them all having Christmas Eve dinner together," John Lind remarked, laughing.

"Jesus, Captain Lind, you are a blood thirsty bastard. Besides, I don't think you will find any of these people celebrating Christmas, at least not in the Castro camp," Gail's voice shook. She rose from her seat and went into the nearby bathroom.

Phil Avery brought their attention back to the program. "If I may, I did some calculations just now. The way I figure, after the Unicorn leaves the scene with Seaduce, or Drummer, she will be under way around 2300 hours. She won't make her port at Guadeloupe's Les Saintes islands, until 0900 to 1000 hours. We feel that whatever Castro is demonstrating, if it requires that it be in the water, he most likely won't be doing it in daylight hours. That means he will be spending Christmas Eve in the cove. If we go for nearly the maximum time on those timers, we could have detonation around 2100 on Christmas Eve, does that make sense to you, Captain Chen?"

Captain Chen nodded in agreement, and added, "I would rather not guess at that right now, Phil, we will just have to wait. That decision can only be made at the time of intercept, and when I get under Castro's hull. Once this time is established, I can determine when we can get the maximum charge and the time for the best kill. You want maximum damage, that means maximum body count, that's what I will deliver for you."

The room became deadly silent, nobody spoke, they just looked at O'Brien, who squirmed uncomfortably. He reached for his cigarettes sitting on the counter and lit one. Still nobody spoke. Others lit up.

"Hey, that's what it's all about. I didn't plan this trip, Castro did."

Suddenly the impact of what was going to happen in that small island cove took hold. In everyone's minds, a picture of the devastation and death began to take place. A deadly incident that would forever be a part of that small island's history.

Admiral Koster saw the symptoms and took charge. "Congratulations, O'Brien, it's a winner. Congratulations to all of you, it's a good exercise, good planning. Think of all those wonderful Cuban people, who will have their island back. If we are real lucky, we may even get rid of a few major drug lords. Maybe, just maybe, somebody may sit up and take notice, and get the message that no one, not even a head of state, is safe from real justice, and I am sorry if you don't agree, but to me this is true justice. Maybe, Operation Yuletide can make the difference in our losing battle with this growing cancer in our country. Come, let us all raise our glasses to this mission."

The Admiral did not get any support in a toast, but all joined in congratulating Rudolf.

South Bay, Florida
Altitude, 6500 feet
2010 hours

Gail Townsend watched the tiny moving white and red lights below disappear beneath the wide wing of the Piper Archer. They were like fluorescent ants moving head on at each other, but somehow surviving. Just ahead she could see a small town illuminated by a variety of colored lights at the edge of a massive dark area. She guessed it was South Bay, located on the south end of Lake Okeechobee on Route 27. She remembered a great Bar-B-Q restaurant in the heart of the town, called the Old South that featured great cat-fish and ribs, a treat she enjoyed many times when driving across from Miami to Tampa or St. Petersburg.

She decided to break the silence of the hypnotic drone of the engine. She turned to speak to Phil, but his attention at that second was listening to Miami radar giving him new instructions. The Piper banked to port and Phil increased the throttle. Gail could feel the lift as the plane began to climb. In seconds, Phil had the Piper level again two thousand feet closer to the stars.

He made some adjustments on the mixture and throttle, changed some frequencies on his radios, then switched on the autopilot. He removed his headset and switched on the overhead speaker and adjusted the volume.

"Hey, how are we doing?" Gail asked.

"Doing fine. I was hoping to pick up O'Brien talking to Miami, but he's probably not using radar tonight. Jesus, look at those stars out there. I don't think I have ever seen it this clear over here before."

"Phil, we haven't had much time to talk lately, I mean about you and me, personally. I really owe you a lot, you got me out of the fires of St. Thomas, but I have not been honest with you, I lied to you, Phil. I was messing around with some substance, not a lot, but enough."

Avery looked at her. She looked away letting her long hair hide her expression of shame.

"Gail, I knew about the drugs. I was counting on you to get yourself straight once you were off that rock down there, and you did it, right?"

"Oh yes, I have no problems now. Totally clean, is what I believe they say. I was lucky, Phil. Carlton was able to help me. He introduced me to a close friend who is a doctor, and he, well, it's over. I just want you to know, you can count on me. I won't fail you on this operation. I am a little scared, I will admit that, but I will make it. Funny, until today's meeting, I guess I never thought of what the outcome could really be. "

"I don't think you were alone. Everyone got a real shot in the ass today on just how deadly this could end up, for a lot of people we don't really know. I had a little chat with Captain Chen about this new plastic explosive we will be using. He claims the plastic is great, it's half the volume they have been using with C-4, and has twice the power. He is still concerned about the plastic boxes that were designed to hold the explosives. He did not bring it out at the meeting, but they did have some failures in their tests with the adhesive they were using on the containers."

"Does O'Brien know about this?"

"Oh yeah, so does Koster. At this point, they are ready to take the gamble, plus, there is still some time to get it right."

"I really like that young Captain Chen, don't you, Phil?"

"Yeah, he is going to be a pleasure to work with. He's a real professional. Do you know, he is full blooded Hawaiian?"

"No, but hum me a few bars, maybe I will recognize it."

Avery glanced over at Gail, her head was turned away from him and her right hand was covering her mouth. She couldn't hold back any longer, and burst into laughter. She turned and looked into Phil's sober face. "I just had to do it."

Avery joined her. They both laughed loudly until their eyes began to water. The real emotion that was behind their laughter was the emotion they wanted to vent and share. They wanted to cry, but didn't. It was the toughest day yet of Operation Yuletide.

For nearly a quarter of an hour Gail and Phil sat in silence, each with their own thoughts, each with their own imagination running wild on what it would be like on that night when they would meet with the Unicorn. Gail broke the silence for the second time.

"Buckwheat was telling me after the meeting that he feels we should have some fire power aboard the Drummer, just in case."

"Fire power, like guns?"

"Yes, like guns. He was concerned that when you are negotiating with Castro's crew and Chen's team is in the water, what happens if they are spotted or something goes wrong with someone's equipment and they have to surface, or the big search lights pick them up underwater. He just feels that you and the team would be sitting ducks."

"I don't think they would resort to open warfare. They have too much at risk. We are positive that Castro is doing this on the QT and doesn't want publicity or complications. Keep in mind his nearest landfall, if he needs to run at this point, is owned by the U.S. of A.. Naw, they won't use guns. However, we will be in international waters, they would be in their rights if they thought they were being attacked."

"That is exactly what Buckwheat was talking about. I think we should mention this to Dan. Hell, I don't know of any charter yacht down there that doesn't carry a weapon on board."

"Oh, you bet. I always carried a revolver with me on deliveries. But Commander Buckland is probably talking about having serious weapons on board, like M-16's. That could lead to some serious problems if we get searched down there."

"I have the perfect spot to store any weapons, if you and Buckwheat decide it's good insurance."

"Oh really, and were would you hide the arsenal?"

"In the washer and dryer, where else? All they are is dummy face plates, there are no guts in them, just an empty cabinet."

Phil laughed. "Yeah, that was some of the so-called weight that they removed that bugged me. I hated to lose those conveniences. The weight they represented couldn't have amounted to fifty pounds, if that. I will talk to Dan about that tomorrow. Speaking about tomorrow, you have to make reservations for Larry Keene. He's coming in from Houston. He wants to check on his two iron ladies. I suppose he will want to take the Drummer out for some more tests."

"Personally, I think he is coming back hoping that Dan will find him a berth on the operation. I would feel better if he was with us, at least for the trip down to St. Thomas, don't you?"

"After I ask for the cannons, I will ask Dan for Larry, o.k.?"

Gail smiled and sat back in her seat, looking into the black sky ahead.

Thirty miles behind Phil Avery's propwash flying the same course, a chartered Cessna 172 Cutlass was fighting a strong cross wind at 6500 feet, and the pilot was requesting more altitude from Miami Center for cleaner air. In the rear seat, Ted Collins managed to get his long legs folded so he could curl up and sleep. In the right front passenger seat, Commander Buckland struggled with a dim flashlight, trying to study the sectional chart. At the controls, Dan O'Brien was cursing the blackness outside his cabin windows, he hated to fly at night.

CHAPTER 17

Connie Simmons stood on the starboard deck holding onto one of the steel shrouds that held the main mast. The sun was high in the cloudless blue sky, and the strong easterly winds were creating white caps outside the harbor. A number of charter yachts with their sails reefed down were heading to their bases in the harbor. She squinted her eyes as she fought the sun's reflection off the water hoping to see the island of Virgin Gorda to the southeast, but it was blocked from view. She turned and looked back into the cockpit where captain Mel Spencer was doing repairs on the portable cockpit table.

"You know Captain Spencer, this past week visiting all these lovely islands was like taking a step back in time. The whole week seemed like living a fairy tale. These wonderful island people appear so happy with life. It seems they don't depend on anything. If it happens, it happens, if it don't, it don't. When I think how upset I get even if the TV goes on the fritz, it makes me feel almost embarrassed. What an education this has been for me. At first I thought everything here was sort of crude and I felt sorry for these people. Now, I feel they really do have a wonderful life, it is us who have forgotten how to live; we take so much for granted, don't we? Am I making sense? Do I sound crazy?"

"No, not at all, ma'am. Most folks, like yourself, who come to these islands for the first time find a new meaning to how life could be, if they were not so spoiled. You would be surprised how many women really get turned off seeing how most of these islanders live. They can't possibly understand how they could live under those conditions. Those are the people I'd just as soon leave on the dock. Their kind need to stick to cruising on the Queenie Two or the Norway."

Mel Spencer smiled at the young woman as he admired her lengthy slim body. She was younger than her shipboard friend, Betty, but not nearly as attractive. Connie had a clean honest look about her, more like the girl next door. Betty was more sensual, and loved to flirt.

289

Connie leaned into the open companionway and yelled. "Hey you guys, let's get moving. I'm getting hungry." She turned and looked at Spencer. "And they say women take time getting dressed. You would think those two guys were going to the prom the way they fuss with their hair."

Spencer cracked a smile, shook his head and then looked aft to make sure that his first mate, Paul Gransaull, had removed the outboard from its stowage bracket on the rail. The outboard was gone.

"Hey, Paul, are you ready back there?" Spencer cried out.

"All set," came Gransaull's response.

Spencer moved the toolbox from the cockpit seat so the guests would not trip over it when they came up topside. He threw the screwdriver he was working with into the toolbox and closed it.

"Did you get it fixed this time, Captain?" Connie asked as she stepped up on deck.

"I think so, see, it doesn't rattle anymore." He took hold of the varnished teak table and shook it.

"It just needed a longer deeper screw." He waited for a reaction to his remark, but Connie ignored him.

"Hi, folks," Cal Tucker said as he stepped on deck out of the companionway. His wife, Betty and Frank Simmons followed him.

"Well, for better or worse, here we are, ready to go play tourist," Betty said as she pulled a large straw hat down over her jet-black hair.

Shielding the sun from his eyes with his hand, Spencer pointed towards the stern. "Paul is at the stern in the dinghy waiting to take you to Village Cay, where you can pick up a taxi if you want to tour the island. When you are ready to be picked up, just tell anyone behind the bar that you want to reach us. They will get on their VHF and call us."

"Captain, is there anything we can pick up for you in town?" Cal asked.

"Cal, let's go, o.k.? Captain Spencer's a big boy and I'm sure if he needs anything, he can get it, right Captain?" Betty said as she looked at Spencer over her sun glasses, then placing her hand on Spencer's forearm, she passed by him brushing her breasts against his arm. Deliberate or not, it stimulated Spencer and he instantly remembered how long it had been since he felt a women's firm breasts against him.

"You folks have a good time. Now remember, talk to a couple of taxi drivers, and ask what they will charge to take you around the island, then pick the one with the best tires."

"Gotcha, Captain. Oh, what about that neat store and restaurant you were telling us about, you know, the one with the English pub? Where is that located?" Frank asked.

"You see that two story building with all the flags flying out front? It's the yellowish one with the upstairs balcony? That's Pussers Store, a great place to browse and shop, and they have great food. Later, you may want to have dinner over there, on the other side of the harbor where all those sailboats are? That's the famous Moorings Charter Company. They have an excellent restaurant on the waterfront, and another on the hill above them called Treasure Isle."

"Thanks, Captain. See you later this evening," Cal said as he motioned for the party to get moving.

The foursome walked aft and one by one stepped down into the inflatable where Paul Gransaull patiently waited. In a few minutes, they were skimming across the water towards the marina.

Spencer watched as they headed in towards shore. He couldn't forget Betty's deliberate act rubbing her breasts against him. "You wanted to arouse me, bitch. Its a shame you didn't stay behind. I wouldn't mind rolling around with you in my bunk a few times.." he said to himself.

"Penny for your thoughts? and I bet you were thinking just how nice it is to have the ship to yourself for a few hours, right?"

Karen Goodson stood on the top step of the companionway. Her golden hair flew wildly around her face, still wet from her shower. She had a bright yellow towel wrapped tightly around her. Suddenly she realized how she was dressed and had second thoughts of stepping on deck. She had seen that look in Spencer's eyes before, and she was becoming uncomfortable.

"Come on, pretty lady. Let's have a cold one. It's our day off, isn't it?"

"Ah, sure, why not. I'll get us some cold ones out of the fridge." Karen started down the stairs thinking it would be a good time to put something else on.

"Don't move that pretty little body, I have them right here."

Spencer flipped up the canvas seat cushion and opened the ice chest that was built into the port cockpit seat.

"Two Beck's coming up."

Karen stepped up into the cockpit, took the bottle of beer and deliberately sat on the opposite side of the cockpit, keeping her knees tight together. She knew this could be a mistake, but would make the best of it.

"Damn, Karen, you outdid yourself this week. Jesus, you came up with some great dishes. You been reading some fancy books on cooking or something?"

291

"No, just ideas on menus and fun dishes I picked up from the other gals when we hit port. What did you think of that shrimp and pork stir-fry last night. I had to substitute a little and used chutney when I ran out of soy sauce. Which reminds me, as soon as Paul gets back I need to get into town and get some groceries."

"Ah, relax. It may be awhile before Paul gets back, I sent him on a few errands, and to pick up some pulleys at the rigging shop."

Karen became nervous and started to move towards the main cabin companionway. Anticipating her move, Spencer stepped in front of her blocking the companionway entrance.

"Mel, don't do anything stupid. Things are not what they used to be. I have changed, Mel. Now please, let me pass."

"Come on, Karen, it's been a long time. You know how I always felt about you? When I arrived at Charter Services and saw you on the phone that day, well, all those sweet memories came back, those great nights we had."

"No, Mel. The answer is no. Now please, don't cause a scene. Let's finish this charter with respect for each other. I'll leave now if I am causing a problem for you, o.k.?"

"It's the kid, isn't it? Paul's got you all hot and bothered. Shit, Karen, you got him by ten years."

"Five years, and no, it's not Paul. Yes, I gave him opportunities, but he is a gentleman, plus, he's not interested."

"Bull shit, he's been jumping your bones since we left, hasn't he? You both spend a lot of time at night on deck, and the other night over in Virgin Gorda you guys didn't get back aboard until three in the morning."

"I told you, Mel, nothing is going on. He's a nice guy, and he hasn't laid a hand on me."

Spencer took one swipe with his big hand, caught the large towel over her right breast and pulled. It spun Karen nearly around. She reached out and grabbed the end of the cockpit table with her right hand as she held on to the towel with her left. With lightning reaction, she swung back around, lifting her left elbow and catching Spencer under his bearded chin. He tried to recover, but couldn't. He dropped the bottle of beer on the deck and fell backwards into the open hatch. He grabbed hold of the teak frame around the companionway door, which saved him from tumbling backwards down the companionway and landing seven feet below on the main cabin floor.

Seeing that Spencer was straining to hold on, Karen braced herself against the bulkhead, grabbed both his wrists and pulled back with all her strength. Spencer's tail went down, hitting the steps of the ladder, then scraped across the threshold and onto the cockpit floor. The yellow towel was under him. Karen, totally exhausted, released his wrists and collapsed against the cockpit table.

"What the hell's going on here?"

Karen looked up. Gransaull was standing on the starboard deck outside the cockpit. Spencer was totally exhausted, chin on his chest, taking deep breaths. Karen tried to pull the towel out from beneath him, but couldn't. She pulled herself up, pushed Spencer to one side and stepped over him. She went down the staircase into the main cabin and walked forward to the crew quarters and into her cabin.

"Spencer, what happened?"

"Nothing, we had an accident, that's all. Did you get that new block for the traveler?"

"They were closed for lunch, until 1400."

Gransaull could guess what had happened by the expression on Karen's face. She was angry, not embarrassed. He reached down to help pick Spencer up, then stopped. What he wanted to do was tear his head off. Spencer was physically fit and strong, but Gransaull knew he could take him. He also knew he was on a mission with this man, and this was not the time and place to settle differences. That could come later. Instead of helping, he stepped over Spencer and went below. On his way to his cabin he stopped in front of Karen's door.

"If he lays another hand on you, I will break his fucking neck." He opened his cabin door, went in and fell down across his bunk.

Yacht Haven Marina
St. Thomas, USVI

Friday, November 21st
1030 hours

Cal Tucker was stacking the awkward dock cart with the remaining pieces of luggage and shopping bags, silently swearing at the women for buying so much junk at every port they had visited.

Karen was below decks gathering up the soiled bedding and packing the sheets into pillow cases. Gransaull was collecting the empty scuba tanks to take up to the dive shop to be filled. Frank and Betty were in their stateroom counting cash, putting together a sizable bonus to give the deserving crew, a customary contribution at the end of a charter. Connie

293

was standing on the bow, finishing a roll of film on one of the most photographed sights in St. Thomas, the port of Charlotte Amalie.

"Well, I see you're just about ready there, Cal. I just made your transportation arrangements up at the hotel lobby. Your taxi will be up in the circle at the head of the stairs in fifteen minutes. Is everyone ready?" Spencer asked as he stepped off the dock onto the Seaduce.

"Yes sir, oh by the way, Captain, I want to thank you. This vacation, has been without a doubt the best vacation Betty and I ever had and the best part, you made Betty a real believer in sailing, something I have been trying to do for years."

"My pleasure, Doc. I just hope you all come back."

"Don't need to ask twice. We are already planning next summer, hoping to do two cruises this year."

"Mr. Tucker, you're a man after my own heart."

A few minutes later, the four charter guests were on the dock. They hugged, shook hands and said their farewells to Spencer, Gransaull and Karen Goodson. Simmons handed Spencer a ragged looking envelope and apologized for its condition.

"We just want to thank each of you for a spectacular ten days, and want to give you this gift as a token of our appreciation, o.k.?"

"Thanks, folks. We appreciate your thoughtfulness, and hey, we had a great time too," Spencer said.

The two couples waved and started walking down the dock followed by Gransaull with the overloaded dock cart.

Karen Goodson went below and returned with her bags and put them on the dock. She looked at Spencer and smiled. "Ah, just leave my share of the tip with June at the clearing house office. I'll pick it up with my check tomorrow. Thanks for the ride, Mel, see you around."

Spencer gave her a salute, but said nothing.

Halfway down the dock, Karen met Gransaull returning to the Seaduce. He stopped her, and took her two duffel bags.

"I'll walk you up."

Spencer watched his crew as they continued down the long dock. He laughed out loud, as if to say he didn't care, then he turned and stepped down into the Seaduce's cockpit, lifted the seat cushion over the cooler and took out a bottle of beer.

Paul and Karen stood at the main entrance to the Yacht Haven Hotel. They stood silently looking at each other.

"I'm sorry you're leaving the boat and I want to see you again, how can I do that?"

Karen slipped her hand inside her jeans pocket and pulled out a small folded piece of paper. "It's all on here. I'm staying with a girl friend out on east end, near American Yacht Harbor. Please call me, Paul, anytime." She handed Paul the note, reached up and kissed him lightly on the lips, then turned and walked out to a waiting taxi.

Paul watched her as she left in the van. She never looked back. He walked back through the lobby and out to the docks. Half way out on the dock heading for the Seaduce someone called out his name.

"How was your charter, Paul? It is Paul, isn't it?"

Gransaull turned and saw a big barefoot man standing on the bow pulpit of a large ketch moored alongside the dock. He had a deep dark tan and wore a badly bleached unbuttoned oxford blue shirt and stained tan shorts. His uncombed hair was full of silver streaks. Paul guessed he was about fifty years old. He studied him for a second, then responded. "Yes, my name is Paul, Paul Gransaull. Who.."

"Rick, Rick Van Wagner. We met briefly when you and Spencer came in from the States a while back. How was your charter?"

"Ah, it was just fine thank you. We had some real nice folks on board, why do you ask?"

"Well, I noticed Karen Goodson jumped ship earlier, did Spencer chase her off?"

"Ah, I really don't know, Mr. Van..."

"Van Wagner. Listen, Mr. Gransaull, if you have any problems with Spencer, and I mean any problems, you let me know, alright?"

Gransaull was getting a bit annoyed, and wanted to end the conversation. "What interest does this guy have in us anyway?" he asked himself, then replied. "Ah, sure, thanks. I better go, ah, thanks for your concern, Mr. Van.."

"Rick, just call me, Rick."

Gransaull nodded his head, turned and continued down the dock 'til he reached the Seaduce. Once on board, he went aft to gather the scuba tanks from the locker. He was coming forward with two tanks in his hands when he noticed Spencer standing on the dock. He had a beer in his hand and grinning at him.

"Well, my young warrior? Being we don't have any new charters scheduled, what's say we stock up in the morning and start working our way to St. Lucia? We can make a few stops on the way, like St. Martin, St. Barts, Antigua."

"Ah, I thought we were supposed to hang in here until we got word from the clearing house."

Spencer reached into his shirt pocket and produced a folded piece of pink paper. "Here it is, son, hot off the Avery Charter Company Press."

He handed Gransaull a note, which said to call Gail Townsend, Avery's Charters, Area Code 813 555 6657.

"I just talked to Ms. Townsend. We are to go directly to St. Lucia, don't pass go and don't collect $200. However, I told her I was going to make a couple of stops anyway. We have to be at Marigot Bay in St. Lucia on the 15th to pick up a party of four, then make way for Jamaica via Antigua. It's a Christmas package."

"Sounds good to me, Captain. What about a new cook?"

"Oh, Gail doesn't feel it necessary for the trip down. She said she'll have one waiting down in St. Lucia. Of course, this all comes as a surprise to you, right?"

"I don't follow you, Captain."

"Sure you do. Who the fuck are you kidding, Gransaull? You know more about this trip than I do, don't you? Why don't you just come clean? Hell, I don't know who you really are nor do I care, but we're in this together, whatever it is we are involved in, so why fuck around, right?"

"Captain, I don't know what you want from me, and I don't know what the hell you're talking about, o.k.? Maybe you shouldn't be drinking in the hot sun. If you want me to follow Karen, let me know and I'll get off this barge right now, just say the word. I'm sure I can pick up a another boat."

Spencer was a bit surprised. "This kid was either telling the truth or he was one cunning bastard," he thought.

"O.K., forget it. You go get your tanks filled and meet me in about an hour at the Bridge. We'll discuss our provisions and set a time to leave. I plan to go to St. Maarten for a couple of days to see some friends."

Spencer walked off heading for the Bridge. Gransaull waited a few minutes than followed him carrying the two air tanks. He dropped them off at the dive shop below the Bridge, and walked up to a bank of public phones located near the small hotel arcade.

The phone rang twice. A woman's voice answered. "Good morning, Avery's Yacht Management, this is Gail, how can I help you?"

"Ms. Townsend? This is Paul Gransaull."

Suddenly, Paul felt a stinging pain between his shoulder blades. He nearly dropped the phone from the impact of the blow that hit him from behind.

"Give that bitch, Gail baby, my love, shithead."

Gasping to catch his breath, Gransaull watched Spencer as he kept walking towards the arcade. All he could think about was to run and tackle him, then crush his face into the concrete walk.

"Paul? What is going on?"

"It was Spencer. He caught me. He knows I'm talking to you."

"So what? We hired you, Paul. Just tell him you had a personal problem you needed taken care of and called us, that's all."

"No, that's not all, Ms. Townsend. He is very suspicious of me. He challenged me a little while ago when he told me about your message to go to St. Lucia. He thinks I know more about this charter out of St. Lucia then I will admit. I don't think I can take this guy much longer, Ms. Townsend. I came close to punching his lights out yesterday."

"Don't do anything dumb, Paul. Let me get hold of Dan O'Brien and ask him what he wants you to do. Jesus, we are so close now. Listen, you call me back, around six your time. That will give me enough time to talk things over with O'Brien and Phil Avery, O.K? Call me, Paul. I will be waiting right here."

"Roger that, Ms. Townsend." He hung up the phone and walked over to the small grocery store in the marina complex and went in. He was walking down an aisle when Rick Van Wagner confronted him.

"I just saw Spencer give you that whack at the phone bank, kid. I would say you just might have a serious problem with your captain. Why don't you gather your things and come on board the Piccolo with me. You can stay until we head out on charter."

"Ah, I can't, captain. We leave tomorrow for St. Lucia. We have a charter to pick up there in a couple of weeks."

Van Wagner turned and pretended he was reading the label on a bottle of sun tan oil he took from the shelf. "You're one of Ian Billing's boys, aren't you?"

"I beg your pardon? Ian, who is Ian?"

"Ian Billings, the Agency? Washington? Come on, lad, I should have guessed before now. No wonder you're taking such abuse, and I bet that Spencer doesn't know who you really are, right? You know, I told my wife, Colleen, you were just too squeaky clean to be what you say you are. What's going on? Is there something going down around here we don't know about?"

All Gransaull wanted to do now was disappear. "How does this guy know Ian Billings? This operation was to be top secret, and why haven't they explained more to Spencer?"

297

"Ah, Captain, I really have to go. Thanks for the offer, and I'm sorry, I don't know your friend, Ian."

Gransaull got out of the store and kept walking until he left the hotel complex. He headed for the nearest public phones and called Gail Townsend back to tell her about the run in with Rick Van Wagner. She gave him O'Brien's number and after a number of tries, he finally located O'Brien.

"Jesus Christ, this thing is getting out of hand, where are you now, Paul?"

"In a small shopping plaza near the cruise ship docks. This captain, Rick Van Wagner, who is he?"

"He is a retired agent, one of the best I've been told, before Billings' time. I had a long talk about him with Billings last week. Van Wagner called Billings to tell him that Spencer was down here bragging about the Seaduce belonging to the U.S. Government, and that he was on some kind of mission that he wasn't briefed on yet."

"Holy shit, you mean Spencer knows about Van Wagner's background?"

"Yeah, he knows about Van Wagner. Shit, I was sort of warned about this and I should have paid it more attention. I was told Spencer had a couple of old cronies down there, and when he drinks he gets diarrhea of the mouth. Van Wagner overheard him running his mouth and reported it to Billings. Of course, Billings denied any knowledge of Spencer or the Seaduce. He told Van Wagner to forget it, but it appears he is not buying Billings' story. We better have a chat with Van Wagner, matter of fact, I'll call Billings right now. You'd best stay clear of Van Wagner, and Jesus Christ don't get caught talking to him if Spencer is around. When are you planning to leave for St. Lucia?"

"Tomorrow, at least that's what Spencer said earlier. We don't have to be there until the 15th of December, but he wants to leave now. He did say he wants to make a few stops, one being in St. Maarten to see some friends. Mr. O'Brien? Just when are you going to talk to Spencer and tell him about the rest of the operation? I'm afraid at the rate he is drinking and with his present attitude, especially towards me, he may screw this mission up for you. I will do what I can, but I can't sail that yacht alone, at least not yet."

"I know Paul, I know. Listen, I will make some calls tonight and make a decision about Spencer. Shit, I should have never let Commander Buckland talk me into keeping this asshole on board. Listen, Paul, you go back to the yacht, while Spencer is still off the boat, and see if you can screw something up that could delay your leaving tomorrow. You know, something mechanical. Can you do that?"

"I guess so, I don't know what I could, wait, there is something I might be able to do. We had some problems with the water pump on the engine. Spencer cracked the casting of the pump housing when he replaced the impeller. He sealed it with some shit, but it's leaking. I could back off the nuts and break the seal; that might hold us up. He mentioned that he would probably have to get a part from the States or Puerto Rico, if it got worse."

"Good, try that. If that doesn't work, screw up the fuel filter, or a couple of fuel injectors. I'll get working on what we can do up here to solve this problem. I might even come down and have a chat with Spencer, if that's what it will take. Call me tomorrow as soon as you can and let me know what's going on. At any cost, do something to stall, but don't do anything that will put the Seaduce out of commission permanently, Jesus, that's all I need."

"Roger that, Mr. O'Brien. I'll take care of it, and now that I know more about Van Wagner I can handle him better."

"Good, talk to you tomorrow, Paul."

O'Brien called Ian Billings and brought him up to speed on the Van Wagner problem and the situation with Gransaull and Spencer.

"Dan, another call to Van Wagner from me would only wet his appetite and he would know that there is something big going on. Let's wait until he calls me again, and then I will explain everything to him, especially about Gransaull. Keep in mind, Dan, Van Wagner was one of our best, this guy can see through a lead curtain. It's spooky how he can read people. Now, how is everything else shaping up?"

"Right on schedule, so far, Ian. Lind and the Sonar left yesterday for the Bahamas and should be in San Juan a week from today. Ted Collins, Phil Avery and Larry Keene are going to be doing some test runs on the Island Drummer this weekend out of Sarasota, and Commander Buckland is due in here tonight with the communications package we have been waiting for. Personally, I am ready for a double something."

"When is the Drummer scheduled to leave?"

"Phil wants to head out of Sarasota the Friday after Thanksgiving, stop in Key West, then make a straight run to St. Thomas. He would like to clear Key West no later than December first. His plan is to spend maybe three days at Key West getting ready, figures he can make it to St. Thomas in seven to eight days, weather permitting."

"What are your plans, Dan? Have you decided where you'll be during the operation?"

"No, not exactly. Right now I would like to be on the Sonar, as she will be the center for all communications. Buckland is working on the systems right now with the Navy and Bollman's command center in Miami. When he gets here tonight, we should have all this worked out. So far, it appears that we can pretty much just go with our standard VHF radios, setting different channels for each day. We are not too concerned about landfall picking us up, but maritime shipping is another thing. We are in the middle of a highway, so to speak, for all the inter-island freighters and some cruise ships. We will have a complete update come December 22nd of what and who we can expect in the shipping lanes around our intercept point."

"Dan, there must be a better way you can communicate, isn't..."

O'Brien, frustrated with the subject of communications, and aware it was a very weak link in his plan, interrupted Billings rudely.

"Avery and I feel certain that our code names and messages will confuse anyone listening. Only a six year old might figure out what the hell we are talking about."

Billings heard O'Brien's tone of voice, and decided to change the subject. "Well, I do have some good news for you from the Defense Department. You won't have any Soviet eyes in the skies over you for the 23rd encounter. Admiral Koster even announced this morning that there will be no Navy or Marine maneuvers taking place in the Caribbean for the last two weeks in December. That should even make Castro happy, knowing he won't be running into the USS Kennedy or Eisenhower carrier groups on his cruise."

"That is good news, Ian. You know, right from the beginning of this operation, I thought old iron pants Koster would call in the cavalry at any sign of trouble. At least I can sleep better tonight. Thanks for the info."

"Listen, Dan. You've worked hard on this operation and I know that the time is almost here. For what it's worth, I think you did a hell of a job, and whatever the outcome, well, you have all our respect here for your efforts, and I wish you the best of luck in your hunt."

"Thanks, Ian. Thank you for all your help and I hope I don't let you down. I can live with Koster. All I would like to do now is to pull this caper off."

"Take care, Dan. Give me a jingle when you decide what you're going to do and where you plan to be, will you do that?"

"You bet. See, ya."

Caribbean Marine Suppliers
St. Thomas, USVI

Saturday, November 22nd
1020 hours

"Listen, friend, I can only do what I can do. Our wholesale store in San Juan is closed on Saturday, o.k.? I can't do anything for you till Monday, sorry. Have you checked near east end with Antilles boat yard? They have all kinds of junk engines out there, maybe you can find an old Volvo water pump cover in their yard. If you have to leave right away, that's my only suggestion. Sorry, Captain. Next?"

Spencer took the broken part from the counter and walked out of the marine store. It began to rain. He couldn't find a taxi, so he started to walk. A half-hour later, soaked to his skin, he was sitting in a waterfront bar down near the old sub base. The two pieces of the broken water pump housing sat on the bar in front of him, and he was picking them up, putting them together where they separated, then separating them again.

"Water pump cover, lousy casting. Volvo six, right?"

Spencer turned around and looked into the bearded face of large man sitting two stools away. From the looks of his hands and nails, he was no brain surgeon. He wore a dirty banlon shirt, stained khaki shorts and ragged boat shoes. His hair, like his eyes, were black. The most noticeable thing about him was the real Rolex Mariner watch on his right arm.

"Gimme my regular, Boots," he called out to the young black barmaid.

"How'd you know it was a Volvo?"

"Easy. I was a Volvo dealer down here one time. Replaced a lot of old engines with them six bangers, they were tough, top of the line at one time."

"I don't suppose you would have some spares around like this, would you, pal? I'm hurting bad. Supposed to go on charter, and I can't get another part until Monday out of San Juan."

"Can't help ya, sorry. You might try Antilles yard. They have done a lot of repowering out there." The stranger downed his double gin, dropped three dollars on the bar and left.

Spencer ordered another beer. The rain continued to fall.

Yacht Haven Marina
B Dock
2115 hours

301

Paul Gransaull was lying in his bunk reading, when he heard a light knock on the cabin topside. He kneeled on his bunk and opened the overhead hatch. He recognized Karen's silhouette against the marina lights. She was standing on the dock in the light drizzle.

"Hi," she called out when she saw him appear in the hatch.

Gransaull was surprised to see her. "I called earlier, but there was no answer."

"I know, I was out with friends. Are you alone?"

"Yes, I haven't seen Spencer all day. He left to find a part for the generator this morning, but hasn't returned yet. Hold on, I will be right with you, come on board and get out of the rain."

After closing the hatch, he ran to the companionway and opened the hatch. Karen was standing in the cockpit, with water dripping around her face and down onto her yellow slicker. Gransaull moved up to her and put his arms around her. They kissed, softly at first, then as his arms pulled her closer, they kissed harder.

"I was afraid we would leave, and I wouldn't see you again."

"I know, that's why I'm here. Paul, I missed you."

A blinding light that flashed into their faces interrupted them. "Paul Gransaull? Are you Paul Gransaull?"

The man's voice was deep and carried a heavy native accent.

"Yes, I'm Gransaull, would you mind taking that fucking light out of my face? Who the hell are you, and what do you want?"

The tall man stepped closer to the edge of the dock and turned out his flashlight. Gransaull could see that he was a young policeman. Standing a few feet behind was another officer in a long black slicker.

"Mr. Gransaull, there has been an accident. Your captain, Mr. Spencer? He is in critical condition at the hospital."

"What? When, I mean what happened?"

"I can't say, sir, it's under investigation. It seems he may have been a victim of a hit and run; that's all I know. If you would like a ride to the hospital, we will be glad to take you."

"No, that's fine, officer," Karen said. "I have a car and I know where the hospital is. Can you tell us how badly hurt Captain Spencer is?"

"Ma'am, I just know he has a fractured skull and a broken leg. There was some talk that he may have a punctured lung. He was hit pretty hard, ma'am."

"Where was he? I mean where did this happen?"

"Some people who live at the Shibui condominiums down near the airport spotted him lying in the bushes about two hours ago. If it wasn't for those bushes, he would have rolled down a 300-foot cliff. He would have not survived."

"Thank you, officer. Come, Paul, we'd better get over there. I'll help you lock up."

"Sorry to be bringing you such bad news. Good night."

St. Thomas Hospital
2300 hours

"Hello, I'm Dr. Jerome. I understand you're friends of Mr. Spencer? Do you know if he has any family here?"

"No sir, we both work with Captain Spencer on a yacht. I don't know anything about his family. He never spoke of any, but I can find out for you in the morning."

"That would be a good idea, Mr. Gransaull. Your captain came out of surgery about fifteen minutes ago. We did the best we could here, but he needs more blood, and his face and head injuries should be looked at by a plastic surgeon. We have removed some of the bone splinters from the skull and relieved the pressure on the brain. He had three broken ribs, one of which punctured his right lung. His left leg had two compound breaks and he has a fractured right wrist. We expect there could be more internal damage, maybe some bleeding, but without exploratory surgery, well, like I said, we are not really set up here to handle a trauma situation like this. We should move him while he is fairly stable."

"I understand, doctor, thanks. I will make a call right now and see what can be done."

"There is good air ambulance service available to San Juan and the States, but I recommend he goes to San Juan. I will be here for the next, oh three hours at least. Let me know what you decide."

"If he stays, doctor? I mean if we can't find.."

"He could die, ma'am, possibly within six to eight hours. I would get him out of here for his own good."

The young doctor turned and walked off.

"Phone. I have to call O'Brien."

Karen grabbed Gransaull's arm, and asked, "Who?"

"Ah, nothing, there has to be a phone by the admitting desk. Do me a favor, Karen, get a phone book and find out about air ambulance service. I hope they are right here on the island."

They both ran to the emergency room entrance, where they separated and began their long ordeal to save Mel Spencer's life.

The Bridge Restaurant
Yacht Haven Marina

Sunday, November 23rd
1210 hours

Paul and Karen sat at a table at the Bridge restaurant going over the information they had on Mel Spencer. Paul had to make a call exactly at 1300 hours to O'Brien to update him on where Spencer was taken in San Juan, the name of the doctor who he talked to at the hospital, and explain how he had set up the financial arrangements.

"How are they doing locating Mel's ex-wife and children?"

"Don't know. Maybe, O'Brien will have some news when I call him in a few minutes."

"What more did you learn when you went over to pick up the police report?"

"They won't give me one yet. When I talked to the investigating officer he said that in tracing Mel's whereabouts yesterday, it did not make sense that he was hit by a car up that steep road up to Shibui. A barmaid over near the sub base said he left there about three. He was seen down near the Normandy restaurant around six, and again getting into a white pick up truck near your favorite restaurant, that Gregory's East place."

"You know, Paul, I wondered about that last night when the police said he was found up at Shibui. There are no bars up there. Shibui had a bar when it was a hotel, but that was years ago. Why would he be all the way up there, unless he had a friend up there."

"Mind if I join you?"

Paul and Karen both looked up into the wide tanned face of Rick Van Wagner.

"Ah, I guess not. I suppose you know about Captain Spencer?"

"Oh, yes. Terrible accident. How is he doing? I understand he is over in San Juan holding on a thin string."

"You know something, fella? What ever your problems are with Mel Spencer, I could care less. But, he is human, and he is my boss, and he is hanging on by a thread. I don't like you, Van Wagner, and I don't care for your fucking attitude towards Spencer, so why don't you just take a walk."

Van Wagner grabbed Gransaull's wrist and nearly put his fingers through the skin. Gransaull felt sheer pain throughout his entire arm. He thought for a second that his wrist might even be broken.

"Listen up, macho-man. I will be joining you when you speak with O'Brien in a few minutes. As a matter of fact, I will be with you for the next few weeks. I will be taking the Seaduce down to St. Lucia, friend, and you are going to start acting your age." He released Paul's aching wrist.

Paul grabbed his wrist. He was speechless.

Karen reached out and grabbed Paul's hand, then turned and confronted Van Wagner. "Do you mind telling me what's going on here? Rick, you are not welcome here, leave us alone, and who the hell told you that you were the new captain on Seaduce, anyway?"

"His boss, that's who, Karen. Now, I am going to ask that you leave Paul and I alone, even if you do mind. Why don't you go down to Seaduce and relax. I will bring Paul down in an hour. Oh, if you don't mind, I left my shit in Seaduce's cockpit. The cabin was locked. Would you mind throwing them in one of the staterooms?"

Karen said nothing. She stood up, picked up her purse and left. Paul was about to say something, but Van Wagner shook his head. "Let her go."

Van Wagner looked around for the waitress, then cased the nearby tables for anyone within earshot. "Paul, I got a call from Billings this morning at 0600. It was an urgent call, and he had me call your friend, Dan O'Brien. After a few calls back and forth, we had things settled on my taking over the Seaduce. My immediate problem was getting another skipper to take my charter. I got lucky and found one whose yacht is hauled out getting repairs. He took the Piccolo on the charter an hour ago. Now, you and I have some serious things to discuss. How much does Karen know about the Seaduce and the operation?"

"How much do you know, Captain?"

"Santa Claus, Snoopy, Dumbo, Red Sleigh, Rudolf, Yuletide, and we going to eat a fruitcake on Christmas Eve, is that enough?"

Gransaull studied the man for a moment. He had to believe him, he had no choice, and it appeared that what O'Brien said of the man must be true. The one thing still on his mind needed to be settled, he looked straight into Van Wagner's cold eyes and asked. "Spencer, tell me what really happened to Spencer?"

"Nothing to tell, Paul. He had an unfortunate accident. He will be alright, if that's worrying you."

"What worries me, Captain, is will I ever know the real truth about his, ah, accident?"

Van Wagner smiled and shook his head slowly, never losing eye contact with the young sailor. "Come, let's go. We have to get up to Havensight and use the phones up there, more privacy." Van Wagner got up from the table and Gransaull followed him out to the parking lot behind the hotel.

"Here, we'll take my wheels, save some time."

Gransaull stopped in his tracks and examined the small pick-up truck. Van Wagner's "wheels" was a rusted out Toyota pick-up truck, an old white pick-up truck.

He got in the cab as Van Wagner fumbled with the keys. "A pick-up truck? Somehow I figured you for a Volvo wagon."

"Oh, this ain't mine, it belongs to a friend. I just borrowed it. You're right though, I do own a Volvo. My friend picked it up this morning to work on the transmission. It's not a wagon though, it's an old 69 two door. You mean Billings even told you what I drive?"

"Naw, seems like all old sailors seem to own old Volvos."

The two men began to laugh as they entered onto Long Bay Road, and headed for the small shopping plaza at Yacht Haven.

CHAPTER 18

Fun & Sun Apartments
St. Petersburg Beach, Florida

Monday, November 23
0920 Hours

Dan O'Brien sat at his small kitchen table looking at the coffee stained chart he had pondered over since early August. He took his rule and went over the Unicorn's course again, putting in new time increments based on his rough estimates of the Unicorn's cruising speeds, head winds and known tides. He changed the Unicorn's ETA at the interception point to sometime between 2300 and 2400, which was later than his original estimate. Phil Avery had found some errors in O'Brien's figures when they were going over the plans in Ft. Lauderdale. He knew these numbers would be computed again as soon as they had a visual contact by the SR-71 on departure day, December 21st. He was hoping that the times he was posting would be close to the actual times that the Unicorn was located. This would put the time of interception near midnight on the 23rd.

The phone on the wall rang causing him to jump and drop his felt pen. "O'Brien here."

"Hi, Dan. It's me, Buckwheat."

"Hey buddy, where are you?"

"Up here at the Pentagon Penthouse since 0630."

"Koster's office

"You got it, and is he giving you a run for your money on who is running the show. I'd better warn you, he has all the magic buttons right on his desk that can make things happen up here."

"And what has he done for me lately?"

"Dan, your communication troubles are over. The old man has all the communications worked out, and exactly what you wanted. No military, no high-tech black boxes, just plain old VHF's with some frills."

"What do you mean, frills?"

"Dan, did you know you could put scramblers on VHF radios?"

"Of course, ah, well, let's say I knew it had been done."

"Well, listen to this, Koster came up with a better idea. We are getting new VHF frequency hoppers.

"Say what?"

"Frequency hoppers, they look just like any marine VHF radio, but they hop all over the channels."

"Cut the shit, Buckwheat, what the hell are you talking about?"

"We are talking specially tuned VHF radios that are used by the DEA and U.S. Customs. Each of our players, with the exception of Castro, of course, will have a new VHF radio. These radios will start out on a given channel, say number nine. When you begin transmission they start switching to other channels automatically during the transmission. All radios assigned to Operation Yuletide are matched, so they all switch channels at the same time in the same sequence, get it?"

"I think so, where and when do we get them?"

"They will be on the way before the end of the day. I already called down to St. Thomas for captain Rick Von something, what ever his name is, on the Seaduce? But I got Paul Gransaull. I told him the equipment was being air freighted today out of Richmond, Virginia. It will arrive St. Thomas on Eastern's first flight from Miami around 1130 hours tomorrow. Caught them just in time, they were leaving tomorrow for St Lucia. As far as getting the equipment to Captain Lind on Sonar, we will send the radio down with Captain Chen and his crew, when they fly out of Homestead for St. Croix. The radio for Island Drummer should arrive tomorrow. I couldn't reach Phil Avery, just his machine. Will you follow up for me and advise him?"

"Of course. Well, sounds like the old man came through again, doesn't it?"

"That ain't all, Dan, and you're going to go ballistic on this. Koster is not trusting the VHF ranges even if you are sending signals from the top of ninety-foot mast antennas. He is bringing in two Lockheed P-3 sub killers from Moffett Naval Air Station in California."

"Son of a bitch, I knew it. One way or other, Koster has to get his fucking Navy involved in this thing. Shit, we don't want any, what the hell is a P-3?"

"A P-3 is a four engine Lockheed Electra, remember them? Well, the U.S. Navy bought a bunch of them and put some real neat sophisticated electronics on them so they can hunt Ivans, what they do is hunt subs, Dan."

"So, why do we need them?"

"Koster feels we should have sub hunters around the area with the special VHF hopper equipment to act as boosters just in case, that way they could take radio signals between our guys and boost to their signals making sure they are getting received. In other words, they would be a flying amplifier over our small fleet to insure communications.

"I don't suppose it would do any good for me to call the Admiral and tell him it won't be necessary, would it?"

"Nah, chances are the two birds are already lifting off into the sunrise over San Jose and winging east. They will be flying into Key West, refuel, then head down to St. Croix and San Juan, where they will be stationed. Dan, there is nothing unusual about these birds being down there, they frequently fly around the Caribbean basin hunting Ivans and dropping sonar transmitters or aggravating the two old Cuban subs when they are on missions and not leaking. Another thing, Dan, Koster says we may need these birds to fly spotter for us between the Blackbird flights. They can get closer to Castro's yacht and broadcast positions more often."

"Yeah, the old man is right, as usual. You know, I wouldn't put it past him to show up on the fucking Island Drummer on December 23rd in full scuba gear with a stick of dynamite in his hand and looking for Castro's yacht."

"Now that you mentioned it, he did radio his buddy Captain Lind and told him to have plenty of yogurt on board, vanilla yogurt, his favorite."

O'Brien chuckled. "Happy Thanksgiving, where are you spending the holiday?"

"At home with the family and the wife's folks. What about you, Dan, are you coming up to D.C.?"

"Nah, I'm going to hang around and get caught up on some sleep. Next week is going to be rough, and from here on in it's going to be nerve wracking."

"Well, I'm going to play daddy for a few days, see you on Friday morning."

"Fly into Sarasota and call Gail, let her know what time you arrive, she's made all your arrangements. You are supposed to be a prospective buyer for the Drummer, so try and look like an intelligent civilian."

"Oh, that explains why I leave the dock with Gail and Phil, with all my bags, and never come back, right?"

"That's the way Phil wants to handle it, pal, see you on Friday." O'Brien put the phone down and looked at the calendar on the wall. He noticed a picture of a turkey on the date of November 26th. The next square, November 27th had a small note in the box written in pencil. "Yuletide departs North Pole."

The phone rang again. "O'Brien."

"Well, I didn't expect to catch you, Mr. O'Brien."

"Who is this?"

"It's Mel Spencer, remember me?"

"Mel, how are you feeling?"

"Alive, O'Brien, does that surprise you?"

"Why should it? The last report I had on you last week, was that you were coming along just fine."

"Well, now that's a surprise. I had no idea you were checking on me, O'Brien."

"Look, Spencer, you got into this mess yourself with your damn drinking, so don't try and put this off on anyone else."

Spencer chuckled. O'Brien could hear that he was having difficulty breathing, ending his phrases with deep breaths.

"I take it you have been told that I was beat up and robbed. At least that's what it was supposed to look like."

"That's what I have been told. You were hit in the head and rolled out of a car into a ravine."

"Well, don't believe everything you hear, O'Brien. A detective came over this week from St. Thomas. He, like the investigating officer, is very suspicious about the incident. They feel like I do, that I was set up, so to speak, and that I was not expected to survive."

"You actually think that, Captain?"

"You bet, and I think I know who hit me from behind and hauled me off."

"Did you tell this to the police?"

"Of course, and they are going to check out my suspect. I had met him, coincidentally, earlier that day."

"Well, I'm sure, Mel, if there is any basis to what you think happened, they will get to the bottom of it."

"You bet they will, and I have nothing but time now to give them. My doctor told me it would take another week for the swelling in my skull to go down before they install a plate, and at least two more weeks before I can get into therapy for all my broken bones. I am thinking of demanding some protection down here, O'Brien. I still feel like a target for your friends."

"That's ridiculous, Mel, and you know it. Do you want me to arrange to have you brought to the States? Maybe you would feel better up here in Florida? I promise we will get you the best care there is to get you healthy again."

"No thanks, O'Brien, I feel safer here. I have written a letter, O'Brien, that explains everything I know about you and Ted Collins, Commander Buckland and Van Wagner. It's been mailed to a friend, with orders to open it and take it to a lawyer or a newspaper should anything else accidentally happen to me."

"That's fine, Mel, do what ever you feel you have to. I have to go now, I will try and stop down to see you in the next few weeks. Meantime, I will make sure everything is being taken care of for you through Avery's Management Company, including holding your paychecks until you call for them. Think about moving to the States, o.k.?"

"Yeah, sure, I'll give it some thought. By the way, I heard that Van Wagner and the Gransaull kid are going to take the Seaduce down to St. Lucia. Of all the captains on the beach over there, how come you picked one that is booked solid and doesn't need the work? A retired government man, right? Just coincidence I suppose."

"Mel, you knew this was a special job from the beginning, when you took an oath of secrecy. Instead, you elected to run your mouth down there. I knew nothing about Rick Van Wagner until I received a call from Washington. He's a retired agent, and with you out of commission, he agreed to help us out, at least for the next couple of weeks."

"I suppose you're not going to believe me, but I never told anyone what I was doing, and who for. I may have suggested that it was a government operation, but never said what, or who. But I bet my sweet ass, that's why I'm lying here with part of my skull missing."

The phone went dead. O'Brien placed the phone on its receiver, then lit a cigarette. He focused his eyes again on the calendar. He picked up the phone and dialed Ian Billings at his home in Maryland.

Avery's Yacht Management Office
1035 Hours

Phil Avery was on his phone with his St. Lauderdale office manager going over last minute business arrangements. Gail Townsend was at her desk talking to two young women Avery hired to do detailing and cleaning on customers' yachts. After they received their work sheets they left.

Gail looked over at Phil, who was off the phone and leaning back in his wing back chair, smiling at her.

"Well, you look like you just received some good news. Did Lauderdale give you a raise?"

"No, just wondering what everyone over there is thinking about us taking off on a charter."

"Well, let's let them imagine what they want, now, how about some coffee?" Gail said as she stood up and walked from behind her desk, interlocked her fingers, turned her palms out and stretched.

311

Phil was amused just watching her. In so many ways she was like a fragile young girl, then, with a simple change of expression, or a movement, she became a very sensuous woman.

"Gail, hate to ask, but you did talk things over with Carlton last night about the trip?"

"No, I did not. Do you want coffee?"

"Yes, I do. Gail, today is Monday, Thursday is Thanksgiving, and we leave for the Caribbean on Friday, you are cutting this a little close, don't you think?"

"I wish you would not concern yourself with this, Phil. I will tell him, when the time is right. I have not been avoiding doing this, honest. I want to use this trip, in a way. I know it sounds unfair, but after tomorrow night, I would not be seeing him for nearly a week anyway. He is taking the family up to his parents' home in Connecticut. I have to stay here, spend Thanksgiving alone, waiting for phone calls. I would have done it, don't get me wrong, but now I can tell him that I have the right to, oh, I don't want to get into this, Phil. I promise, Carlton will not be a problem. I know you're worried he will show up in St. Thomas and make a scene. I promise you he won't. He will just have to trust me, won't he?"

"Yes, he will, and you're right, I don't want him in St. Thomas, which reminds me. Are you getting nervous about going back down there, now that it's getting closer?"

"No, I can handle it."

The phone rang, it was O'Brien. Gail left to go get coffee. When she returned, there was a note on her desk. "Be back in five, went down to the Drummer."

Phil went over to the navigation station and examined the radio installations. There were two VHF radios stacked into the custom cabinet. Just below, there was a large pigeonhole that was being used for tech books, logbook and operational manuals. He felt that the new VHF radio mentioned by O'Brien could easily be installed in this space. After a brief walk through, he went topside, locked the cabin door and returned to his office.

"Hopping frequencies? I never heard of such a radio,"
Gail remarked.

"Neither have I, but we are getting one delivered today, according to O'Brien. It's the Admiral's goodbye gift. He is also arranging to have a couple of innocent sub hunters flying around the area with VHF repeaters aboard to ensure we are getting our messages back and forth."

"What an angel that man is. His wife must adore him, he thinks of everything, doesn't he?" Gail said.

"Jesus, he'd better, that's why he's the Chairman of the Joint Chiefs."

Aboard Island Drummer
Sarasota City Marina

Friday, November 27th
1340 hours

Ted Collins stood over the stainless sink, twisting the small wire that secured the cork. The cork exploded out of the dark green bottle, followed by a stream of fizzing foam. Collins tried to stop the flow of the expensive champagne with a towel, then he placed the bottle in his mouth.

"Ted Collins, you gross thing," Gail yelled.

"Jesus, you don't expect us to drink that stuff now, do you?" Buckland cried out.

Almost choking, Collins released the bottle and picked up one of the plastic champagne glasses and poured.

"I don't have anything that you couldn't catch in a whore house."

The four men and the lone women stood in a small circle in the middle of the spacious main cabin, each holding a plastic glass filled with champagne.

O'Brien smiled, lifted his plastic glass, "To the team, and what a team you are. To Ted Collins, probably the world's greatest naval architect of our times, and builder of this magnificent ship. To Phil Avery, what can I say? He's about to become a very undecorated and unknown hero to his countrymen and free Cubans all over the world. To Gail Townsend, a woman with class, style, brains, courage, guts and the greatest legs since Grable. To Buckwheat, a true gentleman and an officer, so we have been told."

"Hear, hear", the small group responded as they raised their glasses, touched them in a toast and downed the wine."

"Who the hell is Grable?" Buckland asked. "Clark Grable's wife or something?"

Not a word was said as eyes shifted back and forth to see who would respond to the young commander.

"You probably never heard of Harry James, right, Buckwheat?"

"Sure I have, he had a big band, played the trumpet, right?"

"Bingo, Commander. Now who was Harry married to?" O'Brien asked.

313

"Mrs. Harry James, right? Do I win the prize now?"

"Hey, nobody recognized Dan O'Brien here, doesn't someone have something nice to say about this old fart?" Buckwheat said aloud.

"I do," Gail said softly, as she put her arms around O'Brien's neck and kissed him hard on the lips.

"Damn, it must be nice to be old enough where girls can trust you," Buckwheat continued.

"I would follow this gentleman, anywhere," Gail responded.

O'Brien placed his glass down on the nearby counter, looked at his watch and addressed the crew. "O.K., it's time." O'Brien led the crew topside into the cockpit.

"Sorry I couldn't work things out for Larry Keene, Phil. The old man shot me down. He wants to keep..."

"It's alright, Dan. We can make it, don't worry. If either of those two iron ladies down there start acting up, we know where he is at all times, stop worrying."

Avery went back down to the main saloon and started converting shore power to ship power. He started the ship's generator, switched power sources, turned on the electronics and made a final check of the engine room. Everything was ready.

He returned topside and started the port engine, then the starboard. Needles began to move and lights came on and off. In seconds, all the instruments confirmed the engines were running normal and all systems were working properly.

Gail went forward and released the two bow lines from the large cleats, as Buckwheat ran around midship releasing all the spring lines. Collins uncleated the two stern lines and tossed them onto the dock. He stepped off the Drummer onto the concrete dock and joined O'Brien, who was leaning against a piling watching. Avery turned and looked at his two landlocked friends. He threw them a snappy military salute, then he moved both clutches forward. The huge sailboat responded, moving slowly out of her berth. Gail and Buckwheat fended off at midship, as Drummer passed through the outside pilings.

O'Brien and Collins walked to the end of the finger dock and enjoyed the awesome sight and the beauty of the classic yacht as she slipped silently away, leaving hardly a ripple in her wake.

Gail and Buckwheat both came to the stern rail. Standing below the large American flag that was waving from the backstay, they looked like Mr. and Mrs. America. They were both dressed in matching white shorts and

Navy blue pullovers. Embroidered on the left breasts of the shirts, the logo and name ISLAND DRUMMER.

"See you soon," Gail yelled, as she and Buckwheat waved.

O'Brien gave a weak wave, he was suddenly overcome with a feeling of a great loss, as a lump gathered in his throat.

"Well, Danny old man, she's the last one to leave. Operation Yuletide is now officially on the waves," Collins said.

"Yeah, hard to believe, isn't it?" O'Brien could not believe the emotional strain he felt inside. He found himself fighting off tears. He turned away from Collins and started walking down the dock.

"Come on, Ted. Let's go in the lounge and get us a double something, I'll buy."

Collins and O'Brien sat at a small table as far away from the luncheon crowd as they could get, and sipped on their drinks.

"You know, Dan? All at once I feel absolutely useless. I mean there is nothing for me to do now. I didn't think it would bother me, I mean not having a part in the real action, but it does. I wish I could be doing something more."

"You have done enough, Ted. My God, man, look at the miracle that just left the dock? Eight weeks ago it was a worthless hunk of fiberglass and wood, an ugly skeleton in an old airplane hanger in Immokalee. Now it may just be the most unusual sailing yacht in the world."

"It's a one of a kind, that's for sure," Collins said laughing.

"Well, I can appreciate how you feel. I feel the same way. Kinda like the general who never gets to the front lines, he just keeps sending in the troops. Hell, I sent out a trooper on the Seaduce yesterday, who I don't even know."

"Oh, you mean Van Wagner? No problem there, Dan. I know him, well. I sold him his first charter yacht. You do know, he bought one of my first 52 Citations, don't you?"

"No. I didn't know that. How come you never brought it up before now?"

"You never asked. I have known Rick for at least ten years, he's one of the most popular captains in the charter business down there."

"Did you know that Van Wagner is a retired CIA agent?"

"A what?" Collins replied.

"That's why we hired him, or I should say needed to hire him. Van Wagner, who knew Spencer, heard him running at the mouth that he was working for the government, that the Seaduce was purchased by the taxpayers, and they were on some kind of mission. Van Wagner reported this to Billings, Billings advised me, and when Spencer had his accident, we put Van Wagner on the Seaduce."

"I'll be a son of a bitch. Rick told me he was a retired building contractor, or something like that. I'll be damned. Does he know the whole plan yet? I mean does he know about, ah, the Christmas party?"

"No, I will tell him when he gets to St. Lucia. I want to paint him in a bit of a corner, so he won't jump off the operation. He was complaining that taking over the Seaduce was going to hurt his business. He has hired another captain to take his next two charters. He expects to leave the Seaduce when they reach St. Lucia and fly home."

"Jesus, Dan. You like to call things close. Man, if he jumps ship on us we are screwed. Gransaull, or what ever his name is, won't be able to take over the job, he's not ready, is he?"

"No, he is not ready, nor will he be in time. I'm counting on selling Rick on staying with the mission once he learns what we are really up to. Billings feels he will stay on, he said it's Van Wagner's kind of mission."

O'Brien waved his hand to get the attention of the waitress. "Two more doubles here, please."

Antigua
Friday, November 27th
1620 hours

The small Avon inflatable vibrated as it skimmed across the choppy waters. Rick Van Wagner, controlling the outboard at the stern, had Paul and Karen holding on for their lives. He took a few circles around the many, anchored yachts resting in the peaceful harbor looking for friends or yachts he had shared anchorage with over the years.

Karen recognized a number of crewmembers on yachts that she was familiar with, and hoped that she could get time to visit with them. Meanwhile, Paul Gransaull was thoroughly enjoying seeing the magnificent yachts in the historic harbor, surrounded by satin green hills, and the remains of hilltop forts that protected the harbor hundreds of years ago.

After parking at the dinghy dock behind the Copper and Lumber Store, the threesome joined a joyful group celebrating someone's birthday at the Copper and Lumber's famous pub. The big round bar was nearly full, but Rick found a single seat and was able to squeeze Karen in. They all ordered beers and started scouting the many faces around them. It did not take long.

"Hey, Rick, Jesus, what are you doing down here? I thought you and the Piccolo were banned from these waters."

Rick turned and came face to face with Captain Charlie Lake.

"Shit, I heard you went down to Argentina, or someplace exotic."

"It was Belize, and it was far from exotic, man. I took a job driving an old wooden ketch built in Germany in the twenties, for some rich Mexican who was supposed to own some fish canneries. He was fishy alright. I loaded up with some of his friends from Panama one weekend for a short overnight sail? Next thing I knew I was in the pokey, the yacht became part of the Belize navy, and the owner and guests disappeared."

"How long did the keep you locked up?" Gransaull asked.

"Nearly two years, son, long enough to get sober." Lake turned and yelled across the bar. "Hey innkeeper, I would like to buy this crew a drink, if I can charge it to me wife's account."

Gill Macaulay, who managed the Copper and Lumber Store with her husband Allan, responded to Captain Lake's request.

"You don't have an account here, Captain. Your bitch wife went back to Australia with your six children, leaving us with a bloody bill and your fleabag dog. You owe me more than your Clorox bottle yacht is worth. Now, you ask if you can charge four beers?" Gill smiled as she leaned over the bar and addressed Karen. "Hi, I'm Gill, I run this place. What's your pleasure?"

Gransaull broke out in laughter. "Does this guy really have six children and a wife in Australia?"

There was dead silence. Gill tried not to laugh. She finally offered a controlled smile, and in her sexy Scottish brogue said, "You bettcha, laddie, or, it's six wives and one child in Austria."

Nicholsons Clearinghouse
Antigua

Saturday, November 28th
1010 hours

Rick Van Wagner sat by the telephone waiting for the operator to ring him back on his call to Dan O'Brien in Florida. The phone rang and he picked it up. The operator told him to wait. He could hear the phone ringing.

"O'Brien here."

"O'Brien, it's Van Wagner."

317

"Yes, Captain, where are you?"

"We are in Antigua, got in late yesterday. Listen, I need to get more information from you. Ian Billings was not very clear on dates and times. When do you need the Seaduce in St. Lucia? Paul Gransaull told me you don't have a charter until the 10th, and I can't stay that long, O'Brien, I have a boat to run."

"Captain, where are you calling from?"

"Ah, Nicholson's clearing house at English Harbor."

"Listen, we need to talk, but I would prefer you were somewhat more private, if you understand?"

"Of course, but not to worry, these lines are clear."

"I understand, however, I would prefer if we could talk in total privacy. Do you know where the NASA tracking station is on the island?"

"Of course, it's at the airport, why?"

"I want to have you go there, how long would it take you?

"Well, if I had a car, maybe a half hour, a taxi would be about the same. Who should I ask for or see when I get there?"

"Don't know yet, standby there, I will call you right back. What is your number?"

Admirals Inn
English Harbour
Antigua
1045 hours

Van Wagner spotted Paul and Karen on the outside patio at the Admirals Inn, drinking coffee and enjoying the fresh morning air. There were many guests in the area, too many in fact, and seated too close to have a private conversation with Gransaull.

"Well, looks like I'm a bit late for breakfast."

"Nope, we waited for you." Gransaull motioned for a waitress.

"Well, what do you think of this place, Paul?"

"I can't believe how well they have preserved everything around here. Karen was giving me a crash history lesson about this Inn and that dug out boat slip over there, where they brought in the long boats, it's fascinating. I'm expecting Admiral Nelson to come stumping out of the hotel any minute."

"You're right, Paul, I don't know anywhere else in the entire Caribbean that can compare to this wonderful corner of Antigua," Karen commented, in a melancholy voice.

"Ah, listen up you two. I have to go out to the airport for a while on some business. Why don't you come with me. We will jump in a cab, go out to the field where we can rent a car, then you both can go touring for the day. This island has some fantastic beaches and resorts on the east side. We can set up a time to meet back here, say at happy hour."

"Hey, I'm for that. Karen says she has a special spot she wants to take me to, called Shirley's tights?"

Karen and Rick both laughed.

"Well, that's what you said, Karen."

"Heights, Paul, it's called Shirley Heights."

"You settle up here, Paul. I'm going to run out to the Seaduce and check on things and pick up some papers. I'll get us a cab on the way. You come down and pick me up at the Copper and Lumber Store. I shouldn't be gone longer than fifteen minutes. Oh, Paul, can we speak in private for a second? Please excuse us, Karen."

Gransaull and Van Wagner walked down to the waterfront and sat on the small stone wall.

"I talked to O'Brien a while ago. He wants me to find a very private phone somewhere and call him back in an hour. Just what do you know about this operation, Paul?"

"Ah, not much. I understood from Spencer that we would be getting our final orders and information when we got to St. Lucia. I think it has to do with our charter guests, they were bringing the orders with them, I think."

"Well, I'm really getting fucked up. Seems like your friend O'Brien wants me to stay on the yacht longer that I planned. Hell, I just thought I had to get her to St. Lucia. Ian Billings never told me anything more. You know, this is typical bullshit from these guys, they couldn't get organized if they were in charge of a one car funeral."

"What about Karen, Captain. Did you ask if she could stay on?"

"No, sorry about that, the original plan from Billings said she will have to fly out of here, Paul. She can't go any further."

"O.K, I'll tell her. She more or less knew it was coming."

"Tell you what, I'll ask again later, maybe I can change their mind."

"Thanks, Captain." Gransaull returned to the table and joined Karen. Van Wagner walked out of the Inn onto the main road to where the taxi drivers congregated under a shade tree and hired one. After giving the driver instructions on where to find Paul and Karen, he went down to the dinghy dock behind the Copper and Lumber Store and headed out to the Seaduce.

Copper & Lumber Store
1830 Hours

Van Wagner entered the crowded bar and worked his way through the crowd of tourists, locals and yacht crews. He spotted Karen and Gransaull in a small booth.

"Well, did you have a good day on the island?"

"You bet, Captain, we hit every pub and beach known to the tourists. Come, join us."

"No, you two will have to go solo tonight, I'm afraid, I have some things I have to do. Why don't you spend the night here at the Inn, I'm sure there's room." Van Wagner smiled. There was no response. "If you change your minds call me on the radio, I'll leave it on channel nine, o.k.?"

"Ah, sure you won't join us, Rick. We are all going up to Shirley Heights to watch the sunset, and have dinner. They have a great restaurant up there and lots of your kind of atmosphere."

"Oh really, and just what is my atmosphere, Miss Karen?"

"Jazz, rhythm and blues. I understand the owner of the restaurant is a swinger and has the best collection of jazz tapes in the entire Caribbean."

"Oh really? Well, ask him if he's got some Earl Garner. If he does, tell him to put him on the machine, and turn him up. I'll should be able to hear the music down in the harbor, that's if he has any real amplifiers."

"See you later, Captain."

"Ah, Paul, I will need you on board early, we need to tackle that water pump again, and install that new radio we got in St. Thomas."

Gransaull got the message. He had already checked on flights back to St. Thomas for the next day.

Aboard "Seaduce"
English Harbour, Antigua

Sunday, November 29th
0635 Hours

Van Wagner lay on his bunk, resting his head in the palms of his hands, looking out the port window as daybreak began to lighten the deep purple skies above the eastern hills surrounding the harbor.

Halyards slapped inside tall metal masts of a dozen yachts anchored in the popular anchorage of Freemans Bay. At times it almost sounded like church bells, all ringing together, then they would fall off, and maybe just one, or two would keep the cadence. There was little breeze, and few wind shifts all night. A small shower came over, and Rick felt the cool spray from drops that were hitting the brass frame of the open port light. He did not stir, and it did not last.

The sound of a distant rooster echoed in the harbor. A barking dog, close by, probably in one of the cottages that were located up the hill above Galleon Beach. A sudden gust of wind, and the halyards began to chime as the Seaduce moved slowly around to starboard. Small vibrations sang through the hull, as the anchor line rode through the hawse pipefitting. Seaduce was making small groans, as if she, like all the life around her, was beginning to waken.

Rick sat up, threw his legs over the side of the bunk, scratched his scalp vigorously and left his stateroom. He went to the galley and felt the small six-cup percolator coffeepot on the stove. It was still warm. He poured what coffee was left in a fresh cup and walked up on deck. He flipped a cushion over to avoid sitting on the wet surface and sat down, only to be startled by the coolness of the vinyl cushion through his light cotton shorts.

As he scanned the harbor, he checked the position of the other yachts around him. Most of them were riding on the same heading. Two small sailboats, closer to the beach near some beach apartments, were moving wildly. Off the bow of the Seaduce and anchored close to shore was a custom Hinckley 50 sloop. Its name was "Wings" and its hailing port, Boston.

Through the maze of davits, stainless stanchions, life lines, stowed outboard motors on special brackets and a dew soaked American flag, Rick could see life moving about in the cockpit, and hear metal hitting metal. Rick guessed it was the coffeepot banging against the stainless sink in the galley, someone was up and making the coffee.

The first rays of sun were now reaching out and licking Fort Barclay Point, directly astern of the Seaduce. In the distance, an outboard engine was whining and cavitating as it sped out of the channel towards the Seaduce. Rick watched as it came closer. He could see two people were in the small rubber dinghy. In a few minutes, the dinghy pulled up along portside and stopped.

"Thanks, skipper, owe you one." Paul Gransaull pulled himself up on the small rope ladder and onto the deck. The outboard revved up and went back out into the channel heading back to Nelson's Dockyard.

"Morning, Rick."

"Morning, Paul. Didn't expect to see you out here this early."

"Couldn't sleep, one of those nights, ya know?"

"Yeah, I tried two double scotches, a beer and five aspirins, still no sleep."

Gransaull stepped slowly into the cockpit and sat down across from Van Wagner. His face was sober, almost sad. His eyes searched hard into Van Wagner's looking for some unanswered questions. Van Wagner wasted no time.

"You know all about this mission, don't you, Paul?"

"I know what I have been told, now I need to know what you were told by O'Brien yesterday."

"Castro? Does that ring a bell?"

"Yes."

"Do you know what is expected of us?"

"Yes, we are part of a plot to blow him out of the universe."

Gransaull pointed at the coffee mug in Rick's hand. "Can I get some coffee?"

"It's all gone. Just how much to you know, Paul? For example, do you know where all this takes place and when?"

"Somewhere down around Guadeloupe. But, we won't have anything to do with that. We will be on a freighter heading for Puerto Rico when Castro's yacht blows, at least that's what I have been told. The explosion is to take place on Christmas Eve."

"So you do know the complete operation? You're a jet jockey, how the hell did you let your friend, Commander Buckwheat, talk you into this?"

Gransaull laughed as he looked into Van Wagner's puzzled face. "Yes, I'm an F-14 Tom Cat driver, and according to my orders, I am on a TDY assignment for sixty days. My name is not Gransaull, by the way, it's Bill Cumberland. Now, can I go make some coffee?"

"How much did Mel Spencer know about this mission?"

"Not much. He was told that we were going to be playing in a hunt and seek game, tracking some suspicious yachts that were suspected of running drugs. He was also told to get us to St. Lucia and that he would be further briefed by this phony charter group we are picking up. These folks are really agency people, but I guess they told you that."

"Shit, how did I get in this mess? Now I can't get out. Your friend, Mr. O'Brien? He is the one who designed this entire caper, according to Billings, and the guy's a novice sailor, right?"

"That's right."

"Do you know who else is involved?"

"Well, not personally, but I do know there is this freighter, code named "Red Sleigh", and another sailboat code named "Yuletide" that we need to meet somewhere west of Antigua on the 23rd. This Yuletide yacht will be code named Music Box, when it meets Castro's yacht. It will be acting out a charade as a distressed vessel. Castro's yacht is expected to come to its aid, and provide some parts and food. During the exchange of goodies, a navy seal team will plant explosives under Castro's yacht that will explode some twenty four hours later when it's anchored off Guadeloupe."

"Stop, Jesus Christ, I can't take anymore, your version is worse than O'Brien's yesterday. This guy O'Brien is mad. He really thinks he is going to stop Fidel Castro in the middle of the ocean, borrow a fuse and some water, while a seal team is under his yacht sticking silly putty on the hull?"

"Actually, Rick, when I first heard the plan laid out by Commander Buckland and Ian Billings, it made sense. After a while though, it became rather complicated. The whole operation is based on one key play, Castro falls for the bait that a sailboat is in distress, and needs help."

Gransaull got up and walked towards the open companionway. He stopped, turned and looked at Van Wagner.

"This Dan O'Brien somehow convinced Washington his plan would work, that it could be done, leaving no trace back to the mission players. That's why this beautiful yacht has to be destroyed with all of us lost at sea. Well, not really, just pretend stuff."

"Well, that was the original plan, Paul. But now Mr. O'Brien has a new problem, me. I can't get killed, I am too well known, and now I have been connected to this yacht. Even if I leave now, any good investigation will have to come back around to me. Who is O'Brien afraid of? Shit, the worse that can happen, the insurance company haunts me for a while, who else would care?"

"Well, I would have to think O'Brien is not concerned about insurance companies. He is concerned about the Russians and the Cubans, who will be looking for a smoking gun. He just wanted a fail safe program built in as he promised the White House."

"There's got to be an easier way, and maybe we need to try and find it. Jesus, how do you think O'Brien found out all this shit, I mean about Castro and this private cruise?"

"I don't know, I wasn't privy to that information. I was just told to keep an eye on Spencer, make sure we got down to St. Lucia by the 10th of December, meet our charter guests at some resort hotel in Marigot Bay. We would get our final orders there. I know, we are to come back here before we leave for the meeting with the freighter."

"Go make some coffee. There's some instant if you don't want to wait. Jesus, I can't believe what I got roped into here."

Gransaull went down the companionway and into the galley.

"When do we leave, Rick?"

"Ah, tomorrow, sometime, maybe even Tuesday."

"What about Karen?"

"I picked up a ticket yesterday to get her back to St. Thomas. There's a Liat flight out around two o'clock. O'Brien wants her gone, and he wants to know if you were smart enough not to tell her anything about what's going on."

Gransaull came back on deck and sat down, he stirred the cup like a chef folding heavy cream. He reached up into his shirt pocket and withdrew a small black covered notebook. He tossed it over to Rick.

"That's all your codes, and information on the communications. That new VHF radio, the one Mel put in at St. Thomas? Well, that's the hopper, did O'Brien explain?"

"Yes, I'm familiar with the radio."

"Did O'Brien give you your code name?"

"Doc."

"Not bad. He gave me, Dumbo, supposedly because I can fly."

Van Wagner carefully scanned the small loose-leaf notebook. "Shit, we are not even entered in here."

"I know, I came in late, like you."

"Fruitcake? Castro's yacht is called fruitcake?"

Gransaull chuckled, "I love this shit, don't you?"

"To get back to Karen, she knows nothing, and I am not in love. Infatuated, yes. You see, I have a wife in D.C. She's sharp, beautiful and taking some post graduate courses at Georgetown University. Going to be a lawyer someday, like her famous daddy."

"You don't sound too thrilled."

"I'm not, I'm really losing her, it's been going on for over a year. We, well, the Navy is what I want, and that is no longer important to her."

"Hey, you're not the first, pal. I lost one after eighteen years, and threw in four kids, just to get away. The agency killed us. Now, I'm forty-seven, a newly wed with a wife twenty years my junior and a six month old son."

"And you're going to stay on this mission?"

"Yeah, I have to see how this one turns out. This caper is going to get nominated for a Academy Award for sure. We just have to come up with a better plan for O'Brien on how you and I are going to be survivors after this beauty gets deep sixed. Did they ever explain to you what was going to happen to Spencer had he stayed on as captain?

"No, but it had crossed my mind. His accident in St. Thomas has been on my mind too. Sometimes I feel like the whole thing was planned to eliminate him."

The sound of an engine starting broke over the water, and a puff of white hazy smoke formed around the Hinckley's stern. There was movement on deck, and the sound of a grinding windless as it began to retrieve the long anchor line. "Wings" was getting underway.

Rick stood up and stretched. "I'm going to take a shower and get dressed. We'll go pick up Karen and head over to the Inn and get some breakfast."

"Sounds like a winner. Ah, Rick, I feel much better now that you are going along on this. I don't mind telling you, I'm not often nervous hitting a rolling carrier deck at one hundred and thirty knots, but I was starting to lose a lot of sleep over this operation. Now with you on board, well, I can maybe get some sleep."

Van Wagner, standing clad in his boxer shorts, looked more like a retired Marine drill sergeant than a retired CIA agent. He was broad chested, with a reasonable spread in the middle, but solid, and very muscular. He stood admiring the young navy flyer, admiring his youth and the sincerity in his gray eyes. He smiled at the airman and offered his hand.

Fun & Sun Apartments
St. Petersburg Beach, Florida

Sunday, November 29th
0830 Hours

The call O'Brien waited so patiently for, finally came in. Phil Avery advised him that the Island Drummer had arrived in Key West.

"Hey, Rudolf, we thought we would see you waiting on the dock down here to greet us."

"I would have liked that, Phil. Now, tell me about the shake down cruise, all went well I take it?"

"Everything worked perfectly. We have some minor things we need to adjust and tighten, but nothing serious. We did, however, get a little pumping action on the mast the first night out. We had everything out, taking a steady wind off the port bow with fifteen knots over the deck. Once in a while it would go to eighteen and twenty, and we had to dump some sail, but it was livable. The pumping came when we were hard on the wind, but it was nothing serious."

"I'll advise Ted, and see what he says. Now, what are your plans to leave Key West? Will you still be going straight to St. Thomas?"

"Well, that's up to the weather now, Dan. There is a small low-pressure building up west of Puerto Rico that we will want to keep an eye on. We may change our plans and run to the Bahamas if it hangs around there, or moves west and north towards Cuba."

"So you may run through the Bahamas after all, o.k. I understand."

"Well, like I said, Dan, I wanted to head out and run down off Cuba's north coast then swing down and go straight for the Virgins, but if we need to go east for while and run the Bahamas, we will do that."

"Listen, Phil. It is nearly 0900. Can you get back to me tonight and let me know for sure about your time of departure? I should have news on Captain Lind later. He is in the Turks and should be leaving there sometime today. I talked to the Seaduce yesterday in Antigua and the new captain, Rick Van Wagner? He's ready to start down to St. Lucia."

"Did you have a problem keeping him on the mission? I mean, you told him what he's involved in now, right?"

"Oh yes, and he, well, let's say he's going along with us, but he thinks I'm some kind of basket case."

"He's a good man, Dan, and he will do what has to be done, don't worry about him. Well, listen, I'd better get back to the crew, I'll call again this evening."

O'Brien put the phone down, picked up a cigarette, lit it and walked to the stove and poured coffee into his mug. He went to the kitchen door, opened it and walked outside. There was a cool nip in the air and a chilling breeze that came down the road from the beach. He looked over at the cottage where Eileen lived. The Mercedes was gone. After looking at his watch, he returned to his apartment and turned on the TV. Some preacher was telling a story in some tropical gardens, somewhere in Florida.

The phone rang, startling O'Brien, nearly dropping his coffee mug. "Got to calm down," he thought as he reached for the receiver.

"Hey, Dan. Heard from anyone?"

"Hey, Ted, yes, I just talked to Avery. They are on the hook behind some hotel in Key West. They couldn't get into a slip last night."

"How were they, did they have any problems running down?"

"No, everything is fine, they did have some pumping on the mast at one point, blamed it on overloading the sails. Phil will go over that with you later tonight when he calls you."

"Are you going anywhere today, Dan?"

"No, I think I'll start getting my stuff together, do some packing. There's nothing much to do now but wait and keep our fingers crossed that all the equipment stays together."

"How's Van Wagner doing on the Seaduce?"

"Oh, just fine, I talked to him yesterday. They arrived in Antigua and plan to leave Tuesday for St. Lucia. John Lind is in the Turks and heading out later today. Avery and the Drummer will leave on Tuesday also, weather permitting.

"Listen, I'll call you later around two or three, o.k.?"

"O.K. You have a good one, Ted. I'll be here, and if you want to come over later, maybe after dinner, we can talk to Phil and go over the Drummer's problems."

Collins paused for a moment. He did not like the sound of O'Brien's voice. It sounded weak and strange.

"Dan, would you like to join us? I could come over and pick you up in a few minutes. We can watch the Giant and Eagle game and drink a few beers."

"Naw, thanks, Ted. You go ahead, enjoy your family today."

O'Brien put the phone down and for the second time that morning, he felt a cold hand on his shoulder. For the first time, he felt a loneliness he could not shake, he wanted to be somewhere. It did not seem right that everyone was on the move, while he sat in a rented apartment praying something would happen, like the phone to ring, or maybe Eileen would come through the door. He looked up at the TV screen. Now there were six beautiful young women in full length yellow gowns, and young men in blue tuxedos singing. O'Brien turned the volume up expecting to hear a chorus of "Hello Dolly." instead they were singing "He will forgive your sins today, if you let him in your heart to stay."

The small tube went out, as did the sound. O'Brien lit another cigarette and walked out the door.

CHAPTER 19

Castro's Mansion
Varadero, Cuba

Monday, November 30th
1100 hours

Fidel Castro sat in the shade of the small umbrella that shaded the glass top table he was using for a desk. The small flagstone patio once used as a private sun deck, was located just outside his large office at the rear of the mansion. He was studying the list of crew and staff members who would be traveling with him on the Unicorn in three weeks. He looked at his watch, it was 1113 hours.

The first list provided by Unicorn's new captain, Carlos DeTorre, consisted of only four names. Two of them were engineers, one a master of electronics, and the other a senior navigator. All of the men were out of DeTorre's "Dragon" Squadron and all of them had been thoroughly screened before being approved.

The next list showed the names of Yang Lo, General Vincetta, Captain Carmen Amadore, Major Taymo Diaz, Vincetta's aide, and Raoul, his brother. The name, Juan Luis Cantillos, Castro's oldest friend, was crossed out, as was Dimitri Sorokin.

"Good morning, Comrade President."

Castro looked up to see General Vincetta walking through the open French doors. "Buenos dias, General. You are late, I expected you an hour ago."

"Yes, I apologize, I was delayed at headquarters. I received a call from Captain Chenaves at communications. He advised me about a strange communiqué that took place at 0610, between comrade Sorokin and Soviet Fleet Headquarters at Sevastopol."

Castro looked up over his reading glasses into the bewildered face of his first General. "What business would Dimitri have calling Soviet Fleet Headquarters?"

"It seems he was inquiring about the Kompas research ship. If you recall, it was in Havana for months, then went to Murial for new electronics. About three weeks ago, it left for the south Atlantic. I investigated through Navy Intelligence, and learned that the Kompas was sent to relieve the Chukotaka.

Castro looked puzzled. He stroked his beard lightly as he stared out onto the calm seas of the Bay of Cardenas.

"I called over to Admiral Santamaria's office. All they had on the Kompas was that it was taking up position off Antigua to monitor down range activities on shuttle missions from Cape Kennedy, and to relieve the Chukotaka. Chukotaka was being called back for maintenance, and was heading for the Black Sea."

"Who did Dimitri talk to?"

"Admiral Gorshkov."

"Gorshkov? Admiral of the Atlantic Fleet?"

"Yes, but evidently an old friend of Dimitri and his family. They spoke a long time about personal things, and Dimitri's parents. He told Gorshkov that the captain on the Kompas is a friend of his, and that he wanted to contact him sometime, but did not know the procedure. Gorshkov told him he should have no problem, that he could contact a Captain Syvy at Cienfuegos Headquarters, who would give him instructions."

"Strange, but then most of our Russian friends are, aren't they?" Castro smiled and motioned to Vincetta to join him.

"Sit, sit down. We should go over our list of who will be traveling with us. I just noticed that we have neglected to take care of food for the voyage. There is no cook on the list, or what ever they call them on ships. We need to have someone to cook and provision the boat, do you have any ideas on this?"

Just then, the phone sitting on the table began to ring. General Vincetta glanced at Castro for approval to answer. He nodded his head, yes.

"General Vincetta, can I help you? Oh, yes, Comrade Sorokin, so pleased to hear from you. Did you have a peaceful weekend? Good, yes, he is right here." Vincetta handed the phone to Fidel.

"Buenos dias, comrade, I was just about to call you. But of course, what is it I can do for you?"

Fidel's eyes shifted to Vincetta. He bobbed his head, as if approving what Dimitri was saying. "Of course, I am honored, comrade. This is good. You will enjoy the sea vacation. We will work out the details on where you will be for these days. Actually, you can be included in our journey into the hills. That would be most natural, if you were to join us, no? Good, that is what we will do. I will have this announced just before we leave."

Castro picked up his pen and wrote a message on a blank piece of paper from his legal pad that read, "He is going with us."

"Did we hear about what? No, this is news to me. When did this happen? Hold on comrade, hold on."

Castro put his hand over the mouthpiece of the phone and said to Vincetta, "Did you hear anything about two American carrier groups being sent to the Caribbean in December?"

"No, comrade President, I have heard of no such announcement."

"No, my friend, we have not heard anything. When was this announcement made? I see. Well, we will have to be especially careful then, won't we? Ah, speaking of receiving news, has there been any word from your headquarters, I mean, have you heard anymore about Kotov? I see, that is good. I will call you later, meanwhile General Vincetta and I will work on your plans to vanish for a few days. Goodbye, my friend."

Castro put the phone down and smiled at Vincetta. "Something has changed. Dimitri wants to go with us on the voyage."

"That is strange, I wonder what changed his mind? Maybe the call to Gorshkov had something to do with it. I'll look into this new problem about the American carriers, I will call Admiral Santamaria as soon as we arrive at Headquarters."

Castro sat back in his chair, shielding his eyes from the sun with his hand, as he stared out upon the glistening bay. "Where did you say this Kompas is stationed?"

"Most of the time, they patrol south of the Turks and Caicos down to Barbados. They stay around Antigua and Barbuda most of the time. As you know, the NASA tracking station is located on Antigua."

"Well, whatever Dimitri is up to, we will eventually find out. Dimitri is not one to keep secrets. It might be that he feels more at ease now that he learned that the Kremlin is not sending him a new assistant, at least not until after the new year."

"Now, what do you have for me in your magic case?"

Vincetta opened his brief case and pulled out a black covered binder notebook. He then pulled out a folded chart and opened it. It was a nautical map, taken from a cruising guide, showing the island of Guadeloupe and the islands nearby. Castro helped him spread it out on the small tabletop. Vincetta opened the book and began to explain plans for their arrival aboard the Unicorn.

"We will have two advance men, posing as tourists, in position on Guadeloupe no later than December 22nd. They will arrive from Venezuela with their female companions and take the ferry over to Terre de Haut, this island, right here." Vincetta put his index finger on the small island that lay just south of Guadeloupe.

"Once they check in into their hotel in the town of Bourg De Saints, they will contact our local agent, who will have a small boat chartered, ready to take them over to the island of Grand Islet."

Vincetta took his index finger and placed it on the small island just southwest of Terre de Haut. "They will set up their camp on a high hill at the south end of the island where, I am told, they will have a perfect view of the cove we will be anchoring in. They will have their small transceiver working and monitoring our frequencies no later than 1200 hours on the 23rd. Their code name for the operation is La Mer, the sea. Their radio code name is Pawn."

"What about our guests? Have we received any new word from Señor Chiba?"

"Yes, finally. Your guests will meet in Martinique during the day of December 22nd. Their chartered yacht, the Bonaire, is an American built Bertram Yacht, a sport fishing type, and is 46 feet long. It is owned by Carlos Fabrico, Fabrico Meat Packing Company, in Chile."

"Yes, I remember him, a good old friend, go on."

"They will be arriving on different airlines during the day, and are to meet in the town of St. Annes, at a hotel called the Caritan."

"How do we communicate with them, General?"

"We don't. Our agent will direct their captain to these islands off Guadeloupe, and our outpost on the island will direct them to the cove. They are going to try to arrive around 1100 hours to have maximum tide to enter the cove. Our team will have their boat ready to assist if needed."

"Who do we have on Martinique?"

"I don't know if you remember him, his name is Tomas Puros. We have brought him down from New Orleans."

"Puros, Ah yes, he served us well in Nicaragua. I thought he was sent up to Panama last year?"

"He was, but he requested to be returned to New Orleans, he has family there, and heads up one of our most successful party organizations."

"What time do you estimate we will arrive at the island? Have you discussed this with Captain DeTorre?"

"Yes. We should be arriving at the island around 0900 hours on the 24th, however, we may have to slow our speed, as the tide may be too low at that hour to enter the cove. We will not need to clear customs, unless we are forced by weather to land on the main island of Guadeloupe. Should this happen, we will put into Basse Terre at the River Sens, right here." Vincetta put his finger on the chart.

"If we need to go into port, all our necessary documents will be ready. If comrade Sorokin is joining us, we will need to work up his papers. Now, most important. Our contingency plans call for an emergency escape out of Guadeloupe by air if needed. Comrade Puros is taking care of this, too. A chartered jet out of Mexico City will arrive Guadeloupe by way of Jamaica, on December 24th. It will standby with its two pilots and be ready to leave with our party should anything go wrong. Puros will make all the arrangements on Guadeloupe to get us to the airport, and will take care of all the communications. I will notify our Air Defense Command prior to our departure that a flight may possibly enter our air space from the east. They will be given aircraft identification, time of entry and destination. It will be coded as a priority flight under your orders, and it will be allowed to land at Santiago with no security needed."

"Good, very good. Not like the old days, huh? You did a fine job, General. I must meet with comrade Puros and.."

Vincetta interrupted. "If I may, I do have some bad news. We have lost two of our expected guests, I'm afraid. There was a misunderstanding between two of the Colombian representatives, only one will be coming. We have also lost a representative from Chile, he was called to Spain, something to do with his family and the holidays."

"I offer a golden opportunity to these stupid bastards, and they ignore us? So, that means we have only four?"

"That is correct, but, that is all we need for now."

"You may be right, General. I stay up nights now, wondering if we should consider building our dolphins out of the country. It could be our oriental friend is right, China undoubtedly can produce the dolphins cheaper and faster with no risks. We would always be looking over our shoulder if we built them here, and we would always have the problem of working under the noses of the KGB, unless Sorokin can keep them out of our hair."

"I was hoping, comrade President, that you would consider this. I think we should talk to comrade Lo about this matter before we leave. I have to admit, I have been nervous about the idea of building them here, right from the beginning."

"Good, then we both agree, General. We shall speak to comrade Lo before we leave. We will need some idea of his costs too. We don't want to let our guests know of this arrangement, and will advise comrade Lo of the consequences if he should try and go around us with a better deal, do you agree?"

"Of course. I will personally take care of this with comrade Lo."

"Speaking of Lo," Castro raised his voice. " He asked if it would be possible to do a test launch from the marina some evening. He would like to make sure everything is operational before we leave. We don't want anything going wrong during the demonstration."

"I don't know about that. It is secure enough there, but there is little depth around that part of the harbor. Did he want to move the Unicorn out in the bay?"

"No, I would not allow that. If he wants to launch, he will have to do it from the overhead gantry. Unicorn does not leave the shelter until we are ready to sail for Guadeloupe. I even turned down Captain DeTorre's request for sea trials. It would arouse too many questions if the Unicorn was seen in the bay."

"Yes sir, I agree. Oh, which reminds me. Captain DeTorre did mention he would like to move his men down to Santiago as soon as they are cleared. He wants his engineers to go over the engines and electronics, if this is possible?"

"Of course. You make the arrangements for quarters at Monacada Barracks. See that they get everything they need. Anything else?"

"Yes, one more request. Major Lucia, your new pilot? He wanted to know if it would be at all possible during one of the supply flights to Santiago, if he could bring his wife and children along. It would be one of the trips that no other personnel were on board, of course. They were married in Santiago, and he wants to show the children the city and the bay by air. December is their twelfth anniversary".

"What do you think, General?"

"I see no problem, but it will take a special permit from you. He would have to get them on the base and cleared properly. However, as it is your personal plane."

"Take care of it, have the papers drawn up for my signature and I will sign them."   .

Fun & Sun Apartments
St. Petersburg Beach, Florida
1245 hours

Dan O'Brien had just put the phone down, after talking to a local travel agency looking into flight schedules to San Juan, St. Thomas and St. Croix. On the small island counter top, he had his charts and navigation tools neatly together, ready to slip into an old pilot's flight case. In the bedroom, spread across the bed was a hanging bag with his favorite light weight blazer, two pairs of light cotton slacks and a half dozen oxford shirts, and in a soft duffel bag, containing briefs, shorts, socks, T-shirts, two bathing suits, a work-out suit were carefully packed.

The phone rang. "O'Brien."

"Dan, Admiral Koster. How are you today?"

O'Brien did not like the tone of the Admiral's voice. He had become good at predicting Koster's moods from the tone of his voice.

"I'm just fine, Admiral. I was just heading out the door."

"Were you now? And I suppose you were planning to take a little trip, like down to the Caribbean?"

O'Brien could not believe it. How the hell did he know?

"Can't do it, Dan, not yet, I need you up here pronto. If you can, get on a flight to get you here within four hours. I will have a unmarked pick you up. If there are no flights, I'll send my plane down, where's the nearest Air Force Base, Tampa, right?"

"Ah, is there something wrong, Admiral? I mean, I haven't.."

"Call me back in ten minutes with your flight schedule. I am with the Secretary in my office."

The phone went dead.

"Jesus, what the hell could have gone wrong?" O'Brien began to break out in a sweat. He picked up the phone and before he realized what he was doing he dialed the Citation Yacht Company. So he asked for Ted Collins.

"I don't know Ted, but I don't like it. Listen, I have to make flight plans to get to D.C. Do me a favor. Here is Bollman's number in Miami, 305 555 8090. Call him and ask if all is all right in Christmasland. See if anyone has called in, like the Sonar with some problems or something. If he wants to know why, just tell him that, well I'm en route to Washington, and just wanted an update when I land. Tell him what you want, but see if there is anything wrong that we don't know about, thanks."

O'Brien put the phone down and called the travel agency back. He learned there was a Delta leaving Tampa International at 1420 hours, arriving in Baltimore at 1710. He called the Pentagon and left word with Admiral Koster's aide.

Baltimore/Washington Airport
Baltimore
1750 Hours

O'Brien stood next to the Delta baggage conveyer and watched intently for his bags to appear out of the leather skirted opening in the wall.

"Mr. O'Brien?"

O'Brien turned and looked into the soft hazel eyes of one of the prettiest faces he had ever seen in a Navy uniform.

"Ah, yes?"

"Hi, I am Lieutenant Brooks, and I am here to take you to Washington, sir."

"I don't suppose we could take a wrong turn and go to Atlantic City, or someplace exotic, would you?"

The young navy officer blushed. "No sir, we are on a tight schedule I'm afraid. Can I help you with your things?"

"Ah, no, that's alright. Where are you parked?"

"Just outside the door. Here, at least let me take your flight bag."

The drive into Washington was slow, but O'Brien appreciated the breathing space before his meeting with the Admiral. He enjoyed the young Lieutenant, listening to her tell the story of her life. She was the youngest of four, all navy brats, and the only one to follow her daddy's footsteps, a retired Vice Admiral, living in Richardson, Texas. Alice, after completing two years of college at the University of Delaware, enlisted in the Navy, and was now on Admiral Koster's staff. Before the wheels of the gray Chrysler staff car crossed the threshold counter of the Pentagon guard gate, Alice had agreed to meet O'Brien for a drink after his meeting with the Admiral. She handed him her beeper number, and home number, as he left the car.

Admiral Koster, sleeves rolled up, tie pulled down, hair tossed wildly around his small ears, was not his social self when O'Brien entered his office. "Put your shit down there somewhere, and come over here."

O'Brien dumped his bags on the floor inside the door and walked over to the large table where Koster stood bending over an all too familiar chart of the Caribbean and South Atlantic.

"Sir, what is the problem?"

Koster turned and looked O'Brien dead in the eyes."

"We may be getting into a fucking frying pan here, with your operation, my boy."

"I don't understand, Admiral, what is happening?"

"We are not sure, yet. Captain Valdimar Smirnov, our Soviet Naval Attaché' here in Washington, informed us, in a nice informal way at a party last night, that there would be a major exercise taking place in the eastern zone of the Caribbean basin in mid-December. There will be no less than two battle groups participating, estimating thirty war ships and at least fifteen support vessels. The groups are supposed to be getting assembled, right now. Departure times have not been released by their Atlantic Fleet Headquarters in Sevastopol, at least not as of 1700 hours Zulu."

"I don't understand, Admiral, what does all this mean? Surely this can't have any connection with Castro's activities; that would be crazy. He is working behind the Soviets' back on this operation."

"That's what you say, or what your spooks have been selling you from down there, but what if they are pulling your chain? For a worst case scenario, let's say the Reds know about Castro's plan. Maybe they want him to get into something more comfortable than their pants, like drugs. It could be they want to be rid of him as much as we do. No telling what they know about his operation, is there? Wouldn't it be ironic if they were the ones who found a way to run into him, or better yet, through him on his yacht? They could be playing our game, with the same intentions, just using more sophisticated equipment."

"Sir, these maneuvers they talk about. Isn't this a bit strange? I can't recall the Russians bringing any kind of a fleet of warships to the Caribbean. When was the last time they brought any of their major warships down into the south Atlantic? Not even in October '62, that I recall, the freighters that were bringing the missiles into Cuba were unescorted."

"You are correct, and surprisingly observant, Mr. O'Brien. The Russians have never come this far south with a battle group of any size, anytime."

Koster pulled a folded handkerchief from his hip pocket and wiped his moist brow. "How much faith are you putting into your two moles down there, Dan? They stopped broadcasting, didn't they? The Cubana pilot, didn't he end up back in the Cuban Air Force? Maybe he had a change of heart, maybe he turned on us, and just maybe, the Russians are going to be in the neighborhood waiting to catch you with the smoking gun. Think about that, O'Brien."

"Sir, I can't believe that the Reds know. I can't believe that they would go though this much trouble. It has to be coincidental, something else. The messages we were getting were real, and I believe them, sir."

"Do you know how I feel right now, O'Brien? I feel like I have been conned, Danny boy. You made this big stink about having the pond clean down there, you don't want any Navy hanging around. I let you sucker me in, now look what we've got, the best part of the Soviet Atlantic fleet maybe heading our way, and all I have is two P-3's on watch dog duty. If I had stuck to my plans, not yours, I wouldn't have the blue Caribbean getting covered in red flags. They wouldn't have come near us with a force this large if we were in the neighborhood."

"Admiral Koster, have you made a announcement recently, or what ever it is you do, to let the press know that the Navy is going on maneuvers in the Atlantic?"

"Last Friday, no, it was Thursday, CINLATIC announced the movement of two carrier groups attached to 2nd Fleet, would be taking part in training exercises in the Gulf of Mexico, mid December. Navy will be releasing the names of the carriers and support ships later this week from their Information Bureau in Norfolk. One of these groups I wanted in the Caribbean, remember? But no, I listened to you instead."

"Sir, is it possible that this is the reason why the Soviets decided to come into the Caribbean at this time, knowing you would not be there as originally planned?"

The Admiral turned his large body and rested his backside on the chart table. He looked across the spacious room.

"I don't know, Dan. This is a very unusual move by Admiral Mikhailovsky to begin with. Shit, they know we won't be tracking with satellites, and they won't pay any mind to the SR- 71 Blackbirds, and they know our subs will be busy playing grab-ass with theirs. Jesus, I just don't know. It's got me going nuts. I haven't even talked to the Joint Chiefs on this. I have a meeting with them in the morning, that's why I wanted to see you tonight. Dan, I think we should scrub Operation Yuletide. Let's pull in our horns and retreat while there is time. Hell, if Castro decides to go ahead with his meeting, there will be enough Russian hardware and traffic down there to walk on without ever getting your feet wet. How the hell could you even think of pulling off your mission in those busy waters?"

O'Brien just watched the tall man before him physically collapse from within. His eyes were swollen, pale skin seemed to be showing shadows of gray. He stood, hands flat on the table, head deep between his shoulders, staring down at the floor.

"I'll do whatever you say, Admiral. I am sorry if I caused this, I mean by not agreeing with you, and pushing so hard to keep our Navy out of the way, I had no idea.."

"Shit, O'Brien, nobody could have predicted this one. Where are your troops right now?"

"Captain Lind and the Sonar just left the Turks, can't be more than sixty or seventy miles out. He's heading to San Juan, but we can reach him out of Miami. We can have him back in Miami in three days. The Seaduce and her new captain are in English Harbor, Antigua, waiting to sail for St. Lucia. The Island Drummer arrived in Key West, and plans to start down to the Virgin Islands, maybe as early as tomorrow."

"O.K. Dan, Here is what we will do. I will meet with the Joint Chiefs at 0800. They will be advised that we are on hold. I will be meeting with the Vice President at 1030 hours and advise him the same, and he will advise the President, who has just returned from his first summit with Gorbachev, I might add. You get your ass up early tomorrow morning and wait for a call from me or Admiral Tom Coons. You do remember the Admiral from Navy Intelligence, don't you?"

"Yes, sir."

"Good, I will call Tom tonight and pull out the stops to see what we can find out. There is time here, some time, and maybe, just maybe we can find an explanation to the Russians' intentions, maybe not, but we will be a little patient. This whole damn scene is beginning to haunt me, like it's happened before, ah, I think they call it deja."

Suddenly, Koster stood up straight, spun around and faced O'Brien. He looked like he just received a transfusion. His color changed, and his bright gray eyes seem to bounce with excitement.

"Where will you be later?"

"Ah, my apartment, sir."

"Damn, I forgot, this is your home, isn't it? O.K., you stand by there. Here, write your number down on this paper, I will give it to one of Tom's people. You get home, don't leave until you hear from me or someone at Intelligence."

"Ah, yes, sir. Do you?"

"Get, shoo, your driver will be waiting outside. You tell the Lieutenant to take you home, in her car, not a company car. Get her beeper number and when you hear from us, be ready to move."

"Yes, sir. Should I call any of the team and advise them that there could be a change in plans?'

"No, damn it, just do as I say, go home and wait."

O'Brien picked up his luggage and flight case and went into the outer office where the pretty Navy officer waited.

"You have to take me home, sir, and in your car. Admiral's orders. We will have to make one quick stop though. Happy-Lee's take-out in Georgetown, they do great egg rolls."

CINLANTIC Headquarters
Norfolk Navy Yard
Norfolk, Virginia

Tuesday, December 1st
0734 hours

Commander William "Will" Shock, CINLANTIC Fleet Information Officer read the teletype report that had just been handed him by Captain Tom Hathaway, Chief Communications Officer.

"Thanks, Tom. This is everything we have, no surprises?"

"That's it, Commander. If there is any truth in your report from the Soviet naval attaché, it's a deep dark secret to all his folks at home in the Kremlin, and Soviet Navy Headquarters."

The tall lanky officer put a handful of papers down on the Commander's desk and walked over to the large world map on the wall. He studied it for a minute, then turned.

"It doesn't make sense, sir. The Russians have never taken a battle group into the South Atlantic. Why would they do it now, especially when all we are hearing is they are cutting back on exercises. Another thing, why do this on the eve of a very successful first summit meeting between the President and Mr. Gorbachev?"

Hathaway, a communications expert and specialist on Soviet naval operations, walked back to the desk and stood relaxed before his superior.

"We are running some update stats, sir, on just how inactive the Reds have been in the past six months. Sir, here is another fact. There is no activity that even looks like preparations for mobilization at their Atlantic Headquarters at Sevastopol, at least not that our intelligence can find. Hell, Commander, if they were going to move that many major war ships anywhere, the yards would be bustling with activity, and supply trains would be pouring in. Sevastopol and all the ships in port are covered in five inches of snow, and there are no signs of major preparations, or anyone even shoveling snow. They are definitely in a stand-down mode, not even on alert status."

"Thank you, Captain. Now if you will excuse me?"

"Yes, sir. I will be standing-by down at com-central should anything new develop, I will call you, sir." He snapped a short salute, spun on his heel and left the office.

Commander Shock picked up his phone and dialed Admiral Koster's residence. "It's just like you figured, Admiral, it's some kind of bluff, just like they did during Grenada invasion week. Evidently, when they heard you were going with two carrier groups into the Gulf, they decided to give you something to sweat about. I would be willing to bet that this entire brainstorm was executed by a low-level official, or maybe even the young attaché' himself. Are you going to counter with any comment? I see, yes, I can do that. I will have the report sent up to you in time for the meeting. Yes, sir, thank you, sir."

Commander Shock put the phone down and walked around his desk to a large display board on his office wall, that listed all the active ships attached to CINLANTIC fleet. It gave each ship's current state of readiness, maintenance schedule, work in progress, and their berth locations. It also listed all active ships currently operating in the 2nd and 6th Fleets. The list of aircraft carriers also showed where all their air wing squadrons were based and their readiness. Other information included crew strengths, leave status, etc. He put his finger on the carrier, USS JOHN F. KENNEDY, CV 67, Norfolk.

Back at his desk he made another call to Vice Admiral Tom Coons at the Pentagon. "Morning, Tom, tell the old man he can have the Kennedy, tell him before the meeting. She can be ready to sail in six days. We can put together enough ships to make up a standard carrier battle training group. Remind him, we will be seriously taxing the fleet and the Kennedy will be short one frigate. Her only frigates will be coming out of Mayport. Advise the Admiral that if this meets with his approval, we will notify Fleet Air Wing immediately and begin alerting the squadrons."

"Will that be all, sir?"

"Yes, that's affirmative. I will wait until I hear from the Admiral, talk to you later, Tom."

Dan O'Brien's Apartment
0810 hours

"What the hell was that?"

"It's just my beeper, relax, Dan."

O'Brien could feel her warm body move gently away from his, as if she were slipping out of his skin. Through the eerie velvet shadows of the room, he could see her move past the foot of the bed to the chair were her clothes had been neatly draped. She picked up her small black leather purse and stepped out the bedroom door. He looked at the glowing red numbers on the nearby nightstand clock, 0814. He reached for his cigarettes and found only an empty collapsed package. In one swift move, he slipped off the bed and walked into the bathroom, closed the door, and without turning on the lights, stepped into the small-enclosed shower and opened the two valves. His body shook as the cold water sprayed over him. The bathroom light suddenly came on and the shower became crowded. "They want you over at Vice Admiral Coon's office in one hour, I won't have time to even change."

"You look fine, just the way you are." O'Brien pulled her close and kissed her gently on her forehead.

Outside the brownstone apartment building, the brisk northern winds were driving the chill factor down to twenty-five degrees. The skies above Washington were heavy and gray. A policewomen, standing behind a 1981 Pontiac Grand Prix, was having difficulty with her pen as she attempted to fill out a parking violation. After 7 a.m. the car was illegally parked on Wisconsin Avenue. The officer finally gave up on the pen, and chose the comfort of her heated patrol car and left. The owner of the Pontiac was enjoying the comforts of a warm shower.

Vice Admiral Coon's Office
The Pentagon
0930 Hours

"Sit down, O'Brien. Would you like some coffee?"

"Ah, no thank you, Admiral. Do you mind if I smoke?"

"Yes, if you don't mind. You are welcome to go out that door over there, which will take you to a small hallway where you can enjoy your smoke. I gave them up nine years ago, and now can't stand the smell."

"You're are lucky, sir. I had quit, almost, until I had my first meeting with Admiral Koster."

The Admiral chuckled as he looked down at an open file folder on his desk. He brought his big hands together and entwined his fingers and rested them on the file. He looked straight into O'Brien's eyes.

"Dan, we think the Russians are bluffing about sending war ships to the Caribbean. We are certain that this was the work of one man, possibly, Captain Smirnov, the attaché' here in Washington. We can't figure the rhyme or reason for his fabrication. We do know that there is absolutely nothing going on at their Fleet Headquarters, and absolutely nothing moving through their communications network regarding any fleet movements. I almost have to agree with Admiral Koster, that Captain Smirnov may have had too many Shirley Temples at that party the other night."

"Well, this is a relief, sir. For a minute, I had visions of a D-Day invasion taking place off the coast of Puerto Rico."

"Mr. O'Brien, here is what the new plan is, and Admiral Koster wants to be sure you understand this.

"As you know, we released a story last Thursday that two carrier groups were being alerted to go on a training exercise in mid December and that they would be attached to 2nd Fleet, and would be operational in the Gulf of Mexico. The two carriers were to be the Eisenhower and the America. We are about ready to send out another release within the hour, that a third carrier group will be alerted, and will be going down to the Caribbean with a PR stop at Ft. Lauderdale."

"Jesus, he's going to do it? Just to call their bluff?" O'Brien said in a startled tone.

"Well, not so much calling their bluff, but hopefully they won't call ours."

"Damn, sir. That could put Castro's operation on hold. I don't think he would..."

"Hold it, Dan. I clearly said, alert, surely you haven't forgot what alert status is?"

O'Brien studied the man behind the desk. Tom Coons was a senior officer, and like Koster had the experience of three major conflicts on his sleeve.

"Dan, none of these groups will move when the departure date comes due. By then it would be too late for the Soviets to make a move. However, we are going to go through the readiness mode, and act like we are going to sea. It is going to be super expensive. Without even leaving the docks, this caper will cost us a few million dollars.

"Now, here is how it will be spelled out. The Kennedy and the America will be scheduled to depart Norfolk on December 12th and head for the Gulf of Mexico. The Eisenhower and two nuclear cruisers, two frigates, four destroyers, one oilier and one supply ship will leave Norfolk on the 15th. Each carrier will be carrying their maximum complement of squadrons, making up the largest air wing ever to put on an exercise in the Gulf and South Atlantic."

"If I may ask, what happens when all this is canceled? Won't that look strange, sir?"

"Oh, yes, and a lot of fine sailors, their families, their friends and relatives are going to be pissed, not to mention all the government service agencies. Everyone will want a piece of the Admiral's, ah, backside, when all this is canceled. Lucky for us the guy who lives at 1600 Pennsylvania

Avenue is in on the deal, but of course Koster will take the heat. The cancellation will be addressed as part of Navy's cut-backs for the end of the year."

1055 hours

O'Brien sat silently and took in the sights of Washington, as Lieutenant Brooks wove in and out of the traffic working her way to Washington National Airport. For the first time he noted that the city was already decorated and prepared for Christmas. There were colorful large candy canes attached to the street lamps with big red bows, and colorful strands of decorations stretched across the streets overhead. Occasionally, a Santa Claus stood ringing a bell near a small stand with the famous Salvation Army signs asking for help for the needy.

"I wish it would snow," the young officer murmured.

"You what?"

"Wish it would snow, I hate days like this. Just look at those ugly gray clouds. If the sun isn't going to shine, and it's just going to be cold and damp, I would rather have it snowing."

"I think it may be too cold to snow, pretty lady. But, I agree, this weather does bring out the doom and gloom and lowers the spirit. I'll be glad to get back to warm sunny Florida in a few hours."

"Well, thank you, Daniel O'Brien, it's nice to know I will be missed."

"Oh, I didn't mean."

"That's alright, Dan, I know what you meant. I wish I could join you."

"Are you serious? Would you come with me?"

"I would if I wasn't on call this week. We are short on personnel right now, and probably will stay short right through Christmas. Are you going to be in Florida for Christmas?"

"Ah, don't know yet, still working on that."

"Why don't you come back up to D.C.? My roommate is going home to Indiana around the 20th, and I would have a spare room?"

O'Brien stared at her youthful face. She looked like a poster girl for the Navy. Her short brown hair clung tightly to her milky white complexion. A wide bridge, and a pixie nose separated her big brown eyes. Her mouth was small, and lips thin, with just a touch of color. She had a special beauty about her and O'Brien was totally bewildered as to why he was attracted to her. He wanted to continue this relationship, but knew that in a few minutes they would separate and it could be a long time before he would see her again.

"Do you want me to park the car and come in with you?"

"Ah, no, you better just go on. I, ah, won't have a lot of time, Alice, and, quite frankly, I hate those movie type good-byes at airports and bus stations."

She laughed and shook her head.

"That's better. Do you know how beautiful you are when you laugh?"

"No, but hum a few bars and I'll see if it sounds familiar."

The Pontiac pulled up behind a Hertz mini bus in front of United Airlines. O'Brien reached over the seat and lifted his flight bag. Alice got out of the car and went back to the trunk where she released the lid, exposing O'Brien's bags. A Red Cap walked over and asked if he could help.

"I will call you tonight, if that's alright?"

"Of course, but make it after 2100 hours. My roommate goes to bed early."

O'Brien wrapped his large arms around her small-framed body. They kissed hard.

"I will miss you, Dan," she whispered in his ear.

"You're going to have to move that car, Lieutenant, Ma'am," came a strange voice from out of nowhere.

A snowflake drifted slowly down before their saddened eyes. They smiled.

Island Drummer
Whistle Buoy, Main Ship Channel

Five miles south of Key West
2350 hours

Phil eased the Drummer past the large whistle buoy in the middle of the ship channel. Gail sat looking at the distant glow of lights reflecting on the low clouds that crowned Key West. Two sets of flashing collision lights could be seen moving about beneath the clouds. Like lost eagles, the two small planes circled, searching for their roost. To the east, more lights could be seen glistening from the small islands that formed the lower keys.

"Kinda pretty isn't it?" Buckwheat announced as he stood in the companionway, resting his elbows on the cabin roof. He looked up at the large boom overhead and followed the huge main sail up to the top of the

345

mast. Only the wind singing through the steel shrouds disturbed the stillness. The graceful hull of the Drummer silently knifed through the light seas as she drove deeper into the blackness where the heavens and ocean became one.

Avery looked at his watch. "We will take two hour watches starting now. Here Gail, you take the helm and Buckwheat will relieve you at 0200 hours."

Gail stood up, stretched and made a small groan. "Yes, Captain, what is our heading?"

"One-twenty-six-true," Avery answered as he stepped from behind the helm and walked around to the starboard side of the cockpit. Gail took the helm, looked down at the compass on the top of the console. She reached down and turned up the lights on the instrument panel located on the cabin bulkhead, that displayed the ship's speed, magnetic heading and wind direction.

"Any one want coffee or something to drink?" Buckwheat asked."

"No, not me. How about you, Gail?"

"Uh, uh, not just yet. The coffee should still be hot though, I put it on low when I came up an hour ago."

Buckland started down the steps of the companionway. "See ya in a couple of hours."

Avery moved up beside Gail and reached for the mainsheet that was coiled on the lounge seat behind them. He gave the sheet a small jerk releasing it from a jam lock and let the wind take the mainsail out to starboard a few degrees. After checking the trim, he reset the sheet.

"She feels great, Phil. Do you think we will lose this nice breeze later into the morning?" Gail asked.

"Naw, it should hold steady. It is starting to swing down some though, it's coming in about zero-six-zero now." Phil moved out of the cockpit onto the starboard deck and checked the huge jib. It was full and needed no adjustment, neither did the mizzen sail. He climbed back into the cockpit, sat down and lit a cigarette.

"Hey, down below, how about some noise up here? I put those two new tapes on top of the TV, Buckwheat, put that Herb Alpert tape on."

"He may have already crashed, Phil."

Suddenly, the four speakers in the cockpit started to crackle and pop, then as if John Souza and the United States Marine Band appeared with one hundred and six trombones, the cockpit shuddered under the ear splitting sounds of guitars. Gail and Phil started screaming down to Buckwheat. He finally located the volume controls for the tape deck. After a few seconds of adjusting, the softer sounds of guitars were strumming to a Latin beat, and the familiar melody "Amor."

"Now, isn't that more romantic than listening to "Tee-a-wanna-taxi?" Buckwheat yelled from below.

"You have my vote," Gail yelled back.

"You know, Phil, I am hardly moving this helm. This lady is really a queen. It's hard to believe we are actually on our way. Looking back, not too many weeks ago in Fort Myers we all thought the Drummer would be a total disaster, that it would never fly. Now look at us, we are on our way to make history with her."

Avery smiled. He studied Gail as she stood square behind the large stainless wheel. Her legs were braced, her feet well set, expecting the unexpected. She was quite relaxed and comfortable in her preferred stance, a definite sign of her experience on a sailboat.

"Are you warm enough, Gail?" Phil asked.

"Ah, I could use something. Would you mind getting me a windbreaker, or better yet, there's a gray sweat-shirt on my bunk."

Phil got up and disappeared down the companionway. He returned in a few minutes with the sweatshirt and handed it to her. He took the helm as Gail slipped into the warm cotton shirt, with Gators printed in orange letters on it.

"Thanks, now, why don't you get some rest, you only have three and a half hours left."

"Yeah, but I think I'll curl up here in the cockpit for awhile if you don't mind." Phil had brought up a blanket, and he had put on a jacket down below. He picked up one of the cockpit cushions and put it up against the backrest of the lounge seat, sat down and rolled his legs up on the seat, put his head back and threw the light blanket over himself. Pleased he was comfortable, he looked over at Gail. She was scanning the view ahead. Her profile, even in a sweatshirt, and against the dark starless night was very easy on the eye. Phil closed his eyes, and took a deep breath through his nostrils. The salty sea air was clean and welcome as he slipped into a pleasant new world, serenaded by hundreds of guitars playing the song, Feelings.

Avery was still sleeping when Buckwheat relieved Gail, and did not stir until Buckwheat woke him at 0400 to take his watch.

At 0600, the noisy buzzer on Gail's alarm clock filled the small stateroom. Gail sat up on the bunk in the darkness, and wiped her eyes while she began to gather her wits. She slid off the bunk and stepped into the small compartment that offered all the conveniences of a modern bathroom, just scaled down to fit everything in a small space. One could sit on the head, run the portable hand held shower with one hand, and brush teeth over the stainless sink with the other. When she arrived on deck, Phil was sitting relaxed in the cockpit behind the helm. The wheel was operating under the influence of the autopilot.

"Morning, Captain. How are you feeling?"

"Super. Did you sleep alright?"

"Like a tick. What's happening?"

"Still on course, no change, winds coming down some, shifted to zero eight-five." Phil looked at his watch. "We should start to see some dawn breaking in about forty minutes. I'm going down and look at the charts. Do you want some coffee?"

"Oh, yes, thank you and if you can find some crackers or cookies, that would be nice."

"You got it," Phil said, as he disappeared down the companionway.

After preparing a new pot of coffee, he went over to the navigation table, where he had the chart of the Bahamas and Cuba already laid out. He found his first waypoint, Cay Sal Bank, and estimated the Drummer's time of arrival to be around 1140. He figured the winds would be nearly on the nose when they changed course to head eastward at this point. After starting both engines, they would drop the sails and set up a cruise speed of about ten knots. Avery went along his penciled in course line to the next waypoint, Cay Guinchos, then continued on for forty miles until he located Lobos Light. He calculated that running at ten knots they could be at Lobos light in nineteen hours, or about 0900 in the morning. It was another 240 nautical miles to Great Inagua Island and Matthew Town, arriving there around 0900 on December 4th. He made up his mind that this was not a good time to pull into that port and decided he would continue on to Puerto Plata. He also decided not to share his plan with Gail. The coffee was ready, and he found an unopened bag of chocolate drop cookies.

12 miles off Cuba's northern coast
1430 hours

The Drummer was sailing on her new easterly heading, with Cay Sol Bank ten miles back in her turbulent wake. Buckland toyed with the small throttle levers, bringing the powerful twin engines into perfect sync, simply by listening to the pitch of the exhausts and feeling the vibrations on the cockpit sole beneath his feet, a typical trait of multi-engine pilots, who never rely solely on tachometers.

A heavy sea mist hugged the deep green water and a well-spaced three-foot swell greeted the Drummer's clipper bow from the port quarter. There was a slight roll on the Drummer and Buckwheat had to constantly apply correction to the heading, but she was far from uncomfortable. Visibility was fair under the high overcast, and the winds were gentle from the east at seven knots.

Avery sat on the aft cabin roof with his 750 power binoculars pointed south towards Cuba, approximately twelve miles away. He started to scan the limits of his vision, when he spotted a shadow in the mist about two o'clock. He stood up and turned the focus adjustments to see if he could improve on the image.

"Bogie, Buckwheat, at one o'clock, looks like a freighter, maybe three miles heading our way, mark your heading."

"Ah, one-three-zero."

"Come up one-two-five and hold."

"Roger, I don't see her, Phil. Oh, yes I've got it now. Maybe I should come up one-two-zero?"

Avery just looked at Buckland over his glasses.

"Right, one-two-five, steady as she goes."

"What's going on up here?" Gail asked as she entered the cockpit with a plate full of sandwiches.

"We have company coming at us at one o'clock," Buckwheat responded.

Gail looked towards the target, which was taking on more definition.

"It's a freighter alright, and most likely a Russian from the looks of its lines. Gail, how about taking down our Stars and Stripes until we pass the bastard."

"Why Phil, we have every right to be out here, we're not in Cuban waters are we?"

"Shouldn't be, but I would just as soon keep that captain guessing for now. I have been told by a lot of people that the Cubans could board us regardless how far out we are out of their waters, it has happened. No sense in advertising, he will be too far to make out our name or hailing port, just do it, o.k.?"

Gail went aft and removed the American flag from the backstay and brought it to the cockpit.

"Steady there, Buckwheat, he seems to be shying away, changing his course a bit. Still too far to make out any identification. I would guess she is going to be around five hundred feet, maybe less, not a large tonnage ship, and now I'm having doubts she's a Soviet, more like a island trader."

349

"O.k., I see her flag, she's flying a Panamanian."

"Good, now can I put our colors back?"

"Nope, she's heading for Havana, I'm sure, let's just wait. What kind of sandwiches do we have?"

"Deviled ham with egg, or tuna with tomato on wheat."

"Didn't we buy some good ham and cheese?" Avery remarked as he remained watching the freighter.

"Yes, we did, Captain Bligh, but I couldn't find them, who ever packed the ice box put them in some special hiding place, or we have gnomes on board who raid our stores in the wee hours."

"I cannot tell a lie, I ate all the ham and cheese, guys."

Gail and Phil looked at Buckwheat standing proudly behind the helm smiling. "Can't help it, I get nervous at sea when I can't sleep, so I eat."

49 miles west of Lobos Light
December 3rd
0640 Hours

Avery lit a cigarette as he made a slight course change on the helm. The temperature had fallen in the past hour, and the skies above were burdened with low hanging clouds. The Drummer was closed up tight on deck hours ago, when they went through a light shower. A quick glance at the engine gauges satisfied him that the two iron ladies were performing perfectly. A foot above his head the long boom swayed slightly back and forth, neatly wrapped in a giant sail cover. The bowsprit jutting out above the sleek clipper bow, rose and feel in a soft rhythm as the black waves disappeared quietly beneath the Drummer's deep hull.

There was something bothering Avery, he sensed someone looking over his shoulder, watching him. He was almost too nervous to look behind. He even swore that he could hear strange voices from behind, but blamed that on the constant changing of the exhaust sounds as they released their hot vapors of gas and water into the cooler waters of the Caribbean.

"Want anything from below, Phil?" The voice of Commander Buckland came from the darkened companionway. Avery had to strain to see Buckwheat's tanned face in the darkness.

"I'm o.k., thanks, Commander."

Buckland moved around the starboard side of the cockpit and stood next to Avery at his right side.

"Skipper, I told Gail to stand down this watch. I couldn't sleep, she can relieve me later, if that's o.k. with you?"

"Of course, I will probably stay on deck with.." Avery suddenly spun around, his eyes squinting aft into the darkness. "Take the helm, Buckwheat," Avery commanded as he leaped up onto the cockpit seat, then stepped over onto the port deck. He took hold of the lifeline and walked slowly towards the stern.

"Buckwheat, kill the navigation lights," he yelled back.

Buckwheat had some difficulty locating the right switch on the console panel. He finally found it. The bright white glow from the stern light located on the transom, went out, leaving only the pitch-black night surrounding the Drummer. It took a few seconds for Phil to adjust his eyes, but then he finally saw what had been haunting him for the past few hours. He could see the white foam of disturbed water separating in the wide wake behind the Drummer, and now he could hear the slapping of waves hitting a surface some distance behind. Then he saw the dark shadow of the immense hull coming right at him. It was black and deadly looking. He wanted to yell to Buckwheat, but his throat seemed to close around his words. The huge bow came to within fifty feet of the Drummer. Avery could see the silhouette of a deck-mounted cannon, with its shiny wet steel barrel pointed at him. There were shadows of at least two people in wet dark slickers standing just aft of the cannon. There were no markings on the bows of the giant hull. Avery could not figure out if it was Bahamian or Cuban. He knew one thing, it wasn't American. He was about to yell back to Buckwheat to turn the lights back on, as well as the spreader lights that would illuminate the entire deck for identification, when the mysterious craft slipped back into the darkness and disappeared.

Avery watched for a few seconds, then made his way back to the cockpit. "We had company back there just now, but I couldn't figure out what it was, Cuban or Bahamian."

"No shit? How close were they?"

"Close enough to see they had at least a three inch something pointed right down our throats, or to be more polite, up our ass."

"What do you figure, Phil, Cubans?"

"Yeah, more than likely in these waters. We wouldn't have anything that small patrolling down this far, and I don't think the Bahamas Defense Forces have any black hulls on their patrol boats, besides, they would have boarded us, or at least shined some lights on us. Naw, I think these guys know who we are, they saw us earlier today, I'm sure. We were probably reported by that freighter that passed us just before dusk, remember?"

"Yeah, you mean the one west bound for Havana? It passed us at exactly two miles south, at 1935 hours. I logged it."

"O.k. Bucko, I am going to hit the sack, you've got it. If you should encounter our friends again, keep cool, stay on course and don't flirt with them. If they hit you with lights, just smile and wave, throw on all the spreader lights, and stamp your feet hard on the deck. I will come up and help you, got it? And no mooning either."

"You got it, Captain."

Aboard Cuban Torpedo Boat, P-4 PA 903
Captain Justo A. Carrillio, Commanding Officer
0705 hours

The young Cuban Captain, Justo Carrillio, removed his foul weather coat and hung it on a hook in the small cabin. Rego Urutia, the ship's radio operator was talking with Patrol Fleet communications at Punta Alegre, eighteen miles south of their position. Carrillio leaned over the small chart table and marked his position and that of the Island Drummer, some five miles ahead. He confirmed the course the large ketch was on and determined its heading and destination, Great Inagua Island. After checking the radar screen and recalculating the distance between his craft and the target, he wrote down his findings and handed them to the radio operator, who transmitted the coordinates, description, direction and speed of the Drummer and ETA for Inagua.

Carrillio picked up the small mike from the intercom box and called to his first officer on the bridge. "Come to two six zero degrees, all engines attack speed. I will be back on deck in one hour."

As the young captain began to move towards the small bunk against the aft bulkhead, the small room vibrated as the engines increased their rpms. Then the entire cabin shifted downward and rolled to starboard as the giant steel patrol craft turned into her new heading. The twin M-50 diesels easily drove the Soviet built P-4 attack boat to speeds over forty knots. As he sat down on his bunk, the sixty-two foot steel hull began to groan and roll harder to starboard, as the helmsman hunted for his new heading. Carrillio was about to reach for his intercom and yell at the first officer when the ship leveled off, the engines began to sound like they were running in sync, and the vibrations subsided. He squinted as he checked the large magnetic compass mounted on the overhead panel of the navigation station. The large needle looked close enough to the two-sixty reading. He could finally rest his head and close his eyes, it was nearing the end of his long twelve-hour patrol, and soon he would be approaching the Port of Havana, where for two days he would rest and enjoy his family.

CHAPTER 20

December 8th
1510 hours

Phil Avery checked the autopilot and made a small adjustment to compensate for the currents and increased the throttles on both engines two hundred rpm's to maintain a ten-knot speed. The seas, running four-foot swells were meeting the Drummer's clipper bowhead on as warm gusty winds crossed the deck out of the east.

"We should have Culebrita in sight in an hour," Avery yelled to Gail and Buckwheat who were lying on air mattresses on the foredeck. He looked to the southwest and noted the huge clouds building up over the eastern part of the island of Puerto Rico, and was pleased that he had none of the thunderheads in his path.

Nineteen miles due south of Island Drummer the U.S. Navy Mine Sweeper, AG 521 (Sonar) was riding the same rolling seas. She was one hour out of San Juan on a heading of 120 degrees, and three hours from Christiansted, St. Croix, where Captain Lind and his crew would drop anchor.

Aboard Sonar
1515 hours

"You sure blew my socks off this afternoon when you showed up, O'Brien. Don't tell me, you're here to make sure I keep this tub on schedule?"

"Nothing like that, Captain. I just couldn't sit up there in Florida and not be part of the operation and since you are going to be in the hub of the mission, I felt being aboard Sonar I would be in position to hear what's going on."

"Does Admiral Koster know you're here?"

"Oh, yes."

"Who's watching the store in D.C., or isn't that necessary now?"

"Our communications center at FBI Headquarters in Miami is keeping us all together. Agent Bollman has a team working with us on every piece of communication equipment available, telephones, VHF, UHF and single side band. Didn't you read your instructions, Captain? All this was in the package I gave you at the Lauderdale meeting?"

Lind smiled as he ran his big hands over the large stainless ship's wheel, never taking his eyes from the deep blue seas ahead. He knew he made O'Brien uncomfortable, and enjoyed it.

"How did you know I would still be in San Juan? Hell, I loaded up those cedar shakes you set up for cargo two days ago."

"I took a chance that you would be there, but had I missed you I would have found you in St. Croix. FYI, I rented a condo in Christiansted until we leave."

"Oh, you don't like the stateroom we gave you? Hell, I moved my first officer just to accommodate you, Dan. Charlie will be offended when I tell him that you're staying on the beach."

"Fuck Charlie, Lind and let's cut the horseshit."

"O'Brien, you're too up tight, you need a few days on the beach to relax. By the way, is your super yacht in St. Thomas yet?"

"Not as of last night, but she should be there today. They called from the Dominican Republic two days ago and said they should arrive in St. Thomas on the 9th and Seaduce has made it to Antigua."

"Antigua? I thought she was in St. Vincent or St. Lucia?"

"We had a change of plan and decided it would be wiser to stay in Antigua and work out of English Harbour."

"Any changes in my itinerary?" Lind asked.

"No, you go to St. Croix and wait. The UDT team should be arriving from Homestead on the 21st. They will be billeted at the reserve barracks at the airport until the night before you leave."

"So, what do we do in the mean time? We won't be leaving for nearly two weeks, O'Brien."

"Yeah, I know, just do what you need to do to look innocent. Do maintenance jobs, like paint, scrape, polish, whatever crews do on their ships while in port."

"I'll tell you what we do when in port, we go out, get drunk, get laid and come back and trash the heads and plumbing."

"There will be none of that shit, Captain Lind. You and your boys are on a secret mission, we don't want any drunks running like loose cannons getting in trouble down here. That's an order, Captain."

"Piss-poor planning, O'Brien, I take it you never planned any military activities before, right?"

"Had my share, now if you don't mind I would like to take the wheel for a while."

"Sure, be my guest, heading is one-twenty."

"Ever handle a ship his size before, O'Brien? Ah, this is a first, but I guess for you this must be like running a Tinker Toy."

"You don't like me much, do ya, O'Brien?"

O'Brien turned and looked into Lind's tanned face. Lind forced a smile as he leaned against a large communication cabinet his arms folded across his barrel chest. He was dressed in his old Navy khaki uniform bare of any rank. On his feet a pair of well-abused boat shoes, with no socks.

"Let's put it this way, Captain. You were Koster's choice; that's good enough for me. Whether I like you or not has no bearing on why you are here, Koster assured me you had the talent and the experience we needed and anyone who could run his sinking destroyer through an entire Jap fleet and live to tell about it is good enough for me."

Lind laugh and moved next to O'Brien, rested his big hands on the instrument panel and looked seaward.

"Old Koster has a bad habit of twisting war stories, Mr. O'Brien. Did you ever hear of a Destroyer called the Johnson?"

"No, can't say I have."

"You heard about the battle of Leyte Gulf though?"

"I recall we won a victory that should have been won by the Japs, if my memory serves me."

"No, wrong battle O'Brien. The Johnson, DD 557, a Fletcher class destroyer built in Seattle in October '43 was sent right into the Pacific action. She was 375 feet long, displaced 21,000 tons and her steam turbines pushed her at thirty-five knots. She was loaded too, had five 5-inch guns, four 20-millimeter Oerlikon anti-aircraft guns, two twin 40 millimeter Bofors and ten torpedo tubes. She was light, fast as a tiger and sleek as a panther. It took three hundred and twenty seven men to harness this lady, and I was one of them. I was a young gunnery officer." Lind paced back and forth keeping his attention focused on the seas ahead. He continued. "It was October 25th, 1944, the Johnson was celebrating her first birthday and we were part of an escort that was baby sitting six jeep carriers off the island of Samar in the Philippines. We were spotted by a large Japanese flotilla of battleships and cruisers. Our fleet commander, Admiral Sprague, ordered the carriers to turn and run, knowing the carriers did not have a fighting chance against that Jap armada. To cover the carriers' escape, our captain turned the Johnson into the Jap cruiser line and ran head on into them laying down a smoke screen to cover the carriers. We had two sister destroyers join up with us and we got a little help from the Lord, who gave us a couple of blinding squalls that hid the carriers. We were able to get the carriers out of range from the Japs 18 and 16 inch guns, however, their 14's easily found us. We got off about 200 rounds on their cruiser squadron before they concentrated their guns on us tin cans. Our boilers were not up to full steam and were only giving us about twenty knots. When we got inside the cruisers line we dumped ten torpedoes at the Jap fleet and scored one hit on the lead cruiser before they caught us, man, they were good. In a matter of minutes all our guns were out of action. There were dead bodies lying all over, fires burning from bow to stern and our two stacks were blown away. Then a miracle, another squall line came through and we got fifteen minutes to recover and take up new positions. We mustered anything that could shoot including M-1 Carbines and 45 automatics. When the rains cleared the Johnson and our two sister destroyers went in for the final kill. We didn't know at the time that the pride of the Japanese fleet, the battleship Yamato was in that fleet. Fearing getting torpedoed Yamato turned and ran for Japan, but left us to face off with the battleship, Kongo. We dueled for about fifteen minutes ducking her big guns and scoring a few minor hits, but nothing serious." Lind's voice suddenly began to weaken as he fought his emotions, then continued. "Our skipper noticed a fast cruiser and four destroyers were in pursuit of the carriers, so we went after them with all the steam we had. What happened next was another miracle of the battle. The Japs, not knowing we fired all our torpedoes, fired their torpedoes prematurely at the carriers so they could turn and face us in their defense. Their torpedoes missed our carriers, but their guns found all three of us and after twenty minutes of getting our ass blown out of the water our captain sounded the order to abandon ship. The battle for the Leyte Gulf was over. The Japs lost three cruisers, but more important they lost what could have been an easy victory. They could have easily sunk our six carriers along with our tin cans, but they could not defeat the courage and bravery of a few sailors and marine pilots who saved the day. My captain, a full blooded American Indian, went down with the Johnson and I lost one hundred and eighty-seven shipmates out of the three hundred and twenty seven that I shipped out with."

Lind stepped away from O'Brien and began scanning the horizon. His watery gray eyes were fighting his deepest emotions as he turned to face O'Brien.

"Yes, it was quite a day, O'Brien. Our entire crew faced death in that battle, fifty or so were the lucky ones, they got it quick while fighting on deck never knowing what hit them. Some forty-five or so with severe wounds died slowly in the oil soaked seas. Ninety of our crew drowned immediately, never found and the few of us that did survive considered ourselves very lucky, the sharks had full bellies eating our wounded and dead shipmates and left us alone."

"Here, Captain, take your helm." O'Brien said silently, then away from the helm and walked out of the wheelhouse. He stood on the starboard outboard station inhaling the cool sea air flow deep into his lungs as he fought the sour bile rising in his throat and his own emotions. His newfound new respect for John Lind, things would be different between them from now on.

St. Thomas, U.S. Virgin Islands
Charlotte Amalie Harbor

Wednesday, December 9th
0710 hours

Phil Avery stepped out of the companionway onto the empty cockpit of the Island Drummer. He balanced his mug of hot coffee as he made his way back to the helms wheel and the pack of Winstons he left sitting on the lounge seat. He picked them up relieved the pack felt half full as it was his last pack. He sat down, lit up and began to survey the anchorage.

The sun was just beginning to break over the hills that rose above the eastern shoreline of the harbor. It was a typical and welcome sunrise over the island of St. Thomas that Avery had seen many times before. The early morning sounds also familiar to him began to amplify as if somehow controlled by the sunrise included crowing roosters, numerous barking dogs and the sounds of heavy burdened trucks with engines straining challenging the torturous grades of the winding steep hills. Anchored in the harbor nearby, sailing yachts created a chorus of sounds as the clanging of unattended halyards played their unscored melodies within their metal masts.

Avery made a wise decision to slip into St. Thomas at night and get a good night's sleep. He knew the sight of the Drummer entering the harbor during the day would attract many curious crewed yacht charter captains who sailed older models Ted Collins designed.

Gail appeared on deck with her coffee mug in hand. She smiled at Avery and said: "I have the perfect excuse to keep the curious from asking for tours, Phil. We tell them that the owners are on board and want complete privacy, no visitors." Avery smiled. "Beautiful, that's it Gail, we'll spread that word as soon as we get on shore."

Gail smiled, turned and looked eastward into the sun breaking out of the clouds floating on the hilltops. Avery sat and admired Gail's hourglass figure silhouetted against the sun. Her long dark tanned legs were accented by the short yellow terry-robe, and his nostrils filled with the sent of her flowery bath oils. He thought about how she performed on the trip down and how professional she handled her seamanship skills. He was grateful for her talents and her company.

"Well, here we are, back on this miserable rock." Gail said softly as she walked towards Avery. Her eyes were searching deep into his looking for a little compassion, waiting for the question, "are you sorry you came back?" It did not come. Avery just smiled at her and lit another Winston.

"What's our schedule, Phil?"

"Well, soon as Buckwheat rises and we have some breakfast, we'll draw straws to see which one of you stays on board while I report to our clearing house and call O'Brien."

"You know, Phil, I was thinking, why don't we get out of here, drop hook at Secret Harbour or American Yacht Harbour. We wouldn't be so damn visible and could relax a little. Worrying about uninvited visitors showing up is going to drive us nuts, we'll never be able to leave the Drummer alone."

"You're right and a good idea. We will tell everyone that our owners want no visitors, and as soon as we get our guests on board we'll sail to Caneel Bay, or to West End in Tortola. We have nearly two weeks to kill here before we head down, my God, we're just two weeks away."

"Phil, what's wrong, you look like you just saw a ghost?"

"It just hit me, I almost forgot what the hell we came down here for, I guess I put it out of my mind concentrating on getting here."

"You know, we should have stayed in Puerto Plata a few days longer, Phil. If I had known that we would have made it here so fast, I would have bribed you to stay longer."

"Yeah, sorry about that, I was so worried about getting here by the 10th, I will make it up to you, I promise."

"That's two you owe me captain, you wouldn't let me see Matthew Town either, but, I forgive you. How's your coffee?"

"Cold and would love a warm up and would you mind while below, bang on the Bucko's door, I want to get over to the marina and register with the clearing house early."

"Right, I'll go get dressed, but first I'll get you a coffee." She smiled and went below.

Charter Services Clearing House
Yacht Haven Marina
0915 hours

Avery guided the small Boston whaler around the yachts on anchor as he headed for the dinghy dock at the Marina. When he got close to the docks he started looking for familiar faces.

"Jesus Christ, the damn crewed yacht boat show is going on." Avery cried out.

"What does that mean, Phil?" Buckwheat asked.

"It means every damn yacht charter broker in the world is here at the hotel and we could be in deep shit."

He had to park the Whaler at the dinghy dock next to the ramp that lead to the marina docks where every yacht broker and agent would be passing by heading to the show boats.

Avery found a spot between two inflatables and Buckwheat tied the Whaler off. They jumped on the cement dock and headed straight for Charter Services clearing house. Avery noted a number of women in pairs sporting lily white legs and pale faces, all definite tell-tales of just arrived charter brokers or travel agents. So far so good, no one recognized him, although a couple did notice the handsome young tanned young man tagging along with him.

They entered the offices of the Charter Service Clearinghouse.

"Hello, I'm Captain Phil Avery on the yacht Island Drummer checking in, are you holding any traffic for me?"

The attractive black girl behind the counter looked up, smiled and went back to writing on a note pad.

"Ah, ma'am, I'm Captain Avery, yacht Island....."

"Yes, sir, I heard you, I will be with you in a moment." The young girl volleyed never looking up.

"Jesus, this place is a zoo, Phil. What the hell goes on here?" remarked Buckwheat.

"This is where the crewed yacht skippers and crews get their mail, messages, make phone calls, hire crews and check on their bookings, that's why they call it a clearing house."

"Looks more like a PX communication center. Jesus, just look at all this young stuff, and man, none of them wearing puppy binders."

"Puppy binders?"

"Bras, man, you know those Maidenform things."

361

The receptionist waved to catch Avery's eye. "Captain, I have two messages for you, one from a Rudolf?"

Avery looked puzzled at first. "Rudolf? Oh, yes, Rudolf, ah, he's my brother-in-law, thank you."

Avery looked at the message. Call 447 5678 ASAP RUDOLF.

"Ah, where is this area code for this number, miss?"

"That's a St. Croix number, Captain, area code 809."

"Yes, o.k., here, ma'am, here are my insurance papers, registration papers, license numbers and would you mind getting me processed and give the papers back to this lad, tell him how much you need and I will give you a check later. His name is Buckwheat, my mate, just tell him how much you want ah, I need to make a call.

"Buckwheat, you stay here with Miss.."

"Athenia."

"Ah, yes, Athenia. She will tell you what we need. Just sign my name to anything she needs, and wait right here."

Avery stormed out of the charter services glass doors and headed for the hotel lobby. All he could think about was something had gone wrong. "What the hell was O'Brien doing in St. Croix? What the hell was going on?"

Avery went to the lobby public phone and called St. Croix.

"Dan, what the hell are you doing in St. Croix?"

"I came in on Sonar two days ago. Listen Phil, I want to call a meeting, fast; I really messed up. I have all the gear in place but too much time to kill, how is everything on the Drummer, any problems?"

"No, the Drummer is fine. But problems, yes. We got some super problems over here, we just landed in the middle of a fucking crewed yacht show."

"What the hell are you talking about? What's that got to do with you and the Drummer?"

"Dan, this show is an annual thing, its when all the crewed yachts come here to Yacht Haven and play host to hundreds of international travel agencies and the world's best known charter yacht brokers."

"So. What's that got to do with you?"

"Dan, the Drummer is the latest thing in a mega yacht, Its also one of Ted Collins designs and every broker and captain over here will want to get aboard and see what Ted has created. His yachts are very popular down here, as you know. The brokers expect to see her so they can sell charters on her, understand?"

"Yeah, I guess so. So what do you want to do?"

"I want to get her out of this harbor as fast as I can and move to a place where we won't be harassed by anyone. We can't show her to anyone, my God, we would be the laughing stock of the industry, these folks like to open things like cabinets and refrigerators and they will see air condition vents but no compressors, freezers with no guts.."

"O.k., I understand, Phil. Can you hide over there someplace?"

" We think so, we are going to check out a place called Secret Harbour. We are telling everyone here that the owners are on board and don't want visitors."

"Good, o.k., now let's talk about this meeting, Phil. I want to get Rick Van Wagner up from Antigua. We have ten days before we start heading south and we need to talk about all this idle time we have. Lind wants to send his crew home for a few days, they're getting restless and this damn tugboat looks strange hanging out on the hook in this harbor. I have also decided to keep the Seaduce in Antigua and I want to set up new times for getting those charter guests down and go over our codes and communications procedures."

"Do you want me to work on that meeting over here, Dan?"

"Yes, pick a place we can all meet, make it private. Then get back to me so we can coordinate everyone getting over there, I want to meet on this coming Friday, if possible."

"Roger that, Dan. I will take care of it. I will call you later tonight, probably around ten or eleven, if that's o.k.?"

"I'll wait to hear from you."

Avery hung up the phone and headed straight back to the clearinghouse where he found Buckwheat sitting with a very attractive red head in a very small bikini sporting a very big pair of puppies.

"Mr. Avery?"

"Yes?"

"Hi, my name is Betty Little, I'm the assistant manager here. Could I see you in my office for a second?"

"Of course, is there something wrong, Miss, did my mate here fill out some wrong papers?"

The young commander leaped up from his chair, excusing himself from his lady friend.

"Ah, everything alright, Captain Avery?" Buckwheat asked.

"Ah, don't know, but stay here for a few minutes while I talk with Ms Small." Avery responded.

"That's Little, Captain Avery, the name is Little, Betty Little."

"Oh, excuse me, ah, she's the assistant manager here and I have to go with her, so you stay here."

Buckland watched Avery walk away. He couldn't believe the changes in Avery ever since they landed on the Island. He became suddenly nervous and jittery.

Avery followed the shapely women into a small office at the rear of the busy large room that was crammed with desks, computers and an army of young women working at computers and answering telephones.

"Sit down, Captain. I may have some disturbing news for you."

"Disturbing news? What is it? Are my papers not in order?"

"No, nothing like that, your papers are fine. It's about a strange man who has been hanging around here for nearly a week, inquiring about your yacht and your crew. He is here almost every day asking if anyone has heard from you, even talked to the Coast Guard, according to one of my receptionists. Did you file a float plan or something? Could he be the owner of your yacht?"

"Jesus, I don't know, Betty. It certainly has nothing to do with the owner, I can assure you that."

Phil suddenly sprang to his feet and put both of his hands against his temples as if he just took on a migraine.

"Holy shit, excuse me, Betty. Tell me, is he about my height? maybe a little larger in size, with dark black hair, well dressed with lots of gold, like a real Rolex watch and nice gold bracelet?"

"Ah, yes, now that you mentioned it. He is rather attractive, a little broader than you, I'd say in his early fifties maybe. He was very well mannered and he does dress very well. I think he is staying right here at the hotel."

Avery walked over and opened the door then turned and smiled at Betty. "Thanks Ms. Little, and not to worry. I know who he is. He is a friend of my first mate. I will find him and let him know we arrived safely, thanks for your concern."

Avery went through the outer office and walked right past Buckwheat who was still engaged with his little red head lady friend.

Avery went through the open courtyard of the hotel, praying he would not meet any more old acquaintances. He arrived at the hotel's registration desk dripping in perspiration.

"Pardon me, ma'am, do you have a Carlton Tucker registered here?"

The clerk behind the registration counter looked over at another clerk who was flipping through some invoices.

"Sarah, do we have a Carlton Tucker registered?"

"Sure do, but he is not in. He went over to St. Johns this morning to meet some friends."

"Are you sure, ma'am?"

"Positive. He asked me about transportation. I sent him out to Red Hook to catch the ferry over to the island."

"Thank you."

Avery ran back to the clearinghouse and got Buckwheat. In a matter of minutes they were skimming across the bay heading out to the Drummer, that now stood out like the statue of Liberty in the middle of the busy harbor.

"We have to get the Drummer the hell out of here," Avery yelled to Buckwheat. Buckwheat was doing all he could to hold on in the bow of the jarring boat.

Aboard Island Drummer

"Oh God, I don't believe it. He is here?"

"I hate to be the one who said I told you so, Gail. But I know this guy. I knew he would come down and look for you. And from what I heard, he has even contacted the Coast Guard looking for us. Shit, wait till the old man hears about this."

"Oh, God, O'Brien will ask me to get off the Drummer, won't he?"

"You can ask him yourself. He's here. He flew down and met the Sonar in San Juan. He is in St. Croix and wants us to meet on Friday. He was concerned about all of us being down here with too much time on our hands, and I have to agree with him. This place is turning into a hot-pit, and now we have Carlton to deal with."

"Phil, I will go ashore and settle with Carlton. It's my problem and I will handle it."

"No, I need you on board. We have to move out, and now. We will take our chances and go over to Secret Harbour. I'll get the charts, you and Buckwheat get ready to move out. Buckwheat, I'll hit the circuit breakers below, you get the engines running."

Avery went below and found the local Virgin Island cruising guide and brought it up on deck. In a matter of minutes, both engines were idling and Buckwheat and Gail were working the windlass bringing up the anchor. Once it was secured, Avery spun the Drummer around and headed west along the busy waterfront of downtown. He did not want to go past Yacht Haven Marina and the cruise ship docks. Instead he would take the long route, slip out of the harbor on the west end, then swing around back to head down the south shore and look for the entrance to Secret Harbour, which was about half way down the island.

Secret Harbor
1420 Hours

The harbor was exactly how Avery remembered it from many years before, when he brought his Morgan Out Island 41 here for a three day rest from chartering. It is a peaceful harbor, and normally not visited by many transient yachts. It was perfect.

Avery had made arrangements by radio to have a rental car brought over from a small leasing firm in Red Hook. He agreed with Gail that they would both confront Carlton later in the evening to try and settle any problems. Buckwheat had plans for the evening to meet the young bikini at the Bridge restaurant. Avery had one late call to make later, and he was concerned about Gail and her problem. Maybe, he would not even have to tell O'Brien.

The meeting, it was decided, was to be down at the west end of the island near the airport at the Islander Inn Resort. There was a small outdoor bar there, and a secluded beach where they could meet and not look suspicious. The hotel was a haven for businessmen and contractors who were working on the airport properties. The meeting would be set for noon on Friday, December 11th.

Yacht Haven Hotel
Room 407 .
1925 Hours

"Gail darling, where are you? Yes, wait there. I will be right down.

"He is on his way down. Phil, please, let me handle this alone. I don't need you here. You will only aggravate him and nothing will be settled. I can handle him, Phil. Please, go."

Avery said nothing. He looked into Gail's eyes. He knew what she said was true, she could handle Carlton, and truth be known, all he wanted to do was to re-arrange Carlton's face. There would be another time for that.

Avery winked at Gail, spun around and walked out of the hotel lobby. He went over and located the rental car, and left the hotel. He drove down towards town, then, remembering a few back streets, drove up the hill to

Bluebeards Castle, where he found a pair of friendly couples vacationing together from Cleveland at the outside bar.

The piano player, Toby, a popular local chap, was quite talented on the keyboard. His idol was Earl Garner, and he was easily swayed by Avery's ten-dollar bill into playing some famous Earl Garner's famous creations, like "Misty." A five dollar bill in a highball glass on top of the baby grand, got "Misty" played a couple of more times.

Avery stood on the balcony that looked out towards the waterfront business district area of Charlotte Amalie. The red and white lights of the slow moving traffic moved along the waterfront main road in silence, and the lights of small businesses and houses sparkled like gas lanterns, spreading up the steep hillside surrounding the harbor. All across the great harbor, ships of all sizes swung at their moorings. Their lights sparkled and reflected on the soft restful black mirror that cradled their hulls. "This undoubtedly is one of the most spectacular views in the entire Caribbean," Avery thought to himself.

"It looks like a Christmas tree that just fell down, doesn't it, Phil?"

Avery did not have to turn around, he knew it was Marilyn Swayer. He was almost pleased.

"Still take your scotch on the rocks with a splash?" she asked.

"Still sleep with two pillows?" Avery responded.

Avery turned and rolled right into her waiting arms. They kissed hard. His hands slipped down along her arched bare spine and pulled her closer, her lips parted and her tongue lightly tickled the corner of his mouth.

"Here for the show?" He asked.

"No, I heard you were here and I needed an affair. Why are you here, Phil."

"Delivery and a charter, favor for Ted Collins."

"Interesting. Did you bring down his new citation?"

"Uh-huh."

"Can we go see her?"

"Uh, no, owners on board."

"I have a room with a great view of the hotel's kitchen."

"I love kitchens."

Yacht Haven Hotel
Room 407
0810 hours

Gail pushed the sliding glass door open and took in a deep breath. From her fourth floor view she looked down over the marina. Even at this early hour, the ramp heading out to the docks and the Bridge restaurant was busy with crews preparing for the boat show that opened at 0900. A number of brokers could be seen in their colorful shorts and halters heading for breakfast at the Bridge, some going to yachts that offered them breakfast. Over at the cruise ship docks, one of the largest frequent visitors to St. Thomas, the SONG OF NORWAY, was echoing door chimes, calling for the first seating for breakfast. Behind her, the popular CARNIVAL was getting some touch up work done on her gleaming white hull. Two workmen, standing on a small floating raft were rolling new paint on her scars from fending off rubber tires at the many ports she visited.

"Great view, isn't it?"

Gail felt Carlton's arms surround her and his body tighten against her back. She closed her eyes and relaxed as he moved his mouth up and down her neck, breathing warm air over her ear. She turned and embraced him, kissing him softly, then harder. Carlton tried to move her back towards the bed, but she stood firm, then relaxed her arms and stepped back away from him.

"I'm going to take my shower now, then I am getting dressed and leaving. We agreed last night that it had to be this way. No questions, no arguments. I go back to my work, you go back to Sarasota and I will see you as soon as this charter is over."

"That was the agreement, and I will not argue with you, Gail. I just want you to know that I trust you, honey. You have convinced me that I can trust you."

"That's all I ask, Carlton. I love you, you know that. I just had to get away, I had to take this cruise. It will be better for me and you, with Christmas week coming, it's just too.."

Carlton reached out and took her in his arms and held her. "I know, I know. But, I promise, after the first of the year..."

"Don't, Carlton, I don't want to hear any promises, not now."

The Islander Inn Resort
St. Thomas
1310 hours

O'Brien was getting nervous. He looked at his watch for the second time in ten minutes. "Where is he? He told me that he would be here at noon on the dot."

"Relax, Dan. Sometimes these island airlines have big delays. He's probably gone home to see his family. He's been gone for a while, remember? And he does have a new baby."

"Yeah, I guess you're right, Phil."

"I'll be happy to call his home, does anyone have his number?" Gail asked.

Avery had been lying down on one of the hotel chaise lounges. He sat up and said, "Ah, why don't we give him a few more minutes. Hey, Buckwheat, how about going up to the bar and getting us another round."

"Sure, Phil, does everyone want the same?"

"Ah, not me, I'll wait for a while," Gail responded.

"Yeh, I'll have another beer, ah, see if they have Red Stripe."

"Red Stripe? What the hell kind of scotch is that?"

"It's a Jamaican beer, best in the Caribbean, nice and light."

"I'll take one of those too, if they have it," Avery said.

"Mount Gay and tonic, more lime, tell the girl more limes."

"Gotcha, Dan."

Buckwheat stood up from the lounge chair and ran through the palm trees up to the bar.

"You've already met this guy, Van Wagner, haven't you, Phil?"

"Yeah, many years ago."

"You'll know him when you see him then?"

"Oh sure, he looks like a line backer, can't miss him."

Gail rose from her lounge and pointed up towards the bar. "Hey, gentlemen, would that be him coming back with Buckwheat?"

"That's him, friends, Captain Rick Van Wagner. I take that back, he is no longer looking like a line backer, he looks like the entire line," Avery chuckled as he rose to meet their new recruit.

"Here he is, Dan. He was sitting at the bar," Buckwheat said laughing. "He saw us gathered over here, but didn't recognize anyone."

"Dan O'Brien, pleased to meet you, Rick." O'Brien shook hands with Van Wagner and began introductions.

"This is Gail Townsend, over here John Lind, and Phil Avery, who says you have met before."

"Oh, sure, how are you, Phil? It's been awhile, didn't recognize you. You skippered the old "Glass-Slipper," a Morgan Out Island, right?"

"Right, you have a good memory."

"Ah, you're starting to look familiar to me now, young lady. Gail Townsend, that name, wait a minute, sure, you were crew on, ah, Golden Touch, right?'

"Yes, a couple of years ago." Gail was praying that Rick would drop it right here. She knew that he was a close friend of her ex-captain and lover.

"Well, now that we all know each other, let's get down to business folks," O'Brien said.

"Here's our first concern, and it's all my fault. I wanted to get all our gear down here with plenty of time, just in case we had mechanical problems. Now it seems we have more people problems, and too much time on our hands, so we need to cure that. Our departure times for the mission are still going to be controlled by the sighting of our target by the Air Force Blackbirds, and we don't expect that before the 21st. John Lind here has a serious problem. He has a crew of old salts who like to take liberty. They are getting antsy over on St. Croix, so we decided to split them up and send half of them home and some over to San Juan, keeping just two or three on board for security. We may bring the Sonar over here for awhile, she looks like the Queen Mary sitting over there, and the locals are starting to ask questions."

"Dan, you're getting paranoid. No one is asking questions over there, you're just nervous one of my guys will get juiced and get put in the slammer, and the police will ask all kinds of questions, and..."

"I don't give a shit what you think, Captain Lind. We need to do something."

"When are Captain Chen and the UDT team due in Dan?" Phil asked.

"Not until the 19th. They will be flying in from Homestead on a C-130. Plans are to billet them in a Army reserve center at the airport.

"Hell, Dan, I would bring the Sonar over here. You could park down by the old sub base, or drop your hook right down town. You could always say you're waiting on some parts to be flown in."

"That's what I told Dan yesterday, Phil. I told him I could order a couple of exhaust manifolds. I'm going to be needing them soon any way. It would look perfectly normal for us to be hanging around."

"O.K., do it, John, just don't start tearing something apart that can't be put back together in time."

"Hell, Dan, those manifolds have to come from Michigan, and I doubt if they will make it by Christmas, but at least it looks like we are waiting for something other than a report from some spy plane."

"What about my problem, Dan? I can't stay on the Seaduce. I have my own problems right here. My boat comes back in tomorrow, and it goes out again on Monday. I am booked solid right through New Year's"

"Yeah, but you have a skipper doing your charters, don't you?"

"Yeah, but these folks coming in for the next few weeks are old friends. They charter with me almost every year, and they expect to have me on board, not a stand-in."

"Jesus, if you leave us, Rick, we are fucked. I was counting on you."

"Hey, I told that asshole, Ian Billings, I could take your ship and green crew down to St. Lucia, that was it. I had no idea what you guys were up to until you called me a week ago."

"How about the new kid, Paul Gransaull? Do you think he could take over the yacht? Hell, all he has to do is sail out to meet the Sonar. He will have almost a straight shot due west out of Antigua."

"Too green yet, Phil. He tries hard, but, well, I would be concerned about his ability. I know he is a hot shot Navy pilot and all that, but.."

"Rick? God man, you got to help us out here. Can't you tell your guests you have the flu or something?"

Van Wagner looked at O'Brien's pathetic face. Everyone was silent, no body spoke or looked at each other.

"Shit, O.K., I'll work it out some how, but I am not going to be very popular at home or with my crew and friends. I also have another problem. Why am I sailing this old wooden ketch in the first place? Taking it down on delivery is one thing, but now I am taking her on a charter to doom, and speaking of doom, how do I survive this, this explosion we are all supposed to die in during this unfortunate accident."

"No, no. You and your mate are going to be thrown clear when she blows. You will be the only survivors, because you were both on deck when the explosion occurred. You were both thrown overboard with the first explosion. Your guests were all trapped below, enjoying some of the food that you managed to get from Castro."

"O.k., now you have Gransaull and me as survivors. Lind here, picks us up, right? He is supposed to take us to San Juan with the recovered bodies and parts and pieces of the "Seaduce.""

"That's right, that's how we have it planned. Of course, you won't be aboard when she goes. Captain Chen's UDT team will set the charges and the Seaduce will be set on autopilot. When she is clear of the Sonar, someone pushes a button and boom... it's gone."

"That leaves two prime witnesses though, doesn't it? I thought you were trying to cover all your asses here. Gransaull and I will have to be questioned by the Coast Guard, and the insurance company and whomever, isn't that risky? Back in my day at the agency, we wouldn't leave this kind of, ah, stuff around, if you know what I mean? You also have another problem, the Seaduce doesn't have an autopilot, but that's no big deal, we can tie the helm off."

"Well, Captain, we will have to take our chances on you being questioned, I don't know what else we can do. We lost our main plan when you put the finger on Mel Spencer, remember?"

"Of course I remember. He was about to show your hand, and he would have. Speaking of Spencer, where is he and how is he?"

"He's recovering over in San Juan. Ah, he's doing just fine."

"Are you a little nervous about this guy, Dan? If not, you should be. He has a real attitude problem, and a super hard-on for you, O'Brien, ah, pardon me, ma'am."

"I know he has, he has already threatened me. But, for now, we have him under glass, I'm not too concerned with Spencer right now. When he gets his financial reward, I don't expect any more problems."

Avery interrupted. "You know, I might even hire Spencer, just to show good faith. I can find him something. He is a good skipper, and this way we can keep an eye on him."

Van Wagner looked at Phil and shook his head. "Good luck, pal. Personally, you better hope he catches pneumonia and is allergic to antibiotics."

"Captain Rick, that's terrible. Doesn't this man's life have any meaning to you?" Gail asked.

"It's not me I'm worrying about, Ms. Townsend. It's the U.S. Government."

"O.K., enough about Spencer. Let's go on to the next problem, the Seaduce. I think it would be wise to have her stay in English Harbour rather than head down to St. Lucia. I'm concerned about communications down there. We don't have that problem in Antigua. What are your feelings on this, Rick?"

"Well, you're right. I am much better off staying around Antigua. You will also be saving about five to six hundred sailing miles, and in that old ketch, that's a lot of miles. Plus we have the December weather to worry about. We can day sail out of Antigua, go to any of the many close by islands and look busy, don't worry about that. When you're ready, we will be there waiting in the harbor. You mentioned December 23rd? Is that the date you want us to leave?"

"Ah, yes, that's if our information sticks."

O'Brien lit a cigarette and continued. "Alright, that's settled. We will make the arrangements for your charter guests to arrive in Antigua. Now, you will be working through that Nickerson's clearing house is, right?"

"Correct, and it's Nicholson's. Yes, they will contact me when you need me."

"Good, you do what you need to do to get registered with them, and make sure they know the hour you leave for Jamaica. Get logged out somehow, Rick. Now, let's look at your problem, Mr. Avery. What do you want to do now that we have all this time?"

"Well, Gail, Buckwheat and I have a problem of just staying out of the way of visiting brokers right now. We can hide for a few days where we are, but we will have to move again. My suggestion is that you get our charter guests down here as soon as possible. We will notify the clearinghouse that the owners are coming in and want to remain private, this is not unusual. We can go over to Caneel Bay, or run up to the BVI and stay out of harms way. We will come back to St. Thomas on the 22nd and wait."

"I have no problem with that. I will call Ian later and get him going on the charter folks. I did explain to you, these guests are going to be living and answering to phony names, so don't even ask what they do, who they are, or where they come from. All these folks belong to Ian Billings, and they have strict rules, O.K?'

"Now, let me bring you up to date with new toys from old Scrooge. He has made arrangements for two P-3 patrol planes to be flying umbrella while we are on maneuvers. They are, for those who don't know, U.S. Navy sub hunters. They have four engines, are prop driven and easily recognized by all the antennas and radar garb, and naturally, their Navy markings. These planes will be flying out of Puerto Rico, and St. Croix."

O'Brien reached in his pants and took out his wallet. He pulled a small folded paper out. "The code names for these two birds are "Peter Pan" and "Dumbo." Make note of this. One or the other will be in radio reach at all times when we are under way. They are equipped with booster amplifiers that will assure us that we are receiving each others messages. They can also do visuals if needed."

"I take it these types are well known down here in the Caribbean area?" Lind asked.

"Oh, yes. Navy told me they are part of the scenery down here. They are always training, or tracking someone down here, theirs and ours."

O'Brien returned his wallet to his pocket, then looked around at his team. "Now, does everyone have their code books up to date? Remember, we are all going to code when we get under way, except when Phil is broadcasting his plea for help, and having conversation with the Unicorn. Naturally, we, or I should say Captain Lind will also be off code when in contact with Castro."

"Dan, what if the Unicorn doesn't show? I mean, what if they have difficulties, or we have some foul weather and we miss them, or heaven forbid, we lose the nighttime advantage for the interception. Is there any back-up plan to do anything? Castro is going to a secluded island. Would we get another chance to maybe sneak in and set charges there? We have the team and the talent."

"I hear you, Phil, but no, there is no back up plan. If we miss our shot, for any reason, we put our tails between our legs and head home. We have no other plans, and attempting anything on or near those French islands, well, it would be damn risky."

"What we may be able to do is get close enough with the Drummer on a innocent cruise by, and see if we can see anything. What ever those devices are that Castro is demonstrating, just may be seen by us through our glasses or at night with infra-red."

"You know, Dan, it may be wise to take a few of the UDT guys with me when we make our run for Antigua. We can wait out the explosion, and be down there in no time to see what we can learn. Like you said, Dan, if we miss an opportunity in open seas, or something goes wrong with the charges, we may just possibly get a another shot at them at anchor. Hell, we can't just let him go."

O'Brien interrupted Avery. "I'll think about it, o.k.?

"Alright, we all have things to do. Let's get back to our ships and start getting ready. Now, if you need me, here is my land number in St. Croix. If all else fails, you all have your direct lines to Miami and to Bollman's operators. I want a landline report from each of you every time you move. Remember, I have no way of knowing what's going on down in Cuba until the first report reaches McDill Air Force Base, then on to Koster and back to Bollman. We need to be on our stations no later than the 22nd, and ready. Don't use your VHF's to locate each other. When the time comes, we go to code, remember that. I will notify our Navy air coverage, and they will be checking in with you as soon as they are in the area, so keep your new hopper radios on, and before I forget, put them on channel two. Use your primary VHF's for any chatting to other ships or to your clearinghouses, is that understood?

"Gail, I hope you got your little problem all solved and your visitor is off the island. We don't want any more interference from here on in. If he shows up again, you will have to leave the operation, is that clear?"

Gail was dumbfounded. She looked at Phil, but he just offered a shrug with his shoulders. She looked back into O'Brien's cold gray eyes. "How did you?"

· "We knew the minute he flew to Miami, and he'd better be home in Sarasota tonight. He is supposed to arrive at Sarasota airport at 1930 hours."

"Jesus, you guys."

"Let's go folks, ah, let's not leave together, o.k.? Commander, you and I will hop up to the bar and kill a beer. Lind, why don't you go up to the hotel entrance and get a cab. I will meet you at the seaplane ramp downtown for the 1630 flight back to St. Croix."

"Oh, good luck to all of you, keep your equipment ready and don't forget to call."

Van Wagner stepped over to O'Brien and whispered in his ear. "I see some signs about you that disturb me, friend. I know the pressure is on, but if I were you, I'd stay a little more clear of that bottle if you want to get through this operation."

"Mind your fucking business, Mr. Van Wagner. I don't have a problem. Even if I do, I will make it through this operation, so don't you worry, o.k.?"

Van Wagner just smiled, then put his large hands on O'Brien's broad shoulders. He looked straight into O'Brien's eyes, and in a very low voice, said, "You mess up here, Mister, and screw any of these folks up? I will personally see your ass hangs for it. So, you may want to start worrying about it."

Van Wagner turned and walked down towards the beach. O'Brien turned around to find that he was standing all alone.

Morningside Condominiums
Apartment 4
St. Croix, U.S. Virgin. Islands

Saturday, December 19th
0840 hours

The next eight days seemed to drag on for O'Brien. He would spend most of his day going over the charts, again and again. He would make too many phone calls to Washington, and was told to back off by Billings and Admiral Koster.

He did learn that the Navy called off their exercises in the Gulf and in the Caribbean, as he was told they would do. He also learned the Russians' threat was just as suspected, a young Russian Captain with too many martinis, mouthing off. He was called back to Moscow, and a new attaché had already arrived.

Phil Avery had gone up to the British Virgin Islands with his new charter guests, who arrived on December 13th. He was due back in St. Thomas on December 21st.

The Seaduce got her charter guests on the same day, Sunday, December 13th. Van Wagner left Antigua on Monday morning and was going to sail south for a few days, maybe down to Guadeloupe, and be back at English Harbor on December 21st.

The Sonar, with Captain Lind and four of his crew were over in St. Thomas. He ordered his exhaust parts and they were expected to be in on the 19th. He too, would be back in St. Croix on December 21st, with his full crew.

Captain Chen and his team would be arriving Sunday, December 20th. Dan wanted to go down to the airport and meet them, but thought twice. He would wait Captain Chen's phone call, or maybe go down and hang out in the lounge at the airport, just to watch them arrive. This too was discarded as a bad idea, as he had no idea what their ETA was. After making the rounds of some of the local pubs, he fell into his bed and slept until 1420 that day, and never heard the phone ring.

CHAPTER 21

Captain Carlos DeTorre installed the last cross-point screw into the varnished mahogany panel. Satisfied the panel was secured, he stepped back and checked to make sure it was lined up with the other panels on the large instrument bulkhead.

"Have you checked your instruments yet, Captain?" asked Gayo Rodriguez, Unicorn's communications officer.

"No I haven't, Gayo, but we can do that right now. If you don't mind, flip that master switch to "on" for the 12-volt systems. It's right there, behind you."

Rodriguez went over to the electrical panel on the aft bulkhead. He threw the double switch lever and two red lights above the switches came on, declaring that the ship's 12-volt system was live.

"I hope there is no one working on the 12 volt system anywhere," DeTorre said laughing, as he checked the voltage meter that he had just replaced.

"It's working fine, comrade, one less problem. How is all your equipment, Gayo? Did you find out what was wrong with your radar motor?"

"Yes, Captain, it was only a burned out fuse, it's been replaced and the unit is spinning like a new top."

"Good, are you concerned why the fuse blew out?"

"Well, Captain, it could be a number of things. There was quite a bit of water in the motor housing that leaked in around some worn seals. I resealed it carefully. I believe this was the problem."

DeTorre moved over behind the large stainless helms wheel and looked out through the blue tinted bridge windows across the long narrow bow.

"She is a beauty, isn't she, my friend? I am like a little child with his first new toy, I can't wait to get under way." He reached over and picked up a portable mike, pushed in the intercom button marked "engine room."

"Attention, attention, all engine room personnel. Be ready to start all engines, standby to go to maximum rpm's for military speed." He looked at Rodriguez, who looked a little bewildered. DeTorre began laughing. "Can you imagine what's going on down in the engine room right now in the minds of our two engineers? Listen, just listen." He pointed to the speaker grill that was right over his head.

The overhead speaker began to crackled. A soft voice responded. "Is that you, Captain DeTorre?"

DeTorre hesitated for a few seconds. "Yes, Antonio, it's just me," he said laughing. "How are you and Manuel coming along, do you have those oil filters changed yet?"

"We are almost done, Captain. The port engine is finished, and we should have the starboard finished in about a half-hour."

"Good, I want to do run-up tests, and apply full pressure checks. We will take the engines up to maximum rpm's and hold them there for two minutes so you and Manuel can inspect every hose connection and every engine seal. I do not want any mechanical breakdowns on this mission. When we are finished with the engines, we will run the two generators and pressure check them. This may be the last time we can thoroughly go over all our systems, comrade, we could leave at anytime, understood?"

"Yes, sir. We will call you as soon as we are secured, Captain."

DeTorre, still giggling about his little joke with his crew, noticed that Rodriguez had walked over to the open bridge door and stepped out on the catwalk. He was leaning against the railing looking down at the dock below, watching two soldiers uncrating new MK 47 automatic rifles.

Rodriguez turned towards DeTorre, and with great concern in his voice, said, "I thought that our President said we were not going to take any arms along with us."

"What he may have said and what General Vincetta ordered me to do, are two different things. President Castro was planning to bring his brother along too, but now I understand he may be too ill to leave Cuba."

"Captain, I don't suppose that we are cleared to take the ship out for a trial run before we leave?"

"No, General Vincetta told me that our President does not want anyone seeing us in the bay until we leave. I tried, but the answer is no. I would love to give those drive shafts some exercise. This yacht has been sitting too long, we will have our hands full with the stuffing boxes and shaft leaks when we get under way."

"Captain, we could put extra spring and stern lines on, and put the engines in gear and run them up. That way we could check the shafts and make our adjustments."

"Brilliant, Gayo, good idea, and that is exactly what we will do as soon as we have all our gear on board."

"Yes, sir. If you will excuse me now, I'm going aft and see how the crew is doing bringing the little submarine on board."

"Wait, I'll go with you." DeTorre went over to the metal toolbox, dropped the screwdriver in and closed the lid.

The two officers walked aft down the portside catwalk until they reached the end of the main salon. A crew of five men was huddled around the miniature sub that was sitting on its wooden cradle. One man was standing on top, legs braced and reaching for the large hook that was being lowered from the overhead crane.

DeTorre entered the main salon through the double doors that led to the aft deck. A carpenter was just finishing tacking down what appeared to be some old red carpet on the makeshift cradle that would support the sub. DeTorre looked up through the large gaping hole in the cabin roof. The two large doors that had been installed were open, and two workers were standing on the cabin roof ready to guide the submarine down through the opening into the salon.

On Castro's orders, the varnished oak parquet floor had been covered with cardboard, heavy vinyl cloth and wood planks to protect it from any mishaps. He wanted no damage to the beautiful finished floor.

The hook was attached to the lifting cable eye, which was suspended above a spreader-bar. There were only two lifting points on the sub, one forward of the vertical sail and the other nearly at the base of the tail fin. Two smaller hooks, suspended on short cables from the spreader bar, were put into the two lifting eyes.

An order was called to take up the slack of the spreader bar. Another order was given and the mini-sub lifted off the cradle and began its slow journey upward. Four tether lines were attached and manned by four soldiers on the ground, who guided the sub as it swayed overhead.

Mr. Lo was giving all the commands to the hoist operator. When the sub was high enough, he ordered the hoist to move slowly forward on the traveler. He began screaming at the soldiers to keep pressure on their lines, so the sub wouldn't travel, or sway too far forward and smash into the large exhaust funnel or hit the davit booms on the cabin top.

It took nearly an hour, but the sub was finally settled on its new cradle and secured. DeTorre was pleased that it had been brought aboard without doing any damage to the submarine, or to the Unicorn.

The next test was to close the two large roof doors, and to make sure they would not leak. The doors would be opened again to make sure that the two forward davits could hoist them easily without straining the hinges. Then the two portable cradles for the two auxiliary tenders would be put in place, although only the lighter of the two, an open outboard skiff, would be actually brought on board. The larger, heavier inboard\outboard runabout would stay on the hangar floor because it would be in the way when the Dolphin was lifted in and out of the cabin.

The Unicorn was ready to sail. Fuel, water and provisioning were on board. All she awaited were her passengers.

Fidel Castro's Mansion
Varadero
0950 hours

General Vincetta put the phone down gently. He looked up into Fidel Castro's curious black eyes.

"Well comrade, what did General Rogelio say?" Castro asked.

"He is very disappointed, Comrade President, but he understands."

Dimitri Sorokin, standing at the open door looking out across the bay, turned towards them. "He should not feel hurt, comrade, he will still be in charge of the country. Your brother will not be well enough in four or five days to leave the hospital and take on his duties. Pneumonia is nothing to fool with, Fidel."

"I know, Dimitri, I don't like leaving him like this. I only hope when the time comes for us to leave he will be past the worst."

General Vincetta changed the subject. "Comrade Sorokin, you have never been to the Lesser Antilles, or to Guadeloupe before, have you?"

"Ah, no, General, I have not."

Castro, still somewhat concerned about General Rogelio's feelings was not listening to Vincetta's conversation with Sorokin.

"I will talk to him, General, he will listen to me, he will understand," Castro said. He got out of his large chair and slowly walked over to the open French doors that opened onto a small garden and the neighboring grounds of the old DuPont mansion. It was cloudy and a light rain was starting to fall. "What do we hear from our friend, comrade Chibas, General?"

"Nothing new, sir. Everything is still the same. All our guests will be on board a fishing yacht and should arrive at the island around noon. We told them we wanted to be in the cove prior to their arrival as we may need more room to maneuver."

"How does Captain DeTorre, that is his name, correct?"

"Yes comrade Sorokin, that's correct." Vincetta responded.

"How does he feel about the limits of this anchorage? Has he had time to study the charts and to speak to someone who is familiar with the island and the cove?"

Castro turned and stood erect, as if at attention. He stared straight ahead at a large oil painting that hung on the wall behind his desk. It was a painting of Admiral Nelson, lying on the deck of his flagship being attended to by his officers after he had been fatally wounded during the Battle of Trafalgar.

"I have a lot of faith in Captain DeTorre, Comrade Sorokin. He has been to this island many times with his father and uncle. They spent many years fishing around Guadeloupe. His uncle lived and died on Guadeloupe. He designed and built many of the fishing boats that are still used by the commercial fishermen."

"That's good, now I shall rest easier," Sorokin said smiling. He glanced up at the painting, then back at Castro, who was still studying it as if he had never seen it before.

"Comrade President, tell me. What is it you see in this painting that seems to disturb you?" Sorokin asked.

"I see myself in this picture, comrade. I see myself surrounded by my officers, dying from a wound caused by one of my own soldiers, an accident, of course."

Sorokin looked over at General Vincetta, who was sitting directly across from him, spinning a gold pen between the tips of his two index fingers. His eyes rolled up into their lids and back. Sorokin got the message. It was not unusual for Fidel to start talking about his life's end. He often became a little melodramatic, when he was about to be put in a situation of risk. In a few days, he would be on the open seas on a small yacht, and possibly heading into harms way. He was looking for compassion and support from his two companions, waiting to hear one of them say that he would reign forever. Those words never came.

"Comrade President, have you decided if you are going to replace your brother on this trip?"

"No, I have not decided. I don't think that I will. It is probably just as well he does stay behind, just in case something should happen to me."

"Comrade, nothing will happen to you. We have a excellent team on board, however, I wish you would change your mind about letting me put weapons on board. A few hand guns are hardly..."

Castro interrupted Vincetta. "No, I don't want any incidents or accidents. We are taking all the precautions we need. We have our new identities, new papers. Just think, I will probably look like some Jewish lawyer from New York, after I cut this beard off." Castro laughed at himself. "And you, Dimitri, you are supposed to be cutting your hair and dyeing it black. But, you will never look like a Cuban."

"Monday, comrade President, Monday morning. I have an appointment with a young lady over in old Havana that will give me my youth back."

Castro smiled and winked at Sorokin. "Angie, right? Little Angie, yes, she will give you your youth back, comrade. She will blow the wax right out of your lily white ears for a carton of American cigarettes." Castro laughed out loud, then turned to Vincetta. "General, do you have Dimitri's papers ready?"

"They will be as soon as we get his new photograph. We can't finish until he gets his hair dyed and cut."

"Alright, but let's start to move on these things, comrades." Castro walked back to his desk and sat down. He opened a large notebook and started to run down a list of items he was planning to discuss at the meeting.

"Oh, yes." Castro remarked as he flipped through pages in the notebook. "I was to ask you about Doctor Sanchez at the University. He was supposed to get a large supply of this antibiotic "Amoxil?" What do you have on this?"

"This Amoxil is one of the more effective drugs we need to fight this terrible flu we have spreading throughout our country."

"Where are we getting this Amoxil?" Castro asked.

"From friends in Panama, Costa Rica and Mexico."

"It comes from America, no?"

"Oh, yes, comrade, and it is expensive."

"I want to be sure that our military is given the drugs first. Do you understand? No drugs will be issued to anyone without authorization from me. After all our military personnel are taken care of, then we will distribute to civilians, do you understand, General?"

"Of course, comrade President. I will take care of this as soon as I leave this meeting."

Sorokin watched General Vincetta. He was getting a bit edgy and nervous. Castro was displaying a side of his personality not often seen by Sorokin.

"Do you want me to check with our doctors, comrade? Maybe we have something that will work as well."

"Ha, your countrymen are responsible for bringing us this plague. You don't even make good aspirin in the Soviet Union. I would never take any pills that your doctors send to us. Vodka? Now that's different. Drugs? Horseshit."

Castro closed the notebook and pointed his finger at Vincetta. "We have to be careful ourselves, General. As soon as you can get some of this flu drug you make sure we have a supply aboard the Unicorn."

"How about a doctor? Maybe your doctor, Major Morales?"

"Horseshit, no doctor," Castro said. "Now, let's talk about our plans for getting to Santiago, and how you're planning our so-called vacation in Oriente Province."

Vincetta cleared his throat. "We will be going to Sagua De Tanamo, at least that is what security will be told. It is an old base site, that you once named Fajardo's Forest after our old friend, Carlos Fajardo. Remember?"

Castro laughed. "Oh, yes, do I remember that camp. Sergeant Fajardo had a severe case of dysentery for three weeks. There was not a leaf, plant or lizard in the entire northern forest that escaped his attention."

The three men laughed. Vincetta continued. "This is where you will be spending a week or more, doing some planning and relaxing. Naturally, I will be with you, as well as the usual security staff."

"General, you mentioned yesterday there was a change in our escape plan, something about changing airplanes and islands." Castro shuffled papers around on top of his desk, looking for something.

"The plane, yes, there has been a change in the plane that was to stand-by in Guadeloupe. Thomas Puros informed me that the jet he was going to charter out of Mexico was not available, and in any case it did not have the range we would need. He has made other arrangements to have a Beechcraft twin engine prop plane, a model 402 I believe, standing by instead. This plane can land and take off on Terre-de-Haut, which would be easier for us to reach and get on board without French authorities looking over our shoulders. This airplane is equipped to take more passengers and it has the longer range we will need."

Castro looked at his watch then pushed himself away from the desk. He stood up and walked over to the open French doors again. It was raining harder and the sound of thunder rolled in from across the bay. "We are still flying down to Santiago at midnight on the 21st, correct?"

"Yes, sir," Vincetta replied.

Castro looked at his two most trusted companions. He reached into his fatigue jacket pocket and pulled out a freshly wrapped cigar. After he lit it, he blew a large cloud of blue smoke into the air and smiled. "My friends, we are going to be rich. We will have money and security the likes our country has never known. We will no longer have to borrow or beg for our existence, and we won't have to answer to anyone ever again."

Castro returned to his desk and sat down. He gathered a bunch of papers and slid them into a weathered old briefcase. He looked up and smiled.

"This meeting is over, comrades. I must go see my brother now," he rose, stepped from behind his desk, picked up his sweat stained fatigue hat and without another word, walked out of the room.

Island Drummer
West End
Tortola, British Virgin Islands

Sunday, December 20
0845

The peaceful cove on the west end of Tortola is one of the famous landmarks of the British Virgin Islands. It is also the most popular port for visiting yachts and tourists who arrive daily on ferries from the U.S. Virgin Islands.

A large wave went under the Drummer's hull and startled her crew. It came from the wake of the Bomba Charger 0830 ferry, which had just arrived from St. Thomas.

"Jesus Christ, what the hell?" Gail yelled from her stateroom.

"It's alright, one of the inter-island ferries just came in to the customs dock."

"Well, we are rock'n and roll'n down here, let me know when the hurricane has passed."

Gail came up on deck laughing about the crew below complaining. She was wearing a brief navy blue bikini and had a bath towel rolled around her neck. It was time for her morning swim.

"I forgot to put the board down, sorry about that," Avery said quietly.

"Hey, Captain, you can't think of everything, especially after we killed two quarts of Pusser's Rum. You may want to check our guests, I haven't heard one of their heads flush this morning."

Avery laughed as he stepped out of the cockpit onto the starboard deck. He released the lifeline gate for Gail.

"I even left the boarding ladder out for you, just in case you decided to take a moonlight swim."

Gail chuckled. She knew the truth, he just forgot to bring it in the night before. "Nice work, Captain. Damn, we are getting sloppy, don't you think? Anyone could have come aboard last night and helped themselves to something, ah, what do we have of value?" Gail said laughing.

"Buckwheat? He looks expensive," Avery said.

They both giggled like children. Avery held Gail's hand as she took hold of the steep boarding ladder, took a few steps down then slipped into the deep blue water. She disappeared for a few seconds, then Avery saw her just below the surface doing a graceful breaststroke. She broke water about fifteen yards away, waved at Avery and started her swim towards the docks on the south side of the cove where a small bareboat charter company docked their yachts.

An hour later, the cockpit was full of groaning bodies, each telling their private tale of how terrible they felt and describing how many times they made it to the rail during the night. One by one they asked Buckwheat what it was he mixed with the rum?

Pat Brewster and Linda Star managed to put together what they called the last breakfast.

"We have to get to a grocery store, Captain, before we all start killing each other for the last package of Ship Ahoy cookies," Pat remarked as she gathered up the breakfast dishes.

Almost like a well tuned choir, all the voices in the cockpit screamed, "Ship Ahoy cookies? We have some cookies?"

Linda Star, standing next to Avery asked, "What's our plan, Phil? Do we head in today?"

"Yeah, we have played hide and seek long enough here in the British Virgins, we'll head back to St. Thomas today. Tomorrow is check in day." Avery looked at his watch. "We have to call O'Brien and be ready to take off at a moment's notice, which means we have to fuel up and provision this afternoon."

1105 Hours

The large Danforth anchor was secured in its stainless steel cradle. Avery gracefully spun the Island Drummer in her own length, as he used his twin engines to minimize her turning radius. Buckwheat and Gail began preparing to hoist sails, as the Drummers' new crew, Don and Pat Brewster and Jack and Linda Star added their limited assistance.

Avery looked back at the anchorage, it was still quiet and peaceful, only a single bareboat was heading out. He glanced up at the sun, which was nearly overhead. There were some clouds that had built up to on the east end of Tortola and a few over St. Johns, but nothing threatening. He thought it would be a pleasant downwind run all afternoon to Charlotte Amalie. The wind was light, but would pick up as soon as he cleared West End.

St. James Club
Antigua

Sunday, December 20th
1235 Hours

The outdoor patio restaurant overlooking the marina docks was filled with tourists, mostly Europeans, enjoying lunch.

Rick Van Wagner and Paul Gransaull thought this would be a nice setting to get acquainted with their new charter guests, who had arrived from the States the night before and checked into the St. James Hotel for their first night.

Steve and Evelyn Rodis were a very attractive couple, somewhere in their early fifties. Dennis and Rose Miller appeared younger, more physically fit. Van Wagner and Paul Gransaull could not understand how the two couples had been selected. None of them had ever sailed, nor had they been to the Caribbean before.

"I know I am not supposed to ask you questions, ah, I mean I know I can't ask your real names and all that, but, are you all with the agency?"

Steve Rodis looked at Dennis Miller, then shrugged his shoulders. "We are, that is, Dennis and I are. Naturally, our wives, well they both have other duties, I mean they both work elsewhere."

"Yes, fine, I was just curious. You know, I was with the agency for nearly.." Van Wagner was suddenly interrupted by Gransaull who gently stepped on his foot."

"Ah, would you ladies like to have a tour of St. Johns after lunch while Rick goes over the yacht with your husbands? I would be most happy to take you up to the market."

"Well, that would be nice, Paul, don't you agree, Rose? I would like to see St. Johns, I read about it on the way down yesterday."

"Fine, we leave right from here. Rick, you can grab a taxi if you don't mind, and we will meet you back at the Copper and Lumber Pub, say fiveish, O.K?"

Van Wagner laughed to himself. Paul was learning fast.

"Tell me, Rick. Are we going to just stay here on Antigua until we get some word to leave?"

"Yes, we are sort of on standby. Tomorrow I will be talking to our contact in St. Croix, to let him know you are here. I will also inform the clearinghouse here that you arrived and are on board. We may have to do some day sailing to kill time, just to look like we are on a normal charter, before we sail for Jamaica."

"Jamaica? We are going to Jamaica? That's an awful long way from here, Captain."

"Yes it is, Rose, but we are not really going there. We want certain people to think that's where we are heading. I take it you all haven't been briefed, have you?"

"We pretty much know what we need to know. We were told that you or Mr. O'Brien would fill us in. By the way, just where is this meeting place, where we transfer to this freighter?"

Van Wagner looked around at the nearby tables. The patio restaurant was full, mostly guests of the hotel and Van Wagner was getting uncomfortable.

"Ah, I think we better talk about this later, if you don't mind."

The Careless Navigator
Kings Alley
Christiansted, St. Croix, U.S.V.I.

Sunday, 1335 Hours

JoJo Delugo folded the small white cotton towel and patted her forehead. She had been cleaning and rinsing glasses in the steaming hot sink and placing them on towels on the small bar.

"Nice to see someone else sweat down here."

"Mr. O'Brien, no lady should ever be seen sweating, don't you know that?"

O'Brien laughed as he poured the remains of the Red Stripe beer out of the bottle into the glass.

"You have taken quite a liking to that Red Stripe, Mr. O'Brien."

"Yeah, it's nice, good day drinking beer, but at night, I prefer one of the heavy German brews."

O'Brien was just about to mention to JoJo that it was too quiet, not another soul had come in the bar since she opened. Then a slender young man entered the bar and took a seat by the door. The sun was blinding coming in through the doorway, and O'Brien could not see his face right away. When the stranger asked for a Bud there was no question that the voice belonged to Captain Jack Chen. Now O'Brien had to strike up a conversation, as two strangers would do.

He called out. "Say, are you on a cruise ship visiting?"

Chen looked down the bar at the well-tanned man talking to him. He recognized the man he met in Key West, barely three months back.

"Ah, no sir. I'm down here with some friends to do some diving and relaxing."

"Diving, that's great. Have you been over to Buck Island yet?"

"Oh, yes, that was one of our first stops."

"My name is O'Brien, by the way. I just retired, and I'm kinda bumming around, you know? This here is JoJo, JoJo DeLugo, she owns this establishment, and a great little B&B a few blocks away."

"Pleased to meet you, JoJo. My name is John, John Koto."

"Koto is that Japanese, John?" Jojo asked.

"Yes, and a little Hawaiian, so I am told. I was actually born in Chico, California."

O'Brien moved down from the back of the room and sat next to Chen. They talked for nearly an hour then left the pub, telling the barmaid they were going touring and would be back later. They got into O'Brien's rental Toyota and headed down Strand Street, which led them out of town and into the open country.

"How are the troops, Jack?"

"They are fine, Dan, except for Billy Allen, he has been fighting some kind of flu-bug."

"How's the housing, o.k.?'

"Oh yeah, it's comfortable. We have everything we need. We would like to get in some more training with our special diving gear, but that's difficult. We have been going over to Sugar Bay, as much as we can. The diving is great there, and it's pretty isolated."

"Anyone asking questions?"

"Nah, not so far. We are just acting like a bunch of American G.I.'s goofing off, getting drunk and doing some diving."

"Yeah, wish I could join you, I'm getting cabin fever hanging around waiting."

"Where is everyone? I mean are all your boats were they are supposed to be?"

"Ah, they will be by tomorrow morning. Our plan is that everyone is to be ready to leave anytime after tomorrow, the 21st."

"I take it you have no new word on the intercept?"

"No, all we can do is wait word from the Blackbirds when Castro is on his way. Then, all we have to worry about is the Sonar blowing a manifold or the Island Drummer blowing one of her engines, or the Seaduce losing its aging rudder or its keel or some asshole ship enters the killing zone during the intercept."

"Cheer up, Dan. You left out a few things, like the failure of the last test we did with the so-called new mounting devices. We brought the prototypes, we know they worked."

"I really don't want to hear this shit, Jack."

"O.K., how about some good news? We have a new timer, that will give us up to thirty hours, not twenty-four."

"That is good news, but we still have to work out the problem of how much time we need so we can set the timers, and we can't work on that until we see what kind of speeds the Unicorn will be running at. We have to keep in mind that her speed should be increasing as she gets closer to us. She's burned off a lot of fuel in that first twenty-four hours. By the time she meets with you guys, she will be considerably lighter and faster. I doubt if we will have our surveillance working after we make contact."

"Not to worry, Dan, all we need to do is to roughly calculate her speed from our intercept point to the island. We should have plenty of time to have the timing devices set to go off on the evening of the 24th. That is when you wanted the detonation, right, on Christmas Eve?"

"That's it."

"Sounds good to me, Dan. Now, before we run out of island, where are we going?"

"Frederiksted, I want to show you the pier. Captain Lind and I decided it's best to bring you and your team out here and board the Sonar, rather than Christiansted Harbour. We can use the pier. There's a lot of commerce moving around and we would look less conspicuous. Naturally, we will do this at night. It won't take long. I will pick you and the team up at the airport and take you to the pier."

"We'll be ready, Dan. Now, if you will drop me off near the airport road, I'll hike back to our quarters. I'm concerned about Bill Allen. If he is still running temperature, we may have to check him in somewhere. I have some antibiotics, but so far they haven't done anything to help him."

"How is this flu affecting him?" O'Brien asked.

"It seems it's all in the throat and chest now. It started out as a simple head cold, you know, like a sinus congestion."

"Let me see what I can do, standby your phone tonight. I will see if I can get some proper medication."

O'Brien drove to the south side of the island and joined the main road that ran from Frederiksted to the airport. He dropped Chen outside the gates that led to the military area on the east end of the airport.

Dan O'Brien's Apartment
2030 hours

O'Brien picked up his ringing telephone.

"Scrooge here, how's your Christmas party coming?"

"I got all the presents I need, unless you have a few you can deliver tonight?"

"Negative, but there are two great Disney movies on TV tomorrow. Dumbo and Peter Pan. You should be able to see them on your local TV."

"Ah, thanks, I will check the local listings."

The line went dead.

O'Brien, wishing he had not mixed that second rum and tonic, lay down on his bed and concentrated on the Admiral's Disneyland lingo. Dumbo and Peter Pan, the two Navy P-3 sub hunters must be arriving in St. Croix tomorrow.

O'Brien rested his hand over his eyes, then massaged his forehead. "In twenty-four hours, the show would finally be on the road," he thought, as he reached for the glass on the nearby nightstand, it was half full of watered down scotch. He raised his head and put the glass to his lips, but he did not take a sip. He threw the glass against the far wall, just missing the small black and white TV on the dresser.

Beal Air Force Base
California

Monday, December 21
0400 Hours

The large steel by-pass doors of hangar five opened. Staff Sargeant Bob Landon put the small yellow tractor into low gear and began to pull the

large black aircraft attached to a tow bar behind him. Landon looked back over each shoulder to check his two crewman who were walking next to each wing tip, guiding the giant plane onto the cold wet ramp. Parked nearby in a Air Force staff car, Lt. Colonel Harry Barrett, Captain Eugene Winters and Captain Jack J. Sloan waited patiently. They watched as the long black plane moved silently across the wet tarmac behind the tractor. It came to a stop directly in front of their headlights.

"She may be nearly twenty years old, Harry, but she still makes my skin tingle when I see her, especially at night."

"Yeah, I know what you mean, Jack. I'm going to miss flying these birds when I check out next month. You two guys just make sure that the new kids take care of them, we're down to four now and I haven't heard anyone talking about replacements."

Sargeant Landon stopped the tug and his crew installed wheel chocks at the two main gears. As the tow bar was released from the nose wheel, Master Sargeant Norman Weijlard stepped out of the cockpit onto the hydraulic platform stand that had been rolled up next to the aircraft's port side, and ran down the stairs to the ground.

A pick-up truck arrived towing a A-1 generator. One of the ground crew took a heavy cable from the generator cart and plugged the end into a receptacle in the belly of the aircraft. He started the generator, threw a switch and watched for the light that would tell him the aircraft was receiving power. The Crew Chief checked for auxiliary power input, then he checked the external circuit and secured the selector switch. Two turbo-jet J-58 engines powered the 107 foot long aircraft. The United States Air Force officially lists this aircraft in their inventory as the SR-71A, nicknamed "Blackbird." It is one of the fastest piloted aircraft in the world and the pride of the Strategic Air Commands Reconnaissance Squadron.

0417 hours

Seated in the compact cockpit, Colonel Barrett and his RSO (Recon Systems Officer) Captain Winters carefully went over their pre-flight systems checks. Captain Sloan and Sargeant Weijlard hooked them up to their communications systems, life support systems and harnesses. Sloan took them through their cockpit pre-flight checklist. With the flight crew satisfied, two ground crew stood by to remove the mobile platform and tow it clear of the aircraft. The pilot received a signal from the crew chief that the area around the aircraft was clear, then he closed and sealed the canopy.

Captain Sloan gave his superior a snappy salute, got into the staff car and drove away from the ramp.

Eight minutes later, the powerful twin J-58 turbo-jet engines were pushing the 170,000 pound aircraft nearly vertical, at 550 miles per hour to an altitude of fifty-five thousand feet. Once level flight was achieved, Barrett brought the two throttles to cruise settings. He selected his radio frequencies, navigational frequencies, checked his compasses and banked the Blackbird in a steep port turn, until he reached a heading of 121 degrees. It was nearly 1230 statute miles to his destination, San Antonio, Texas. He would arrive there in eighty-one minutes, land, refuel and depart again. He would then head due south to the Gulf Of Mexico.

0748 hours

Fifteen minutes into the flight, the two airmen began preparing the aircraft for the mission ahead. They would be photographing nearly 150,000 square miles of the Caribbean Sea, including the islands of Cuba and Hispaniola. Their first waypoint was 1003 miles ahead, the most western end of Cuba. Staying just outside of Cuba's protected airspace at seventy-five thousand feet, the Blackbird would be cruising just under 1600 miles per hour. Captain Winters started to prepare his cameras for the mission run. He turned on his radar and activated his anti-defensive systems. Circuit breakers were pushed in to activate the camera selection switches, which were all in a stand-by mode.

When Barrett reached the first waypoint, he banked eastward and flew just off Cuba's south coast. Winters moved the switches on selected cameras from the stand-by mode to the run mode. Ten miles west of the port city of Santiago Del Cuba, his next way point, he banked hard right and headed for the next waypoint, the western end of Haiti. Once this waypoint was reached, he banked due east and flew along Haiti's southern coastline. In a few seconds, he flew over the city of Port Au Prince. He looked ahead into the crystal clear sky and searched the horizon where he located his next waypoint Santo Domingo, nearly 150 miles due east. At Santo Domingo, Colonel Barrett banked his Blackbird in a hard port turn and took a northwest heading for the Bahama Islands. He picked up the VOR at Nassau and flew directly to the city on the island of New Providence. Once overhead, he banked westward and began a long descent that would take him over Fort Lauderdale, Lake Okeechobee, Sebring, Bradenton, out over the Gulf of Mexico. One hundred miles southwest of Tampa Bay, he turned again and

began a long descent that would take him to McDill Air Force Base, Tampa, Florida.

McDill Air Force Base
Tampa, Florida

Air Force intelligence personnel removed all the film canisters from the Blackbird's cameras and took them to the laboratory for development. The developed film would be studied closely by Major General Fredrick Metz and Master Sargeant Tony Mazda. They were particularly interested in studying about 3,000 square miles of the entire film. This being the route that they were told the Unicorn would be taking.

The entire flight from Edwards Air Force Base to Tampa, 4600 miles, took less than four hours. The crew arrived early enough at the officers' mess to enjoy a late breakfast of eggs, and biscuits with sausage gravy.

1130 hours

After breakfast and a short briefing, the two officers stepped back into their Blackbird, A/C # 17952, took off from McDill, climbed to 50,000 feet and headed southeast towards the Bahamas.

They climbed to 75,000 feet over Nassau, turned south and flew to Puerto Rico. Over San Juan, they headed southwest to the city of Ponce on the southern coast. From this point, they went west again and began photographing the same route they had flown earlier, only in reverse. This time, however, the Blackbird ended its mission at Laughlin Air Force Base in Del Rio, Texas, headquarters for the 9th Strategic Recon Wing. Their mission was completed.

Two hours after Colonel Barrett landed, SR-71A, A/C # 17950 lifted off at Laughlin piloted by Major Christopher Jack, with his R\O, Lieutenant Ross Stocker. Major Jack, a seasoned pilot with over 2000 hours in U-2 and SR-71A type aircraft, had flown more missions over Cuba than any pilot in the squadron. He was going to see Cuba again. The search for Fidel Castro, officially began at 0400 hours.

Santana Marina
Santiago de Cuba

Monday, December 21st
2050 Hours

The lights in the huge hangar building were turned off. Only a few portable work lights lit up the port side of the Feadship yacht, where the boarding ramp was located. In the main salon, Captain DeTorre was showing Fidel Castro, General Vincetta and Dimitri Sorokin the cables that tied down the Dolphin to the deck. The cables that secured the large cradle were a hazard to step over. DeTorre commented that four crewmen had already sustained bad shin injuries tripping over them. Castro made no comment.

At 2100 hours, a meeting was held of all hands in the owner's cabin. Four bottles of French champagne and two boxes of special cigars were opened.

"I congratulate you on this the eve of our exciting adventure. In a few days, we will become victorious again, in our continuous struggle to protect.."

A cabin door slowly opening into the room interrupted Castro. Everyone in the cabin watched as the short man stepped into the cabin.

"Colonel, where have you been? You were supposed to be here ten minutes ago?" Castro asked loudly.

"I'm so sorry, comrade President. I was having troubles with the toilet. It won't, ah, I don't know how to make it go down, sir."

Castro burst into laughter. General Vincetta, standing close to the small man, put his arm around his shoulders. "Colonel Navarro, this was not exactly your day, was it?"

Navarro smiled and nodded his head in agreement.

General Vincetta said, "I called Colonel Navarro before the sun rose this morning and told him to pack some clothes and get his house in order, as he would be leaving on a secret mission with the President, and would not be home for maybe ten days. When I sent a jeep for him early this evening, he was gone. Nobody, not even his beautiful wife, Melinda, knew where he was. We thought he had deserted. Then he shows up at Camp Columbia, having coffee with our President's pilot, Major Lucia, who is also his brother-in-law. I was quite surprised, and I would still like to know, Colonel, how you knew to go to the airport at Columbia, without knowing where you were being sent on the mission. I had not issued you any instructions at that time."

"You forget, General, you told me to pick up a package at the University Hospital. You said it contained special medications, ah, antibiotics, I believe, for our President. If you look at that package I handed you at the airport, it was clearly labeled to be on the President's flight at 1800 hours. I had car trouble and by the time we got it started again, it was late, so I figured I would go directly to the airport and find my brother-in-law, Major Lucia. He told me you and the President would be on the flight, and, well.."

"You see, General? That is why this young man is a Colonel today, he plans ahead and that is why I chose him to serve in my special security squad." Castro said, as he smiled at the Navarro.

"Here, take this." Vincetta handed Navarro a plastic tumbler. He picked up a bottle of Champagne and filled the glass. "To our voyage."

Everyone raised their glasses, except Mr. Lo, who was not drinking. Castro moved over to the forward bulkhead wall where a chart of the Caribbean had been pinned up. A small red circle was drawn around the island of Guadeloupe. He put his right index finger inside the circle.

"Here is our destination, a small island just south of Guadeloupe. It is approximately one thousand miles away. Captain DeTorre has told me that it will take us somewhere between fifty and sixty hours to get there, pending sea conditions. Captain, would you take over, please?"

"Yes, comrade President. This wonderful yacht is one of the world's finest. She was designed for long range cruising and can easily reach destinations nearly three thousand miles away. We have two very large turbo diesel engines, which can push us along smoothly at sixteen knots. As we burn off fuel, we can increase our speed to eighteen, or even twenty knots. However, with the currents and winds, we will be averaging more like fifteen for the trip." Captain DeTorre went over to the chart.

"You see, we are here, at Santiago. We will run down here, to a point just off the coast of Haiti, then turn east and run along the southern coasts of Haiti and the Dominican Republic. If you follow this line it is pretty much a straight course all the way to Guadeloupe. Since this is going to be a long voyage for many of you at sea, you may be concerned about seasickness. Not to worry, it happens to all of us professional sailors at one time. We have medication for you to take and my First Officer can give you advice on what to do. We do have plenty of safeguards aboard in case we should have an emergency. We have a twelve-man raft, plenty of emergency rations, radios and one of our own emergency military beacons, should we need it. Your life jackets are in your cabins, along with instructions on what do in case we have an emergency. Any questions?"

"Yes, Captain. Weather, what kind of weather can we expect for the trip?"

"Of course, comrade Sorokin, let me introduce our navigator and weather expert, Lieutenant Varas."

"As of 1800 hours, the Navy Weather Center at Murial reports no unusual activity taking place in the area of our route. There is a low pressure to our west, east of Honduras. It is heading east, northeast. Presently, we have two high-pressure areas, one just east of the Bahamas, and one down over Barbados. There is no expected change for the next twenty-four hours, and we will get updates all along our route. We will also be getting advice from American sources, as we go."

"Captain, what about, well the worst case scenario. Say we get into a serious problem while we are, say, just outside of Puerto Rico and have to be rescued. Wouldn't they send the United States Coast Guard looking for us? They have a number of patrol boats I under stand, operating out of San Juan and the Virgin Islands, don't they?"

"Please, Captain, let me explain to comrade Sorokin." Vincetta interrupted. "Comrade Sorokin, that is why you have all those new identification papers with you, in case we do have a serious problem. If the Americans rescued us all, they would take us to San Juan and in twenty-four hours we would be home. Of course, we would have to travel to Mexico, but we would make it."

"Dimitri, my friend, look at me, the New York lawyer. Here, look at my new name and photo on my new passport." Fidel Castro took the Mexican passport from his hip pocket and handed it to Sorokin. "Now, do I look like someone to fear?"

Sorokin opened the document and studied it for a second and laughed. "You really do look like a lawyer." The entire crew laughed.

Up until this point, nobody had commented about the President's new look. He had shaved his beard and left only a small mustache. His hair was close cut and looked much younger and even leaner. The most comforting thing about his new look was the mystery behind the beard no longer intimidated anyone, he looked rather peaceful, happier.

Dimitri Sorokin had also undergone major alterations. His hair was dyed black and he had it waved. However, he still didn't look like a natural Latino.

"How about you, Mr. Lo, how will you fit in if we get caught by the Americans?" Sorokin asked. "Are you going to play the part of our cook?"

Lo just smiled and shook his head.

"He commits suicide, from what I understand," General Vincetta replied.

"Are you serious, General?" Sorokin asked.

"Mr. Lo, you take the knife and stick it like this?" Vincetta took both his hands, pretending he had a knife, and pulled his hands into his stomach.

Lo, with his right hand formed an imaginary pistol. He put his index finger on his right temple, raised his thumb and said, "Bang."

There was dead silence in the cabin as everyone stared at him. Nobody dared ask if he was serious.

Fidel Castro broke the silence. "Nothing is going to happen, my friends. We are going to have a good voyage. We are going to meet some interesting people and we are going to get rich. Cuba will be rich." He looked at his watch. "Captain DeTorre, I believe it's time?"

"Yes, comrade President," DeTorre responded.

Castro looked at Colonel Navarro. "Colonel, you will be under Mr. Lo's command and assist in any way during our voyage and see that our project stays secured at all times, understood?"

Navarro looked at Castro and responded with a positive nod.

DeTorre walked to the front of the room, "Comrades, we will now prepare to depart. My crew will handle all the dockside cables and lines. We would appreciate if you would all take positions where you won't interfere with the crew. We will be keeping the yacht in a black out, except for running lights. Please do not turn on any lights until we are clear of the harbor and the escorts. Thank you."

DeTorre began to leave the cabin, when he suddenly remembered to explain the escorts. "I might add, comrades, we will be meeting two of our own patrol boats at El Morro near the entrance to the harbor. They will be escorting us for about five miles out to sea. They have been ordered to do this by General Vincetta and Admiral Santamaria. They were told that our Navy was releasing us after being cleared of suspicion of drug and gun running. You will note that we are flying the flag of Panama on the stern. We are a registered Panamanian vessel, owned by a wealthy oil baron in Peru. It would be best that all of you keep out of sight while we are being escorted. We don't want our Navy to know who we really are, now do we?"

Antonio Lopez and Manuel Fajardo went right to the engine room and began preparing to start the engines. Captain DeTorre went up to the fly bridge to take command of the vessel. Cabino Varas and Gayo Rodriguez went down the ramp onto the dock and began disconnecting power cords and dock lines. Castro and General Vincetta went into Castro's quarters just aft of the main bridge.

Dimitri Sorokin looked at his watch, it was 2145. He looked at Colonel Navarro who still holding on to his full glass of champagne. He seemed a little perplexed. Sorokin walked over to him.

"Colonel, you look bewildered. This trip must have come as quite a surprise to you, no?"

"Yes, quite a surprise. Comrade Sorokin, can you explain something to me?"

"I will try, comrade. What is your problem?"

"That big black thing in the back room, back there. It looks like a long bomb."

"I guess it does in the dark. No, it's not a bomb, although it does have enough explosive power to blow us all to another planet if someone fucks around with it. It's a submarine, a radio controlled mini sub. Your President hopes to sell them to major drug lords who we are meeting in Guadeloupe."

"Jesus, I mean, how did our President get into this business? A submarine? Who built it? I mean, we did not make this machine in Cuba, where did it come from?"

"You will have to ask the oriental man, Lo, about that, Colonel. Now that you have been ordered to work with him, you will be able to learn more about the machine. Personally, I think that your President is making a serious mistake trying to deal with these drug people. We are going to have to be on our toes when we meet with them." Sorokin leaned close to Navarro and practically whispered in his ear. "For your information, Colonel, there are a few weapons on board, General Vincetta saw to that, but don't breathe a word, Comrade Castro forbade him to do so."

"You don't think we will have a problem with these men when we meet, do you?"

"No, I hope not. They will be coming to meet us on a big powerboat. I don't think they would do anything stupid, especially around a French island. There is supposed to be a very well trained and equipped French Navy patrol and rescue squadron based in Pointe-a-Pitre, only a few miles from our meeting place."

Sorokin and Navarro left the cabin and walked back to the stern on the starboard side. They felt the engines start up as the well-oiled teak deck beneath their feet began to vibrate.

Santiago Harbor
Fort El Morro
2200 Hours

It was exactly 2207 when the Unicorn was intercepted by two Soviet built P-6 Soviet torpedo boats. Their modern 85-foot hulls were designed to travel at speeds in excess of 50 miles per hour, powered by four M50 diesel engines. A crew of fifteen sailors maintained the ship's readiness as a defensive or offensive weapon. Two 21-inch torpedoes were mounted on her side decks, and four 25-millimeter cannons were mounted fore and aft.

Although often criticized by the Cuban Navy crews for its shabby and crude workmanship, it was tough, fast and a dependable ship that earned their respect. The Cuban Navy had only six of this type of patrol boats and took exceptionally good care of them.

The two escorts occasionally flashed their powerful searchlights across the Unicorn's superstructure as they moved in on both sides to within fifty yards. The curious crews were all on deck taking a close look at the capitalist luxury yacht.

DeTorre kept his face to the dark and reminded the crew and passengers to keep their faces well hidden from the curious sailors.

After a half hour, the escort patrol boat on the port side picked up speed and made a wide port turn and headed back towards the lights of Santiago. About fifteen minutes later, the other escort slipped away in the darkness heading west. At 2300 the Unicorn was cruising comfortably on a light choppy sea at fourteen knots. DeTorre set his course at 154 degrees true and would maintain that heading for the next eight and a half hours, until he reached his first waypoint 30 miles south west of the town of Coteaus, Haiti. At this mark, he would bring the Unicorn to a easterly heading of 090 degrees true, and maintain this heading until he reached their destination, Grand Islet, in the Isles Des Saintes, just south of Guadeloupe, nearly eight hundred and eighty miles away.

Dan O'Brien's Apartment
St. Croix

Tuesday, December 22nd
1231 Hours

O'Brien had just finished packing the last of his magazines, charts and notebooks when the phone rang. "O'Brien here."

"Dan, it's Bollman. Get to a pay phone." The line went dead. O'Brien ran out of the apartment around to the carport and got into the rented Toyota. He sped down Kings Cross Street, turned left on Company Street and pulled into the parking lot of the large marketplace. There were two public phones there. He placed a call to the number in Miami, and after a few minutes Bollman was on the line.

"McDill called, 1120. They picked up what they believe is the Unicorn, Dan. She is right on schedule, heading right on the course you predicted."

"Lou, they're sure, no doubts, right?"

"Dan, if you gave them the right photos and description, they are positive. They will try and get a transom shot this afternoon on the late flight to guarantee that the name Unicorn is on the stern. They did say that, unlike your original photos, that there is only one auxiliary boat up on deck, not two, but the one matches the photo. She is flying a Panamanian flag."

"It's got to be her, Lou. Jesus, where is she? Don't give me the fucking numbers, just reference. I need to get the coordinates later. The P-3's will give us exact locations when they pick her up later. Shit, am I supposed to call?"

"Easy, man, it's all taken care of. Both P-3 crews were already alerted and one of them is already winging its way out of San Juan, and heading down the trench to pick the Unicorn, south of Haiti."

"Have they been able to calculate anything yet? Where did they actually spot her?"

"Ah, they spotted her about twenty-five miles due south of Coteaus on the western end of Haiti. Best estimate right now, with two passes, is that she's doing close to fifteen knots. She was first spotted at 0850. We took a quick guess, and estimated she should be at the intercept tomorrow around 2300 hours, maybe a little sooner."

"God damn, it's perfect. We will have her in the middle of the night, just like we hoped."

"Listen, Dan. I will make the duty calls to your friends in D.C. Is there anything you need or want me to tell the old man?"

"Yeah, tell Scrooge, I'm about to sail up the Mississippi without him."

"Huh? Is that some kind of coded message?"

"No, Lou, just a joke. He will understand. Hey, I have to go. I will call you later, I have to contact the Drummer and the Seaduce, pronto, and get the UDT team alerted. If you need me sooner, call the Careless Navigator, ah, 809 555 4332. Tell JoJo you need me to call. Use the name Kevin; that's my brother. I will be checking in with JoJo all day, o.k.?"

"Right, Dan. Hey, congratulations, and good hunting."

O'Brien drove down to Church Street and then turned right on King Street, where he parked near the waterfront. He could see the Sonar sitting quietly on her anchor, some hundred yards out. He walked out on the old seaplane ramp and tried to see if he could spot anyone on deck or in the wheelhouse. He was lucky. Captain Lind was standing on the foredeck under a canvas awning, watching three drop-lines he had baited earlier. He looked up and saw Dan O'Brien, and somehow he knew it was time.

Ten minutes later he was walking along the ramp with O'Brien planning their departure. They decided it was best to get the Sonar moved down to the west end of the island, near the pier at Frederiksted later in the afternoon. O'Brien would call Captain Chen and alert him to have his team down at the pier with their gear around 0100. O'Brien would check in his rental car and take a taxi out to the pier earlier and wait for Chen at a local pub. Lind returned to the Sonar to get his crew ready.

O'Brien walked back up King Street and found another pay phone. He called Charter Services in St. Thomas and left the code word for the Island Drummer to call him immediately. He then called Nicholsons in Antigua and asked them to radio the yacht Seaduce, giving them their coded message. He then drove up to Kings Alley, parked, ran into the Careless Navigator and had two cold Red Stripes. He explained to JoJo that his brother, Kevin, might call and would she tell him to call him at the apartment.

As O'Brien opened the door to the apartment, the phone was ringing. He picked it up, it was Phil Avery.

"Well, Phil, it's that time, Fruit Cake is on its way. Is the Yuletide ready to go?"

"You bet, Santa's helpers are a little strange but willing to work. Is it safe to say approximately when the Christmas party will take place?"

"Ah, it's too early. Right now, we are guessing that the first guests should start arriving about 2200 to 2300 hours on the 23rd."

"Good, O.K., we will make our plans and should be heading your way tomorrow. Ah, you will most likely be leaving around 1600 hours tomorrow, correct?"

"Ah, that's about right. It's about five hours before the party, right?"

"That's the way I figured, we should be out of here say around 1400 hours, heading your way. We will flash you if we see you, if not, we will send a message to you through Peter Pan or Dumbo."

"That's a roger, Phil."

O'Brien moved his gear off the bed, stripped down to his shorts and lay down. He looked at his watch. It was 1424 hours. "Where was Rick and the Seaduce, he should have called by now, he had a long way to go... damn, I hope he is ready."

The phone rang and O'Brien got it on the second ring.

"Dan, it's Rick, got your message."

"Yeah, Rick, use your codes, o.k.? The FruitCake has been shipped and on its way. Are you ready to go?"

"Just as soon as you give the word, Dan. Remember, it's going to take me twelve to fourteen hours to.."

"Yes, I know, you should be heading out no later than, say, 0350 tomorrow. That will give you plenty of time to find Red Sleigh. The Christmas party is going to begin around 2200 or 2300 hours tomorrow night."

"Roger that, Dan. Ah, should we check in with Peter Pan or Dumbo?"

"Ah, yes, good idea. We will be using Peter and his friend for long distance calls and any changes until we get closer."

"What about weather? I can't get any good info down here, it's almost as bad as the Virgins."

"I will check it out. This afternoon my report from the Red Sleigh said that we will have a no snow for the next few days, perfect for the holiday."

"Gotcha, Dan, O.K. I will be in touch, count on me heading out at 0300. I will have the wind on my back, so figure maybe I can get her up to ten knots, o.k.?"

"Good luck, Rick."

"He has to travel about 170 miles, that's seventeen hours, putting him in the area at 2000 hours, damn, he's calling that close." O'Brien began the long vigil, trying to run the entire program in his head.

CHAPTER 22

San Juan International Airport
San Juan, Puerto Rico

Tuesday, December 22nd
1305 Hours

The vintage Lockheed P-3C Orion rumbled down the runway building up the speed it would need to lift the awkward looking aircraft into the air.

To a layman watching the P-3 take off, the four-engine prop plane looked like some kind of a experiment with its long probe extending out of the tail section. The word NAVY on the vertical tail and the insignias on the wing and fuselage clearly declared the strange looking aircraft belonged to the United States Navy.

In the Orion's cockpit, Commander David "Lank" Parker was at the controls. To his right, co-pilot Lieutenant Greg Tombline and at the flight engineer station was Chief Petty Officer 1st class, Kevin Brown. It would take the combined effort of all three men to convert the noisy vibrating machine into a graceful smooth flying bird. The four powerful Allison Turbo-prop engines producing 4900 horsepower each played the major role lifting the giant aircraft into the air.

The United States Navy found the Lockheed Electra to be the perfect candidate to meet their criteria for a long-range submarine hunter. It could carry tons of electronic gear, including special radar and sonar devices, as well as air-to-surface missiles and mines for submarine hunting. It was strong, dependable and could stay aloft for eighteen hours. The P-3 is the Navy's ultimate submarine hunter.

"Navy 165, maintain heading one-four-zero to 5,000. You're clear to fly the coastline southbound. Squawk two-zero-three-zero, and contact tower on frequency one-two-one-one-zero."

"Roger, Departure. Heading one-four-zero to Angels five, squawking two-zero-three-zero, changing to tower frequency, one-two-one-one-zero, have a good day, Navy 165 out."

"Shit, Lank, look at that stuff building up over the mountains. I was hoping to scoot over them and head down to Ponce and save us some time."

Commander Parker looked past Lieutenant Tombline through the portside windows. A formation of clouds were already topping out at 25,000 feet over the rain forest at the western end of the velvet green island. He checked the color radar screen in the middle of the instrument panel and set

403

the range on zero to fifty miles. There were a number of large cells inside the formation, but to the south and west it looked clear and that was were they were headed.

"Commander, what's your feeling about this super yacht we are looking for and these other boats with funny names?" Tombline reached over and showed his commander a notebook that contained a list of names typed on a page. "Look at these code names, the Yuletide, Red Sleigh, Fruit Cake, Scrooge, Santa Claus, it looks like we're flying cover for Disneyland."

Parker smiled. "I have no idea, Greg. I do know one thing, in my sixteen years of flying patrols, I have never had an assignment like this one and I really can't answer your question."

"I wonder if the President is having some high level secret meeting with someone down here," Tombline mumbled as he scanned the coastline ahead. "I saw a movie once where the President did exactly that. He met with his Soviet counter-part to sign some secret pact, or something."

"Whoa there, Tonto," Parker remarked laughing. "Let's not get carried away here."

"Well, think about it, skipper. We get word from the Pentagon to bring two of our birds down here and stand by. Then, you get this special code book delivered by courier and a phone call from Headquarters telling you to send our sister ship to St. Croix to operate out of there. Hell, we're working with half our normal crew, not doing standard operating procedures hunting Ivans. Instead, we go looking for a private yacht called Unicorn; but, we have to call it FruitCake and when we find it, send messages on a special VHF radios to the other yachts with the nutty Christmas names."

"Whatever is going on, Greg, it's highly classified and has top priority. Sorry I can't answer your questions, partner, but look at it this way, the pay is the same, the weather's great, we have all four fans running and we get to play in San Juan, so we do our thing and ask questions later, o.k.?"

"Yeah, I guess." Tombline leaned back in his seat and rested his head against the headrest. "I guess it could be worse, our code name is Peter-Pan, we could have been called Dumbo. Boy, I'm not letting Captain Blackfoot's crew off the hook on that one and I am going to like calling them up, hey Dumbos." Tombline began to laugh. "Do you want to hear something funny, Lank? I asked Bill Coats yesterday before he left for St. Croix if he ever saw the movie Dumbo? He said he didn't think it had come to any of the theaters around San Jose yet."

Parker laughed. "Ya know, he probably doesn't realize that the movie was first shown in 1943, or 44. It's probably older than his father."

"Hey, we're at angels five, level off and take us around the backside of those thunderheads."

"Roger that, Commander."

The young officer rolled the P-3 out and leveled off again, flying almost due west. After making trim adjustments, he brought the aircraft to a new heading. Commander Parker read through his orders. They were to scout the southern coasts of Puerto Rico, the Dominican Republic and Haiti to locate and report on the position of the motor yacht, Unicorn. The yacht had been spotted earlier that morning by an Air Force U-2 southwest of Haiti. Once the Unicorn was located, Parker would contact Guantanamo communications center using his code name, Peter-Pan and report the yacht's position, speed and course. At 1800 hours, Parkers radio operator was to start doing radio checks using the special VHF "hopper" radio to locate the other mission vessels.

Parker decided to climb to higher altitudes for a better view of the weather, it was clear but hazy. They passed fifteen miles south of the popular port city of Ponce, partially covered in low clouds. Directly ahead, the large island of Hispaniola.

"Hey, Gary, do you have those photos of the yacht handy?"

Lieutenant JG, Gary Wells, TACO (Tactical Air Coordinator Officer) appeared with a large brown envelope and handed it to Parker. He opened the flap and pulled out four black and white 8 by 10 photographs of a luxury yacht taken at different angles. He glanced at them and handed them to Tombline.

"That is the Fruitcake, Lieutenant," Parker said.

Tombline studied the photos. "It says here, on the back of these pictures and on this memo, that the yacht is one-hundred and twenty four feet in length. Jesus, that may be a small target for us, but that's a lot of fucking ship for a private yacht."

Parker laughed. "Trouble with you, Greg, you're from Kansas, you're not used to seeing these boys with their big toys."

"She shouldn't be to hard to pick out, Commander. They told you at briefing that she was already spotted by Air Force earlier around Haiti's west end?"

"Yeah. The way I figure, according to Air Force coordinates." Parker reached down and picked up a chart that was folded and stuck between his seat and the console. He continued. "I figure she should be somewhere between Jacmel and Grand Gosier when we arrive there, say about 1445. They will be running out here, maybe forty miles to pass this point of land here called Cabo Beata." Parker put his finger on a small peninsular on the south coast of Dominica.

"Roger that, sir. but it looks like we are going to run into some weather ahead."

"Yeah, I just hope we can get down and get a good visual. Air Force said she's doing around fifteen knots.

Altitude, 12,000 feet
56 miles southeast of Port Au Prince, Haiti
1447 Hours

"Commander, we have a number of targets, seven to be exact in the immediate area, but I think we have your fancy yacht 35 miles northwest, bearing three-one-two degrees. Speed fourteen knots, on a heading one-zero-two degrees. Thirty-two miles south of Jacmel."

"Thanks, Lieutenant." Parker sat up in his chair and made adjustments to his shoulder harness. "O.k., Greg, let's go down and take a peek."

Parker pushed his intercom button, "Captain to crew. We are descending to six thousand, buckle up and secure your equipment, we have some tumblers coming up. O.k. Greg, here is where you earn your pay, it's all yours."

Tombline took the wheel with his right hand and placed his left hand on the four engine control levers. He applied right rudder and rolled the control wheel to the right. The P-3 responded with ease. When he reached the heading of three-one-five degrees, he rolled back, leveled off and began to descend, applying elevator trim, nose down, while bringing back power settings, bleeding off the increasing airspeed.

A thousand feet ahead and rushing up to meet him were thick gray clouds that would soon turn the warm sun filled cockpit into a cool dark dungeon. For the next ninety-five seconds, the Orion would be tossed around like a leaf in the wind. The crew would be praying that all the black and gray boxes mounted on rubber washers throughout the cabin would stay on their shelves, along with the heavy TV monitors. In the cockpit, six hands were busy holding onto flight controls, engine and prop levers, while three pairs of eyes were scanning vibrating instruments watching for warning lights and all ears were listening to the groans and creaks of the airframe, praying they wouldn't hear the sound of metal tearing away.

At fifty four hundred feet, the Orion broke out of the darkness and into a new world of pale grays, above and below them. They were between cloud layers in a light rain flying level and in relatively smooth air.

"Where is she now, Lieutenant Wells?"

"Ah, about seventeen miles behind us, sir, moving on the same heading."

"I've got it, Greg," Parker took the controls. "We're going to head west for a little while and let this weather move out. It's clearing behind us, so we'll come back and see if we can get that visual on Unicorn."

"Ensign Phelps?"

"Yes, Commander?"

"Contact Guantanamo, confirm our contact with Fruit Cake and give them the position report. Tell them, no visual yet. Remember, we are.. Peter Pan. If they ask any questions, or don't recognize your code, get me on the horn."

"Roger, Commander."

Navy A/C 15216 continued west at its cruising altitude of 12,000 feet. About forty miles west of Haiti over the Jamaica Channel, Parker was about to bring his plane back on a easterly course when his headset came alive.

"Commander, we have company. Two bogies coming in fast from three o'clock high position, about twelve miles and closing at 500 plus."

"Roger that," Parker confirmed in a cool voice.

Tombline was searching to the north out his side windows.

"Got anything, Greg?"

"Not yet."

"I'm going to turn into them, keep your eyes open." Parker dropped the starboard wing and rolled the P-3 into a steep turn. When he reached his new heading of 090 degrees, he rolled out and leveled off at 9000 feet.

"They went south right over us, Commander. They are ten miles out and turning left. They are definitely coming back, sir. Looks like they are going to turn into us and give us a look see on the starboard side. Yep, that's what they're doing."

"Sir, I've got 'em," Wells reported as he looked out of the surveillance window over the starboard wing. "Looks like a pair of MIG 21's."

"The Lieutenant is right, sir. I see 'em. They are two Cuban Air Force MIG 21's, both Fishbeds, C series. They should be right outside your window, Lieutenant Tombline."

"Yep, they're here," Tombline responded.

"Ah, Wells, look in my flight bag, the old canvas one, in the head. There's a white plastic bag inside, take it out and bring it up to me, fast."

Lieutenant Wells stepped behind Commander Parker and handed him the small white shopping bag. Parker reached in and brought out three rubber masks. He threw one over on Tombline's lap, and handed one to Lieutenant Wells. "Put them on," Parker commanded.

Tombline pulled the heavy rubber mask down over his head and adjusted the two holes for his eyes. He looked over at his commander. He had converted himself to Richard Nixon. Wells was Ronald Reagan, and Parker was John Kennedy.

Parker reached down and engaged the auto pilot. He came out of his seat and the three of them found a place in the cockpit windows looking out at their uninvited guests. The two Cuban pilots were in formation flying about twenty yards ahead of the starboard wing.

"Boy, them 21's are sure big and ugly, Commander," Wells commented.

"Yeah, and they look pretty ragged, just look at all those oil and fuel stains running under their bellies," Tombline said."

"Hold on a second, guys. Let's see just how bright these two jocks are," Parker announced. He reached over to the center console, took all four throttles and brought the power off slowly. The two MIGs crept ahead and had to use their spoilers to slow down. About the time they were in position again, Parker reached up and increased the throttles and air speed. The MIGs drifted back and had to throttle up to get abreast again.

The outside MIG suddenly climbed and did a slow roll over the top of the P-3, and took position off the port wing. Parker hurried over to his seat, sat down and started to wave to the young pilot.

"I've got it," Parker yelled. He added some right rudder and dropped the left wing, slipping the P-3 into a port skid, closing on the MIG. When the MIG pilot reacted and banked away, Parker immediately rolled back to a starboard skid and forced the other MIG to break off. When the two MIGs came back to position, they were greeted by three middle finger, birds.

Unknown to the three Presidential characters on the flight deck, the Cuban pilots were interested in what they thought was a strange pink balloon appearing in the portside window over the wing. It was actually Petty Officer Larry Steiner's big pink bare ass.

The two MIGs broke off, went to afterburners, climbed and headed north across the channel towards Cuba.

The rubber masks came off and laughter filled the cabin.

"Can you imagine what those two pilots are going to tell their comrades when they get back to their base?" Parker remarked.

"When did you think about pulling off this caper, Commander?" Wells asked.

"Oh, when I was told I would be coming back here on this mission, I guess. It's something a few of us old Neptune pilots thought about doing for years, but never pulled it off. Last October, my oldest girls had a costume party on Halloween, and, well, the masks were sorta hanging around the girls room, and..."

"Commander? Do your daughters know where you are? And what you do for a living?"

At 1745, Commander Parker called the mission off because of weather and headed back to San Juan. They could not get a visual due to low cloud cover, but were certain they had their target on radar. Unknown to Parker and his crew, at 1614 hours, they and the Unicorn were photographed from seventy-thousand feet by infra red cameras. The SR-7l's mission films at that very minute, were being developed at Laughlin Air Force Base, Del Rio, Texas and within the hour Washington would be notified that the Unicorn was still on course and on schedule.

At 1850 hours, forty three miles south west of the San Juan Airport, Commander Parker ordered Chief Petty Officer Larry Steiner to activate the VHF hopper radio and start sending Peter-Pan radio checks to any vessels in the area. After a dozen calls, Steiner was about to shut down the radio, when he received a weak, but clear response.

"Peter-Pan, Peter-Pan, this is Red Sleigh, Red Sleigh. How do you copy?"

"Red Sleigh, this is Peter-Pan, read you loud and clear. What's your position? Over."

"Five miles north of Frederiksted, departing for Christmas Party at 1600 hours, Yuletide close by, do you copy?"

"Roger, Red Sleigh. Peter Pan is heading for the barn, Dumbo on standby at 1900. Peter Pan, Out."

Steiner switched to intercom and called his Commander.

"Commander Parker, I just raised the Red Sleigh over at St. Croix. He was rather weak and told me he was leaving at 1600 hours, that Yuletide is close by and will be heading for the Christmas Party."

"O.K. Steiner, got it, good work." Commander Parker looked at his watch. According to plan, Dumbo should be just about to take off over in St. Croix for their eight hour patrol. He reached inside the damp chest pocket of his flight suit, and pulled a small notebook out. He began to thumb through its pages. He stopped and studied the list of yachts involved in the mission. 1. "Sonar", a Navy minesweeper, code named Red Sleigh, commanded by Captain John Lind. 2. "Island Drummer", a seventy-five foot ketch rigged sailing yacht code name "Yuletide" commanded by Captain Phil Avery. 3. "Seaduce", a seventy-two foot ketch rigged sailing yacht code name "Music Box." commanded by Captain Rick Van Wagner. 4. "Unicorn", a one hundred and twenty-four foot Feadship motor yacht code named "Fruitcake", commander Cuban unknown. "Christmas-Party" Point of down range rendezvous for Red Sleigh, Yuletide and the Music Box. This location to be determined when course of Unicorn is finalized on December 23rd..

He went to the back page where he had written. "Mission contacts." Commander Bentley G. Cummings, mission operations officer, Central Command Strike Headquarters, McDill AFB, Tampa. 813 555 0045. Mission Communications Office, Miami, Florida. Lou Bollman. 305 555 8990, 555 8779.

Parker closed the notebook and returned it to his pocket. He looked out ahead at the dark shadows that covered the valleys through the mountains as sun rays caught the higher mountain tops The glowing lights of San Juan reflected off the clouds in the distance. A cruise ship, with its strings of white flickering lights above its superstructure could be seen far out to sea.

"Time to check in, Commander."

"Yeah, go ahead Greg, the pattern looks pretty quiet, maybe we will get lucky and be able to go straight in. Request a right hand approach anyway, we'll stay west of the city."

"Roger." Tomline responded. "San Juan Approach, this is Navy 165 inbound, twenty miles southwest, descending through five thousand, requesting landing instructions."

St. Croix Airport
St. Croix, USVI

1802 Hours

Captain William J. Blackfoot moved the four throttles forward and locked them. He released the brakes and the P-3C Orion, A/C 152171, weighing nearly 670 tons began to move down runway 9. Sitting in the co-pilot seat, Lieutenant Bill Coates reached up with his left hand, secured the throttles and called off the airspeed numbers.

Two minutes into the flight, Captain Blackfoot banked the P-3C to starboard and came around to a two-eight-five heading, which took him directly over Frederiksted. He would head his plane to the southern coast of

Puerto Rico and follow the flight plan that Peter Pan had flown earlier. His orders were to locate the Unicorn, record and report its position. His radio operator was to begin broadcasting radio checks immediately after take-off and locate any of the mission's vessels.

At the cruise ship pier in Frederiksted, Captain John Lind was calling out engine commands to his helmsman as the Sonar moved slowly towards the huge pier on her starboard side. Two black men were standing on the dock waiting to catch the docklines from Sonar's crewmen standing on the forward and aft decks.

Lind's attention was suddenly disturbed as he heard the sound of a large propeller driven aircraft overhead. He looked up and caught the underside of the Lockheed P-3 as it headed westward into the sunset. He knew it was one of the two P-3's that would be watching out over him for the next couple of days, and that made him feel good. His special VHF radio was off and he did not hear the first radio check being sent out from Dumbo. His thoughts were on docking his ship.

"All engines, reverse," Lind called out from his starboard bridge rail.

"All engines reverse, sir," Pete Corrigan yelled, as he reached up and brought the two large steel clutch levers back into the reverse position.

The Sonar began to shake and vibrate as the two huge bronze propellers attempted to stop the forward motion of the old mine sweeper.

"A little more throttle, Peter my boy, a little more throttle," Lind demanded.

Corrigan reached up and opened the two throttles to increase the speed of the props. Sonar was not slowing down as fast as Lind wanted, the pier was coming in fast on the starboard quarter.

"Give it hell, Peter."

Corrigan opened both throttles to full travel. The Sonar shook and rattled harder. The waters at the stern were so churned up by the prop wash it looked like the stern was coming up out of the water.

Sonar hit the pilings with a thunderous crash and bounced off. Sounds of splintering wood and cracking timbers were painful to Lind's ears.

"Engines neutral," Lind yelled. "Get those lines up," was his next command. "Jackson, get two springs on this tub, and get up there and check those two assholes on the dock, make sure they secured those lines. After they saw this docking, they probably tied our lines in square knots."

"Sorry about that, Skipper," Corrigan murmured as he began to shut down the two engines.

"Not your fault, Pete. This old tub skates like a surfboard. What we need is more fuel on board, we need weight, we're too damn light, but we need the speed.   Crazy O'Brien wants this tub to maintain at least fifteen knots tomorrow."

Lind was about to go below when he noticed the mooring lines had gone slack, and Sonar was no longer against the pier. The current was pulling her out.

"Johnson, Williams, O'Leary. Where the fuck are you? Get on these lines up here before we drift back to San Juan."

Yacht Haven Marina's Fuel Dock
St. Thomas, USVI

Tuesday, December 22nd
1630 Hours

Avery and Buckwheat checked the dock lines while Gail helped the dock-boy bring the heavy fuel hose over to the port side filler.

"Gail, you'd better collect the ladies and head up to the market. I'll go up to Charter Services and advise them we are heading out at noon tomorrow for St. Maarten. Buckwheat, you check out the engines and make sure we have plenty of spare oil, and check all the fresh water tanks. As soon as you're finished, meet me at the ships store, and we will go over our want list."

"What about Don and Jack, Phil? Are they staying on board?"

"Yeah, they're fine, ah, Buckwheat, you stay with that young man and make sure he tops both tanks, we don't have any tankers out there and we will be eating up the juice tomorrow."

"Sure, Phil, you get going, I'll catch up with you."

Charter Services Clearing House

"Hello, is Cathy around?"

The young black receptionist responded, "No, Cathy is at a meeting in town and won't be back until tomorrow. Is there anything I can do?"

"Yes, I'm Captain Avery, can you give her a message?"

"Of course." She picked up a pen and began to write on a small white note pad.

"Ah, tell her Captain Avery, yacht Island Drummer came by to advise her we will be leaving tomorrow with our charter, we are going direct to St. Maarten."

"Is this a float plan, Captain?"

"Ah, yes, and I will call in on the radio when we are clearing the harbor tomorrow and give you our ETA."

"That's fine, Captain, you have a safe trip."

"Thanks, I'll just pick up my mail now, thanks again."

Avery went over to the pigeon hole mail boxes, and found the box marked "Drummer". There were a couple of printed flyers, A bill from Hertz and a letter for Gail. It was a plain white envelope, with no senders name, just a post office box in Sarasota, Florida. Avery studied the letter as he walked over to the telephone bank. He slipped it into his pocket, lifted the receiver of the pay phone and dialed for the operator.

"Yes, operator, I would like to make a credit card call to the States. Yes I will hold." Avery dreaded these next few minutes, as he would be talking to his offices and he expected the worst. Much to his surprise, it turned out that both offices were doing fine without him, with one exception, his friend Ray Bergy had quit the Immokalee job and Sam Levin had taken over the operation.

Avery went down to the ships store, which was about to close and ran around with Buckwheat buying last minute items they would need including four sets of slickers. The charter guests had not thought to bring foul weather gear.

It took fifteen minutes for Phil to get his crew together, get the Drummer's engines started and move away from the fuel dock. He took the Drummer out in the harbor and found a nice secluded area away from the marina, and dropped the anchor.

It was decided that the entire crew take the dinghy to Gregory's East restaurant for their last dinner together in St. Thomas. It was midnight before Avery was able to get everyone back on board. An hour later, the last cabin light went out. Everyone was in their bunks except Gail and Phil Avery, who decided to sit on deck for a while.

"Wow, I need a drink, can I get you something, Gail?"

"No, unless you know a good lawyer?"

"What's up? Something to do with the letter I gave you today? It's from Carlton, isn't it?"

"Yes, it's from Carlton and it's good news and bad news, which do you want first?"

"C'mon, no games, he ain't coming back here is he?"

"No, Phil, it's over for us. He is convinced that I am down here because this is the life I really want and more important, the men are here that I would rather be screwing, to put in his own words."

"So much for the good news, what's the bad?"

"The bad news, Carlton has gotten religion. He told his wife about me and she forgave him. It probably cost him a new Jaguar, or a face lift. Anyhow, she wants blood, and wants me out of Sarasota. He says he plans to do it, one way or another."

"Gail, you're not leaving Sarasota, unless you want to. Personally, I never did like the man, but you knew that. I always felt you could do better."

Gail stood up turned and stepped out of the cockpit and up on the aft cabin roof. She leaned against the mizzen mast, head down, facing away from Avery. He knew she was crying. He wanted to go to her, but felt she needed to cry it out. Nothing he could say was going to heal her wounds, he had seen her go through this before.

Avery went below, mixed a double rum and coke, drank it down, then mixed another. He went to his stateroom, stripped down, fell across his bunk and listened. A few minutes later, Gail came down the stairs and he heard her stateroom door close. Now, he thought, he could get some sleep. Then he remembered it was December 23rd, departure day, the day when he would challenge the Unicorn. Would he actually see Fidel Castro? What will it be like out there in twenty two hours? Maybe it would rain, maybe a storm would come in. Maybe Unicorn had a mechanical problem and headed back. Maybe Seaduce wouldn't show up, maybe, maybe.

Avery got up and turned on the cabin lights to find his cigarettes. Two minutes later, with another rum in his hand, he went back up to the Drummer's cockpit. The sky was as black as the water. He watched the headlights of a car speeding along the main road that ran along the waterfront. He began to think about the mission again. "What is it going to be like? Will the Unicorn take the bait and stop. Would he be able to hold their attention long enough for the Navy Seals to attach their deadly explosives?"

Thirty seven miles south, tied to a long pier, another man sat alone on his ship looking into the same black waters and cloudless black sky. He too had a glass of spirits in his hand watered down from the melting ice. The only light on his face came from the security light on the end of the long pier. The only sound he heard was the slapping of water between the steel hull and the dock pilings. Like Phil Avery, this man was thinking about his life and the lives of many around him and how the next twenty four hours could change them for ever. Like Phil Avery, Dan O'Brien's eyes would not close and would see the first light of dawn.

414

Aboard the yacht Seaduce
English Harbour, Antigua, W.I.

Wednesday, December 23rd
0315 Hours

The gurgling sound of the small exhaust pipe expelling gasses and water was irritating Rick Van Wagner as he skillfully maneuvered through the large fleet of yachts moored in the peaceful harbor. He was trying hard not to disturb his fellow sailors and grateful that the long narrow hull of the Seaduce produced only a slight ripple as she glided towards the entrance of the harbor.

Paul Gransaull, who had been standing on the bowsprit since he hauled in and secured the heavy plow anchor, walked quietly along the teak deck.

"Not a creature is stirring, not even a drunk," Gransaull remarked in a whisper as he stepped into the cockpit.

"Hard to believe, it's only two more days to Christmas, isn't it, Paul?"

"Yeah. Don't seem right, Captain Rick. But, you know? I have to hand it to the people on this island, they have the real Christmas spirit. They know how to make the season bright and cheerful, don't they? Just goes to show you don't need mittens, icicles, snow drifts, fireplaces and Budweiser horses running through the snow pulling a sleigh loaded with beer to make Christmas official."

The Seaduce passed under the historic walls of Fort Berkeley at the harbor's west entrance. Van Wagner increased the throttle and the engine responded. Gransaull looked back over his shoulder at the peaceful harbor setting. Anchor lights swayed gently at the tips of the tall masts. A glow from a match or cigar lighter flickered and disappeared in the distance. He looked up to the crest of hills on the east side of the harbor. He could barely make out the outline of the small stone building on Shirley Heights. "A special place with a special woman," he thought, as visions of Karen became alive in his mind.

"Better get down and check on our guests, Paul. I told them to take a Bonine before they crashed last night. Just make sure they're not moving around. We are going to be getting into swells in a few minutes. Make sure everything is nailed down."

"Right. Oh, by the way, what was the weather report you got from that skipper on that schooner last night?"

"Oh, nothing to be concerned about. We may get lucky. There are two highs taking care of us right now. One north of the Bahamas and one down

415

around Barbados. Only bad stuff, a low pressure system out west heading east for Jamaica. We will probably see some choppy seas out there today, may even get a few showers later. The good news, we are going to have a tail wind all the way out to the rendezvous. We need to keep this lady up to and over hull speed for the next seventeen hours or so. If we have to lighten up later, we'll strip her down and deep six everything that isn't holding the bottom on."

"I'll go check the guests. Want some coffee?"

"Yeah, that would really help right now. Listen, I'll keep the helm till 0500. You come back and take the next shift. Now, fetch me a coffee with a wee bit of Irish Cream, lad. Then you had better put your dreams away for a couple of hours. This is going to be a long day."

"Yeah, and to think, this is the last voyage of this grand old yacht. It seems a disgrace to destroy her, doesn't it?"

"Yeah, they don't make these anymore. Oh, before you go, bring up that Rube Goldberg speaker you put together and let's see if it's going to work. Put the VHF on, that new one with the hopper in case they may be trying to check in with us."

Gransaull placed the small teak box on the cockpit seat, went down and turned on the radio. It began to crackle, the first sign that it was working. This meant that they could hear any messages topside, without disturbing the sleeping guests below.

"Well?" Gransaull asked from the companionway.

"It's crackling, so it must be working."

Gransaull left the coffee on the lounge seat next to Van Wagner, and disappeared down below.

The Seaduce passed through the harbor entrance, and Van Wagner set his course. His first heading would be 268 degrees, which would take him to the island of Redona, some twenty seven miles ahead. He estimated his time of arrival around 0630, near daybreak. He would sail north of Redona, leaving the island of Nevis to the northwest, then change course to 260 degrees, checking his drift every two hours. He estimated that they would reach their intercept point with "Solar" (Red Sleigh) at 2030 hours. If all went well, this would put the Seaduce about fifteen miles north of the interception point between the Unicorn and the Island Drummer.

For the first time since he accepted the assignment, he began to question his own abilities. Did he leave with enough time to make his intercept? What if the Unicorn got there earlier than estimated? How soon would he have communications with Dumbo, or Peter-Pan? The radar, they hadn't checked the radar since they left St. Thomas. He looked down at the large compass on the top of the varnished steerage box, it read that Seaduce was on a heading of 260 degrees.

Unicorn
Muertos Trough
72 Miles south of Isla Sanona, Dominican Republic

December 23
0745 hours

Fidel Castro stepped out of his cabin onto the busy bridge. Captain DeTorre was leaning over a chart table. Cabino Varas was at the helm and Gayo Rodriguez was drinking a cup of coffee and watching two radar screens. Before anyone noticed his presence, Castro decided the blinding sun coming directly through the bridge windows was too strong for his eyes and he returned to his cabin to look for his sun glasses.

The portside bridge door slid open and Dimitri Sorokin stepped in. He was wearing a gray sweat suit and a baseball cap.

"Good morning, comrade," DeTorre said as he smiled at Sorokin. "Sleep well?"

"Not really, Captain. I'm still having trouble getting use to the vibrations. Is there something out of alignment, maybe a damaged prop or bent shaft?"

"Possibly, Comrade, but I think the major cause of the vibrations during most of the night was our helmsman, Antonio Lopez. He decided he would change the engine rpm's, he said they did not sound right and he put them out of synch, they even woke me up," DeTorre laughed.

Sorokin stepped over to the chart table. "Just where are we, Captain?"

"We are right here, a little over seventy miles from the Isla Sanona." DeTorre put his pencil point on the point of land so designated on the chart. "We are about twenty six hours from our island, and we have good news, especially for comrade Lo's sensitive stomach. The weather is going to be perfect all the way. We will have some seas to deal with later and some headwind, but this magnificent machine will keep you as comfortable as if you were in your car."

"Ha, that's not saying much, Comrade. My car needs new shocks."

Castro came back onto the bridge.

"Good morning, comrade President," Captain DeTorre yelled, and came to attention.

417

"Good morning, gentlemen. Dimitri, my friend, you slept well?"

"Ah, no, but that's alright, I will nap later."

Castro looked around the spacious cabin, then walked up to the large window looking out over the bow. The sun was strong and the windows were covered with salt spray.

"Captain, you should have one of your men clean these windows, they are terrible," Castro said as he ran his finger across the glass. "This is from smoking, this is cigar residue."

"Could be, sir, I will get the windows cleaned today."

"How are we doing on time, Captain?"

"Very good, Comrade President. We have increased our speed by two knots since yesterday, however, we may lose some headway later when we get into heavier head winds and larger swells."

"Has anyone checked on Mr. Lo?"

"Yes, Comrade President, I did," Gayo announced. "I brought him some coffee around 0700. He was doing better, but he still won't come out of his cabin. Ah, it is rather messy in there too, it smells bad, sir."

"We have to get him out of there, I want to have a meeting with him before noon and Dimitri, I want you there too."

Dimitri nodded yes.

"How do I call General Vincetta on this thing?"

"Let me show you, sir." DeTorre pushed down the selection button for the General's state room and handed Castro the telephone receiver.

"Comrade, what are you doing? Come up to the bridge and learn something. Captain DeTorre wants you to do your part today and run this fine ship. You have what?"

Castro put the receiver down on its cradle and started laughing. "Looks like we have two cabins that we may have to burn when this trip is over. General Vincetta can't get off his little white pot and would appreciate someone could bring him some black coffee and toilet paper."

Terre-de-Haut, Isles Des Saintes
December 23rd
0815 Hours

The tiny, but popular island of Terre-de-Haut was beginning to come alive. The beauty of the island lay in its steep hills and deep valleys, surrounded by peaceful bays and beautiful beaches. In the small settlement, Bourg De Saintes, the clean red roofed houses were like post card photographs. On the north end of the town called Mouillage, there were a number of handsome villas. An American, named Thomas Porter (Puros) rented one of these villas for his wife and four other members of her family. They had arrived in Guadeloupe on the afternoon of December 20th. The three couples had toured the main island, shopped in Point A Pitre, did some diving on Terre-de-Bas and explored the small uninhabited island of Grand Islet.

Puros made a deal with a local fisherman and chartered one of his sturdy wooden fishing boats with a small Honda outboard motor.

On the morning of December 22nd, Puros, Marcel Belisteri and Carlos Mesa took the boat to Grand Islet. They hiked up to the highest point on the island, which was located on the southern most tip. They were five hundred and fifty feet above the clear sandy bottom cove where the meeting between Fidel Castro and his guests would take place.

Puros removed a portable Sony radio/tape deck entertainment center out of his canvas backpack. It looked like any other store bought appliance, but this one has been rigged with a special VHF Transmitter-transceiver and set on a special fixed channel, so it could be used to talk with the Unicorn and the Bertram sport fishing yacht. Puros plugged in the small hand mike and tested the frequency. There was no response, nor did he did not expect one, contact was hours away. He was told that the radio would have a range of fifteen to twenty miles on fully charged batteries.

Belisteri had taken the field glasses out of his small back pack and scanned around the island. They had the perfect view. He could see the two sister islands of Terre de Bas and Terre de Haut. Most important, he could monitor all the waters around the islands, including the southern end of Guadeloupe. They had learned that the area around the Isles De Saints would be swarming with tourists on Christmas Day. Hundreds of boats would be moving about the islands, especially around the main island of Guadeloupe, about five to six miles north of them.

The trio decided that they had best plan on coming back to their lookout early on the morning of the 24th and to look as if they were camping out. They had brought a small tent, and would buy some large beach towels should anyone fly over, they wanted to look like tourists camping out.

"Who is that?" Carlos whispered.

Puros and Belisteri turned around and saw the figure of a white man standing below them about one hundred yards away on the path back to the beach and to their boat.

"Give me those glasses," Puros ordered.

Carlos handed him the binoculars.

"He may be just a tourist, he is very pale and young. Looks American to me."

"Anyone else with him, Tomas?"

"No, unless they are down by the beach. He is heading back down now. He has a pair of binoculars around his neck, or it may be a camera."

"What do you think, Tomas?" Marcel asked.

"I think we should go back to the villa, get drunk and fuck the brains out of those beautiful women, no?"

Carlos and Marcel both laughed as they picked up the back packs and dusted them off. Puros did not laugh; he kept his eyes on the tall stranger as he disappeared below the crest of the hill.

After docking their boat in the small fishing harbor, the three men headed back to the villas. Puros took one of the scooters they rented and went around to the airport road. He noted that a twin-engine Cessna 441 Conquest was sitting on the north end of the field. Someone in a white mechanic's uniform was working on the port engine. There was another man sitting in the cockpit. He moved up closer so he could see the large numbers on the side of the fuselage. They were the right numbers, HH 0030 Z. The aircraft was painted light beige with orange and dark brown trim stripes. It was the plane he was waiting for, although it was not the aircraft that was originally described to him. He was expecting a Beechcraft twin, however, the phony registration numbers did match. He decided to wait until later in the evening to come back and talk to the pilots.

Instead of returning to the villa, Puros decided to have a look around the waterfront shops in Bourge Des Saints. He stopped at the ferry dock where he met the fisherman who rented him the boat. After a short conversation, the fisherman told Puros of an American who had inquired about him and his friends. The American also rented a boat. The old man told Puros that the American was staying out at the LeBois Joli Hotel, a little over a mile west of the village.

Admiral Koster's Office
The Pentagon, Washington, D.C.

December 23rd
1034 Hours

The small buzzer on the telephone rang. The Admiral took off his glasses, wiped his eyes, then picked up the phone.

"Yes, I will have another coffee, thank you, Ms. Knowles."

"You had your limit today, sailor-boy. Mr. Billings is on line one, and I will get you a half a cup."

"Ah, you're a angel. While I talk to Billings, please try and get me Admiral Mac. He is supposed to be down at Sixth Fleet HQ this morning."

"Yes, sir."

Koster leaned back into his high-back leather chair and pushed the speaker phone button down. "Morning, Ian. Have you got something for me?"

"Yes, but you're not going to like it."

"Shoot."

"Last week, we received a report from our New Orleans office that one of our favorite Cuban expatriates was getting somewhat active. On Thursday, he quit his job at a shipbuilding company, drew out some savings and drove down to Grand Isle. He came back with a young lady, put her up at a motel near the airport. On Friday the 18th, he left home, picked up the little lady, then boarded a Delta to Atlanta, changed planes and ended up in Miami. He stayed at the Miami International Inn, left the next morning on a Eastern to San Juan and we lost him there."

"So? What has he got to do, ah, what did you say his name was?"

"I didn't, sir. His name is Tomas Puros, one of Castro's old time friends and trouble makers. He has been doing many favors for the Cuban Government in the past five years, mostly down in Panama and Nicaragua. We continually keep close tabs on him."

"You think maybe he is tied into the Yuletide operation?"

"We know he is, Admiral. We played a hunch and found him, his lady and four other friends two males and two females in Guadeloupe."

"Well, that sounds a bit interesting," Koster said as he moved up closer to his desk. He reached over and put the phone on private and lifted the receiver.

"I sent a man down and he arrived in Guadeloupe Saturday afternoon. He already located Puros and his friends and has them under surveillance. I will be hearing from him again tonight around 1800 hours."

"Why do you think this Puros is there, Ian?"

"Oh, maybe just as security, I really don't know."

"What about his associates, who are they? Are they some of the drug people that Castro is meeting?"

"Ah I doubt it, however, they did come in from Venezuela. They are all staying at a villa on one of the islands south of Guadeloupe, Terre de

Haut. It may be some time before we know who they are, sir, my man is trying to get photos of them."

"Your man, is he on the same island too?"

"Yes, Admiral. He's made plans with a private pilot to charter a Cessna tomorrow on Guadeloupe. He wants to fly around and scout the area, especially the island where the meeting is to take place."

"Good, Ian, that's good. We need to know what this Puros is up to. Does your man know what is taking place down there? I mean, did you tell him?"

"No, sir. He was told to report on all of Puros' movements, that's all."

"Are you going to advise the French authorities?"

"No, sir, that would be risky, Admiral. We don't want to be tipping our hand. We would have to explain to them that we are down there doing surveillance on possible drug suspects. We don't need the French getting involved and definitely don't want them to know that we have agents on their soil."

"Of course," Koster interrupted. "Good work, Ian. Keep me posted. Ah, call me at home tonight with that report when it comes in."

"Yes, sir. By the way, how are things going so far?"

"Well, I decided took the Air Force off the detail after this afternoon's sortie. We won't need the Blackbirds, unless weather becomes a factor. I have decided to use only the P-3's we have flying cover for the mission. They have all the electronic equipment needed to find and track Castro and if they are seen, no one cares, they're a familiar sight down there. This way they can report directly to O'Brien, plus it's a hell of a lot cheaper."

"It's hard to believe, Admiral, that in the next forty- eight hours one of this country's most infamous enemies could be erased off the planet by a small group of mostly civilian volunteers."

"Yes, scary isn't it?" Admiral Koster hung up his phone. He stood up, stretched and walked over to the chart table. He took his finger and put it on the island of Guadeloupe, then found the small cluster of islands called Des Saintes. There was a red pin stuck in the smaller of the three islands.

He looked up at a small yellow paper that was pinned to the chart with the Unicorn's last reported coordinates. Another red pin was located on a route line that O'Brien had given him. He looked at his watch. He should be getting an update in the next half hour from McDill.

The intercom buzzed again. He ignored it, knowing that in less than ten seconds Ms. Knowles would come bursting through the door to see if he was still alive and breathing. The large door opened and the concerned woman appeared searching the large room. When she saw the him, Koster could see the relief on her face.

"Admiral, I have Admiral McKenzie on the line and Admiral Halprin's office just called to inform you that his ETA at Guantanamo is 1940 tonight."

Koster looked down at the silver pocket watch he was holding in his hand. "Seven seconds, not bad pretty lady, you're getting better."

"I beg your pardon?" she said with a warm smile. "I'll practice more, sir. These sixty-two year old gams don't fly like they use to."

Koster headed for his desk. He gave his trusted secretary a wink. "They were never designed to fly, madam, like two fast destroyers, they were designed to look sleek and stay in shape."

Care De La Marine, Bourge Des Saintes
Terre De Haut

December 23
1235 Hours

Tomas Puros handed Julie a fifty dollar bill. She leaned over and kissed him gently on the forehead. His hand slid up under her cotton cover up and his fingers worked under the tight fitting swim suit until his hand held the firm roundness of her buttock. "Buy something nice. Where are you going?"

"Just across the street," she responded smiling. "I told the girls I would meet them at the Mahogany Boutique."

"Is that enough money? You want more?"

Julie smiled. She grabbed his wrist and tried to push it down. Puros tightened his grip, digging his fingers into her soft flesh. Then he released her.

"I have earned more, no?"

He slapped her hard on the backside as she whirled around and headed between the surrounding tables and out the open door to the street.

"She's a tiger, Tomas, where do you find such a beauty?"

"Fishing. I went down to this place called Grand Isle, on the Gulf of Mexico with a friend. We stayed at this old fisherman's motel and next door was this great Cajun restaurant, or at least it served great Cajun food. Julie was working there. It was, as they say in New Orleans, "sex at first bite?"

Puros waved for the waiter. "You want another rum, Carlos?"

"No, I am fine."

"You, Marcel, another beer?"

"No, I will wait. What are we going to do now?"

Puros put his finger to his lips. Marcel got the message. Puros looked around. The small restaurant was crowded with tourists enjoying lunch, most of them French. What Puros was looking for was a tall young blonde man, but he was not in sight. He looked into the curious eyes of his comrades and spoke. "I have reason to believe our visitor on the island yesterday could be an American agent, most likely watching me. I thought I was being tailed out of New Orleans, but I thought I lost them in Miami."

"What do we do, Tomas?"

"I don't know yet. He can't possibly know what is going to take place tomorrow. It would be impossible for him to know about the meeting and who will be there."

"You think maybe he followed you to see what you are doing?"

"That's possible. They watch me like a hawk, all the time. He most likely has pictures of both of you by now and the girls."

Marcel laughed. "He will have a tough time getting any background on me or Carlos. He may get lucky with the whores though. Carlos's friend, Tina, mentioned she worked Vegas a few years ago, and I'm sure she has a .."

Puros interrupted. "It would be easy to eliminate him. He looks young, and not too experienced. He let himself get caught yesterday. He is also too loose with his tongue with the locals. We could take him out at his hotel, or lure him back to the island later and take care of him there," Puros said as he looked about the room again.

"Would he come to the island?"

"Oh, yes. We will invite him, Marcel. We will load up the boat, put all the gear on it and head over. He will follow. When we get there we'll set a trap and kill him. We put him in the tent and keep him there until dark. Later, we can wrap him up in the tent, take him down to the boat and deep-six him."

"His boat, what if.."

"We will bring his boat back with us and park it at the dinghy dock. It will be dark, nobody will know the difference. But we need to get the boat back. If the boat showed up missing, there would be search parties out looking and we can't afford to have that happen during the next two days."

"By the time that they discover he has not returned to his room, it will be too late, right, Tomas?" Marcel asked.

"Right. I figure, if nobody gets nosy or worried about him, it will be Christmas Day and we will be in Barbados or Caracas that night. The only thing I worry about, is he here by himself? If not, who is he reporting to, when and where?"

"Too risky, Tomas," Carlos said, shaking his head.

"Fuck him. What can he do?"

"What do you mean, Carlos?"

"I mean, we came to do a job, that was to watch over the cove, make sure this boat the Bonaire finds the damn thing. We keep an eye out for any problems and in an emergency, get our President and his people off the boats and to the airport, that's our job, let's not take any chances with this watch-dog of yours."

"You may be right, Carlos. He doesn't know what we are doing. He can't get close enough to us on the hill to hear what we are doing. We will make sure we are shielded. We can communicate from inside the tent if we have to."

"Very wise decision. We will ignore the asshole. If we have a problem, if we have an emergency and if he gets in the way, well, then we do what we have to do, is that agreed?"

"Yes, Tomas, we agree. However, maybe it's best we leave the women at the villa tomorrow. Better yet, send them over on the morning ferry to Pointe a Pitre, tell them we will meet them later at the Marché Central or the Gare Maritime. If they miss us, they can just come home on the late ferry."

"You are right, Carlos, as much as I felt they would look good for us on the island posing like tourists, if we do have a problem it's best they don't know what is going on. We will leave them behind."

Puros pushed his chair back from the table and stood up.

"Good, now, let's pay this bill and find the girls. I would like to take a swim this afternoon, how about you two?"

Carlos looked at Marcel. They both laughed.

"No my friend, we have other plans."

The three men left the restaurant, stood out in the busy street for a few minutes then started walking slowly to the villas. Edward Cameron stood in the shade of the awning outside the small boutique. He watched as Tomas Puros walked away with his arm draped over one of his companions. The three women were still inside the shop. He had no idea what to do next. He decided he should call Langley. So far, he had not seen any suspicious activity. However, he had no idea who the two friends were, or the women. The agency had not filled Cameron in on what was going to take place there in the next twenty four hours or who was involved. This information would be given to him as soon as he confirmed to Washington, that Puros was somehow connected with the arrival of Castro's yacht. He was only told to watch and report on all Puros' activities.

CHAPTER 23

Bourge Des Saintes
Terre De Haut, Iles Des Saintes

Wednesday, December 23rd
0920 Hours

Tomas Puros and his two companions, Carlos Mesa and Marcel Balisteri, left the dinghy dock in their small outboard skiff and headed west towards the small point of land called Pain De Sucre, about three quarters of a mile away, hugging the shoreline's calm waters. They brought along all the equipment and stores they would need for the long day. Their women companions had agreed to go shopping in Point-a-Pitre on the main island of Guadeloupe and would meet them later in the afternoon at La Darse, a popular market on the waterfront.

Puros guided the skiff close to shore as they headed for Pointe De Bois Joli three quarters of a mile southwest. As they passed the small cove where the Les Bois Joli Hotel was located, they did not take notice of a young man in a outboard fishing boat begin to follow them. They continued on towards their destination, Grand Islet, two miles away.

After reaching a the island, they secured their boat on a secluded sandy beach bordered by two large volcanic rock formations. They unloaded most of the gear and started the quarter mile hike to the top of the island's highest point, 550 feet above the sea. Once they reached the crest of the hill, they agreed it was the best place to set up their look out post. In a matter of minutes, they set up a small camp. Puros took out his high-powered field glasses from his back pack, stood up and began to scan the entire scene around him. It was somewhat hazy, but he could see the island of Dominica to the south nearly fifteen miles away. To the north he could easily see the two islands that make up the Isles De Saintes, and the big island of Guadeloupe. There were countless boats moving about, most of them sailboats. Due west of the island, he spotted a large passenger liner four miles out heading north. He counted three large freighters between three to five miles offshore heading southward..

"I'm going back down and get the ice chest, Tomas. Do you want me to bring up those two lanterns?"

"No, Carlos, just the ice chest. We will be leaving before dark. If we don't have any communications today, we will come up at daybreak tomorrow."

"I would be willing to stay, Tomas, if I can bring Maria up here. She would go crazy making love beneath the stars."

"She would go crazy all right, Marcel, looking for a man to make love to her."

"Fuck you, Carlos. That whore you brought here? I think she served in my old regiment in Nicaragua. Only in those days, they called her "red-balls Maria." The three men laughed loudly.

"Carlos, go get the ice chest, we need a drink."

"Si, but Marcel, you come wait for me at the top of the hill and you carry the chest up here."

Marcel shook his head, smiled and started unpacking the small tent.

Carlos worked his way down the narrow rocky path to the beach. When he reached the bottom, he had to walk around a large formation of rocks. As he came into the clearing on the beach, he noticed there were two boats pulled up on the sand. Standing off to the side of the small beach on a rock ledge was a tall blonde haired man. His back was to Carlos and he was looking through a pair of field glasses. The man was dressed in long tan trousers and short sleeved blue oxford shirt. He was barefoot, and had a camera hanging over his left shoulder, resting on his side.

Carlos walked gently towards the two boats, careful not to disturb any loose stones. He watched the man with every step. He knew who he was. He was the same young man who been watching them, the man that Puros said might be following him.

"Buenos dias, Señor," Carlos yelled out.

Startled, the man turned quickly to face Carlos. He started to lose his footing and slip down the side of the sharp rocks. After pushing off boulders and carefully choosing foot holds, he managed to get down to the beach without seriously hurting himself. He looked up at Carlos and smiled.

"Good morning, sir. You surprised me."

"Oh, I did not mean to scare you, Señor. You are not hurt, are you?"

"No, I'm fine. I left my soft shoes back at the hotel." The young American walked slowly in the hard sand towards Carlos. He realized that he had been caught. He studied Carlos as he got closer. He noted the man was short and overweight. His greasy black hair was thinning on top, with long wavy strands that touched his collar. His eyes were hidden behind reflecting sun glasses. Beneath his black bushy mustache, he had a warm, friendly smile with large white teeth.

The tall American extended his long arm to shake hands.

"Hello, my name is Bill."

Carlos shook his hand. He could see the young American was in very good physical condition, with broad shoulders and a thick wide neck. He looked to be in his thirties. His eyes were light gray and his hair sandy blonde and his face was sunburned, especially his nose and forehead.

"What brings you to this little island, ah, Bill?"

"Oh, just sight seeing. I've been coming here almost every day since I arrived. I was told there are some great iguanas on this island. I have been taking pictures of them, when I can find them."

"Yes, I noticed them, but, well, they give me the creeps. I stay away from them."

"Yeah, they are pretty ugly."

"Listen, Señor, I have two friends up on the hill setting up camp. I have good wine and cold beers over here in the ice chest. Why don't you join us for a drink?"

"Ah, no thanks. I'd better get back to my hotel. I have a young lady waiting for me, ah, she's not too adventurous. She prefers to hang out at the hotel pool, in the shade and, well, I had better start back."

"Nonsense, you must have one drink with us. Besides, I need help getting this heavy chest up these fucking cliffs, I would appreciate it, Bill."

Carlos went over to his boat, stepped in, picked up the heavy ice chest and handed it to the young man.

It took a few minutes to make the climb to the top of the hill. Marcel, sitting on a rock smoking a cigar waiting for Carlos nearly choked on the smoke when he saw the young man walking up the path with Carlos.

Carlos was quick to explain.

"Marcel, don't stand there like a frozen jackass, take the chest. My friend Bill was kind enough to help me bring it up this far."

"Hello, Marcel, is it?" The young man asked.

"Yes. Who are you?"

"His name is Bill." Carlos remarked. "Bill, you never did say your last name."

"Oh, ah, Williams, Bill Williams."

"This here is Marcel Balisteri. Our other friend, up there you see at the top of the hill? He is Tomas, Doubting Tomas."

Cameron looked up the hill. Puros was standing, hands on his hips, silhouetted against the light blue sky, looking down at him. He could not make out Puros' face, but he already knew what he looked like. Now he was actually going to meet him.

Marcel took the chest from Cameron and the three men began to walk up the hill. Puros watched as they came closer towards him. He had no idea how Carlos met the American and was trying to prepare himself. He knew that this man was tailing him and knew who he was. Now, he thought, "What have these two fools said to him?"

Carlos was the first to reach Puros. He took off his glasses so Puros could read his eyes.

"Tomas, meet my new friend, Bill Williams. He is an American."

"Oh really?" Puros said as he reached out to shake Cameron's big hand. "And where are you down from, Mr. Williams?"

"Ah, actually, High Point, North Carolina."

"Oh, yes, I know High Point. There are many furniture companies located there, isn't that right?" Puros asked as if he were testing the American.

"Yes, you could say that."

"Hey, my friends, look what I have here." Carlos opened the ice chest and took out a bottle of 1978 Pouilly Fuisse.

"Nineteen seventy eight? My God, Carlos, where did you find it?" Marcel asked.

"I brought it with us, you stupid ass. Why do you think Maria has such a wide ass when she came here, man? I had six more hanging from a special belt she wears under that big skirt."

Cameron laughed together with the three men.

Carlos opened a small cotton blanket and spread it out in front of the tent. They all sat down in a small circle in front of the tent.

"So, why are you gentlemen up here and your women back at your villas?" Cameron asked. He suddenly realized he had just made a terrible mistake. He waited for one of them to ask how he knew about the villas and the women, but the question never came.

"Oh, we sent them over to Guadeloupe on the morning ferry to do some Christmas shopping. We are going to join them later. We had some business to talk over, and wanted to sit up here and watch the boats go by and get drunk."

Carlos moved around on his hands and knees behind Cameron to get access to the ice chest. He opened it and removed a few plastic glasses. He reached down through the freezing cold chunks of ice and found the rough wooden handle of the rusty ice pick, resting on the bottom.

"I sure hope I am not interfering with your business? I will have a drink with you and then I must get back to my boat. I too have a young lady waiting at my hotel, and it's that time of day, you know? You lay down on the cool cotton sheets, the fan is turning overhead, you start to smell the fresh scent of her cologne." Suddenly the young mans voice collapsed. There were no more words, just a muffled gargle sound coming from deep down inside his open mouth. His eyes began to water as his head began to fall backwards. Just above his adams apple, a small sharp pointed object appeared surrounded by blood that trickled down his sweating neck. His arms suddenly sprang out, then fell at his side. Carlos placed his hand between the young man's shoulder blades and pushed. Cameron fell forward, his face hit the blanket and the rocky surface beneath. His nose crushed inward splattering his blood on the clean white cloth. The rotten wooden handle of the six inch ice pick was protruding out of the back of his neck, just below the skull.

Nothing was said. Puros and Marcel placed their hands under his heavy upper arms and pulled him forward into the opening of the small tent. They pushed him in the rest of the way, and dropped the tent flaps.

"Now we have to wait. Shit."

"We had to do it, Tomas, you know that?"

"No, I don't know that. Now we will never know what he does, who he works for, why he is here, and who he has been talking to."

Marcel opened the tent and worked his hands around the man's large body, looking for his pants pockets. He found no wallet. He did find seven American dollars, and sixty cents in coins and a room key to his hotel. Room 7.

"I will go to his room tonight, Tomas. Give me the key, Marcel."

"You will take the boat back too, Carlos, when we leave. Now we must think of how to get his body to the bottom of the sea," Puros said as he wiped the sweat off his brow on his shirt sleeve.

"There is line in the boat, Tomas. We can use the blanket, we can tear it in strips and tie him up."

"Good, yes. We will have to roll him in the tent and weight him down with rocks. Then we can take him out in the middle of the pass and drop him. It must be a couple of hundred feet out there. Carlos, you drop his boat off at the fishing dock where he rented it. Let's hope nobody will be looking for him until after the weekend."

"Tomas, why don't one of us call the hotel pretending to be him. We can tell them he decided to go to, ah, Dominica for a couple of days, and ask them to hold the room."

"Good, as soon as you find his belongings in the room and get his real name, that's what we will do tomorrow. Good thinking, Carlos, that will give us the time we need."

Marcel looked down at the bare foot partially sticking out of the tent. "Who do you think he really works for, Tomas?"

"CIA, FBI, it don't matter. What will matter is that when I get back to New Orleans they will be all over me. As long as Mr. Williams here keeps the fish happy, I'm safe. They can't prove anything even if he surfaces, come to think of it. Nobody has seen him with us, and as far as the French getting involved with any of these agencies, forget it. The French hate Americans, especially the government."

Puros reached over and pulled his backpack to him. He opened it up and took out the Sony radio. After plugging in the small microphone, he pulled the two telescopic antennas up and turned the radio on.

"Bonaire, Bonaire, this is Hilltop, do you copy?"

"Unicorn, Unicorn, this is Hilltop, do you copy?"

Puros picked up his field glasses again and looked to the south towards Dominica. The haze was getting heavier and the island was obscured. He looked westward and saw only a few boats passing close by, and all of them heading north. No sign of a large luxury power yacht, just sailboats and a couple of small fishing boats. He looked at his watch.

"We will check again at 1500 hours. Carlos, where are the cheese and crackers?"

"In my pack, Tomas."

The body of Edward C. Cameron, father of two sons, husband of Cecilia Cameron, Severna Park, Maryland, would be sent to the bottom of the Passe Du Sud Ouest, between the islands of Terre De Bas and Terre De Haut in 90 feet of water, and would never be recovered.

Island Drummer
Charlotte Amalie Harbor
St. Thomas, USVI

December 23rd
1205 Hours

The skies above Charlotte Amalie were overcast and the winds were gusting up to 20 mph, coming out of the southeast. Phil Avery had checked all the weather reports available to him all morning. There was no mention of any severe weather in the eastern Caribbean. The only trouble spot was a low hanging over Jamaica causing some high winds and heavy rains.

"Gail, get on the horn to Charter Services and advise them we are leaving St. Thomas at 1230 hours. Tell them we are heading to Antigua, and estimate our arrival at 1200 hours tomorrow. Tell them we are expecting calls on Christmas Day, and they should advise the callers to contact us at Nicholsons clearing house in English Harbour.

"Right, Phil. What about the jib, do you want us to roll it out?"

"Naw, not in this breeze, let's just power out of here. When you get below, ask Buckwheat to come up and take the helm for a spell, I want to check the charts."

Gail went down the companionway. Pat Brewster and Linda Star were in the galley cleaning up the lunch dishes. Jack Star was sitting on the long sofa listening to his walkman and reading a St. Thomas tourist guide. Don Brewster was not visible, neither was Buckwheat.

"Has anyone seen Commander Buckland?" she asked.

"Here I is," came a voice from the forward cabin doorway. Buckland walked into the salon with a big apple stuck in his mouth. He was in his cutoffs and an old faded Michigan State sweatshirt.

"I bet Captain Bligh wants my body topside, right?"

"You got it, baby, it's your turn to drive."

The main cabin suddenly vibrated with a demanding voice that came over the VHF radio. "Yuletide, Yuletide, Peter Pan, how do you read?"

Buckland walked over to the navigation station and picked up the mike on the special hopper VHF radio. "Peter Pan, this is Yuletide, read you loud and clear, over."

"Yuletide, the Music Box is almost half way to the party. Fruit Cake may be running a little late. Will have new invitation coming from Dumbo at 1500. No word from Red Sleigh, can you deliver his present?"

"Roger that, Peter Pan, we copy, out."

Buckland hung the small mike on its clip, turned and looked into Gail's expressionless face. "Well, all our guys are on schedule, well, all but Captain Lind. I wonder what's wrong over in St. Croix?"

"Well, we'll know in a couple of hours. You better get topside and let Phil know about the report. I have to call and let Charter Services know we are leaving and get us officially logged out, for the record."

Buckland relieved Avery at the helm and told him about the report. Phil also appeared concerned about Captain Lind and Sonar as he gave Buckland the heading for St. Croix.

The Island Drummer moved quietly out of the harbor and into the deep Atlantic waters. Buckland glanced over his left shoulder and looked at the huge white modern hotel, Frenchmans Reef that dominates the eastern side of the inlet to the harbor. Two modern looking sailboats, both reefed down, were heading into port, and one of the large inter-island ferry boats was about to cross the Drummer's bow.

Avery was sitting at the navigation station going over the route to the intercept point. He refigured their ETA in Fredriksted when they would join up with Captain Lind, O'Brien and the Sonar.

"How's it looking, Phil?"

Avery looked up to see Gail's warm face smiling at him. "Fine, we should be over at the pier at 1530. I'm about to try and contact Peter Pan to see if he can get a visual on Sonar. I don't think they have their hopper radio on, which doesn't really surprise me, especially with O'Brien aboard."

"Maybe he's not on board yet, and it could be they may be busy picking up that DUI team."

Avery picked up the mike on the special VHF receiver. "Peter Pan, Peter Pan, this is Yuletide, do you copy?"

"Yuletide, this Dumbo, you got the Dumbo, read you loud and clear."

"Roger, Dumbo. We need an eyeball on the Red Sleigh. Do you copy?"

"Roger that, Red Sleigh is O.K. Standby Yuletide for message."

"Roger, Dumbo, standing by."

"Huh, I guess they had contact with Lind after all."

"Yuletide, this is Dumbo."

"Roger, Dumbo, go ahead."

"Red Sleigh loaded with all the presents. Waiting for you to join guests, all is ready for the party."

"Roger that, Dumbo, Yuletide bringing presents around 1500."

"Roger, Yuletide. Invitations delivered. Will be on standby."

"Roger, Dumbo. Yuletide standing by."

"I take it, Captain Avery, those are all our other crew members out there with all those funny names?"

"That's right, Pat. Sounds a little weird, but it's Greek to anyone who may eavesdrop. Not that they could, these special radios won't let them."

"What about other ships listening to your mumbo jumbo, Phil, don't you think they could figure out what you're talking about?"

"Not hardly, Jack. You see, these radios we are using have special "hoppers" built in. They don't stay on one channel. All the players in this operation have this equipment, and we are all tuned alike, no human could manually keep up with us if they tried to listen."

"Hoppers, of course. I've heard of them."

Avery went back to his charts. Gail went topside and joined Buckwheat. The Stars also went topside to take some pictures, and the Brewsters sat around the large teak table and began to play a card game they called "Nerds."

Sonar
Frederiksted, St. Croix

December 23rd
1310 Hours

"Come in, the door's open."

O'Brien opened the narrow varnished door to John Lind's cabin. "Just got word from Dumbo that the Drummer is due here around 1500 hours. Did you get that earlier message about the Seaduce being half way to our intercept?"

"Sure did, Dan. Well, it looks like everything is on schedule, so far, except your friend Castro. It sounds like they may be slowing down a bit."

"Could be they are hitting heavier seas. The winds have picked up, haven't they?"

"Yep, feels like it. We have some weather out west near Jamaica, nothing major, but it could possibly affect us later. There is some shit coming right down the chute from St. Maarten to San Juan, but we will be well out of its path."

"That's all we need, fucking bad weather. They've been saying all week that the weather was going to be perfect through Christmas, now we have this shit coming in."

"Easy there, man, it's only some squalls. They blow out fast. Like I said, twenty miles south of here it's probably beautiful. Don't sweat the small stuff, Dan. You may want to worry about those five young warriors and their Hawaiian Chief down in the galley. They are messing around with those plastics. I wish they would go up on the dock and stuff that shit."

O'Brien smiled. "I'm sure Captain Chen knows what he is doing, John. All they are doing is packing the explosives in their special magnetic boxes, nothing gets wired until they get attached to the Unicorn."

"What's with that young kid, Billy? Is he still going on the mission tonight? He looks like death, and that cough sounds like advanced TB or something."

"Yeah, I hope he's alright. Again, it's not our call. Chen knows his men and I'm sure if he's that sick, he will be grounded."

"If you ask me, he should get off right now and get his ass over to Roosevelt Roads in Puerto Rico. They have a good dispensary over there."

435

P-3C Orion A\C #152171
Dumbo
30 Miles West of Haiti's South Shore

1330 Hours

Captain Bill Blackfoot checked his watch. "O.K., Mr. Coats, let's turn her around. We'll check on Fruitcake, then head east till we find the Music Box. He should be, oh, about 90 to 100 miles out of Antigua by now. After locating him, we will swing up and find these other two, Red Sleigh and Yuletide at St. Croix."

"Right, Captain, do you want to maintain twelve-thousand?"

"Naw, tell center at San Juan we are dropping down to 7000 and give him our heading. They will most likely give you a new squawk number. We'd better look like we are earning our living, let's get her down on the deck and pretend we are looking for trouble."

"Roger, Captain."

Lieutenant Coates rolled the giant Lockheed to starboard and began a steep descent. He pulled back the power on the four big Allison engines as the airspeed began to build.

The aircraft commander hit his mike button. "Jack, need you up here for a second."

Lieutenant Jack Wilkins came up behind Captain Blackfoot.

"Yes, sir?"

"We are going back around to the east. We will pick up that Fruitcake target and get another fix, don't call it in just yet. We are going over to check on the rest of the players. There's that sailboat, the Music Box, that came out of Antigua, and the two ships up at St. Croix, the Yuletide and the Red Sleigh. Now, these guys in St. Croix, according to my orders, are now going to leave the Fredriksted area around 1500 hours. Commander Parker told me that Washington is concerned about this Music-Box boat. Evidently, he has a long run to get to his destination, so we will have to get a good fix on him, Roger that?"

"Right. Say, Captain? Did you learn anything this morning as to what the hell this is all about? I mean what's the purpose of all these boats coming together later?"

"Nope, our job is to patrol, and keep our distance on the Fruitcake boat. They don't want us to be noticed by them if we can help it. The other three guys, well, we keep passing their messages back and forth until they come closer together later tonight."

"Then what, Captain?"

Before Captain Blackfoot could respond, the young Co-Pilot in command of the aircraft sang out. "Then we go back to San-wonderful-fucking-San Jose," Coates cried out as he leveled the P-3 at 7000 feet.

Ian Billings' Office
CIA Headquarters
Langley, Virginia

1402 Hours

"No, sir, I have no idea. As I told you yesterday, I was to hear from Cameron last night around 1800 hours and so far no contact. No, Admiral. We have no plans to send in anyone else, but we will consider that if we don't have contact by 1800 hours tonight. Yes, sir, I will, good afternoon, sir."

Ian Billings put his phone down, looked up at his desk clock, then opened a file on his desk labeled "Cameron, Edward C. CIA, File #3557899 DOB 9\12\54".

Admiral Koster's Office
The Pentagon

1421 Hours

Admiral Koster stood over the familiar chart. He was getting to the point where he had committed to memory the distances between every point of interest involved in Operation Yuletide. He took his calipers and started re-checking the latest position reports he had received from McDill Air Force Base in Tampa. The first report, pinned on the board, read, "PETER PAN REPORTS: FRUITCAKE, SPOTTED 0807. 73 MILES SO. ISLA SANONA, DOM REP 200 MLS WEST SAN JUAN 228 MILES WEST INTERCEPT 68DG 20MI LON WST 17DG 0MI LAT NO RAD CONT MUSIC BOX 0935. 70MI WEST ANTIGUA ON SCHED. RAD CONT YULETIDE 0955 ST THOM ETA RED SLEIGH 1500 ETD SAME. RAD CONT RED SLEIGH 0958 ST CROIX ETD 1500. PETER PAN SJ PR 1123HRS. DUMBO, REPORTS FRUITCAKE ID 1105. 68DG 10MI LON WST 16DG 55MIN LAT NO 200 MILES WEST INTERCEPT 14KTS AVG ETA INTERCEPT 2335HRS RAD CONT YULETIDE 1240

437

INFORMED DPT ST THOM ETA ST CROIX 1500 RAD CONT RED SLEIGH 1255 ST CROIX INFORMED ETA 1500. RAD CONT MUSIC BOX INFORMED ETA INTERCEPT 2155-2200.

Koster took his rule and pencil and made the new location marks for the Fruitcake and placed a pin on the mark. He did the same with the Music Box's estimated position. He went over to Guadeloupe and studied the small island for a minute, then opened a chart torn out of a guide book on the Leeward Islands that gave good details on the Isles Des Saintes. He studied the small island labeled Grand Islet and tried to picture in his mind what it must look like. He then went back to the large chart and studied the waters around Guadeloupe.

Unicorn
83 Miles South-West of Ponce

1430 Hours

Captain DeTorre, standing on the fly-bridge, was pleased at the performance of his new command. He had just gone over the fuel consumption reports with Antonio Lopez and they had 400 more gallons of fuel at this point than estimated. DeTorre increased his speed to nearly eighteen knots to start making up for the heavy seas they had encountered earlier. So far the only real major problem that had presented itself was the primary radar dish was frozen again. Lopez was working on the drive motor up on the mast.

Castro had called for a meeting with General Vincetta, Sorokin, Navarro and Lo.

"Comrades, I am told we are close to our schedule, maybe a few minutes late, however, as you all heard a few minutes ago, Captain DeTorre increased our engine speeds. He says we can make up the time we lost early this morning." He looked over at the frail oriental. "Comrade Lo, after a lot of thought and consideration, I have decided to accept your offer to build my Dolphins in your country."

"That is a very wise move. I found it very difficult to imagine you building them in Cuba without being caught, especially by the KGB."

Sorokin smiled at Lo's comment.

"I can provide you with well-built subs, and further more, I can deliver them to other countries, something you would have had a problem with in Cuba."

"You must understand, Mr. Lo, that this arrangement is only temporary. When that time comes, I don't expect to have any problems, if you know what I mean?"

"Comrade President, I am here to help you and your country. You have no reason to not to trust me. I built your first Dolphin, didn't I?"

"Yes, and we appreciate that, and you will be well rewarded after this trip."

"I am curious, Mr. Lo, how will you be able to produce these machines in China with your government's eyes watching you?" Sorokin asked.

"My dear comrade, how does anything get done under any government's nose, including yours, I might add? The right people get their reward and the job gets done, that's all."

"What kind of production are we talking about? I mean, when we place orders with you, how many can you build and how often?"

"General, I won't really know that until we are set up to go into production. I would guess that with a minimum crew we should be able to build maybe two a month?"

"That will never do, comrade. That is only twenty-four subs in one year. We can't live on that, we need ten times that many."

"Comrade, let us not get too concerned about this now. I will promise you that I will fill your demands. You must let me worry about this."

Castro studied the little man. He hated Lo's manner. He was always too cool, always smiling, which annoyed Castro. Down deep inside he did not trust Lo, but for now he had no choice. Castro changed the subject.

"Well, Dimitri, now you know what it is like to be a capitalist. Here you are on a two million dollar yacht, eating like a king, smoking Cuba's best cigars, drinking French and Italian wines, and heading for a romantic French resort island. How does it feel?"

Sorokin smiled. "Not bad, comrade President. I could get used to this life. I imagine it's a bit like the way Jack Kennedy must have lived before he became President, wouldn't you say?"

"I don't talk about Kennedy, comrade. Nobody around me talks about Kennedy." Castro reached into the top pocket of his guayabera, and pulled out a cigar. It took four stick matches to light it.

Sorokin saw a total change take place in Castro, his skin even seemed to change color, as if all his blood had been drained out. His face went pale white.

Vincetta stood up from his seat and walked over closer to Castro. "Comrade President, I'm sure comrade Sorokin is unaware that the name Kennedy is never mentioned in your presence."

439

Sorokin did not understand, but it was obvious from General Vincetta's attitude that the subject of Kennedy was not to be raised again.

Castro stood up, walked over to the small wet bar, picked up a bottle of tonic water, opened it and poured it into a large glass. He took some ice from the small refrigerator and dropped the cubes into the tonic. He turned and faced the four men, whose attention was still on him. Castro's voice was quiet at first. "There was a time when I thought he was almost magic. He had a special way about him with people. I watched the crowds around him when he was campaigning on television. I would watch the faces in these crowds. How they would glow with excitement, like he had hypnotized them. What warmth he must have felt coming from them. He could see and feel that love. I know what he felt. I know how the feelings are inside you when they touch you, chant your name. I know the power that fills from within, the strengths, the burning of pride inside, the total fulfillment of knowing you are needed. The United States Government would like me to believe that this man, Jack Kennedy, personally wanted to take my life. I did not believe it then, and I still don't believe it today. Jack Kennedy was many things, but a man who would plot a murder of another man? No, he was not a murderer."

"But comrade, there was proof that Jack Kennedy had authorized a plan to have you executed," Sorokin said.

"What proof? There was no proof, just talk, comrade, political talk. It was the CIA and his military leaders that wanted me dead. It was the military leaders that wanted war with Cuba. It was also the politicians, the powerful men in congress and the senate. It was the men who ran the wartime machinery, business men, who made millions on their government contracts. Killing me was just the excuse to invade Cuba. Comrade Khruschev saw this, so did General Konstatin Butuzov. That is why we decided as early as May 1961, to start installing ICBMs."

"General Butuzov was not in favor of this move. He feared that too many skilled technicians would have been killed if the United States attacked. He was a good friend of my father, that's how I know about it," Sorokin remarked as he stood up. He walked over and stood in front of Castro. He raised his arm and rested his hand on Castro's shoulder.

"Do you feel comrade Khruschev sold you out when he made the deal with Kennedy? Do you think this was all Khruschev's doing? It wasn't, my friend. There were many, including General Butuzov, Admiral Mikhailovsky, General Sergei Olegski who pleaded with Khruschev to take Kennedy's offer. We turn our ships around and bring back the missiles and Cuba would not be invaded, that was what Kennedy promised Khruschev.

Comrade Khruschev would have tested the young Kennedy, you know that. And you must also know, we would not be standing here today had Khruschev had his way that terrible Sunday morning."

"Comrade Sorokin is right. Kennedy would have sunk the freighters and destroyed our military installations in a matter of hours. Our defenses were almost non-existent against the firepower that the States would have brought to bear. Tell me, comrade Sorokin, would Khruschev have ordered retaliation had the Americans attacked us?"

"Most definitely. We considered then, as we still do, any attack or aggression on Cuba was an attack on the Soviet Union. However, if the truth be known we were not ready for that kind of offensive, that was another fact we faced. The United States had full advantage over us in ICBM's. I sometimes wonder if the world really knew just how close we came to a nuclear holocaust in those few hours. I had finished college that summer, and was working for the Central Committee as a runner when the threat came. I remember women in the offices crying. We all had to work that weekend. None of us had any sleep or time off. Moscow was totally deserted, even the underground was closed. It was a time I will never forget." Sorokin returned to his chair and lit a cigarette.

"Maybe back then you would have retaliated if we were invaded or attacked, but not today, not with this new leader. And save me from explaining the agreement that we signed nearly twenty six years ago. If for any reason, we are attacked by the United States today we would be left in the alley like a rabid dog. The great mother country won't come to our rescue, not today, my friend."

"I'm sorry you feel that way, comrade, really sorry, but I know you are wrong."

"Huh, I have been very much right, comrade, on most of my predictions over the years. And I am right about your new leader. He is weak, and I don't trust him."

"Tell me, comrade President, you seem to be, shall we say, soft on Kennedy. Do you consider him some kind of American hero? After all, he was a known playboy, cheated on his wife, screwed movie stars. He was hated by most of his general staff, and was executed by some sicko in Texas for reasons still unknown."

"He was executed alright, he was also murdered, my friend, by the same people who wanted me dead back then. They even tried to connect me with his death because of the Bay of Pigs, and the so-called contract that he put on my life. Do you know why he was killed? I will tell you why. He was killed because he was stepping on the wrong toes in Washington. He was about to clean house in the Pentagon, taking away the military influence over the government. Kennedy had made many outside enemies too, businessmen wanting to get richer on their war machine contracts. It was well known that Kennedy had a plan that he was about to introduce to pull out of Vietnam. That meant the cancellation of billions of dollars on big defense contracts. Then there was the Mafia, they were pissed because Kennedy did not send in the Marines when the Bay of Pigs battle had failed. Last but not least, the undercover agencies. Kennedy wanted to close down the CIA, and eventually retire his most dangerous enemy, the little fat fag that ran the FBI. They wanted the world to believe that a lone gunman shot Kennedy? Bullshit. The United States government tried to wrap my flag around Kennedy's murder and sell their so called investigation on the "lone killer" to the gullible Americans, and they did it, they got away with it."

"I suppose you know who killed him?" Sorokin asked.

"Of course, and if you all live long enough, you may someday learn the truth. Then again, there are those in Washington, who are still very powerful and who could keep the real story behind Kennedy's murder buried forever."

"Who do you think killed Kennedy?" Sorokin asked.

"They all did." Castro turned and walked over to the door. He stopped and looked at General Vincetta. "They all did." He stepped out and closed the door.

Sorokin put his cigarette out in the ashtray. He looked over at General Vincetta who was slumped in his chair, with both hands resting on his inflated stomach.

"Well, General, that man continues to amaze me."

"Yes, that is only the second time I have heard him talk that much about Kennedy. You see, comrade, he fears that his fate will be the same as Kennedy's."

"You mean, he fears his own people?"

"No, comrade, not the people. He fears our own government, especially the military. He feels there is someone waiting to become Cuba's next leader out there holding the gun with the bullet that will take his life. That is why he has to find new ways of financial independence. That is why we are here. He does not really like meeting or working with these bandits, believe me. He just feels it's the only way for the present, just until we can..."

"Save your breath, General. I have heard this before. I think your President is fucking crazy for getting even this close to these bandits as you call them. He may be making the biggest mistake of his political career and his life. I hate to see this happen. Excuse me, gentlemen." Sorokin walked out of the cabin leaving Vincetta and Lo sitting alone.

St. Croix
16 Miles South of Fredricksted
1610 Hours

"Yuletide to Red Sleigh, need to talk to Rudolf, do you copy?"

"Roger, Yuletide, standby."

"Yuletide, Rudolf here."

"Roger, we should get a traffic report from Dumbo, don't you think? It would be nice to know where all the players are, and how many ships we have out there on our course."

"Roger that, Santa Claus. Are you going to be staying close by?"

"Negative, that. We will give you space to starboard. Maintain your heading, we will start moving out for a few miles, but we'll keep you in sight."

"Roger. Standby Santa."

Unknown to Red Sleigh and Yuletide, Captain Blackfoot and his crew were monitoring the special VHF radio. They were nearly thirty miles southwest of the Island Drummer and the Sonar, making their next large loop between all the ships in the operation. The only one they kept totally clear of was Fruitcake.

"Red Sleigh, Red Sleigh, this is Dumbo, we are on the air and have your request. Have already done homework on your problem. You have no less than eleven, repeat eleven, ah, strangers on the course. Three heading to the north pole, on your highway. ETA's, 1630, 1700 and 1915 for sightings. Four moving south, out of the game. There are two possible problems, both heading east, twenty five miles south of P.R. They are five miles apart, heading zero-niner-zero, and six miles south of Fruitcake. Fruitcake should pass them on same heading, about 1730 hours, they are moving at 10 knots. ETA six miles south of intercept point, 0240 hours, if they maintain course."

"Roger that, we copy. We will need to keep an eye on those east bounds, Dumbo. Have you contacted Music Box lately?"

"Roger. He has picked up head way. His new ETA with you is 2115, copy that?"

"Roger, Dumbo, Red Sleigh, out."

"Yuletide, did you copy?"

443

"Affirmative, suggest we go to max on all our radar and watch for all targets."

"Roger, Yuletide, out."

Avery went up on deck and looked out to port. He saw the Sonar moving gently over the calm seas. On her stern deck, he could make out a number of men, who were doing exercises. He felt a bump on the arm and turned to see Gail standing next to him with his binoculars. He took them and looked out again towards the Sonar. He laughed, "Quite a sight, six nude studs jumping up and down. You wonder if that can't hurt a little. Here, want to peek"?

"I already picked mine, smart ass," Gail turned around and went over and joined the Stars sitting on the starboard side of the cockpit.

"How ya doing there, Buckwheat?"

"O.K., skipper, I'm heading down on one-nine-zero, getting away from the Sonar. How far out do you want to go?"

"Far enough so Gail can't enjoy Captain Chen's stud show."

They both looked over at Gail who was ignoring them, but she managed to shoot them a inconspicuous bird while holding up her plastic tumbler in a salute, while at the same time carrying on a conversation with Linda and Jack.

"I'm going down and turn on the radar, I will relieve you in an hour."

"Right. Hey, Phil, it's getting close to showtime. How are you feeling?"

"Oddly enough, I feel fine. I think I got it all out last night, yep, I feel good today. How about you?"

"As long as nobody gets hurt, I'm ready."

Avery took another look at the Sonar. He saw another figure on the foredeck sitting alone on the trunk cabin. He was sure it was O'Brien.

"I wonder how old O'Brien is feeling about now."

"I bet he's excited, Phil. Think about it, his plan is still working, isn't it?"

"Yeah, it's still working. Speaking of working, how's that port engine temperature doing?"

"Ah, about two-ten, two fifteen, still ten up over the starboard."

"Don't forget to change those crossfeeds on the forward tanks. See you later."

Avery went below and ran into Don Brewster, who was chopping up lettuce in the galley. "What's on the menu tonight, Don?"

"Pat has her special meat loaf in the oven. She said you all may want to eat early, since things will be getting busy later."

444

"Pat's a woman with good sense. Is she resting?"

"Naw, she's in the head, again. I don't think she's going to be a big fan of ocean voyages," Don began to laugh. Avery joined him.

"How about a Mount Gay and tonic?"

"Sure, skipper, It's kinda early, but, sure."

Avery went over to the navigation station, turned on the primary radar set and set the range to maximum. He went over to the wet bar and took out the Mount Gay, and a bottle of tonic water.

"Hey, cut me a couple of lemons, there, chef."

Sonar
1710 Hours

O'Brien walked into the galley, where Chen and his five crew members were sorting out their gear on the Formica tables.

"Well, Captain, how are things going down here?"

"Fine, Dan, we are putting our gear together and getting ready for the transfer. What time will we be moving over to the sailboat?"

"Ah, I would say about two hours, around 1900 hours. We want to be sure we are in clean air, or I should say clean seas. We don't want anyone catching us out here together."

"That's fine, Dan. We need about another thirty minutes and we'll be ready."

"Hey, Mr. O'Brien, we will get a chance to have dinner before we move out, won't we?"

"Jesus, Dowd," Chen cried out. "You just finished lunch less than three hours ago, and you just polished off half an apple pie, what's with you?"

"Don't know, must be the salt air, I guess."

"Not to worry, I'll see that Kelly gets a good meal in you before we transfer." O'Brien moved around the table and stood close to Bill Allen. "Billy, how are you feeling?"

"Ah, lots better, Mr. O'Brien. Still a little congested, but I'll be ready, right, Captain?"

O'Brien reached over and picked up one of the breathing apparatuses that the team would be using.

"That's the LAR-V re-breather I showed you in Key West, remember?"

"Yeah, of course, it looks smaller for some reason. Just how deep can you go down with these, Captain?"

"Oh, twenty, maybe twenty-five feet, tops. They are designed for sub-surface operations, totally undetectable, no bubbles."

"You have all your cases ready with the explosives?"

"Right here in this back pack, along with all our tools."

"Well, I wish I could be going with you, but, well, I smoke too much, and these re-breathers call for good lungs, that let's me out."

The crew all had a laugh with O'Brien and joked about his black lungs. He agreed with them as he left the room and made his way back to the bridge.

O'Brien found Captain Lind leaning over the chart holding a pair of calipers. "Well, Captain, how we doing?"

"Just fine, Dan, just fine. How are the boys in the back room?"

"Oh, they are ready. They're getting their gear in order." O'Brien looked at his watch. "What time do you figure we will be getting together for the transfer of the props and the team?"

"Oh, 1930ish. We will be pretty much out of sight from our last northbound bogie, a small freighter that will passing on our port around 1900 hours. I figure she's probably heading for San Juan. I would like to get all the transferring finished while we still have some natural light to see by."

"Are you going to have the Drummer lay right alongside?"

"Oh, sure, the seas are pretty mild. We will take her on the starboard side. We have plenty of large fenders on board. We'll just head up into the seas and go dead in the water. I figure it shouldn't take us more than fifteen or twenty minutes, tops to make the transfer."

"Yeah, I guess you're right. Well, do you want to give the Yuletide a call and advise them?"

"Sure, we can do that. Why don't you talk to them, Dan."

Lind reached up and took the mike off its holder.

"Yuletide, Yuletide, this is Red Sleigh."

"Yuletide here, come back Red Sleigh."

Lind handed the mike to O'Brien. "Ah, Santa, we want to get together around 1930 to exchange goodies. Do you copy?"

"Roger that, Red Sleigh. We will begin to close around 1900. Will watch for that northbound bogie, so far I have nothing on radar at this time, maybe target changed course?"

"Roger that, Yuletide. We have negative contact. My guess is she may have sailed more westward towards Puerto Rico."

"We should be getting a word from Dumbo pretty soon, shouldn't we?" Avery asked.

O'Brien looked at his watch. "If we don't hear from him by 1800 hours..." O'Brien was interrupted.

Captain Blackfoot's voice came over the ceiling speaker, "This is Dumbo reading you both loud and clear. As of 1630 hours, Fruitcake is on schedule, new estimated ETA at intercept, 2345. Music Box is on schedule, ETA 2130, we had a visual on him. They request that you have some food ready, they threw everything overboard and have one soul on board who is very sick."

"Roger that, Dumbo. How about the two eastbounds, running south of Fruitcake, over?"

"New headings on those targets. One heading one-two-fiver, the other, one-one-fiver, heading down stream, no longer part of the problem, over."

"Roger that, thanks, Dumbo. Red Sleigh, out."

"Red Sleigh, you have some weather southeast of you, twenty five miles out, moving west at ten, looks like a couple of isolated T-storms that you might want to keep an eye on. We will check back in with you at 1930 hours."

"Roger, Dumbo. Look for you at 1930."

"Well, O'Brien, now you have nothing to worry about. All our traffic seems to be cooperating out here, they are all gone-zo. But we better take a...." Captain Chen interrupted Lind as he entered the pilot house.

"Captain Lind, Tony is reporting some cells down range, twenty miles, moving west at ten miles an hour, bearing one-six-zero."

Lind reached up from the helms wheel and turned on the radar set that was mounted into the ceiling above the windshield. It would take a few minutes for the tube to light up. He turned the range selector to the maximum range. When the tube lit up, the cells showed up clearly. Three hot ones, measuring nearly five miles across, running east to west about fifteen miles long.

"Shit, this might fuck us up. There's bound to be some strong winds ahead of these bastards, and they will definitely stir up some foam down there. We may have a problem with the transfer after all. O'Brien, take the helm, steady on one-eight-zero."

"Yuletide, Yuletide, Red Sleigh, over."

"Yuletide, here."

"Ah, check radar. We have some cells south east an hour plus away. Could cause us some problems. They are moving about fifteen. We could get lucky and fall behind them if we slow down a little, or just head for their backside."

"I like the latter, Red Sleigh. You pick a number and we will fall off and follow you eastward, but let's keep up the speed. The seas down there may be a little more to deal with within the next hour or so."

"Roger that. Let's go to one-sixty five for a while and hope for the best."

"Roger, Red Sleigh, going one-sixty five, out."

Avery increased the speed of Island Drummer, and decided to close the gap between the two ships. Within a half hour he was nearly abreast of the Sonar heading towards the east end of the line of thunderstorms that was directly off their bows.

Seaduce
1845 Hours

Rick Van Wagner leant over the chart table, recalculating his arrival time to meet Sonar approximately fifteen miles north of the intercept point. He had picked up some speed and estimated that he should have the Sonar on his radar screen not later than 2100 hours. For the past six hours, he and Gransaull had thrown everything they could overboard, providing it would sink. His only concern now was not with the performance of the yacht or his navigation. He had a guest on board who could not get out of her cabin. Rose Miller had become sea sick at dawn, and refused to leave her cabin. The only person she would let near her was Evelyn Rodis, not even her husband could get her to come out.

At 1800 hours, Van Wagner got his report from Dumbo that Sonar and Island Drummer were making good time and should be at the interception point as planned. Unicorn was also making good time and would be at the interception point between 2330 and 2350 hours. The next report would come at 2000 hours from Peter Pan.

CHAPTER 24

Caribbean Sea
82 Nautical Miles south of St. Croix

December 23
2120 hours

The three luxury yachts and the former Navy mine sweeper began to close the distances between them. Each captain and his crew were on full alert as their ships moved cautiously through the black night across the endless swells of the Caribbean Sea.

The streamlined Feadship with her tireless Cuban captain at the helm was averaging nearly seventeen knots. The plan was to have his ship at anchor off the island of Grand Islet at 1200 hours, on December 24th and Captain DeTorre was determined to be on time. He sat comfortably in the tall padded helmschair behind the large steel wheel on the open fly-bridge. The only light that disturbed the blackness came from the cluster of instruments located on the large console before him. This greenish light reflected on his face giving him a sickly look, which was noted by his only companion, Dimitri Sorokin, who was sitting nearby enjoying the last of his after-dinner cigar. There was no conversation, only the sound of the wind whistling through the shrouds that supported the ship's mast and the low rumble of exhaust escaping through the exhaust pipes hidden within the large funnel behind them.

Fidel Castro, General Vincetta and Yang Lo had returned to their staterooms after dinner and a few after dinner drinks. On the main bridge directly below the fly bridge, Cabino Varas and Gayo Rodriguez monitored two radar screens, while listening to the two VHF radios for any traffic. They were both relieved that most of the radar targets that had surrounded them earlier had moved off the screens and there had been little VHF traffic for the past two hours.

Nearly forty miles east northeast of Castro's yacht on a bearing of zero-six-eight degrees, the Island Drummer and the Sonar waited patiently for word from the Seaduce. Their bows were headed east south east into the light wind and rolling seas, drifting with their engines in neutral. Their powerful radar were searching at their maximum range.

Barely out of radar range, with her single diesel engine running at full speed, the Seaduce sliced through the warm waters trying to make up time. All her lights were out and would not be turned on until Sonar or Island

Drummer contacted her; or if she came in view of another ship. Rick Van Wagner was sitting at the navigation station watching the slow sweep of the radar signal reaching out at maximum range for contacts. Paul Gransaull was at the helm and the four guests were down below in their staterooms.

Aboard the Island Drummer, the crew was busy preparing to take on the appearance of a severely damaged yacht. The fake props built in Florida and brought down aboard the Sonar had been transferred to the Drummer waiting to be put in place.

Phil Avery and two of Captain Chen's men wrestled with the Drummer's large boom. With the help of the topping lift, they lowered the boom carefully onto the main cabin roof, where Gail Townsend had stacked cockpit cushions to prevent it damaging the cabin. Commander Buckland and Tad Frisoski began installing the shredded and torn main sail. They attached it to the main halyard and ran it up the mast. It looked convincing as it fluttered uselessly in the light breeze, unattached to the boom. Meanwhile, Jack Star and Don Brewster were attaching three large teak name plates with the name "Seaduce" in gold leaf engraved on them. One on each side of the bow and one the transom.

Linda Starr and Gail Townsend, armed with cans of black flat water color paint, sprayed around the top edges of the opening ports along the hull sides giving the impression that smoke had vented out the ports. Glen Sellers and Jack Dowd were on the Drummer's bow preparing an old spinnaker, which would be used as a floating sea anchor.

After completing his chores on deck, Commander Buckland went down to the navigation station, turned up the volume on the VHF radio and continued listening for any word from the Seaduce while watching the radar for contacts. Captain Chen and Pat Brewster went down to the Brewster's stateroom to check on the ailing Bill Allen. The young sailor had a relapse earlier breaking out in cold sweats and running high temperatures. Chen told Allen that he would have to be returned to the Sonar, but that if he felt up to it, he could inspect the explosive charges on the SEADUCE with Captain Van Wagner once his charter passengers were transferred.

Fifty yards off the Drummer's port beam, Sonar was in total black out, except for instrument lights and the radar monitors glowing on the bridge. O'Brien and Lind watched, waiting for word from the Seaduce. O'Brien put his left wrist near the green radar tube and tried to read his watch.

"It's 2201, Dan," Lind said.

"Where is he, John? Where the fuck is Van Wagner and...."

The bridge suddenly echoed with static from crackling speakers and a roll of thunder vibrated off the ship's steel plates.

"Yuletide, Yuletide, this is Peter Pan, do you copy?"

Buckland and John Lind hit their mike buttons at precisely the same time to respond. All that the crew on Peter Pan could make out were the words, "over...over."

Lind raised his voice with authority. "Peter Pan, this is Red Sleigh, standby. Yuletide, stand down," he ordered. "O.K., Peter Pan, you've got Red Sleigh, go ahead."

"Red Sleigh, you have company coming, Music Box is closing fast, you should have contact bearing zero nine fiver."

Suddenly every window on the entire bridge of Sonar began to vibrate. The four thundering Allison engines of the P-3 Orion drowned out the radio message, and sent crewmembers diving under tables and bunks as the huge Lockheed passed over the two blacked-out vessels. Avery looked up in time to see the blue and orange flames coming out of the exhaust pipes on the sides of the engine nacelles. He estimated the P-3 had missed the top of the Drummer's mast by less than twenty feet.

"Jesus Christ, Peter Pan, you nearly got my stick," Avery screamed out. Then he screamed down to Buckland at the navigation station. "Buckwheat, get on the horn and tell that stupid asshole he damn near got our mast, I'm putting on the mast light."

Buckland reacted and began yelling into his mike. "Peter Pan, this is Yuletide, come back."

"You got Peter Pan, over."

"Little close there, Captain. You nearly circumcised our mast just now, do you copy?"

"Roger that, we have you on the scope, not to worry, Yuletide."

"Roger that, Captain, but our stick is sixty-five feet above the waves, does your scope show that?"

There was a slight pause, then a response. "Whoops, ah, sorry about that, Yuletide. Ah, listen, Captain, we are going to fly down to the southwest until we pick up Fruitcake we think we may have him on the tube right now, but we will confirm. Music Box will be on top of you shortly. We will come back to you in about thirty minutes and give you a new position on Fruitcake and any other bogies that might have come into your front yard, do you copy?"

"Roger, Peter Pan, we copy. See you in thirty minutes."

Buckwheat's voice was suddenly cut out, as a louder voice came over the speakers.

"Yuletide, Yuletide, this is Seaduce, ah, make that Music Box, do you copy?"

Before Buckwheat could respond, John Lind had the mike button down and happily greeting the Seaduce crew.

"Seaduce, this is Red Sleigh. We have you buddy, you just came on the screen. Welcome to the party. You need to come up five degrees, heading two-seven-five, do you copy?"

"Roger that, two seven-five, have you on the tube now, be alongside in about forty-five minutes."

"Roger, Seaduce. Sonar standing by."

The relief of knowing that the Seaduce had finally arrived was written all over O'Brien's glowing face. He turned to John Lind and winked, then reached over and picked up the VHF mike.

"Yuletide, Yuletide, this is Rudolf, proceed to the party place now, advise when contact is made with Fruitcake and let's keep the chit chat to a minimum, Fruitcake will be listening I'm sure, let's not give him any reason to get nervous. Contact us when you reach party place, we make your ETA, ah, thirty minutes. Can you do that?"

"Negative, negative, Rudolf, need to make emergency transfer, we have a very sick dwarf, do you copy?

O'Brien guessed it was the young navy diver, Billy Allen.

"Roger that, come up as soon as you can, will be standing by for the exchange, move now"

"Red Sleigh, this is Music Box, best put a light in your window, its thick out here and you don't want us climbing down your chimney."

John Lind began laughing. "Captain Rick is right, Dan. We better give him something to see us by, or he might run right through us."

Lind reached over and flipped on the anchor light that was located on the top of the pilot house masthead, then switched on his navigation lights.

"Yeah, we don't have any unfriendlies out here, might as well play it safe. We need to get the Drummer over here and make the transfer now and get her out of the way before the Seaduce arrives."

"I agree, Dan," Lind reached for the mike and pressed the key down. "Yuletide, this is Red Sleigh. Proceed immediately for the transfer, copy?"

"Roger that Red Sleigh, we are heading for you right now."

"Phew," O'Brien said as he reached in his shirt for his cigarettes. "Now, Captain Lind, I could use a stiff shot from your Mount Gay bottle now that the gangs all here." O'Brien clapped his hands together and smiled.

"I think you should wait, Dan. We have a few tough hours still ahead." Lind said cautiously avoiding eye contact with O'Brien.

Lind was interrupted by his first mate. "Captain, the sailboat, Yuletide is coming alongside."

452

Lind and O'Brien turned and walked through the open door on the starboard side. O'Brien could hear the sound of the Drummer's exhausts as the large pipes took turns being muffled as they rolled beneath the water. He watched as the graceful clipper bow accented by its massive bow sprit moved slowly towards the high steel sides of Sonar's hull. She began to roll slightly as she came close. Captain Lind assembled a number of hands to fend off the Drummer and transfer the stricken sailor.

The transfer only took a few seconds. Bill Allen was aboard the Sonar and taken down to the crew quarters. The Island Drummer moved out and away from the Sonar to begin her short journey to the interception point, less than fifteen miles away.

O'Brien watched as the Drummer silently slipped into the darkness. He could see the huddle of bodies standing in the cockpit around the helm and waved at them, but nobody noticed or heard his words. "Gods speed, young warriors, and good hunting."

Avery advanced the throttles and adjusted the hydraulic struts as he eased the Drummer up to hull speed. Gail and Buckwheat ran around the decks making sure all the gear was tied down. Below in the main salon Captain Chen and his young team were putting on their wet suits.

"I'm going down below, Phil, to watch the screen for any targets. I'll keep the radio turned up so we can hear Peter Pan when he checks in." Buckland headed for the companionway.

"Good idea. You might want to call O'Brien and advise him that we may want to terminate Peter Pan after his next report if its a good one. We don't want any low aircraft flying around us as we reach zero hour."

"Roger that, Captain," Buckwheat disappeared down the companionway.

"How are you feeling?" Gail Townsend's soft voice broke over the whistling winds singing through the steel shrouds.

"Like a woman in labor." Avery responded.

"That's what I like about you, Avery, you have a lovely way with words."

"I'm scared shit, does that answer your question?"

"Yes, at least you're being honest. Now, is there anything I can do for you up here? If not, I'm going below and see if I can help Commander Chen's young studs get into their wet suits, o.k.?"

Avery laughed. "You know, you have a way with words too, and speaking of words, there are a few I owe you."

"Really now, like what?"

"Gail, I know I haven't said so, but, well, I am sure glad you're here."

Gail moved closer to Avery's side. She placed her left hand gently around the back of his neck. Her long fingers began to massage his neck muscles, while her other hand grasped his right forearm and squeezed lightly. He felt her firm breasts rub against his arm as he turned to look into her eyes as he put his arm around her waist and drew her closer, then kissed her gently.

Aboard the Music Box, Paul Gransaull was instructing the crew on the transfer that would take place when they reached the Sonar. For the first time since they left Antigua, over fifteen hours ago, Rose Miller came up on deck. Her only comment when she sat down to join her husband and the Rodis' was she had never seen stars so bright. Other than that, she complained that she thought she smelled a little sour. All the water in the tanks was totally exhausted, they were deliberately drained overboard during the voyage to lighten the yacht for speed.

Van Wagner maneuvered the Seaduce around the stern of the Sonar and came up on the starboard side. In no time, the crews had the yachts secured to each other and more names were added to the Sonar's guest list.

Van Wagner and Gransaull helped the weakened Billy Allen transfer the plastic charges over to Music Box. Allen and Van Wagner went right to work setting the charges. A simple detonator was placed in the cockpit and wires were brought up from the engine room and attached. Allen explained to Van Wagner that once the timer knob was turned clockwise to the full stop, they had sixty seconds to clear the yacht. The three charges in the engine room were installed so they would blow outward and downward. Three charges were placed in the main salon. One charge was placed in the middle of the main salon floor beneath the rosewood coffee table, which would blow the entire main cabin skyward in a large explosion that would easily be seen by the Unicorn miles from the interception point. Once the explosives were in place, Allen returned to the Sonar and went back to his bunk.

PC3 Orion, Peter Pan
8000 Feet
Westbound, 93 miles south, San Juan

2218 hours

Captain Dave Parker thumbed his mike button on the control wheel. "Hey, Jack, do you have a fix yet on that, ah, fruitstand?"

"Ah, that's Fruitcake, sir."

"Right, that Fruitcake?"

"Roger, Captain, he's nearly twenty nine miles south southeast and well behind us now. Still on a heading of zero-nine-nine degrees."

"Speed?"

"Ah, maybe eighteen knots. I estimate he is about twenty-six miles from the intercept point. I give him an ETA of, ah, one hour and twenty minutes give or take a few. He's fighting some wind and current now."

"O.K., crew, let's turn this bus around. Greg, you got the bird. Jack, get those longitudes and latitudes worked out pronto, so I can give them to Yuletide, Red Sleigh and Music Box on the hopper. Hell, they should have the Fruitcake on their radar screens, wouldn't you think, Jack?"

"Roger that, skipper, especially the Yuletide. There are only twenty six or seven miles between them now."

Dave Parker pulled his pipe out of his flight suit pocket, and pointed it at his co-pilot. "Do it, Greg."

"Yes, sir." Greg Tombline took control of the wheel and went into a standard right bank, maintaining his altitude.

"Should I set up for San Juan, Davie?"

"Roger that, somehow I feel that when I give this last report, they are going to kiss us off. Shit, we may still get home for Christmas." Parker twisted around in his seat and called back to his R\O.

"Jack, give us a heading for San Juan while you're at it."

Jack Wilkins finished his navigation and handed it to Parker. "Home is three-five-three degrees."

"Roger, skipper."

"O.K. Jack, patch me through on that special VHF and let's see if we earned our wings tonight. Man, I can use a shooter."

"You're all set, skipper," Jack Wilkins reported.

"Yuletide, Yuletide, this is the Peter Pan, do you copy?"

"Peter Pan, you have the Yuletide."

"We have your Fruitcake, on the way to the oven."

Parker could hear the slight laughter in Buckland's voice as he tried to respond. "Roger, Peter Pan."

"Your target is heading, zero-niner-niner. ETA interception, one hour twenty minutes. Approximately twenty-four miles out, located two-two zero same miles your station. Latitude, sixteen point two five degrees north, longitude, sixty-five point three-five degrees west. Do you copy?"

"That's a Roger, Peter Pan, I copy and I've got a bogie, twenty five miles, bearing two-two-six degrees, looks like the Fruitcake to me."

"Red Sleigh, Red Sleigh, this is Peter Pan, Yuletide has the Fruitcake on the stove."

"Roger, Peter Pan, this is Red Sleigh. We heard the news. Stand-by for orders."

O'Brien and Lind agreed that it was a good time to release the P-3 and its crew.

"Peter Pan, Red Sleigh here, this is Rudolf. Terminate mission, repeat, terminate mission. Advise North Pole and Scrooge ASAP when you reach your nest, do you copy?"

"Roger, Rudolf. Good hunting, Yuletide and Merry Christmas."

"Merry Christmas, Peter Pan, and pass on our holiday greetings and best wishes to the Dumbo, and thanks."

" Roger Yuletide, Peter Pan is out of here."

Parker placed his hands behind his head and locked his fingers together. "O.K. gentlemen, let's get this bird back to its nest and get our asses over to that beach club, I'm treating tonight."

"Hey, skipper, this was one of the craziest missions I have ever been on, what do you figure is going on down there tonight?"

"Got me, Jack. But I've got a feeling that sailboat, the Yuletide, isn't exactly a welcome wagon. Evidently they are going to have some kind of confrontation with that boat they call the Fruitcake, that's for sure. What those other two are doing staying out of harms way is anyone's guess."

"You know, skipper, I've been thinking. I wonder if it isn't just some big drug bust. You know, our guys going out to catch some major shipment heading for, who knows, someplace."

"Our guys playing pirates? Well, maybe. After all, they are in international waters. Shit guys, I don't know, but it must be important to Uncle. They got our ass out here, didn't they? I promise you when we get back home, I will call some friends in D.C. and rattle some bones and see if I can find out, O.K.? Meantime, get me to that fucking beach."

Dave Parker reached up and advanced the four throttles to max-power. The four engines responded and the sub-hunter began its next leg to San Juan.

Yuletide
19 Miles due East of Unicorn
2315 Hours

On Buckwheat's command from below, Avery brought the Drummer to idle and turned the bow into the light wind coming in from one-five-five degrees. Gail, Chen and Don Brewster were on the bow ready to cast off the huge spinnaker that would act as a sea anchor. Avery put the engines in reverse and backed down slowly.

"Cast the sail," he yelled to his crew forward, then went over to the companionway. "Buckwheat, this had better be the spot. Where is he now?" Avery asked, as he stooped down at top of the companionway.

"Nineteen miles, bearing two seven six, no, make that two seven nine degrees."

Avery stood up, his eyes opened wide and his mouth dropped open. "Shit, the radio, we forgot the damn radio," Avery cried out. "Buckwheat, in the nav table, lift the top, the portable VHF, Jesus, get it up here. Oh, shit, did we ever check that thing for batteries?" He thought a minute, then yelled again. "Did we ever try it to see if it works?"

Buckland flew up the stairs into the cockpit with the hand held VHF radio. He fumbled with the small plastic cover on the back that gave access to the battery compartment. He had four double A batteries in his hand. Avery grabbed the radio, from Buckland's hand, pulled out the antenna and turned the small switch to the on position, turned up the volume and the squelch knob. He got what he wanted, the squealing and scratching sounds only an empty frequency could provide. He had power, it had batteries, now he had to use it.

Buckland took the radio from Avery, put the small battery panel back on the set and dropped the spare batteries into Avery's shirt pocket. The two men stared at each other for a moment. Avery could see that Buckland was concerned, but Avery offered no apologies for his unprofessional behavior.

"Gail, get back here and take the helm. Buckwheat, you and Don get the dinghy down in the water." Avery ran over to the companionway and shouted down into the salon. "O.K., gang, it's time to get to your stations, on the double. You, the seal team, get your shit up here, on the double."

Captain Chen stepped onto the companionway staircase and put his face right into Avery's. "Easy, there Phil. We have time, man, don't panic. We have lots of checking to do. I won't rush my team, do you read me, Captain?"

Avery knew Chen was right. "I read you. Just bring them up as soon as you can, o.k.?"

Tad Frisoski was the first diver on deck and he began taking the gear handed to him from below and putting it on the starboard lounge seat. Chief Dowd came up, followed by Glen Sellers. They were all in their black wet suits, only their eyes, nose, mouth and cheeks were visible. They put on their strange looking special breathing devices. Each man had a small bag attached their belt, which carried their explosive charges and tools. They also carried a small TAC board and a wrist compass. As his men checked each other's equipment, Captain Chen launched the dinghy then went below and put on his suit. He would lead the team tonight in Bill Allen's place.

Avery gave the helm to Gail, took the small handheld radio and walked back to the stern. He stood against the stainless life rail and looked into the black night, searching for the first sign, the first lights of the UNICORN. The palms of his hands were clammy and the back of his neck at the hair line and his temples were sweating. He tuned the radio to channel 16, brought the radio up to his cheek and pushed the mike button in. "Mayday, Mayday, to any vessel in the area. Mayday, Mayday, this is the yacht Seaduce, the yacht Seaduce, Mayday, to any vessel." He released the mike button and waited. There was no response.

Below him, attached by a tether line, the small rubber inflatable dinghy banged into the transom as it waited for him.

"We're ready, Phil, want us overboard?" Captain Chen asked.

"No, hold it, that fucking dinghy won't work, we need to get the whaler down. Gail, get Buckwheat back here."

Captain Chen responded. "Easy, Captain, we can lower it, you just stand clear of the davits, o.k.? Keep that radio going."

Avery was not doing well at all and he knew it. He was scared and making stupid decisions. Putting in the small inflatable dinghy was dumb. He had to haul supplies back from the Unicorn and he would have had to row. The Whaler had a outboard.

The Boston Whaler was lowered into the water with Frisoski sitting in it. He fended off the small dinghy and released the two davit cables. He then pushed the small fifteen horsepower outboard down into the running position.

"Want me to start the engine, Mr. Avery?" Frisoski asked.

"No, not yet," Avery replied.

Captain Chen yelled out, "Phil, the Mayday, get on it, man."

"Mayday, Mayday, Mayday, any vessel, this is the Seaduce, Mayday." He released the transmitter button and waited.

Unicorn
17 Miles West of Island Drummer
Heading 099 Degrees

The speaker on the flybridge intercom crackled. "Captain, from the bridge."

DeTorre reached over and picked up the remote microphone.

"DeTorre."

"Captain, we are getting a Mayday signal, fairly strong.

"Mayday? What are they saying?"

"Ah, just a mayday call to any vessel, I think they said they were the something duce?"

"Standby there. I am transferring control back down to the main bridge. I'll be right down."

DeTorre had just reached the main bridge when the radio began to broadcast again. " Mayday, Mayday, any vessel, Seaduce calling any vessel, Mayday."

"What have we got on the tube, Carlos?"

"I have two targets, Captain, both stationary. Here, this one up here? It looks like a small freighter, hard to tell though. This one, almost directly on our course, it too is not moving."

"I don't like this," DeTorre said, as he looked closer at the radar screen. "Go to a deeper sweep, what else is out there?"

"Sir, our main radar motor is out, we can only get a forward picture, less than a forty degree sweep. I am on maximum range now."

"Shit, how soon before we get in sight of that target ahead?"

"Oh, ten, fifteen minutes, maybe less. We should pick up his lights any minute if he has any, Captain."

"Get me my glasses."

DeTorre went over to the radio rack and picked up the small microphone. He checked the channel window on the VHF radio for the frequency, it was set for channel 16. He turned up the volume, then turned the squelch knob until static cut in, then backed off. He pushed in the mike button. After clearing his throat, DeTorre began to speak into the small mike.

"Vessel calling Mayday, vessel calling Mayday. What is your emergency? Over."

459

Aboard the Island Drummer

"Phil, did you get that?" Buckwheat yelled from the navigation station. "It's got to be the Unicorn, what do you think?"

Avery was frozen. He could hear the voice coming over the small speaker and he could hear Buckwheat yelling, but all his muscles seemed to be frozen.

"Shit, Phil, he's calling, talk to him," Chen pleaded.

"This is the Seaduce, the yacht Seaduce, calling a Mayday, how do you read me?"

"You're loud and clear, Captain. What is your emergency?"

Avery could hear the strong Spanish accent in the commanding voice. "Storm damage and engine room fire. Fire is out. We are not in danger, we are not sinking, repeat, not sinking. Need food, water and fuses."

"Seaduce, what kind of vessel are you, over?"

"Sailing yacht, seventy five feet. We are on charter out of Antigua, heading to Jamaica. We hit a storm, lost all our sails, had electrical fire in engine room. Need fresh water, food and a couple of 30 or 50 amp fuses. Operating on spare battery, can you assist?"

"Stand-by Seaduce." DeTorre thought for a minute. "Can you give me your position?"

"Ah, just an approximate. I can fire a flare if that would help. You can't be too far, Captain."

"Standby, Seaduce."

DeTorre went over to the helmsman and looked down at the large compass. "Steer one-four-zero degrees, reduce to 500 rpms. What are those two targets doing now?"

"Still stationary, Captain."

"Stay at this heading and keep your distance. I must talk to the President."

"Yes, Captain."

Sonar
17 Miles due North of Island Drummer

John Lind was watching the radar screen and noticed the Unicorn changed her course. "What the fuck? He's changing course on us, Dan."

O'Brien looked up at the screen. "Oh, shit! What's Avery going to do now? He was depending on Castro approaching from the west, not the south. It looks like Castro is staying well clear of them."

"Dan, do you think it could be us? Surely they got a radar fix on us, and we aren't moving or talking, they may be getting suspicious. I'll bet they do an end run, just watch."

Unicorn

DeTorre stood in the doorway of Fidel Castro's stateroom as he explained to him the events that were taking place up on the bridge.

"Please accept my humble apologies, comrade President. How do you want me to respond to this ship?"

"He is a sailing craft you say? Out of Jamaica?"

"No, comrade President. He is heading for Jamaica. He hit a storm and lost his sails, then had some kind of fire. He claims he is on a spare battery now and his signal is pretty strong. We are almost sure we have him located just a few miles ahead on our course, but there is another larger target less than twenty miles north of him, also stationary and not responding to any radio calls."

Leaning on one elbow, Castro reached over, took the light cotton blanket and threw it aside. He sat up and swung his legs over the side of the bed. He rested his elbows on his knees and pushed back his hair. He reached over and picked up the used cigar sitting in an ashtray. DeTorre picked up the small gold cigar lighter, flipped the small wheel twice. A small blue flame appeared and was presented.

"What do you think, Captain? How's our time?"

"We are on schedule and making good time. I would like to stop and help this sailboat, but I am very nervous about the other boat to the north. He must hear the sailboat's call for help, yet he is not responding."

"Go call the sailboat, Captain. See what we can help him with. I don't want anyone to board the sailboat, nor do I want anyone on board this boat. We can put one of those inflatables over with one of your crew and keep the rest of our crew out of sight. I don't want any one seen other than yourself and Carlos on deck, he's the one who looks more like a Mexican, right? I will wake General Vincetta and meet you on the bridge, go, go."

Aboard the Island Drummer

"Mayday, Mayday, this is the Seaduce. We are sending out a flare, repeat, shooting off a flare now."

Avery spoke to the sailor holding onto the short barreled flare gun. "O.K., Tad. You fire that thing almost horizontally. We don't want to attract anyone else who may be in the area, keep it low, understand?"

"Right, sir."

Frisoski held the small flare gun with two hands. He cocked the hammer and fired. The flare arched about thirty feet above the water and flew nearly a quarter of a mile.

"Do you think they saw it, Phil?'

"Don't know. We'll wait. If that didn't work, we'll send one in their direction. Shit, I wish I knew what he was doing. I don't like the course he is taking. I needed him on the leeward side off our stern." Avery shouted, "Buckwheat, where the fuck is he now?"

"Seven miles, bearing two-two zero, moving slow, on one-four zero."

Unicorn

"Well, that's him, Captain. The flare was not too bright, and it was low, but that's him, bearing zero four zero, sir. Wait a minute, look at the radar, Captain, look at the other target to the north. It is moving now. Yes, he is heading, ah, three-five-five degrees, he is turning. Now he is steady at three-five-five."

DeTorre rested his hands on the large navigation table as he stared out the windscreen into the black night. He turned and looked at Castro who was standing next to him.

"Comrade President? What do you think?" DeTorre asked.

"It's your call, Captain. I feel we should help them if we can," Castro said cautiously.

DeTorre walked over and stood behind his helmsman.
"Carlos, take us back around to port, zero one zero, both engines half speed. Go up above the target, then turn and head into him, keeping him to starboard. I want to stay above him, let him drift into us, so we can keep an eye on him. I don't want him any closer than thirty yards. We will put Manuel in the rubber raft and he can take the supplies to them."

DeTorre spun around and pointed at Manuel. "You go up and uncover the big search light on the bridge. See if you can find the switch for it up there."

"Yes, Captain." Manuel left the bridge.

DeTorre picked up the mike again. "Seaduce, this is the vessel Unicorn. Do you read me?"

Avery waited a moment, then responded. "Unicorn, this is Seaduce. We read you loud and clear. Can you tell me if you saw our flare? Where are you?"

"Affirmative, we saw your flare. We are close and will be approaching you from the west. What are your needs? Call them out slowly, do you understand?"

"Unicorn, we need fresh water and any food you can spare. I need two fuses 30 to 50 amps. I believe I can get my auxiliary engine running again and charge the main batteries. When I get my engine running, I can motor to San Juan. Over."

"Are you American?"

Avery froze. "Shit, what do we do now?" Avery mumbled.

"Tell him the truth, Phil," Chen whispered to him.

"Yes, I am."

"How many people on board?"

"I have four Canadian guests and a first mate. My yacht is registered in Panama."

"Stand-by, Seaduce," DeTorre ordered.

Vincetta arrived on the bridge and DeTorre gave him an update and pointed out the targets on the radar. The target to the north had made another heading change, it was heading two-seven-zero and had slowed down again.

"Can you raise this other ship?" Castro asked.

"Not so far, they have been quiet, Comrade President."

"Let's get this captain what he needs, or what we can spare. Then let's get going. Are we still going to make the island on schedule?"

"Yes, comrade President, with plenty of time to spare."

"Good, let's get this over with. I think we should all go back to our quarters and let Captain DeTorre deal with this interruption."

Castro, Vincetta and Sorokin had started to leave the bridge, when Castro turned around and addressed DeTorre, "Captain, I want you to keep a close eye on that other vessel up north? If he stops or turns south, I want you to get us out of here immediately, do you understand?"

"Yes, Comrade President."

Outside the bridge, Sorokin stopped Castro and Vincetta. "Comrade, don't take me wrong, I know you mean well, but don't you think this is a bit risky? You don't know that this is not some kind of trap. What if this is a set up? That vessel up there could be a warship for all we know. This vessel in distress, it could be a floating bomb."

"Dimitri, you are so paranoid. Nobody knows who we are, remember? How could anyone set us up out here? There wasn't time. Nobody in Cuba knows where we are."

"Your friends, comrade President, the ones we are meeting at the island, they know. What's to stop them from ..."

Castro broke out in laughter. "My friends, you say? I don't know these thieves. But I do know one thing, they want to make money, and they will want to see what I have to offer, so why should they want to harm me, comrade?"

"Comrade Sorokin, if you prefer you and I will remain on the bridge and keep an eye on things, if that will make you feel better?" Vincetta said in a sarcastic tone.

"It won't, General, but I will take you up on the offer." Sorokin walked back through the door to the bridge. Castro turned and walked down the deck to his stateroom. His last words of advice were that Sorokin and Vincetta were to keep out of sight of the sailboat's crew.

Once back inside, Sorokin asked Vincetta why Castro would want to help a strange ship at sea, and possibly put himself at risk.

Vincetta gave Sorokin, what he felt might be the explanation. "When Castro was returning to Cuba in 1956 to begin recruiting for the revolution, he came back aboard a very old American built wooden yacht called the Granma. You know, Comrade, the one in the Museum in Havana? Well, sixty miles south of Cuba, they ran into some bad weather and high seas and the Granma was taking on water. They thought it would sink, and all their rations were ruined. A large American commercial fishing boat that had left Santiago two days earlier just happened by, and ended up coming to the Granma's rescue. The Americans gave them a portable pump, food and water. I think maybe the memory of that event might have something to do with his compassion for this sailboat tonight, Comrade. He is a compassionate man, comrade, once you really know him."

Aboard the Seaduce

"I see them, Phil, there, on the horizon, see their lights?" Gail shouted.

Avery responded. "Yeah, O.K. Captain Chen, you had better get your men in the water. Ah, Buckwheat will have to come up here. Gail, go down and take Buckwheat's place on the radar and radios. Ah, Don, Don Brewster? You take the helm, just hold on to it, o.k.? The rest of you get into your positions along the port side cat walk. When that yacht gets close enough, start waving and yelling. If you know any French, use it. Chances are they are going to hit us with strong search lights, so look the part, just like the movies."

Avery handed the portable radio to Chen and went over to the stern. He stepped over the life rail, and started down the ladder and into the Boston Whaler. Chen tossed the small VHF radio to Avery. He ordered his men to check their CO_2 gauge on their Lar-V re-breathers, to insure each diver had a minimum of 200 bars showing. Next they inflated their special vests, which would enable each diver to remain positively buoyant. Each diver climbed down the transom ladder onto the swim platform, then slipped into the cool black water next to the small fiberglass boat.

Avery leaned over the stern of the whaler and spoke to Chen as he floated nearby with his team. "I'm going to start moving out, Captain. I want to be at least twenty to thirty yards away from the Drummer. They won't want to come too close, I'm sure. You and your men better watch for their big search lights. I saw the photos of this baby, and she has some serious spot lights on the bridge."

"Roger, Phil. You may want to give them another shout, tell them you see them, keep him happy, man, and let's hope they stay off our port side."

Taking Chen's advice, Avery picked up the small radio off the seat and began to transmit. "Unicorn, Unicorn, this is the Seaduce, we have you in sight."

"Seaduce, we are two miles due west of you. I will be coming up on your stern. Have all your guests and crew on deck where we can see them, do you understand? If you have any kind of lights, please put them on now. We will have you under our spot lights. I repeat, we want all your passengers and crew on deck. We are armed, Captain, and will shoot if we see anything suspicious, do you understand me, Captain?"

"Jesus, what do you make of that?" Avery asked.

Chen was holding onto the side of the whaler along with his team, while they watched the lights of the Unicorn draw nearer.

"They are giving us a warning in case we are pirates, I guess. Hell, I think I would do the same if I was him. Yep, this guy is cool, don't get him nervous, Avery," Chen said in a cautious tone.

Avery's radio came alive again. "Seaduce, we will put supplies in bags and boxes and pass them over to you. We will have a man deliver the supplies in a raft."

"Negative, Unicorn. Our Captain is already in our auxiliary skiff moving out to you."

DeTorre thought about this for a second. Then decided this was a better choice. He would not have a man off the yacht in case there was an emergency.

"Seaduce. Advise your Captain we will pass him the supplies, but we will not permit him to come aboard, do you copy?"

"Unicorn, that's affirmative. Our captain feels we may still have problems in our engine room. It is still smoking, and he would prefer that you don't come too close, just in case."

DeTorre had to give that some thought. "Yes, this was good thinking, the American knows his business."

"Seaduce, this is a wise decision, tell your captain we appreciate his concern. We will look for your dinghy. Is your Captain carrying a light of some kind?"

"Negative, Unicorn, we will try and guide you. He is about twenty yards off our stern drifting towards you."

De Torre went out the door of the bridge and yelled up to Manuel on the flying bridge. "Manuel, did you find that light switch?"

"Yes, Captain, but it does not work. Maybe there is a circuit breaker down there somewhere."

Carlos reached over and handed DeTorre a small hand held one mile spot light. "This should work, Captain."

DeTorre walked out on the starboard cat walk and looked towards the direction of the stricken sailing vessel. His eyes squinted and strained looking into the black night. Then he saw her. He also saw a flash of some kind on the water.

"Seaduce, fifty yards dead ahead," DeTorre called out. He went to the open bridge door and gave orders to his helmsman. "RPM's, two hundred, standby to reverse all engines. Watch for a man in a small boat somewhere off the starboard bow."

"I found the circuit breaker," Carlos shouted.

"Manuel, switch on the light up there," DeTorre ordered.

The big search light came on, its long thin beam reached out into the blackness high above the sea. Manuel guided the beam downward to the sea directly ahead. The tall mast was caught in the brilliant white light. Manuel brought the beam down until it reflected off the bright white hull of the large sailboat sitting dead in the water straight ahead. DeTorre looked through his glasses as Manuel moved the light from bow to stern along the yacht's port side. He could see women and men waving.

"Bring that light down, Manuel and look for the small boat, I think it is to the right, about thirty yards out to starboard."

The light hit Avery in the eyes and he had to turn his head to protect his eyes. He reached down and put the throttle in neutral, then began to wave frantically back to the Unicorn to move the light away.

Captain DeTorre ordered Manuel to move the light away from the small dinghy. Manuel swept the light back to the Drummer in the distance.

Captain Chen and his team had reacted automatically when the light began looking for the whaler. They released their hand holds on the whaler, ducked below the surface, and swam close together in a westerly direction putting distance between them and the dinghy. When they surfaced, Chen motioned for the team to begin to start their sweep in a semi-circle away from the whaler, and close in on the Feadship from the starboard side. They hoped this would keep them out of the search light's beams.

Avery stood up carefully, spreading his feet to keep his balance, and began to wave at the Unicorn while shielding his eyes from the blinding light.

"Jesus, that fucking light is strong," he called out, knowing he could not be heard, but hoping they would see he was being blinded.

Chen and his team were about fifteen yards west of Avery and he called to Avery in a low voice. "Phil, we are going to move out, heading to target, do you copy?"

"Yes, I understand." Avery responded, trying to speak without moving his lips. "You stay well off to my port. I will see if I can get him to turn that fucking light out for a few minutes, standby."

Avery started waving harder with his arm while holding his hand over his eyes and yelling. De Torre got the message.

"Manuel, take your light off the small boat and hold put it back on the sailboat. I will handle the small boat and the man with my light."

Manuel moved the light back onto the hull of the Drummer.

"Reverse engines," DeTorre yelled.

The Unicorn's giant hull was silent for a moment, then the entire yacht began to shutter and vibrate as the water at her stern began to boil from the two large propellers reversing their bite into the dark sea.

Chen carefully guided his men on the wide sweep westward, putting distance between him and Avery. He kept his eye on the silhouette of the Unicorn as it came closer. He was about thirty yards off the Unicorn's starboard bow when she began to slow down. He could hear and feel the large props slicing into the water as they reversed their pitch. Large black and gray clouds of smoke rose above the Unicorn's superstructure as her engines protested the sudden demands for full power.

Captain Chen took a heading to the Unicorn with his wrist compass. He then gave the hand signal for the team to submerge. Each diver placed their re-breather mouth piece between his teeth and opened the valve to purge their systems of C02 by breathing in the pure o2, then exhaling through their nose. They pulled their face masks over their eyes and adjusted the tension straps. Next, they purged their special dive vests, making it possible for each diver to become negative buoyant, and letting their weight belts take over and allowing them begin to descent. Chen watched the depth gauge attached to his wrist. When he reached twenty feet, he signaled for the team to level off. Each diver adjusted the valve on his special diving vest, charging it with just enough air to stabilize his descent and neutralize his buoyancy. Once they were all level and assembled, Chen gave the signal to hook-up the buddy lines. Chen and Glen Sellers were a team and were hooked to each other with a tether line. Dowd and Frisoski connected theirs. Chen then signaled he would take the lead and head out towards the Unicorn, which was about twenty five yards away. The currents were starting to take the swimmers westward away from their target. Chen picked up the pace, time was definitely not in their favor now. They needed every minute they could buy to set the charges.

Avery was drifting too. He realized that he had to put the engine in gear and head closer to the Unicorn, or he would be carried behind her. He looked around, saw no sign of Chen's divers and put the throttle forward into gear.

The large search light on the Unicorn's flying bridge shone on the Drummer, scanning her decks. Then another light came on, this time from the lower bridge starboard side. It was less intense, and unsteady. Avery figured it was a hand held light. It darted around him for a few seconds. He took a long drag on his cigarette, almost burning his lips. It worked. Who ever was holding the light saw the cigarette glowing. The light flashed into Avery's eyes. He decided to see if he could be heard on the Unicorn.

"Ahoy, Unicorn, can you hear me?"

DeTorre could hear Avery, but he hesitated before he responded. "Do we have the supplies ready to hand over?" DeTorre asked his crew.

"Just about, sir, " came the response.

DeTorre located the lone man in the whaler with his light.

"You there, in the boat," DeTorre yelled, while cupping his hand around his mouth. "Come over closer, we will throw you a line, then hand you the supplies, do you understand me?"

Avery heard him, even over the sound of the noisy outboard, but elected to pretend that he didn't. He needed to stall for time. He wished he had checked his watch when he was spotted. Chen had told him that he would need at least ten minutes. The light was in his eyes again and he lost direction. He raised his arm to break the bright beam. DeTorre reacted and moved the beam into the water just ahead of the whaler.

"Cut your engine, sir," DeTorre yelled again, louder.

Avery moved the throttle lever to neutral. He was about ten yards out looking up nearly vertically at the figure on the bridge some twenty feet above him. A line suddenly came down along the hull just aft of the bridge at the main deck level. He saw two men standing next to the rail. One was holding a large box, the other pulling the line back up over the rail. Avery moved the throttle to forward and moved closer to the hull, turning the helm and aiming at the dangling line coming down from the rail. When he looked up at the bridge the light hit him again and his eyes slammed shut.

"Sir, my crew will hand you the supplies. I hope that these will help you. There are two fuses, I hope they are the right size. Do you want me to radio to anyone about your distress?"

Avery was about to answer when the whaler collided with the hull of the Unicorn and almost tossed him on his back. He grabbed the whaler's gunwale, as he turned the ignition key off on the control box. The line hit him on the side of his head and he grabbed it with both hands, then stood up. His eyes were at the deck level, looking at the black hard shoes of the two crewmen. He looked up into their sober faces.

"Hello, I'm Captain, ah," Avery drew a blank, he forgot what his fictitious name was.

"Buenos noches, Captain, here is the food and supplies you asked for." The young Latin got down on his knees, and pushed the cardboard carton beneath the center rail on the life line, into Avery's waiting hands. Avery took the carton and placed it on the seat. He looked up to see another carton waiting.

"I can't thank you enough."

"Here, Captain, some fuses. We have two of each. I hope these will do."

Avery took the long round fuses from the man. He looked up towards the bridge. There were two faces looking down on him now.

"Captain, do you want us to call for assistance, or notify anyone?"

Avery had to think for a minute. "Ah, I would appreciate when you get into port, ah, just where is it you are you heading, Captain?"

"We are heading to Guadeloupe, but that is still twelve hours away. Your closest port would be the Virgin Islands, due north from here, about 100 miles. There is another ship, only seventeen miles north west of us, he appears to be heading this way. We think he is a freighter or a small tanker. We cannot raise him on the radio. If you still have problems, you may want to signal him."

"Yes, and thank you for everything, Captain. As soon as I can work on my generator and get these fuses wired, I should be in good shape. Once my batteries are up I will have the main engine running and will head for San Juan for repairs. I can't thank you enough, Captain. If you will give me your name and home port, I would like to reimburse you for your trouble."

"Nonsense, Captain, we were happy to help. I repeat, is there any message or anyone you want us to contact for you?"

"Ah, negative. Once I get my main engine running, we will be just fine. I have charter guests on board, they are just a little hungry. We have been drifting for, ah, several hours, all our food went bad."

"Good luck, Captain," DeTorre said. "Standby to move out," he yelled to his crew.

Avery started to push off, then hesitated. "Got to stall for some more time," he thought to himself.

"Captain," he yelled.

One of the men on the bridge returned and stood silently looking down at Avery.

"Yes, if you don't mind, sir. There is someone you could call for me when you reach Guadeloupe?"

"Wait, I will get a pencil," the man responded. He disappeared for a minute, then returned. "Go ahead, Captain."

"Would you contact my Clearing House for me? The number is 809 555 5640. Tell them that I had some difficulty and will be in touch with them from San Juan tomorrow afternoon."

"Where is this, this clear-house you speak of?"

"St. Thomas. It's in St. Thomas."

470

"I will do this, Captain. What is your name, sir?" DeTorre asked again. Avery quickly threw the line up to the closest crewman, reached over and started the outboard. He sat down and yelled to the two crewman. "Thank you, thank you." He hoped that the Unicorn's captain figured he did not hear him. Suddenly the light was back on him and he had to look up. He smiled and waved as he yelled to the top of his lungs. "Buenos noches, gracias, gracias," he shouted. The two Cuban crewman started yelling too.

When Avery glanced up again at the bridge, the man and the light were gone. Only the big search light remained on, scanning the Drummer and its crew. Avery pointed the whaler at the Drummer, opened the throttle and started skimming over the tops of the rolling seas.

"Jesus, I hope they had enough time under there," he kept saying to himself, as he glanced back at the Unicorn. He could see the exhaust smoke rising over the large funnel, and white water cresting around its bow. The Unicorn was moving out.

CHAPTER 25

Aboard the Sonar
0126 Hours

O'Brien looked up at the bright green radar screen above the helm station. He could see the Drummer and the Unicorn clearly. It looked like they were parked side by side.

"Goddamn, what's going on, anything on the radio?"

"Cool it, Dan, you'll hear it when we do. We have to start heading down there pretty soon, or the explosion could be too late. The Unicorn will have too much distance between us. We are about eighteen miles apart right now."

"Head back south, head for the Drummer," O'Brien said.

"Are you nuts? We don't know what's going on down there, Dan."

"I said turn this fucking tub around and head for Avery. If something is wrong, it's wrong. We will do something else. If we can get close enough to that red mother fucker, we'll ram the son-of-a-bitch."

"O'Brien, you are losing it, man," Lind said worriedly.

"Helmsman, I just gave you an order, get this tub on a course to the Drummer, now," O'Brien screamed.

The sailor looked at his captain for approval. Lind nodded his head, the sailor spun the wheel to port.

Lind turned to one of his crew standing in the door way. "You, go back aft and let Van Wagner on the Seaduce know what we are doing. Tell him to speed up if he can and stay close on the starboard side, we are going to head south." Lind turned his attention to the young sailor at the wheel. "Helmsman, both engines ahead one-third."

"Both ahead one third, yes sir," the sailor said.

Beneath the Unicorn

When they reached their target, Captain Chen and his team immediately went to work. Chen and Sellers went amidships and attached their charges next to the keel on the port side. Dowd and Frisoski planted their charges further aft on the starboard side of the keel. Frisoski placed his charges next to the starboard strut that the shaft ran through. Dowd set his near the raw water intake of the starboard engine, then he swam over to the port side and placed the timing device.

473

Once Chen had his two charges in place, he pulled out the detonation wire from his gear bag, installed the bayonet-type metal detonator into the plastic charges inside their plastic magnetic boxes, then worked his way back with Sellers to the rear team. He continued to install the detonators into each secured charge, then attached the wire to the timing device which was attached to the port strut, set the timer, descended to twenty feet and started swimming north away from the Unicorn for at least twenty yards before surfacing.

Jack Dowd was surprised at the amount of suction near the screened raw water intake. He fought off the thought that the engines were being revved up to move out. He decided the charge would be best set behind the large grilled opening. Struggling to open his gear bag, he drifted close to the intake and his arm was sucked up against the steel screen. This startled him, and he began to push away, but got pinned flat against the hull. He placed his charge on the hull and pushed and kicked hard to get away from the hull. Tad Frisoski had finished attaching his charges and was swimming forward along the keel to join him. Tad did not see the large rubber fin that came out of nowhere and slapped him in the face, smashing his face mask against his nose, and knocking the re-breather mouthpiece out of his mouth. This flooded the Lar-V re-breather making it useless. Frisoski screamed as pain bolted through his head from the impact of Dowd's foot. He expelled the air in his lungs. Now he was pinned under the hull, next to the keel. He clawed at the rough blue anti fouling paint, tearing his gloves to shreds. Feeling the impact of his foot hitting something, Dowd spun around only to find his teammate in serious trouble. He attempted to offer Frisoski his mouth piece. Shutting off the mouthpiece valve, he tried to put it in Frisoski's mouth, but Frisoski was too excited and was thrashing wildly about, trying to push away from the hull. He was fighting for his life, trying to pull himself along the slimy hull. Dowd put his mouthpiece back in his mouth, opened the valve and wrestled with Dowd. He needed to get to the co2 valve on Frisoski's vest. Once inflated, Frisoski would be able to float to the surface. He found the valve, turned it and heard the air charging into the jacket's chambers, and Frisoski floated upwards along side the hull. Dowd held on to his teammate and began to rise with him, while pushing away from the hull. He then located Tad's weight belt release and pulled it. The belt fell off, and Frisoski headed for the surface only five feet above them. Dowd released his weight belt and grabbed onto Frisoski's arm to ascend with him. He applied pressure to Tad's stomach to ensure Tad expelled any air that could possibly cause an embolism.

They broke the surface together and Dowd immediately attended to his buddy, who was gasping for air. He pointed upwards to remind Tad that they were right under the stern of the yacht. Dowd feared there might be guards on the aft deck and he did not want to alert them. Frisoski heard his friend's warnings and regained his composure. They began to surface swim on their backs, slowly away from the yacht, watching for any signs of life on deck that might detect them. The decks were clear, the Unicorn was totally blacked out. They swam harder drifting with the current over the choppy seas.

Chen and Sellers came to the surface on the starboard side of the Unicorn. They drifted back along with the currents, keeping their eyes on the railing above. When they floated past the transom and were well behind the stern, they were pleased to see there was no sign of security guards standing watch.

The water at the stern began to churn, sending vibrations back to Chen and Sellers. The Unicorn was moving off. The mission was complete, and they quietly watched the huge yacht slowly move away.

"We've got to find the guys," Chen yelled. Sellers pointed to the north, where they had agreed to meet. They spread out and began surface swimming in search of their teammates.

Avery tried to stand up in the bouncing Whaler as it headed away from the Unicorn, but he was forced to sit down. The small search light came on again, and found him. He waved and yelled, "Thank you, thank you." The big spotlight was still flashing back and forth along the white hull of the Drummer. For the first time, Avery was able to look at the condition of the yacht. The tattered sail was blowing wildly, the boom really did appear to have smashed into the cabin and each porthole appeared to have soot around their openings. Avery could hear screams and yelling from the Drummer's crew above the noisy outboard motor. He slowed down and watched the Unicorn making headway, increasing its speed. Then the two search lights were turned off. He looked behind him and noticed how deadly black everything was. He had to find Chen and his team. He spun the wheel around and headed back in the direction where the Unicorn had been and started yelling. It took nearly fifteen minutes to locate Chen and Sellers. Chen had brought a small flash light and was able to signal Avery when he came close to them. It took another fifteen minutes to locate Dowd and Frisoski. Chen figured they would have drifted west and that's where they found them.

By the time Avery and the team reached the Drummer, Buckland, Gail and the crew had the Drummer pretty much back in order. The main sail was unwrapped from the boom and ready to be run back up the mast. The boom was lifted by the topping lift and the main halyard connected to the main sail. The water color paint was easily washed off, and the wooden "Seaduce" name plates were removed. The Sonar and the Seaduce were four miles north and closing fast.

Avery called everyone into the cockpit.

"O.K., everyone, you know the drill. Captain Chen will take his team and their gear in the whaler and transfer them over to the Sonar. He will come back, pick up the Brewsters, the Stars and Buckwheat. Buckwheat, you get your ass back here. Everyone understand? Let's do it."

Avery checked the Drummer's throttles and made sure the two clutches were in neutral and started the two engines. Chen and his crew put their gear in the whaler and headed out to meet the Sonar. In less than ten minutes, the Sonar was idling twenty yards off the portside of the Drummer, with her bow headed due east. About thirty yards off her stern, Rick Van Wagner carefully moved his yacht into position along the portside of Sonar. He eased up carefully to the steel hull, as Sonar's crew members stood ready to fend off.

"As soon as you're clear, Gransaull, go for it. Don't slip or fall, we'll never find you," Van Wagner yelled.

Gransaull was standing at the starboard life line gate, holding onto one of the spreader shrouds. The Sonar's hull was within arms reach and he waited as the Sonar slowly rolled and dipped to port. Two sets of hands appeared about Paul's head. He leaped and was caught and pulled onto Sonar's deck, landing on his feet. He spun around as the Seaduce pulled away. He looked down at Van Wagner standing at the helm, with only the pale green light from the compass reflecting in his face. Gransaull commented later that Van Wagner had the look of a victorious crusader, smiling and waving wildly. Van Wagner pulled ahead and cleared Sonar, began a sharp port turn, then headed westward. Gransaull thanked the two crewmen who helped him on board, then ran up to the pilot house. O'Brien was just about to get on the VHF, when he saw Gransaull enter the bridge.

"Why aren't you with Van Wagner?" O'Brien asked.

"He wanted to go solo, Dan."

John Lind entered the cabin after searching the horizon from the outside bridge. He went right to the radar screen, put his finger on a small blimp, then turned to O'Brien. "Dan, Unicorn's on the edge, he'll soon be out of radar range, let's move." Then Lind noticed Paul Gransaull.

"Gransaull? What the hell?"

"Van Wagner wanted to go alone, Captain. I lost the argument," Gransaull said.

O'Brien took the VHF mike from its bracket and began to broadcast. "Yuletide, Yuletide, this is Red Sleigh. Are you ready to run."

The overhead speaker responded instantly. "Red Sleigh, standby."

O'Brien turned to Gransaull and handed him the mike. "Here, take this. As soon as they come back, tell Avery to swing around and pick me up. I'll be at the stern." O'Brien turned and went down through the door to the crew's quarters.

"What the fuck is going on here?" Lind yelled. "O'Brien, you asshole, get back here." He grabbed the mike out of Gransaull's hand. He knew that he had no control of O'Brien now.

"Yuletide, this is Red Sleigh. You have a bundle of toys to pick up, get in close, watch for Rudolf on the tailgate, he is coming on board."

Lind threw the mike up on the console and slammed his fist against the instrument panel. "I don't believe that asshole. What a time to leave. What's he trying to prove?"

Gransaull had no answers for Lind, he was too concerned about Van Wagner. He went over to the portside catwalk and stared into the blackness that Seaduce had disappeared into.

Aboard Yuletide

"Steady as she goes, Phil, this current is murder," Buckwheat said as he watched the Drummer's bow as Avery closed on the Sonar's stern.

"Where is Dan?" Avery called out.

"There, Phil, at the stern," Gail responded.

Buckland ran up and stood amidships. He could see that O'Brien was going to try and jump from the Sonar's large hand rail. He carried a bag of some kind, which flew out of his hand and landed on the Drummer's foredeck. As the Drummer came within two feet of Sonar's hull, O'Brien jumped and landed on Buckland, who was waiting to catch him. They both fell on top of the cabin roof and had the wind knocked out of both of them.

Lind, watching the radar at its minimum sweep, picked up the VHF mike again, and tried to reach Van Wagner. "Music Box, Music Box, this is Red Sleigh, you are in position about one mile west."

Aboard Island Drummer

"What's taking him so long, Phil? The Seaduce should be history right now, there must be something wrong. Van Wagner isn't even responding to Lind's call. Damn, why didn't he keep Gransaull with him, now he's..." O'Brien never finished his sentence.

Aboard the Seaduce

Van Wagner made one last check on the engine room and salon charges, then double-checked their wires. Satisfied that all the wires were connected properly, he went back on deck. He had prepared two dock lines to hold the wheel steady on course. He tied one line from the wheel to the port jib winch, then took the other line and tied off the helm from the starboard winch. With the wheel now stable, he started to prepare the timing device. He picked it up from the cockpit seat and studied the wire connections. After looking around the cockpit to make sure that everything was ready, he reached up and put the engine in gear, then pushed the small throttle handle forward. The aging six cylinder engine revved up. Holding the timing device in his left hand, he turned the knob between the thumb and index finger of his right hand until it hit a stop. He dropped the metal box on the cockpit seat, turned and ran aft towards the stern along the narrow deck. He heard the radio begin to squawk calling him, but it was too late to respond. He never saw the unsecured mizzen boom and sail swinging wildly back and forth through the wind. The end of the boom caught him in his right shoulder and upper chest, breaking his collar bone, and spinning him around. He fell backwards, landing flat on his back, hitting his head on the teak deck, knocking him unconscious.

The explosion was spectacular. As planned, the main cabin roof blew skyward, taking most of the wood mast and the boom and main sail high into the black night. The mast snapped in two in the main salon as the hull sides blew out and the bottom tore open, releasing the heavy lead keel. The big six cylinder engine and all the running gear followed the massive keel as it tumbled to the deep caverns nearly three thousand feet below. The red, yellow and white cloud that flashed like a giant flash bulb lit up the sky. It hung in mid air for a few seconds cremating canvas and wood, then vanished into a grayish blue vapor. Flaming pieces of the Seaduce landed close to the Drummer and Sonar.

John Lind wasted no time. He reached for the standard VHF radio mike and began broadcasting the news of the disaster over the emergency channel. "Mayday, Mayday. This is the freighter, Sonar, reporting a ship explosion in our vicinity. Mayday, Mayday, to any vessel in the area, a ship just exploded. Mayday, Mayday, to any ship in the area, a ship just exploded in our vicinity."

DeTorre stared at the VHF radio. Its small crackling speaker held the undivided attention of everyone in the wheelhouse.

Standing in the port doorway to the bridge, Manuel Fajardo yelled, "Look, Captain, look at the sky behind us."

DeTorre ran over and stepped out of the door of the wheelhouse onto the catwalk. Looking back to the horizon, he could see the brilliant yellow glow against the black sky. DeTorre squinted his eyes, as if he would be able to see the disaster taking place on the horizon. He felt a cold chill come over him. "I wonder if it was that sailboat we helped? Jesus, do you think it could be them? What do we have on the small radar?" De Torre yelled.

"We are picking up what looks like two targets, Captain, it's hard to tell because they are very close together and almost off our screen."

DeTorre went back inside and picked up the small VHF hand mike. "Sonar, Sonar, this is the motor yacht, Unicorn, do you read me?"

"Unicorn, this is Sonar, read you loud and clear. What is your position? Over."

"Sonar, we are about seventeen miles due east your position. We have reason to believe that the ship you are reporting on may be one that we gave assistance to an hour ago. The vessel was called the Seaduce, it was a sailboat, I repeat, it was a sailboat. Do you copy?"

"Unicorn, this is the Sonar. You say it was a sailboat called the Seaduce?"

"Sonar, that is correct. We intercepted this yacht a little over an hour ago. It had been damaged in a storm and had a fire aboard. Her captain claimed the ship was sound. We gave him some food and fuses. She was carrying Canadian passengers, heading to Jamaica. Home port was Antigua, over."

"Roger, Unicorn. We are half a mile from the burning wreckage. We will look for survivors and report. Can you join us and help in the search for survivors?"

Drummer's crew was listening to the conversation between Unicorn and Sonar. Castro's crew was reacting exactly the way O'Brien had predicted.

"Jesus, that Lind has a fucking nerve," O'Brien commented.

Lind got the response they were hoping for. "Negative, Sonar. We are too low on fuel. We will start broadcasting for help to any vessels in our path, over."

"Roger, Unicorn. We are attempting to call U.S. Coast Guard in San Juan on our single side band. We will be looking for survivors. If we find any, we will head for Puerto Rico, do you copy?"

Captain DeTorre responded. "We copy you, Captain, and we wish you good luck. We will try to communicate with the authorities in San Juan when we reach port tomorrow. Good luck, Captain."

DeTorre had no intention of calling anyone when he reached port.

"Captain DeTorre, I wonder if this freighter, this Sonar, is the target that we saw hanging around up north earlier when we were helping that sailboat. Remember, he went north, then west, then came south?"

DeTorre thought a minute. "You are right, that was a bit strange, wasn't it. Well, let's ask."

"Sonar, this is Unicorn, do you still copy?"

"Roger, Unicorn."

"Captain, where you by chance in the vicinity of this unfortunate yacht an hour ago? We had a radar fix on a large target to the north of us, less than twenty miles, that seemed to be turning in circles?"

Lind had an answer to this question. There was no question in his mind that the Unicorn had been watching him on their radar and his maneuvers must have looked suspicious.

"Unicorn, that's affirmative."

Back on the Yuletide, the crew waited to hear Lind's explanation.

"Ah, huh," O'Brien commented. "Let's see how the wizard Lind gets out of this one."

Lind continued. "We picked up some cables from abandoned long line nets. They got wrapped around my starboard wheel and rudder, had to send a diver over. Good thing we were delayed, we wouldn't have been here to help."

O'Brien held his breath. "That Cuban ain't going to buy that line of shit, Lind," he thought.

There was short pause.

"Unicorn, standby. We are at the site. Stand-by for additional information."

Lind sailed the Sonar around on the leeward side of the floating burning remains of the Seaduce, and called for both engines to stop.

"Any sign of Van Wagner?" Lind yelled from the bridge.

"Not yet, Captain Lind," Captain Chen reported as he, his crew, and the Sonar's crew stood at stations all around the Sonar's decks looking for Van Wagner.

"Gransaull, was Van Wagner wearing a life vest?" Lind yelled out.

"Jesus, Captain, I can't remember."

"We need to put a raft overboard, Captain Lind," Chen yelled out.

"Right, get my men to help. I'll run through the middle of the wreck and split it up. All hands on those lights, start yelling, he may be hurt."

Lind took the Sonar at a crawl through the scattered burning wreckage of the beautiful classic yacht. There was little fire around the wreckage because the Seaduce had been nearly out of fuel, and there was no oil slick to burn.

Aboard Island Drummer

Phil Avery looked into Dan O'Brien's concerned face.

"We have to go, Dan, they will find him, we will keep in touch, o.k.? We have a long trip ahead, and we'll be running into a lot of traffic in the morning as we get close to Antigua, which means we will have to slow down and cruise at regular speeds. We only have six hours."

O'Brien raised his arms over his head, and began to shake his hands. "You're right, Phil. Go ahead, open them up. This is what she was built for. This is it, the true test, right? We built this thing to be in two places at once, so we could catch Mr. Castro and we wouldn't be caught. You know, I planned this mission and now we're here, and it's working, but so far, it's killing the wrong people, isn't it?"

Gail saw O'Brien starting to come apart, and she figured he had probably been drinking all day. His eyes were glassy, his voice was weakening. He began to laugh loudly. She moved to his side.

"It's alright, Dan, they will find Rick. He's tough, he'll make it. Come, I'll treat you to a big Mount Gay and tonic, and you and I will listen to the radios, alright?" Gail caught Buckwheat's eye and signaled to him for help. They each took one of O'Brien's arms and led him down the companionway into the main salon. Gail took him over to the large sofa on the port side and told him to rest, while she got him a drink.

Avery dropped the hydraulic struts and slowly opened the throttles. The Drummer pulled herself away from the ocean's firm grip and began to pick up speed. It was going to take Avery and the Drummer nearly twelve hours to reach Antigua. It would take the Sonar two more hours of

481

searching, before they discovered that Rick had been killed in the explosion. Jack Dowd and Tad Frisoski found him floating face down in his life vest.

Sonar began its long journey back to San Juan, but they would lose still another sailor before the sun came up on Christmas Eve, 1985. Lieutenant Billy Allen, age thirty one, died in his sleep of pneumonia, at 0421 hours.

Unicorn
0335 Hours

December 24
119 Miles West of Guadeloupe

Fidel Castro walked into the quiet, semi-darkened bridge. Antonio Lopez was at the helm and Manuel Fajardo was sitting on a stool with a headset on and watching the small radar screen. There was no traffic within the twenty-five mile range.

"Where's Captain De Torre?" Castro asked.

The two young engineers were startled by Castro's presence. They were still having difficulty recognizing him without his beard and dressed in shabby street clothes.

Lopez smiled and responded, "Comrade President, Captain De Torre is sleeping, he said to wake him at 0400 hours."

"How's it going, are we still on time?" Castro asked.

Fajardo quickly answered. "Yes, Comrade President, we are maybe a little ahead of schedule, according to Captain DeTorre. You can see, sir, there is nothing out ahead of us, and, oh, we never did hear anymore about the sailboat after it blew up, either."

"Sailboat? What sailboat? What are you talking about?"

"The sailboat that we stopped and helped a couple of hours ago? It blew up, and everyone was killed. I am sorry, Comrade President, I thought they told you."

"How you know this?"

"It was on the radio, Comrade President. A freighter that was close by saw the explosion and went to help them. He began to radio for help and reported the accident. Captain De Torre talked to the freighter's captain. The freighter reported again later and said the ship was completely destroyed, and that they were picking up the bodies, there were no survivors."

Castro's face showed concern. He rested against the bulkhead and looked out into the endless black night.

"How terrible. Captain De Torre must have felt terrible. Such a shame. How many people were lost, did they say?"

"No, Comrade President," Lopez said. "We figured there must have been at least six on board. We saw that many when we gave them the supplies."

"We saw the light of the explosion in the sky too, Comrade President," Manuel added.

Castro moved over and sat down on the tall helm seat. He continued to look out into the empty seas.

"It was terrible, Comrade President, such a shame. But we did try and help, didn't we?" Lopez said quietly.

"Yes, yes, Lieutenant, we tried to help." Castro stood up and walked towards the port side door to the outside deck. He stopped, and without turning around, said, "Pray for their souls, my friends, they no longer need to worry about this miserable world, do they?"

"No, Comrade President," Fajardo said.

Castro went to the door. He stopped, turned and said to the young helmsman, "Tell Captain DeTorre to call me at 0600."

"Yes, sir. I will tell him. Buenos noches, Comrade President."

Castro said nothing, he left the bridge and returned to his stateroom.

Admiral Koster's Residence
196 Winding Hill Road
Fairfax, Virginia

0345 Hours

Admiral Koster walked quietly into the small bathroom, trying not to disturb his wife. He did not have to switch the light on, he knew what he wanted in the medicine cabinet, and exactly where it was located. He opened the small bottle, removed three of the round tablets and put them in his mouth. They had a nice minty flavor, and within a few minutes the aggravating heart burn would vanish from deep down in his chest. He walked back into his bedroom to the double set of French windows that looked out across the front yard of his modest colonial house. The light frost around the window panes, where the wood frame met the glass, looked like a kaleidoscope of sparkling designs created by the street lamp. The new snow that had fallen earlier in the evening left everything clean and crisp, except for the footprints on the old brick walk way connecting the street to the house, left by guests at his Christmas party. He pulled up his favorite wingback chair and sat down, and propped his chilled slippered feet close to the base board heating element. He sat back and looked out the windows into the black sky. The snow had stopped and he could see a few stars. He thought about the mission and about O'Brien and his old friend, John Lind. "Where would they be right now?" He asked himself. He thought about Fidel Castro. "This could be his last Christmas, what a gift that would be for thousands of Cubans." He thought about Washington, the White House and the chiefs of staff. "Wonder if the President will ever tell anyone what really took place down there?" He sat back and closed his eyes. The tablets were working. He pulled his flannel robe tighter around his large frame, rested his chin on his chest and fell off to sleep, confident that Operation Yuletide was being professionally executed.

CHAPTER 26

2310 Hours

Tomas Puros, Carlos Mesa and Marcel Balisteri walked down the quiet path to the main road. Puros wanted to get away from the villa and its open windows where their companions could hear their conversation.

"Marcel, if you don't get that fucking sorry look off your face, I will give you something to worry about. You have your women asking me questions about you, what's wrong with you anyhow? I told them you are sad because your children are not here to celebrate Christmas, then I find out you lied and told that whore that you don't have any children."

"I am sorry, comrade. I, I'm just nervous. I can't get my mind off the American. I worry that those ropes will come loose, we should have put more weight in that tent, Tomas."

Carlos grabbed Marcel's shoulder, forcing him to stop walking and turn to face him. "Marcel, trust me, he won't come up, at least not right away. Listen, we only have two more days on this damn island then we all go home, O.K.? So, stop worrying about the American, he is dead and he is at the bottom of the sea."

Puros removed a pack of cigarettes from his shirt pocket, and lit one. He looked into Marcel's dark eyes and smiled, hoping to get him to lighten up. Marcel did not respond.

Puros continued. "By the way, exactly what did the lady at the hotel say when you called? Do you think she believed you when you told her you were the American calling?"

"I did not say I was him. I was worried about my accent, so I said that I was a friend and that he told me to call. I explained that he had left the island and would return sometime Sunday afternoon. The lady I talked to just thanked me, that's all."

"You see?" Puros said laughing. "Nobody will miss him. You put his boat back at the dock and nobody saw you, right? He had no woman with him, he was bullshitting us, right? So, let's forget about him and start planning for tomorrow. We will tell our women we are going fishing early and will be back around noon. They can go to Guadeloupe and do more shopping, we have to be on that island early in the morning. I don't want anything to go wrong, our President will be there in less than twelve hours.

We will leave the villa about eight o'clock and be in position on the island by nine. We will need some food and water and without the tent we are going to be in the open, so maybe we take some sheets or a blanket from the villa and build a shelter of some kind."

"Don't forget those extra batteries, Tomas, for the radio. I put them in the kitchen, on the counter, earlier."

"Thank you, Marcel, I did forget about them. I will put them in my back-pack as soon as we go back."

"Tomas, what about those two pilots? You were going to visit them last night, but.."

"We will do that on the way out this morning. Better yet, I will take care of that while you begin loading our boat. They are staying on the beach at the Grand Anse Apartments. I will go by there first and see if they are alright, and give them a walkie talkie radio so they can monitor us in case of an emergency. As a matter of fact, the beach where they are staying is right on the south end of the runway. That is the beach we will use to evacuate our President and his people if we have any problems. We can take the boat right up on the beach where the plane will be waiting to pick him up. Keep in mind, this is Christmas Eve, there are a lot of tourists around and the beaches will be crowded. We must act naturally and walk through everything. Nobody will take notice, not to worry, my friends."

"Well, I am ready to get some sleep. I am satisfied with our plans. Is there anything else, Tomas?"

"No, Carlos, and you're right, we should go now. Marcel, are you feeling better?"

"Yes, I will be alright."

The three men walked back to their villas as a light rain began to fall.

Island Drummer
161 Miles West of Antigua
December 24th

0305 Hours

The crew on the Drummer didn't speak as they left the area. Only a few waves were exchanged between the them and the crew aboard the Sonar. Avery took the Drummer's helm and set course for the long sweeping route that would take them to Antigua.

All systems on the Drummer were working perfectly and the two big Chevy engines were running smoothly. Avery guessed they were averaging about twenty-one knots even with the strong currents and the moderate swells.

Three hours later, Commander Buckland was standing the last hour of his watch at the helm. In forty seven minutes, he could finally close his eyes and get some sleep. Like everyone on the crew, he was totally exhausted. Down below, Dan O'Brien was passed out, thanks to Mount Gay rum. He had not taken the loss of Rick Van Wagner very well, nobody had. When Gail suggested that he call Rick's wife when they reached Antigua, he had snapped at her saying that he couldn't do it. It was agreed that Phil Avery would call her, only after the Coast Guard out of Puerto Rico had officially contacted her.

The next shocking news that O'Brien would have to deal with later would be the death of the young Navy Seal, Bill Allen.

Phil Avery lay awake in his bunk and listened to the muted sounds of the smooth running twin engines just three feet below his bed. He identified each and every groan, squeak and clang that took place throughout the entire hull. The slow rocking horse motion as the great hull knifed through the seas, accented by an occasional roll, would have normally put him to sleep, but the night had been far from normal. He was devastated by Van Wagner's death in the explosion. He looked at his watch, it was 0516 hours. Gail would be relieving Buckland at 0600, so Avery decided he would join her topside if he was still awake. He would have to relieve her at 0800 anyway, since O'Brien would not be in any condition to stand his shift.

He heard a metallic click that came from his cabin door and he raised himself until he was resting on his elbows. He squinted as the door slowly opened. Gail stepped in and closed the door. Small beams of light passed over her body as she came closer to the foot of the bed. She was wearing a short yellow silk robe with green patterns on it, which she let slip off her shoulders and fall to the floor. She put her hands on the bed and crawled towards him. When she came within inches of his face, she relaxed and fell limp on his body, her head resting on his broad chest. He sank deep into the bed and tightly wrapped his arms around her.

Grand Islet
Isles des Saintes

1023 Hours

Tomas Puros stood on the treeless hilltop under the blinding sun, focusing his binoculars on a vessel that was heading north about three miles south of the island. There were the usual sailboats and fishing boats cruising about, but so far this was the only one that looked like the yacht he was expecting. He could see it had a large flybridge, a small tuna tower and outriggers. It was definitely a sport fisherman and it was coming quite fast towards the island. He looked below to see if there were any boats in the cove below. It was mid-tide and the sandbar that surrounded the cove was visible through the clear green waters 500 feet below.

"Tomas, do you think that's him?" Carlos asked.

"Yes, I think so, Marcel. Get the radio out of my field pack, quick."

Marcel had the portable radio sitting on the canvas field pack. Puros plugged the microphone into the radio, pulled the telescopic antenna to its full length, turned on the radio and brought up the volume and it began crackling. With one hand he held the binoculars steady on the fast moving power yacht and the other hand he held the mike and pushed the button in.

"Pawn to Bishop, Pawn to Bishop, do you hear me?"

The radio remained silent. Puros turned up the volume.

"Pawn to Bishop, Pawn to Bishop. Do you read me?"

The small black Sony radio responded. "Pawn, this is the Bishop, you are loud and clear."

"Bishop, I have you in sight. Are you south of the Castle?"

"Si, we have Castle in sight."

"Stand by Bishop," Puros ordered. He turned to Carlos and Marcel standing next to him. "Our first visitors are here. Marcel, you work your way down to the cove and stand on the south end so they can see you. We need to guide them close to the rocks where the deep water is. I will guide him from up here, go on."

Marcel reached over and picked up his back pack and started walking down the hill on the south side. He would eventually get just above the cove, where he would have a good view of the sand bar and the narrow passage that the large Bertram yacht would have to challenge. Once inside the cove, it was a perfect anchorage with nearly twenty feet to the sandy bottom.

"Pawn to Bishop. When you reach the castle, look for a pawn over the castle wall, watch for his signals. It is very close at this time, tide is not high, and only five feet at the entrance."

Bonaire
46' Bertram Sportfishing Yacht
1050 Hours

Captain Jose D'Amato understood what Puros was telling him. Through his binoculars, he could see one of Puros' men working his way down the small mountain and Puros and another man standing on up at the top.

D'Amato reached up and brought the two throttles back, and the yacht began to settle down in the stern as she came off plane.

"Rojo, get me the chart," D'Amato yelled to his black mate. In seconds, Rojo had the chart sitting on the console in front of his captain. D'Amato studied the island and the small cove that he was about to enter. There was little information on the chart relating to the cove and the sandbar that ran from the northern end, bowing in a crescent shape and tapering off at the south end, leaving a small passage close to the rocky wall. The cove itself was about 250 feet across and over 300 feet long. According to an old guide book, the cove had twelve feet of depth at mean low tide.

D'Amato ordered Rojo to stand on the bow and watch the water as he worked his way closer to the island. There was a strong current that ran clockwise around the island's southern end working against the Bertram's broad hull. D'Amato would use the current to keep him out of trouble should he get too close to the rocky sides of the cove on his starboard side.

"You're looking good, Bishop, watch my Pawn down there, he will guide you."

"Fuck your Pawn," D'Amato mumbled to himself as he eased the throttles forward. The two Detroit diesels were hardly laboring as the yacht moved cautiously over the shallow water coming into the cove. The depth recorder was showing nearly seven feet, as the deepest part of the Bertram's keel passed over the sugar white sands.

"He's in, beautiful!" Puros said out loud. Carlos clapped his hands. "Pawn to Bishop, you are in the castle, nice work, Captain."

"Gracias, Pawn, gracias," D'Amato replied. "We will set our anchor now. Will you be joining us?"

"Negative. I will remain to watch for the King, who should be in the area within the next two hours, over."

Puros was about to light a cigarette, when the radio came back on. "Have you heard from the King? Is all well?"

"Negative, Bishop. Will not hear until they are in the area." Puros laughed and shook his head. "What the fuck does he think I have up here? A fifty-thousand watt radio station? Have we been in touch with the King?"

Carlos Mesa laughed, then replied. "Well, remember, he has very important cargo aboard, keep that in mind. You know, we have no idea if Castro is really coming, do we? They could have turned back days ago, how would we know, comrade?"

"I would know, believe me, he is coming and we will see him as planned when the sun is the highest."

Aboard the Bonaire

Captain D'Amato, not one for taking chances, decided that since he was the first to arrive, he would take the anchorage closest to the only exit. When Castro's yacht arrived it would have to go beyond him and anchor.

D'Amato shut down his two engines and turned on his auxiliary generator for power. His passengers were all inside the main cabin enjoying their favorite drinks and playing poker. In the ships galley, Carla D'Amato was preparing lunch.

The four Latin men had no interest in where they were, or what time their host was arriving. Their card game had begun nearly sixteen hours before and the stakes were high. Aldo Rivia from Colombia was losing nearly a half million American dollars.

Captain D'Amato entered the main salon, went over to the air-conditioning panel and placed the fan selector in "full-high" position.

"Captain, you are freezing our asses off," Roberto Calva yelled as he held his cigar between his badly stained teeth. Calva was an attorney from Panama. On his right was Ramon Cantillo from Colombia. Sitting next to Cantillo was Jorge Armando, born in Cuba, residing in Chile. Aldo Rivia was one of the most successful drug negotiators in Colombia.

"Forgive me, gentlemen. The smoke in here is ruining the interior of this yacht. Señor Fabricio, my employer, your good friend and owner of this very expensive yacht, does not smoke. Señora Fabricio is allergic to smoke, she would die if she walked in here right now."

Cantillo laughed. "You tell our friend, Fabricio, that it's time he gets a new yacht anyway and Señora Fabricio, shit, she never shares his bed on this floating play-pen, who are you kidding, Captain? She hates the water." Cantillo never looked up at D'Amato.

Totally disgusted with his guests, Captain D'Amato reached up and put the air conditioning selector to maximum cold. He ignored the grunts and complaints from the table and went down into the galley to join his wife, who was about to serve lunch.

Unicorn
26 Miles due West of Grand Islet
1109 Hours

Fidel Castro stood braced against the teak capped windscreen. The strong wind tore at his loose shirt and the bright sun reflecting off the water forced him to squint. Next to him, Captain DeTorre sat in his helmschair holding onto the large stainless wheel. Dimitri Sorokin was relaxing in his favorite lounge seat, clad only in his swimsuit and a pair of aviator sunglasses. General Vincetta occupied another lounge seat, dressed in white cotton slacks and a red pullover cotton shirt. He was reading a book that had been left aboard the yacht by its previous owner, "Bring on the Empty Horses" by David Niven. Occasionally, Vincetta would laugh, but he would not share the joke when they asked what was so funny.

"How far out do you put us, Captain?" Castro asked.

"We are maybe twenty five miles out, Comrade President.   We have the islands on radar. We will be sending messages out in fifteen minutes to advise Puros of our ETA. I have left orders below to call me as soon as we get any calls from him."

"Is the main radar fixed now?" Castro continued.

"Yes, comrade President, the motor is back working, but for how long, well, we don't know. We expect it may happen again."

Castro turned and looked down at Sorokin laying back on the lounge chair. His body was that of a much younger man. Castro deeply admired him for his physical appearance, but more so, for his wisdom and intelligence.

"You are beginning to look like a tourist, my friend, too much sun is not good for the skin, especially on that new tissue on your leg scars, Dimitri."

Sorokin opened his eyes and looked up at Castro. He thought Castro looked like a refugee or some poor immigrant. His hair was greasy and matted. He had on an old olive drab long sleeved shirt soaked with sweat, and a pair of wrinkled khaki trousers. He wanted to say something to Fidel about his appearance, but knew it would only make him angry. He decided to smile and close his eyes.

"We will be at the cove no later than 1200 hours, Comrade President," DeTorre yelled over the wind.

"It's been a good voyage, Captain. You like this ship, don't you?"

"Yes, comrade President, she is magnificent. I would like to see about ten or fifteen more knots, that's all. May I ask what happens to her when we return to Cuba?"

"We will have to put it all back together and send her back to the Mediterranean to be sold. However, if we do well at this meeting who knows, maybe we will bring her to Havana and I will give you a permanent new job as her captain. How do you like that?"

The young captain reached down and grabbed his crotch in his hand. "I would chop all this off for that opportunity, Comrade President."

Castro laughed, but he was shocked at DeTorre's crude gesture. He bent down and yelled to Sorokin that he was going below for a while.

Sorokin removed his glasses and smiled. "You need some sun, comrade, stay up here and relax a while. I will go make us a drink."

"No, I want to read, my friend. I will see you when we get to the island." Castro looked over at Vincetta. His book was lying on the deck, pages fluttering in the breeze. He was fast asleep.

1124 hours

"Captain, we are getting a message from the island, somebody is calling for the "king", isn't that our call sign?"

"Yes, that's it. Call Puros, tell him that we should be reaching the island around 1200 hours. Ah, wait, you have to tell him in code. Say King takes the Pawn, King Takes the Pawn. Will be in the castle at 1200. Repeat that to him, understand?"

"Yes, Captain." Manuel left the flybridge and returned to the wheel house below. When he reached the radio, he picked up the mike and began to broadcast.

"King takes the Pawn, King takes the Pawn. Do you copy?"

"Pawn to King, Pawn to King, read you clearly. What is your position?"

Manuel hesitated. "Negative on that. We will be at the castle 1200 hours. Copy?"

"Pawn to King, affirmative. Do you have visual yet of the castle?"

Manuel looked at the radar monitor. He could see the large island of Guadeloupe and the targets just to the south, which would be the Isles De Saintes. He looked out the large windshield. The brilliant sun was bouncing off the seas with endless flashing lights, as if millions of rhinestones were playing on the waves.

"King takes Pawn, yes, have visual."

Aboard Island Drummer
Redonda Island
1140 Hours

"How are you doing, Gail?" O'Brien asked.

"I'm fine, Dan. Maybe a little weak in the knees though, wondering what is taking place about now down in Guadeloupe."

O'Brien looked at his watch. "Well, if Chen did his job, we should hear about the explosion in about nine hours, that's if there is any kind of communication between Antigua and Guadeloupe."

Avery and Buckland came up on deck. "O.K. Gail, you have the island of Redonda over there on your port, can you see it without the glasses?"

Gail squinted and shielded her eyes with her hand from the sun. "Yes, I can see it, about eleven o'clock."

"Good. Now, over here, about two o'clock you have Montserrat. We want to stay on this heading closer to Redonda, that way we can minimize boating traffic. As soon as we pass Redonda, we will head on down and shoot for the southern end of Antigua and English Harbour."

"What time do you estimate we will arrive in Antigua, Phil?" O'Brien asked.

"Well, if we powered all the way, we could get there around 1430. However, we will probably have to cut our speed down as we get closer to Antigua. My guess is that there will be a lot of traffic sailing along the west side of the island between St. Johns to the north and English Harbour to the south. Most of the yachts cruising around here will be under the command of very experienced captains and crews. We don't want to show them a seventy five foot ketch that cutting through the waters like a jet ski at twenty-five knots."

"Phil, why don't we raise the sails when we have Antigua in sight. It would look better, after all we are supposed to be out on charter. I bet we could make it all the way on one tack, right to the harbor's entrance," Gail suggested.

"Good idea, Gail. At 1200 hours we'll call Nicholsons clearing house on the radio and tell them we have arrived, so they can log us in. We will tell them that we are staying outside the harbor, day sailing. That way, it makes no difference when we drop anchor." Avery looked at Gail with admiration. "Now I know why we brought you along, since we knew you couldn't cook. Good thinking, lady." He laughed and put his hands on her bronzed shoulders.

"Gail, if you're tired, I'll be happy to relieve you. Why don't you and Phil go and study the charts. I think I can keep us out of harms way for the next few miles."

"Sure, thanks, Dan. You got it. Heading is zero eight five."

Gail stepped back from the wheel as O'Brien put his hands around the metal ring. He smiled and winked at her as she left to join Avery.

Grand Islet
1209 Hours

Puros was trying to keep calm, but the excitement of seeing the giant Feadship yacht in close was evident in his communications with Captain DeTorre.

DeTorre had his hands full trying to maneuver the large yacht so he could take a straight in approach at the narrow opening between the rocks and the sand bar. Puros kept screaming over the radio giving DeTorre unnecessary orders. Finally, DeTorre had to tell Puros to stay off the radio.

Without the luxury of thrusters to help him maneuver the lengthy bow close to the rocky wall to his starboard, DeTorre had to work carefully, using his engines to keep him in control of the bow. At this point, his rudders were almost useless. Despite all his efforts the current, working against the massive starboard side of the hull, was pushing the Feadship slowly into the shallow waters over the sand bar. DeTorre knew that he would be very close to the soft sandy crest of the bar and hoped that he could get over without contact. He wasn't that lucky. Only forty feet of the giant hull had passed over the bar before DeTorre felt the soft bump.

Carlos was running up and down the deck looking over the port side of the yacht for coral or rock heads under the fine sand. DeTorre felt no resistance as he continued forward at slow speed. He knew the keel was dragging through the fine sand and he prayed that he wasn't sucking too much sand through the raw water engine intakes. He felt certain that the filters would take care of a reasonable amount of sand that was drawn in and that the props and rudders would clear the bar easily.

In a few short minutes, the Feadship had cleared the sand bar, leaving in its wake a brown foaming cloud swirling around in the once crystal clear blue water. DeTorre was not concerned about damage. There were no unusual vibrations or rise in engine temperatures, and both depth recorders were still sounding, which meant his underwater electronic gear was intact. He began to pay attention to the next job at hand, getting past the large sport fishing yacht that lay anchored just ahead.

Although concern was written all over the faces of Sorokin and Vincetta when the Unicorn bumped crossing the sandbar, they did not make any comment to DeTorre, nor did they hear any word from Fidel Castro, who was still in his stateroom.

Although there was no structural damage when the Feadship's keel and bottom plates moved through the soft sand bar, large areas of bottom paint were scraped off together with a lot of parasites; including a number of plastic boxes that were magnetically held in place against the plates and keel and connected by a small wire to a timing device.

As DeTorre maneuvered the Feadship carefully past the stern of the Bertram, he noticed the captain and a crew member standing in the large open cockpit. They were waving and smiling as the Unicorn passed by less than fifteen feet away. DeTorre responded with a military salute and continued into the large basin ahead of him. He maneuvered the bow of the Unicorn slowly towards the rocky face of the island. He ordered the anchor to be released then he backed down, leaving a comfortable distance from the island and keeping his stern over 10 feet of water and twenty yards away from the sand bar. He was well into the lee of the island and did not expect the Unicorn to swing into trouble, but to ensure his position, he ordered that a stern anchor be prepared to be released just in case.

After dropping anchor, the Unicorn's crew set up security around the yacht, while Sorokin and Vincetta held a conference with Fidel Castro in his stateroom. There had been no communication with the Bonaire since the Unicorn arrived. They had been instructed to keep off the radio, unless there was an emergency. They were close enough to each other to communicate with bull horns.

After the meeting, Castro sent a message over to the Bonaire asking her passengers to come over to the Unicorn at 1700 to discuss plans for the demonstration. Lo had been working on the Dolphin all morning, charging up the batteries and adjusting the control surfaces. Now that the Unicorn was anchored, he was able to run static tests on the Dolphin's control servos using the two transducers already in use in the Unicorn's electronic depth sounders.

DeTorre was pleased to see that both transducers located at mid-ship were still working properly, and he decided that it would not be necessary to send a diver beneath the Unicorn to check for any damage.

"Captain, we are a bit concerned about the confines of this cove. Should we have to leave in a hurry when the tide is lower than it was when we came in, are we going to be able to get out safely?"

"Yes, comrade Sorokin. When we leave, we can get closer to the rock wall where the deeper water is and get out easily. I had some trouble with the currents as we were coming in, they kept pushing us over into the shallow water. We should have no problem as long as that sportfishing boat doesn't get in my way. I will be having a meeting with its captain later to discuss our of emergency plans. Tomas Puros is due to join us, he should be here any minute. He has worked out all the emergency plans. You, comrade, General Vincetta, our President and Mr. Lo will be taken out in a small boat to a nearby airstrip, where a plane is waiting to fly you back to Cuba."

Sorokin was speechless. He had no idea that these plans had been made. Castro had said nothing to him.

"General Vincetta, did you know about this?" Sorokin asked.

"I should think so, comrade. I made the arrangements a month ago."

"Well, I'm impressed," Sorokin remarked as he smiled and nodded his head. "Ah, Captain, this radio, this one here?" Sorokin pointed to one of the many small black boxes on the communications rack. "This is a VHF radio, is that right?"

"Correct, we have four of them on board. This one here, one over the helm station, another in the navigation station, and the one on the fly-bridge that has not been working too well, oh, I think there may be another in the captain's stateroom, why do you ask?"

"Oh, nothing, I just wondered which one was the VHF, just in case. You never know, something could come up and we may need help. We would use this radio, correct, I mean here in this area, this is how we would communicate?"

"Correct, comrade, everyone here in these islands uses this radio. Now, if you will excuse me, I have to lower our runabout and clear the main salon roof for the demonstration latter."

"Of course, Captain, can I help you?"

"Thank you, that would be kind of you."

The two men excused themselves and left the bridge. As they walked forward on the main deck, the sound of a small outboard engine got their attention. They went over to the rail and saw the small open boat with a man steering the outboard heading for the Unicorn's boarding ladder. He was waving at the people standing in the Bertram's cockpit as he passed by their stern.

"That is Tomas Puros, comrade Sorokin. He is one of the President's favorites, I understand. Come, we will go greet him, then we will take care of the small boat topside."

Antigua
English Harbour
1248 Hours

The Island Drummer cruised down off the west coast of Antigua under full sail, heading towards English Harbour. Avery had all the sails eased off as the brisk wind blowing out of the east was becoming a concern, the Drummer was becoming too sensitive and rolling. He decided to drop the main and reef the jib.

Antigua lay about three miles east. They could see a large cruise ship leaving the harbor at St. Johns, and there were more sailboats cruising about than they expected to see. Avery commented that most of the yachts were probably crewed charter yachts sailing out of English Harbour, doing their Christmas week charters.

The rolling green hills under the bright sun gave way to moving dark shadows as low clouds swept swiftly over the island. To the crew aboard the Drummer, Antigua looked like a painted postcard.

Avery had checked in with the clearing house at 1205 hours. He told the young lady at Nicholsons that he had sailed directly from St. Thomas, which would put his sailing time at twenty four hours, which was perfect, and right to plan. Nicholson's advised him they were holding three messages for him. Avery requested they not be relayed, that someone from the yacht would come up and pick them up as soon as they cleared customs.

"Phil, are we going to have any problems explaining where your charter guests disappeared to?" O'Brien asked.

"No, we don't need to account for them here, nobody at Nicholsons is going to care who is on board, or why. Stop worrying, Dan, we will get through this, believe me."

"Yeah, I guess I'm just..."

Avery interrupted, "I know, Dan. Oh, by the way, I have your phony passport and I.D. in an envelope down in my luggage, compliments of

Admiral Koster and Ian Billings. Koster knew you would get on the Drummer somehow, so he sent your stuff down with our charter guests."

O'Brien forced a smile. He reached for his cigarettes and found only an empty pack, rolled it up and was about to throw it overboard, but he stopped and put it into his pocket. He walked over to the companionway and went below.

Avery was concerned about Dan O'Brien, he watched him age over the past two months. He had lost a considerable amount of weight, which added to his aging appearance. Avery looked towards the bow, looking for Gail. She and Buckland were sitting on the main cabin roof doing a little sightseeing. He hated to disturb her, but he thought O'Brien could use some of Gail's special medicine about now. He called her over.

"Phil, Dan is more than I can handle right now, I will talk to him, smile at him, even get high with him, but I can't get his mind off of what is taking place a few miles south of here. It's beginning to drive me crazy too, I keep seeing people screaming, trapped in the yachts. Maybe I saw the Poseidon Adventure too many times."

"I know." He leaned over and kissed her gently on her forehead. "See what you can do anyway, and bring me up a very light rum and tonic, with a lime, if there are any left."

Freeman Bay
English Harbour, Antigua
1431 Hours

The Island Drummer swung peacefully on her anchor in the crowded bay. There were celebrations already taking place throughout the harbor. Many of the yachts were displaying all kinds of Christmas decorations and crews were still busy working on stringing lights and long green garlands in the rigging of their yachts.

The Drummer's crew was sitting in the cockpit enjoying the view and the sights and sounds of the festivities around them, while they waited under their yellow quarantine flag for customs agents to come and clear them. They had been told that they would be boarded between 1400 and 1500 hours.

"Jesus, Phil, does it always take this long to get customs out to clear?"

"Patience, Dan, I'm sure they have their hands full. Just take a look around, man, there must be two hundred yachts parked between here and Falmouth Harbour."

"How far is the airport?"

"About a half hour, maybe twenty minutes in a good cab."

"We need to get out there and find someone who will charter us a small plane. We need to get down and take a look, make sure that the Unicorn and their friends arrived. Shit, for all we know, Castro may have been handed a no-show. Suppose the other guys didn't make it?"

"Dan, as soon as we clear, you and Buckland can take a cab from over at the Dockyard and go on out to the airport. There are plenty of charter flights available, but we need to have a plan. We have to set up land communications between us and ah, whomever. What we need to do is find a couple of rooms over at one of the hotels and get a telephone number. That's the first step."

"Why don't I get on the radio and contact the Copper and Lumber Store and check for rooms. If they are full, I'm sure they can tell us where we may find some housing."

"Good idea, Gail, go ahead, get on the horn and see what you can muster up."

Avery continued. "Dan, let's say we get the housing, and now we have a phone to use, or at least we are be able to get messages. If I recall, there are no phones in the rooms of these hotels, it's all done at the front desks, know what I mean?"

O'Brien stood up and walked around the cockpit. "Jesus, how are we, shit, this is crazy, wait, I've got it." O'Brien snapped his fingers. "There are some Air Force personnel out at the airport, right?"

Avery looked at O'Brien with concern, "Yeah, Air Force, and I think maybe some Navy. They run the tracking station out there. We talked about this up in Washington with Admiral Koster, didn't we?"

O'Brien went behind the helmswheel and grabbed the large steel ring. "Yeah, why didn't we think of that sooner? I will call Koster as soon as I can get to a phone and have him introduce us to whomever we need to know at this tracking base. We can work from out there. They must have plenty of communications, may even have quarters up there that I can stay at. I'll pack a bag, just in case." O'Brien walked towards the companionway, stopped and turned. "Now, as far as chartering a flight to go to Guadeloupe? If I recall correctly, the distance from here to the Isles Des Saintes is about eighty miles. A Cessna 172 should be able to get there and back in a little over an hour, right?"

"Right, Dan, but why not wait until we talk to Koster. We have messages to call him. It could be they have already sent someone down there to take a peek, you know how Koster works, Dan, he's been full of surprises on this whole mission. I would be willing to bet that while we have been bouncing all over the Caribbean Sea, he has had someone down there photographing the whole operation."

Gail and Buckland started laughing along with Avery. O'Brien looked at their cheerful faces and for the first time in days, he began to laugh.

"You know, you're right, Phil. Old Scrooge is probably down there in Guadeloupe himself. Remember how he looked when he showed up at your condominium in Lauderdale? He looked like some lost tourist who had fallen off his yacht."

The cockpit of the Drummer rang out with laughter and tears were seen running down O'Brien's cheeks. For the moment, at least, they had taken his mind off the mission.

Copper & Lumber Store
1550 Hours

It was decided that after the crew cleared customs they would dinghy over to the Copper and Lumber Store. Avery talked O'Brien into staying at the Pub until he and Gail got back from Nicholsons, where they needed to check in and pick up their messages. Commander Buckland would stay with O'Brien and keep him entertained.

Avery and Gail were only gone an hour. They picked up their messages and Avery called San Juan and talked to the Coast Guard. John Lind and his crew had already departed for St. Thomas. A Captain Lindquist briefed Avery about the death of the Navy Seal, Bill Allen. On the drive back to the Pub, they decided that they would not tell O'Brien about Allen, at least not yet. The only thing that troubled them was the message for O'Brien to call Scrooge. They felt certain that Koster would tell O'Brien about Allen's death, which could put him over the edge.

The taxi pulled up in front of the Pub and Gail and Avery got out. Just before they entered the door, Gail turned to Avery and told him not to mention the message from Koster to O'Brien. Maybe they would get lucky and O'Brien wouldn't ask about the messages. They decided not to mention it and hope for the best.

Buckland and O'Brien were mixing it up with two couples at the bar. O'Brien had already downed three rum and tonics, and was ordering rounds for the bar.

"Hi Carl, we are set for hotel rooms but we need to leave now.." Gail said smiling at O'Brien

"Hi Phil, hi Gail.." O'Brien moved off his stool and put his long arm around Gail's waist and pulled her into the bar. "Gail, I want you to meet some fine folks from Texas. This is Pete and Honey and Jack and Maureen, did I get that right?"

"Sure did, ah, thought you said your name was Dan?" the young Texan man remarked laughing.

Avery responded before O'Brien could open his mouth. "Oh, his nickname is Dan, it's short for dangerous. He is supposed to be our navigator and we are supposed to be in St. Maarten right now, but Carl's compass was off...so we made a wrong turn, right Carl?"

Buckland moved himself between O'Brien and the attractive blonde Texan women. "Hey, we had better get going. I have to get back to my watch." Buckland put his arm around O'Brien and moved him away from the bar into the crowded aisle shoving him through celebrating patrons talking and singing carols.

Avery placed a fifty dollar bill on the bar and smiled at the Texans. "This should take care of the tab, I hope. If it doesn't, tell the barmaid and I will stop in later..."

Gail had already alerted a taxi and was waiting at front of the hotel. After getting in Gail ordered the driver to take them to the Inn Hotel.

"What's going on, what does Scrooge want?" O'Brien asked.

Gail, nearly sitting in Avery's lap in the back seat, responded, "Oh, just wanted to wish you a happy Christmas, Dan."

"Yeah, I bet. That miserable old bastard, I bet he is over at the White House right now, downing some Christmas cheer with Ian and ..."

"Hey Dan, ask the driver about transportation out to the airport. How much will it cost, and is there an FBO or a charter company out there where you can rent a plane," Avery yelled.

"Hey, what's your name, friend?" O'Brien asked.

"Pepe," the driver responded.

"Pepe, did you hear my friend? How much will it cost to take me to the airport?"

"Twenty EC," Pepe replied.

"EC?, oh, that's right, Caribbean rates, right?"

"That's right, and that's a good price, Dan. Pepe, how do we get in touch with you later?"

"You can get me on the radio at the front desk. Just tell them you want Pepe."

"Right, we will do that later," Avery said.

501

The taxi pulled up to the entrance of the small stone front building. Buckwheat got out and helped O'Brien. Avery paid Pepe and told him he would call him later. Gail had O'Brien's small overnight bag. They walked up the stone steps into the hotel's modest lobby where Gail confirmed she was the woman who called on the radio and reserved two cottages for two nights.

After some convincing, O'Brien was talked into laying down for a while in his cottage, which overlooked Freeman Bay. After getting him settled, Buckwheat joined Avery and Gail on the hotel patio, where they had a drink and discussed their next move, and their new problem, a drunken Dan O'Brien. They decided to let him sleep it off and forget the scouting mission over to Guadeloupe. They agreed that if all went well, the mission will be all over by 2100 hours. Getting information from Guadeloupe would be a problem without the scouting mission, particularly since it was Christmas Eve.

Gail managed to get her hands on O'Brien's small black book with all the codes and numbers. Avery had a tough time making the decision, but he thought it was worth the gamble. He took the book and went into the lobby, where he placed a call to Admiral Koster. It took nearly a half hour calling all the listed numbers, but he finally reached the Admiral at his home.

"Are you concerned, Mr. Avery, that O'Brien won't be able to function properly?"

"No, Admiral, he's just, well, so tense, but then, we all are. These next few hours of waiting are going to be hell, and we don't have any way of knowing if the operation went off. I don't know why, but we never thought about how we would find out."   "Yes, I know. Listen Avery, you have a good head on your shoulders. You just keep O'Brien horizontal for the next few hours. When he gets up, get him to a phone and have him call me. I will straighten his ass out, don't worry about that. I will not say anything about the Allen boy's death, I agree that can wait. However, we do have a problem down in Guadeloupe. Ian Billings sent a young agent down there to follow some Cuban who came down to Guadeloupe from New Orleans. This guy is one of Castro's troubleshooters, which means he is somehow tied in with the meeting on Grand Islet. Ian said he hasn't heard from his man in two days. As soon as the dust settles, you may have to go down there, or maybe we'll send your young Navy man, Commander Buckwheat, and have him look for this guy."

"Roger that, Admiral. Do you know the agent's name?"

"Negative, I do however, remember the name of the Cuban. His name is Puros, Tomas Puros. Get back to me later, Avery, I'll get that name for you."

"Yes sir, thank you. I guess all we can do now is wait, right sir?"

"That's it, Mr. Avery, we wait."

"Oh, before I forget, Admiral. Having those two Navy P-3 sub-hunters down here really helped. We appreciated their services."

"What P-3's? I don't know of any P-3's that flew out of San Juan and St. Croix. You must have been seeing things. Have O'Brien call me later tonight, ah, we did not have this conversation. Watch your fingers, I'm hanging up the phone, good day, Mr. Avery." The line went dead.

Bonaire
Grand Islet, Isles Des Saintes
1400 Hours

The five men stepped down into the hard bottom inflatable for the short ride. Captain D'Amato put the outboard in gear and moved slowly towards the Unicorn.

Standing at the top of the aluminum boarding ladder, Carlos Mesa waited patiently with Captain DeTorre to greet the guests. In Castro's roomy stateroom, Castro, Sorokin, Vincetta, and Tomas Puros sat waiting.

The door to the stateroom opened, and the first one to enter was Jorge Armando, followed by Roberto Calva, Ramon Cantillo and Aldo Rivia. Standing next to the door, General Vincetta held out his hand and introduced himself, then introduced his President, Sorokin and Puros. After some small talk, the eight men made themselves comfortable, while Carlos acted as bartender and waiter.

Roberto Calva had been chosen by his shipmates to be their spokesman in their discussions with Fidel Castro.

"Señor Castro, you have come a long way to tell us that you have some new method of delivering our products to the United States without detection and which could save us millions of dollars. Well, we are here to learn about this method, Fidel, however.."

Calva was sharply interrupted by General Vincetta, "Señor, it is President Castro to you, nobody calls our President by his first...."

503

Castro moved forward to the edge of his seat and raised his hand as if he were stopping traffic. "That's alright, General." he said smiling. "We are friends here, please, comrade Calva, continue."

Calva relaxed back into his chair and crossed his arms, but only for a second. He moved forward again to the edge of his seat and pointed an index finger at Castro. His face took on a look of anger as he addressed Castro.

"You don't want to be called, Fidel? O.K., fine, but you don't brand me with your comrade shit, understand, Mr. President? I am not a communist."

Castro bowed his head slightly, never taking his eyes off Calva and returned a forced smile.

Sorokin caught Vincetta's eye. Neither of them was feeling comfortable with their visitors and were already planning alternative measures should the atmosphere deteriorate any further.

Castro, a master at changing conversations, stood up and brought his hands together, rubbing them vigorously. He smiled.

"Gentlemen, in the next few minutes, I will show you the most advanced method of delivering drugs to any location on the shores of the United States. There isn't an inlet, river or bay that can't be accessed by this new machine."

Armando signaled for Carlos to refill his gin and tonic as he said, "Machine? You are going to show us some kind of new machine?"

Castro stood relaxed and concentrated his gaze on Armando.

"Yes, it is an old idea with new technology added, my friend and it will give you the ability to deliver your goods without losing expensive aircraft and boats, not to mention the pilots and manpower you keep losing to American jails and cemeteries."

Aldo Rivia jumped up from his chair screaming. "This is fucking crazy. I came all the way here to sleep on a stinking crowded fishing boat, then be told by a has-been dictator that he has some kind of fucking new toy to deliver drugs in? I'm out of here, gentlemen, just get me over to the airport on Guadeloupe, O.K. Mr. Dictator?"

Vincetta leaped up from his chair and threw himself on the surprised Rivia. They both crashed through Rivia's empty chair onto the hardwood oak floor, rolling around like two wild animals. It took the strength of Sorokin, Calva and Castro to pull them apart.

Sorokin separated the two men with his outstretched arms, while Castro and Calva restrained them. Sorokin shouted. "What the hell is going on here? We are all here to learn something and hopefully embark on a new business venture together. President Castro is giving you the opportunity to see an almost risk-free new method of delivering your products. The least you can do is see what he has to show you. Can't we do this without violence?"

Sorokin put his arms down, and stood in the middle of the room, shifting his eyes between Rivia and Vincetta.

"Who the fuck are you?" Calva asked.

Before Sorokin could respond, Castro spoke up. "He is a friend and businessman who has invested in my invention."

"You are not Cuban, are you? Where do you come from, Mr. Sorokin?" Calva asked.

"Soviet Union, my family owns the largest contracting company in Moscow. I am investing in Cuba, personally."

Calva was not buying Sorokin's story and did not hesitate to tell him so.

"You're right about one thing, Mr. Sorokin, your family owns many building machines, but you my friend, you are the KGB, don't try and bullshit us. We know who you are and why your here. I am only surprised that half the KGB is not here with you looking for ways to retire, things at home aren't going too well for you right now, is that not right, comrade? Your new leader seems to be wanting to change things, like leaning a little more to the west, don't you agree Mr. Sorokin? Pretty soon we will be doing business in Moscow."

"Señor Calva, your life will be over if your caught sending your shit into my homeland, we don't have high powered lawyers to defend you, or judges and politicians you can buy and don't ever think you would be safe in your own country. We don't work like the Americans, we don't ask questions or wait for permission from your government to find you. We come and find you, your family, your associates and conduct our own trial."

Fidel Castro knew he needed to put an end to the verbal sparring and that he needed to control the situation before it blew up in his face. He thought it would be best to show the Dolphin mini-sub to his prospective customers and give them time to calm down.

"Gentlemen, please come with me." Castro stood up and went to the door.

The seven men entered the main salon and saw Mr. Lo standing inside the mini-sub with only his shoulders and head visible. He had removed the sail panel that housed the transceivers and antennas.

The Dolphin looked most impressive sitting on its wooden cradle. It took up most of the salon, leaving only a few feet to walk around, and even less to the ceiling of the salon. Its dull black satin finish covered its topsides and the bottom was painted a light gray. It looked like its namesake.

"It's a fucking submarine, a mini submarine," Calva spoke out.

"Not quite, gentlemen, it is more like a killer whale, in size and physical character, wouldn't you agree?" Castro commented. "Mr. Lo, there in the cargo section, is getting the Dolphin ready for our demonstration later this evening. Meanwhile, let me give you a small tour and explain how it works."

Castro tapped his knuckles on the hull lightly. "This is high-tech fiberglass called Kevlar. It is light and strong. Note the fins here on the stern, shaped like whale fins. Like an airplane, these vertical fins move and act as rudders. The horizontal fins also move and act as elevators, which give control to dive or surface. Look here, notice this large opening here at the tail cone. That's where the exhaust comes out, better known as the water-jet nozzle. You see, a water jet pump propels this brilliant machine, there are no props. The entire structure is almost totally undetectable, as it uses very little metal. We have a small stainless steel shaft and electric motor, and a few minor metal parts. Everything else is plastic, fiberglass or wood."

Lo climbed out of the sub and came down the ladder to join Castro and his guests. Castro asked him to continue the tour and to answer any questions. Castro and Sorokin stood off to one side, and Vincetta excused himself and went back to his stateroom. He had hurt his wrist in the scuffle and went to find a bandage to wrap it with.

For the next hour, Lo went over the Dolphin step by step with the four curious visitors. Every question asked was met with an intelligent answer. Lo invited each man to climb into the Dolphin and look at the size of the compartments that would house their products. He guaranteed them that the compartments would be water tight. He saved the best till last, when he explained how the explosive charges would be set off should someone try and remove the sail panel without the proper code. They were totally impressed.

The group returned to Castro's quarters where Lo went over the communication system. He explained how the computers would be pre-set on board the mother ship before launching for each delivery and he showed how easily the depth recorders were modified to transmit the proper signals to the Dolphin from its mother ship and the pick up boats.

"In conclusion, gentlemen, let me add that this new method of delivery into the United States is so foolproof that you may have to send in a few regular deliveries occasionally, so that the Americans don't suspect that you are using other methods of delivery."

"I don't follow you, Mr. Lo, what do you mean?" Calva asked.

Sorokin spoke up. "I think what he means is that you will still have to maintain some of your standard methods using aircraft and boats to deliver your drugs to keep them from looking for any new methods you have come up with. Eventually, one of the Dolphins, for one reason or another could be found."

Calva turned and addressed Castro. "Yeah, but what about the explosive charge? Nobody except the person with the combination knows how to open the thing, right? No one who finds a dolphin isn't going to live long enough to talk about it."

Sorokin spoke again. "Yes, but it may be seen and possibly even photographed. Worse case scenario, they may find out about them, but their major problem will be finding a way to catch one, that won't be easy. It will also be very expensive for them right now to pursue new tactics. Most law enforcement agencies are getting their budgets cut. Reagan just announced he would never raise taxes this year, he wants to keep his job."

"You know, I can see these things going right into New York Harbor and sailing up the Hudson," Rivia said laughing.

"You're right, Señor. How about the Mississippi or under the Golden Gate Bridge?" Vincetta added.

"Señor Castro, I apologize. You just may have come up with something, and we look forward to seeing this Dolphin demonstrated later."

The small oriental man interrupted. "Ah, I am sorry to announce that it will be impossible to have a demonstration tonight," Lo said nervously.

"What do you mean, Lo? What is wrong?" Castro demanded.

"The transceiver, I can't get it to function properly. I may have damaged it accidentally this morning when I was removing it from the case. It was jammed and I forced it, and broke some of the circuits on the board."

"Well, that's just fucking fine, isn't it?" Vincetta said.

"Just a minute, comrade Lo. You must be able to work on circuit boards, that's your business, isn't it?" Sorokin added.

"Comrade, I need the proper testing equipment, I don't have that here. I don't have anything that I need, only a small testing light and some solder, that's all. Please, these boards are still in the prototype stage, gentlemen. I don't have spares."

"I don't believe this and you expect us to do business with you? This is incompetence at the highest degree, you stupid yellow bastard, do you realize what this trip has cost us? I should blow your fucking brains out right here and now."

"Easy, General, I'm sure Mr. Lo is telling the truth, it was an accident, and I am sure he will go back and work on the circuit board and see if he can find the problem, right Mr. Lo?" Sorokin asked in a calm voice.

"Yes, comrade, I will do my best. I know I can get some of the controls to function, it will take some time, but I will try."

"These fucking Chinese, you can't trust them," Vincetta said.

"General, we have to give him a chance, meanwhile gentlemen, why don't we all retire for a spell. I'm sure you would all like to return to your quarters and freshen up. Why don't we all meet back here, say around 1900 hours. We are preparing dinner for everyone, aren't we, General?" Sorokin said calmly.

"Yes." Vincetta said.

"Good, we will have a good dinner, drink some wine and I bet that Mr. Lo will have the Dolphin ready to go by then."

"Sorokin, you missed your calling. You should be running some major American corporation," Calva said laughing, then turned to his shipmates. "Let's go back to the Bonaire. We will come back as you requested, Mr. Sorokin and let's hope Mr. Lo doesn't disappoint us."

"By the way, Mr. Castro, have you a price on these Dolphins, providing they work?"

"Ah, we have, Mr. Calva, but we would rather wait until we meet later to discuss purchase prices and deliveries, if you don't mind?"

"No, I guess not Mr. Sorokin, until later?" Calva smiled and left the cabin, followed by his three associates.

"I am sorry for butting in like that, but I thought it best that we negotiate a little more with our friend Mr. Lo, before we start talking price on the Dolphins. Have you talked to Lo at all about this?"

"Of course we have, comrade," Vincetta commented before Castro could open his mouth. "We established our price with the Chink an hour ago when he failed us and he will pay dearly if he can't get us out of this embarrassing situation, am I correct, comrade President?"

"Yes, General," Castro said cautiously. "He will pay, I promise. Now, comrades, if you would please excuse me? I would like to rest for a while. I want to be called if Lo has any news." Castro turned and walked through the door to his cabin.

"I don't like the look of him, General," Sorokin said.

"He will be alright. He doesn't like being made a fool of, comrade. Today he was insulted and severely disappointed. He has also learned what these thieves are really like. He looks upon them as possible leaders of their countries. Do you realize how powerful these animals are? They have money, arms, protection, and absolutely no respect for anyone, and we...

Sorokin wasted no time in interrupting Vincetta. "And you, my friend, are ready to make them even more powerful, more dangerous. You do realize this, don't you, General?" Sorokin spoke in a tone of concern. He turned and walked out of the smoky stateroom, deliberately slamming the door.

The Inn
Antigua
1810 Hours

"Yes, hello, Admiral. Sorry to disturb your dinner."

"That's alright, O'Brien. How are you feeling, son?"

"Oh, a little of everything, Admiral. We are three hours away from making history, but we have no way of knowing if we did, if you know what I mean?"

"Dan, I can understand your frustrations, but you are on the home stretch now. This is what you worked and planned for, don't you dare fall apart on us now. I am giving you a direct order, get your fucking head out of that rum bottle immediately. If this mission is blown by your own hand wrapped around a bottle, you had better look for an island down there where you can hide for the rest of your life, do you read me, Mr. O'Brien?"

"Yes, loud and clear. But.."

"No buts. Listen to me. Did Avery tell you about Ian's man down there in Guadeloupe?"

"Yes, he mentioned it, but he also said you haven't heard from him since.."

"That's right, and that's why Ian has another man heading down right now, but they don't expect him to land in Guadeloupe until 1100 hours tomorrow. He will have your number there at the hotel, and he will call you if he learns anything. You just stay put. You don't need to go sightseeing either. We have some troops there on Antigua that we can send out scouting if necessary. We have the equipment down there to do so, do you copy?"

"Yes, but it would be so easy, Admiral, to take a small plane down there and just take a look see, it's only eighty miles."

"Listen, we take thousands of pictures down there every month of our Russian friends and their trawlers, who monitor our tracking station there.

509

We have the equipment and the talent to photograph anything we need. I will make that decision from up here, do you read me, O'Brien?"

"Yes, I understand. Are you going to send someone out today?"

"O'Brien? I want you to crawl back into your wonderful tropical bunk, pull the mosquito netting over you, turn up the fan and go to sleep. I am going downstairs and join my sons and daughter and their families. It's beginning to snow, so we are going to have a White Christmas here. You are there, where you need to be and where I need you to be. You have done a great job, Dan, and the headlines will prove it in the morning. Get some rest and Merry Christmas. Call me at 0900 tomorrow." The phone went dead.

O'Brien walked through the lobby and into the small bar. There were two couples sitting at a table next to an open window. Another couple sat at the bar, still in their beachwear.

"Yes, sir, what can I get you?" The young black bartender asked.

"Ah, a large coke, lots of ice. Can I charge it to my room?"

"Yes, sir, what is your name?"

O'Brien froze. He could not think of what name he had registered under. "Ah, I will be right back, I'll get you some money, just hold the coke."

1845 hours

Gail and Avery arrived by taxi at The Inn and went to O'Brien's cottage where they found him fast asleep. They left quietly, and walked next door to the next cottage and woke up Buckland. He told them that O'Brien had a long talk with Admiral Koster and all he had said was that the old fart would not let him charter a plane and go down and look at the cove. He also told him that Ian Billings had another man on his way to Guadeloupe to check on the missing agent.

The threesome went up to the hotel bar, picked up their drinks at the bar, then went out on the open patio and sat at a small table, where they discussed plans for Christmas Day, should no word come back from Guadeloupe.

"I think we should get the Drummer ready to leave around 0600 hours and head on down. We can throw up the sails if we have to look good, however, I think most yachts will be staying in port tomorrow, it's Christmas Day, what do you think, Gail?" Avery asked.

"Wrong, Phil. There will be plenty of traffic out there. Maybe not at daybreak, but as long as I can remember when I was working out of St.

Thomas, our Christmas guests wanted to be cruising, not sitting around some anchorage, especially on Christmas Day."

Avery took a long drag on his cigarette and looked out towards the scenic view below. "Well, it's nearly eighty miles down there. Even if we cheat a little and add some power, we could maybe do eighteen or twenty knots; that would get us down there around 1300 hours. Man, without communications this is going to be a bitch." Avery flipped his cigarette over the stone wall, then put his head down into his hands, and began to rub his eyes.

"Why don't we get out of here at midnight, Phil. Turn on the boilers and be down there at daybreak. The weather is severe clear for the next few days, at least that's what they were broadcasting earlier. Why wait until morning? We can make good time and that way we won't have to worry about running into much traffic either," Gail said.

"What do you think, Buckwheat?"

"Hey, Phil, you're calling the shots, whatever makes you happy. But what do we do with O'Brien? Just leave him here?"

"Not a bad idea, Phil," Gail added.

"Jesus, Gail, this is his show, he's busted his ass on this operation. No, we couldn't do that, I mean, I would love to, for his own good, but he would never forgive us, nor could I forgive myself."

"Well, Captain, what do we do?" Buckwheat asked.

"We go." Avery stood up and brushed the ashes off his white ducks. "Let's let doom and gloom sleep for a while. We will come back and get him around 1930 hours. How long did you book the two rooms here for, Gail?"

"Until the 27th."

"Good. We will keep them."

"What if Scrooge tries to contact us, or their guy in Guadeloupe wants to talk to us, Phil?"

"We will leave word here at the hotel to have them call Nicholsons. They can call us on the VHF or the single side band, shit, I'm not going to sweat out anyone calling us. I think we need to be where the action is, sitting here is driving me up the wall."

"I agree, Phil, and I think our friend Rudolf will be most pleased at your decision," Gail said.

"O.K. Gail, you and I will get back down to the Drummer and start getting ready. Buckwheat, you wake up Dan around 1930 hours, get in a taxi and meet us at the Admirals Inn. We will have dinner there, then head out to the Drummer."

Phil was getting excited. For once, he felt he was calling the right shots and so far, he was getting the full support of his crew. His only problem would be O'Brien, but he figured Dan would be totally in favor of the move. Later that night, he would learn he was right.

Aboard the Unicorn
Grand Islet, Isles Des Saintes
1947 Hours

Yang Lo sat on the soiled canvas that protected the oak floor beneath him. Parts and pieces of the electronics that made up the brains of the Dolphin's electronic machinery surrounded him. A steel pot, with a burning candle centered inside and a wire supporting a suspended screw driver over the flame, pretty much told the story that Yang Lo did not have the tools he needed to work on the damaged circuit board. The screw driver was no replacement for a proper soldering iron.

Standing around were Fidel Castro, Vincetta, Cantillo, Calva, Armando and Aldo Rivia. They looked on in silence as Lo made one more attempt with the end of the heated screwdriver to melt the solder he held nervously in his hand.

"Gentlemen, it is very difficult for Mr. Lo to work with us looking over his shoulder. Why don't we go up on deck and enjoy some refreshments and some of President Castro's cigars."

General Vincetta was doing his best to keep his composure. He had already prepared Fidel Castro for the worst, should Lo fail them. Sorokin was busy with Antonio Lopes and Cabino Varas setting up a portable bar topside on the open flybridge to entertain their guests. Sorokin had a plan that he would introduce to the four prospective buyers that he hoped would keep them satisfied until the Dolphin could be properly launched, hopefully before daybreak. If the demonstration had to be completely scratched, Sorokin would suggest that another meeting for a demonstration take place in Belize, sometime in late January. He had a good friend that lived there in Dangriga in a home on the Mullins River, a perfect spot to demonstrate the Dolphin. There was a large dock at the site and plenty of water to bring the Unicorn safely up the river.

2014 Hours

The sunset was spectacular as the Unicorn's passengers and their guests relaxed on the large open flybridge. Castro enjoyed introducing his company to a rum drink. It was a mixture of run and coke, with a taste of brandy and cream de-coco and a squeeze of lime over ice. The conversations ran from politics to jokes, and eventually to women. Tomas Puros was telling entertaining stories about the three women that he had imported for the trip to the island. When Jorge Armando ordered him to go get them and bring them over to the party, Puros got irritated and refused. At this point, things began to get a little testy between Puros and the guests. They all started to demand that the women be brought over to the yacht. Sorokin had to step in and bring everyone to their senses – these women were not to know who was attending this secret meeting and should be left at the Villas. It was finally agreed that Sorokin was right and the subject was dropped.

Vincetta, taking no chances, privately asked Puros to leave the yacht and return to his friends at the Villas. He also told Puros to be back up on the hill with his radio at first light to keep an eye on things. Vincetta walked Puros to his small outboard boat that was tied to the Unicorn's boarding ladder. Before they reached the ladder, Vincetta went into his cabin and came out with a large package, wrapped in brown paper and string. Puros put the package under his arm and went down the ladder. He started his motor and headed out of the cove at top speed. He had only a short period of daylight left, and at least a half hour ride back to the dinghy dock at Bourge Des Saints.

After the sun went down and pesky insects began to draw blood, it was agreed that everyone return to the Bonaire and play cards. Castro and Vincetta asked to be excused. They wanted to stay with Yang Lo and see if they could help. They were still convinced that Lo would have the Dolphin ready to test before dawn. Sorokin thought it would be good to stay with the guests and accepted their invitation to join them in their card games.

It was 0340 when Sorokin got back to the Unicorn, where he found Manual Fajardo and Gayo Rodriguez standing guard. Castro, Vincetta and Yang Lo had retired at 0200, after Lo had convinced Castro that the Dolphin could not be launched.

CHAPTER 27

Aboard Island Drummer
English Harbour
0110 hours

The Island Drummer moved quietly through the crowded harbor as she headed out to sea. Thousands of colorful Christmas lights were still glowing on numerous yachts, giving the historic harbor the appearance of a giant amusement park. There was music echoing off the hillsides, while singing and laughter was broadcast from yachts where parties were in full swing. Once in a while when the winds would float down from the eastern hills, the familiar island sounds of a steel drum band could be heard coming from Shirley Heights.

Avery maneuvered the Island Drummer carefully through the anchorage, while Gail, Buckland and O'Brien stood watch around the deck to ensure that Avery had sufficient seaway. On the bow, Gail stood leaning against the rolled up jib, guiding Avery through the anchor lines and sterns of the anchored yachts. When they had cleared the fleet she looked back at the glistening harbor, then up at Shirley Heights where strings of Christmas lights danced along the crest of the hill. "It is a magical night," she thought. "It's supposed to be special, a night to be shared with someone special." She pulled her windbreaker tight around her body and imagined how she would have dressed, had she been invited to attend the celebration of Christmas at Shirley Heights. She closed her eyes and for a moment and drifted back to Christmas a year ago. The private gala party she had to attend at the Sarasota Country Club, escorted by a total stranger, an associate of her lover. She thought about the dress she wore, and how she was the center of attention for men and women alike. She felt like a queen, until Carlton arrived with his wife. It was the first time they had met. Gail was impressed how this woman glowed in beauty and charm. "It was strange watching her with him, knowing that he did not love her." She thought. "But it's Christmas and husbands and wives were..." Gail lowered her head into her hands, the tears came easy.

"Hey, didn't you see that ocean liner coming at us? Jesus, Gail, want to get us all killed?"

Gail looked up into the handsome young face of Commander Buckland. Even in the pitch black she could see the compassion in his eyes and hear the tenderness in his voice. She opened her arms and they embraced. "Merry Christmas, I know it's tough, Gail. I don't ever remember spending Christmas Eve and being this lonely. It's like I'm in another world looking down on everyone else."

"I should have been more thoughtful, Buckwheat, I could have at least found some kind of Christmas tree, something to remind us. I didn't even think of buying anyone a gift. It's like Christmas is here, but not for us, is that how you feel, Buckwheat?"

"Yeah, I guess that's what I mean."

Buckland released his arms from around Gail. He moved his right hand up to her cheek, and with his thumb gently wiped the tear that was running down from the corner of her eye.

"Come on, let's go back there with our other two lonesome friends and see if we can raise their spirits. Is there anything down below we can eat? I'm starved, and I can use a beer, how about you?"

"No, but I will have a scotch, and yes, we have plenty of cheese and Ritz crackers. I'll go down and put a plate together."

Gail and Buckland were walking back along the deck just as the bow of the Island Drummer rose upward and broke through the first of many swells she would encounter in the open seas.

0230 Hours

"C'mon, Phil, you can't win this war all by yourself, take a break, it's well past my watch," Gail said calmly as she moved next to Avery's side.

His hands slipped off the large wheel as Gail's hands took their place. "One-seven-five is your heading, bright eyes," Avery said, then leaned over and put his arm gently around Gail's waist. She turned and faced him. They kissed.

"Merry Christmas, I wish I could..."

"Don't say it, Phil, I know how you feel, I feel the same, so does Dan and Buckwheat. I guess we could have planned this better, I mean the Christmas thing, but I just couldn't get my head in gear about anything else. This whole damn operation is changing me, Phil, and it's scary."

"It will be alright, Gail. I'm sure whatever happens, well..."

"Phil, you don't want this to happen, do you? I mean, blowing up Castro and these people. This really bothers you, doesn't it?"

"Yes it bothers me. Jesus Christ, Gail, we are involved with a plot to murder people, aren't we? Forget about it being Fidel Castro for a minute. What if it was another man, one who we did not know as a bad guy. Would you have volunteered to participate in destroying a stranger even if your country asked you to?"

"Phil Avery, listen to yourself. It's not like you have Castro in your gun sight and are pulling the trigger. You are not personally going to kill the man. An entire committee is. You might even say, the entire Cuban-American community is and by a direct order of the President of the United States, think about that. I had to come to grips with the possibility there will be others who will die in that blast, innocent people, just obeying orders like we are. Those are the souls I bleed for, not that grease ball Castro. My God, Phil, look at who have already been expended on this operation. That young Navy diver, Bill Allen, we don't know anything about him. I'm sure his family is going though a terrible time at this very moment. And poor Rick Van Wagner, he was just getting his life together again with a new bride and a new son. My God, what a Christmas this is going to be for those families, what a sacrifice they had to make and for what? A chance to exterminate an enemy of the United States who isn't exactly threatening our country. One man, who is politically a thorn in our government's side. These families won't even know that their husbands and sons were sacrificed for his death and if it doesn't happen, what do we charge young Bill Allen and Rick off to?

"O.K. Gail, cool it, and you can get off the soap box, right now. Remember, we have the poor bastard on board in a bunk below, who has taken responsibility for all of these lost souls, regardless of the outcome. Maybe we should start giving more thought to helping him right now."

"You're right Phil, I am sorry. If this whole thing fails and Castro escapes and sails back to Cuba and his drug friends get back to where ever, it will be alright with me, I just want you to know that."

"Watch your heading, pretty lady, you're falling off course."

Phil adjusted the two throttles, bringing the rpm's down from 2000 to 1800. He looked at his watch.

"What time do you figure we will hit Guadeloupe?" Gail asked.

"Oh, about 0600. We could delay that a little too. I worked it out earlier. It's exactly 86 miles from English Harbour to Grand Islet and the cove. I figure it will take us just about six hours at this speed. The southern end of Guadeloupe is about five miles north of the island. As soon as we pick up the north end of Guadeloupe on radar, we can adjust our speed to arrive at the cove just after daybreak."

"That's just three hours away. Why don't I go wake up Buckwheat and let him take the helm until 0500. I'll get up and make us all a good breakfast. I think we should all be up and on deck as soon as we can see Guadeloupe. You will want to run up some sails, won't you? I mean, so we at least look like we are on a cruise."

Avery laughed. He reached out with his right arm and brought Gail close to him. She rested her head on his shoulder, and for a few seconds they just enjoyed the cool breeze in their face. The symphonic sounds of the steel shrouds vibrating in the wind added music to their private moment. Gail turned her head and pressed her nose against his cheek. He turned and met her lips. They kissed hard. He moved his mouth next to her ear, and whispered. "I think I am falling in love with you, Gail." He felt her body tighten. She let out a deep sigh, but said nothing.

0616

"O.K., we have a good fix on Basse Terre." Buckwheat adjusted the brightness on the radar screen. He had a good picture. Guadeloupe was ten miles south, south east, at a heading of 158 degrees. Buckwheat went to the chart and located his position, then drew a line that went along the west coast of Basse Terre, and down to the Isles Des Saintes. He took a reading and wrote it down on a pad. He then took the calculator and worked out the Drummer's speed and time to target, Grand Islet. After studying the small island, he thought it best to let Avery have a look at which approach he wanted to take. They could sail to the west of Terre De Bas, round the island and head east past the small island called La Coche and approach Grand Islet and the cove from west, or go through the pass between Terre De Bas and Terre De Haut and approach Grand Islet from the east side of the island. He took the pad of notes, went over to the galley, poured a cup of coffee and went up to the cockpit.

"Phil, if we stay off the coast, say three miles, and stay with this power setting, we could be at the cove at 0815, give or take a few, depending on what approach you want to take."

Avery looked down at the large compass on the top of the console as he checked his heading, then responded. "You know, I have been thinking. What if we get down the road here another hour, throw up the sails and start making for Pointe A Pitre. We could cruise into the harbor, run up to the Government Dock, take on some fuel, clear customs and see if we can learn anything about an accident, maybe.."

"Jesus, Phil, that's going to take some time. We will have to go around the south end of the island and come back up into the harbor. Let me go down and work that out before we go through that trouble. We would have to clear customs and today is Christmas, or did you forget?"

"Phil, I think Buckwheat is right, why waste our time backtracking into Pointe A Pitre? It's going to be a mess in there today," Gail said as she tried to catch Avery's eye.

Dan O'Brien put his coffee cup down on the seat next to him, and looked up at Avery at the helm. "Phil? I am not familiar with this Pointe Pitre place, what is the advantage of going there?"

"Forget it, Dan, I just thought we might learn something about the explosion, if it happened, and save us a trip down to the cove. I was just thinking it would be best not to be seen down there. I may be too cautious, but I think letting anyone from the Unicorn's crew see the Drummer again, even though it's not disguised, would be asking for trouble."

"Come on, Phil, there is not a man alive that could put the two yachts together. My God, what did we go through that whole exercise for?" O'Brien asked.

"Dan, if there was anyone on that yacht that knew sailboats, they could easily see the similarities between the Drummer now and two nights ago. Besides, the French Navy keeps their patrol boat at the Government Dock, they are called FSMC, similar to our Coast Guard, I believe it stands for the Force De Surface Missions Civiles, something like that. If that ship is out of port, chances are we were successful."

"Jesus, Phil, that's like saying if the lights are on in the White House, the President is home, that's horseshit. Let's just go with our original plan, o.k. and get down and take a look see for ourselves at that cove." O'Brien stood up and walked to the main cabin bulkhead. He rested his hands on the cabin roof and just stared ahead into the graying skies. "I am supposed to call the old man at 0900, shit, now what do I do?" he asked himself quietly.

Commander Buckland walked up and stood next to Avery, and in a concerned voice said. "Dan's right, Phil, and it is his call. I think we should go right for the cove. It could take another hour or more of not knowing if anything happened if we go up into the harbor. I'm sorry, I have to agree with O'Brien, that's how I feel, pal."

Gail moved closer to Avery's other side and placed her hand around his arm and squeezed lightly. He knew they were right. He was stalling, but something deep inside him kept telling him to stay away from the cove. It was the same feeling he had when the Unicorn was coming down on him in the whaler two nights ago.

He smiled and in a whisper said "Alright, you win." But he had to offer a compromise. "As soon as we reach the southern end of Guadeloupe, I would like to put in a call to the FSMC. I'll ask them if there were any problems down around the Saintes, that we had heard from a passing vessel they thought the spotted a ship on fire last night as they cruised by."

"That's a good idea, Phil. What do you think Dan?" Buckwheat remarked. "That way we may find out if the explosion went off on time, or at all. It makes sense to me." Buckland was doing his best to get approval from O'Brien, but there was no immediate response from him. Then O'Brien turned and faced his three companions who were giving him their complete attention.

"Sure, you do that, Phil, that's fine," O'Brien said, then he went down the companionway and disappeared below.

Dinghy Dock
Bourge Des Saintes
0705 Hours

Tomas Puros handed Marcel Balisteri the large package, wrapped in burlap sacks and told him to put in the bottom of the skiff. Carlos Mesa arrived on the small scooter and advised Puros that he had spoke to the pilots over at their apartment on the south side of the airport, and advised them to stand by their radio all morning until they were released, which Puros estimated would be around 1200 hours.

The three men were in the small boat and ready to leave the dock, when Marcel's girl friend appeared. She started to scream and curse at Marcel for leaving her again to go fishing. She reminded him it was Christmas morning. Marcel had to walk her back to the Villa and calm her down, while Puros and Mesa waited.

"You did tell your broad that we are on the 2;30 flight, didn't you, Carlos?"

"Yes, she knows, Tomas. How long do you think we will be this morning?"

"We should be back here no later than noon. The tide will be good for the yachts to leave around 11 o'clock. High tide will be around noon."

"Things went well, I mean the meetings went alright?"

"I have no idea, my friend. All we are going to do now is make sure that the two boats get out of the cove. Then we will come back here, check out of the Villas, get the whores on the ferry to Pointe A Pitre, get to the airport and board an Air France jet to Martinique."

"Tomas, how long do you think it will be before they come looking for that American?"

"Why do you care? You seem to be really troubled by this man, Carlos."

"I just hope that we have covered all our connections to him, I mean that nobody can.."

"With the money you get for this trip, you can hide in the mountains of Venezuela forever, comrade, ah, here comes Marcel, now let's get going, we are late. I will tell you for the last time, forget that American."

Unicorn
Grand Islet
0725 Hours

Sorokin was awakened by the sound of a door closing in General Vincetta's cabin next to his. He looked at his watch then closed his eyes again. He thought about the four characters he had entertained until a few short hours ago. He chuckled to himself as he remembered how much he had won in the last three hands, which would please Fidel. He had left the card game with over seven thousand U.S. dollars. Suddenly another sound vibrated throughout his cabin. Someone was starting the main engines. He slipped out of his bed and looked out his cabin window. He could see the Bertram was still there. There were two people up on the fly bridge, and someone on the davit hoist, evidently bringing their dinghy on board. Sorokin decided to get in the shower, then locate Castro to see if there had been any change in Yang Lo's repairs.

"Good morning, Captain," Vincetta remarked as he entered the bridge.

"Good morning, General. Have you seen President Castro?" DeTorre asked.

"Yes, he is in the galley getting coffee. He will be here in a moment."

"You know, comrade? That little yellow man, Yang Lo, has not gone to bed? He is still working on the submarine back there?"

"Really? Maybe he has finally fixed the fucking thing?" Vincetta said with in a sarcastic voice.

"No, that he has not done. I spoke to him about an hour ago. He said the receiver, whatever that is, it is ruined now."

"Huh, it's a good thing that Sorokin was aboard for this trip, or Mr. Lo would have been feeding the local fish by now. He caused us a lot of grief and embarrassment last night."

"What will you do next, General?"

"Comrade Sorokin convinced our friends over there that we should meet again next month in Belize. Looks like you get to keep the Unicorn for a little longer, Captain."

"That pleases me, General."

"What time do you plan on getting us out of here, Captain?"

"I spoke to the Bonaire's captain earlier, he said the tide will be high at noon, but we can get out earlier. He plans on pulling up anchor around 1030 hours and heading out. We can probably make it out behind him."

Vincetta looked up towards the top of the hill.

"And Puros? He is supposed to be up there now, isn't he?"

"Yes, comrade. I have been waiting for his call on the radio, but so far I have not seen or heard from him."

"Well, I will be most happy to get out of here as soon as possible, Captain. Keep me informed. When Sorokin comes in, tell him to join me in the President's stateroom."

"Yes, comrade General," DeTorre snapped a quick salute, forgetting for a minute where he was. Vincetta just smiled and returned a more relaxed salute, then left the bridge.

Sorokin sat and sipped on his hot tea, as he watched Castro walking back and forth looking out his cabin windows.

"You think they will come again, my friend? I mean, do you think they will trust us if we can set up another meeting in Belize?"

"Yes, of course. They are definitely interested in the Dolphin. The more we talked last night about the possibilities of the machine, the more excited they got. My only problem was keeping their mind off what price you will be selling them for."

"You did not tell them?"

"No, I did not. However, Aldo Rivia mentioned, joking of course, that you probably had a million dollar price tag on the machine."

"He is right, I expect to get just that."

Sorokin looked over at Vincetta, who was lying stretched out on the sofa, smoking a cigar and reading another book.

"What do you think, General? Will they pay a million dollars for the Dolphins?" Sorokin asked.

"They have no choice," Vincetta responded, without looking up from his book.

"It looks like it is getting cloudy, the sun has gone away," Castro commented as he looked out again into the quiet cove.

Just then, the second main engine could be heard starting up.

"This is good. We are getting ready to leave," Castro said.

Vincetta put the book down and stood up. He walked over and joined Castro, who was looking at the large Bertram yacht fifty-some yards away.

"Yes, soon. We just have to wait for a little more water to cover the sand bar. You know, comrade President, you have the option to fly out of here this morning. We have the plane standing by."

Castro looked at Sorokin sitting in a captains chair enjoying his cigarette. "What do you think, comrade?" Castro asked Sorokin.

"Me? I have become spoiled, I am enjoying this luxury, like an American capitalist. I would just as soon stay on board for the cruise home, unless you order me to do otherwise."

"We all stay then," Castro remarked with a light laugh. "Let us go up to the bridge and join our Captain. I would like to watch how he takes us out of here." Castro headed for the cabin door, Vincetta was right behind him.

"Are you coming, comrade?"

Sorokin put his cigarette out in the ashtray and followed his companions up to the main bridge.

Island Drummer
0805 Hours

"I think it's time to put on that second pot of coffee, if you will excuse me." Gail stepped around the small cockpit table and headed for the companion way. She stopped for a second and placed her hand gently on O'Brien's back. He did not respond. She went below.

It only took a few minutes to bring the Drummer into the wind and hoist the mainsail and unfurl the large jib. Guadeloupe lay less then three miles off her bow.

"There are the Saintes." Avery said as he brought the Drummer back on course. The main and the jib sails were set and trimmed. Avery decided not to put the mizzen sail up. The winds were light, less that ten knots and the seas were fairly calm. There were a few clouds hanging over Guadeloupe that were blocking the sunrise. High above, a thin layer of clouds began to form, moving in from the east.

Gail brought the binoculars out of the cockpit locker and took them out of the case. She handed them to Phil.

"Here, you can see Terre De Bas now, Grand Islet is not visible yet, but it won't be long."

O'Brien took the binoculars from Phil and held them to his eyes.

"I don't see any smoke or any sign of unusual activity down there."

"Dan, had there been a fire, it would be out by now. The explosion should have gone off nearly eleven hours ago."

"Yeah, I guess you're right." O'Brien handed the glasses back to Gail.

"Are you going to call that French Coast Guard station?" O'Brien asked.

"Naw, we'll wait. We should be close enough to see the cove in about fifteen minutes." Phil reached up and advanced the throttles and the Drummer responded picking up speed.

"Thank God, there's no traffic out here yet. We just might get lucky and get close enough to see the cove."

Grand Islet
0810 Hours

Puros was the first one to arrive at the top of the small hilltop. He immediately looked down at the two majestic yachts resting calmly below. He could see the anchors in the clear waters, and on the foredeck of the Bertram, two men were wrestling with the small dinghy dangling on a cable from the davit.

Light gray smoke was visible coming from the two large pipes in side the funnel of the Unicorn. Both engines were running. Now he had to find out what time the yachts planned to leave, and to make sure they were aware of the tide schedule.

"Quick, Marcel, get me the radio out of the back pack," Puros ordered.

"Pawn to King, Pawn to king, do you read?" The small speaker in the portable radio crackled, then came alive.

"This is King, read you loud and clear."

"Pawn to King. We are in position. Have you set a time for departure?"

"Roger, Bishop leaving at 1030. We will be right behind."

"Roger that King. Best tide at 1200. Also, the flamingo is standing by in case."

"Roger."

DeTorre figured out that Puros was referring to the emergency plan, the flamingo must be the airplane he had standing by on Terre De Haut.

Puros put the mike down, lit a cigarette and got comfortable. Marcel and Carlos spread the small sheet out on the grass and sat down next to Puros. All they could do now was to watch and wait.

Island Drummer
0841 Hours

Avery was looking through the binoculars towards Grand Islet. "Son of a bitch, I don't believe it," he bellowed. "They are both there, what the fuck went wrong?"

"Give me those glasses," O'Brien ordered.

"That's them, and they don't seem to be suffering any damage." O'Brien dropped the glasses from his eyes and turned to Avery as if waiting for an explanation.

"Gail, here, take the helm." Avery reached up on the console and pulled both throttles to idle. The Drummer immediately started to slow down. "Here, let me have those, Dan."

Avery took the binoculars and stepped out of the cockpit and made his way forward. He leaned against the port rail and focused the lenses on the Unicorn. "That's her," he yelled back. "It's the Unicorn, I can read the name on her transom."

Avery looked back at Gail and pointed to the south. "Gail, head on down for a few miles. We will turn and tack back towards them, we need to get closer."

"What the hell do you think happened?" O'Brien kept repeating.

"Maybe those charges couldn't stick to the hull, Dan. Wasn't that one of Chen's major concerns? He kept questioning those magnetic boxes they gave him," Gail asked.

"Captain Chen did not say anything the other night, but chances are the bottom of that Feadship may have been slick with some kind of sea growth, you know, barnacles. Shit, all this for nothing." O'Brien ran his fingers through his hair. "I don't believe it."

Avery came back to the cockpit and threw the binoculars across the cockpit, fortunately hitting the padded seat cushion before falling on the floor.

"What do you want to do, Phil?" Gail inquired.

"I told you, keep heading down, didn't I? I'll tell you when to change course," Avery snarled. "Shit why wait, move over, give me the helm, we are going over there now."

Avery looked around at his crew, then began yelling. "Buckwheat, standby the on that port winch. Dan, take the slack up on that starboard winch. Gail, you handle the main sheet. We are going to head right at them."

Avery advanced the throttles and started turning to port. "Standby to release the jib as soon as we pass through the wind, Dan. There it is, let it go." Buckland started cranking in the huge jib. Gail set the mainsail. The bow of the Drummer was aiming right for the two yachts clearly visible against the islands dark gray walls.

0851 Hours

The small rocky islands just to the west of Grand Islet were now visible. Avery checked the chart. He estimated he was about 350 yards from the Unicorn and was preparing his next move to turn south.

"O.K. crew, listen up, we are going to tack again back to our original course to see what's going on over there."

"Phil, look, I see smoke coming out of the Unicorn's funnel and exhaust around the stern of that sportfisher, see it? It looks like they may be getting ready to leave," Gail yelled out.

"Buckwheat, what's the tide situation, do you remember?"

"I think it's high around noon, don't know for sure, I'll go down and check."

"Forget it Buckwheat, need you up here for the next tack," Avery said as he tried to estimate his distance for the tack. "Dan, you'd better get back here too, I'm going to need you on this next tack."

0854 Hours

It was like watching a film in slow motion. The stern of the Unicorn lifted into the air on a giant bubble of water, followed by a tremendous water spout that shot up fifty feet in the air. There was a roll of muted thunder that echoed off the steep sides of the cove and for a few seconds both yachts were totally invisible behind a shield of gray mist and swirling black smoke.

Without hesitation, Avery pulled the two throttles back slowing the Drummer's speed. He brought the bow into the wind, relaxing the sails. He was trying to get a better view of what was going on in the cove.

"Something blew, Phil, something blew, big time," Gail screamed.

O'Brien holding on to the headstay stood on the bow sprit while the large jib flapped wildly behind him. He was straining to see through the swirling mist if both yachts were still there. The sportfishing boat turned with it's bow facing the Unicorn and a small boat was running between them.

"Let's get these sails secured," Avery shouted.

In seconds, Gail and Buckland had the main down and wrapped, while Avery hauled the jib in on the roller furling. O'Brien never moved. He hung onto the bow rail and kept his eyes on the two yachts, now less than one hundred yards away.

The Unicorn was obviously going down in the stern, and smoke was pouring out of the aft portside hatches. Then came another explosion. The Unicorn's stern rose again and began to sink more rapidly.

O'Brien started yelling back to the crew. "She's going down, she's going down."

Gail picked up the binoculars from the cockpit seat and looked closely at the activity taking place between the yachts. She could see a number of people in the water swimming for the sportfisher.

"Phil, it looks like everyone is heading for the fishing boat. I can count at least three people in the water, and six or seven standing in the cockpit."

"Hang in there, Gail, keep reporting on what's happening. I'm going to ease in closer."

"O'Brien," Avery yelled out. "I'm heading for the Unicorn, keep your eyes open for any signs of shallow..."

Avery never finished his warning to O'Brien. There was another explosion, this time the Unicorn's stern rose nearly out of the water, then it sank. Pieces of debris flew into the air and came crashing down all around the cove. Heavy black smoke and orange flames could be seen along the port side of the salon. A small wave generated by the explosion was broadcasting outward towards the bow of the Drummer.

Buckland ran forward and joined O'Brien on the bow, while Gail called out what she could see through the glasses.

"Shit, that fishing boat is moving, Phil. It's going along the wall, heading south, can you see it?" Gail yelled.

"I got it," Avery responded. "It looks like they're making a break for it."

"Wait, they just stopped. Damn, I can't see, the smoke is,... wait, they must be hard aground," Gail cried out.

"They're aground, Dan," Buckland yelled, as he pointed towards the Bertram yacht. "Wait, he's backing down, he's free."

"They got off and moving out and looks like they are heading right into the wall," Gail cried out in disbelief.

"I'm going in closer," Avery cried out. "You guys keep alert, we are going in closer." Avery ran back and took over the controls of the Drummer.

As the smoke began to clear, they could see that the entire stern of the Unicorn was now under water and the aft deck was awash. She was starting to list heavily to port. White and gray steam began streaming from the funnel, and a cloud of black smoke was steadily pouring out of the main deck cabin doors and windows that were blown out on the port side.

"What the hell is that, Dan? Look, something is coming out of the rear of the main cabin," Avery yelled.

"Jesus, it looks like the bow of a submarine," O'Brien said.

The Dolphin, released from its cradle, was no longer secured to the cabin hold downs and slid into the two French doors of the main salon. After the second explosion, the two French doors leading to the aft deck could not hold the small submarine back. The doors broke outward and the Dolphin began to slide out of the cabin. Directly under the salon, a fire that started in a electrical panel, reached one of the fuel tanks for the auxiliary generators. When the tank exploded, it blew the Dolphin completely out of the Unicorn, igniting the Dolphin's explosive charges.

The third explosion nearly knocked O'Brien and Buckland off the bowsprit. They saw parts of a large black and white object being thrown like a giant football into the air, spinning wildly. Buckwheat and O'Brien saw the strange fins like a killer whale's, then it blew up, tossing pieces of its black shell all over the water in front of the Drummer.

The Unicorn was totally engulfed in smoke with red and yellow flames pouring out of her forward section. The large funnel surrounding the huge exhaust pipes collapsed and fell off the top deck. The mast, antennas and radar dishes began to collapse. The small Whaler that was covered in a cradle slipped off the cabin and rolled into the sea upside down. The Unicorn rolled over and lay on her port side with her bow was out of the water and her anchor chains taut. It appeared that the Unicorn was resting on the shallow bottom. The once beautiful classic yacht, finally stopped its death dive into the boiling sea.

"Dan, look, about thirty yards left of the Unicorn, in the water. Is that someone waving to us?" Buckland said.

At first O'Brien did not see the man, then he saw an arm waving wildly. " Yes, I see him. He's swimming away from the yacht, he sees us, Buckwheat. He's waving at us."

Buckland turned and yelled to Avery and Gail. "There's a swimmer heading for us, about eleven o'clock off our bow."

"Gail, get up here with those glasses," O'Brien yelled.   "Go ahead, Gail," Avery said. "I'll keep an eye on the Bertram, he's still working his way over that sand bar, go find out what Dan's yelling about."

528

Gail handed O'Brien the binoculars. He searched for a few seconds then spotted the man in the water, about thirty yards west of the Unicorn and swimming hard towards them.

"He's heading for us, Gail. Go tell Avery quick, we need to pick this guy up before the Unicorn blows us all to kingdom come."

O'Brien started to scream at the swimmer. "Get away from the boat."

Buckwheat looked over at the Bertram. It was definitely moving out and it looked like it was beginning to turn in the direction of the Drummer. "Phil, the fishing boat." Buckwheat yelled to Avery as he pointed towards the oncoming yacht.

Avery brought the throttles back. He kept his eye on the Bertram, now coming up on plane and closing. He was about a hundred yards away. Phil saw a flash come from the bridge. The first two rounds whistled over Avery's head, one hit the mainsail with a loud poof sound. The third shot hit somewhere behind, in the aft cabin or the hull.

At the top of his voice, Avery yelled to his crew. "They are shooting at us."

In one swift move, Avery hit both throttles and swung the helm over hard, turning the Drummer's bow directly into the path of the oncoming yacht. It was a defensive move, and Avery was counting on the head on challenge to spook the Bertram's captain. It worked. The sleek Bertram swung to port in a tight turn then headed for the south end of the island.

During the frantic maneuver, Avery did not notice that he nearly threw O'Brien and Buckwheat overboard. Gail was half way back to the cockpit, when the deck moved out from beneath her feet. The only thing that saved her from going over the rail was one of the spreader cables. She caught it, spun and crashed into the lifeline, which kept her from going overboard.

Avery brought the Drummer back around and continued to head for the stricken Feadship. The fire had spread throughout her structure. Flames were beginning to come up through the salon roof, where the two doors had been installed.

"We have got to get out of here, her tanks might go any minute, we are too close," Avery screamed.

Buckwheat came flying back along the deck catching up with Gail. "Give me a hand, Gail," he yelled. "We have to throw the Avon over."

As they passed Avery in the cockpit, Buckland explained his intentions. "Phil, we're going to put the Avon over. I'll go get the swimmer, the water is getting too shallow for you, be careful."

Avery responded. "Alright, understood, Gail, you give Buckwheat a hand."

O'Brien began to panic. Phil could see him waving wildly throwing his arms about.

"What's wrong, Dan?" Avery screamed.

"Sandbar, stop, stop now, too shallow, stop."

Avery heard him this time and responded. He pulled the throttles back and ran the clutches into reverse, then opened the throttles again, full bore.

Buckwheat and Gail had just pushed the Avon over the stern rail, when the Drummer reacted to Phil's commands. They were both thrown overboard, barely missing the large teak swim platform. Gail hit the Avon before she hit the water, cutting her head just above her right eye. She was bleeding badly. Buckwheat swam over to her and got her back to the swim platform and was trying to push her up, when he felt the suction of the giant propellers pulling the water away from him and pulling him down. He barely made it up on the platform before he was pulled into the propellers. As soon as the Drummer stopped backing down, he dove into the water and swam after the drifting inflatable. He caught up with it and climbed aboard, picked up the oars and started paddling towards the bow of the Drummer. He yelled at Avery. "You crazy son-of-a-bitch, you damned near killed us." But it was to no avail, Avery did not hear his cries, he was busy yelling at O'Brien.

"Phil, Gail is hurt, help her," Buckland screamed. This time Avery did hear his cries and looked aft. He put the clutches in neutral and ran to the stern. Gail was just about to start up the stainless ladder when she spotted Avery looking down at her. Her face was white, and a river of blood covered her temple cheek and neck.

"I'm o.k., Phil, get back to the helm."

He looked at her blood soaked face and hair and realized he must have caused the accident. He leaned over the rail and reached for her hand.

"I did this?" he asked.

"I'm alright, Phil. Now get back up there before we all get killed."

Aboard the Unicorn
Before the first explosion.
0853

Fidel Castro, General Vincetta and Sorokin were standing on the main bridge with Captain DeTorre and Manuel Fajardo. The impact of the fist explosion was so light that DeTorre at first thought he must have drifted over something, or the stern ran up on the bottom. He looked at his instruments and could see nothing wrong. Both engines were running smoothly, all temps and pressures normal. Everyone on the bridge felt the small impact, but not a word was said. It wasn't until he got a call from the engine room that he learned of the disaster. Lopez had just finished examining the engine room and was going through the forward engine room bulkhead when the explosion went off. He was thrown against one of the generators, and a section of a steel grate that was part of the overhead catwalk, fell on his head, putting a large gash over his ear and knocking him unconscious for a few seconds. The engine room was filled with smoke, but the exhaust fans were clearing it out. When he made his way towards the rear of the engine room looking for where the trouble was, he opened the aft bulkhead door and saw the water coming in. Part of the port strut, still attached to a twisted frame, had been pushed up through the hull. An electrical panel was burning and sparks were flying everywhere. He noted that the fuel tank for the auxiliary generators was located just a few feet away. He made his way to the forward intercom station and called the bridge.

DeTorre pushed down the flashing plastic button on the intercom panel. "Go ahead, Lopez," he said.

"Sir, we have a serious problem in the aft generator room. The port strut has come up through the bottom of the hull. We are taking on water, and there is a fire in one of the main electrical panels."

"Can you extinguish the fire, comrade?

"Too dangerous, captain, the generator's running and the fuel tank is right there."

"Get out of there, and shut down all the main engine fuel valves and kill that generator, now. Make sure the aft bilge pumps are running. I have green lights up here. I will switch to batteries for power. Is there anyone else with you?"

"No, captain, but, sir, there was an explosion under the boat."

DeTorre slammed his fist down on the steerage console.

"Get out of there, comrade, as soon as you can."

He turned and looked at Castro. "Comrade President, we may have been sabotaged."

"What do you mean sabotaged?" Vincetta asked.

"Sir, you heard Lopez. He has just reported we have been holed somewhere near the props. We are taking on water fast. He also says there is a fire in..."

Those were the last words DeTorre was able to say. The second explosion occurred, this time knocking almost everyone on the bridge to the floor. Castro was thrown against the forward bulkhead. Sorokin fell backwards into the radio racks, then crashed to the floor. Vincetta was thrown partially out the port doorway and DeTorre was thrown against the helmswheel and over the control levers to the engines, fracturing two ribs.

Back in the main salon, Yang Lo and Colonel Navarro were just beginning to secure the Dolphin to the hold-down brackets when the first explosion came. The Dolphin's cradle moved forward, and the sub's tail fins slammed into the oak wood bulkhead, smashing all the movable surfaces. Lo and Navarro immediately took two of the forward tie down lines and started to pull the Dolphin away from the wall, when the second explosion came. The Dolphin came out of the cradle and hit the ceiling, then fell back into the cradle. This time, the Unicorn slipped down in the stern and the Dolphin and the cradle slid across the floor and rammed into the two French doors that went out to the aft deck.

Yang Lo, who was on the starboard side of the room, could no longer see Navarro through the smoke. Navarro was trapped on the port side of the salon, where two of the large windows had just blown out. He got on his hands and knees and crawled towards the side door to the main deck. He was about to step outside, when he felt the Unicorn begin to roll to port. There was too much smoke forward to see what was ahead, so he climbed on the rail and vaulted as far out into the water as he could. Not knowing what was going on or who was killed or hurt on board, his only plan was to swim as far away from the Unicorn as he could. When he stopped swimming, he noticed the large sailboat coming right at him. He wiped his eyes and stared at the familiar red and white stripes and the blue corner on the flag flashing back and forth in the rigging. "The Americans are here," he thought. He began to wonder, if the explosions on the Unicorn could have been planted, maybe this was the plan that the Americans had designed to destroy Castro. This meant that all his messages had got through and they had came here to kill him. He started to yelling and waving wildly at the sailboat, hoping they would see him. He began praying to be saved. He was also praying for freedom for his wife and children, he thought about Carlos. "Today is Christmas, Carlos was going to have our families on board his plane and fly to Florida, oh, God, let this be our day."

Aboard the Unicorn

Captain DeTorre grabbed his right side, he knew he had rib damage. "Is anyone hurt?" he asked, but there was no response. It seemed everyone on the bridge was in shock. "We must get off this ship now."

"Comrade President, the door, go out the door," DeTorre yelled. He picked up the mike for the special UHF radio and began calling Puros. Puros saw the second explosion clearly and had already sent his two men down to the boat to head out around the island and prepare to pick up the President's party.

Knowing it was going to take Puros' two men a long time to make the trip around the island to the cove, Bonaire's captain, listening to DeTorre and Puros on the radio, interrupted their conversation and advised Puros to catch his men and tell them that Bonaire would meet them in the Passe Du Grand Islet, near the east end of the island. There they would transfer Castro's party.

General Vincetta was pushing Castro along the deck to the boarding ramp ladder. Gayo Rodriguez stood at the top of the platform, dropping AK-47 automatic rifles down to Manuel Fajardo, who was standing in Bonaire's inflatable with Rojo. Cabino Varas came running up from the starboard cabin area. He was yelling to Gayo that Lopez was still down below. Yang Lo followed directly behind him. When they reached the ramp, Rodriguez held everyone back until Fidel Castro was down the ladder and safe aboard the inflatable. Vincetta looked back towards the bridge. He did not see DeTorre or Sorokin.

"Cabino, go up to the bridge and find out what is happening to Captain DeTorre and comrade Sorokin," Vincetta ordered. He turned to Gayo and told him to let Yang Lo by so he could board the raft.

Lo stopped to address Vincetta. "I think your Colonel Navarro was hurt, or maybe killed in the salon back there, General."

"You go down, get in the boat, we will find the Colonel," Vincetta commanded.

"I'm going down below and find Antonio, General, he may be hurt," Gayo said, and started to head aft towards the open salon door.

"Look for Colonel Navarro, Cabino. He must be in the salon somewhere," Vincetta yelled out.

While DeTorre was shutting down the Unicorn's engines and electrical systems, Sorokin turned on one of the VHF radios and selected channel 72. DeTorre looked over at Sorokin and heard him talking in Russian on the mike. He heard Sorokin calling for "Kompas". The name sounded familiar, but DeTorre could not remember where he had heard it before. When the speaker responded, DeTorre heard a man also speaking in Russian. He heard him say Captain Gorshkov and there was something about Antigua and twenty kilometers. DeTorre waited at the door for Sorokin. Finally, Sorokin dropped the mike and headed for the door. He followed DeTorre to the ramp where they met Vincetta.

"Hurry, we must get out of here, there are bound to be more explosions," DeTorre said. Vincetta headed down the ladder, followed by Sorokin. DeTorre spotted Lopez and Rodriguez coming out of the starboard galley door. He did not have time to call out to them. They went right to the rail, stepped over it and jumped overboard.

"Come on, Captain, there is nobody left," Vincetta yelled up to DeTorre.

"Where is Colonel Navarro? Did anyone see him?"

"We think he may have been killed in the salon, they can't find him," Vincetta responded.

"Please, Captain, jump, jump now, she is about to blow," Lopez was yelling from the water, as he swam along side of Rodriguez near the inflatable.

DeTorre leaped off the platform and hit the churning water. He nearly landed in the inflatable. Sorokin and Rojo pulled him into the raft. There was no room for Rodriguez and Lopez. Rojo told them he would come back and pick them up. Meanwhile, they were swimming as hard as they could towards the Bertram.

Aboard the Bonaire
0916 Hours

Captain D'Amato secured his anchors and was maneuvering the yacht around. He spun the Bonaire's stern around towards the Unicorn, so the Unicorn's passengers could board easily. Ramon Cantillo and Jorge Armando had threatened D'Amato a few minutes after they saw the Unicorn was in trouble. They had ordered him to leave immediately. When DeTorre radioed that the Unicorn had been sabotaged and was possibly sinking, he also ordered D'Amato to standby. He figured that the Bonaire's four guests may have wanted to leave the Unicorn's crew hanging. DeTorre warned D'Amato that he would order his crew to open up with automatic weapons and sink him and his guests, if he did not wait for Castro and the Unicorn's crew. At this point, DeTorre suspected that the four drug dealers may have had something to do with the Unicorn's disaster.

D'Amato prepared to argue with his four passengers, but they did not interfere. He called Puros on the VHF right after DeTorre ordered him to execute the emergency plan. He advised Puros that the easiest way to get

Castro safely out of there was to get him on board the Bonaire. He would take Castro out of the cove and meet Puros' men and their boat behind the east end of the island and make the transfer. He convinced his four passengers that their other option was to be shot and possibly killed by the Unicorn's crew, reminding them the Bertram had over 600 gallons of fuel on board. Although the four were armed with small weapons, they knew they would be no match for Castro's guns. They agreed that taking Fidel Castro with them was the smart choice.

Rojo headed the dinghy straight for the Bonaire's stern. The transom door was open, and Carla D'Amato and Pauli were waiting to help Castro's party get on board. Armando and Cantillo were standing in the cockpit watching, while Rivia and Calva remained on the bridge with Captain D'Amato.

"Where did these come from?" Castro asked Vincetta, pointing to the five Soviet made automatic weapons on the floor of the boat.

"It was my idea, comrade," Sorokin responded.

"We may still need them, Comrade President. I figured that our guests may have threatened Captain D'Amato. It looked like they were getting ready to leave us. I told the captain that we would open fire on him if he left the cove."

Rojo spoke up. "They are mean, señors, very mean. And, you are right, Captain, they did threaten us. They wanted to go without you."

"Do they have weapons?" Vincetta asked.

"I think so, they are small though."

Sorokin reached down and picked up one of the AK-47's, then handed one to Vincetta. Varas and Fajardo reached down and took two other guns, leaving one. Castro looked at the gun, then looked up at Sorokin.

Sorokin motioned Castro with his eyes to pick up the weapon. Castro shook his head, turned and watched the Bertram as they approached.

"We will hold these guns and cover each other as we get aboard," Vincetta said. "If any of them so much as reaches in his pants, shoot them."

Navarro was getting tired and started to tread water. He noticed the big sailboat had slowed down. Then he noticed for the first time a man standing on the bow waving. He waved back, and could feel his heart beating with excitement. "They see me, they see me," he thought. He then turned his attention back to the Unicorn. He couldn't believe his eyes. The once beautiful yacht was dying before his eyes. Then he noticed the small rubber life boat. He could pick out Castro and Vincetta, the others he was not sure of. He saw the people standing on the bridge of the sportfishing boat. His heart sank. If this was the attempt to kill Castro, it had failed. His thoughts went back to his family and he started to pray again. "Please, Luis, be safe in America." He looked around and spotted the small boat with the blond headed man rowing towards him.

Aboard the Bonaire

It took five minutes to get the Unicorn crew on board. Carla D'Amato rushed Castro, Vincetta and Sorokin into the main salon.

Captain D'Amato yelled down to the Unicorn's crew. "Take those guns inside, quick, get them out of sight. The French Navy will be all over us in a few minutes. Someone must have called them by now. The smoke must be visible from Guadeloupe."

DeTorre told his crew to hold on to the weapons and sit on the deck, out of sight. He then walked into the main cabin and joined Castro, Sorokin and General Vincetta who were sitting on the small sofa. He noticed something out the cabin window and walked over and pulled the curtain back. For the first time since the rescue, someone noticed the Island Drummer.

Up on the bridge, Jorge Armando also noticed the large sailboat moving in close to the burning Unicorn.

"Captain, do you see that giant sailboat?" Jorge Armando asked.

"Yes, I have been watching her. She looks like she is trying to come in and help."

"Most likely she has notified the French authorities, si?"

"I don't think so, I heard no calls on the emergency frequency."

"Then why is she getting so close, Captain."

D'Amato reached over and picked up his binoculars and scanned the decks of the sailing yacht. He felt a light bump and realized he was hitting bottom.

"Here, you watch that fucking boat, I've got to get out of here."

Aldo Rivia took the glasses and began to search the sailboats deck. He saw two men standing on the bow, one man driving the boat and a woman walking forward on the deck.

"The men in the bow, they are pointing at something. Now the boat stops, the men almost fell off. They must be aground, no, wait, there is someone in the water, off the stern of Castro's boat."

"Give me those." Armando took the glasses. "You are right, Señor, there is someone in the water waving at the sailboat."

Armando walked to the aft rail at the back of the bridge and looked down in the cockpit. "You there, with the gun, ah, Lopez? Are you missing a man from your crew?"

Antonio Lopez looked up at the short stout man. He thought for a second, then remembered Colonel Navarro. "Yes, yes we are, one of our crew was caught in the explosion, we believe he was killed. Why?"

"He is alive, Señor, and there's a big sailboat near your boat about to pick him up."

Lopez jumped up and went into the main cabin where he explained to DeTorre what he had been told. DeTorre climbed the ladder up to the bridge and grabbed Captain D'Amato by the arm.

"Please, your glasses, I need your binoculars, Captain."

It took a few seconds for DeTorre to find the swimmer. It was Colonel Navarro. He was waving, but not at the Bonaire. DeTorre focused on the sailboat and noticed the two men on the bow. One of them appeared to be yelling and waving at Navarro. It was then that DeTorre noticed the large flag flying from the back stay.

"They are Americans," he turned and looked at Captain D'Amato. "They are Americans, Captain, we must get our man before they do."

D'Amato looked puzzled for a second. "Captain, they won't hurt him, they are just trying to help, I'm sure they will let him go to the authorities when they arrive."

DeTorre grabbed D'Amato's arm and screamed into his face. "We don't want the Americans to have our man on their boat. I said we go get him, now, or I will start putting holes in this fucking barge, do you understand me, comrade."

D'Amato did not open his mouth. He reached for his engine levers. He pulled back on his port engine clutch while advancing the starboard engine. The huge sportfisher spun like a top in her own length. He threw the port clutch forward and headed for the south end of the cove. He figured he would have about the same water over the sand bar that he had yesterday, so he was going to go for it.

DeTorre went back down to the lower deck and entered the salon. "It's Navarro, Comrade President, he is alive, but there is an American sailboat heading for him. We are going to try to stop them."

Castro jumped up from the sofa and went to the large glass sliding doors the separated the salon from the cockpit. He spun around and faced the young officer.

"Captain DeTorre, you forget, we can't get involved here. If we tangle with that American boat we will have too many complications, possibly with the local authorities if they show up here, don't you agree, comrade Sorokin?"

Castro looked at Sorokin for support.

"What can we do to get him back safely?" Castro asked.

"Nothing, I'm afraid," Sorokin said.

General Vincetta moved in between Castro and Sorokin and faced his leader. "Comrade President, we can't afford to be caught out here. The French authorities must be on their way by now. We must get you to the airport. Colonel Navarro is no fool, he will not tell those American assholes anything. All he needs to do is to get to the Guadeloupe airport. He will be alright." Vincetta was trying to be convincing and cool, but Castro and Sorokin were looking right through him. Each of them was giving Navarro second thoughts.

Suddenly the Bertram's engines began to wind up and the bow begin to rise.

"What's happening? " Castro asked.

Sorokin looked out the glass cabin doors. They were clear of the cove. He went over to the port side window and pulled back the drapes. He saw that they were heading straight for the huge sailboat.

"My God, somebody warn the captain topside, we can't do this." Sorokin started for the large smoked glass doors of the cabin. There were two sharp reports from above, rifle shots, then another.

Sorokin and DeTorre collided trying to get out of the cabin and climb the ladder to the fly bridge. Sorokin got to the top first. He saw Manuel Fajardo with a AK 47 resting on the stainless rail of the bridge, he was kneeling and aiming.

"Stop," Sorokin yelled as he made a flying dive for Fajardo. He hit him in the small of the back with his shoulder, spinning him around. The gun fell forward and slid down the front of the bridge, bounced off the main cabin and slid off the port side catwalk into the water.

"Get out of here, Captain, now. Don't get any closer to that sailboat, forget about it." Sorokin drew his small Berretta from beneath his shirt. "Turn this fucking boat around, now, Captain."

D'Amato had no desire to challenge Sorokin, and felt relieved that the crazy man, Fajardo was disarmed. He spun the wheel over to port. The big deep-vee hull of the Bertram rolled into a hard banking turn.

"Captain DeTorre, get on that special radio and contact Puros, tell him what's going on here, and tell him to keep us advised of what is happening to Colonel Navarro."

Dimitri grabbed D'Amato's arm. "Where's your VHF, Captain?"

Rojo reached down and opened a door below the instrument panel. He took out a microphone and handed it to Dimitri. "What channel, sir?"

Aboard Island Drummer
0912 Hours

Avery ran up to the bow, where he joined O'Brien. He told Gail to standby the helm.

"What are you doing up here? You better get this thing backed up, look over there." Avery did not have to look twice, they were about to run aground. O'Brien started to yell at the swimmer, who was floating on his back. He was only twenty yards out. Buckland was rowing hard and only ten yards away from the swimmer.

Avery yelled back to Gail to put the engines in reverse. O'Brien suddenly felt the vibrations in his feet as the powerful engines began to pull the yacht backwards out of harms way.

"He's there, Buckwheat's got him." Avery yelled. "I'll go back and help them get on board. Dan, why don't you get on the VHF and see if the French authorities have been called and from what direction they coming. We need to know which way to go to get out of here, we don't want to fuck with the Frogs at this point, agree?"

"Take it easy, fella, I'll have you on board in a jiff," Buckland hollered at the smiling swimmer.

Buckland pulled in the oars and crawled up to the bow of the inflatable. The swimmer's hands came over the top of the rounded rubber tube and grabbed the life line. Buckland leaned over and came face to face with the handsome smiling Cuban.

"Kick, kick hard." Buckland ordered as he tried to get his hands down into the man's armpits so he could pull him up. Suddenly Buckland's eyes were stinging, something splattered all over his face and into his eyes, he couldn't see. He fell backward against the transom, he could feel pieces of something on his arms and face as he wiped his eyes. When he opened his eyes the front part of the raft was covered in bright red blood. He saw one hand still clinging to the life line on the top of the raft. He could not see the swimmer. Buckland fell forward against the hull and grabbed hold of the hand. He looked over the side and saw that the man was face down in the water in an ocean of blood. After locating the swimmer's other arm in the water he pulled again. This time he was getting no help, the swimmer was either dead or unconscious. He had him almost halfway into the raft, when he noticed that the mans entire right shoulder was missing. He was looking into a gaping hole surrounded in torn away flesh and muscle. There was bone matter all over and hunks of muscle hanging by threads. Buckland reached over and got hold of the man's belt and was just about to bring him all the way in the raft, when the swimmer's body jumped again, and more blood splattered over Buckland's face and arms. There was another hole in the man's lower back, a small hole, but it was bleeding badly. Then Buckland noticed the tube that the Cuban was lying on was deflating fast and water was pouring into the bottom of the raft. He pulled him as far back as he could, then turned to see that the Drummer was almost on top of him. O'Brien was standing on the port bow ready to throw him a line.

There was another explosion, this time from the starboard side of the Unicorn. Flames and smoke went skyward for a thousand feet along with thousands of pieces of debris as one of her near empty fuel tanks exploded.

O'Brien did not hear the first shot, but he saw the explosion of red matter blow up in the raft. He looked over at the Bertram. It was nearly out of sight. He searched the Unicorn, listing nearly 45 degrees on her port side. There was too much smoke to see anything, or if anyone still on board.

"What was that red splash?" he asked himself. Then he heard a sharp report, it came from the cove somewhere. It was definitely a rifle shot. He noticed that the raft was going down in the bow.

"Phil," O'Brien yelled at the top of his lungs. "Someone is shooting at Buckland and the swimmer, get us up there, move up, now, we need to help them."

Avery shoved the two clutches forward and pushed the throttles ahead. Gail ran up the deck to see if she could help Buckland. O'Brien saw her coming and told her to go back and get another line, the raft was sinking. Gail went back to the cockpit, grabbed a dock line out of a stowage box and ran forward again.

"Dan, where are they? I can't see them," Avery cried out.
O'Brien pointed off the port bow. "About five yards, stop, shut her down," he screamed.

Avery reached up and pulled the throttles and clutches back, and felt the keel bump. At the same time the bow of the Drummer rose and she came to an abrupt stop. Avery went to reverse and full power. The Drummer did not react to the pulling propellers, and she began to roll slightly to starboard.

Gail climbed over the bow rail, took hold of the anchor platform, swung herself out away from the bow and dropped into the water, where she immediately hit bottom with both feet, it was barely six foot deep. With the line still clutched in her hand, she swam the short distance to the sinking life raft. Buckland grabbed the line as O'Brien began to pull on his end. He towed the raft as he moved aft down the deck, working the tow line outside the masts rigging. Gail took hold of the small wooden transom of the raft and kicked with all her might, attempting to tow it backwards. Buckland started to yell that he needed some rags.

The Drummer was hard aground, but at this point, nobody cared. O'Brien and Avery got down on the teak swim platform and helped transfer the lifeless and bloodied man onto the swim platform. Buckland climbed up to the aft deck, took the tow rope and made a make shift sling. He dropped it down to O'Brien. Avery carefully wrapped it around Navarro's midriff. O'Brien and Avery supported the man from below, while Gail and Buckland pulled from above. After a few long minutes, they had the limp bleeding body lying on the rear deck. Gail went below and gathered up sheets and the first aid kit, while Buckland used his own shirt as a compression bandage on the open wound where his shoulder once was. The other wound, just below his belt where a bullet exited, was large, but was not bleeding as badly as the shoulder.

"Phil, you'd better see if you can get us out of here. We will take care of him," O'Brien said.

Avery went back to the helm and looked at the instruments. Both engines were still running in the green. He put the clutches in reverse and opened the throttles to full rpm's. The Drummer vibrated and the huge exhausts bellowed, throwing water and white smoke for fifteen feet behind the transom. Avery ran the big rudder back and forth. He moved the clutches forward and repeated running the engines up. He took the clutches to neutral, moved the hydraulic strut levers to the full down position, put the clutches in reverse and added power again. On the next cycle of maneuvers in reverse, the Drummer began to move, slowly at first, then suddenly, like a giant hand let her go, she began to pick up speed. A sigh of relief was shared by all. As soon as Avery had room, he spun the Drummer around and headed for the open sea.

"I don't think he's going to make it, Dan, he's lost a lot of blood. That second bullet must have done some major internal damage." Buckwheat murmured. "Something big came out of that stomach wound that floated away."

"Gail, get me some of the smelling salts from that kit, would you?" Gail searched around in the small plastic container.

"Here Dan, this is all I could find." Gail said. She took another sheet, rolled it in a small ball and held it against the open wound, only to see that putting pressure on the wound seemed to increase the blood loss.

"My God, he's bleeding to death, what can we do?" Gail began to sob.

The silent man's eyes suddenly opened and blinked. Buckwheat moved his hand over his dark motionless face to shade his eyes from the sun.

"Mister, can you hear me?" Dan asked.

The Cuban's eyes looked right into O'Brien's. He nodded his head.

"You are on an American yacht, and we are going to get you to a hospital, do you understand?" O'Brien asked.

He nodded again and opened his mouth.

"He's smiling, Dan, he is trying to smile." Buckland cried out.

The Cuban opened his mouth slightly, and in a whisper, began to speak in perfect English. "You did not get him, he is leaving by plane, you must hurry."

Buckland looked up into O'Brien's puzzled face.

"Who is leaving, what do you mean, sir?" O'Brien asked

"Castro, President Castro. He is escaping, now, a plane on a nearby island."

"Jesus, what is going on here? How did he..?"

O'Brien continued to question him. "Sir, there was a submarine on board your ship, we saw a submarine come off your yacht, am I right?"

"Si, it did not work. It is made to carry drugs, it is supposed to go into your rivers and inlets. Castro plans to build them and sell them to the drug families. He will be building them in China, but it did not work and Castro is mad, so are the drug people."

"Who are the drug people, can you tell us?"

"Don't know, please, I am getting cold, I can't feel my feet, Señor."

"Yes, ah, we will get more blankets for you. It won't be long, we are heading for the hospital in Guadeloupe."

"No, Señor, no Guadeloupe, they are there, they will get me. I go with you to America. My brother-in-law, Carlos Lucia, he flies my wife and children to Florida today on Castro's plane. You must tell my Melinda, that I love her and will be there soon, you do that for me?"

"What the hell is he talking about, Dan? Who is Lucia?"

The Cubans eyes widened, his lips parted and a small sigh expelled from his mouth, followed by a stream of blood that began to run down his cheek. His head went limp and rolled to its side.

O'Brien put his fingers on the man's neck arteries to feel for a pulse. Then he put his ear against his chest and listened.

"He's gone."

"Oh, no. Oh, my god, why did they have to shoot him?" Gail cried out, then dropped her face into her hands and cried.

"Dan, he was saying something, he was telling us.. "

"I know, I know, Buckwheat. He knew who we were, somehow he knew we were here to get Castro, but how could he..." O'Brien raised his right hand to his face, as if he was feeling for whiskers. "Wait, Jesus Christ, Lucia, Carlos Lucia, of course, the airline pilot, he was the pilot that was getting us the information out of Cuba. Holy shit, he is flying out of Cuba today, Christmas Day, on Castro's plane."

"Dan, then this guy must be the Cuban officer who was working with Carlos, this is his brother-in-law, the officer on Castro's special guard. That's why he is here, that's why he wanted to escape. He somehow figured we were on a mission to get Castro when the Unicorn blew up."

"You're right. Shit, I wonder now just how much Castro knows about us. They shot this poor bastard, why? Unless they knew he was working with us. Shit, we've got to get out of here fast." O'Brien jumped up and ran forward to the cockpit.

"Phil, pour the coals to her, man, we may have been made. This Cuban fellow was one of the pair that was getting us the information about Castro and this trip."

"How is he doing?" Avery asked.

"He ain't, he's dead. We have to start thinking about our next move."

"Better start thinking fast, pal. If I am not mistaken, that fast moving boat up ahead looks like it's heading our way, and I will bet my Thunderbird, it's the French Navy.

O'Brien picked up the binoculars from the seat and trained them on the high speed vessel coming at them.

"You're right, Phil. It's some kind of French patrol boat. Now what do we do?"

"Well, the only one that saw us in the cove was that Bertram, and I'm sure they don't want to talk to these guys. We just play it by ear. Here, take the helm, let me slow this thing down a little." Avery brought the throttles back.

"What are you going to do, Phil?"

""I am going down and report on the big yacht that we just passed burning near a little island. But first, I am going to help Gail and Buckwheat get that poor Cuban below. We don't want to be boarded with our friend lying around."

Carefully wrapped in blankets, the body of Luis Navarro was taken down below and placed in one of the forward staterooms. His face was cleaned up and he lay in the bunk as if he were sleeping. Should the French want to board, they would tell them he was crew, and pray for the best.

Avery picked up the standard VHF radio mike and turned to channel 16. "Mayday, Mayday calling the Force De Surface in Pointe A Pitre. Mayday."

A very French voice, speaking very good English responded. "Vessel calling Mayday, this is the FSMC, state your emergency please."

"Yes, I am the captain on a chartering sailboat, and have just noticed a large yacht on fire, near one of these small island south of Guadeloupe. I believe the island is Grand Islet in the Saintes?"

"Yes, we are aware of this fire and have a patrol boat en route to the scene. What is your location, Captain?"

"Ah, I am about three miles west of the island, heading around Terre De Bas on my way north to Antigua."

"Captain, did you see any activity near the burning vessel or any other craft nearby? Over."

"Yes, sir. We noticed a large sportfishing boat that came from that same area as we arrived, it was heading south around the island, then went eastward at full speed. There was too much smoke around to see anything else, and my keel is nearly 10 feet, so I couldn't get too close."

"What is your yacht's name, and your calling port, Captain?"

"Ah, my yacht is the Island Drummer, and I am out of St. Thomas on charter for Christmas week. Over."

"Thank you, Captain, for your cooperation and reporting. Have a safe holiday."

"Thank you, Oh, I think I see your patrol boat now. It's about to pass by. I hope there were no casualties on that yacht. Merry Christmas to you, sir."

Avery ran back on deck and watched as the sleek Sterne P680 Air Sea Rescue ship pass to starboard. The one hundred and sixty foot ship was moving at better that 20 knots to the scene. A few crewmen waved as they passed.

"That was a smart move, Phil, acting like a innocent by-stander and calling them before they challenged us, smart."

"Thank you, Dan. Now, let's talk. Where do we go from here, and what are we going to do with that poor dead Cuban?"

"Phil, behind you," Gail shouted.

O'Brien, Avery and Buckland turned and looked back towards the island. The patrol boat was crashing through the seas still under full power. The smoke from the Unicorn was still very visible. But it was the outline of a twin engine aircraft that caught their attention. It was close to the water and coming straight at them.

"Jesus, what do you make of this?" Buckland yelled.

The Cessna Conquest pulled up and banked left, then right and came at stick height right along the port side of the Drummer, dropping its right wing momentarily. It passed at a moderate speed, but the faces in the windows were easily seen. The plane then banked left and started to climb at a high rate of speed.

"Three-zero, three-zero Zulu, she's a U.S. plane," Avery said. "Remember those numbers, folks."

"I'll go down and write them down, Phil," Gail ran down the companionway.

"Dan, you don't think?"

"You bet your sweet ass I do, that was him, I know it was."

Grand Islet
0914 Hours

Tomas Puros unwrapped the M-l Carbine from its brown paper and started to work his way down the face of the steep hill. The smoke from the Unicorn was making any visibility on the waters around the vessel difficult. He could see the Bertram as it moved out of the cove. He had been watching the large sailboat from the time it first arrived.

Now, following orders from DeTorre, he had to find the missing crew member, somewhere in the water off the stern of the Unicorn and the American sailboat, which was moving slowly towards the Unicorn.

He finally found a shelf that he could walk along with good footing and was able to get past the bow of the stricken Feadship, which now lay hard over on her port side. He could see the anchor still in position. Then the wind shifted so he could see the small inflatable moving out from the sailboat.

"There he is, I got him," he said out loud as he spotted Navarro on his back kicking towards the small life raft. The wind shifted again and the black smoke came up the rocky wall surrounding Puros. He began to choke. He pulled his shirt up and covered his nose. Finally, the smoke dissipated, swirling off to his left. The field of view was open to him again. The swimmer was climbing into the raft. Puros squatted down and rested the small carbine stock against his cheek and supported his elbow with his knee. He didn't adjust the sights. He pulled off the first round and he saw it find its mark, the entire front of the raft was covered in blood and the swimmer was falling off the raft. Again the black cloud blocked his view. When he could see again, the swimmer was hanging over the raft and being pulled in by the blond man. Puros brought the carbine back up and fired again. This time there was no explosion of blood and matter, but he knew he hit the man again as his body had jumped from the impact of the bullet.

Satisfied he got his man, Puros stood up and watched for a second and noticed that the raft was now sinking. He took the carbine up again and sighted into the raft, but before he could squeeze off the next round, a ball of heat and smoke came up to meet him, burning his arms and stinging his face. He tried to step back, but he was too close to the wall. His heel hit the wall throwing his balance off. He dropped the carbine while trying to cover his face from the heat, but the next blast of heat and flames went right into his nostrils. When he opened his mouth to gasp for air it was like someone poured molten lead down his throat. He tried to scream, but nothing came out, he fell forward, holding his throat as he tumbled nearly 250 feet, bouncing off the jagged stone wall. He landed head first onto a bed of rocks in shallow water only a few yards away from the stately bow of the dying Unicorn.

CHAPTER 28

Passe du Grand Ilet
0937 Hours

Captain D'Amato moved the Bonaire's throttles to their maximum limits. The Bertram plowed eastward around the southern end of Grand Islet, 75 yards off shore. He did not notice the small outboard boat crashing through the waves close to shore carrying two men. Suddenly he felt a sharp pain in his left arm. Captain DeTorre had a vice grip hold on his upper arm and was shouting and pointing.

"There they are, the pick up boat, turn us around, Captain."

Marcel Balisteri, fighting to keep the small boat stable in the rough seas near the island, happened to look seaward and recognized the sportfishing yacht. He pulled the outboard tiller into his stomach and spun the small boat. A rolling wave came under the hull and nearly threw the two men overboard. By the time Balisteri got control, the Bertram was heading directly towards him.

After seeing the size of the small skiff, DeTorre felt it was too risky to transfer the Castro party on the open seas. The small open boat only sixteen feet long could not handle all of the Unicorn's crew. It would have to make at least three trips, furthermore, the sea around them was alive with small boats. A number of them were headed for Grand Islet, possibly to investigate the giant black and gray cloud of smoke boiling above the island.

DeTorre ordered Captain D'Amato to get the Bertram closer to Terre De Haut, where they would use the Bonaire's inflatable as well as the small outboard skiff to transfer Castro and his crew. D'Amato did not like this plan. He could see a lot of activity on the beach including sunbathers and swimmers plus a number of small boats operating near shore. Sorokin was holding the small 9 millimeter automatic and Castro's crew were holding guns on the guests below. He didn't argue. He moved the throttles forward and headed for the beach on the south end of the island.

DeTorre returned to the cockpit and yelled to Mesa and Balisteri, who were trying to stay a safe distance behind the Bertram's huge wide wake. They finally understood DeTorre's screaming orders to go back to the island and pick up Tomas Puros.

Sorokin went into the main salon, where he found Castro and Vincetta huddled on a sofa speaking quietly. The rest of the crew were outside sitting on the cockpit floor holding their weapons. Bonaire's crew, Calva, Rivia and

Cantillo were sitting on the transom, silently taking in all the activity going on around them.

Vincetta looked up at Sorokin and spoke quietly.

"Comrade, we think that maybe our trusted friend Colonel Navarro may have been involved with the explosions on the Unicorn. At first, we suspected our guests, but that did not make sense. Colonel Navarro, however, seemed to desert us. He swam away from us towards the American sailboat, correct? Well, we think he may have caused the explosion. You see, Colonel Navarro has family living in the United States."

Sorokin studied Castro for a few seconds. Castro's eyes, like the general's, were glassy. He rested his head against the back of the sofa, looking up at the ceiling. Sorokin wanted to leave him with his thoughts, but he also wanted to know his feelings about Navaro.

"What do you think, comrade President?" Sorokin asked.

"I don't know, Dimitri, General Vincetta may be right. But I can't believe that this soldier, this devoted soldier, who I learned to trust and who served me like a son, could do anything like this." Castro turned and looked at Vincetta.

"You forget General, Navarro did not know he was going on this operation until the last minute. He wouldn't have the time to plan such a thing."

Sorokin responded. "Comrades, he had plenty of time. Didn't he disappear for a period of time before he left Havana for Santiago? It seems, General Vincetta, you made a joke about it when Colonel Navarro first came on board. You said something about him getting lost, then finding him having coffee with his brother-in-law at the air base. If I understood correctly, the brother-in-law is your private pilot, isn't that correct sir?"

Castro did not respond. He sat staring at the cabin ceiling.

Vincetta shook his head, put his hands on his knees and pushed himself up from the sofa.

"Yes comrade, but that was in Havana. He was nowhere near the Unicorn until he arrived with us at the marina on the day we left."

Sorokin went over to the wet bar, picked up a glass and filled it with water.

"General, I talked to Lopez when we were leaving the cove and he told me the explosion came from outside the hull, not inside. The shaft strut and the frame it was attached to were blown inside the hull. It could be the Colonel somehow dropped the bomb over the side. After all, he was with Yang Lo most of the time and no one was paying any attention to him. As a matter of fact, for the entire trip Colonel Navarro kept to himself, claiming he was seasick, didn't he?"

Sorokin became silent. There was something bothering him, gnawing away in his brain. Without a word, he spun around and ran to the glass sliding door, pulled it open and stepped out onto the cockpit. Without saying a word to the startled passengers he climbed up to the bridge and walked over to DeTorre.

"Captain, what did you tell Puros to do about Colonel Navarro?"

DeTorre flashed his eyes towards Captain D'Amato and the four men surrounding him at the helm. He motioned Sorokin to step away, out of earshot from the others.

"Comrade Sorokin, I told Puros to stop Navarro from being rescued by the Americans. Puros has the means to do this. I am no fool, comrade. What happened to the Unicorn was well planned. We were deliberately sabotaged. I knew it wasn't my crew. That left you, General Vincetta, Yang Lo, Colonel Navarro and the President. Navarro was the only one who decided not to join in our escape to safety, wasn't he? He also knows too much, comrade, don't you agree?"

Sorokin said nothing. The cold emotionless face before him said it all. He sidestepped the tall officer and walked up behind Captain D'Amato and spoke directly into his ear.

"Turn on your VHF radio and set the frequency for channel 72. I need to use your radio again, Captain."

1023 Hours

In less than ninety minutes after the first explosion aboard the Unicorn, Fidel Castro, Dimitri Sorokin, General Vincetta, DeTorre, Varas, Lopez, Fajardo, Rodriguez and Yang Lo were on board the Cessna 441 lifting off from the short runway on Terre De Haut. Much to their amazement nobody challenged them, or even talked to them as they walked over the crowded beach of sunbathers, through a hedge bordering the airstrip and boarded the waiting plane.

Captain D'Amato wasted no time getting out of the area. He pointed the Bertram's bow due south towards the island of Dominica, twenty-five miles away. In less than three hours he dropped off two of his guests, Jorge Armando and Ramon Cantillo and continued on to Martinique where he dropped off the rest of his guests. Unfortunately for D'Amato, while clearing customs he was boarded by the French police. They had orders to hold him, his crew, his passengers and the yacht at the request of the French Navy. Armando and Cantillo had been arrested by French authorities at the airport on Dominica and were being flown to Fort-de-France. It was learned that the Bonaire had been reported leaving the scene by a passing vessel just before the luxury yacht Unicorn exploded, burned and sank.

As soon as they were airborne, Fidel Castro told Vincetta that he wanted to do something special for Tomas Puros. Castro was pleased with the efficient way that Puros had planned their simple undisturbed escape.

DeTorre, sitting behind the Mexican pilot, ordered him to circle and drop down so they could take a look at the cove where the Unicorn was burning. He also wanted to take a closer look at the American sailboat that was on a westward heading leaving the small island of Grande Islet.

The pilot rolled the Cessna and came around the small island until he spotted the large sailboat. He dropped down to one hundred feet and flew right at the yacht. A few hundred feet away he pulled the Cessna up and dropped the starboard wing so the passengers in the cabin could get a close look at the sailboat. The flyby was fast and Sorokin guessed there were at least four men standing on deck staring at the plane. He was interested in the sailboat, but more important, he wanted to search the seas to the north of Guadeloupe, particularly the passage between Guadeloupe and Montserrat. After a discussion with DeTorre, the pilot was asked to fly north off the west coast of Guadeloupe for a few minutes so Sorokin could search the waters north of Guadeloupe.

"What is it, comrade? What is it you are looking for?" DeTorre kept asking.

Leaning his head and shoulders into the flight deck between the two pilots, Sorokin squinted as he scanned through the light haze ahead. There were many boats moving about, but the one he was searching for should be easy to spot.

"There," Sorokin touched the co-pilot's shoulder and pointed out his windscreen. "There, at one o'clock, see that large ship? Go over there."

The co-pilot looked at the pilot, who was flying the aircraft. The pilot turned and looked at the smiling Russian.

"Over there, see that large ship coming around the island up there, just get me closer." Sorokin, excited now was nearly sitting in the co-pilot's lap.

"Do it, Captain," DeTorre yelled out.

The Cessna banked slightly to starboard and dropped its nose. Sorokin noticed the altimeter begin to unwind as they left twenty-two hundred feet.

"That's it, now we can leave," Sorokin said as he moved back into his seat smiling. He looked at DeTorre who moved up to take a better look at the ship Sorokin was so interested in.

"Comrade, that looks like one of your..."

"That's right, comrade, it is the Kompas, my friend."

"Is that who you were talking to when we were leaving the Unicorn, Comrade? Is that what all that Russian talk was about when you were on my radio and you talked to him again from the Bonaire, just before we left for the island. Just what is it you are doing, comrade?"

Sorokin smiled, and said nothing. He reached in his pocket and pulled out a damaged, but intact cigar.

"So, comrade, you had your own plan all this time? I am impressed." DeTorre laughed, then turned to look back at Castro, sitting two rows back.

Sorokin was quick to get DeTorre's attention.

"No, Captain, let your President rest, I will explain when we get back to Cuba." Sorokin rolled the cigar slowly between his lips, then put it back in his shirt pocket.

"Captain, how long before we get to Cuba?" Sorokin asked.

DeTorre moved up between the pilots and spoke to them in Spanish. He was handed a chart, which he brought back to his seat.

"Our pilot says we will be in Santiago in four hours and twenty minutes, providing we have no problems with the air space over the Dominican Republic or Haiti. It's about 940 miles to Santiago."

"Good, now I can get some sleep." Sorokin slumped down in his chair and rested his chin on his chest.

"Comrade, aren't you going to tell me about the Kompas?"

"Nothing to tell, comrade. Kompas is on assignment, that's all."

DeTorre handed back the chart to the co-pilot, took another look out his starboard side window but could no longer see the Russian spy ship, Kompas. He sat back down and glanced to the rear of the plane and noted all had fallen off to sleep.

Sorokin was pleased that "Operation Dolphin" had failed. Now maybe he could convince Fidel Castro to stay away from dealing in drugs and involvement with the drug cartels. He tried to piece together the day's events. "Did Navarro set the bomb, if it was a bomb. Why did he do it? That American sailboat, was it coincidence that it was in the vicinity? How long had it been out there? Where did it come from?" He thought about the sailboat that they stopped to help. "What was its name? Oh, yes, the Seaduce, and that captain, he was American, yes, and what was the name of that freighter's?" Sorokin's head began to throb as one unanswered questions followed another. He finally gave in to exhaustion and fell off to sleep.

Island Drummer
1037 Hours

Gail brought the coffee pot from the galley and filled the waiting mugs.

O'Brien, in a Tee shirt and shorts, was lying down across the port cockpit seat, smoking a cigarette. Buckland, sitting on the port lounge was cleaning out the cuts in his hands with peroxide and cotton. Avery, with feet wide apart stood leaning his weight against the helmswheel, staring into the open sea ahead.

"Well, I guess this is just about the most exciting Christmas day I have ever had," Gail said as she sat down next to Buckland.

Buckland chuckled. "You know, when I get home I'm going to take Meg up to Vermont, find the coldest most isolated cabin in the woods, climb between two comforters and screw her brains out."

Gail snapped her head around.

"Buckwheat, I'm surprised at you. What a way to talk, is that all you can think about right now?"

"Gail, that's all I want to think about right now. I want to pretend this entire trip was just a bad dream. Meg can help me forget, she's wonderful."

"Yeah, I know how you feel, Commander. I feel like I fell off the face of this fucking earth, I can't remember my employees' names and I wonder if they even remember mine. I haven't talked to anyone in almost, what, ten days?" Avery said.

"Oh, Phil, you have the least to worry about, my God, you have some of the best in the business working for you and you know it. with one exception, your buddy Ray who walked out on your yacht repair business in Immokalee."

Avery started to laugh. "Funny you should mention Immokalee, I was just thinking about that fat slob, Levin, the comptroller? Boy, I wonder where he is today, he was something else. You know, I wouldn't mind having him taking care of my books."

O'Brien rolled over on his side and took a cigarette out of the pack of Winstons in his pocket. He began to babble.

"I keep thinking of those two young kids they found on the Tamiami Trail, with holes in the back of their heads. Do remember him, Phil? You know, that crazy blonde haired hippie truck driver we had at the manger, the

552

one who got caught spying on us? I wonder if he had any family. Then there was Rick Van Wagner. His baby boy is what, two now? It's really ironic. Here we are, Christmas day, sailing on this super yacht off the coast of a beautiful Caribbean island and below we have a dead young Cuban soldier named, Navarro. Strange, he is the sole reason why we are all here, right now this minute, think about that my friends. Navarro was the stranger who brought all of us together, he made this super yacht possible and the reason for creating Operation Yuletide. Now he is dead and his family, for all we know, may just might be free for the first time in their lives in Florida."

"That's enough, Dan." Avery shouted. "We did what we had to do. It was a good operation, well planned and executed. We did the best we could."

"Phil is right, Dan. We did the best we could. It was a brilliant plan, it wasn't your fault something went wrong with those charges." Buckland was trying to ease O'Brien's pain and guilt.

Avery removed a cigarette, lit it and looked over at O'Brien.

"Look Dan, what's done is done. We have some new problems we need to address, like where do we go from here?"

"Good question, Phil, I did not make any plans if we failed, so, we just go home." O'Brien said.

"Dan, in a few hours we will be outside the mouth of English Harbour and we have to decide what we are going to do. We have a dead Cuban on board and we can't sail into port with him. How do we explain him to the authorities? We could continue on up to St. Croix, St. Thomas, or Puerto Rico and dispose of him there, but that's twenty four, maybe thirty hours away and we don't have that much fuel if we plan to power all the way. We need to fuel up at Antigua. Now, what do we do with Navarro?"

"Phil, I don't think we have a choice, do we? We have to deep six him between here and Antigua," Buckland said.

"Jesus, Commander, how can you even think of throwing that man overboard, what about his family? There must..."

Avery interrupted. "Gail, Buckwheat is right. We will have to bury Navarro out here, we can't get caught with him on board."

"Phil, it's not like he is a deep dark secret. Castro's people saw us take him on board, remember?" Gail cried out.

"Sure they know, but just who do you think they are going to notify? They certainly aren't going to call in the frog-fleet on Guadeloupe, which would mean getting themselves involved. No, Castro will give us no trouble on this. I'm sure all they're thinking about right now is getting their scorched red asses back to Cuba."

O'Brien sat up and swung his legs down into the cockpit. Without looking up at the crew, he said in a low voice. "I say we go for the Virgins, Phil. We'll sail all the way, makes no difference when we get there now. I would feel better if we could be on our own turf. We can get things done there. Navarro will keep for the next twenty-four hours. We will have to wrap him up good and air tight. We can put him in that storage locker back in the stern."

"Well, if you want my opinion," Buckland said. "We hide Navarro, go into English Harbour, get on some phones and talk to someone like Admiral Koster and ask him what he thinks we should do."

"Oh, my God, Navarro's poor family. How will they ever know?" Gail said.

Avery reached down and placed his hand on Gail's shoulder. "We will find a way to tell them, Gail." He turned to face O'Brien. "Folks, I have to go along with Dan, I think we should hoist up the rags and start heading up for St. Thomas. We should make it there by noon tomorrow if we don't lose this breeze. It will be a lot easier to get things done up there. Hell, I can sail right into the Coast Guard dock and get Navarro taken care of while Dan calls Washington."

Buckwheat moved around the cockpit and sat down next to O'Brien. "Dan, tell me. Do you think we really got away with it? I mean, do you expect any retaliation?"

"Shit no, what can Castro do? We may think we know now what he is up to with his little submarine. Our little disaster back there may have spared his life, but we hopefully ruined his business plans for a while. He knows our guys will be looking for little mini subs now and he'll think twice about using them. Keep in mind, he also knows we have Navarro, what he doesn't know is whether he is dead or alive. I don't think the person or persons who shot Navaro could tell how serious his wounds were. Naw, we won't get any grief from Castro."

"Yeah, I guess you're right. Can you imagine that guy building mini submarines to carry cocaine into our waters?" Buckwheat said.

"I never thought of it before today, but now I think it's scary as hell. I just wish we could have gotten more information out of Navarro on how the fucking things worked," O'Brien replied.

The Drummer's smooth running engines suddenly began to slow down and began acting sluggish, then the port engine died. The Drummer started to make a rolling turn to port. Avery brought the starboard engine to neutral.

"What the hell? We just lost an engine," Avery said as he studied the instruments. He turned the starter key and the port engine caught and fired up again. He put both engines in gear and continued moving the throttles up slowly. After a few minutes, he was sure everything was back to normal.

"What do you think happened, Phil?"

"I don't know, Dan. They acted like they ran out of gas. Here, Buckwheat, take the helm, I'm going down and check on the tanks. We should have plenty, but we may want to get ready to put up the sails, just in case."

"Right, I'll start getting the sails ready," Gail said, then ran forward to the mast and began to untie the cloth straps from around the mainsail.

"Hey, what's this?" Buckwheat yelled out.

Avery stopped on the companionway stairs and came back up into the cockpit. All eyes were looking towards the starboard bow.

"It looks like a freighter, or a large trawler," O'Brien said.

"Yeah, she just came out from the north end of the island. Isn't there some kind of passage over there separating the island of Guadeloupe?" Buckland asked.

"Sure is, it's a river dividing the island, but that baby didn't come through there, she draws too much. She may have been over at Port Louis on Grande Terre. Lots of big commercial stuff comes and goes out of there," Avery said as he turned to go back down to the cabin.

"Wait, Phil," O'Brien ordered. "Where are those glasses, Gail?"

Gail went over to one of the lockers in the lounge seat and took the binoculars out and handed them to O'Brien.

O'Brien raised the glasses to his eyes. "Hey, Phil, you might want to see this," he said.

Avery looked at O'Brien's concerned face, took the binoculars and focused them on the trawler, which was about three hundred yards off the starboard bow, heading due west.

"She's a Russian, I'll be damned. From the looks of all her antennas and radar, she must be of those spooks that we always hear about. They follow our shuttle launches and anything else we send up out of Cape Kennedy. They usually hang out around Antigua so they can monitor the radar tracking station, you know, the one at the airport?"

"What do you think he's doing down here heading west?" Buckland asked.

"Well, Cuba is due west of here, right? She's probably heading for Havana for some R and R." Avery handed the glasses back to O'Brien and went back down the companionway.

"What's your heading, Buckwheat?" O'Brien asked.

"Three fifty five."

"Let's come over to port, say zero-two-zero, and drop your speed a little."

"O'Brien, what the hell are you doing?" Buckland asked.

"Just do it, I want to see something." O'Brien held the glasses on the trawler, now sitting about two o'clock and two hundred yards out. O'Brien gave a quick look over his right shoulder at the northern end of Basse Terre. He figured it was maybe five miles away.

"What's he doing, Dan?" Buckland asked.

"I don't know, it seems he slowed down a bunch. His closing rate fell off considerably. Like he doesn't want to cross our bows. That son of a bitch is slowing down, he's up to something."

"I'll go down and get Phil," Gail said, as she headed down the companionway.

"Good idea, Buckwheat, go back to your original course and push those throttles up again."

"O'Brien, why are you fucking with these red bastards? They're a little bigger than we are, pal, maybe not as fast, but bigger."

"Little more speed, Buckwheat, head out more, go to three-three-zero."

Buckland noticed what was making O'Brien nervous. The trawler appeared to be tracking them, changing speeds and course along with the Drummer.

O'Brien put his head in the companionway and yelled. "Phil, get your ass up here, now, we may have a problem."

Avery came flying up out of the companionway and joined O'Brien.

"Take a look, Phil, look at the two guys on the bridge, and the one just behind that forward deck house, do you see him? Does he have some kind of rifle in his hand, or am I seeing things?"

"They are giving us a good look see and from the looks of the lenses on their glasses, I'd say they could tell how many cavities you have in your mouth, O'Brien."

"Buckland, give me the helm." Avery stepped behind the wheel and brought the Drummer back to port again.

"Shit, he's moving back over, Phil," O'Brien shouted.

"Are these guys playing with us or what, Dan?"

"I don't know, Buckwheat, but we better start thinking strategy here. I would guess they are planning to scare the shit out of us, maybe even bump and run. They have been known to use this tactic with our Navy ships, or they might be just going to run over us. Either way, I don't like it."

"Gail, get on the VHF and advise the French Navy, ah, what ever they call themselves, the FSMC people. Advise them a Soviet trawler, five miles northwest of Basse Terre, is harassing us. I want this to be on their record."

Gail started down the stairs to the navigation station. She was about to pick up the mike, when she heard someone on the radio speaker calling for the Island Drummer.

She picked up the mike and responded. "Island Drummer here, come in. This is Island Drummer, come in."

"Island Drummer, this is Captain Franco Benvenisti, aboard the patrol vessel, P 680, do you understand?"

"Roger, Captain. I was about to call you. Sir, we seem to be having a problem with a Russian trawler about five miles west of Basse Terre."

"Island Drummer, if you hear me, we want you to return to Pointe Pitre. We need to get a statement from the captain about the accident on Grand Islet."

"Captain Benvenisti, did you understand me? We are being harassed out here by a large Soviet ship."

"You are breaking up Island Drummer, sir, please, return at once to port."

"Fuck you, captain," Gail screamed, threw the mike down on the navigation table, and ran up the stairs. She stood directly in Avery's face but did not get a chance to report on her conversation with the French captain.

O'Brien was standing on the starboard lounge seat screaming. "Jesus Christ, Phil, he is coming right for us. What are you waiting for, get our ass out of here."

Avery's eyes were glued to the huge black bow of the 190 foot Samara Class survey ship boring down on the Drummer. He was less than thirty yards now and turning slightly to starboard. The Russian was setting a collision point and planned to hit the Drummer at mid ship.

"For Christ sake, Phil." O'Brien screamed. He was just about to punch Avery out and take over the helm. He thought Avery had frozen at the wheel.

"One, two, three, now baby," Avery screamed as he pushed opened both throttles. He had already dropped the two hydraulic struts. The two four bladed bronze wheels bit hard into the disturbed waters beneath the Drummer's hull. The two 454 Chevy engines were red lined at 6000 RPM's and the two exhausts pipes began belching clouds of black smoke from beneath the transom. The Island Drummer reacted like a race horse leaving the starting gate.

The trawler's helmsman could not compensate for the sailboat's amazing speed. The trawler was committed and while her twin Skoda diesels labored to push the old research ship to its maximum speed of fifteen knots, it wasn't fast enough to counter the Drummer's actions. The huge rusty hull passed through the Drummer's wake, fifteen feet from the Drummer's stern, cascading mountains of water over her own deck and lifting the Drummer's stern.

"Son of a bitch, I don't believe those guys. Did you see the looks on their ugly faces?" Gail yelled.

"Nope, I was too busy trying not to mess my shorts," O'Brien yelled as he turned to Avery. "Man, you are one lucky bastard. I don't believe this thing just got up and leaped out of the way," O'Brien said as he watched the departing trawler.

"I was counting on it, Danny, old boy. We are almost out of fuel, which means we are real light in our sneakers."

"Gail, did you get hold of those French Navy guys?"

"Yes, and no. They want us back at Pointe Pitre to give a statement. They would not listen to me about the trawler."

O'Brien moved directly in front of Avery and looked him straight in the eyes. "Shit, Phil, did you just say we are nearly out of gas?"

"Well, not completely, we have a couple of gallons sloshing around down there in the aft tank. Maybe enough to get us up to Falmouth Harbour." Avery turned and looked over his left shoulder. "Where are those Russians heading now?"

"Looks like they are heading west. Man, I don't believe those guys, what fucking nerve." O'Brien said as he picked up the binoculars and put the trawler in his range finder.

"Phil, they are starting to turn to port. My God, it looks like they may be coming back."

"Son of a bitch," O'Brien cried out. "Phil, turn us around and head for Guadeloupe, we can't be more than six, maybe seven miles, we can out run that bastard, can't we?"

Avery looked over his shoulder at the Russian trawler.

"Gail, get back on that radio, call out a May Day," Avery yelled out.

Gail went back down and tried again to contact the French Patrol boat. She did not realize, she was using the special "hopper" VHF radio mike, not the standard VHF radio.

"Dan, I don't think we can outrun him, not in these seas, and not with the fuel so low. I'll have to try and out fox him again."

"Shit, Phil, that captain ain't no fool. He knows you can move out fast from a dead stop."

"I know, I'll just have to do something else. Just keep me posted on his closing speed and distance."

Buckwheat had gone down to his stateroom and came back up on deck with a gun that looked like something that may have won the west. He held in securely in both hands.

"What the fuck is that?" O'Brien asked.

"It's a Ruger Blackhawk, single six, twenty two caliber."

"Just what are you going to do with that toy, Commander?"

"I'm going to blow off a commies head if I can get a bead on him. I got magnum long rounds in here."

"Not on my watch." O'Brien grabbed the pistol by the barrel and pulled it out of Buckland's hand and threw it overboard.

"Are you crazy, O'Brien? That was the only gun we have on board, and it was mine, it cost me over two hundred bills."

"I don't care if it belonged to John Wayne. The last thing we want to do is start a shooting war with these bastards. They most likely have some serious cannons on board, wouldn't you think? Listen, Buckwheat, if you want to do something, get all the damn docking lines you can muster and put them on the aft deck, now."

"What are you doing, Dan?" Phil asked.

"Well, if you can get that son of a bitch to pass by our back porch again, we may be able to foul up his screws, if our timing is good and we can get the lines out in front of his bows. Maybe, just maybe, some of them will get sucked into his props."

"Good idea, and it's worth the try." Avery looked to port. "And, here they come again."

"Phil, slow down, let him set up their collision course. We have to try and fool him again. Are your shafts down?"

"Roger that, but he isn't going to buy it twice, Dan. Maybe I should take him on bow to bow. I can steer off at the last second and let him sideswipe us. We'll roll badly, and probably lose all the rigging, but at least we'll stay afloat."

"No, we would all be knocked silly, maybe even overboard and we won't be able to get any lines under him. We'll let him go for the broadside again."

"O.K., only this time I'm going to let him get in a little closer."

Gail came back on deck frustrated and crying. "I can't get anyone, Phil, nobody is responding to my Mayday." She looked towards the west. "Oh my God, Phil, they're coming right at us again."

559

"It's alright, go help Buckwheat, quick, he's getting all our lines together on the aft deck. O'Brien is going to try and screw up their props with our lines, I think he's crazy, but if we can get them to pass close to our stern again, who knows?"

"Right." Gail responded and jumped up on deck and went back to help Buckland.

"Here he comes, look at those funnels blowing soot. He must have those diesels red lined. Maybe we'll get lucky and he'll puke both of them," Buckland said.

Avery advanced his throttles to 4000 rpm's and dropped the struts half way down. He could feel the Drummer's bow begin to dip. Just then, all hell broke loose. The Drummer took a rolling turn to port. Avery recovered steerage. He looked down at the instruments. "Son of a bitch, the port engine is gone again."

Avery pulled the starboard throttle back. He fumbled with the starting key to the port engine. No response this time. He could see the tachometer jumping, he knew the engine was turning over, but it wouldn't start. He cracked the throttle, opened it, closed it, nothing, no fire. He looked over at the Russians. They were about three hundred yards out setting up for a better angle. It was as if they knew the Drummer was in serious trouble.

"Dan, we can't get out of his way this time. All I can do is turn into him with the starboard engine and rudder."

"No, Phil, stay put," O'Brien yelled at the crew. "Everyone get on your life jackets, now. Buckwheat, release that whaler from the davits and bring it around on the starboard side towards the bow, we may need it."

O'Brien ran down into the main cabin and returned a few seconds later with a rusty long barrel rifle that he had smuggled on board when the Drummer was in Sarasota.

"Jesus, Dan. What the hell is that?" Avery asked.

"Old faithful? It's just a cheap old Remington 30\30, but I got me over a hundred deer with it and I'm about to get me my first red bear, if they don't spot me first. Now, all of you go forward, get on the bow and get ready to jump when they hit."

"What the hell do you think you're going to do? Lord Jim?" Avery asked sarcastically.

"I'm going to throw all those lines overboard, then I'm going to rest this cannon on the mizzen boom and get one of those red stars in my sights, you know, the ones they wear on their fucking hats. I am going to shoot, run and dive off the stern and hope it's not me instead of our dock lines that foul up his screws."

"If you think we are going to let you do this, you're crazy. You're coming up on the bow with the rest of us, forget about playing Daniel Boone. You said it yourself, no shooting. What if you got lucky and hit one? You better believe, they won't take any prisoners. They'll stick around until they run us all over, Dan."

O'Brien agreed. "O.K., let's get these lines over along the portside. If he plans to ram us, he'll do it midship. You know, I saw this scene in a movie once, I think it was PT 109, the story of Jack Kennedy in the Pacific? The Japs ran right over his PT boat, but the bow stayed afloat, and he saved his crew, so that's where we go."

Avery could not believe O'Brien could think about a movie at this time, it was almost as if he was trying to be funny. After throwing the dozen heavy lines over the port side, Avery turned and yelled at Gail and Buckwheat to get their asses forward away from the rigging. He waited until O'Brien got ahead of him, then he followed. When they reached the bow, he took the rifle from O'Brien and passed it down through the open hatch over Navarro's berth.

"Shit, I should have grabbed the cable cutters. I could have cut the starboard spreaders and lower shrouds and let the mast fall right on them as they approached," Avery said.

"I would guess that's exactly what will happen anyway, Phil, when they take out the portside chain plates." Gail said. "Everything will go overboard to starboard, right?" She asked.

"Don't really know, never been hit by a trawler midship before," Avery responded.

The Drummer's crew stood poised, hanging onto each other, and onto the flexible lifeline on the starboard side of the bow. They watched in silence, as the trawler lined up on its collision course, which appeared to be aimed directly at midship of the doomed sailboat.

The trawler was less than two hundred yards away and coming fast. The massive black hull, with the rusty fluke anchors protruding out its sides, plowed though the deep blue seas, rolling tons of white water ahead of its bow.

Suddenly, for the second time this day, the crew of Island Drummer witnessed another spectacular scene. About fifty yards off the port stern a huge black dome, covered in cascading water, came out of the blue-green sea. It was like a giant water balloon escaping from the depths. The dome rose fifty feet out of the ocean followed by a large vertical superstructure with giant horizontal wings. The outrageous looking machine poised in mid air for a moment then it crashed back into the sea, sending a six foot wave across the boiling waters.

O'Brien fell to his knees screaming, "Koster, you magnificent son of a bitch, you bloody old war hog, you lying mother-fucker, I love you."

"Commander Buckland, that is one of ours, isn't it?" Avery cried out.

"You bet your sweet ass she is, she's a nuker. A beautiful Los Angeles class nuker. Sweet mother Mary of mercy, the United States Navy is here." Buckland grabbed Gail and began hugging and kissing her.

The USS Memphis, SSN 691 sat nearly motionless in the turbulent water. The top of her massive round hull was barely visible. Her tall black sail and the large vertical fin at her stern were the only parts of her structure totally out of water. Two heads suddenly appeared at the top of her sail. Then a small American flag appeared, hoisted up on one of her vertical towers.

The metallic sound of a portable megaphone broke above the sounds of the choppy seas slapping against the Drummer's hull.

"Ahoy there, aboard the Island Drummer, are you alright? We are the United States Navy attack submarine, Memphis. I am Captain Peter Meredith. Please have Dan O'Brien, if he is on board, get on the VHF hopper, I need to talk to him. If he's not there, have Commander Buckland contact me. We are standing by."

"Dan, I don't see the damn Russians. Where did they go?" Gail asked. Suddenly the trawler appeared from behind the Memphis broad black sail. It was turning hard to port, running almost parallel with the Memphis, about sixty yards off her port beam. One of the officers, wearing a baseball cap, could be seen shooting the Russian crew a bird.

Avery smiled and shook his head. He looked at O'Brien and said, "That sub captain is one gutsy son of a bitch, he must have known he was right in the path of that Russian scow. Man, that took some brass ones."

O'Brien chuckled and took a cigarette from his pocket.

"Gutsy is putting it mildly, keep in mind he is a nuker. But, I have to give that Russian captain some credit too for his maneuvers, he had to get that tub turned fast and he didn't have much room to work with either. Look at him now, he's really starting to haul ass and heading straight for Cuba. Don't you know, he's going to have some tall tales to tell his leaders when he gets back to port? Somebody had to give him the order to track us down and run us over, which leads me to believe, that someone in the Soviet Navy must have known about this meeting and what Castro is up to."

"You know, I never gave that a thought, but you're right, Dan. I wonder if the captain on the Memphis will report the incident?" Avery remarked.

"You bet your sweet ass he will. I would be willing to bet that Norfolk has already been advised and a teletype is on its way to the Kremlin," O'Brien said, as he made his way towards the companionway.

O'Brien went down to the navigation station, turned on the hopper radio and called up the Memphis. He congratulated the captain on his spectacular entrance and the life saving rescue.

Captain Meredith informed O'Brien that he had been shadowing the entire operation since the Island Drummer left St. Croix. He was only a hundred and fifty yards south of the interception point, where the Drummer and the Unicorn met. He saw the entire show and recorded it all on tape. He sat submerged at periscope depth, three miles off the island of Grand Islet and watched everything and moved in even closer after the first explosion on the Unicorn. They recorded the sinking of the Unicorn, the escape of the Bertram sportfisher. They also saw a man with a rifle come down from the top of the island, but lost him in the smoke from the Unicorn. Last but not least, they noticed the small twin engine plane that flew over the Drummer then headed westward. The messages between Sorokin and the trawler were also intercepted on the Memphis and the tracking station in Antigua. The taped conversations had been sent to Norfolk, then onto Navy Intelligence in Washington and to Admiral Koster. They had been waiting patiently, sixty feet below the surface, five miles west of Guadeloupe, for the Russian trawler to make its appearance, as well as guarding the departure of the Island Drummer.

"Mr. O'Brien? My orders are to contact Atlantic Sub-fleet Headquarters as soon as we connect, sir. I have, ah, another strange order, I am to recover Rudolf and Pinetree, or an Evergreen?, I forget which, from the Drummer and take them to Roosevelt Roads in Puerto Rico, where they will be flown immediately to Washington. As soon as Rudolf is on board, I am to put him on a direct line to speak with Mr. Scrooge?"

O'Brien had to restrain himself from laughing. "Sorry about that, captain, it's sort of a code for the operation. I will explain when I get on board. I'm Rudolf, by the way. Obvious, we can't tie up to each other, how do we handle the transfers?"

"No problem, Mr. O'Brien, two of my men have recovered your drifting whaler. We can use it to get Rudolf and that tree over here."

"Roger, captain. Oh, there is one more thing, we have a dead Cuban soldier on board wrapped in blankets, but.."

"Not to worry, I will have my men bring him over. We have the proper means to care for him until we get to port."

"Thank you, Captain, that will certainly please the Drummer's crew."

"Mr. O'Brien, when you're ready to come over, call us, I would like to get under way as soon as we can, we don't like staying up here on the surface. We attract a lot of curious sailors down in these parts and my exec just informed me there is a big target coming this way from the southern end of Guadeloupe, most likely it's that French Patrol boat and I would like to be gone, sir."

"Roger, send your men, Captain. Oh, one thing I would like to know, can you find out if there was a defection today out of Cuba, it would be a plane with women and children on board?"

"I will ask Fleet when I confirm you're on board, sir." O'Brien went topside and informed the crew of the conversation he had with the captain of the Memphis. O'Brien took Avery by the arm and walked back to the stern, just as two of the Memphis crew members pulled up to the Drummer's swim platform in the whaler.

"Commander Buckland, will you show those gentleman where Colonel Navarro is quartered and you'd better get your gear together."

"Well, Phil? It looks like you get to keep the two ladies, I have to take Buckwheat and leave you now, orders from old man."

"Yeah, well, don't worry, Dan. Gail and I can take care of the Drummer, did the old man say what he wanted us to do with her?"

"No, but I will be talking to him as soon as I get on board the sub. I'll have the skipper stay surfaced until I can talk to him and relay the info to you. If I don't get through to him and we have to dive, just do your thing. You'll want to go on up to Antigua and fuel up, so why don't you and Gail just hang out up there until I get more information. It wouldn't be more than a day at best. Maybe you can just leave the Drummer there in one of the harbors, and you and Gail go home. We can send someone down later to bring her up."

"Don't sweat it, Dan. I'll get her up to Antigua and we will wait to hear from you. Maybe I can talk Ted Collins to come down and take her on up to the States later."

"Well, Mr. Avery? I just want to say, it's been one hell of a Christmas and you're an ace in my book. I hope we can keep in touch, matter of fact, I really liked Sarasota and I know this cute little lieutenant who works for Scrooge and I would like to bring her down for a few days and let you and Gail show us around."

"I would like that, Dan, would like that a lot." Phil opened his arms and embraced the big shy Irishman. O'Brien put his arms around Avery and hugged him. He had never hugged another man before, except maybe his father.

"Permission to leave your ship, sir?" O'Brien smiled and saluted.

"Permission granted, Rudolf."

Gail was waiting at the stern rail by the open gate.

"You are one beautiful woman, Gail Townsend, and if I can hug your captain, I guess I can hug you too."

O'Brien and Gail embraced. Tears came fast running down her dark brown cheeks. "You're not going to believe this, but I am going to miss you, Dan O'Brien, miss you a lot."

"We will be seeing each other soon enough, I already set a date with Phil. Now, you take care of him, go and relax for a few days on the taxpayers."

Avery made the last trip with the whaler over to the Memphis, where he deposited O'Brien and Buckland and said goodbye.

O'Brien was about to enter the open hatch on the sub's aft deck and descend into the bowels of the Memphis, when he looked across the sea towards Guadeloupe and saw the huge sprays of water flying around the dark silhouette of a fast moving power vessel. He stood up, cupped his hands around his mouth.

"Oh Santa Claus," he yelled at the top of his lungs, but Avery could not hear him over the outboard motor. Gail, however did hear him and waved.

He cupped his hands around his mouth again. "Tell Santa that the Froggies are coming, the Froggies are coming." He pointed towards Guadeloupe. Gail heard him, turned and saw the patrol boat closing. She signaled with her fingers making the sign O.K., meaning she understood. She threw a kiss and waved.

O'Brien went down the steep ladder into the submarine, followed by a young sailor who closed and secured the hatch. At the bottom of the ladder Lieutenant Wahn greeted him.

"Follow me, sir, the captain is waiting for you."

O'Brien followed the young officer down to the next level, then through the narrow passage toward the bow of the ship. He could hear a symphony of strange sounds inside the pipes surrounding him. He could feel vibrations in the steel plates beneath his feet as the huge propeller began to move the Memphis forward and downward into the depths of the Caribbean Sea, a terrifying thought that did not sit well with him.

O'Brien entered the Captain's modest quarters, where Captain Meredith was seated holding a telephone to his ear.

"Yes, sir, he just walked in. What is that? Oh, yes, and a very Merry Christmas to you too, sir." Meredith looked up at O'Brien with a curious expression on his face. He put his hand over the mouthpiece of the phone.

"It's Admiral Koster, says, he's Scrooge. The Chairman of the Joint Chiefs of Staff, Admiral Koster, is Scrooge?"

"Yep and I am Rudy, or Rudolf, to the Admiral and my friends. May I?"

"Oh, sure." The bewildered captain handed O'Brien the phone, stood up and offered his seat, then moved out into the narrow hallway closing the door behind him.

"Merry Christmas, Admiral."

"Merry Christmas, Dan. Listen, I know the Memphis wants to get down and scoot over to Puerto Rico as soon as possible. He says he can be there in less than four hours. I will have someone waiting to pick you and Commander Buckland up and bring you up to Andrews. With a little luck, you should be home by 1900 hours and have time enough to clean up before a car picks you up and has you at my home by 2100. Mrs. Koster is holding Christmas dinner for you two. We will talk then. Oh, and bring the tape that Captain Merryweather, or whatever his name is, has of your vacation. We can look at it together in the morning."

O'Brien, not sure if he could still broadcast back to the Drummer wanted to at least answer Avery's question about the fate of his yacht. "Sir, what is going to happen to the Drummer? I promised Phil Avery I would call him in Antigua later tonight and let him know."

"It's Christmas Day, O'Brien, Avery's a big boy, he can survive another twenty four hours. I haven't really decided on that yet."

"Yes, sir, but.."

"O'Brien?"

"Yes, sir?"

"Watch your fingers, I am hanging up the phone." He did.

Roosevelt Roads
Puerto Rico
1640 Hours

O'Brien and Buckland were rushed off the USS Memphis minutes after docking and escorted to San Juan International Airport. They immediately boarded an unmarked DC-9 and took off for Washington landing at Andrews Air Force Base at 1912 hours. At 2130 hours, Avery stepped into a black Chrysler outside his apartment on Wisconsin Avenue, and was greeted by Commander Buckland and his wife Meg.

When they arrived at the Admiral's house, the Admiral and his wife warmly greeted them. They moved into the formal sitting room. Sitting next to the open fireplace was Alice Brooks.

"O'Brien? You remember Lieutenant Brooks? Lieutenant, this is Commander Buckland and his wife Meggy. Lieutenant Brooks volunteered to hang around the office for Christmas, so some of her friends could go home. She had nothing to do, so I invited her for dinner, besides, we needed another beautiful woman to decorate our home, right dear?"

Alice Brooks stood up and shook hands with the Bucklands. Her heart began to beat harder as Dan O'Brien walked up to her. Their eyes told each other all they needed to know.

"Hello, Ms. Brooks," O'Brien murmured as he came close to her. Their hands touched, and a silent intimate message was passed.

"It's Christmas, Mr. O'Brien. Why don't you call me Alice?"

"Fine, I'm Dan."

A loud cough got everyone's attention.

"Ladies, I know it's very impolite, but these two gentlemen and I have a few things to discuss before dinner. If you don't mind, we wish to be excused." Koster looked at his wife and winked. "I need ten minutes, that's all, I promise."

She gave him a gentle smile, then picked up a small tray of hors d'oeuvres and offered them to her women guests.

Koster led O'Brien and Buckland down a narrow hall to the rear of the house into a small den. The walls were all beautifully finished in dark mahogany and decorated with many framed photographs and flags hanging about. A pair of leather chairs faced the small fireplace and a large oriental desk trimmed in carved dragons that sat in front of a three window alcove. Behind the desk a large high back maroon leather chair.

The Admiral went over to a small bar and turned on the light in the cabinet. "What's your pleasure, gentlemen?"

"Oh, VO and soda, sir," O'Brien said.

"No VO, how about, ah, Canadian Club?"

"Fine, sir."

"Commander?"

"Ah, Scotch on the rocks, sir."

"A man after my own heart. Do you want Cutty, Dewars or Bells?"

"Oh, Bells, sir."

"You got it, sailor."

After serving the drinks, Koster took his seat behind the desk. He opened the top drawer and took out a folder and opened it.

"Well, fourteen hours ago, you two were living in hell. I'm sorry things did not go as planned, however, I am a believer in fate and if it isn't meant to be, well, there's good reason. Whatever failed, failed, what's worse, we probably won't ever know, personally, I don't care."

The Admiral stood up and went back to the bar and added more ice to his drink. "O'Brien, you put together a hell of a mission. You had all the right ideas and your plan, well it nearly worked. Your people worked even better and I realize it cost some lives, that is something we are never prepared for, however, it was a mission and you have to accept the results. We unfortunately, may have tipped our hand. We have received some flak from the French authorities down in Guadeloupe. The French Embassy has been calling the State Department all day, would you believe on Christmas day? They want to know more about the Drummer. Why was it at the accident scene, why did it leave and rendezvous with a United States submarine?"

"Admiral, what about Avery and Gail Townsend? Where is the Drummer now?"

"She should be anchored in Antigua. The last word I received was the French let her go, sometime around noon, after a little pressure from the State Department. Avery gave them a statement that only a novice sailor would believe. He told them that his keel hit the sub, and he made them stop and surface to check for damage. Then he tells them he plans to sue the U.S. Navy. He may have to go back to Guadeloupe for a hearing on the Unicorn disaster, but we'll worry about this later. I'm sure we can get this settled with the French."

"What about the rest of our team, sir?"

"Well, I don't know too much. The Sonar is back in Puerto Rico tied up at the Coast Guard station in San Juan. All the crew and passengers are home safe celebrating Christmas. I tried to get hold of Captain Chen at Key West, but he had left for California. He is escorting the body of the young sailor, Bill Allen home to San Francisco, then he is going on to San Diego."

"Bill Allen? Bill Allen the navy seal, died? What.." O'Brien began to rise out of his chair. His face turned white. "What the hell are you talking about, Admiral?"

Commander Buckland placed his glass on the nearby table and slid up to the end of his seat.

"Ah, Admiral, sir? I had better explain." Buckland turned and looked at O'Brien. "We never told you, Dan, about Bill Allen, I'm sorry. You were, well, we felt it was best you didn't know, especially after the news about Van Wagner." Buckland dropped his head down. "I'm sorry, Dan."

"What happened? O'Brien asked.

"I believe they said it was complications with pneumonia, or something like that."

"I'm sorry, Dan, I had no idea you didn't know." Admiral Koster said with concern.

O'Brien tossed down his drink and stood up. "Do you mind, Admiral?"

"Help your self, son."

O'Brien went to the small bar and poured a double rye. "Admiral, I know there were some glitches, and I probably could have been more careful, especially at the cove, but, well, things just began to happen not like we planned, you know? I just want to..."

Koster raised his hand and interrupted. "O'Brien, there will be plenty of time to go over what could have been done, later at our briefing with the VP. You and your team did a commendable job and don't worry about any consequences, the Cubans or the Russians are not going to make any waves over this, believe me. What Castro will do is anyone's guess, he escaped this time, only because the good Lord has some kind of special ending waiting for that man, I just hope I am still around to see it."

The large cheerfully decorated table dominated the Koster's formal dining room. Each place setting was perfect, with beautiful china and sterling silver. Crystal glasses sparkled in the candlelight, and the sound of Christmas music drifted in from the living room. The entire room was tastefully decorated with cheerful holiday ornaments and garlands. It looked like a Norman Rockwell painting.

During dinner, Admiral Koster made an announcement that brought a lump to everyone's throat.

"Earlier today, at 1235 hours to be exact, an old twin engine transport, I believe it was a Convair 440, escorted by two F-4 Phantoms landed at Homestead Air Force Base. The aircraft, we learned, is Fidel Castro's personal plane and the pilot his personal pilot. His name is Carlos Lucia. He had on board his wife Theresa and their three daughters. Also on board was his sister-in-law, Melinda Navarro and her two children. The Vice President interrupted his day with his family and flew down to Homestead this afternoon on Air Force One to personally welcome the two families to freedom."

O'Brien pushed back from the table and stood up. He looked at the Admiral and said, "With your permission, sir. I would like to make a toast."

"Of course, Dan, be my guest."

O'Brien raised his wine glass. "To a man I knew for only a brief moment. He made this a very special Christmas day for his family and loved ones and changed my life forever." O'Brien fought back the tears as his voiced cracked. "To Luis Navarro."

Epilogue

Six months had passed since Operation Yuletide and life for some of the participants on the mission had changed considerably.

Phil Avery went back to Immokalee and reopened the small yacht rebuilding company, which became an instant success. His yacht management business also increased and he bought another vintage Thunderbird. He was spending most of his time at his Sarasota office with Gail Townsend. She made only one major change. She gave up her condominium in Bradenton and moved into Avery's small bayside home on Siesta Key, as Mrs. Phil Avery.

Commander Buckland was re-assigned to the Pentagon to Admiral Koster's staff. He never did get to Vermont, but he did have a long weekend with Meg in Ocean City, Maryland.

Paul Gransaull was transferred to San Diego and was attached to Pacific Fleet Air Wing. He was promoted and given a new assignment as a squadron commander on the aircraft carrier, Bunker Hill.

John Lind returned to his home in Ft. Walton Beach, Florida. He bought a new 30 foot center console open fishing boat and started to do day charter fishing trips. He had written to Admiral Koster and offered to return to San Juan and pick up the old Sonar and bring it back to Jacksonville. His request was denied. The old mine sweeper was passed on to the Coast Guard at St. Thomas, to be used as a work boat in the Caribbean.

Captain Jack Chen re-enlisted for another tour and was given command of the prestigious Navy Seal training center at the Key West Naval Station.

Jesus Souza moved into international marketing, and was promoted to a Vice President.

Dan O'Brien retired from the Government that spring and returned to St. Petersburg Beach to renew his old friendship with Ted Collins and his family He took a small apartment on the beach, where he had a frequent visitor who flew down almost every weekend from Washington. On one of her visits, O'Brien made a commitment he could not get out of. He moved to Venice, Florida, where he purchased a modest home near the beaches overlooking a golf course. He also leased a small shop in downtown Venice, where his new bride opened a small gift shop on the main street. It offered mainly Christmas things, like tree ornaments, toys, stuffed animals and special greeting cards. It was called "Alice's Yuletide Place".

On January 7th, 1986, Ted Collins, his wife Karen and their two children flew to Antigua and boarded the Island Drummer. They sailed her from English Harbour to St. Maarten, then to Tortola, St. Johns, then up through the Bahamas, where they ended their three week voyage at Marsh Harbour in the Abacos. Somewhere along the voyage, the name Island Drummer had been erased from the varnished transom and the yacht's proud bows. A new name had appeared, "September Morn". Ted Collins would go on to build many new seventy-five foot super yachts as a tribute to the success of his prototype, the Island Drummer.

In an agreement with Admiral Koster, Ted Collins managed to keep his yacht from reaching the depths of the deep Atlantic ditch, where Koster suggested she be retired. With a little help from O'Brien, the Drummer was saved and would begin a new life under a new flag, and its new name in the Bahamas.

The final chapter of Operation Yuletide came on March 18th. On St. Patrick's Day, March 17th, there was a party that was sponsored by a number of the crewed charter yachts that worked out of St. Thomas. The party was held at one of the island's favorite out of the way pubs, "For the Birds," at Compass Point. In the early morning hours of March 18th, a small rented jeep taking three party goers back to their yachts at Yacht Haven Marina missed a turn at the intersection that went to Frenchmans Reef Resort. The Jeep crashed into the guard rail, rolled over and tumbled into a deep ravine. Two passengers were thrown and survived. The other was DOA at the St. Thomas Hospital at 0340 hours. The death certificate read. Captain Melvin R. Spencer, age 54, Single, white male. Resident: West Palm Beach, Florida. Cause of death: Fractured skull/broken neck. In his personal belongings, a large brown sealed envelope was found. There was a hand written message on it from Spencer. "In case of my accidental death, this envelope and its contents must be presented to the Editor of the Washington Post."